ACCLAIM FOR THE BOURNE THRILLERS

"[The] endless deceptions reliably lead to the extravagant action scenes that are Lustbader's hallmark. Series fans will eagerly await Bourne's next adventure."

—*Publishers Weekly* on
The Bourne Initiative

"Lustbader brings his A game.... *The Bourne Initiative* is just the type of explosive, fast-paced thriller that Robert Ludlum's fans crave."

—**TheRealBookSpy.com** on
The Bourne Initiative

"Lustbader has produced a novel unlike any other in the series.... *The Bourne Initiative* has it all....[It] allows us to experience the complex and very satisfying end to a thriller that succeeds on nearly every level."

—**BookReporter.com** on
The Bourne Initiative

"Written with the same heart-pounding suspense fans have come to expect from Lustbader, Jason Bourne returns to action in splendid, breathtaking fashion....A pedal-to-the-floor spy thriller that plays up everything readers have come to love about Jason Bourne....Lustbader knows just how to keep fans on the edges of their seats as he lays out the story's plot, sucking them in and setting up for a climactic ending that doesn't disappoint."

—**TheRealBookSpy.com** on
The Bourne Enigma

"*The Bourne Enigma* is a rollicking roller-coaster ride of spy games and colorful characters set against the expected multiple international locales. . . . an enjoyable and fast-paced read that faithfully continues the enigma that is Jason Bourne."

—BookReporter.com on
The Bourne Enigma

"In the highly able hands of author Eric Van Lustbader, Bourne has seen a resurgence of terrific proportions. . . . What Lustbader does best is to step into the shoes and skin of Jason Bourne, breathing life into a character who readers of espionage thrillers cannot get enough of. *The Bourne Ascendancy* will not disappoint."

—BookReporter.com on
The Bourne Ascendancy

"*The Bourne Ascendancy* is everything you'd think a Bourne novel should be: relentless action, over-the-top deaths, moral ambiguity, and the fate of the world hanging in the balance. . . . This is one you'll want to snatch up quickly."

—LifeIsStory.com on
The Bourne Ascendancy

"Eric Van Lustbader has once again taken the Bourne saga to another level of greatness . . . filled with non-stop action. Fans of the superspy will find themselves rooting for him right up until the last page is turned."

—BookReporter.com on
The Bourne Retribution

"Action-packed thriller...The unrelenting action in the novel clearly shows how this series has become so popular both in print and on the screen."
—*Suspense Magazine* on
The Bourne Imperative

"Fans of the book and movie franchise will love this new plot-driven international thriller....This is classic Bourne."
—*USA Today* on
The Bourne Dominion

"The twists, the nonstop action, and the multilayered plot that Ludlum fans expect are here in abundance. Fans of the Bourne films will eat this one up."
—*Booklist* on
The Bourne Dominion

"A wealth of information flows as smoothly as a swallow of single-malt scotch. With more twists and turns than a Napa Valley of grapevines, the nonstop action and resourceful Bourne plucked a fourth from my Star Jar."
—**BookReporter.com** on
The Bourne Dominion

"Thriller addicts who love intricate webs of conspiracy mixed with an adrenaline rush of action and global adventure will snap this one up."
—*Library Journal* on
The Bourne Objective

"Breathless writing that makes the pages fly."
—*Kirkus Reviews* on
The Bourne Betrayal

"A cleverly plotted, incisive thriller with a hero I'm glad is on the good guys' side. In an amazing work of fiction, Lustbader takes us into the minds of terrorists."
—NightsandWeekends.com on
The Bourne Sanction

"Lustbader is an excellent storyteller and is not afraid to keep the twists and turns coming in this sequel. . . . This is an explosive addition to a series with an unrivaled heritage and storied pedigree."
—BookReporter.com on
The Bourne Betrayal

THE
BOURNE
INITIATIVE

ALSO BY ROBERT LUDLUM

ALSO BY ERIC VAN LUSTBADER

ROBERT LUDLUM'S™

THE
BOURNE
INITIATIVE

A NEW JASON BOURNE NOVEL BY
ERIC VAN LUSTBADER

GRAND CENTRAL
PUBLISHING

NEW YORK   BOSTON

Grand Central Publishing
Hachette Book Group
1290 Avenue of the Americas, New York, NY 10104
grandcentralpublishing.com
twitter.com/grandcentralpub

Originally published in hardcover and ebook by Grand Central Publishing in June 2017
First oversize mass market edition: November 2017

Grand Central Publishing is a division of Hachette Book Group, Inc. The Grand Central Publishing name and logo is a trademark of Hachette Book Group, Inc.

The publisher is not responsible for websites (or their content) that are not owned by the publisher.

The Hachette Speakers Bureau provides a wide range of authors for speaking events. To find out more, go to www.hachettespeakersbureau.com or call (866) 376-6591.

ISBNs: 978-1-4555-9799-4 (oversize mass market),
978-1-4555-9797-0 (ebook)

Printed in the United States of America

OPM

10 9 8 7 6 5 4 3 2 1

For Victoria, my one and only,
my everything.

THE
BOURNE
INITIATIVE

Prologue

THERE IS SOMETHING *about a man on his knees,* Keyre thought, *that stirs my very heart.* Keyre, the Somali magus, a Yibir whose lineage stretched back through time to the days of the Ajuran Empire, predating all the subsequent failed sultanates, stood on the hard shingle twelve feet from the soft rumble of the Indian Ocean. He breathed in the salt air, the familiar scents of the sere desert behind him, the sunbaked brick of houses destroyed by bazooka blasts and rocket fire. But all these clean scents were at the moment overwhelmed by the stink of human sweat, excrement, and terror.

Ah, but terror is what Keyre fed upon, lapped up like mother's milk since he was a child of eight, in the aftermath of his first kill. The first taste of blood was always the sharpest, but, for him, the blood didn't matter as much as it did to his compatriots. But then they weren't Yibir, weren't steeped in the Stygian darkness of his family's ancient sorcery. Their nostrils dilated as the fresh blood flowed from the newly dead. But for Keyre, the blood was an adjunct, as necessary as shooting dead the man who, on his knees, waves the white flag.

It's the white flag, you see, he told himself. *The white flag stinks of fear. I want to inhale its scent, savor its taste before I put a match to it and set it afire.* Where he stood now, on the shore of Somalia, between the desert of destruction and the Indian Ocean on which he often enough plied his particular brand of terror, he was immersed in the stench of death.

Before him thirteen men knelt, backs bowed, heads bowed further. Some stared in stony silence at the shingle on which they knelt, its shifting layers slicing like razor blades into their knees. Others wailed their fear in pitiful ululations. One or two had tear streaks along their dust-caked cheeks. None of them murmured a prayer—further confirmation, if any was needed, of what Keyre already knew.

He was a tall man, cadaverously thin, all muscle and bone, with a long, triangular face and a saturnine countenance. He was both as athletic as a swimmer and as graceful as a dancer—not only strikingly handsome but possessed of a charisma gifted to very few. He had dedicated himself to many things, not the least of which was creating a dazzling smile that fooled everyone.

Thirteen men, on their knees, bowed down, wrists tied behind their backs. In Keyre's left hand a large German Mauser restored to all its World War II glory. *Who was its original owner? A member of the Gestapo, or the Abwehr, maybe, their mortal enemy. What did it matter anyway?* Keyre asked himself; it was his now, unlocked and loaded.

Stepping up, he placed the muzzle of the Mauser against the back of the first prisoner's head and pulled the trigger. The sound of the hammer falling was as loud as a thunderclap. As one, the line of men flinched. But there was no detonation, no bullet. Stepping to his right, Keyre placed the muzzle against the back of the second man's head. When he pulled the trigger, the man's head exploded, and what was left of him pitched forward, sprawled awkwardly onto the shingle.

Blood, the stench of it rising up to mingle with a terror that, to Keyre's heightened senses, was palpable. Above, black birds wheeled, calling to each other, dinner bells announcing another feast. High above them, the vast sky rippled with clouds, like a weight lifter flexing his muscles.

Another step to the right brought him to a spot directly behind the third man in line. Keyre shot him, with more or less the identical result. In all, there were twelve corpses lying facedown on the bloody shingle when he reached the end of the line. That left the first man. Keyre had reloaded two-thirds of the way down the line; his Mauser was still itching to inflict more death. He could feel the sensation run up the nerves of his left arm, like the output of a live wire. His hand twitched briefly in just the way a female lion's paw twitched when she was dreaming of running down an okapi or a gazelle. Jaws at the throat, clamping down, blood and viscera overrunning her teeth as the males loped up to feed.

Keyre took his time returning to the one remaining kneeling man. He stood in front of him, staring down.

"Look at me," he said. He could see the man shaking. "Look at me!" he said more sharply.

The man's head came up. Keyre locked his eyes onto the prisoner's. "I know who you are," he said, his tone conversational now. "I know what you and your kind have been up to. Their death sentence has been carried out, as you can see." He crouched down so suddenly the prisoner flinched. He was a thin man, short in stature, but with plenty of upper body strength. He was dark of skin, his nose long and sharp. His brown eyes were set close together. His lips were chapped, the skin flaking off as if he'd been out in the sun too long.

He's been here with me too long, Keyre thought. *That's for certain.*

He stared hard into the other's face as he said, "Here, your death sentence will be carried out in the blink of an eye." There were smears of dried blood on the prisoner's cheek; he stank of sweat and terror, and there was about him a certain fecal stench. "But for you, my friend, that death sentence can be commuted. Your life can continue." Keyre left it there; it was time to keep silent.

The prisoner's jaw muscles worked spasmodically. His tongue, gray as ash, appeared, then slipped back between his teeth. "H . . . how?" he asked in a thin, reedy voice, and Keyre knew the man would tell him what he wanted to know.

Despite the miasma the man wore like a cloak, Keyre leaned in and said in his ear, "What I want to know is this: who do you work for?"

The prisoner's mouth worked as if he was trying to summon up the courage to answer or enough saliva to speak clearly.

Before he could say a word, Keyre said, "His full name and position. Nothing less will save you."

The prisoner swallowed hard. His eyes flicked from one side to the other, as if frightened of being overheard, even out here in the Somalian wilderness. "Not out loud."

Keyre nodded, giving him permission to lean forward. He placed his lips against the opening of Keyre's ear and whispered six words.

Those words—the identity of the man who trained these thirteen to infiltrate his cadre—caused a profound change in Keyre's demeanor. His face darkened, his lips compressed, his eyes seemed to cross. Then, in a flash, he turned his head sideways and with his open jaws and his bared teeth, he ripped the man's throat out.

Part One
MEME

1

MORGANA ROY WALKED briskly to work at precisely 8:36 in the morning. As a creature of habit, she always walked a mile from the public parking garage to her office in the rear of a half-derelict building, on the flyblown main drag of Bowie, Maryland. Bowie was just southwest of Fort Meade, where the black-glass NSA colossus rose seemingly out of nowhere. As usual, she had arisen at six in the morning, driven to the dojo where she had been a member for seven years, and worked out vigorously with masters of two different martial arts disciplines for more or less forty-five minutes each, before showering and changing into her work clothes.

Her apartment, twenty miles southwest of the office, would seem to an outsider like a perfectly sterile environment: apart from appliances, there were two or multiples thereof of everything—sofas, chairs, lamps, coffee and side tables, laptop computers at two different workstations. On the dining room table stood two vases, each equidistant from the center. Six chairs. Everything was symmetrical. She lived a compartmentalized life; order was important to her. Chaos made her uneasy, though the truth was she found the concept intriguing.

She made this walk in all seasons, all kinds of weather, without fail, and at a speed that would make most others huff and puff and clutch the stitch in their side. There was about this walk something of a challenge, so grueling in summer heat and winter sleet, that those who occasionally had to walk with her privately called it the Bataan Death March. It was a joke, of course, but a decidedly grim one.

Morgana Roy worked in a small suite of offices hard by a gymnasium, and those new to her unit were assaulted by the smells of stale sweat, underarm odor, and worse, which insinuated themselves through the baseboards of the wall that separated the offices from the gym. Twice a week these would be temporarily overpowered by the acrid stench of Lysol and bleach. Morgana seemed unaware of these odious smells, or perhaps she had become accustomed to them.

Using a magnetic key card, she passed through the door marked with a small, discreet sign: MEME LLC, printed on a sheet of plain white paper. It looked as unsettled as Morgana's state of mind, and in bad weather it had to be replaced almost daily. Still, there was no plan for anything permanent to take its place. Across the street was the smallest post office Morgana had ever seen, a tiny brick building with a sadly draped banner, RENT A P.O. BOX TODAY, hanging off the iron railing of the cement handicap ramp.

At Morgana's entrance, a heavyset young woman of twenty-three in a distinctly non–government issue gabardine suit got up from behind a desk, said, "Good morning," and went to fetch them both cappuccinos.

"Good morning, Rose," Morgana said when Rose returned.

Beside Rose's desk a rubber plant's leaves shone as if polished daily. To the right was a cabinet, closed and locked, that, in fact, contained nothing at all. To the left stood a row of three chairs that had never been sat on, a low table on which were scattered copies of *Vanity Fair* and *Wired*, never read but nevertheless kept current. There were never any visitors to Meme LLC, ever.

At thirty, Morgana was the oldest member of the crew. She had seven people working for her in the office, seven more out in the field. All of them were young and ruthless; they had, to a person, lean and hungry looks, which was just the way she wanted them.

There were two doors in the wall behind Rose. The one on the right led to a break room, complete with a refrigerator-freezer, a two-burner stove, a sink, food cabinets, a coffee bean grinder, and the cappuccino-espresso maker. Farther along lurked a warren of store-rooms that eventually led to a basement.

The left-hand door was locked with a retina-recognition system. Morgana, cappuccino in hand, looked into the display, opening the door. She took a judicious sip of her cappuccino before stepping across the threshold.

She entered a large, windowless room. Across the left wall was a mosaic of LED flat-panel screens, but instead of showing feeds of CCTV cameras in airports and street corners in cities around the world, or images of desert encampments relayed from various drones, these screens contained images from computer terminals, hard drive data folders, dynamic malware firewalls. The images kept changing, often so fast they became a blur. Most of the writing on the screens was in Russian Cyrillic or Mandarin Chinese, but there was one in Persian, others in Hebrew and Arabic, still another in Urdu, a final one in Pashto.

The right-hand wall was a 4K video loop of aerial footage of the Swiss Alps. An hour from now, it would be scenes shot from a boat prowling the Maldives, and the hour after that, the crowded streets of midtown Manhattan. And so forth. No one ever complained about the lack of windows; no one looked up when Morgana strode in, which was just the way she liked it. Her cadre of six had eyes and minds glued to their laptop screens.

There were no partitions between workstations. Thick cables rose from each station to tracks hung just below the ceiling, which allowed Morgana's staff to move around at will, huddle together for impromptu conferences, exchange vital information in real time. Everything on the flat-panels was in real time. Real time meant everything to the operators of Meme LLC; being current was their currency. Morgana fostered a cluster method of cryptanalysis, hence the screens. All Meme's projects were collaborative efforts. This led not only to one success after another but to a close-knit comradeship among the team impossible to achieve inside the federal government's myriad clandestine services.

Morgana passed through a narrow door set discreetly in the far wall. There was no nameplate beside it. This was Morgana's sanctum. From here, she could monitor everything that went on in the outer room. She also had the freedom to turn it all off, and in the semi-darkness contemplate algorithms and her future.

Setting her cappuccino down at her workstation, she removed her jacket, slung it over the back of her ergonomic task chair, sat down. The moment she did so, the screen on her laptop flared to life. Her thumbprint was scanned, and she was in.

There was the usual slew of email messages waiting in her in box, but there was also one that was flagged.

Uh oh, she thought. *Black Star.*

She knew what Black Star meant, and it wasn't usual in any way, shape, manner, or form.

She clicked on the icon. Instead of opening the message, she was taken directly to the office of General Arthur MacQuerrie. His wind-burned, time-lined face filled the screen. His baby blues stared out of the screen as if he were Dr. Strange, who, along with Wonder Woman, was one of her favorite comic book heroes. The analogy was apt. Her boss at NSA was something of a magician. How he kept her unit secret from the mandarins floating at the top of the governmental alphabet soup—NSA, CIA, DIA, FBI, DOD, DHS, you name it—was a complete mystery to her. And that was only the top layer of his legerdemain. Meme was well funded—there wasn't one thing Morgana had ever asked for that the general had ever refused. They had bleeding-edge technology to the point where all their equipment was upgraded twice a year. Obtaining vast sums of money from Marshall Fulmer, former senator and head of the Joint Armed Services Appropriations Committee

(JASAC) who had just been confirmed by Congress as the incoming president's national security advisor, without letting on what the funds were for, seemed an impossibility. And yet the general managed it.

"Morning, Mac," she said, as she took another sip of her cappuccino. "What's up?"

The general was possessed of a wide brow and beetling eyebrows. One could tell a lot from those eyebrows, which were the most mobile aspect of his diamond-shaped face. "It seems our old friend, Boris Illyich Karpov, has climbed out of the grave."

"General Karpov is dead," Morgana said. "His throat was slit from ear to ear, in Moscow last year at his wedding."

"And yet, he keeps bedeviling us." The general shook his head. "As you are well aware, Boris Karpov trod a fine line between doing the Sovereign's bidding and working for himself. That is more difficult in Russia than it is anywhere else in the world, save North Korea. It seems that in the months before he was killed, Karpov was working on several clandestine initiatives."

Morgana's screen split. MacQuerrie remained in the left half, while the right half was filled with a rain of vertical lines of computer code so complex they took her breath away.

"What in the name of holy hell is that?"

"No idea," MacQuerrie said. "Which is why I've brought it to you."

"We'll get right on it."

"That's just what you won't do," MacQuerrie said. "This is for your eyes only. No one is to see or even catch a whiff that this code exists. Got that?"

"Of course, but what do you think it is?"

The general seemed to age a decade before her eyes. He ran a hand across his face, and to her horror, she noticed a slight tremor in the fingers.

"My best guess: a cyber weapon, something so sophisticated that it's far beyond anything we've seen—or even dreamt of—before. For some time, this *thing,* this weapon, was a rumor, nothing more. But because some of the stories attributed fantastic powers to it, I kept my ear to the ground, collated even the most outlandish of the rumors.

"And, then, out of the blue, an hour ago, this shard appeared in the wild. My people found it quite by accident while trolling the dark web for intel on a certain arms dealer we've been after for years, but have yet to pin a single misstep on, let alone a crime. When leads do surface, the people behind them vanish as if into thin air. We never even find a body."

"What's this arms dealer's name?"

"Keyre. He's a Somali pirate—or was, anyway, until we took Viktor Bout into custody." She knew Bout was the most notorious illegal arms dealer of the last decade. "That left a giant hole in the illegal arms trade, and Keyre was first into Bout's territory, killing off whoever was left from the Russian's own network, replacing them with his own people.

"Keyre has proven himself to be smarter, better connected, and far more slippery than Bout ever was. The story goes that his network is larger, more far-flung, and, most crucially, contains contacts inside governments worldwide. Bout had customs and immigration people in a dozen countries in his pocket. By contrast, Keyre's network makes Bout's look like a kindergarten class.

"Whether that's the emmis, I don't yet know, but it's this cyber weapon that's giving me a migraine for the ages. You need to make sense of the fragment and you have to find the rest of the code."

Morgana sat back, absorbing the information Mac was throwing her way. Something was nagging at her, and she voiced it: "Mac, have you thought about why this fragment suddenly showed up on the dark web?"

"What d'you mean? There are any number of ways—"

"No, there aren't. Not something of this level of sophistication. No, Mac, my guess is that it was released on the dark web deliberately."

"But what for?"

"I think it's a strong possibility that whoever took possession of the cyber initiative following Karpov's murder is putting it up for auction."

"Auction?"

"What better way to whet potential buyers' appetites, and drive up the bids, than to let them take a peek behind the curtain, so to speak."

"Christ, I hadn't thought of that." MacQuerrie was sweating now, droplets forming at his hairline, rolling down the sides of his cheek.

"Could this Keyre be running the auction?"

"Possible. Even likely. Somalia is just the place for such things." The general frowned. "But I'm thinking he's only the conduit. Someone else is the mastermind. And knowing Karpov as I did, it would have to be someone he trusted implicitly as well as explicitly."

"That rules out just about everyone in the Russian government, doesn't it?"

MacQuerrie nodded. "Yes, it does."

"Someone from within the initiative itself, then."

"Again, knowing Karpov, he wouldn't trust anyone like that with the big picture. His operations were meticulously compartmentalized. That was his first rule of keeping his work absolutely secure. No one could betray him if they didn't know what was really going on."

"In that case, I'm willing to bet several people wrote this code, each one unaware of what the others were doing. Could Karpov himself have stitched all the pieces of code together?"

"The general was a man of many talents," MacQuerrie said. "It's possible, I suppose, but, frankly, not very likely."

"Well, no programmer could direct Karpov's initiative as a whole. The best ones are like idiot savants: they know their stuff backward and forward, but that's all they're good for. They couldn't direct themselves out of a paper bag." She pursed her lips. "So again, I have to ask, who is running the operation now?"

MacQuerrie did not answer right away. It seemed to Morgana that now they had come to the nub of the matter, his face had gone even grayer. Perhaps it was the lighting in his office, but she doubted that. His right eyebrow twitched, which meant he was under extreme stress. *What could cause such a thing?* she asked herself.

"One thing before we go any further, Morgana."

She said nothing. Even for her, who was more or less inured to such things, waiting for the second shoe to drop was a mighty unpleasant experience. This was General Arthur MacQuerrie, not some fatuous NSA type who didn't know his ass from his elbow.

"I have no doubt that Karpov's operation is aimed squarely at the United States." He paused to wipe at a growing film of sweat on his upper lip. "It could be the national electrical grid or even, God forbid, the president's bank of nuclear missile codes."

"What? But that's impossible. The code data is buried so deeply behind a phalanx of firewalls...and then the codes are changed hourly."

"All true. But Karpov's operational language is so obscure, so utterly unknown, I and my people believe the nuclear codes are its target."

"If the Russians access our nuclear codes..."

"You see the nature of the extreme danger we're in."

Morgana stared at the lines of code, cascading down her screen. *Good God,* she thought. *What we have here is the ultimate weapon of mass destruction.*

Black Star. No wonder.

"This is a superworm," she said. "A form of malware no one's ever encountered before."

"Tell me something I don't know. This is catastrophic. You had better come up with the answer, *stat*."

Morgana didn't like the tone that had set into his voice. This had happened more than once before, when Mac started treating her like a low-level gofer, his voice hard and threatening. She bit her lip, but bile built up in her stomach, churning, as if a whirlpool had opened up inside her.

"Horrifyingly, there's more," Mac was saying.

She tensed even more as the code vanished, to be replaced by a grainy black-and-white photo, obviously taken with a telephoto lens. A surveillance shot, then. Men in tuxedos, women in fancy floor-length gowns, jewels and beading glittering. Over their heads an ornate crystal chandelier, spilling light down on them.

"Moscow." MacQuerrie gave her a date from last year. "On the occasion of Boris Karpov's wedding."

"I see Karpov," Morgana said. "In the center."

"D'you recognize anyone else? He has his arm across the shoulders of the man to his immediate right."

"Yes."

"Do you recognize that man?"

She leaned closer, zoomed in a bit, but not too much; the images would become too vague to accurately glean features and expressions. "I'm afraid I don't, Mac."

The general sighed. "Well, I suppose I shouldn't be surprised."

She felt the whirlpool congeal into an icy ball. She wanted to vomit it up and throw it at Mac. Instead, fighting to keep her cool, she said: "Karpov looks genuinely pleased to be with him. But, as you've told me, he didn't have any close friends in the Russian hierarchy."

"That's correct."

Now she was sure that MacQuerrie was in serious distress; his eyebrows were knit together in a dreadful expression of anxiety.

"That man isn't a Russian, Morgana. He's one of ours—or at least he was. You're looking at Boris Karpov's best friend, the only one he would trust to continue his operation in the event of his demise.

"The man Karpov is embracing is Jason Bourne."

2

THE AEGEAN SEA was a pure cobalt blue in the late afternoon sunlight. The boat plowed through the waves, on its way west. *Nym*, Boris Karpov's hundred-foot motorboat, whose captain and crew were Greeks and Cypriots, was the only asset of the late FSB general that hadn't been confiscated by the Russian government following his murder and the death of his new bride. The only reason it hadn't been confiscated was that Boris had wisely kept the boat in international waters, out of reach of even the Sovereign's avaricious clutches.

These thoughts were uppermost in Jason Bourne's mind as he stood amidships, leaning on the polished port railing, staring at the smudge on the horizon that even at this distance he recognized as the island of Skyros. To the northeast and days behind them was the Sea of Marmara and, beyond, Istanbul, where they had briefly anchored to take on supplies, fuel, fresh food, and water. Istanbul was no longer a safe haven for Westerners. And yet he knew so many people in and around the city that he, rather than the captain, did all the bartering.

From Skyros, he had no idea where he would go. At the moment, he was content to be at sea, to feel the salt wind in his hair, to have it cleanse him of Boris's horrific murder and its exhausting and perilous aftermath. Boris had been involved in a myriad of strategies, initiatives of which neither the Sovereign nor his comrades in the FSB were aware. Perhaps they would all unravel now, or even had already died along with the spymaster who had conceived them. It was a relief not to have to think of tomorrow, of ticking clocks, of countdowns toward one catastrophe or another, of outrunning life or deadly deadlines.

His best friend was gone, had left him the boat as a remembrance. In truth, he had no use for this huge boat. Nevertheless, here he was. It was a matter of honoring both his friendship and Boris's memory to accept the gift, to use it as he saw fit. Boris trusted him to do that; he had every intention of respecting that trust.

Behind him, too, was the Russian Federation. Last year, he had fallen so deeply into a nest of vipers he'd be quite happy never to set foot in Russia again. All this brooding about the past—the part of it he could remember—was making him melancholy. But what else should he feel? Every time he thought he'd had enough, that he should return to the professorial life of David Webb, the person he had been before the Bourne identity had been imprinted on him by the people running Treadstone, he knew it was useless. He'd tried that—twice, in fact—only to become bored within weeks. He was who he was now. He couldn't outrun it; senseless to try.

The *Nym* slowed to quarter speed. Captain Stavros appeared out of the wheelhouse, descended an outside ladder, and approached Bourne. He carried a bottle of chilled vodka, two glasses, and a pepper shaker.

"Berth or anchorage?" he asked in his typical short-hand.

In the days since Bourne had come aboard *Nym*, the two men had come to know each other, as much as two strangers in close quarters can know each other. They ate their meals together, drank together, afterward exchanged stories about the boat's former master, for whom Stavros had a deep and abiding affection. Despite his formidable personality, his studied cruelty, Boris had often been astonishingly genial. Despite his dark and brooding Russian soul—or perhaps because of it—he had loved good food, fine drink, and laughter. Lots of laughter, the perfect anodyne for the bleak profession he had carved out for himself.

Boris had felt things deeply, made friends for life, would do anything for those friends. These qualities, mirrored in Bourne, had formed the basis of their abiding friendship. Even though they often found themselves on opposite sides, many were the times they helped each other out, finding common enemies to defeat. Bourne would miss their camaraderie, but he missed the heightened experience of shared danger most of all.

"Anchorage." Bourne gave him coordinates, and Stavros nodded. He was used to being told the minimum about where his master was headed and why.

Handing Bourne one of the glasses, he gave them both generous pours of the vodka—a very fine Russian brand, Bourne noted. Before they drank, Stavros dotted the surface of the liquor in each glass with pepper. He grinned at Bourne, who returned the expression. This was a silent tribute to Boris, an old-school Russian, if ever there was one. Back in the day you always used pepper before you drank your vodka. Often, the liquor would contain fusel oil, a product of poor distillation; the pepper would bind with the oil, sink it to the bottom of the glass. The word *fusel*, Bourne knew, was German for "bad liquor."

"To our great general!" Stavros cried, holding his glass high. His voice was a deep basso, clotted by years of too much drink and cigarette tar.

"To Boris Illyich." *Long may his memory live on,* Bourne thought.

"We will never forget him!"

They clinked glasses, downed the vodka in one.

Above them, the sky was an inverted porcelain bowl, light-blue and white, the colors of the boat's master stateroom. Gulls wheeled and called plaintively, having flown out from the island's rocky cliffs on the eastern shore to beg for food.

"Will we be staying in Skyros long?"

"Several days," Bourne said evasively, and the captain nodded, understanding: it was none of his business.

He refilled Bourne's glass, then took his leave, heading back up into the wheelhouse to guide *Nym* the last half mile to the anchorage two hundred yards offshore. The water was quite deep on this side of the island.

Bourne moved toward the bow, the better to watch the craggy cliffs and the curved shingle coming into focus. Details, he thought. Everything was in the details.

So many of his foes had forgotten to take care of the details; so many had lost their lives because of that lapse.

Bourne called for the speedy runabout with its over-clocked dual diesels. As he descended the accommodation ladder, he saw the captain staring down at him.

"Sure you don't want one of the crew with you, sir?"

"Positive."

Stavros held up a Steyr M automatic pistol in a sign of query.

"Thanks, but there's no need."

"You never know." Stavros grinned. "The general used to say that."

True enough. Bourne raised a hand, caught the Steyr, then made his way down to the waiting runabout. The captain had dropped anchor at the precise coordinates Bourne had given him. Bourne had been to Skyros only once, and that under extreme conditions. But in light of what was about to take place he supposed his return could be considered a homecoming of sorts.

The crewman who had been preparing the runabout for him leapt up onto the accommodation ladder and cast off. Bourne fired up the outboard engine and headed to a spot just left of the headland that jutted out into the Aegean like a questing nose. Gulls peeled away from the boat, circled him for a while, then wheeled away, calling their disappointment.

When he was close enough for the runabout to enter the shadow of the looming promontory, he steered it farther left. By this point, the headland was between him and the *Nym*. No one on board could see what he was doing or who was waiting for him.

She was sitting on a rise on the shingle, smoking a cigarette, watching him beneath half-lowered lids as he cut the engines, dropped anchor, and leapt into the shallows.

She made no move to help him, stayed where she was, giving him that peculiar sideways glance of hers as he picked his way up the shingle to her. She wore a revealing swimsuit of a metallic plum-colored fabric. She was turned so that he could see the ugly scar that ran along the outside of her right calf all the way up to her hipbone. It was clear the wound had been inflicted in many stages, a form of torture. He knew what had been carved into her beautiful back.

Her magnificent legs were very long, her waist thin. A scattering of freckles dusted the bridge of her nose. Her eyes changed color with the light—either midnight-blue or black. In all, she was staggeringly beautiful.

"Do you think what I'm wearing is appropriate?"

"For the beach, you mean."

She smiled a thousand-watt smile. They were more or less repeating their lines from last year, when they had met in Nicosia. Before that, Bourne hadn't seen her since he had spirited her away from Keyre's camp in Somalia. She had been younger then, no more than a girl, but Keyre had spent months torturing her, indoctrinating her as dictated by his Yibir traditions. What he had meant to do with her, Bourne had no idea, and if she knew she had never told him.

Her name was Mala Ilves, an Estonian by birth. No one but Bourne called her Mala now; few even knew the name. These days she was known only as the Angelmaker.

"For what we are here to do," she said.

"How can I answer? I don't know why you asked me to come here, to such an out-of-the-way place."

She turned her face up to the lowering sun. "It's peaceful here, isn't it?" That sideways glance again. "But it's also bloody."

"That was a long time ago, Mala."

"Not for me, it isn't." She ran her fingertips down the length of the scar. "It's only yesterday."

Bourne came and sat down beside her. "I don't believe that." She smelled of licorice and the sea and clean sweat. A far cry from the stench of blood and rotting flesh that rose off her when he had brought her here from Somalia.

She ran her hands through her thick hair. "I've never lied to you, Jason."

"How many times have you wanted to?"

She wet her lips with the tip of a pink tongue and laughed softly. "I cannot count the times."

He waited a moment before he spoke again. Sunlight glanced off the waves, spreading the last of its warmth toward them. A cormorant vanished from sight, returned to the surface a good three yards away with a silvery fish in its beak. Lifting its head to the sun, as Mala had, it swallowed the fish whole.

"So tell me, why have you brought me here?"

"Are you in such a rush? Do you have somewhere to go? Or someone to see."

The last was not a question, and a tiny curl of warning reared its head in the pit of his stomach. How much did she know about his recent life? Perhaps everything. He knew he would have to begin with that assumption and work his way back to the truth. One thing he would never do is underestimate her; everyone who had made that mistake was dead.

"No," he said. "I'm all yours."

That sideways glance and a sly smile. Did she believe him, or was she as wary of him as he was of her?

"You belong to no one, Jason. Not even the Israeli."

So she did know about Sara. He was angry; it felt like a violation of his private life. But he was not surprised. There had never been anything about Mala that honored privacy. All of that had been systematically stripped from her by Keyre. Lacking her own boundaries, she observed none in others.

"Is that why you brought me here, out of jealousy?" His tone was bantering; nevertheless, his question contained a sub rosa strata of intention.

"Would that be so bad?" She leaned against him, her skin warm, the pulse of blood beneath like a song. "But then I'm a bad girl. No one knows that better than you."

"The ones who knew that better than me are all dead."

She laughed. "Yes. I suppose that's true." She slid her leg against his. More warmth as the sun began to melt into the western horizon. "There is no time but time."

He knew what she meant by that. Time was what you made of it, how you apportioned it, what you trained yourself to remember. And to forget. Is that why he couldn't remember any further back beyond the point when he'd been shot and pitched into the black Mediterranean? He had almost died then. Or was there an incident far worse—so dreadful that his mind had blocked it out of self-preservation? Something even worse than what Mala had been through? What if he never knew? What if it was better for him not to know? But not knowing was a purgatory in and of itself.

"Poor Jason, a man without a history," she said, as if reading his mind. "At least I know who my parents were."

"And how much has that helped you?"

"Ouch. Right. Needling each other is not such a good idea, after all."

"Then why start?"

"Because I'm the scorpion."

She meant the old story: a scorpion found itself on the wrong bank of a river. It asks a frog to carry it on its back across the river. The frog wisely says, *But you'll sting me.* The scorpion replies with perfect logic: *Why would I do that? If I sting you we'll both die.* Frogs being logical creatures, it agrees. But halfway across the river, the scorpion stings the frog. As they're both about to drown, the frog cries piteously, *Why?* And the scorpion replies with perfect logic, *I'm a scorpion. It's my nature.*

Mala shrugged. "But what d'you care? You're no frog."

The failing light seemed to have congealed, and, strangely, the island they were on seemed to shrink into the oncoming darkness, the night being dominated by the black sea, the high brittle dome of stars, the rising of the moon, lanternlike low in the eastern sky.

They rose, Mala leading him up the steepening shingle and over a hummock of rock where she had stashed her hiking boots, her striped beach bag, and a midnight-blue cover-up, which she shrugged on as they began picking their way up and over the rock face.

"Are you hungry?" she asked.

"We could eat on the boat," he said. "There's a fine chef."

"I already made a reservation." Which hardly seemed necessary on this isolated spot in the Aegean; Skyros was not a particularly popular tourist destination.

A packed earth path appeared before them, wending its way over a rise and down. Soon enough paving stones heralded the advent of what passed for civilization here.

The tavern, when they came upon it, was lit up with strings of electric lights crisscrossing its cement patio, where tables and chairs were strewn as if at random. A smiling Greek greeted them with glasses of retsina and showed them to a table at the lip of the patio. From the edge, the fall-off was steep, and they had a picture-perfect view down past the promontory on their right to the cove off which the *Nym,* lights ablaze, lay at anchor.

"That's some legacy your friend left you," Mala commented as she settled into her chair. "He must have had many millions of petro-dollars stashed away."

Bourne stared at her. Was she deliberately baiting him again, or was she just making idle chatter? Either way, he didn't care for the topic. Food came, lots of it. Presumably she had pre-ordered. Everything was sea-fresh and delicious. She did not look at him while they ate, staring out at the mysterious night as if waiting for a communication only she could hear.

As it turned out, she was momentarily at a loss as to how to broach a subject she knew would be delicate, would raise any number of red flags for him. She waited until the plates had been cleared, coffee and more retsina served, and they were once again alone in the night.

"Your friendship with the late General Karpov has caused consternation—not to mention anger—in a number of quarters."

He stared at her, silent, wondering where this was going. Fireflies danced in the shrubbery, moonlight turned the rocks a metallic silver. The crash of surf against the shore was a dim rumble, running up the hill toward them.

She smirked, reached into her beach bag, drew out an eight-by-ten blowup, which she placed before him. "You never should have accepted Karpov's invitation to his wedding. There you are, for all the world's clandestine organizations to see, with the general's arm slung across your shoulders. Bosom buddies, that's the phrase, isn't it?" She laughed. "The Japanese would say 'huckleberry friends.' But they get all these odd translations from American pop songs." She meant, in this case, "Moon River."

"Jason, in all seriousness, this photo has caused a hornet's nest of angst within your own secret services. And as for the FSB, now that the general is gone, now that Timur Savasin discovered you made off with Ivan Volkin's ill-gotten gains, the first minister is also out for your blood."

"Someone's always out for my blood."

"And what about your Israeli inamorata?"

Bourne briefly thought about not answering her, but then realized that might be just what she wanted. "She met Boris, several times."

"Enemies . . . or friends?"

"Boris Illyich was not like that. If you knew him—"

"Little late for that, isn't it?"

He was about to go when she put her hand over his. "Sorry." She looked him straight in the eye. "Really." Still he remained half-risen. She lowered her voice: "You know every wound, every scar . . . you know how hideous my body is."

Bourne sat back down. "Which is what makes me sad."

"You see," she flared. "I knew it!"

"Mala, you misunderstand me. What Keyre did to you, the rituals he performed on you. You became his. But that doesn't have to be. You're stronger than that."

"But, as you see, I'm here with you. Now. Jealous of your Israeli who, I am certain, possesses a flawless body."

Bourne was determined to say nothing more on this subject.

She sighed. "I suppose I feel possessive of you. Our history. And then there's what you've done for Liis."

"Then the two of you have spoken at least."

Mala shook her head. "I tried, but Liis won't speak to me."

"What happened? She was hoping you'd make one of her performances."

"I did. I was in New York in the winter, when she performed at Lincoln Center."

"And you didn't come backstage to see her?"

"We're not cut from the same cloth. I'm death to her. I won't come near her."

Then he understood: that was when she had seen him with Sara. He frowned. "How long have you been surveilling me?"

She pursed her lips. "I strive to know as much about you as you know about me."

"But you never can."

"It doesn't stop me from trying." Then she tossed her head again. "Oh, come on, I have no evil designs on your Israeli."

Sara. Her name is Sara, Bourne thought. He had met the Mossad agent five years ago, had saved her life in Mexico City, had worked with her on and off since then. Last year, she had been falsely accused of murdering Boris. The idea of speaking her name in Mala's presence, of hearing her say it, seemed intolerable. These were two separate areas of his life. Instinct told him that bringing them together in any form was a recipe for disaster.

"Who *do* you have evil designs on?" he said, wanting to steer the conversation in another direction.

"The people who are now out to terminate you with extreme prejudice. And I do mean *extreme*."

"It's been tried before."

"I know, but this is different."

"How?"

"The Americans and the Russians are coming after you simultaneously. If you're not careful, they'll have you in a pincer movement, west and east converging on one target."

He considered this for a moment. "So you brought me here to warn me?"

She nodded. "Partly. And partly to—"

At that instant, the *Nym* was consumed by a series of oily fireballs. The rolling thunder of the detonations reached them seconds after the boat was engulfed.

And then its fractured components spewed high in the air, an infernal fountain.

3

"HAVE THEY FOUND ANYTHING?"

"Nothing, sir."

First Minister Timur Savasin, second only to the Sovereign himself, stood on the grounds of Boris Illyich Karpov's dacha, in the dense woods north of Moscow, hands on hips, sucking on a cigarette stuck in the corner of his mouth. In front of him a squad of men were digging, burrowing, banging on walls and floorboards, checking for false backs in cupboards, secret niches under the stairs, in other words tearing the interior apart. Off to his left, a bulldozer sat idling, while its operator smoked a cigarette. Behind that was the huge flatbed that had transported the machine out here from Moscow.

"No money, no log books, no lists? Not a fucking thing?" he asked in a voice made brittle by frustration.

"No, sir."

He was answered by Igor Malachev, a Kremlin *silovik* who was his second-in-command. Karpov had muscled his way to become the head of both the FSB, the successor to the Soviet KGB, and FSB-2, the anti-narcotics organization. Never again would one man wield such power; the Sovereign had purged all of Karpov's people from the nine FSB directorates. He had named Konstantin Ludmirovich to head the FSB. As for FSB-2, that posting was still vacant. The appointment had come as a shock to Savasin. He had not spoken to Konstantin in five years. Perhaps this was the Sovereign's attempt at a path to a rapprochement. On the other hand, it was just as likely the Sovereign's way of pointing out to both men who really pulled the strings in the Russian Federation. General Karpov had gotten far too powerful right under the Sovereign's nose; clever Karpov had found a way to game the system. That kind of clandestine disobedience would never happen again, the Sovereign's action had made that perfectly clear. Either way, having to deal with Konstantin on an almost daily basis returned to Savasin the old, ugly, and humiliating nightmares. However, with the Sovereign's blessing, Savasin had elevated Colonel Alecks Volodarsky to head of *spetsnaz*, the FSB's Special Forces.

"All right. Go ahead and bulldoze the fucker."

"Really? It's such a beautiful dacha."

Savasin laughed under his breath. Malachev was so transparent—one of his assets, as far as Savasin was concerned: *"Keep the reins tight on your horses; feed them only oats you grow yourself,"* his father had taught him; the old man might have been cruel, might have loved his vodka a bit too much, but he was no one's fool. It was a good lesson for Malachev to learn: seeing the dacha he coveted leveled, and he himself giving the order for its destruction.

Afterward, in the plush backseat of the armor-plated

limousine transporting them back to Moscow Center, Malachev said, "Sir, what was it exactly you were looking for?"

Savasin sat back, thinking that if it were Karpov sitting next to him, after having searched a rogue general's dacha, he would already know the answer. But then Karpov was nobody's lapdog, not even the Sovereign's; that sonuvabitch did whatever the hell he pleased, including marrying a Ukrainian with dissident ties. Clever people like him had no business wielding so much power in the Federation; they were far too dangerous.

He sighed now, staring out at the blurred landscape, which was becoming more muscular with Brutalist buildings shoulder to shoulder like staunch Russian soldiers the closer they got to the ring road that girdled the metropolis.

"It seems that the general had any number of secret initiatives he was commanding before he died."

"Without the Sovereign's knowledge?"

Malachev seemed shocked, but was he really? Savasin asked himself. "Precisely. I am assured we've dismantled them all."

"Why do I sense the other shoe is about to drop?"

"You're right," Savasin said smugly. "General Karpov's best friend, the American Jason Bourne, was in country several times over the last year."

"He was at the general's wedding, I recall."

The first minister nodded. "Indeed. But he returned later on, around the time that Ivan Volkin died. I have no doubt Bourne murdered him, and took with him an enormous amount of money I believe Karpov had stolen from who knows where."

"So Bourne is ground zero for answers," Malachev said, finally getting with the program.

"There is no question in my mind." Savasin shifted from one buttock to another to ease a cramp in his calf. "Which is why I would dearly like to dispatch a Vympel *spetsnaz* death squad to take Bourne out—if we only knew where he was. With his termination we will finally be able to bury the last of Boris Illyich Karpov."

"That's Volodarsky's bailiwick," Malachev pointed out. "I've warned you about him."

"Stop." Savasin had taken out his mobile. "Volodarsky has assured me he's close to pinning Bourne's location down." He began to text as they arrived at their destination. "But just in case, Igor, I wish you to make your own inquiries. Discreetly, of course."

"Always," Malachev said, letting himself out.

Savasin did not miss the wolfish smile on his second-in-command's face.

Françoise Sevigne heard the knock on the hotel room door and, with one last emoji, sent her last text before dropping her mobile into her oversize handbag. Françoise came away from the window overlooking the marina in Kalmar, Sweden. Kalmar was in the southeast of the country, with easy access to the Baltic, via the Kalmar Strait, a narrow body of water separating the Swedish mainland from its largest island.

She opened the door for Justin Farreng, a slim, sandy-haired man with a perpetually harried expression. He slipped into the room, and she closed the door after him, double locking it. He was on her in an instant, his need overwhelming. She welcomed it as a mother welcomes the need of her child, as a totality, as something only she can assuage.

He took her up against the wall, as he often did, a breathless time when they made love like war, their clothes rucked, the fabrics rubbing skin to red welts, their voices rising and falling like a tide. The second time was in bed, naked, comfortable and comforting, slower but also fierce, in the way they threw each other around, like wrestlers grappling. Then rest. Perhaps twenty minutes of deep sleep for him, a letting go of the anxieties he carried around as a salesman clutches his samples case. The third time was languid, warm water cascading down on them from the showerhead. He lifted her as easily as he would lift a child, hands cupped against her buttocks, their heat rebuilding itself from glowing embers, heating the water as well as themselves. Steam enveloped them.

Later, reclining on the bed, propped up on one elbow, she watched while he dressed. "You're leaving early."

"I have a tight schedule."

She laughed softly, scrambled over the bed, sat at the foot, legs spread, thrilling to how instantly his gaze was magnetized.

"Stay," she said.

"I can't. I'm meeting—"

She spread her thighs further. Their insides were still wet. "A man like you . . ."

Half dressed, he came toward her, close enough for her to unzip his trousers. She pulled him down on top of her, guided him into her.

She stared up into his eyes but saw nothing of interest. Weeks ago, she had realized there was nothing but shiny surface frosting. What lay beneath was nothing—nothing at all. Justin had been born into poverty. His father took six weeks to die from a factory accident that took his leg and part of his hip. No one could be bothered to reduce his pain, let alone try to save his life. As a consequence, Justin had one holy mother of an axe to grind with the world at large. He was a very determined man; this made him incautious, even reckless. Foolish, in other words, though there could be no doubt that in matters of getting his revenge he was smart as a whip.

When they were done, she rolled him off her. Stretching full length, she reached under a pillow. Farreng had good reason to feel harried; he was wanted in a number of countries for publishing damning documents hacked off government, corporate, and institutional servers. These leaks had already caused consternation and chaos across the world—hence Farreng's status as a wanted man. LeakAGE, Farreng's organization, was proudly reliant on third-party whistleblowers, whose identity it protected with the ferocity of a lioness with its cubs. The trouble came in vetting the LeakAGE sources, of which Françoise Sevigne was one. He'd never give her up, she knew that even before the first time she had slipped her arms around him and pressed her body against his, felt his instant arousal. That was six months ago, and nothing had changed. His ardor for her burned just as bright.

Smiling, she handed him a thumb drive filled with files painstakingly manufactured expressly for him by agents of First Minister Timur Savasin.

4

THEY REACHED THE runabout at breakneck speed. Neither of them had said a word following the *Nym*'s violent demise. Mala climbed into the runabout first, began to bring up the anchor. Bourne took the helm, started the engines. As soon as the anchor cleared the water, Bourne went full throttle. If Mala hadn't been braced she would've been tossed head over heels.

The sky above where the boat had been was a livid bruise. They could smell the aftermath of the explosions. The stink of marine fuel was in their nostrils. The moon and the stars had vanished into the spreading cloud of smoke and debris blown apart into what amounted to nothing more than grains of sand.

"Jason, what are you doing?" Mala asked as soon as she realized Bourne was heading directly toward the area of the disaster. "You can't believe anyone could have survived those explosions."

"No," he said grimly. "No one's survived."

"Then why are you—?"

"Quiet." His gaze was fixed on the way ahead. "Just be quiet."

She stared at him for a moment, shook her head, then, with a shrug, directed her attention to the debris field. She tried to see what he was seeing, without success. This journey was a mystery to her, and this made her uncomfortable.

They came up on the landward perimeter of the debris field quickly. Bourne still had the outboard at full throttle. Their eyes began to burn from the residue in the air. There was still a good deal of heat; at one spot the water appeared to be boiling, but the smoke made it difficult to see anything clearly. It was like entering a low-lying fog bank.

Mala could see debris bobbing all around them, most of it unrecognizable, until they passed a human arm, twisted and blackened, all the hair burned off. And then a foot, bones poking through. The stench was momentarily sickening.

Bourne plowed through all this at high speed. The instant they breached the far side of the debris field, they saw the patrol boat, lying to, motionless several thousand yards from them.

"Why are they still here?" Mala asked no one in particular. "What are they waiting for?"

"The last diver," Bourne said, cutting the engines.

Guiding her behind the wheel, he handed her the Steyr. Stepping to the gunwale, he removed his shoes, jacket, and trousers. Pulling up one of the cushions, he opened and felt around in the storage cabinet and removed a flying gaff, used to bring large fish up onto the boat. Pulling the hooked head off, he filled his lungs, then dove into the water.

Beyond the debris field, the smoke had risen, then dissipated in the freshening wind driving westward. Shimmering silver light from the full moon slanted down through the water. Almost immediately, he saw the piercing light emanating from the forehead of the diver as he headed away, toward the boat rocking gently on the surface. Bourne had rightly figured that divers had attached explosives to the hull of the *Nym* under the waterline. It was the most logical route to destruction; it was the one he himself would have used. Plus, no one had come onto the boat when they had briefly docked to resupply in Istanbul; he'd taken care of that himself. The process of elimination had been short and to the point.

Powerful swimmer though he was, the diver was too far away for him to make it without fins. He was about to kick up to catch some air rather than catch the diver, when a dark shadow appeared below him. It was as if the sea floor were rising toward him. A ripple of great wings told him all he needed to know. He waited as the creature rose, then he reached down and grabbed onto the upper part of the reef manta ray's mouth. The manta jetted forward with such speed that Bourne's arm was almost pulled out of its socket. Like its close cousin, the shark, the creature was all muscle. He could feel the power of the ray rippling the currents around it, sending patterns outward like a rock thrown into a lake.

Bourne's lungs ached, but he had been repeatedly waterboarded as part of his Treadstone training; his lungs held air as well or better than most free divers.

As if sensing its passenger's mission, the manta put

on even more speed. The diver's silhouette bloomed in front of him. He was very close when the diver, feeling the pressure of the manta's approach, turned toward the disturbance. He saw the manta first and jerked in shock. That was when Bourne let go of his perch, pushed himself upward, and slammed into the diver.

The diver already had his knife out, and he slashed at Bourne wildly, disconcerted by both the ray and Bourne's sudden appearance. With a froth of bubbles, Bourne swept the diver's mouthpiece off, jammed it into his own mouth. He felt the serrated blade slide down his chest, opening a wound from which blood drifted. He grabbed the underside of the diver's mask, ripped it off. The diver flailed at it, and Bourne drove the hooked end of the gaff into the meat of his right arm. He let go of the knife in an automatic gesture to cover the wound with his hand.

The diver was done. Bourne turned him, grabbed him around the neck, dragging him back toward where Mala was standing watch on the runabout. He surfaced farther away than he had calculated, then saw that Mala had wisely backed the runabout into the debris field to keep herself hidden. A few more powerful strokes brought him to the side of the runabout. He spat out the mouthpiece, drew in the rich night air.

Mala ran to the nearside gunwale. Setting the Steyr down, she knelt to help keep the diver against the runabout while Bourne unhooked the diver's oxygen tanks and other scuba gear, which he hoisted into the runabout.

Mala heaved the diver aboard, and Bourne followed, launching himself out of the water and over the gunwale. She saw his chest wound first, but he waved her away toward their prisoner.

"Just a scratch." He put one hand over the diver's mouth, then wrenched the gaff out of his arm. The man's shout was muffled to a deep grunt.

Meanwhile, Mala was examining his wet suit and equipment. "American government issue," she said. "Part of a CIA hit team, I would imagine."

"Not necessarily." Bourne pulled off the diver's neoprene cap, stared down at his unfamiliar face. The man seemed to be going in and out of consciousness. Bourne slapped him hard across the face, then again when the diver gave no sign of coming around.

His eyes opened; he stared up at Bourne, and said, "Where the hell did you come from?" In the same instant, he drew a thin-bladed knife from inside the cuff of his neoprene sleeve and jabbed it upward toward Bourne's throat.

There was no time to pull away, but Mala interjected her forearm, her scars so hard and tough the knife point, driven fast but, owing to the diver's position, without much energy behind it, glanced off them. Bourne drove his fist into the diver's face, fracturing his nose. Blood fountained. Bourne snatched the knife away, threw it across the width of the runabout.

He glanced up for a moment, caught Mala looking at him. He took her arm, checked. Not even a scratch to her scars. He nodded and she smiled. Then she jammed the same forearm against the diver's throat. He looked up at her and laughed, spitting out blood pouring from his ruined nose.

Mala didn't like that. Scrambling over the deck, she

retrieved his knife, brought it back to where he lay, Bourne pinning him in place.

"Time you told us who you work for," Bourne said.

"Some nerve." The diver's voice was thick and half-strangled by blood. He had a Tennessee mountain accent.

"Reconsider."

"Fuck you and the bitch you rode in on."

Mala liked that even less. With one swift, practiced motion, she slit the diver's neoprene suit lengthwise. Reaching down, she plucked at delicate things like a fisherman about to gut her catch.

The diver's eyes flickered. His face had gone unnaturally pale in the smoke-hazed moonlight. "What's happening?"

"You killed my captain," Bourne said. "You killed my crew."

The diver spat pink. "It should have been you."

"But it wasn't." Bourne leaned closer. "I'm still here, and you . . . well, you know where you are." Closer still. "But not what's going to happen to you."

"What is—?"

His voice was cut off by a scream. Mala had made an economical but very deep horizontal cut. She held her prize up for the diver to see. "I don't like being called a bitch," she said with remarkably little malice in her voice. "This is how much I don't like it." She threw the bloody sac overboard.

The diver shuddered and shook. Soon enough, Bourne knew, he would go into shock, and then he'd lose the opportunity that had been afforded him. Mala should never have cut off his balls. He suspected that making a preliminary incision would have been enough. But this was the Angelmaker, not Mala. He had to keep that firmly in mind going forward. Whatever she had been, the person he had saved, tended to, had been warped beyond all recognition by Keyre and his Yibir rituals.

The diver was starting to convulse. Bourne had only a matter of minutes before he passed into unconsciousness and, unless they could stop the bleeding in his nose, arm, and between his legs, which he thought unlikely, he'd bleed out in a matter of fifteen or twenty minutes at the most.

Pressing down hard on the diver's shoulders, he said, "You know my name. What's yours?"

"Smith..." He tried to laugh, blew blood bubbles. "Or Wesson."

Using his name would help focus him, keep him in the here and now. Who knew, maybe delirious as he was becoming he'd think he was among compatriots.

"Who do you work for?"

His eyes, red-rimmed and dull with pain, peered up at Bourne, as if through a hailstorm; it was impossible to tell who or what he was seeing. "Go fuck yourself." His voice was a reedy whisper.

"Who sent you after me? Who gave the termination order?"

The diver arched up. His eyes were going in and out of focus. He produced a macabre grin; his gums were bloody.

"Tell me. Who's your boss?"

"Right, yeah." Smith's eyelids began to flicker. His eyeballs were rolling up.

"Smith. Smith!" Bourne slapped him hard across the cheek. "Stay with me."

"Right."

"Can't do that until you give me the name of your—"

A froth of blood bubbled from between Smith's lips. "You'll never . . ." One shuddering breath. More blood. Then everything stopped, most significantly Smith's heart.

5

MARSHALL FULMER DID not like Sweden—
too namby-pamby for him. The Swedes had no back-
bone, in his not-so-humble opinion. Cowards, all of
them. And he liked Kalmar even less than Stockholm,
where he could never get his bearings. It wasn't like a
real city, let alone the capital of a country, but perhaps,
he reflected during a lull in the meeting, it was just what
the Swedes deserved.

Kalmar was nearest the Baltic States, nearest the
western tip of the Russian Federation, which, Fulmer
supposed, was why it had been chosen by NATO to
hold the Baltic Alliances Conference. As national security advisor, it was incumbent on him to monitor
this high-level conference hastily assembled to form a
strong and united response to Russia's increasing bel-
licosity toward the Baltic States, and to offer support
as part of the American contingent that included a
four-star general from the Pentagon and a mandarin

from the DoD, amusingly masquerading as a military attaché about seven levels below his actual pay grade. Well, that was the way the DoD worked, manifesting mysteries and obfuscations all over the ranch.

Fulmer, seated between the Pentagon general and the DoD mandarin, kept his own council. He was from Western rancher stock—Montana, to be exact. He continued to maintain his family ranch outside Bozeman, and over summer recess spent his time out there riding, herding cattle, hunting, fly-fishing the stream that ran through the north side of the property, and genuinely unwinding.

With his leathery skin and wind-crevassed face, Fulmer looked the part. Mounted on a horse, he could have passed for any number of renowned cowboys out of history. And he had built a reputation inside the Beltway of being a bit of a cowboy. Which meant he shot off his mouth almost as often as he shot his collection of sidearms at his gun club range. Out on the Bozeman ranch he was a crack shot with a scoped rifle.

His colleagues put up with his shenanigans, his media-hogging sound bites primarily, because of the power he had accrued throughout the right corridors in Washington. He was friends with all the right people, all the movers and shakers, left wing as well as right wing. He, better than anyone else, had honed the spectacularly difficult art of walking the political tightrope between parties. He certainly knew how to twist arms when he had to, but he could also charm the pants off just about anyone whose vote he needed.

Now, as the joint session was about to resume, his mobile buzzed. Not his official office mobile—the other one he switched out twice a month. Removing it from his pocket, he looked down at the screen as he held the phone below the table.

A time and a local address. He glanced at his watch. The time was twenty minutes from now. He gathered the papers laid out before him, which he'd barely glanced at, and stuffed them into his slim calfskin brief-case, pushed his chair back, and asked the men on either side of him to carry on while he attended to business back in D.C. They nodded their understanding. Both of them had business back in D.C. from time to time. It was business as usual.

Max, his bodyguard, was at his station just outside the door to the conference room. Naturally enough, he started to dog Fulmer's tail as Fulmer headed for the private elevator that whisked attendees directly to the floor the conference had taken over.

"Stay," Fulmer said, as he punched the down button.

"But, sir—"

"This is Sweden, not Syria."

The elevator doors slid open, and Fulmer stepped in.

"Make yourself useful," he said, dismissing Max. "Go check to see that the Russians haven't tossed my room or something."

Outside the post-modern, anonymous building at which the meeting was being held, he paused to take several deep breaths. The security was duck-ass tight; not a creature was stirring that wasn't connected via wireless earwig to central station trucks just past the human perimeter. Fulmer ignored them all—they had become such a part of his life he scarcely noticed them.

By far the worst part of his job was the endless meetings he was obliged to attend, not to mention chair. Meetings were a waste of time, period. They were the sinecure of the indecisive and the weak-minded. And yet, he was more than willing to put up with the constant irritation in order to reap the myriad benefits of his powerful position.

What would his simple rancher father make of the place his son had carved out for himself in the world's most potent seat of power? Probably wouldn't have believed his son until Marshall toured him around his domain. Sadly, that was impossible; Marshall's parents had died in a barn fire twenty years ago. They'd both rushed into the barn to save their prized horses; neither horses nor his parents had made it out alive. Were their deaths a testament to the high esteem in which they held their horses or to their foolishness? Marshall had never been able to figure that out.

He waved off his car, set off to the west at a brisk pace. Using the GPS on his burner mobile he made his way to the Baronen Köpcenter, a vast mall near the water. Inside, he checked the directory for Stars and Bars, a sports café on the second floor. He took the escalator up. He saw the open entrance to Stars and Bars right away, but he turned on his heel, heading in the opposite direction. For the next seven or eight minutes, he wandered in and out of shops and storefronts. Inside each, he checked every person who entered after him, looking for individuals who repeated. He saw none.

Certain that he hadn't been followed, he retraced his steps, entering the café within thirty seconds of the time sent to him. He prided himself on being a man of promptness—something else his father wouldn't have recognized in his adult son. On the ranch, chores got done, but no one looked at their watches.

The young woman sat with a straight back and a certain sense of herself that Fulmer found extremely attractive. She was sitting at a table by herself, sipping at a cup of coffee into which she periodically poured what appeared to be a clear liquid—possibly vodka—from an old-fashioned glass. For long moments, he stood, transfixed, regarding her with curious concentration. Then, as if making up his mind about something, he strode through the crowded café, sat down in the molded plastic chair opposite her.

His face creased in a smile. "*Bonjour*, Françoise."

She wrinkled her nose, set her cup down with no little energy. "How many times have I asked you not to mangle my native language," Françoise Sevigne said.

"*Vous ne voulez pas la façon dont je parle français? Comment provincial!*"

"You're laughing at me in terrible French!"

"What of it?" His smile broadened. "Are you so thin-skinned?"

"You know that I'm not."

He nodded. "Indeed, I do."

"Then why do you do it?"

He grinned. "Try as I might, I cannot help myself." He spread his hands. "You French. I can't help thinking of the Maginot Line: what you considered impregnable the Germans turned to paper."

Her expression hardened. "You think this is amusing?"

"*Mademoiselle*, that is history. On a more personal front, what we have here is so far from amusing I find I must joke about it in order to keep my mind on an even keel."

This response seemed to mollify her—even give her food for thought. Pouring the rest of the liquor into her coffee, she stirred it with a spoon, then pushed the cup across the table to a spot between his two hands. Before she could withdraw, he traced a tiny circle on her forefinger with the tip of his.

"I think it best our relationship remain professional, Mr. Fulmer."

Fulmer's expression remained placid. "As you wish, Françoise. But I thought the French..." He shrugged. "Never mind." He raised the cup to his lips and drank it down in one.

He cleared his throat. "So," he said in his best congressional hearing voice. "How is your friend?"

"That one is no one's friend," Françoise said shortly. "Especially mine."

"Yes, yes. I know all about what he does to little girls."

"I don't think you know the half of it," she said. "Otherwise you wouldn't be doing business with him."

Fulmer inclined his head. "And you?"

Françoise shuddered visibly. "I'm a go-between."

"To interface with anyone."

"I go where the money is."

Fulmer pursed his lips. "You see, that's the difference between us. I go where the power is." He regarded her from under hooded eyes. "Do you really believe your road is higher than mine?"

She turned away, her eyes searching past the customers coming and going. A young woman entered

pushing her baby in a pram; three men in suits, all staring into the faces of their mobiles, sauntered slowly out.
Beyond, the agglomerated sounds of the mall, echoing
as if they were underwater, filtered into the café between the shouts of those at the bar. The flat-screen
was showing a football match between Real Madrid and
Manchester United.

Since it seemed clear Françoise had chosen not to answer, Fulmer opted to push on. "Back to our—to Keyre."

Françoise swung her head back toward him. "Everything's on schedule. But there are new players in the
field. Circumstances have dictated a higher price."

His eyes narrowed. "How much higher?"

"Double."

"That's nosebleed territory."

It was her turn to shrug. "I don't set the price, I just
report it."

"Tell him I agree. But that's the limit. Tell him he's
hit the ceiling. I'm done negotiating."

"Don't worry. I'll make him see your point of view."

"That's what I'm paying you for." He pushed the
coffee cup away. "Now I have another job for you."

"I'm full up."

Fulmer extracted a small leather-bound notepad
from his breast pocket, wrote a figure down with a
Mont Blanc pen. Tearing off the sheet, he pushed it
across the table to her. "Half of that is already in your
Gibraltar bank. All that's required is a phone call from
me to have it transferred to your account."

Françoise crumpled up the paper, stuck it in a plastic
ashtray, burned it. "Pretty sure of yourself, aren't you."

"I make it a point to know the people I hire."

"Bien," she said softly. "What's the assignment?"

"I want you to find out where Justin Farreng is getting his recent leaks."

Françoise sat stock-still. After a long, agonizing moment, she regained her ability to think clearly. "I'm a go-between, not a detective."

"From where I sit, knowing what you've accomplished for me, there's scarcely any difference."

"Still..."

He shrugged again. "If you don't want the money, I'll find—"

"I didn't say that." Her fingertips turned the ashtray around and around.

"Too much money to leave on the table. So much this could be your last score. You could get out of the game, lie on a beach in Bali or Phuket. Attract the muscled surfer boys. Sleep to your heart's content."

She licked her lips. "Why do you want to know...Farreng's source?" *Good God,* she had almost said "Justin."

"LeakAGE has always been a pain in our asses," Fulmer said. "But as of late Farreng has been spilling open some unpleasant business regarding Reade and Dunlop."

"The law firm in Panama." She regarded him carefully. "Are you a client?"

He shook his head. "But one of my shell companies uses another Panamanian firm."

"Name?" When he hesitated, she said, "I can't help you if I don't know their name."

"Musgrave-Stephens."

"Have you had any indication that Musgrave-Stephens has been hacked?"

"No, but I'm figuring it's just a matter of time."

"Then get your shell company out."

"Getting the company out is a snap. But then where to?"

"I suggest Fellingham, Bodeys."

"Never heard of them."

"That's the point, isn't it," Françoise said with a sly smile. "They take very few clients; they're extremely exacting, conservative to a fault."

"Sounds like just the ticket."

She produced a gold-edged card with raised lettering in a flowing script, handed it to him. "Tell them you're a client of mine."

"Is there anything you can't do for me, Françoise?"

"I seriously doubt it."

He laughed, putting the card away.

"I have another suggestion."

"Fire away."

"You want to be the presidential nominee in the next election, yes? I want to be sure you're not derailed."

"And how would that work, exactly?"

"Dirt, Mr. Fulmer. Have you brought the dirt?"

He grinned. "As we discussed." Slapping his briefcase on the table, he opened it, felt around for the hidden compartment, took out a thumb drive and held it up for her to see.

"And where are you getting the material from?"

"The deep, dark web." Fulmer laughed shortly. "That's strictly need-to-know." He twirled the thumb drive between his fingers. "What I want, what you need to tell me, is how you intend to use this."

Without hesitation, Françoise plucked the miniature drive from his fingertips. "I will have Farreng's source

feed LeakAGE this material detrimental to your enemies. In no time, you'll be sitting pretty as the obvious
next presidential candidate."

There was something greedy about Fulmer's smile.
He made the call transferring her fee into her account,
exorbitant as usual, but worth every penny.

"Nous avons toujours fait comprendre mutuellement,"
he said, murdering both the grammar and the pronun-
ciation, as was his wont. *We always did understand each
other.*

———

Françoise's loathing for Marshall Fulmer knew no
bounds. On the other hand, she was determined to take
as much of his money as she could lay her hands on.
This conflict—emotion on one side, practicality on the
other—was not unknown to her. Still, she needed to
consider each episode as it arose. The conflict was uppermost in her mind as she made her way out of the
Baronen Köpcenter and onto the docks.

It was a fine day. The sun shone brightly down on
her, small puffy clouds floated by. Boats, skiffs, and ships
drifted past. She might have been in a scene from a cartoon or a children's book. However, the life she was
living was strictly X-rated. She went to the rail overlooking the harbor, leaned on it with her elbows. One of
the clouds looked like a lamb, which reminded her to
make a dinner reservation for tonight at Aifur Song, a
new buzzy restaurant. Even Kalmar hadn't been left out
of the latest culinary wave sweeping around the world.

Perhaps twenty minutes later, a young man with dark

hair and even darker eyes came and stood near her. He held an expensive Hasselblad with which he was taking what appeared to be professional photos of the harbor. Despite his age, he already had the spidery red cheeks of the inveterate vodka drinker. He was known to Françoise. His name was Nikolay Ivanovich Rozin. Back home in Moscow, a city she had not seen in ten years, she knew him as Niki. Here, outside the Federation, he was Larry London, a freelance photographer for Global Photographics.

"Time," Larry London said as he clicked away on his Hasselblad.

"I don't like to be kept waiting."

"He knows that."

Without uttering another word or waiting for a reply he knew wouldn't come, he strode away, ostensibly to find another perspective on the harbor and its inhabitants.

Françoise waited for more time than she should have, then turned, went through a waist-high metal gate that led down to the marina itself. She felt the wooden slats shifting slightly beneath her feet as she made the transition from dry land to water.

The boat was at anchor three-quarters of the way down the dock, on her left. It was blue-and-white, a motored sailboat with the name *Carbon Neutral* painted across its stern. It had beautiful lines—sleek and trim—a pleasure boat rather than one made for fishing.

No one welcomed her as she stepped aboard. The deck was clear, but as she neared the cabin she heard music. As she closed on the hatch, which was pinned open, she heard Edith Piaf singing and made a face.

"You've dated yourself, I'm afraid," she said as she descended into the cabin.

"I thought the French music was a fine touch."

"I'm more a Mylène Farmer fan."

He grunted, waved her to an upholstered bench that would turn into a bunk this evening.

"Bourne," he said. "Have you found him?"

"He's on the Aegean."

"The Aegean Sea is a very big body of water."

"Not for everyone. The Americans blew up General Karpov's boat."

He raised his eyebrows, thick as hedgerows, expressive as his late father's. "Did they now? Which Americans?"

Françoise laughed shortly. "Dreadnaught."

He laughed with her. "And Bourne was on board?"

"No idea."

"Those Americans." He shook his head. His hair, dictated by the latest fashion, was thick and shiny along the top, shaved close to his scalp on either side. "Can't count on them being the least bit useful. Bad as the British, these days, and that's saying something."

"Turn off that awful caterwauling, if you please." Françoise crossed her long legs. "Something more appropriate."

The man hit a button, then spun the wheel on his iPod mini and the Junkie XL soundtrack to *Mad Max: Fury Road* pounded forth from the surround sound speakers.

"No listening device yet devised can hear us through this," Gora Maslov said. He had taken over from his late father, Dimitri, as head of the Kazanskaya *grupperovka*, the Russian mafia family that ruled Moscow. In Dimitri's day, the Kazanskaya had majored in drug-running and black market cars. These days, under Gora's rule, the family trafficked in the final frontier territories dominated by stolen cyber weapons, virtual currency, organ harvesting, and humans.

"Well," Gora said, "it seems that being away from Mother Russia continues to agree with you."

She laughed, her white teeth showing briefly. "I've been off to see the world."

"And how is the world treating you?"

"Like an empress."

"Impressive." He grinned. "What would the Sovereign think?"

Françoise rose, fetched herself a drink from the built-in across the cabin, since it was clear that Gora wasn't going to do it. "You know, I think he would approve." She splashed vodka over ice cubes she grabbed from the half-size fridge. "I mean, he's also off to see the world, isn't he?"

She took a long swallow, went and stood before him. Then, without any warning, she slapped him across the face.

"What the fuck?" A red mark blossomed on his cheek, but he seemed unperturbed.

"Keeping me waiting."

"Business."

"Bullshit."

"You take everything too personally."

She shook her head. "I'm disappointed. For someone who's ostensibly part of the new wave, you can be disconcertingly old-fashioned."

"I take after my father." He watched her with glittering gimlet eyes.

She almost hit him again, but knew hot anger wasn't the answer. "You've been watching too many American gangster films." She took a sip of the chilled liquor. "*Scarface* is your favorite, if memory serves."

"That's right," he said tightly. "Keep at it."

"Or is it *Wall Street*?"

He stood up abruptly, and she saw the bulk of him, the gym rat physique, the violence that sheathed his muscles just under his skin.

"One day you'll push me too far."

She looked up at him from beneath long lashes. "That will be a very bad day for you, Gora."

His face went tight. "Is that a threat?"

"It's a promise."

His hands curled into fists. She knew he longed to incite her, which was why she stayed where she was, calmly sipping her vodka. To use the terms of one of his obsessions, he often reminded her of Sonny Corleone: quick to temper, a beat-down never far from his mind. Also, his Neanderthal Rat Pack attitude toward women—meant to be used, fucked, then thrown onto the scrap heap. But not before he delivered a good thrashing or three.

She'd witnessed that happen over and over again with all his girlfriends, even one-night stands, observing at a remove. The last few years, when she had been away from everything Russian, she had received her intel on him through third parties. His behavior kept repeating without letup; Gora was incapable of change. He was who he was—but then that was true of so many people it might as well be part of the human condition.

"Brother, sit yourself down," she said in Russian.

"Don't call me brother, Alyosha."

"My mistake, Gora." Having wound him up as revenge for keeping her waiting, it was up to her to get him to throttle back, to defuse the situation. He'd never be able to do it on his own.

As he sat, she poured some Coke over ice, handed him the cooling glass. As he drank, she placed her hand on his meaty shoulder. "There's room for both of us," she said softly and felt the muscles beneath her fingers lose their tension.

He drained the rest of the Coke and set the glass down, leaned his head back, and sighed. "There are days," he said, "when it doesn't seem so bad being away from home."

"Home is lonely, Gora." She sat down beside him, maintaining physical contact. He'd never had that growing up. "I know you miss Dimitri."

"It was that shit Karpov who gunned Father down. In a barber shop!" His eyes flashed. "Let me tell you, Alyosha, all debts will be paid."

She shook her head. "Karpov is dead, Gora."

"Until his best friend, Jason Bourne, is dealt with, my debt to Father will not be paid in full."

Françoise had to laugh at that, but not to his face. "Is that what all your recent maneuvering is all about?"

"To that end, maybe you could help me. It would mean returning to Moscow."

She shook her head. "I like it out here. I'm never coming home, Gora."

"So you think that wise?"

"Wise?" She cocked her head to one side. "I can't

say. Perhaps I no longer know what wise is. But I know I have to stay here."

"Why?" he asked. "Haven't you killed enough people yet?"

She snorted. "What is that, a joke?"

"I've never killed anyone in my life."

"No, you just order other people to do it," she said acidly.

"There's a difference."

She looked at him as if he were insane. But what was she to say? There was no rational response to an irrational statement, so she returned to the previous topic. "The guise of a go-between is perfect for me, Gora. Which is why I've no intention of returning."

"You disappoint me, Alyosha."

She stood, preparatory to leaving. "What else is new?" She'd had enough of him.

6

THE FOG OF death and destruction clamped them tight, kept them safe as Bourne and Mala, using the emergency oars clamped to the inside of the hull, rowed their way forward, away from the island of Skyros, toward the vessel holding the rest of the kill squad. The vessel had switched on its searchlight, which was aimed at the water. It was past time for "Smith" to have surfaced and swum back to his boat.

Reaching the outer perimeter of their cover of smoke, they shipped their oars momentarily, hauled Smith's corpse over the side, guided him toward the bow, then sent him off into the black water ahead of them. Then they rowed backward just enough that they were hidden again, but not so far that they couldn't see beyond the smoke field, which, in any event, was slowly but surely dissipating.

They could see "Smith" floating faceup, moving away from them on the currents. Bourne had been sure to keep him faceup, after he'd filled his lungs with air to keep him floating long enough for his comrades to spot him. Without his tanks, regulator, mouthpiece, and mask, he would keep afloat even longer.

"Will they find him?" Mala asked as she crouched beside Bourne in the bow.

"Wait for it." He pointed to the spot where Smith's bare feet, blue-white, veined as marble, drifted into the edge of the beam.

"There!"

The shout rushed at them across the water, and the beam swung wildly across "Smith," then past him, before swinging back, correcting. Bobbing in the low waves, he became a kind of metronome, his rhythm in tune with the sea.

The boat moved toward an intercept course. Beyond the searchlight's beam, it was lit up like an airport runway. They counted five men, including the driver. The hull struck the corpse, whirling it away for a moment before it was brought back alongside with a long-handled gaff.

"Christ," they heard someone say as "Smith" was hauled on board. "What the hell happened to Stone?"

"Caught in the blast?" someone else opined.

"His suit isn't shredded," a third voice broke in. "And where the fuck's his equipment?"

"Get ready," Bourne said, handing Mala an oar, taking up the other one himself.

"It's like he was stripped after he was killed," the first voice said.

Bourne and Mala were already rowing backward when the searchlight's beam extended outward, scanning the water between the vessel and the debris field.

Reaching farther, the beam hit the smoke, reflecting backward as car headlights will in dense fog.

"The smoke won't keep us hidden for much longer," Mala whispered.

"With luck, it won't have to."

The searchlight beam kept reaching out, closer and closer toward them. But the closer it got, the more diffuse it became, the more the light was reflected back into the hit team's faces. The vessel began to inch forward.

"Here they come," Mala whispered.

"We hold our position."

"But they'll—"

The vessel came on, slowly but surely. They were close enough to make out one man straining to scan the debris field with night-vision goggles. But again the smoke refracted the spotlight's beam into his eyes. He was, in effect, blind.

Abruptly, he held up one fist, and the vessel came to a halt. Then he lifted a forefinger, circling it. The boat's engines engaged with a deeper sound, and with a roar, the boat made a neat one-eighty, its wake bright in the moonlight.

"Okay," Bourne said. Mala shipped the oars while he moved to the helm, fired up the engine, which would not be heard over the larger vessel's roar. They took off after the hit team, all running lights extinguished, the glow from the instrument panel masked by a towel.

Luck was with them: the lowering moon had been occluded by a bank of thickening clouds within which, every so often, flashes, like jagged shards of glass, winked on and off, semaphoring an oncoming storm.

The wind had picked up; it was against their faces.

The chop increased. In their wake, the smoke had vanished. The night was clear, the last of the *Nym* gone to its watery grave. Somewhere back there, dorsal fins would be cleaving the wave-tops. Sharks would be circling.

Bourne's face was grim as he followed the hit team's vessel as it made a wide, sweeping curve to port in what he now believed would be a semicircle heading back to Skyros.

The Americans' pursuit reminded him that the purge of Boris's friends, colleagues, and family was still under way, both in Russia and the U.S. It wouldn't be complete until all signs of him and his affairs had been eradicated, his past achievements credited to others in typical Russian revisionism fashion. In Bourne's heart only would the real Boris Illyich Karpov remain alive.

A change in pitch on the boat they were following knifed through his sorrow. Immediately, he cut the engine on the runabout, listened to the sea and the night. The rising wind was now at their backs; the runabout wallowed in the deepening troughs. Behind them, the first throaty rolls of thunder could be heard. The night was now very dark as storm clouds continued to overrun the starlight.

Bourne could make out the looming cliffs of Skyros, blacker than black, sensed their solidity as the wind struck them and lifted off them. Now he had no doubt that the hit team was headed to the island, rather than to a ship lying to. Anyway, the team had had no time to mobilize a ship, as it had no idea where the *Nym* was headed; even the captain hadn't known until almost the last moment.

Their runabout, having a smaller engine, couldn't hope to keep pace with the hit team's vessel, but that wasn't Bourne's objective. All he needed was to ascertain where the boat was headed. Whether he got them there before or after the team debarked was immaterial.

And, indeed, by the time he guided the bucking runabout into shore, the vessel was deserted, lying to at anchor. The team was on dry land. A sudden gust of wind turned the runabout broadside, nearly shoving it against the sharp-toothed rocks, outliers of the cliff wall. Bourne restarted the engine, confident that it would not be heard over the wailing of the wind and the crashing of the waves. Surely, the larger vessel would bear the brunt of the storm and be smashed to pieces on the jagged teeth. Possibly that's precisely what the team wanted. If so, they had another means of egress off Skyros.

Bourne guided the runabout around the narrow headland, which would act as a natural barrier to the storm. The water was now shallow enough for Bourne to jump out, bring the runabout in via the nylon bow line. Water, pushed by the approaching storm, rushed up his thighs, over his waist, before momentarily being sucked away again. He made the line fast around a rock, hoped that thus protected leeward the runabout would survive.

Back in the runabout, he checked through all the cleverly concealed cabinets under the seat cushions, found fishing rods and rolls of lines, hooks, a scaling knife, which he jammed into his waistband. He stuffed all the rest of these, except the rods, into a well-used waterproof canvas bag, zipped it up. Then he went down on one knee, fiddling with a black box that depended from the bottom of the instrument panel.

"What are you doing?" Mala asked, but he made no reply.

Now both of them were in the churning surf, then onto the slippery rocks, picking their way to what passed for dry land in this inhospitable area of the island; there wasn't even a thin line of shingle to distinguish sea from land.

They ascended the cliff, finding hand- and footholds where they could. They rose into the wind, which, in no time at all, would seek to tear them off the rocks. The rain hadn't yet hit, but, like the pounding hooves of a charging cavalry, it was coming. Bourne knew they had to reach the cliff's summit and find shelter behind its peaks before that happened.

Mala was lighter than he was, which made her faster, but also more prone to being dislodged by the storm. Bourne struggled to keep up with her, prepared to catch her if she slipped or fell. They were nearing the top when the first raindrops, fat and far between, struck his back. The rock face, already slippery, would soon enough become impassable.

Sure enough, in the next instant Mala's anchor foot slipped as her other leg lifted upward for new purchase. Reaching out, Bourne grabbed her ankle, held her foot steady as she found a handhold above.

The raindrops became smaller, more numerous, until they were like needles trying to penetrate the climbers' sopping clothes. Bourne and Mala continued their assault on the cliff unabated; to slow or falter now would be fatal.

With her left hand, Mala grasped a vertical finger that jutted out from the body of the cliff. Using it as a fulcrum, she swung her body to the right, drawing her knees up to her chest just enough to miss crashing into a trio of rocks. Bourne followed her, grasping the rock finger higher up to accommodate his taller body, then swung himself as hard as she had.

He found himself in a small, triangular crevasse, a fault line near the apex of the cliff, pressed tightly up against her. If he reached up, extending his arm to its limit, his fingertips could just about grasp the cliff top. A violent gust of wind threatened to blow him sideways, the way it had the runabout, and a machine-gun burst of rain peppered his face and chest, for a moment blurring his vision. They had to risk moving to a safer spot. The weather was bad enough now, but the storm had not yet reached its full fury. As it did so, it would become more unpredictable.

He turned to see Mala watching him. By the expression on her face he knew she was thinking of another time, another place, another storm as violent as this one. Its ferocity was one of the things that allowed Bourne to rescue her out of the sacred place where Keyre "initiated" his girls, as he termed it. Bourne had been commissioned to fetch her, to bring her back from the "pits of hell," as her father termed it. He had told him that she and her younger sister, Liis, had been abducted by Somali pirates. During the aftermath, in talking to Liis while Mala was still feverish and in and out of consciousness, Bourne had discovered the father's treachery. His business in tatters, his debts run wild, he had sold his daughters into slavery. Delving deeper, information had come to him that their father had done all this in order to abscond with the money, leaving his old business partner and his irate debtors in Estonia behind, to forge a new life for himself.

After Mala was safe, after Bourne had seen to her many wounds, after he had secured for her and Liis a place to stay where they would be fed and protected and loved, he had, without telling them, dealt with their father. Had he really wanted his daughters to join him? Bourne hadn't given him the chance to lie again. Now it seemed as if storms had followed him halfway across the world, like the shrieking of the damned.

A burst of rain slammed them back against the walls of the crevasse, and Bourne knew it was now or never. Nodding to Mala, he waited for a brief lull in the wind-driven rain, rose on tiptoe, reached up as far as he could and grabbed at the highest part of the rock face. His fingers slipped as he tried to put his weight onto his right arm. He spun, feet off the ground like a hanged man, before Mala grabbed him around the waist, steadied him. He drove himself farther, got a firmer grip on the rock, hoisted himself up.

A vicious gust of wind caught him as he was about to roll over the top of the cliff. For perilous seconds he rocked back and forth, scrabbling for purchase as the wind tried its best to suck him out into the black void. His heart beat fast in his chest as he drove all extraneous thought out of his mind, narrowing his focus. Nothing existed save for the ridge of rock on which he vibrated and shuddered like a tree limb. Then, with a superhuman effort, he hurled himself over the ridge, down to a surface of rock rubble. Now the peak served as a kind of parapet, rising over his head, protecting him from the brunt of the storm.

But there was Mala to consider. Rising up over the parapet, slicing rain against his cheeks and in his eyes, he reached over and down. He called to Mala, but the howling of the storm tore his voice from his lungs, flung it far away. Still, she had had her hand up, waiting for him, and now she took him in a Roman grip—fingers grasped around wrist—and inch by agonizing inch, he lifted her out of the crevasse. In the last moments, one of her feet found solid rock, and with his help, she vaulted the rest of the way, landed, crouching beside him on the other side of the parapet.

"Are you all right?" he asked, over the wind.

She nodded. "You remember, right? When you took me and Liis." She could see in his eyes that he did. Her mouth moved, but for a moment nothing came out. "I didn't want to go. I wanted you to take Liis and leave me. With him."

"You fought me."

"Even bleeding all over, I fought you." She swiped the rain from her forehead but it was a losing battle. "But I didn't hurt you." She smiled, touched his cheeks with her fingertips so lightly it took him a moment to realize that she was mapping the configuration of his bones. "You can't imagine what happened."

"There will come a reckoning. One night when the moon is down."

"But not tonight." She blinked rain out of her eyes. "Tonight we have the American kill team to deal with."

"But not in the way you think," Bourne said, and seeing her brows knit together, he laughed softly. "I have a better idea."

MEME LLC'S STAFF did not like to see their boss angry, but this evening Morgana Roy was good and pissed. Her personnel in the field had relayed intel concerning the botched mission to terminate Jason Bourne with extreme prejudice. They could not identify the team, but Morgana had a gut feeling it was part of Dreadnaught Section, what her guys blackly referred to as SAMS—a special action murder squad, which is what the Nazi SS called their kill teams. Her people were an irreverent lot, which was just the way she liked it.

Although Meme LLC was an off-site, way off-the-books organization that was in no way connected to the U.S. government, it was still nominally a division of Dreadnaught, what she privately called "Arthur's Acres"—the untouchable domain he had carved out for himself within the clandestine services. Which was why Dreadnaught was allowed to have a black ops SAMS team.

After trying and failing twice to reach Mac on his encrypted mobile, she muttered, "Fuck it," and raced out of the office. The heated, muggy air drained all promise from spring. Belatedly, she realized that she was in too much of a hurry to return to where she'd parked her car. Back inside the office, she had Rose hand her the keys to one of the company cars. Moments later, she slipped behind the wheel of a Ford sedan parked on the street. She fired the ignition, cursed as a blast of hot air exited the vents.

Morgana liked MacQuerrie as a boss—he pretty much left her to do her own thing in the manner she felt best. That was a major perk of being off-site and so deeply blacked out from the rest of the government's acronymic agencies, who spent much of their time butting heads and snooping into each other's territory to make sure they weren't getting scooped. What a briar patch.

At that moment, she received a three-word text. She bit her lower lip, nodded to herself. She pulled out and raced down the street, heedless of what amber lights might come.

And then there were days like today when she felt run over, betrayed, marginalized, and totally out of the loop. After informing her of the über-secretive Karpov cyber initiative, after putting her in charge of stopping it, after informing her that Jason Bourne had taken it over from his old pal, MacQuerrie had gone out and ordered Bourne terminated.

Bourne's death is the last thing I want, she thought. *The very last thing this shitstorm calls for.*

She shook her head as she overtook a truck, accelerated into the left-hand lane. She had a heavy foot. In the long hours since Mac had given her her new brief, she and her team had parsed the vertical code he had sent her without even an iota of success. All they could tell her—and this she confirmed herself—was that the code delivered to them was a piece of the whole; a very small piece, indeed. Not nearly big enough to be the Rosetta stone to unlocking the full computer code.

As a consequence, she'd had a couple of her team members scour the web, monitoring chatter from the Russian Federation and their known affiliates, hackers lurking in their dark web dens, known purveyors of cyber weapons. They had turned up zero. She was beginning to consider the possibility that they would fail in their mission. That they wouldn't be able to decipher the code at all, and therefore wouldn't be able to stop it before it was deployed.

Two possibilities has occurred to her. One, the code was not yet complete. Two, it was complete but was being held in abeyance for some unknown reason. Bourne, had he been brought in alive, would have provided the answer to that vital question as well as the key to shutting this unthinkable weapon down for good.

Sure, Mac had told her that he was initiating new protocols to keep the nuclear codes safer than they already were. But who was to say those new protocols would be enough to stave off Karpov's cyber weapon? None of them could take that chance, least of all Mac. She had tried to make that crystal clear to him, but for some reason she had failed—or, more likely, he had failed to take her arguments seriously enough. People like Mac, career officers in the intelligence community, had blinders. They heard what they wanted to hear, they acted as they wanted to act, sure in the conviction that they knew best. This was particularly true when it came to ignoring intel on the ground that didn't fit their perception of the situation. She'd seen it happen again and again, aghast that no one learned from past mistakes. The old boys' club rules were rigidly—even obsessively—enforced to ensure hegemony, even when they ran counter to the rapidly changing situation in the field. They had invested themselves in a quasi-religious belief in the rightness of their iron-bound laws.

"Call Mac," she said to her Bluetooth-connected mobile. But, as before, the call went straight to voice mail. This time she didn't bother leaving a message. What was the point?

She raced along Route 175, headed toward NSA headquarters. She swerved around the vehicles in front of her, not caring how far over the speed limit she was pushing the car.

She knew she was spoiling for a fight. Part of her understood why Mac hadn't read her in to what he was doing: Mac was just doing his thing the way he always did his thing. But the fact was, the moment he had revealed that Bourne had taken up Karpov's mantle, he had involved her.

The bulk of the vast NSA complex loomed up before her, forcing her to finally slow down. But instead of heading to the perimeter, she veered off to the left, heading down narrower streets.

OTTO'S FINE EUROPEAN TAILORING, the stenciled lettering on the front window proclaimed. The building had once been painted white, but the pockmarked stucco façade was in dire need of multiple repairs. At cursory glance it looked abandoned, which was more or less the point.

Pushing through the front door, she passed into the tailor shop, where Otto, a balding man in his sixties, sat behind a waist-high counter, chalking up a suit jacket on a dummy. His own suit jacket was on a hanger hooked over the top of a full-length mirror. His shirt-sleeves were rolled up to the elbow, revealing powerful forearms. His vest held his tie close to his chest. The air smelled of cloth sizing and sour pickles. A half-eaten pastrami on rye lay on its waxed paper at his right elbow. No one else was in the shop.

Otto glanced at her through dust-speckled glasses and nodded as she went through the swinging door in the counter and down a narrow, ill-lighted hallway, through to a room at the rear of the building.

A figure sat in a chair behind a desk equipped with a laptop and several other pieces of equipment. A wide pool of light from the desk lamp fell across the face and hands of the shadowy figure.

"Hello, Morgana." A well-modulated female voice with perhaps just a touch of an indeterminate foreign accent. "Thank you for coming."

"I did debate with myself, Soraya."

"Understandable. You live a remarkably ordered life." Her beautiful profile was typical of Egyptian women but at the same time utterly unique.

There was no place for Morgana to sit, so she remained standing.

"And yet you're here."

"It seems my desk is not as comfortable as it used to be," Morgana said.

"Well said. Feel like stretching our wings a bit, do we?"

"An offer like yours . . . " Her voice faded out. Their

eyes locked; there seemed no reason to finish the sentence verbally.

There was a photo of a beautiful girl, age six, Morgana knew, on the desk. It was turned so that she could see it, deliberately, she supposed.

"How is Sonya?" she asked.

"Adjusting to life in America." There was a slight pause. "She doesn't remember her father. I am obliged to show her photos of him, but I'm not sure it does any good."

"I'm so sorry."

"Thank you. She would have loved him as surely as I did." Then, more brightly: "She misses you."

"We'll have to remedy that." Morgana cleared her throat. "Afterward."

"You have a concern?"

"Not exactly, but I'm so new at this."

"One of the things that makes you perfect for this particular brief." She used the British word for *assignment*.

"All right, then." Morgana nodded. "What would you have me do?"

"Go with the flow."

Morgana frowned. "Go with . . . ?" For a moment her alarm showed on her face. "Chaos."

Soraya inclined her head. "In a manner of speaking, yes." Her large, luminous eyes would not let Morgana go. "The brief is still of interest to you."

It didn't seem to be a question, nevertheless, Morgana answered. "It is."

"Saying good-bye to your very ordered life."

"I'm feeling claustrophobic. In a manner of speaking."

"Also frustrated, I imagine."

Morgana blinked. "I beg your pardon?"

"The bit of code General MacQuerrie sent you."

Morgana opened her mouth to ask how Soraya knew about the piece of the cyber weapon but thought better of it. That she knew, reinforced Morgana's decision.

"Frustration, too. Yes."

Soraya favored her with a smile. "Then it's settled."

"Okay, but . . . go with the flow." She shook her head. "I don't get it."

"Not at this point, at any rate," Soraya said. "But, trust me, to tell you more would be a mistake."

"All right." It wasn't all right, but what else could she say. "I do trust you."

"Or else you wouldn't be here." Another slight pause. "Events will be moving quickly now. No matter. Do whatever you have decided to do. Do not alter a thing."

"I understand." Morgana cleared her throat again. "Is that all?"

"Just—"

"Go with the flow." Morgana smiled now. "Got it."

As she made to leave, Soraya said, "One more thing."

Morgana raised her eyebrows. "Yes?"

"It's highly likely that at some point you'll think I've thrown you to the dogs."

"But you haven't."

"Further along, you'll be able to judge for yourself."

There was a distinct note of finality in the comment. The interview was over.

Ten minutes later, Morgana showed her credentials to security. She might not be government, but there were enough occasions when she was required to be at HQ that Mac had had a Dreadnaught clearance created for her. No one inside NSA had ever heard of Meme LLC, and that was just the way both she and Mac wanted it. NSA was PURINT, pure intelligence, meaning surveillance was done from the remove of satellites, wires, remote chatter interceptors. No one in the field. Whereas the CIA dealt in HUMINT—human intelligence—agents in the field reporting back to their controls. Mac believed in PURINT; otherwise he wouldn't have been in NSA. But he also believed in enforcement and interdiction intervention, hence his creation of Dreadnaught neatly hidden inside NSA. She was waved through, directed to park the car in Mac's designated section of the lot.

Morgana was stopped at another security post just inside the front doors. Then she was required to put her handbag through an X-ray and to pass through a metal detector. Even after that she was patted down by a muscular, grim-faced woman who seemed to be channeling a prison guard.

When the woman's hand rose to her crotch, Morgana said, "Try it" with such ferocity the woman froze. "Go on," Morgana said. The woman shrugged, backed off, turning away as if she had more important things to do than fondle Morgana.

The vast lobby was deliberately intimidating—high-ceilinged, hard-walled, and filled with people on missions far more important than yours, whatever that might be. Morgana laughed to herself as she crossed to the bank of elevators.

Yet another security checkpoint reared its ugly head as soon as she stepped off at the fifteenth floor. Passing through without difficulty, she went down the thickly carpeted corridor, passing doors with only inscrutable designations in a number-letter code. Like on an aircraft carrier, you had to know your way around the place in order not to get hopelessly lost.

Righteous fury was a deadly thing, she knew this. It was more likely to defeat you than to bring you victory. Nevertheless, it was righteous fury that had brought her from her station at Meme LLC to Dreadnaught's door—designated NCN-113, for who knew what arcane reason.

Now, at the threshold, she paused not only to slow her heart rate down but to give equal consideration to rational thought. *"Collect your thoughts,"* her father used to tell her when she was a kid and would get flummoxed at school. *"Put 'em all in a basket, then rummage around in there until you pick out the best one."* Damn, if it didn't always work. But then everything her father taught her was of use to her later on as an adult. He was a twice-decorated former Navy SEAL. Everything he knew about guns, about knives, about hand-to-hand combat he taught her as furiously, as completely as if she were a boy. *"I love that you take to your training like a fledgling to the air,"* he said to her one balmy spring evening. And so did she. What would he think of her now? she wondered. Would he be proud of her or disappointed that she hadn't taken the steps necessary to become a field agent? She'd never know; he'd died ten years ago in a fiery multiple-vehicle accident on the New Jersey Turnpike. Her mother lasted six weeks without him before something inside her—possibly her will to live—failed. Morgana was an orphan; nothing between her and the grave.

With the image of her father as teacher vivid in her mind's eye, she collected her thoughts and drew out the best one, knowing that striding into Dreadnaught half-cocked—or, the way she had been feeling, fully cocked—was definitely not the way to get what she wanted.

And then another voice entered her consciousness: *Events will be moving quickly now.*

Taking a deep breath and letting it out slowly, she turned the knob, pushed the door open, and found herself inside Dreadnaught.

Not that it looked much different than what she imagined any other office inside NSA would be like: there were programmers, analysts, many, many computer terminals, the massed whirr of small fans, like moths fluttering against a windowpane, and the hot, metallic smell of electronics firing away at full throttle.

No one spoke—all communication in this place was made through emails, IMs, texts—even in this day and age when, as Morgana knew better than most, all electronic communication was among the most insecure. NSA personnel maintained absolute faith in the imperviousness of their firewalls and anti-malware software. It was naïve, even childish, in Morgana's view, but that was what came of investing yourself in quasi-religious beliefs. It was their hubris; she had no doubt it would be their downfall.

Heads popped up when she appeared. Nerds these guys might be, but they weren't neutered—not yet, anyway. A young man rose from his workstation to intercept her. He was blond, blue-eyed, square-jawed, and as magnetic as a movie star of the fifties, a time of pink flesh and innocence. She imagined the smell of the corn husks he must have been born into. He didn't disappoint her.

"Lieutenant Francis Goode. How may I help you, ma'am?" he inquired in that flat Midwestern accent she knew well.

Flashing him her creds, she said, "I have an appointment with Mac."

"Who?"

"Ah." That's right; he wouldn't know. "Your boss, Arthur MacQuerrie." The blank face remained, affording her a moment of amusement before she pitched herself into the fray. "The general."

His eyes narrowed, which made him look like a kid. "And what would your business be with General MacQuerrie?"

"I'm afraid that's above your pay grade, Lieutenant. What are you, a GS seven?" She saw that she had struck pay dirt. "Far, far above."

He scowled, which made him seem more handsome. But she could see that he was also intimidated. "Above your pay grade" was a trigger phrase that never failed to strike fear into the hearts of GS eights and below.

And then she thought, *Why am I pissing on this guy? He's been nothing but polite to me.* So she smiled until his scowl melted like ice in sunlight. "My apologies, Lieutenant Goode, but need-to-know is need-to-know. I should have phrased it another way."

He grinned hugely. "No problem, ma'am."

She matched the wattage of his smile, making it more than a veneer. "Call me Morgana."

"I don't think I can, ma'am."

She ducked her head. She could be coquettish as well as the next doll—probably a whole lot better. She regarded Goode from under sooty lashes; men liked that. "Not even between us?"

"Well, I suppose . . ." He gave her a goofy grin, as if it were a present.

"What is it, Lieutenant?"

"May I ask you a question?" And he hastily added, "It's not about your appointment with General MacQuerrie."

"Of course." She nodded. "Fire away."

"Do you really call the general 'Mac'?"

She caused her laugh to be high and fluty, like a teenager's. "Yes, Lieutenant, I do." She raised a finger in mock warning. "But that's only between you and me. If I go before a Senate subcommittee I deny all knowledge of the nickname."

They chuckled together. He was on her side now.

"Hold on a moment," he said. "The general has been in communications all day. I'll let him know you're here."

Morgana nodded as he turned away. Luck was with her. Mac could have been at the Pentagon or Capitol Hill or anywhere else, but he was right here where she needed him to be. And now she knew why he hadn't answered any of her three calls.

It was only several minutes later that Goode returned and, with that innocent smile of his, ushered her back to Mac's inner sanctum. He was going to see her even without an appointment—a sign of her worth to him, even though she had never been here before.

He was sitting at the far end of what looked like a football field, but that might have been an illusion caused by the eerie violet lighting that was part of the electronic security net that enclosed the space.

The lieutenant vanished as soon as Morgana stepped across the threshold, closing the door soundlessly behind him. Halfway to Mac's imposing desk, which surely wasn't government issue, was a conversation area, complete with matching leather sofas and easy chair and an inlaid glass-topped coffee table, also not government issue.

"Morgana," Mac said, smiling and extending a warm, dry hand. "To what do I owe this visit?"

Someone must have cleaned up the remnants of the meeting or else it had taken place elsewhere, as the conversation area was spotless enough to eat off of. Mac gestured for Morgana to sit, which she did on one of the sofas. The general chose the easy chair. He sat back, crossed one leg over the other, showing off the knife-edged crease down the center of each trouser leg.

"I tried calling you, but—"

He spread his hands. "I wasn't available." And smiled. "But I am now. I'm all yours."

"I appreciate that, Mac."

"How are you coming with the Bourne Initiative?"

"You mean the Karpov Initiative."

"The general's dead, as we've discussed," he said flatly. "It's Bourne's now."

She nodded. "Right. Of course." She swallowed, appalled to discover her mouth was suddenly dry. It was one thing talking to Mac over their private line or having lunch with him at one out-of-the-Beltway venue or other, quite another to be sitting in his office in the middle of the NSA wasp nest. She didn't like it here; she didn't like it one bit. She felt as if she were about to break out in hives at any moment. She scratched at her forearm.

"The fact is it's Bourne I'm here to talk to you about."

He frowned. "I don't understand. How does Bourne concern you?"

"First, I want to know if you have even linked Bourne with Keyre."

MacQuerrie grunted. "We have, and it's simple enough. He was spotted last year in Moscow with a female operative known only as the Angelmaker. She's a deadly assassin."

"And?"

"And, the Angelmaker was made a freak of nature by Keyre, then Bourne somehow got hold of her and put the finishing touches on her assassin's tradecraft. Just in the last five years, she's been linked to the deaths of no fewer than eleven businessmen, politicians, and the like. A board member of a multinational in Munich, a diamond tycoon in Joburg, a warlord in one of those constantly fomenting African nations, a rising right-wing pol and his two mistresses in Paris, a reclusive cyber-billionaire in Manaus, in the fucking Amazon, no less. Then there was Palermo, where she took out twin brothers, one a Mafia don, the other his high-powered lawyer—that was a doozy. And let's not forget the murder aboard a billionaire banker's yacht off the beaches of Ibiza. How she pulled that off... Well, you get the idea. She's a fucking menace and another reason Bourne needs to be eliminated." He cocked his head. "Is there a second reason Bourne concerns you?"

Morgana ignored the hint of sarcasm in his question. "So far we have been unable to crack the code you gave us."

Mac's frown deepened. "That's not good news."

"No, it's not." Her forearm was itching again; she resolved to ignore it. "Which is why I want to interrogate Bourne."

The general blinked. "I beg your pardon."

"It's now the Bourne Initiative. You said it yourself, Mac. He's the only one who can give us access to the—"

"Let me stop you right there." MacQuerrie held up a hand. "Morgana, you're a terrifically talented software engineer. The cyber weapons you've devised for me, the ones you've managed to dismantle before they carried out their nefarious missions, are legion. You're at the top of your field. But that field is a narrow-beam affair, do you understand me?" He went straight on, not waiting for a reply; she would have to be an idiot not to understand him. "Your expertise in one field does not qualify you as expert in any other."

"I understand that, Mac, but—"

"This clandestine service—any clandestine service—is, by definition, highly compartmentalized. You understand why this must be."

"Of course I do."

"Then let me say you are not qualified to understand what Jason Bourne would or would not do. So allow me to enlighten you. A man like Bourne—if, in fact, we were ever able to capture him, which is highly problematic—would never give us the secret to this cyber weapon. Even if we used the most extreme forms of persuasion, even if we waterboarded him for—"

"Good God, Mac." She was shaken to her core. "I would never encourage anything like that!"

He smiled thinly. "Of course you wouldn't. And neither would I."

"I'm relieved to hear that."

He regarded her for a moment, as if he was in the process of reassessing her. "What you are asking is quite out of the question."

He hadn't yet mentioned the termination order he had given. Could she no longer trust Mac? Had they become adversaries in a weird form of cold war? Only one way to find out.

"I know."

Mac shook his head. "Know what, precisely?"

"That you sent a team to kill Bourne—"

"What?"

"That the team blew up the boat he was on, only he wasn't on it."

"Morgana, I don't—"

"Bottom line, Bourne is still alive. I want him."

Color had rushed into Mac's face. "You don't know what you're talking about."

"I need him, Mac. *We* need him if we're to crack the Bourne Initiative, as you call it."

"Morgana, I don't understand. I did not order anyone to blow up a ship anywhere in the world."

Her eyes narrowed. "Are you saying that you have not put out a termination order on Jason Bourne?"

He spread his hands. "Why is a cyber jockey like you talking about termination orders?"

"You didn't answer my question, Mac."

The general sighed. "This is eyes-only intel, so..." He made a pained face as if he had a sweet in his mouth that had an unexpected sour core. "It was a Russian team that blew up the boat. General Karpov's boat. Out of sheer bloody-mindedness, I shouldn't wonder. Nothing whatsoever to do with Bourne." He seemed to swallow the sour taste. "Now. Stick to your patch of the woods, Morgana. That's my advice to you."

"You made Bourne my patch of the woods when you gave me my marching orders for this cyber weapon."

"Then you misunderstood me." He shrugged. "These things are bound to happen from time to time."

He said this in such a condescending tone that she sat perfectly erect, as if coming to attention while seated. Her entire body tensed like a pulled bow string. She took a beat to reset. "You gave me the impression that this cyber weapon—the so-called Bourne Initiative—is your highest priority."

He nodded. "And so it remains."

"Then you can't tie one arm behind my back. You have to give me all the tools I need to—"

"I *have* to? I don't *have* to do anything." The thunderclouds arrived with frightening swiftness. "Have you forgotten to whom you're speaking? Not to be overly melodramatic, but, dammit, I set you up in your job, I made sure you got every damned piece of equipment you asked for, even your Italian coffee thingy."

"Espresso maker," she corrected foolishly.

He glared at her. "I can take it all away, including your fucking *espresso maker*."

"And who will that hurt the most, General? Me or our country?"

"Morgana, Morgana, Morgana." He shook his head, his expression now mournful. "It's clear to me now that you have risen too far, too fast. You've reached the sun; your wings have melted. I gave you freedom. You mistook that freedom for power. You have no power, not now, not ever. Do I make myself clear?"

"Crystal clear, General."

He rose, turned his back on her, returned to his seat behind his desk, picked up his phone and began to dial. "Get this done, Morgana," he said, putting the receiver to his ear. "Or I'll find someone else who will."

Her tongue seemed stuck to the roof of her mouth. Her hands were shaking, her knees felt like Jell-O, and her heart was on fire.

There is no one else, she wanted to tell him. But of course, this wasn't true. There was no one else he knew of—but that wasn't the same thing.

Outside, the good Lieutenant Goode was waiting to escort her to the elevator.

"How was your meeting, Morgana?" he asked genially.

"Ducky," she said with a wooden smile. "Just ducky."

At least I didn't get shirty with him, she thought grimly.

8

LIGHTNING ILLUMINATED HER face, bone-white and dark-eyed. Her clothes clung to the shape of her body, revealing as much as they hid. The rain continued to pelt down. The air seemed subtropical, and the sky was low and virulent. Wind whistled over the rock face, the fluting now and again sounding like voices in a hellish chorus.

Bourne wanted to move inland, but in the blinding rain and pitch darkness it was far too risky. He had a flashlight he'd taken from the runabout, but using it would only alert the kill team of an unknown presence they would be obliged to investigate. The remaining members had a personal grudge against him now; he'd killed one of their own. That was an offense they would neither forgive nor forget.

The only saving grace of the storm's ferocity was the fact that the team couldn't move, either. How far ahead they might be was impossible to guess, but

Bourne figured they had no more than a ten-minute head start. That could not put them too far ahead. They would have had to seek immediate shelter. He didn't know if coming to Skyros had been their original plan or a spur-of-the-moment decision once the *Nym* had anchored there, but for sure, they had to stay there now to find Stone's killer, which they undoubtedly suspected was Bourne.

"What are you thinking?" Mala asked over the incessant noise of the storm.

"Turn around," Bourne said.

"What?"

Hand on her shoulders, he turned her. The movement was gentle; she did not resist. When she was sitting with her back to him, he pulled off her outer garment. The rain turned the bathing suit black, like a partial suit of armor. Her back was exposed to him. Bourne placed his fingertips at base of her neck, the apex of the complex patterns of scars Keyre had inflicted on her over nine months, the period of time dictated by the Yibir laws of sorcery to complete the patterns.

Multiple flashes of lightning all at once threw the scars into livid relief—dark, ropy runes on an alabaster field. A chiaroscuro of agony.

These weren't just scars; they were written incantations. Spells woven into the fabric of Mala's body to bind her soul to Keyre. After reuniting with her on Cyprus last year toward the end of his previous mission, Bourne had spent hours every day and night learning as much as he could about Yibir sorcery, an almost impossible task, even for him. The problem was that there was an immense amount of disbelief in sorcery in the mod-

ern world, and in Yibir sorcery most of all. So little was
known about it, and what few practitioners had come to
light were, at heart, terrorists, pirates, reavers, and rav-
agers of those who did not view the world as they did.
Keyre was one such terrorist—the worst of the lot—
the smartest and the cleverest, who commanded absolute obedience from his followers and absolute loyalty
from his clients to whom he sold prepackaged coups,
complete with the latest weapons and the best-trained
soldiers. The caveat, which he never mentioned beforehand, was that these well-trained soldiers were absolutely loyal to him and no one else. Any form of
skimming, withholding, or reneging on a deal ended
one way and one way only: the client never saw another
sunrise. So fearsome was Keyre's reputation that such
betrayals happened less and less often, until now they
were virtually unheard of.

These thoughts passed quickly across the scrim of
Bourne's mind as he traced the runes, one by one, and
in the proper order—that is to say, the order in which
they were inflicted upon Mala's flesh. Rather than hori-
zontally, they were read vertically, like original Chinese
or Japanese. But these runes looked nothing like Asian
ideographs—or like any other language, for that matter.
They possessed their own inscrutable meaning, their
own grammar and syntax, their own logic, if one might
call sorcery in any way logical.

Mala turned her head, so that in the next lightning
flash he saw her in profile. "What are you doing?"

His fingertips continued to move down her back, his
hands parting momentarily to trace the runes on either
shoulder blade.

She flinched. "Please don't. I hate those things. I hate that they're a part of me." She had drawn her knees up to her chest. Now she laid her forehead on her forearms. Her back arched like a bow. "You can't do anything, Jason."

He was finished now, the so-called incantations memorized via his fingertips. He wanted to know them because they were lies. But her belief in what Keyre had done to her was what kept her bound to him. He had seen her at her lowest ebb, when she had come so close to death he could feel its chill breath on the back of his neck. He had brought her back from that brink; all the while she had spoken to him as she spoke to herself. He knew she hated Keyre, but at the same time the dreaded Stockholm syndrome had insinuated itself into her mind with each runic cut of his knife. He had led her to a place where hate and love existed side by side, like the most intimate of lovers; in this sinister manner he had made her his creature. Bourne knew that if he was to save her he would have to break the spell she was convinced she was under. If he couldn't, he harbored no doubt whatsoever that one day she would turn on him and, under Keyre's explicit orders, kill him when he least expected it. For these reasons he had determined to keep her close, to follow wherever she led. He would never be truly safe otherwise.

"Thank God you saved Liis before he could start on her."

"Your sister is safe," Bourne said. "I've made sure of that."

"But is she happy?"

"I've set up a trust in her name. She has her career,

about which she is passionate. But beyond that, is anyone happy?"

She turned then, to place her mouth on his. Her lips were slightly parted, the tip of her tongue entered his mouth. She sighed against him, her hard athlete's body melting. He felt himself respond, even knowing she was at her most dangerous when she appeared most vulnerable. Unlike her younger sister, untouched by Keyre, Mala was incapable of vulnerability. If she had ever had it, it was clear to him that Keyre had excised it with the point of his sacred knife.

"Don't talk that way," she whispered into his mouth. Rain struck them out of the turbulent night. "If I thought you'd ever become like me I'd die."

Alarm bells went off in Bourne's head. Mala was not prone to overstatement, to embellishing a moment, wearing a ruffled blouse when she could don a T-shirt. If she said this terrible thing, she meant it. The thought rocked him; he'd been unprepared for such a raw and naked statement.

"Such morbidity. It doesn't suit you."

She shook her head, her solemn expression holding something deeper, darker. "You took me away from him," she said. "But you didn't save me from him."

"You mean the incantation—"

"This has nothing to do with that," she said sharply.

"What has it to do with?"

"When you took me away from Keyre," she said into the drumming night, "I left a part of me with him."

Bourne's throat had gone dry. *This can't be happening*, he thought. But it was.

"I had a child with him," she went on, each word

seeming to be squeezed out of her guts. "A daughter. Giza."

She turned to him, and he saw the tears rolling from her eyes, down her cheeks.

"Her name is Giza, Jason. He keeps her locked away."

He recalled her fighting him, his strong sense that she didn't want to leave. She had begged him to find her sister, Liis, but never mentioned Giza.

"And please don't ask why I didn't tell you at the time," she continued, as if reading his mind. "I didn't know where he kept her then, and I don't know now. After you took Liis and me away...after that night...I've never seen her." Her shoulders began to tremble. "He holds that possibility out like a carrot, if I do what he commands."

Like a plague, the sins of the Somali continued to multiply exponentially: human trafficker, illicit arms dealer, broker between tin-pot despots and fanatic jihadists, brutalizer of girls, torturer. Extorter of the worst deeds from the tenderest and most intimate of emotions. These were the thoughts that swirled around Bourne's mind as he held Mala's shivering frame, wrapping his arms tightly around her. The worst thing in the world had happened to Mala. Her scars were as nothing compared to separating her from her daughter.

"He'll never let you see her," he whispered when she had quietened. "You know that, don't you?"

"I have to believe..." She passed a hand across her eyes. The blue light from a lightning flash struck her, passing like a theatrical scrim across her face. "My mind says one thing, but my heart says the opposite."

He understood her a bit more, but, frankly, it didn't help much. She was someone he'd saved, brought out of the fire of Keyre's encampment. In the aftermath, he had helped to nurse her back to health. And how had she repaid him? He was grateful that she had told him what she surely had never told another soul, but for him the cost was too high. He had been obliged to remove her and Liis from an intolerable situation. Now, in divulging her secret to him, she had obliged him to return to Somalia, find her daughter, and rescue her. She knew this; it was the reason she had engineered this meeting. Her secret was not Giza; it was with velvet gloves coercing him into killing Keyre—something she herself could not, or would not, do. Because, so far as he could see, the only way to pry Giza out of Keyre's clutches was through his cold, dead fingers.

He let go of her before it was too late, before she insinuated herself into him, made him forget completely that she was the Angelmaker, that death was always clinging to her shoulder, that unless he could save her from herself she already had one foot in the grave. He saw now that merely going after Keyre and killing him wouldn't make much of a difference, if at all. The Yibir would have control of her even from beyond the grave. Bourne suspected that the pain and suffering Keyre had inflicted on her had remade her, reconnecting axons, rewiring her brain to his demonic wavelength. For, make no mistake, Keyre was a demon made manifest in the body of a human being. Bourne had been to his camp; he'd seen with his own eyes the depravity he visited on human souls.

The storm had finally exhausted itself, the rain reduced to a drizzle that, without wind, fell vertically. After the last hours of the attack it felt almost pleasurable.

"We should be heading inland," he said, rising. He wanted to be done with this place, with its secrets, its sinister shadows. "The faster we discover where the kill team has bivouacked the more secure I'll feel."

"We should attack them while it's still dark," Mala said, shrugging on her wrap. Her skin was goosefleshed, but she gave no sign that she was chilled. That was not her way. "But you said you wanted to hold off."

"I said I had a better idea."

Her eyes glittered. "What could be better than slitting their throats?"

And there it was, the extreme peril that lurked behind her beautiful facade. The Angelmaker killed for money. Worse, she lived for death, craved it as others craved food and water. Was there, then, no hope for her?

Pushing this question aside, Bourne moved them out, down the high ridge that had been their shelter. The last of the clouds, racing inland, shredded, revealing a star-strewn sky glittering with newfound luminescence. With the starlight leading the way, they soon enough came across a narrow path, the glistening rocks still shedding water. The passing of the storm had brought a lowering of the humidity and, with it, cooler temperatures that rapidly dried their clothes.

Almost immediately the path turned steep, passing between two massive boulders. Pines sprang on their side, gnarled and twisted by the wind, adding to the sense of claustrophobia. At one point, he had to stop them. They were faced with a treacherous rock fall, impossible to navigate. Anything could set it off again.

He moved them off to their right, finding another way down, always cognizant of the unstable rock fall to their left. As they descended, he kept a lookout for a break, to give them a broader view of their locale and, possibly, pick up the glint of movement presaging the appearance of the kill team.

"You said you have a better idea than taking them out," Mala whispered in his ear, mindful that their voices would carry over the rocky terrain. "What could possibly be better?" she asked again.

Bourne halted them. He pointed off to the right, where a break in the pines offered them a view inland down the slope. "There," he said. "There they are."

A fire had been lit, three tents surrounding it. Now and again they could discern in the glimmering starlight the movement of a human being, a quick, dull wink of an AR-15 assault rifle as light from the fire slithered down its barrel.

Bourne signaled silently to her, and they crept forward along the path, breaking off it when they were just above the bivouac. They were close enough to hear voices but were completely hidden from view behind a dense copse of pines.

"Have you made contact with MacQuerrie?" one said.

"Not yet."

"Fuck, you'd better."

There was a pause. "Frankly, I don't want to be the one to tell him."

"About Stone or Bourne?"

"Bourne. He won't give a shit about Stone."

"You're right. He's a fucker. Well, you'll have to do it, and the sooner the better. There's nothing to be done for the poor devil but to bring him back home. Bourne, on the other hand, we can do something about. He's got to be somewhere nearby. The storm must have pinned him down just the way it did us."

The first one made a call, reluctantly enough, on a military-grade sat phone. When he was finished, he wiped sweat off his brow.

"That bad?" the second one asked.

The first one shook off his question. "Break out the night-vision glasses. He won't be able to see us, but we sure as hell will be able to see him."

They heard the rustling as the kill team strapped on their night-vision goggles. The agent was right: the goggles would pick up their heat signatures. There would be nowhere to hide.

"Jason . . ."

Mala's soft voice pulled him out of his silent session with himself. His short-term tactics were settled; it was the mid-term strategy that still had to be worked out.

The American kill team was coming, heading up the slope because they must figure Bourne had made landfall somewhere close by. This part of the coast was forbidding, and there were only a few places to come ashore safely.

Bourne moved them back to a more strategic position. Rocks and water were their only friends now, the only natural configurations that would block their heat signals. The soft pines, no matter how closely clustered, could not be counted upon to keep them hidden for long. Even the slightest move or alteration in their position would leak a signature and give them away. They'd be effectively pinned down.

"Come on," he whispered. "There's a lot of work to do and little time to do it in."

9

JASON BOURNE. WHERE the hell is he?"

Faced with his boss's towering wrath, Igor Malachev trembled. "We don't know, sir."

Timur Savasin, First Minister of the Russian Federation, turned a withering look on him. "What do I have you for, Igor Ivanovich, except to keep an ear and eye out on *spetsnaz*?"

Malachev stiffened. "I do the best I can, sir. But Special Forces is a paranoid group."

"Everyone in Russia is paranoid, Igor Ivanovich. It goes with the territory." He raised a hand, fluttered it. "Find out where Bourne is, and don't return until you have the answer." Malachev was almost to the first minister's office door when Savasin said, "And, Igor Ivanovich, while you're at it, fetch Alecks Petrovich for me."

Alecks Volodarsky. Savasin could have, of course, picked up the internal phone and summoned the new head of *spetsnaz*, the FSB Special Forces, himself, but his ire was such that he had decided to turn his second-in-command into a lowly gofer. He resisted an urge to order him to bark.

Alone in his vast office inside Moscow Center, Savasin stuffed his hands into his trouser pockets, fuming so hard it was a wonder smoke didn't puff out of his ears. *That boat, Boris Illyich's fucking boat,* he thought. *The fucker might have been a traitor six ways from Sunday, but he had goddamn good taste.* He stalked back and forth across the gray tweed carpet like a caged tiger. *I wanted that boat. It was mine. The Sovereign said I could have it. And now we've blown it to kingdom come. I didn't order the boat blown up. Who the fuck did?* He went and stared out the window at Lubyanka Square. Directly across was the forbidding façade of Detsky Mir, Children's World department store, which reminded Savasin that one of his grandchildren was having his seventh birthday next week. He resolved, as further punishment, to send Malachev over there on his lunch hour to buy a suitable present.

"Come," he muttered in response to a crisp knock on the door. And then louder, a second time, "Come!"

Malachev or Volodarsky? He watched an old man on the square, lost in a greatcoat that might have been manufactured during World War II, struggle with a recalcitrant dog. The dog was almost as big as the old man. Savasin felt a quick stab of compassion for the dog's master. The visitor behind him cleared his throat. Savasin didn't turn around.

"Igor Ivanovich said you wanted to see me, sir."

For a moment Savasin said nothing. He was tempted to send one of his men outside to help the old man with his willful animal, but then reflected that would only shame the old man, who might very well be a war veteran, and that would never do.

"Tell me, Alecks Petrovich, have you found Jason Bourne?"

"Uh, not yet, sir."

"But you're close."

"Yes, sir."

Savasin finally turned around to face the man he had appointed as head of *spetsnaz*. "Volodarsky, if you lie to me a second time, I will personally frog-march you downstairs to the cellars." The cellars were where all the myriad terrors of the infamous Lubyanka prison resided. People who were brought down there were never seen alive again. "Is that clear?"

Volodarsky swallowed hard. "Quite clear, sir."

"Now, shall I ask my question again?"

"No, sir. We haven't as yet acquired the specific whereabouts of the target."

The old man, as stubborn as his dog, reminded Savasin of his father, a man—a veteran of the war—whom Savasin had revered all his life. He'd never had enough time with his father, and every moment of their time together was of immense importance to him. When Savasin had finally laid him to rest, he had not spoken for ten days. He had gone away to the Kamchatka Peninsula, where his father had sometimes—not often enough!—taken him to fish. The glittering ice and softly falling snow seemed like paradise to the young Savasin, and later, after his father was dead, he'd think of those times as if encased in a snow globe, a world sealed off, that only he and his father inhabited. He went there in his mind when his duties became too overbearing or the exigencies of his life went against the grain.

"Alecks Petrovich, I told you not to lie."

"But, sir, I haven't—"

"Really?" He sighed. "Alecks, we grew up together, didn't we?"

"Yes."

"We attended the same classes, university and all that."

Volodarsky nodded.

"We break bread together every Friday evening, do we not?"

"We do."

"And get roaring drunk on the best vodka." His voice turned icy. "Then please tell me why you haven't found Jason Bourne. He was the late, unlamented General Karpov's closest friend, though under what circumstances that came about fairly boggles the mind. Though I have learned not to put anything past him."

"No, indeed. We're all learning that."

A knock on the door deterred the first minister from doling out further verbal torture. But that was okay, for this was only the warmup to the main event. His mouth began to salivate, anticipating Malachev entering. Seeing Volodarsky still there, Malachev would no doubt blanch.

Malachev and Volodarsky did not like each other. It was still unclear to Savasin which one feared the other most. The relationship between the two was heavily reminiscent of the one Savasin had with Konstantin. Not for the first time it occurred to Savasin that he had deliberately set these two together in an attempt to get the better of Konstantin.

"Igor Ivanovich," he said as he turned around, but

the sight of the tall, elegant man standing where Malachev should have been stopped him in his tracks. "Konstantin Ludmirovich," he said.

A thin smile curved the other's lips. "Close your mouth, brother. You're apt to swallow the flies on this floor." Konstantin Ludmirovich Savasin glanced around the office with obvious distaste. He sniffed, his delicate nostrils dilating alarmingly. "You really ought to have a cleaning crew in here more than once a month."

Savasin ground his teeth in fury but did not rise to the bait. Instead, he said with a maximum amount of sarcasm, "What brings you into the lion's den?"

"Is that what this is? Oh, well." He shrugged. "For one thing, it's my day for slumming." His laugh was like fingernails on a chalkboard. "For another, you've summoned a high-ranking FSB officer for what appears to be a dressing down."

"If that's what it is," the first minister said, "then you can be sure it's well deserved."

"Can I?" Konstantin circled his brother. "Can I, really?" He shook his head. "The fact of the matter is that Alecks Petrovich knows nothing about the *Nym*."

Volodarsky swallowed. "The what?"

The new head of FSB's smile was as sharp as a razor blade. "You see, brother, he doesn't even know what we're talking about."

Savasin lost it for a moment. "Colonel Karpov's boat, you idiot," he shouted at Volodarsky.

"That's an FSB officer you're yelling at. One you yourself appointed, brother."

"First Minister to you, Konstantin, as well as to everyone else. I can yell at anyone, even you."

Konstantin shrugged, shook out a cigarette, lit it, took a good, long inhale. The hiss of indolently expelled smoke grated on Savasin's nerves. Konstantin was handsome in an odd, saturnine way. His long face dominated by large, liquid eyes that, like their mother's, were set too close together. He had her skin, as well: pale, almost translucent.

Savasin glared at Volodarsky. "You're of no use. You don't even know what your men are doing. Get the fuck out of my office."

Volodarsky glanced at Konstantin, but the other wasn't about to meet his eye.

"Don't look at him. He'll be of no help to you, take my word," Savasin said shortly. "Just get out."

When the two brothers were alone, Konstantin said matter-of-factly, "The Americans blew up Karpov's boat."

Savasin stared at him as if he had grown another head. "Are you sure?"

When Konstantin delivered a withering look, he went on, "Do you have any hard evidence?"

"The Americans are smart enough not to leave anything behind that could be traced back to them. Let the Sovereign make propaganda hay; he's good at that. As for us, pursuing that line will only lead us down a path that never ends. Which is precisely what the Americans want."

"Nevertheless, the boat—a part of the Federation— has been destroyed by a foreign power."

Konstantin glanced around again, and, with the grace of a dancer, stepped to one of the upholstered chairs in the office, inspected it vigilantly before seating himself. He glanced down, admiring the perfect creases of his imported trousers as he did so. "Oh, come off it, Timur. You don't give a shit about that. It's the boat itself that has your knickers in a twist." He looked up at his brother, a sardonic look in his eye. "I know you coveted it."

"The Sovereign promised it to me."

"Oops."

Konstantin continued to draw in tobacco and let it out in aromatic clouds when his lungs had become saturated with nicotine.

"You'll kill yourself with that filthy habit," Savasin observed.

"Don't you wish."

Konstantin tapped ash into a crystal ashtray thick enough to crack a skull open with one blow—at least that was Savasin's thought in the moment.

"Was Jason Bourne on the *Nym* when it left Istanbul? Or was it heading to a rendezvous with him?"

Konstantin shrugged.

"Bourne was Karpov's closest friend. There's a good chance he left the boat to him."

Konstantin lifted a bit of tobacco off the tip of his tongue. "What do I care."

"I don't believe you."

"That's certainly your prerogative, *First Minister*."

Konstantin had the ability to completely exasperate him, just like when they were kids. The fact was, Savasin loved and hated his brother. He also feared him, always had. Perched on the corner of his desk, he folded his arms across his chest, regarded his brother from beneath heavy-lidded eyes.

"As long as we're talking prerogatives, I don't like

Volodarsky." Konstantin plucked a bit of lint off the supple fabric that covered his kneecap. "Volodarsky is your appointment."

"Yes."

"That's what you get for elevating old friends. He doesn't know his zipper from his shoulder boards. I mean, face facts, he can't even find Jason Bourne. But I have. He was on General Karpov's boat."

"What?"

"No, no, no." He waited a beat and, picking his way light as you please through Savasin's glare, added, "You should ask *why*, Timur. *Why* didn't your man know that?"

Savasin was still trying to recover from the news that the *Nym* would never be his. Maintaining an iron façade, he said, "And you maintain you have no interest in Jason Bourne."

"My dear Timur Ludmirovich, you're the one who hated Karpov with a—how to put it best?—a maniacal, near-religious fervor. I can only suppose that you feel the same way toward his best friend." He shrugged. "As for me, I couldn't care less whether Bourne lives or dies." His eyes glittered with mischief. "He hasn't gotten under *my* skin."

He ground out the butt of his cigarette and rose. "Now, if we're clear on the matter..."

A knock sounded on the door.

"It's like the Kazansky railway station in here today," Konstantin observed with one raised eyebrow.

"Come!" Savasin said, somewhat louder than was necessary.

Malachev advanced into the office, but he was brought up short by the presence of the elder Savasin.

After a moment's contemplation during which Savasin could virtually see the cogs in his head spinning dizzily, he soldiered on, one eye on Konstantin as if at any moment the head of FSB would take a bite out of his thigh like a rabid animal.

"I have confirmed that Jason Bourne was on Karpov's boat when it left Istanbul."

Savasin gave his older brother a savage glare. "And was he on it when the Americans blew it up?"

Malachev spread his hands. "Unfortunately, First Minister, I don't—"

"He doesn't know," Konstantin broke in. "No one here knows." His scimitar smile seemed to extend from ear to ear. "Except me, of course."

Savasin felt a headache coming on. He dismissed Malachev with a curt wave of his hand. When the brothers were alone again, he said, "Well, what are you waiting for?"

"I'm waiting, little brother, for you to meet my price."

Savasin felt his blood pressure threatening to go through the roof. Still, he held himself in check, replied evenly, "And what would that be?"

"I want you to fire Volodarsky."

Relief was just a word away. "Done. He's proved eminently incompetent."

"Jettisoning your childhood pal. Just like that." Konstantin sniffed. "Well, I suppose that says something about you."

"I'll be more judicious when I appoint—"

"Oh, no. I want my own man heading up Special Forces. As head of FSB it's my right."

He should have known firing Volodarsky was only the beginning. "As first minister, I can veto any appointment you make."

"You could," Konstantin said. "But then you wouldn't find out about the disposition of Jason Bourne. Is he dead? Alive? And if still alive, where is he?"

Savasin felt as if he were standing at a waterline, the sand washing out from under his feet. "You said you didn't know—"

"I said I don't care. I don't. But you do." Konstantin flipped another cigarette into his mouth, lit it with his oversize steel lighter. "I am aware of *how much* you need to know, little brother," he added in a rush of smoke. "So . . ." He shrugged.

Savasin continued to struggle for equilibrium. Maybe this wouldn't be so bad, he told himself. After all, Volodarsky was clearly the wrong choice to head up *spetsnaz*. Konstantin was frighteningly intelligent. It was entirely possible that Konstantin's pick would be a good one. In that frame of mind, he said, "Who's your man?" The instant he said it, he knew he had capitulated. He realized his mistake. Whoever his brother had in mind would be his man through and through, which would, by definition, make him Savasin's enemy. Konstantin was also frighteningly clever.

"Nikolay Ivanovich Rozin."

"What?" Savasin raised his eyebrows. "Rozin is a field agent."

"Undercover. Yes, he's perhaps the best field agent we have."

"Huh. He's also something of a loose cannon, so maybe taking him out of the field is a wise choice."

"Who said anything about taking him out of the field?"

The disorientation returned. Damn Konstantin to hell. "Then how will he—?"

"I mean to break the mold, little brother. I *want* him in the field." He sniffed. "In my opinion, the *spetsnaz* officials have gotten too complacent, too comfortable milling around Dzerzhinsky Square. That requires a revolution, or don't you agree?"

The damnable fact was that Savasin did agree. Konstantin was dead on in his assessment of Special Forces. It was a problem Savasin himself had been meaning to address. Konstantin had beaten him to it. Nothing new there, he thought bitterly.

"As it happens, I do agree." He bit off each word as if they came from a bar of soap. He nodded. "All right. Elevate Rozin and let's see where that leads." He lifted a hand. "But know that he's on a short leash. If he steps out of line—"

"I'm the wrong person to threaten," Konstantin said. "Have you forgotten so soon?"

Savasin was so angry he almost lacerated his tongue. "I forget nothing," he said thickly.

"Better." Konstantin regarded the glowing tip of his cigarette. "As it happens, your Bourne boarded the *Nym* even before it put in to Istanbul." His eyes flicked up to engage his brother's. "By all rights, he should have been on the boat when the Americans blew it up."

"I thought you had no interest in Bourne."

"Insofar as you do, I have a great deal of interest."

"You wanted to deny me the satisfaction of taking his life."

"Correct."

"But the American team missed him. So he's still alive. Where?"

"In the eastern Aegean. The island of Skyros, to be exact. We have picked up a coded distress call."

Savasin's brows drew together. "Coded?"

Konstantin offered an unsavory chuckle. "Leave it to General Karpov. It's his signal." He beamed. "As it happens there's a *spetsnaz* team ready and waiting in Istanbul. It's only a short flight to—"

"I want control of the *spetsnaz* team," Savasin said, shaking off this latest specter of their shared past.

Konstantin shrugged. "Have at it, little brother. I've got what I came for."

10

NIGHT WAS DESCENDING into the shoals of a glimmering dawn.

"I don't like this," Mala said.

"You don't like anything."

The sea was ahead of them. The closer they came to it, the higher they ascended, until they were above the treetops down below. The harsh salt wind lashed what foliage remained into dwarfs, limbs painfully twisted as if from long torture.

"They're gaining on us," Mala whispered.

"I know."

"We ought to increase our speed."

"And risk exposing ourselves to their night goggles?" He shook his head.

"But at this rate, they're bound to catch up to us before we make the coast."

"Maybe. Maybe not."

She gave him a sharp, sideways look. "What d'you have up your sleeve?"

"It may not work," he said. "I don't want to give you false hope."

Her eyes flashed. "That's what you gave me when you took us out of Somalia."

He couldn't argue with her there.

He led her off the rough track they had been following, and they began climbing the cliff face, clawing for foot- and handholds. The problem of always keeping large enough rocks between them and the kill team added an extra degree of difficulty.

After setting the last of the traps, using the fishing lines and hooks, they reached a declivity in a massive rock formation, in the lee of the wind coming in off the sea. They were approximately halfway up the cliff wall on the other side of which was the Aegean and the boats, theirs and the kill team's.

She let out a small puff of air. "I particularly don't like this sitting here, waiting for the Americans to catch up with us."

"This crew isn't CIA."

"No? Who, then?"

"They mentioned MacQuerrie."

"Yes, I heard."

"General MacQuerrie is in charge of his own piece of turf within the American clandestine services. His group is known as Dreadnaught. His people do a lot of very dirty wet work."

"Isn't all wet work, by definition, dirty?"

"Maybe. But Dreadnaught's is pitch-black filthy."

"All the more reason why you should want to get up close and personal. Tooth and claw." She gave him a particularly piercing look. "Don't you have a personal stake in killing them?"

"Do you?" he said.

"Yeah, they blew up your friend's boat thinking you were on it. Instead, they killed the captain and crew. Now they're hunting both of us."

"They don't know you exist."

She grunted. "That's what this is all about, isn't it? You're testing me. See if I'll abandon you to your fate?" She shook her head. "Our fates became entwined the moment you entered Keyre's camp. The moment—"

"Don't say it, Mala. I'm warning you."

"Someone should have warned your friend."

The most terrible thing about being with her was that it was like looking into a mirror—somewhat distorted, but nevertheless the fact remained that they were both killers. Her unbridled bloodlust, the fierce joy in killing she had learned at Keyre's knee conjured up the spirits of all the people he had killed, no matter the reason. Each life you took diminished you, of this he was certain. Would there, then, come a time when there would be nothing left of him to keep alive? She also engendered in him this nihilism, these black questions that ate at him, not at the edge of darkness, but during the interstices of life in the shadows, the moments of idleness, few though they might be.

"Jason, I need you to know that things are different now with Keyre. These days, he runs a business, everything online: expenditures, profits, transfers to and from accounts held by a mare's nest of shell companies in Switzerland, Gibraltar, Caymans, Bermuda, Iceland, Lichtenstein, who knows where else? Domiciles don't matter, except on paper—and even paper doesn't exist anymore. It's all in cyberspace, all in ironclad clouds." She took a breath. "You wouldn't recognize the place."

"No pools of blood? No heads on spikes, shriveling in the sun? No incantations over guts pulled from the living?"

She said nothing.

"I'll recognize Keyre. There's a face I'll never forget."

She looked away for a moment, her hair streaming out behind her until she lassoed it with her fingers. She seemed to be listening to a sound only she could hear. It was very far away, coming off the sands of Somalia like a mirage.

When she turned back to him, her eyes seemed enlarged, as if she had ingested a drug. Maybe she had, Bourne thought. Maybe that drug was Keyre himself.

"You know," she said in an altogether different tone of voice, "there was a time when I loved you. A time when you were my entire universe."

"You were very ill," he said, not wanting her words to sink in, knowing that she might very well be laying a trap, that he absolutely could not trust her, no matter how much he might want to. She was still very much Keyre's creature, despite all his efforts. It saddened and angered him in equal measure that he had freed her body, but not her mind. He wished to convey none of this to her. "I nursed you back to life. It's only natural. Transference."

"That's one word for it."

"What word would you substitute?"

She eyed him, searching for any flicker of emotion. She was as expert at pulling emotions from people as a fisherman drawing his catch out of the water. She shook her head. "But, you see, Jason, what I learned is that love is beyond your ken. When love knocks on your door you remain deaf, dumb, and blind."

She was talking about herself, of course, but what she said made him think of Sara, of all the time they spent together, how well they knew each other—and yet, Mala was right, he always kept a part of himself hidden, locked away, set apart from even the few people he was closest to: Sara, Boris, Soraya Moore. He loved all three of them in his way. But that was the problem: *in his way*. What was that, exactly? Was he really and truly incapable of loving someone, of giving all of himself? Had living in the shadows, inhabiting all the most perilous fringes of the world, damaged him beyond repair? Had all the betrayals, the paranoia of future betrayals, made him more weapon than human? No answer presented itself, only a blank wall even he was incapable of scaling.

Mala's voice was like a scarf of purest silk winding around him, impossibly soft, impossibly strong. "I held you and Keyre, one in each hand"—she lifted both hands, cupping them—"balancing the two of you like the scales of justice."

"Keyre and the concept of justice are incompatible."

"So you think, Jason. But you're wrong. Justice is paramount to Keyre—it always has been."

"You have found some good in him, is that what you're telling me?"

She bit her lip. "We're—all of us—capable of great good and great evil, don't you think?"

The night, slipping away, was gradually being replaced by predawn light, dirty and wan.

"Right now I'm thinking it's ironic that light is better for us than darkness. Those night-vision glasses are better than the human eye in picking up and homing in on prey."

"You don't really think the traps will injure them?"

"They might—once. After that, no." Bourne moved them to their left, positioning them squarely at the head of the rock fall they had bypassed on the way down. "But it doesn't matter; that's not their purpose."

———

The first tripwire Bourne had set caught one of the Dreadnaught agents at thigh level, the fish hooks puncturing his trousers and flesh. As he reared back in reaction, they tore chunks of muscle out of both thighs. He grunted in pain as his legs went out from under him. The rest of the team abandoned their positions, grouped around him.

"Fucking Bourne," said the lead, a man with a long indentation down one side of his bald skull. He was about to cut the fishing line with his knife when he looked around. Then he put the knife back in its sheath. "Okay, this can't be the only one. Be on the lookout. And don't cut the line. There's no telling what that will trigger. We're dealing with a very clever and resourceful sonuvabitch. You see here a perfect example. He must've seen that we had night-vision goggles, exceedingly fine for picking out living creatures in the night, but of no use at all seeing trip wires."

The man on the ground was writhing in agony. The leader glanced at him briefly. "Give him something."

"He's bleeding like a stuck pig," said another and pointed. "One of the hooks must've torn open an artery."

The wounded man started to scream as the real pain set in. The leader clamped a hand over his mouth. "Give him something to shut him the fuck up," he said.

"We're just going to leave him here?" asked another.

"This isn't the marines. We don't exist." The man dug into a first-aid kit, extracted a hypodermic needle, and drove it into the man's biceps.

As the wounded man calmed, closed his eyes, the leader nodded, then stood up. "Bury him deep, where no one will find him. Then let's move out."

Afterward, they returned to their positions, more or less, trying as best they could to compensate for the loss of their comrade. With two down, there were three of them left: the leader, the boat driver, and one other, the man who spoke up. Their spread was of necessity more compact, covering less territory. That could not be helped, and, as it turned out, it didn't matter, since as they encountered more of the trip wires they were forced to move closer together.

This was the purpose of the trip wires' placement as Bourne conceived of them: to create a funnel along which the Dreadnaughts were forced forward. He did not want them spread out when he sprang his lethal surprise.

———

It took them longer to come into Bourne's view than he had expected. Then, as he counted their number, he understood. The first trip wire must have caught one of them because there were three, not four. He glanced to right and left, but this was inhospitable terrain for a flanking maneuver, plus they couldn't be sure where he was.

That would change in a moment.

Ready? he mouthed, and she nodded. She was ready.

They had briefly discussed how to get the rock fall moving most efficiently. They separated now, growing dim to each other in the ghostly light. Sea birds had awoken, calling and crying as they circled overhead. He welcomed the raucous noise; the clatter as the rock fall began would easily be confused with the clamor of the birds.

They were each now on separate parts of the rock fall, their butts on solid ground, their boots hovering inches above the layers of precariously balanced rock shards. Ignoring each other, they looked to the movement below them as what was left of the Dreadnaught team entered the defile into which they had been herded, beginning the steepest part of the ascent.

Bourne pushed himself back, stood up, fired his pistol at them. The report caused the rock fall to tremble, that's how fragile its stability was. The three men below scrambled as best they could, but the defile afforded them scant cover and, in any event, at that moment, Mala ground her boot heels into the shards with a powerful double kick. The rumble began.

Bourne lowered himself, gave his own mighty double kick—once, twice, the third time in exact concert with another from Mala, and the entire rock fall gave way. The avalanche picked up speed at once, and, as it did so, its sound deepened, widened, became palpable, like an intense atmospheric disturbance, rushing, tumbling, roaring down the defile with such demonic energy all three Dreadnaughts disappeared from view.

It was only afterward, in the stifled peace of the rock slide's aftermath, that they heard the sound of the rotors and, looking up, saw the military helo diving toward them.

11

MORGANA WAS WAITING behind the wheel of the car when Lieutenant Francis Goode exited the NSA complex. When Goode got in his car and fired the ignition, she followed him out of the vast parking lot that surrounded the black edifice like a castle moat.

He took the highway, headed deeper into Virginia. She turned off with him at the Odenton exit, tailed him through local streets, watched him park in the lot attached to the Long Range, a local firing range, and enter the building. Five minutes later she followed him through the front door.

The big guy behind the counter in a red SHOOT FIRST T-shirt looked at her askance until she waved her ID in his face. Then he was all smiles and what-can-I-do-for-yous. She paid for an hour, chose her weapon, and was rung up.

She was given a 9mm Glock, ammunition, and a set of sound-dampening headphones. She entered the range itself, trolled through the row of shooters, looking for Goode.

The lanes to either side of him were occupied. She was on the verge of taking a free lane down from where Goode was firing, but the shooter to his left stopped firing, pressed a button on the partition, and watched as his target headed back to him. Striking it down, he took it and his handgun, and brushed past her as he left. Morgana stepped up into his spot, clipped a new target to the wire, sent it hurtling to the far end of the range. Then she loaded the Glock, took her stance, aimed and squeezed off six shots in rapid succession. She pressed the recall button, but she already knew what she would see: six holes dead center. Having been trained by her father when she was still in her early teens, she had developed into a crack shot.

She was staring at the target when Goode tapped her on the shoulder. She turned, the look of surprise blossoming perfectly, and smiled.

"Hey," she said, taking off her earphones. "Lieutenant Goode, right?"

He nodded, clearly pleased that she remembered his name. "Ms. Roy!"

"Morgana, remember?"

"Ah, yes, of course."

He had a horsey kind of laugh, which meshed perfectly with his corn-fed looks. She wondered whether he'd say "Aw, shucks" if she complimented him. That'd be a hoot and a half.

"What are you doing here, Ms. . . . er, Morgana?"

"Working the Glock, same as you."

"Now there's a coincidence."

"A happy coincidence, I hope."

Here comes the "Aw, shucks."

"Gosh, well, it is for me."

Good enough, she thought with an interior grin.

His gaze slid reluctantly from her face to the target she was holding. "Hello! That's some nifty shooting."

"Thank you, kind sir."

He blushed and grinned, but for the moment seemed to have run out of compliments to give her.

"Well..." She picked up the Glock she had set down when he tapped her. "Nice running into you. Gotta get back to my routine."

She started to move away, thinking, *Is he going to bite, or not?*

"Uh, Morgana."

There's my good boy!

His voice trailed after her. She took two more steps, then paused, turning back. "Yes, Lieutenant?"

He came after her, just like a puppy dog. "If you don't..."

She stood her ground, waiting for him to come to her.

Obedient to her will, he took another couple of steps toward her. "If you don't mind me asking, are you almost finished?—with work, I mean."

She gave him a rueful smile. "Sadly, I'm only about halfway through." She cocked her head. "Why d'you ask?"

"Oh, well." His face fell; it was so pathetic. "I only meant, it's getting to be dinnertime. Mine, anyway. I have early mornings."

Oh, goody, Goode. Her smile brightened. "So do I."

"Well, d'you think you could...you know?"

"Could what?" Such sweet torture for him.

His cheeks were flaming. "Make an exception and come have dinner with me."

She looked around as if trying to decide. "I don't know. I..."

He was right in front of her, eager and terrified. "Please say yes."

"I did skip lunch today, so I am kind of hungry." She nodded. "And I guess I can catch up tomorrow morning."

He didn't hesitate at all. "Really? That's super."

———————

"Frankie. I wish you'd call me Frankie," he said. "All my friends do."

"I like the sound of that," Morgana said. "Frankie." She watched his cheeks color again. He was so transparent, like all men when you engaged their reptile brains.

They were ensconced in a back booth of a jam-packed steak house not far from the shooting range. The restaurant, clearly one of his local haunts, smelled of charcoaled meat and beer. At the bubbling, full-up bar an early season baseball game was playing on a TV screen. The oversaturated colors made her retinas throb. It was odd and vaguely disturbing, she thought, how the screen drew your eye no matter where in the room you sat.

They were drinking beers. Their server set plasticized menus in front of them, then slipped away without a word.

"So, Frankie, how d'you like working at Dread-naught?"

"Are you involved?"

She smiled. "Not married. No boyfriends."

He laughed, relaxing, as she had hoped. "No, no. I meant involved with Dreadnaught. I mean, you call the general Mac."

"Oh, that." She shrugged, keeping her voice offhanded. "I run an off-site enterprise for him. Deep data analytics."

He frowned. "Isn't that what NSA itself does?"

She smiled, took a sip of her beer. "What we do is a bit more specialized."

"Well, that tells me a whole bunch of nothing."

"Uh huh." She set her mug down carefully. "And you never answered my question."

"I can't talk about Dreadnaught." He appeared concerned. "You understand. You can't talk about yours, either."

"No." She waved her hand. "Of course. You're a good soldier, Lieutenant Goode."

"Frankie."

She cocked her head, gave him a quizzical look. "That was a joke."

"Huh? Oh . . . oh, yeah. Sorry."

"Never apologize, soldier."

He gave her a salute. "Yes, ma'am."

She dropped her eyes to the menu but didn't read it. She was thinking that she had already caused him to drop enough clues as to how he liked his women. "What's good here?"

"The New York strip."

"I'm partial to the tomahawk rib eye." She lifted her eyes to him. "Ever had that?"

"Uh uh. I always order the same thing."

Sure, you do. "How about we share the rib eye? It's big enough for two."

"Sure." He grinned. "Why not?"

It was crystal clear he liked the idea of sharing his meat with her. She laughed silently at the double entendre.

She slapped the menu. "It's settled then. You choose the fixings." She was betting with herself that they would be potato skins, loaded, and creamed spinach. The waitress drifted by, he ordered, and she won a million dollars.

"Well, one thing's for sure," she said, when they were alone. "We're in the same business."

"What business is that?"

"Secrets."

He nodded. "I hear you." Tilting his head back, he drained his mug, licked his lips as he looked at her. "So I know you'll get it." He sighed, rubbed a hand across his face. "It's so hard, you know. Keeping the secrets."

"The secrets set you apart. Who can you get close to, right? You can't even hold a decent conversation with most people."

He let go a deeper sigh, relaxing all the more. "You got that right."

"Unless it's with an insider. Someone who keeps as many secrets as you do. Maybe more."

"And even then."

Their steak arrived, along with the potato skins, loaded with butter, sour cream, bacon bits, chives, and creamed spinach, which she despised. They spent the next forty minutes sharing the tomahawk, which was surprisingly good. Frankie thought it had too much flavor, which made her mouth twitch in a sardonic smile. What a plain vanilla guy he was. While they ate, they spoke of things of no consequence to her: where he was raised, went to school, how he became interested in intelligence work while he was in the army. He had two brothers and a sister. He told her where they were and what they were doing, but that information went in one ear and out the other. She reciprocated with her own background. She drew enormous enjoyment from fabricating it on the spot: small family, home schooling, an abusive father—that was a must with this guy; men like Frankie were dying to fix females with broken wings.

"I see you're not plying me with liquor," she said, lifting one eyebrow, "like most men."

"I'm not like most men."

Oh, yes you are.

She laughed softly, throatily. His sincerity was almost heartbreaking. "I'm beginning to get that impression."

Afterward, in the parking lot, with chorus lines of traffic snaking by, he told her he wanted to see her home, as if they were sixteen-year-olds. That was a no-go. She didn't want him to see how far away from here she lived, she didn't want to raise any red flags about why she was at his shooting range.

"My place is being repainted; it stinks to high heaven." She gave him a judicious look. "But, you know, Frankie, I'd like to see where you live."

"Really?"

They were striped in shifting vehicle headlights. A semi's air horn trumpeted a mournful sound, doppler-ing away.

She nodded. "Really." Just a bit shy now. "Unless you don't want me to."

Of course he wanted her to; his eyes were glazed with the thought of her.

His home was in a concrete block building, low-rise, painted a pastel blue, one of many on a street lined with dusty chestnut trees. To her it looked like limbo, lost in the mists between urban and suburban. As they got out of their cars, a teenage kid in a high school varsity jacket bicycled past. He raised a hand to Frankie, who called, "Hey!" after him. Somewhere a dog barked, mournful as the semi's air horn.

"Well, this is it," Frankie said, opening the door to his second-floor apartment.

A bachelor pad, for certain. The living room was dominated by an enormous flat-panel TV. A sofa and easy chair were plunked in front of it with no thought to placement. Opened bags of potato chips and Cheetos shared a low table, cheap and scratched, with an oil-stained pizza box, one forlorn slice, cheese congealed like icing, lying within. No rugs. No pictures or photos on the walls, only posters for *Metal Gear Solid V* and *Call of Duty: Black Ops*. Military video games.

"My goodness," she said, turning slowly in a circle, "this could use a woman's touch."

Frankie flushed. "Sorry. But, well, my job gives me no spare time."

"Except for the shooting range."

"Huh. That's part of my job." He stepped toward her. "Here, let me take your coat."

It was the first time she felt his hands on her. They trembled just a bit right before she let her coat fall into his waiting arms.

"And what about weekends?"

He shrugged. "Weekends I treat myself to a big Waffle House breakfast after I hit the shooting range."

Waffle House, she thought pityingly. *That's his big treat.*

He watched, mouth half open, while she unzipped her dress. It slid down and pooled around her ankles. Very carefully, she stepped out of it; she did not take her high heels off. Men liked their women in high heels, especially with nothing else on.

He seemed to have stopped breathing. Then, as she walked him backward into the bedroom, his breath started to come in little wheezes, like he had asthma. When the backs of his knees pressed against the bed, she shoved him down, climbed on top of him.

"I can't believe this is happening," he said thickly.

"Shut up." She put her lips over his, her breasts pressed against his fluttering chest.

She undid his belt and trousers because his hands were trembling too badly, but when they touched her bare flesh they were terribly gentle, terribly romantic, if hands could be said to move in a romantic fashion, so that she felt some inner cog slip in the machinery of her plan, just for a moment, she felt the dissonance, the potential for change, and then it was back in place and everything was as it had been.

The act was purely physical for her, but not for him. And like the best escort she made it real for him, made him believe what he wanted to believe, helping him wish it into existence. There was an eruption of violent motion, of sweat and intimate moisture, and then it was over. It ended abruptly, and more than a little sadly. But then these things always did, she had found.

She had once seen a film of a cheetah running down a baby Thomson's gazelle while its mother hightailed it. The cheetah had used every last ounce of energy to reach the small gazelle, grab it by the throat, and kill it. For a long time, it crouched above its fallen prey, watching for larger predators, chest heaving mightily until it slowly brought its breath back into itself.

This is how Frankie seemed to her now, his chest rising and falling just as if he had run a great distance. She was still on top of him, thighs spread, hands gripping his shoulders.

"My God, that was good." She looked him right in the eye when she said this, which was the only way to lie successfully. She had learned that particular lesson a long time ago.

"Wow," he replied. "Just wow."

She laughed her soft, silken laugh, and, putting her lips against his ear, she told him how she had felt when he did that to her, and that, and that. She felt him stir beneath her.

"Frankie," she said.

He stroked the base of her spine. "Mmm?"

"I want to tell you something."

"Okay."

"I want to tell you what I do."

"But I thought we—"

She pressed a finger against his lips. "I'm trusting you, yeah? I need to. I've got no one else."

He stared up at her, as mesmerized as he had been at dinner, but for a different reason. Then again, maybe not.

So she told him about Meme LLC, about what they did there, and, saving it for last, about Mac giving her the impossible task of deciphering and intercepting what had come to be called the Bourne Initiative.

"I never heard of the Bourne Initiative," he said. "You sure that's what it's called?"

"Of course I'm sure, and here's why: Mac claimed he didn't send a Dreadnaught field unit to terminate Bourne."

"Well, I know the Russians have a kill team in place."

"That's what Mac said."

"Right."

"I don't believe it. I need Bourne. I want you to help me find him."

"Wow." He lifted her up, moved her aside, rolled to the edge of the bed. He stood up, looked back at her. "As usual, the general was right."

"What?" She experienced the sudden onset of free fall. "What did you say?"

His demeanor had altered radically. The dazzling marquee lights had shut down; the carnival of pink flesh and innocence had left town. His smile was a little sad, but mostly pitying. And that pity—now it was he who was pitying her—was in the instant possibly the hardest outcome of this failure for her to endure.

"You know what a honey trap is, I take it?"

His eyes were alight with a dark and sinister energy. But at the moment she was too shocked to feel fear.

Jesus Christ, she thought.

She wanted to say something, anything, but her

tongue seemed glued to the roof of her mouth. She could not move or breathe. An unbearable weight pressed down on her, forcing the air out of her lungs.

What the fuck is happening? She knew; of course she knew. But her brain refused to process the information.

Her consciousness, lifting out of her body, flew far away. Once, when she was a teenager, her father had taken her hunting up in the Yukon. They had gone hunting for what? Deer, elk? She couldn't for the life of her remember now. It was snowing when they'd come upon the wolf. Its left forepaw was stuck in one of those awful steel traps. It turned, looked at them with eyes that she could swear spoke to her. Then it put its head down and started to gnaw at the trapped leg just above the steel jaws. *"Oh, hell,"* her father had muttered just before he shot the wolf dead.

Lieutenant Goode opened the shallow drawer on his bedside table, took out a pair of real handcuffs. There was a pistol in there, too—a 9mm Glock—which he expertly slid out of its stiff leather holster. Both gestures carried grave portent.

"You're a bad girl, Morgana. Very bad." He pointed the Glock vaguely in her direction. "So this is where you find yourself. I'm the honey, this here's the trap, and there's no fucking way you're getting out of it."

12

IT WAS MEN, not machine-gun fire, that came down out of the dawn. The helo disgorged four men, jumping out of the open bay as the helo hovered over the rocky slope. To a man, they tumbled, unable to hold their initial balance, but soon enough they were up and bounding like mountain goats across the rocks, heading straight for Bourne and Mala.

"At last," he said. "*Spetsnaz* has arrived."

But that wasn't all. Three figures emerged from out of the dust of the rockslide as it began to settle. The Dreadnaughts weren't buried; they were very much alive, and like a nest of wasps that had been swatted they were mad as hell.

"We have no choice now," Mala said. "We have to fight them." She looked from one group to the other. "But we're just where we shouldn't be, caught between them."

Bourne squeezed off one shot at the *spetsnaz* unit.

"That was a lousy shot," Mala muttered.

Turning, Bourne squeezed off a shot at the advancing Dreadnaughts.

"Missed again," Mala grumbled. "What the hell's the matter with you?"

Grabbing her, Bourne crab-walked, picking his way through the spaces between the rocks, moving as quickly as he could out of the line of fire that had just started up between both sides.

And then Mala shut up, because she understood at last what he had meant to do all along. Following his lead, she slid on her backside, careful not to dislodge any loose rocks, making her way by staying completely in his shadow as he advanced along the cliff. The newly risen sun, tearing open a fiery rent in the pinkish dawn sky, was directly ahead of them. Behind them the two warring groups increased their combative fire.

Far enough away from the fray, Bourne slowed them, then halted altogether. They remained flat on their backs, staring up at wisps of cloud reflecting on their undersides the tender colors of the new day, while fusillades of submachine gun fire ripped apart the tortured soughing of the wind.

They lay in a little hollow, completely blind to the action, using their ears in a vain attempt to follow the battle. Beside him, Bourne felt Mala's muscles twitching spasmodically and knew she was itching to bang some heads together—American or Russian, it made no difference to her. Her nostrils flared to the scent of fresh blood. Hearing the moans of the dying, Bourne sensed it was all she could do not to leap up and join the killing.

She started when his fingers wrapped around her

wrist, and she turned her head. A sorority of disparate emotions darkened her eyes to midnight-blue. Rage, frustration, and, yes, love swirled in those eyes. Her lips were half open, as if she were about to reveal something terribly intimate, but if so, it never emerged.

Silence. The sea wind regained sovereignty. The gunfire had ceased as abruptly as it had begun; the calling of the gulls resumed, tentatively at first, then, as a sense of normalcy returned, the morning righting itself, the cries became more plaintive as the gulls appeared over the crown of the rock face.

Just above where they lay, the crest of the cliff began a downward sweep, leading to the lowest ridge to the east. Bourne felt the waves of restlessness in Mala and, turning to her, mouthed, *Wait*.

Why?

Listen. Just listen.

Both were stilled, then, as if they were among the corpses littering the rocks to the west. Their eyes were turned in that direction, as well, which is why they didn't see the lone survivor of the crossfire, a *spetsnaz* assassin, who had circled around to come at them from the east. He held a knife in one hand, his other weapons having emptied themselves during the withering firefight. He was big, muscular, bald of pate, animalistic of eye.

Baring his teeth, he leapt onto Bourne, drove the knife toward him. He meant to rip open his neck, but at the last instant Bourne twisted enough to change the strike point to his shoulder. Mala whipped up and around, one arm swinging wide to catch the Russian on the chin. This was a Special Forces member, hard-trained, wet-trained, with neither conscience nor room for remorse. He withdrew the knife blade, slashed it across Mala's chest, biting through the scarred skin, into the flat muscles between the hollow of her neck and the sharp rise of her breasts.

In the first few seconds, that seemed to be a mistake. The attack allowed Bourne the time to slam the edge of his hand into the side of the Russian's neck. The strike should have temporarily paralyzed him, but he only grinned—more a grimace, a hard surface, revealing nothing, reflecting everything.

As swiftly as the rock-fall avalanche, he crashed against Bourne, driving him backward. Sharp rocks bit into Bourne's back. Using the point of his knife, the Russian opened the shoulder wound he had inflicted, twisting the blade, until Bourne, lips drawn back in a silent snarl of pain, wrapped his hand around it, the edge scoring a line of blood in his palm as he wrenched the blade out of the muscles of his shoulder.

The Russian jammed the heel of his hand against Bourne's chin, pushing his head back until Bourne was effectively blind to what he was doing. Twisting Bourne's hand back on itself he created a fulcrum of pain in Bourne's wrist so acute that Bourne should have been forced to let go of the blade. Instead, Bourne used his free hand to pinch the Russian's carotid artery, temporarily cutting off blood flow to his brain. The Russian grunted and, in that instant, Bourne took charge of the knife blade, pushed the point into the Russian's face.

The point struck the ridge bone just below the Russian's left eye. Because of the upward angle, it slipped off the bone, tore through skin and flesh, burying itself in his eye. He gave out with a bellow, jerking back, giving Bourne full control of the knife, which he pushed in deeper, past the eye, into the Russian's brain.

———

Françoise awoke, as she always did, in a strange kind of purgatory, neither here nor there, but elsewhere. Possibly she hadn't slept at all, although there were intimations of the Swedish dawn sidling through the drapes. In the bathroom, she knelt as if to pray, and vomited up the memory of her abominable meeting with her half brother, Gora.

Françoise, with her face drowned beneath the cold water flow from the sink, heard the opening bars of "Bad Habits" by the Last Shadow Puppets from her mobile's speaker. It was a special ringtone she had edited and installed for only one person, and she lifted her head, crossed the hotel room without toweling off, snatched up her phone from the bedside table. Because of her insistence on dinner at Aifur Song, on squeezing out whatever amount of experience she could from this excuse of a city, she had had her guts mangled. *Oh, well,* she thought. *It's part of the price of doing business.*

"Auntie," Morgana said into her ear, by which code word she knew Morgana was in trouble.

She sat on the edge of the bed, back as ramrod straight as a sentry's, and said slowly and precisely, "What flavor of trouble are you in?"

"Licorice." The worst.

They both hated licorice.

"Where are you?" Knowing the severity of the trouble, there was no point in asking Morgana details.

"NSA HQ. Under armed guard. They allowed me one call, and I—"

"Stop." Françoise knew she needed to get off the line before NSA had a chance to realize they couldn't trace the call and started in on Morgana. That wouldn't do at all.

"I'll take care of it," she said, and broke the connection. Immediately, she opened her mobile, removed the SIM card, crushed it with the high, sharp heel of a shoe. Just in case. After inserting a brand new SIM card, she pressed a speed dial key.

There was hollowness on the line, along with a number of clicks like insects or electronics communicating with one another.

"Yes," the male voice said.

"It's happened," Françoise said. "It worked. Just as I predicted."

"That is gratifying news," Marshall Fulmer, the national security advisor, said, as if he had just heard the local weather report. "Where are they holding her?"

Françoise told him.

"I'm more than halfway back to D.C.," he said. "I'll make a call freezing everything in place."

"She's my friend. I don't want her harmed in any way."

"I promised you that she wouldn't be. Just keep her out of my hair, okay?"

"No problem there."

"You still sound nervous. Have faith, my dear."

"In an American national security advisor?"

He laughed at that. "I like you. I really do. You have what we call true grit back in the old country." He chuckled again. "Sit tight. She'll be with you shortly."

Françoise tossed the phone onto the bed, crawled

between the sheets, and slept like a baby until Justin Farreng knocked on her door with the breakfast he had had delivered to his room two floors above.

She opened the door nude.

"Good morning." He looked her up and down appreciatively. "What would've happened if I'd been housekeeping or the night manager?"

"They would've had a helluva story to tell." She let him into the room, closed the door behind him.

He set the tray down on a table.

"Coffee first," she said. "Black." As he filled cups from the silver carafe she regarded him from beneath hooded eyes. He was not a bad-looking fellow, smart, funny at times, slightly crazy, like all the best people. And his lovemaking was more than adequate. It was a minor wonder to her that she felt nothing at all for him. He might just as well have been a slab of raw meat hanging in a butcher's locker.

He smiled at her when he handed her the coffee, and she smiled back, even while her mind was elsewhere—with Morgana. Had Fulmer arrived in D.C. yet? Had he freed her, set her on a plane to Stockholm? Was she on her way here? Now that she was awake, the caffeine kicking in, she felt on edge, in an entirely different way than last night, waiting for Morgana's call, which, she had had to admit to herself, might not come.

"Toast?" Farreng asked, holding up a freshly buttered triangle of whole grain.

"Revelations?" Françoise replied, holding out the thumb drive Fulmer had given her.

"So soon?" Farreng's eyebrows lifted as they made the exchange. "How good?"

"It will give even you pause," she said, dunking her toast into the coffee, then ripping off a bite between her even, white teeth. She had inserted the drive into her laptop's USB port, using the security code Fulmer had made her memorize, the moment she had returned to her room and before she dressed for dinner. The files therein were real eye-openers, especially the ones pertaining to General MacQuerrie. *Good Lord, what these people get up to,* she had thought while showering off the day's sweat and sticky particulates. Everything online, buried in servers protected by layers of firewalls and malware busters, and yet vulnerable to attacks so sophisticated the cyber weapons morphed exponentially every week, if not daily. *Nothing's safe anymore,* she thought, *unless it's a hard copy locked away in a vault buried in the concrete foundation of a massive office building. And even then…Back to the future, right?*

"Is that so?" He grinned, tumbling the drive between his fingers like a prestidigitator. "I'll be eager to see what your sources have unearthed this time."

"Make sure you're sitting down when you do."

His eyebrows rose again. *Don't do that,* she thought. *It makes you look like a clown.*

"It's not like you to oversell your product, Françoise."

"That's right." She bent, taking another slice of toast. "And this time alert me before it goes live. I want a front-row seat at the freaking firestorm."

———

Mala hauled the Russian off Bourne, unwrapped Bourne's fingers from the knife. "Shit," she said, staring at his bloodred palm, "I can see clear to the bone." She looked at him. "Does it hurt?"

"Don't feel a thing," Bourne said. "Same for my shoulder." But his eyes were going in and out of focus.

Using the knife to make strips out of the Russian's trousers, she fashioned compression bandages by wrapping the strips around his palm and over his shoulder under his armpit. "Not the most antiseptic, but what the hell."

Waving off Mala's help, he got to his feet.

"We've got to get out of here," she said. "Right now."

Bourne nodded. "We'll take the powerboat."

The climb up to the crest taxed neither of them, but the way down to the shingle and the curling combers was dauntingly steep for Bourne in his condition. Nevertheless, they began their descent without hesitation.

Despite the difficulties, their progress was easier than the night before in darkness and the beginnings of the storm. The wind had lapsed to the lightest of breezes, the air was still night-cooled, and the way was sunlit.

Bourne did not give the slightest indication of the level of pain he was in, now that his body's trauma defenses were wearing off. There was no option other than to keep moving.

Nevertheless, two-thirds down, he was obliged to pause. Despite the still, cool air, sweat ran down his face, trickled along his spine and from under his arms. The throbbing in his shoulder and hand was a palpable thing, spiking his heart rate. Black spots danced before his eyes. He realized his breathing was coming in shallow gasps; he slowed it down, taking deep, even breaths, reoxygenating his lungs.

Mala, realizing something was wrong, paused below him, turning an inquiring gaze back at him.

He made a shoveling motion with his good hand, indicating she should continue on. This she did without another word, and, relying on his second wind, he followed close behind.

An eternity of pain accompanied him, during which nothing existed beyond the next hand- and foothold, the search for the best path, bypassing deadfalls, perilous crevasses or cracks, and loose rocks. Following Mala made all this easier and more difficult at the same time. She was lighter than he was by a good margin; sections that held her might not hold him, which made him doubly cautious. On the other hand, this intense concentration kept his attention from the pain, which was so excruciating he was only partially successful in compartmentalizing it.

But, at last, even eternity must end. He slid the last three feet to the shingle, keeping his knees bent as if he were a parachutist landing, in order to cushion the shock to his feet and legs. They were several hundred yards to the east of where the boats had been left. They seemed to have weathered the storm better than he expected.

He and Mala set off at once, with him taking the lead. Mala did not protest. In fact, she had said nothing at all since their brief conversation while she was jerry-rigging his bandages and binding his wounds, both of which were deep, bloody, and angry. He'd need expert medical attention, the sooner the better, in order to stave off infections that would put him in the hospital, weak and vulnerable.

They were a dozen feet from the powerboat when

he collapsed. Mala ran, knelt beside him, and gasped. The wound in his shoulder had bled right through the thick cloth, soaking it. His entire right side was dark and sticky with blood. The wound must have punctured the brachial artery.

She lifted the lid of one of his eyes, said, "Shit," wasted no time in a vain attempt to revive him; it would take too long, and time was now in short supply. She understood the extreme peril Bourne was in. Reaching under his armpits, she dragged him directly into the water, kept him afloat as she swam to the port side of the powerboat. Grabbing on to his bloody shirt with one clawed hand, she levered herself over the gunwale, then, feet firmly planted on the deck, hauled Bourne up and over, onto the deck.

For a moment, she stared at his face, pale and bloodless. Despite her efforts at field dressing, he was still bleeding. In fact, now that she had a chance to study him closely, it was clear to her that he was dying.

Part Two
Keyre

13

AS JASON BOURNE lay slowly bleeding out on the deck of a water-swilled powerboat, purchased by a cutout offshore middleman for Dreadnaught, a veritable shitstorm was exploding in the face of General Arthur MacQuerrie, head of that most secret of government entities, in the form of the latest LeakAGE bombshell, a hacked trove of eyes-only documents from the NSA's very bowels. They revealed that, in the first place, NSA, that most august, feared, and reviled surveillance division of the American clandestine services, which prided itself on its SIGINT, electronic and satellite spying, and turned its nose up at the CIA and its outmoded HUMINT, boots-on-the-ground form of intelligence gathering, had on its blackest of books its own HUMINT division code-named Dreadnaught. In the second place, that Dreadnaught was heavily and, needless to say, illegally, funded from various named sources, none of which, apparently, existed. In the third place, that said Dreadnaught was in the business of targeting enemies of the American homeland—controversial, gray-area entities, to a person—and terminating them with extreme prejudice, without the knowledge, never mind the consent, of Congress. In the fourth place, that these bloodletting assignments were decided upon and meted out solely by one General Arthur MacQuerrie without any kind of oversight whatsoever.

And in the fifth place, and most damning for MacQuerrie, were a raft of files spewed out into cyberspace documenting the eye-opening amounts of money salted away by the aforementioned General Arthur MacQuerrie in a briar patch of shell companies in the Caymans, Panama, Argentina, Gibraltar, and Cyprus. As an adjunct to this perfidy visited upon the federal government and the American people was the treasonous way these shell companies appeared to rub shoulders with those known to belong to certain high-level officials and billionaire oligarchs of the Russian Federation.

The flurry of documents was released at three in the morning, Eastern Daylight Time. Before first light in D.C., emissaries of Homeland Security, accompanied by a contingent of heavily armed military personnel, confronted a sleep-bedazzled MacQuerrie on his front doorstep. Moments later, under the teary gaze of his wife, he was handcuffed, hustled down his McLean walkway, past prize azaleas and rhododendrons, ushered with only a modicum of courtesy into the back of one of three gleaming black Chevrolet SUVs. Four minutes after they had arrived, the modern-day caravan was gone, leaving only faint bluish exhaust fumes that dissipated even before the distraught Mrs. MacQuerrie closed the front door and dialed their lawyer's home phone number.

Meanwhile, the ominous caravan made its next stop at the home of Lieutenant Francis Goode. Goode, having received advance warning of the intentions of the long arm of the federal government, had tried to do a runner, but too late. As the SUVs hurled themselves around the corner to his street, he sprinted back into his house and barricaded himself inside. A fierce firefight ensued, in the midst of which the good lieutenant, having determined beyond a shadow of a doubt that there was no way out, put the muzzle of his pistol into his mouth and blew his brains out.

At around the same time as the LeakAGE barrage began, Fulmer, having deplaned at the VIP side of Dulles International, and true to his word, deployed the full flower of his influence, gaining Morgana her freedom from NSA custody. As dawn broke over D.C., she was aboard a military transport on her way to Stockholm and thence, via a far more comfortable commercial flight, to Kalmar, where Françoise was anxiously awaiting her arrival.

Not many things gave Françoise anxiety; doing nothing but waiting was one of them; meditation was not her thing. Of course, as recompense, she experienced the delightful diversion of watching the LeakAGE shitbomb light up the Internet like a line of napalm detonations. The speed at which LeakAGE stories went viral still astonished her, but this one, as expected, flashed around the globe at what seemed light speed. And why not? Not only was an American general implicated in nefarious dealings, but the NSA itself—everyone's favorite whipping boy since Snowden—was caught with its pants down. As she had foreseen, everyone wanted a piece of that action. And, not so incidentally, the pressure on Fulmer's own not so very kosher interests domiciled in Panama was lifted. This story was so big it would defy the usual mayfly-short news cycle; it would build and build, and then linger for months. More than enough time for Fulmer to leave Musgrave-Stephens and reassign his interests to Fellingham, Bodeys.

Which reminded her. Hunched in front of a laptop shielded from ISP snooping, she began the long, laborious process that would ensure her another airtight get-out-of-jail-free card to play should the necessity arise.

———

The Angelmaker was reluctant to leave Bourne alone on the rocking powerboat, but there was no help for it. Slipping over the gunwale, she swam the short distance to where the shingle came up to meet her just before the creaming surf, if that's what you could call these laughably small waves. But that's what you got in what was essentially a landlocked sea.

Picking her way across the prickly shore as quickly as she could, she approached the area where she had been waiting for Bourne as he drove toward her in the *Nym*'s runabout. Down on her knees at the base of the cliff, she dug beneath the surface, extracting a neoprene waterproof bag, which she unzipped. Inside were a mobile and a sat phone, two different caliber handguns, extra ammo, a serrated knife in a thick rubber sheath, a coil of nylon rope, and a first aid kit in a long red plastic box. After assuring herself that it hadn't been disturbed and that everything was there, she made an encrypted emergency call on the sat phone, not trusting to mobile service here. Then she put back the phone, zipped the bag, and returned with it to the powerboat.

Back on deck, she placed the bag next to Bourne, pressed her fingers against his carotid. Relief flooded through her: he was still alive. Then she opened the bag, took out the first aid kit. First, she applied tourniquets to stop the bleeding. Then she cut off the bloody field dressings and commenced to clean the wounds, first with an antiseptic solution and then with a powerful antibiotic powder. Lastly, she bound them with Elastoplast, sealing them temporarily. Still, there was nothing she could do about the blood he had lost, and that was a real worry.

She sat back on her haunches. Bourne's blue-white face looked like a three-day-old mackerel. It made her sick in the pit of her stomach. Bending over from the waist, she placed her lips against his. They were cold as ice, as if he were already dead. She opened his mouth with hers, breathed warm air into him, as if this were a fairy tale, as if she had magical powers and she could breathe life into him. Why not? She had done everything else she could think of to save him.

Fuck those fucking Russian fucks, she thought. *Their day will come, and when it does I'm going to use their guts for balalaika strings.*

A moment later, she heard the deep, rumbling sound of the heavy diesels, and the ship came into view. On the elevated rear deck of the ship was a helo, which airlifted them to Skyros Island International Airport. There, a newly minted Bombardier 8000 long-haul private jet was ready and waiting for them. Customs and immigration had been arranged following her call, and they wasted no time in taking off. The Bombardier 8000, the company's newest flagship jet, cost nearly $69 million, cruised at a speedy Mach 0.85, and was as comfortable as could be.

Preparations had been made for Bourne to be transferred onto a locked-down gurney. Every conceivable blood type was available. As soon as the surgeon on board had determined Bourne's blood type, his nurse commenced the first of what would no doubt be a number of transfusions. A saline drip was arranged on Bourne's other side, to deal with his dehydration. By that time they were six and a quarter miles high, the sky was a shell of bright purple-blue, and the Angelmaker could finally relax. For a time, from the aspect of her cushy leather seat, comfortable in dry clothing, she drank bottle after bottle of water, observing the surgeon, who looked very grave indeed, and his nurse expertly attending to Bourne. When it was that her eyes closed and she dropped into the arms of sleep she could not, afterward, recall.

It was just over 2,688 miles from the Skyros airport to Somalia. The Bombardier 8000 touched down just over four hours after it had taken off, one of its passengers still more dead than alive.

14

BOURNE, LYING INSENSATE in a spotless room near the center of Keyre's camp, hung suspended between yesterday and tomorrow. The camp, riding the Horn of Africa, still on the shores of the Arabian Sea, would have been unrecognizable to him. Since Bourne had made his first nocturnal visit, it had grown into something resembling a medium-size village, complete with its own airfield with runways long enough to accommodate jet planes even larger than the Bombardier 8000, for cargo shipments were constantly being flown to and from the camp, executing Keyre's arms traffic. Thanks to extensive dredging, the area was now a deep-water port for cargo ships, which came and went with the same purpose as the air traffic. Too, the tents Bourne had encountered when he snatched Mala and her sister had given way to sunbaked brick buildings. Cranes rose into the air, bulldozers, and all manner of earthmoving equipment rumbled and thudded, as more and more buildings were constructed. Cart paths had been widened and paved, altered here and there to form a semblance of a grid within the perimeter of the village, which was protected, like military bases the world over, by high fences, barriered gates, and three shifts of armed sentries. There was even a radar tower, along with a pair of anti-aircraft missile launchers.

But all of this bristling modernization was at present unknown to Bourne. His mind, teetering on the verge of an abyss with no bottom, had returned to the Somalia he had known. To the pitch-black night of an AWOL moon and stars, filled with the ominous rumbling of what would rapidly develop into a monstrous thunderstorm. As if in a grainy film he saw himself planting the two incendiary bombs on the north end of Keyre's tented camp. Detonators set for six minutes, he threaded his way through the darkness, passing up at least three opportunities to break the necks of sentries; he wanted no evidence there was anyone near the camp except in the north.

In the days previous, he had made a map of the camp during a series of clandestine forays at dawn and twilight, when daylight was at its weakest. Mounting the heights slightly inland of the camp, he sighted through powerful binoculars, taking mental notes of the comings and goings of everyone within the camp. Occasionally, he saw the girls, and he determined, sadly, there were too many for him to free them all. He saw the line of wooden spears upon whose sharp tips were jammed severed heads, some fresh, others reeking beneath their crawling carapace of flies, still others meatless, dark and leathery from sun and salt wind. Bony cattle roamed through the compound, heads down, in a vain attempt to forage scraps amid the pyramids of plastic bottles.

One dawn he observed a contingent of jihadists firing machine pistols at a cracked and bullet-pitted Western toilet, lying on its side in an open space of dust and porcelain shards. The next morning, assaulted even at this remove by the horrific stench of rotting flesh, he bore witness amid the wreckage of the ruined toilet to five wooden stakes to which had been crudely bound five headless corpses. The same contingent fired their machine pistols at these targets, making them dance as the bullets struck them. The jihadists laughed obscenely.

The morning before his planned raid, he observed Keyre using a crude but enormous machete to sever a man's head. His men kicked the head around like Aztecs at their ball game before hoisting it onto an available spear. During his twilight recon, Bourne was unfortunate enough to see one of the girls being dragged out of the communal tent. It was not Liis—he had been given portrait photos of both sisters by their father. To his horror, the girl could not have been more than twelve. Perhaps she had been recalcitrant, perhaps she had spat in Keyre's face, or tried to escape. In any event, she now faced the ultimate punishment. Quitting his position, Bourne sprinted as fast as he could manage while keeping himself hidden, but he was too far away to come close enough to do something to save her—though precisely what that might be without getting himself killed he could not say. And yet it was impossible for him to stand by and do nothing. But, apart from attacking the compound with a company of well-armed soldiers, there was nothing to do. And this knowledge pierced him deeply and completely.

The poor girl's death, barbaric and inhuman as it was, served to confirm every horror story Mala and Liis's father had told him about Keyre and his jihadist cult of personality. Feeling helpless in the face of such evil was one of the worst moments in Bourne's life, a nightmare that would stay with him for years to come. There was no good way to bear witness to such an atrocity, except for him to promise himself that the people responsible—especially Keyre—would pay with their lives. And in the here and now, he knew the best thing he could do was to save Mala and Liis from such a monstrous fate.

Even in the dead of night he knew where every tent was and who or what resided inside each. Most important, he knew where Keyre spent most of his time and where his girls were kept. For reasons he had yet to determine, Mala was stashed in a separate tent next to Keyre's, perhaps for easy access. But her sister, Liis, was in with the other girls. It made things awkward—more difficult, but not impossible. It didn't help to see how much other death lay around the camp like so much fallen snow; it made it worse. He wanted nothing more than to rid this camp, this spot of beautiful coastline, of torture and death-dealing. But virtually the whole of the Horn of Africa was an abattoir, a cesspit of tribal warfare and bug-eyed revolutionaries, maddened by their own religious zeal.

The night had come, the darkness around the tented camp absolute. The incendiary explosive devices were in place. Less than ten seconds to go until the twin detonations, causing panic, shock, and chaos.

Seven, six...

———————

"What the hell is going on?" Morgana said when Françoise met her as she entered the small, neat-as-a-pin arrivals hall, after deplaning. "Nobody told me anything." It was clear she was equal parts incensed and frightened from her brief though surely scary incarceration. "I'm sitting on both flights biting my nails, looking over my shoulder, waiting for the NSA to drag me back to holding."

"Forget the NSA," Françoise said, kissing her on both cheeks, then taking the crook of her arm in hers. "At the mo-mo, they have more on their plate than they can handle."

Morgana halted them both, and in the middle of the echoing arrivals hall, Françoise dragged out her mobile, fired up a browser, and showed Morgana the CNN site. Morgana grabbed the phone out of her hand, greedily reading and scrolling down at the same time.

"Good Christ, all hell's broken loose."

Françoise nodded. "MacQuerrie has vanished down the fed rabbit hole, possibly never to return." She grinned. "Ding dong, the wizard is dead."

Morgana looked up into her friend's face. "This is real?"

"Uh huh."

"Wow," Morgana breathed. "Just...wow."

She went back to reading the adjunct articles as Françoise steered her outside, where a hired car was waiting. She managed to get Morgana inside, then slid into the backseat beside her and closed the door. The driver glanced at her in the rearview mirror, and she nodded.

"It's good to have you here," she said as the car pulled out into the exit roadway. "With me."

Morgana, finished reading, for the moment anyway, handed back the mobile. "Did you have something to do with this?" When Françoise shrugged, the grin still on her face, Morgana said, "I don't know what to say."

"I told you I would help you if you ever got into real trouble."

"I know, but..." She took a deep breath, let it out slowly. Relief brought her shoulders down from either side of her neck. "I don't know how to thank you."

"Oh, I'll think of something," Françoise said with a twinkle in her eye. "But first, we take you shopping. You look like Raggedy Ann." She took her friend's hand, squeezed it in a reassuring manner. "Then we eat. I know a great place. The last time I was there I threw up three hours later."

Morgana laughed. "That's a recommendation?"

"In this case, it is." She laughed. "Trust me."

"Always," Morgana said. "Always."

Tick-tock... *Boom!*

The entire tented camp was in a frenzy, revolutionary

zeal temporarily submerged under the twin necessities of putting out the fires and finding the perpetrators. Under cover of the major diversion, Bourne headed in.

Moving fast and low, he threaded his way between the tents, taking as direct a route as he was able, considering all the running troops he had to dodge. Now, with an earth-shuddering roar, the sky cracked open and the deluge commenced. That was both good news and bad news. The thick curtains of rain added to the confusion and helped mask his progress through the camp, but it also went a long way to putting out the fires prematurely.

Inside their prison tent, a dozen girls stood perfectly still. They stood on their mean pallets, legs slightly spread as if they were on a ship rolling on the high seas. They were the only immobile people in the entire camp. Not one of them thought to take advantage of the opportunity to run, not after what had happened at twilight.

Someone had lit a kerosene lamp. By the inconstant light of its flickering flame, they stared at him out of emaciated faces with overlarge eyes, their bodies pale beneath tattered clothes. Once again Bourne's heart was rent. He wanted to save them all, but to save two he needed to leave the others behind. He'd never make it out with all of them in tow.

Stepping to Liis, he grabbed her hand, led her out of the tent, out into the deluge. Already the ground was a muddy morass. The rain was coming down so hard, even the sandy soil could not drain it away fast enough.

He endeavored not to let the girl's stumbling gait slow him down, carrying her under one arm when he had to. Like a waft of air, she weighed next to nothing. Arriving at the rear of the tent in which Mala was being held, he used a knife to rip open the fabric. With Liis in tow, he stepped through the rent to find the older sister.

She was not alone.

Bourne had expected a guard, perhaps two. The person standing between him and Mala was Keyre.

15

"**A**ND LIEUTENANT GOODE,**"** Morgana said, as she sipped her dirty martini. "Ah, Lieutenant Goode."

Françoise, her hands cupped around a vodka rocks, said, "You know this man?"

"He was the one." Morgana took another sip, delighting in how the icy liquid turned to fire in her belly. "The one who MacQuerrie prepped to suck me in."

"A double honey trap." Françoise nodded. "Very clever."

"I was an idiot."

"We're all idiots once in a while." Françoise laughed. "Otherwise, how would we know we're human?"

Aifur Song was packed to the gills, an apt analogy given the preponderance of fish and seafood on the artfully designed menu. Since they had arrived a half hour ago, the noise level had steadily risen, until now it was a dull roar, like stormy surf heard at a short remove.

Their drinks finished, the waiter brought refills without being asked. Shortly thereafter, while the two women were catching each other up in a concerted attempt to restore Morgana's equilibrium, a young man with dark, probing eyes and straight dark hair, slicked back to reveal a widow's peak, appeared out of the crowd, wending his way to their table.

"Ah, there you are," Françoise said, raising a hand. She made the introductions. "Morgana Roy, meet Larry London, a terrific freelance photographer."

Smiling warmly, Rozin, newly minted head of *spetsnaz*, briefly took Morgana's hand before sliding into a chair at their four-top. "Very pleased to meet you, Ms. Roy."

"Morgana, please."

He nodded. "Morgana. And you must call me Larry." He laughed. "All my friends do." His laugh was dry and easy to digest; it drew you to him without any fuss. Their waiter materialized at his elbow; Rozin pointed to Morgana's dirty martini. "I'll have what the lovely lady is drinking."

"Very good, sir," the waiter said, departing.

"Morgana," Françoise said, "you recall the photo of the mother and daughter Afghan refugees being pulled out of the water after their boat capsized."

"The one that won the Pulitzer? Sure. It was the centerpiece of the Global Photographics traveling exhibit a few years back. Everyone's seen it."

"That was Larry's work."

Morgana cocked her head. "Really?"

He shrugged. "Right place, right time."

Françoise scoffed. "He has no ego, this one. That was peak performance, Larry. Everyone knows that."

The anecdote served its purpose; the ice had been neatly broken. When Rozin's drink was set before him, they all toasted "better days," and swallowed the alcohol.

"And what do you do, Morgana?" Rozin asked, setting his cocktail glass down.

"Oh, no, Larry," Françoise cut in. "You mustn't ask her that."

"Mustn't I?" Rozin's eyes sparkled. He knew very well Morgana's specialty, having been read in by Françoise via text message while Morgana was trying on clothes. "How delightfully intriguing."

"Intrigue is just what we seek to avoid." Françoise picked up her menu. "Isn't that right, Morgie?"

Rozin made a face. "Oh, don't call her that; Morgana is such a beautiful name. One you don't hear very often. Welsh. From the compound *Morcant*—a circle or bright sea."

Morgana was impressed. "That's more than I knew."

"Oh, Larry's assignments take him to every corner of the globe," Françoise said, "where he absorbs knowledge like a six-year-old."

"Are you two lovers?" Morgana asked, looking from one to the other.

"Lovers?" Françoise burst out laughing.

"It's that funny?" Rozin exclaimed. It wasn't difficult evincing wounded pride.

"Larry's one of my messengers," Françoise said. "Receiving and delivering vital information." Her eyes flashed merrily. "Number one. *Ichiban*, as the Japanese say."

Rozin shot her a dark look, as if with her bantering she was cleaving too close to a kernel of truth. But Morgana was too entranced by the lighthearted byplay that included her as an instant friend—part of this family, one might say—to notice. Fun was to be had here, and a secure place to rest her still-spinning head, safe and protected from the dreadful events of the last twenty-four hours. Her unwinding had begun when Françoise had taken her shopping. It continued now, at a faster pace, running downhill like water to the ocean. And, oh, it felt so good to finally let her guard down.

That was when the shakes started. She looked up helplessly at Françoise, who understood that her friend was going into delayed shock. Jumping up, Françoise took Morgana by the hand, steered her through the restaurant as quickly as she could.

They made it into the ladies' room just in time. Françoise held Morgana's hair back from her face as, bent double, she vomited up the gin and terror that had been roiling inside her, clamoring to be released. Periodically, Françoise lifted her head past the electronic eye, automatically flushing the toilet over and over.

"Jesus, Françoise." Ripping squares of toilet paper off the roll, Morgana wiped her mouth with shaky hands. "Jesus fucking Christ." She was shaking like an addict in withdrawal. "I'm not cut out for this life."

Françoise cradled her shoulders gently. "None of us is, darling. I'm afraid there's a steep learning curve."

Morgana stood up, but, still shaky, she leaned against the stall's left partition. "Was it the same with you?"

Françoise nodded. "Of course. But, you know, it was Larry who taught me a lot."

"Larry. Really." Morgana allowed herself to be led out of the stall to the line of sinks.

"Uh huh," Françoise affirmed.

Morgana washed out her mouth, splashed water on her face, toweled off. "God, I look a fright," she said, staring into the mirror.

"Nonsense. You're one of those women who don't need makeup to look beautiful." She tilted her head, handed Morgana a tube. "Maybe just a touch more color on your lips."

As Morgana checked out the color, then applied the lipstick, Françoise said. "You know, now I think about it, maybe Larry would do the same for you."

Like the tent that held the other girls, Mala's tent was lit by a kerosene lantern—two of them, in fact, one on each side of the tent. Their light revealed a cheap tribal rug covering the rough ground, a small propane ring on which hunkered a squat iron kettle, beside which were a handleless cup and a square tin canister marked as Russian Caravan tea. Next to that was, incongruously, a wooden rolling cart with six long drawers. One of the drawers was pulled partway out. Bourne could see inside, and his blood ran cold. An array of implements, all sharply bladed or pointed, some steel, but others iron or fire-hardened bamboo, each meticulously nested in its own lined niche. In the center of the tent stretched a curious contraption made of bentwood and dowels, stained almost black in spots, a framework on which a human body could be lain giving access to both front and back. The carpet beneath the thing was black, as well. Many layers of blood, dried one over the other.

At the head—or foot, it was impossible to tell—of this strange and sinister piece of furniture, stood Mala. Keyre was pressed up against her back, holding an instrument much like a scalpel, but with a wickedly curved blade, at her carotid, which pulsed with her terror. Liis, cleaving to Bourne as if he were a rock, gave a little strangled cry.

"Kill her?" Keyre said without preamble in Somali. "No, I don't think so." Was he addressing Bourne or Liis? Perhaps it was both.

The instrument moved down from the side of Mala's neck to a spot just underneath her right breast.

He caught Bourne's eye. "But one of these will come off now." He gestured with his head. "Unless, that is, you let go of the girl so she can be with her sister, where she belongs."

"The girls belong as far away from here as they can get."

"And that is why you're here, one guesses." He was tall but not a big man. Wiry and athletic, one muscle fitted into another without the interference of fat or excess flesh. His mahogany skin appeared to be stretched over muscle and bone with the form-fitting tightness of Lycra. His cheeks were shadowed, deeply sunken—or were they deformed by ritual scars? In the lantern light it was difficult to tell. His tightly curled hair fit like a cap high on his head, the sides and front shaven clean. His eyes radiated the fever-bright light of the fanatic. People like Keyre could not be reasoned with; they had to be dealt with on their own terms or not at all.

"Before anything gets out of hand—"

Keyre tossed his head. "It's already out of hand. Thanks to you."

"And yet here I am. I've got your attention. More than that, I have an audience alone with you." Bourne cocked his head. "How d'you suppose I could have gotten that otherwise?"

Keyre grunted. "You speak very good Somali, for an infidel."

"I'll take that as a compliment."

"Don't take it for fucking anything."

Bourne decided he needed to take a chance. Pushing the cowering Liis slightly away from him, he unwound her fingers from his. For a long, tense moment, Keyre did nothing. Then he lowered his instrument to his side, but kept it at the ready.

"Speak, then."

Bourne produced the deep sigh of a businessman who finds himself at the short end of the stick. "You're right, I did come here for the girls."

"Their father."

Bourne nodded.

"Their father's a shit. He sold them to people, who sold them to me."

It was easy to believe Keyre was an inveterate liar; the talent went with the territory. But this time Bourne felt certain he was telling the truth. "Nevertheless, I'd like to take them away."

"Impossible," Keyre said. "The process is in its final stages."

Ripping off her stained cloth shift, he pushed Mala forward with his chest and knees so that she came fully into the light. Liis's cry was like that of a baby bird witnessing her mother being crushed. Mala's skin down her torso and limbs was a reddened webwork of open cuts, angry wounds, and livid scars. She had been systematically tortured. This was Bourne's initial reaction, not yet understanding the maiming wasn't disfigurement at all—at least, not in Keyre's eyes—but a series of Yibir magical glyphs, whose lineage stretched all the way back to the ancient Ajuran Empire of the 1300s.

"Once it has begun," Keyre said in a frighteningly reasonable tone, "this process cannot be interrupted." He gestured with his chin. "Take the little sister if you must. I will name a price, you will pay it, here, now, and you will depart, never to return."

Bourne had been moving, ostensibly to gain a better look at the extent of the damage Keyre had inflicted on Mala. He stared into her eyes, which looked like depthless pools, dead at their bottoms, and he thought, *She's already lost*. But then the punishment he had witnessed, meted out at twilight to the little girl, returned to him with all the force of a hammer blow. An innocent caught up, like so many innocents, in the tribal warfare between fanatic religious factions. These days, jihadists came in every color of the rainbow, shedding blood and brothers over territory more than two thousand years old.

"Those are your terms," Bourne said, still evincing the businessman's attitude.

"They are."

"Let's see if we can—"

"*Final* terms," Keyre said flatly, and the instrument returned to the soft flesh beneath Mala's right breast. "Rejoice that I have given you any terms at all."

"Oh, I am," Bourne said. "Rejoicing, that is." And with that, he kicked over the lantern closest to him, which was why he had moved in the first place.

Kerosene spilled out of the uncapped reservoir and with a great *whoosh* of heat and light caught fire. The fibers of the rug were dry, perfect fuel for such a conflagration. Bourne pushed Liis backward through the rent with one hand, then, in almost the same motion, stepped through the flames, emerging on the other side like some avenging deity, a god of death.

16

THE NEW, IMPROVED, and far more powerful national security advisor Marshall Fulmer bestrode the D.C. Beltway like a colossus. As the person who had uncovered MacQuerrie's illegal incarceration of Morgana Roy and, by extension, the existence of Meme LLC, a black off-site cyber operation seemingly devoted exclusively to furthering the general's astonishingly far-flung interests, which might or might not sync up with Russian Federation business interests—even before LeakAGE released the slurry of MacQuerrie files—Fulmer received an unprecedented quantity of air time, photo ops, and interviews with the most prestigious of TV's talking heads. He was invited to the White House to meet with the president and his security staff, who solicited his opinion on how to ensure they would not miss even one of MacQuerrie's well-hidden tentacular organizations.

Since MacQuerrie had shut up like a giant clam, they

also wanted to know just what the hell the general was up to. Was it simply greed? Or was there a more sinister purpose at work here?

At no time during these intense sessions did Fulmer mention the Bourne Initiative. Further, he felt confident that MacQuerrie would never, ever divulge the initiative's existence, let alone his almost obsessive interest in it. For Fulmer, since the time when he'd conceived of his plot to overthrow the general, was convinced that MacQuerrie had engaged Meme LLC to uncover where in the cyber-world General Boris Illyich Karpov had stashed the code to build the ultimate cyber weapon, one capable of punching through any firewall in its path and penetrating to the heart of America's final defense: the nuclear launch codes.

What MacQuerrie wanted to do with it was not quite clear—sell it, use it as ransom to scramble to the top of the federal heap, what? One thing Fulmer did know was that Meme LLC was Morgana Roy. It was her mind that ran the cadre; without her, Meme LLC was useless. In fact, as of last night, Meme LLC was finished. Its members had been let go, but not before signing a second document of nondisclosure on pain of being charged with treason and, without access to counsel, tried and incarcerated for the rest of their lives. They were little people; they didn't matter. Only Morgana Roy with her brilliant mind and knack for parsing the most mind-bending algorithms mattered. And now she was where she needed to be, with Françoise. Françoise had her orders. She'd soon put Morgana to work.

In the meantime, it behooved Fulmer to bask in the glow of his newfound notoriety. He had attained hero status. In the best vampiric Beltway tradition everyone wanted to include themselves in the halo effect. But he had been around politics too long to believe it would last. As Napoleon famously wrote, "Fame is fleeting, but obscurity is forever." Soon enough, another hero would come to the fore and be anointed by the press, and he would be forgotten, put on the shelf along with all the other sclerotic pols. Not so when he became president. Every day would be like this one, filled with spotlights and sound bites. He'd make damn sure of it.

One of Fulmer's beautifully self-serving traits was his ability to change course as the situation before him demanded. Difficult enough to do in the slippery business world, almost impossible in the sclerotic political arena, where you were eternally enmeshed in a web of backroom deals, bill riders placating insistent interest groups in your states, flexing moral muscles in the service of amassing a nest egg of favors from your enemies across the Congressional aisle. At this point in time, Fulmer had a larger nest egg than even Lyndon Johnson had had in his heyday.

As a result of this ecstatic flurry of activity, Fulmer found himself at the end of each long day both exhausted and exhilarated. And it was at this time, doubtless because of their ability, akin to the Nazi Gestapo's, to strike their target at the precise moment of maximum vulnerability, that the lampreys swam closest to him, looking to attach their suckers to his flesh without being immediately brushed aside.

Such a person was Harry Hornden, a freelance journo of no small note. He was peculiar inasmuch as he had no trouble straddling both the old and the new worlds of journalism. He wrote award-winning think pieces for prestigious monthlies, while also maintaining a snarky and, in Fulmer's opinion, somewhat subversive blog, read by more than a hundred thousand people, which meant, of course, an alarming number of crazies, idiots, cranks, and professional Internet trolls. That the blog appealed to both far-left anarchists and far-right white supremacists was, Fulmer supposed, some sort of victory, though over what he wasn't at all sure, and possibly didn't want to know. Except that Fulmer wanted in on everything, because if you weren't constantly vigilant, you never knew what might pop up and bite you on the ass.

And so it was that on the fifth day after the MacQuerrie shitstorm clogged cyberspace and even, for a time, overloaded the current LeakAGE site, which, for security's sake, changed ISP daily, Fulmer accepted the invitation to have dinner with Harry Hornden. Hornden himself called Fulmer instead of having one of his flunkies do it, which, to Fulmer's way of thinking, showed at least a working knowledge of political protocol.

And yet he wasn't above tweaking the journo's nose when he arrived at the corner table Hornden had booked at The Riggsby, a newish restaurant that had the feel of old Hollywood.

"Harry, how many times did you get called *whore's son* in college?" he said, sliding into his chair opposite the journo.

If Hornden was offended, he gave so sign of it. "That started in high school, actually." He grinned as the drinks arrived. "I took the liberty of ordering us a brace of Sazeracs. Good for you?"

"Always," Fulmer said, clinking the rim of his glass with Hornden's. He was intrigued; the journo hadn't picked one of the top ten power restaurants in D.C., so he must have something unusual on his mind; he didn't seem to care whether he was seen with the new hero or not.

Hornden was a largish, square-shaped individual, long hair still sandy, eyes still bright blue, but turned down at the outer corners, as if he were eternally mournful. He looked like a college athlete gone slightly to seed. He was on the wrong side of forty and as yet unmarried, Fulmer knew, having leafed through the jacket on Hornden his staff had assembled. There wasn't much to it, really, beyond schools attended. The text would have you believe that he was a genuine boy scout. No arrests, no girlfriends, or boyfriends, though he networked like a fiend. But his contacts were just that: contacts and nothing more. In fact, when you came right down to it, there was startlingly little background on him. This, also, Fulmer found intriguing.

"What shall I call you?" the journo said, ignoring the menus the waiter had left on the table.

"Just think of me as the pope," Fulmer replied.

"I hope you're not expecting me to kiss your ring."

"I'll let that pass." Fulmer held up both hands, free of rings of any sort. "Divorced. Twice."

"Condolences."

"My exes would lap that sentiment up with a spoon. As for me . . . " He shrugged.

The prelims over, they took up their menus as if in response to a call to arms. "I eat here all the time," Hornden said. "Michael Schlow's my favorite chef."

They ordered Caesar salads and the *côte de boeuf* for two, along with a fine bottle of Faust cabernet, an ironic choice if ever there was one, Fulmer thought with a wry smile. Small talk followed, continuing through the meal. Not one word of business, not a single probing question from Hornden. The conversation most closely followed the lines of two old colleagues at a reunion meal.

"I'd prefer to leave the desserts to the pigs and the kids," Hornden said when the main course plates and platters were cleared. "But I'm not averse to an espresso and an after-dinner drink. Averna, perhaps?"

The usual wolf pack of reporters was milling around the restaurant's exterior. A minor frenzy ensued as the two men exited, but Fulmer's driver, with his lineman's body and sharp senses, was expert at keeping the flies away from the meat. Not a word was uttered by either of the principals as they climbed into Fulmer's black SUV, which drove off down New Hampshire Ave, NW, as soon as Max swung into the front passenger seat.

"So," Fulmer said, shooting his cuffs, "what's on your little mind?"

The journo indicated with his chin. "What about the driver and the bodyguard?"

Fulmer pressed a button and sheet of bulletproof glass rose up to seal them off.

"Happy now?"

"Hardly." Hornden seemed to have grown a haunted look. "But then was I ever?"

Fulmer shot him a sideways glance, then looked away out the window. The last thing he was interested in debating was the existence of happiness—a state of mind so ephemeral it did not exist in the physical world. In his opinion, it was something concocted by the wolves of Madison Avenue in order to sell great quantities of useless and expensive crap to people who thought they needed it. Fulmer fervently wished he had come up with that scam. Well, there were always others; that particular magician's hat was bottomless.

"I want in," Hornden said without even a pretense of a preamble. It was go time.

Fulmer was still staring out the window, looking at nothing. His inner gaze was concentrated fully on what was happening as each moment ticked by. "In on what?"

"Whatever it is you have up your sleeve."

Fulmer evinced zero interest. "This is why you asked me to dinner?"

It wasn't a question; no reply was forthcoming.

"I'll say one thing, Hornden. The dinner was excellent. Thank you for that." He waited a beat. "Otherwise, you've wasted my time."

"If you let me in," Hornden said slowly and distinctly, "you get everything."

"I already have everything I want or need."

The journo's tone changed abruptly. "Listen, Mr. Fulmer, I know your fingerprints are all over that last LeakAGE release."

Fulmer grunted. "I don't even know Farreng. Never had any communication with him whatsoever."

"So you used a cutout. Come on, I know you're the origin of the leak that buried MacQuerrie and his team."

Despite his innate caution, Fulmer's head swung around. He tried to stare Hornden down, but the man wasn't giving an inch. "How could you possibly know such a thing?"

"The only way for you to find out is to let me in." Hornden's eyes glinted in the semi-darkness. "Then you get access to every one of my contacts—including the one who knows what you did last week."

The journo's trap had been laid out, baited, and sprung. *Oh, what a lovely night this turned out to be,* Fulmer thought. He took his time running through possible courses of action in his mind. First off, was Hornden bluffing? Had he triggered a lucky shot in the dark? What if it wasn't luck at all? What if he really did have an informant who knew that he was responsible for the leak? Fulmer had been dead careful, which is why he had set up the meet with Françoise in that little city in Sweden he'd already forgotten the name of. But he also knew that no matter how careful you were in this cyber day and electronic age, there was no such thing as air-tight security.

He could dismiss Hornden's claims, kick him to the curb, go on about his business, and forget this meeting ever took place. It was certainly a tempting choice. But if Hornden's contact was real, if he, in fact, knew what was transferred at Fulmer's meeting with Françoise, then there was danger lurking in the long grass Fulmer could not afford to ignore. His new status and what it meant for him going forward would be put in jeopardy. The theft of government files was an act of treason, even if it uncovered wrongdoing. And then there was the NSA—those people would crucify him. He closed his eyes, counted to a hundred while watching the pulse of his heart on the inside of his eyelids.

When he opened his eyes, he had made up his mind. All possible decisions had fallen into line, leaving one at the head.

"I want the name of that one contact."

The journo had the grace not to smirk. "Naturally."

"Immediately."

"Just say the word, Mr. Fulmer, and I'll do better than that. I myself will take you to the source."

"Deal," he said, as much to himself as to Harry Hornden.

———————

Flames leapt like a living thing from the cheap carpet, up Keyre's arm, turning his clothes to smoke and ash. He appeared oblivious. In fury, he hurled Mala to the floor, stamped hard on her forearm. Bourne heard the crack of a bone and saw the girl's face distort in pain.

Keyre or Mala: the choice was not a difficult one. Reaching down, he grabbed Mala off the burning carpet, slapping out the flames snapping at her bare flesh. His momentary focus on the girl gave Keyre all the opening he needed. Leaping at Bourne, he slammed his whitened knuckles into Bourne's right cheek, over and over. Something gave way an instant before the flames reached Keyre's face, climbing his left cheek. He gave them no mind until their tips cindered his eyelashes. Then he withdrew behind what was now a wall of flames.

Bourne, his face a bloody mess, dragged Mala to her feet. Whirling her around, he picked up the other lantern, threw it at where Keyre had been standing.

Then he shoved her out into the night, where her sister was waiting, quaking in terror. The chaos gripping the camp was if anything more intense. The rain still pelted down, thunder rumbling down from the hills that had served as his observation garret. Gathering up both girls, he hurtled through the silvery downpour toward the south end of the camp, back the way he had come.

With a scream, Mala tried to break away, to turn around, return to her tormentor. She was so violent that Bourne was obliged to lift her off her feet, carry her beneath one arm like a sack of squirming snakes while he held Liis with his other hand. Blood sluiced off Bourne's cheek. Beneath the ripped skin, the bone was fractured. As for Mala, she was bleeding in too many places to count. She was holding her broken forearm in her cupped palm.

"I hate you, I hate you, I hate you!" she chanted over and over again, her eyes rolling wildly.

17

KEYRE DID NOT want to look at Bourne; it was the Angelmaker who looked in on him to make certain the doctor was performing his duties to the utmost of his abilities. Not that he had a choice; not that he would jeopardize his life by missing a trick in bringing Bourne back from the dead—or as near to it as you could get without passing over to the other side. The Angelmaker supposed that was why the doctor, whose name was Mure, hyperventilated every time he came near his patient. If she were of another nature, she would have murmured a word or two to calm the physician down. But she would no more think of doing that than she would inhale water in an attempt to breathe.

Keyre was not, however, above asking her, "How is the patient?" every time she emerged from the camp's surgery, no matter how many times a day that happened.

"The same," was her standard reply.

"Still unconscious?"

She nodded. He seemed anxious, and with good reason. He had tasked her with bringing Bourne to him, only not half dead.

"It's been five days." He roamed the sparsely furnished room like a caged tiger. He was naked to the waist; something he only was when they were alone. The same whorls and glyphs that he had incised into her back were weals, raised and hardened, on his own. He had filled out since his first encounter with Bourne. He had the shoulders and upper arms of an American linebacker. His left arm and the side of his face bore the terrible scars, white-blue, twisted like serpents as if with the imprint of each flame separately, of the kerosene fire. His eyelids had no lashes—once burned off, they had never grown back—and the lower lid of one was permanently withered, making that red eye water constantly. The fire, or perhaps the inhalation of smoke, had altered his voice. It was deeper in tone, darker, but at the same time paper thin, like the eerie, wavering notes of a bassoon.

"There should have been some improvement by now."

"There is," she pointed out. "He's no longer at the point of death."

Keyre spun on his heel; the six-sided scar on his chest, the glyph of a Yibir master, seemed to stare at her. "What use if I can't talk to him, tell him . . . " He broke off, wiped a dark hand across his forehead, his eyes, his mouth. The gestures were ritualistic, a Yibir prayer, or invocation, possibly even a spell, the Angelmaker wasn't sure.

"Time is running out," he said, and for the first time she understood fully how isolated he was, how utterly alone, even among his own cadre, even at the heart of this village of gold and diamonds and international legal tender he had built fostering a larger and larger percentage of the illegal arms and human trafficking trade.

He has no one, she thought now. *He's never had anyone.* For the longest time, she had assumed that was what he wanted, what he needed. But she had mistaken him, just as everyone who came in contact with him had mistaken him. And now, for the first time, with the advent of his extreme anxiety, she glimpsed the reason for the violations he perpetrated on the girls, including her. They were the same violations that had been performed on him as a child. He was searching for someone to douse his loneliness, his apartness. Someone like him.

To date, she was the only one who had ever fit the bill, even if it was imperfectly. This was the reason she was so precious to him, why he had fought tooth and nail to bring her back to him, why he always would. Before her, he had always put himself first. With her, that had changed.

And yet, what was he to her? Warden, torturer, artist, collaborator in Yibir with her skin and the flesh just below. A totem, in other words. Something of this world and yet not of it. Something Other, for which she had no words, which, apart from the Yibir, did not exist in any vocabulary.

She took a step toward him, felt the heat from his glyphs, as if they were living things. "What do you want me to do?"

"I want him awake."

"Then use your magic." There was a mocking tone to her voice she knew was dangerous, and yet she would not shy away from it. It hit her, all of a moment, that being near Jason emboldened her, just as it had when he'd first invaded the camp.

"I hate you, I hate you, I hate you." Her own words reverberated in her mind. But what had she really meant?

"He responds to you." Keyre seemed to have ignored her comment. "You're the one to push the process."

"But—"

"No buts. You were the one who got him here; no one else could."

He stared her down, and like always, she acquiesced. "As you wish."

"As *we* wish,"—his eyes grew dark—"isn't it?"

She laughed, because she had to laugh—it was the only way forward now. She had taken only one step on Jason's path, and Keyre's uncanny Yibir antennae were already vibrating. She couldn't afford to make that same mistake again.

"Go," he commanded. "Do what has to be done."

"Whatever it takes?"

"Whatever it takes out of you, Angelmaker."

———

What do you do when you've a brother both older and smarter than you? More clever, too. A chess master who delights in outmaneuvering you?

These were the questions that had plagued Timur Ludmirovich Savasin virtually all his adolescent and adult days. How simple life had been, how happy, before Konstantin revealed his true nature. *Like a strange vampire, drunk on fucked-up nourishment,* Savasin thought, *Konstantin has drained all the enjoyment out of my life.*

From the backseat of his armor-plated Zil, Savasin stared morosely out the tinted window at the garbage-strewn streets, at the pedestrians, backs hunched against the cutting spring wind, shoulders up around their ears, hands jammed deep in the pockets of their flannel overcoats. Except the kids. They smoked, stood splayed on building stoops, hair stiff and glossy, arms tattooed like the evil-looking drawings in Japanese manga, and stared sloe-eyed at Savasin's long, sleek Zil, as if assessing its worth on the black market. Were they armed? Savasin wondered. Did the future belong to them? Not if the Sovereign had anything to say about it. In this, above all, there was no difference between the White Russian czars, the Red Russian Communists, and now the current regime. All used what was to hand, the Cheka, the OGPU, the NKVD, the MGB, the KGB, the FSB. Only the names changed; the orders from the state ministers remained the same.

Savasin, Moscow a blur outside his bulletproof windows, felt a welling up of disgust, not only for his own weakness in failing to find a way to deal with his brother, but for the city, the Federation itself, which was rotting beneath the soles of their expensive foreign-made shoes. The Sovereign would not countenance the truth, and everyone around him—Savasin included—was too terrified of him to clue him in. He still dreamt his dreams of a reconstituted Soviet Union without any thought of how his regime could govern such a far-flung empire when previous regimes hadn't been able to manage it before. Moscow couldn't even manage the

Chechens, not to mention the other Muslim minorities, gorging themselves at the table of the worldwide jihad.

The chattering of his mobile fax startled him out of his increasingly gloomy thoughts. Tearing off the single sheet, he read through the text his office had sent. He was ten minutes away. What was this that couldn't wait until he arrived? Then he read it again. What was the Bourne Initiative?

The intel had been siphoned off of the leak inside Dreadnaught. The fax coughed to life again, spewing out a second sheet. This one had only one paragraph of text, according to which the Bourne Initiative was the designation the now disgraced General MacQuerrie had given to his search for a supposed über cyber weapon a cadre of Russian dissidents had been working on under the supervision of— He now had to break off a moment, pressing his thumb and forefinger against his closed lids in a vain attempt to forestall that tension headache rising like a poisonous toadstool from the hellish depths of wherever it hid itself.

His head throbbing, he took his fingers away, stared down at the four words at the end of the single paragraph: General Boris Illyich Karpov.

Savasin's stomach gave a great heave. Had he not been told that all of Karpov's initiatives had been eradicated as completely as if they had never existed? Hadn't that been guaranteed him? And yet, here was evidence that at least the Americans believed this so-called Bourne Initiative was still alive. Savasin briefly consoled himself with the possibility that this could be a masterful piece of disinformation. But that didn't last long.

Apart from Bourne, the Americans knew next to

nothing about Karpov. Why would they? The general was a mystery even to his own people, and, really, the Americans were idiots. So rule out disinformation. Which left the worst possible scenario: that Karpov had been running a rogue cyber workshop right under their noses, and Savasin's people had not unearthed it.

Savasin was incensed, as well he should be. He had a brief thought of informing Konstantin, but Savasin was still smarting from the news that the *spetsnaz* team he had taken over was, to a man, dead. And where was Jason Bourne? God alone knew, and surely God wasn't speaking to Savasin. Besides, using the FSB had never been the correct method of winkling out what Karpov was up to. There was a better way. More risky, yes, but, as the Americans said, no pain, no gain.

Savasin had barely been in his office two minutes when Malachev appeared. The fact that he had entered without knocking, that the upper eyelid of his left eye was twitching to beat the band, spoke eloquently of his extreme agitation.

Nevertheless, Savasin, whose brother had put him under a very dark cloud indeed, said, "What?"

Instead of being taken aback by his superior's shortness, Malachev grinned as he placed a mobile phone on Savasin's desk. "A short video just came in from one of your agents."

The first minister's ears pricked up like a hunting dog scenting game. *Your agents.* Like General Karpov, Savasin had his own cadre of agents in the field, each one on a specific assignment. "Is it the *right* agent, Igor Ivanovich?"

Malachev gestured. "See for yourself, sir."

Savasin did. In fact, he watched the surveillance video three times before he lifted his head to look at his second-in-command. Their gazes met like fireworks exploding. "You know what this means, Igor Ivanovich."

"Indeed, I do, sir. When are you going to spring it on him?"

"Oh, no, no, no. Nothing so straightforward." His fingers caressed the mobile's screen. "This calls for something ... more elaborate, more byzantine." A crafty smiled curled his lips at their edges. "Igor Ivanovich."

"Sir!"

"An extra thousand in the Cypress bank account of the agent who caught this encounter on video."

"Right away, sir."

When Savasin was alone, he checked the directory on his second mobile, the one he used only sparingly. Then he took his Makarov from his desk drawer, checked that it was loaded, and, rising, grabbed his overcoat and headed for the door.

Back in his Zil, he gave his driver an address in a district a mile away from where he needed to go. The Zil could wait for him there. He wanted no one, not even his driver and bodyguard, to know his destination.

———

When the Angelmaker entered the surgery, she sensed a change in the atmosphere. Nothing she could put a finger on, but something was definitely different. The doctor rose upon her arrival. He gave her a disapproving face when she signaled him to leave her alone with the patient. Clearly, he didn't trust her. She couldn't blame him.

She stepped to the bedside, gazed down at Jason's face in repose. He had regained much of his color but—and here she reached out, moving her fingertips gently over his cheekbone—in this place where, years ago, Keyre had fractured the bone, the skin tone was slightly different, so subtly that if you didn't know what to look for you'd not even notice. But the Angelmaker did know, and she saw that the skin over the repaired bone was the tiniest bit paler, as if it belonged to someone else.

"Jason," she whispered. But all she heard in reply were the rhythmic beeps of the monitor to which he was still hooked up measuring his heart rate, oxygen level, and respiration. She watched the saline and antibiotic solution slowly drip into the vein in the crook of his elbow.

She bent over him, put her lips to his ear. "Jason, it's raining outside," she whispered. "Pouring. Thunder rumbling. You have Liis by the hand, you have me under your arm. We're both bleeding, both hurting. Behind us is the tent. Inside it's burning; the rain hasn't yet penetrated. Liis and I are drowning in a night of chaos. You move quickly and stealthily through the camp, avoiding the armed men. We can barely see what's ahead of us, the rain is so thick. But you know where to go, and I say, 'I hate you, I hate you, I hate you,' over and over and over."

She took his hand in hers. *I've thought about that moment... What did I mean by that?* She squeezed his hand. *I'm desperate to know, but I fear it's a question without an answer.*

And then, to her immense relief, she felt his hand squeeze hers in return.

She raised her head, looked into his face. "Jason, wake up." Then she kissed him, partly open lips pressed ever so gently to his.

Eyes opened.

"Jason."

"Where?"

His throat was dry, and she fed him several slivers of ice from a cooler at his bedside. His eyes continued to study her as he worked the ice around his mouth, helping the shards to melt. She watched him swallow. Such a small reflex, yet she found herself loving it inordinately.

Swallowing the last of the ice water, he said, "Where am I?"

She should have had a ready answer for him, a quick-draw explanation, but she found herself uncharacteristically tongue-tied. This frightened her, though fear was an infrequent visitor at her door.

"Are we still on Skyros?"

This she could answer. "No."

Something changed behind his eyes, a wall forming. She knew that wall, knew once it came down she'd never get past it.

"Tell me this isn't a CIA facility."

This made her laugh. It was a genuine laugh, one that made him laugh as well. *When was the last time I laughed?* she asked herself. At dinner with Jason overlooking the moonstruck Aegean before the *Nym* exploded. Time being more elastic than a rubber band, that seemed like a lifetime ago.

"No. No guards here, Jason."

"Just you and me."

"Not quite."

"No, of course, a medical staff."

She nodded. They were coming closer to a moment she now dreaded. "A doctor, a nurse. Yes." Best to take baby steps now. "And, of course, the emergency team that worked on you while we were in the air."

His eyes regarded her, revealing nothing. She shuddered inwardly. His coldness, his complete apartness, as if he lived in another dimension she could not touch, let alone share, caused her real pain.

"How far have we come?"

And there it was. The question she could not dodge, and lying to him would only make matters worse. If, now, he didn't trust her, all was surely lost.

"We're in the Horn of Africa."

Again his eyes changed, and she felt a bit of life drain out of her.

"Somalia."

Her lips scarcely moved, her voice so low his head lifted off the pillow in order to hear her. "Yes."

18

I DON'T LIKE IT."

"Which part?" Hornden asked. "I mean it can't be the neighborhood." He gestured at the nighttime street. "We're in Dupont Circle." He grinned. "It can't be this beautiful Georgian townhome we're about to enter. You'd be hard pressed to find a tonier address in all of the District."

Fulmer glanced back at the line of Cadillac Escalades and more prosaic limos lined up at the curb, their drivers reading the paper, drinking coffee out of paper cups, or resting their heads against the seatbacks, catching a few winks.

"None of the drivers are on their mobile phones," Fulmer said.

"A strict policy of the establishment their distinguished guests are only too happy to oblige."

A man of no small stature at sentry duty just inside the front door nodded to Hornden—he was very conspicuously known here—and they passed through the small vestibule, pushing through another door into the two-story entrance hall proper. A huge crystal chandelier hanging from the ceiling threw discreet lights every which way. Directly below it was an inlaid fruitwood table, polished to a glassy finish, on which stood a cut-crystal vase bursting with a professionally arranged profusion of long-stemmed flowers that looked like a fireworks display caught in mid-burst. Behind all of this was a grand staircase, curling upward to the second floor.

As far as Fulmer could tell, all the activity was on the ground floor. To their right was a grand salon, furnished with silk divans and love seats. The warmly lit room was devoid of chairs or proper sofas. To their left was a small salon, a library, in fact, with floor-to-ceiling shelves filled with books, no doubt all erotic classics, Fulmer thought acidly, for he had noted immediately that every single woman in both rooms was young, shapely, gorgeously dressed, magnificently jeweled, and coiffed to a fare-thee-well, confirming his suspicions about what sort of gathering he'd been brought to.

"I think I'll take a pass. My wife and kids are waiting for me, and tomorrow is Sunday; we always go to early worship."

But as he turned, Hornden caught him by the elbow, swung him back around. "No need to be alarmed. You won't be tainted here. On any given night half of the most influential men inside the Beltway unwind with appointments here."

And, indeed, it was true. As Fulmer's gaze moved from the female pulchritude so brazenly on display, it alighted on one representative and senator after another.

There were a couple of men from DoD, another from the Pentagon, along with a handful of ex–administration appointees who had maintained or, in some cases, increased, their standing among the District's power brokers.

"You see?" Hornden said. "Nothing to be concerned about."

Fulmer put his back to the crowd. "I don't want them to see me here."

As if he hadn't heard Fulmer, Hornden's smile broadened. "And here she comes."

Fulmer turned around to see a willowy woman in a simple black cocktail dress and exceptionally high heels approaching them. She matched Hornden's smile, revealing small, white, even teeth. Unlike the other women in the rooms, she wore only a modicum of greasepaint, as Fulmer called makeup. Her skin was flawless, clear and dewy as a child's. He was rocked by a sudden, unbidden thought: *She has the face of an angel and the eyes of a devil.* Those devilish tawny eyes regarded him with a straightforward interest, mixed with a certain curiosity. They were so light they gave her skin a burnished glow.

"National security advisor Marshall Fulmer, meet Gwyneth Donnelly. She's the genius behind this place."

"Stop it, Harry," she said as she held out a perfectly manicured hand. As Fulmer took it, she said, "Call me Gwen." She cocked her head. "And what shall I call you? Mr. Fulmer? No, too formal. Marsh?" Her laugh was like the tinkling of small bells. "No. I think not, judging by the horrified look on your face."

Fulmer cleared his throat. He felt a bit dizzy. Was it overly warm in here? "Mr. Fulmer will do quite nicely."

Gwyneth nodded. "As you wish." She lifted a well-toned arm. "This way, gentlemen."

She led them through the library, where their passage went totally unremarked. One of the hallmarks of the place was that every one of the clients kept his eyes on the women. Each to his own, self to self, could have been the business's motto.

Thus heartened, Fulmer crossed to the far side of the library. They looked to be heading toward a wall full of books, until Gwyneth released a hidden latch and a door-size section of the wall swung inward. The three of them went through.

Down a wood-paneled corridor, lined on either side by Audubon lithographs of tropical birds, at the end of which was a door Gwyneth opened. The room was capacious, decorated not as an office but as a den. Lamplight only, turned low, gave the place a nestlike aspect. Oversize easy chairs covered in tobacco-colored leather, an abstract pattern rug under their feet, a glass coffee table, a small sofa upholstered in the same material as the chairs, between them a low cocktail table with a shiny, mirrored top. The papered walls were hung with Currier & Ives prints. In all, it felt like stepping back in time, into a men's club from the nineteenth century.

"Please make yourselves comfortable," Gwyneth said as she crossed to a sideboard holding a dozen or so bottles of liquor. "Mr. Fulmer?" she said over her shoulder.

"It's late. Nothing for me."

"Harry? Your usual?"

"Perfect."

Gwyneth brought two glasses, handed one to Hornden, sipped at the other as she settled herself in a chair directly opposite Fulmer.

Is it my imagination, Fulmer asked himself, *or did she take an extra few seconds crossing her legs?* Either way, he glimpsed more of her than he had before. He liked what he saw, but was loathe to admit it to himself. Instead, he stiffened his spine, like a good soldier preparing for inspection.

"Harry," Gwyneth said, a small smile playing about her lips, "be so kind as to remind me why we're here?" She was looking directly at Fulmer, which she had done since she sat down.

"The national security advisor would like you to answer a question," Hornden said.

"Just one?" That smile, less enigmatic, more playful now. "Oh, dear."

Hornden cleared his throat. "Fulmer would like a bit of clarity as to who told you that he was responsible for the latest LeakAGE debacle that brought down General MacQuerrie."

Before Gwyneth could answer, a repeating noise sounded, growing louder, like an approaching police car, causing Fulmer to start, only to relax as Hornden drew out his mobile. Gwyneth's brows knit together.

"Dammit to hell, Harry, how many times do I have to tell you—"

"Sorry, Gwyneth. Mr. Fulmer." He rose. "I have to take this." And he exited the room without another word.

"Honestly," Gwyneth said, clearly irritated, "I don't know why I continue to tolerate that man."

"Perhaps because he's a good source of income," Fulmer said, feeling more in control than he had since he'd stepped foot inside the townhome.

Gwyneth seemed to consider this for a moment while regarding Fulmer over the rim of her glass. That tinkling laugh rose again. "A pity you're not a drinker."

"I didn't say that."

She graced him with a sly curve to her lips. "You know, late at night, when most of the city is asleep, is the best time to drink, the best time for conversation, the best time for reviewing what went before and planning what is to come."

"For that, I require a clear head."

She drained her glass. "Liquor clears my head."

"Then I salute you."

Leaning forward, she put her glass down on the mirrored table, and Fulmer was treated to the sight of her full, creamy breasts. He was startled to realize she wasn't wearing a bra. Didn't every woman wear one?

"Harry warned me that you were no fun," Gwyneth said, straightening up, but none too quickly.

It took more effort than he would have liked to keep his eyes from bugging out. "Harry knows very little about me."

That smile again, returning to the enigmatic. *When did enigmatic become so erotic?* Fulmer asked himself.

"Don't you ever let your hair down, Marshall?"

He was about to correct her, then decided to let it go. He liked her calling him by his Christian name. "I can't afford to."

"Then what good is living?"

Fulmer felt the ground giving way under him again.

"Tell me who told you I was responsible for supplying LeakAGE with . . . I assume it was in the course of pillow talk."

"It's true," Gwyneth said. "Men like to unburden themselves after sex. One intimacy leads quite naturally to another."

"I wouldn't know, but I'll take your word for it." He sat forward. "Who blabbed?"

"Your bodyguard, Max."

"What?" Fulmer winced as if he had been stuck with a needle. "Don't be ridiculous."

"I pride myself on never being ridiculous."

"But it can't be. Max has been with me for years. He's a loyal—"

"Even guard dogs get fed up with their masters, especially if they're treated poorly."

Fulmer was about to deny that he had done any such thing, when he cast his mind back to how dismissive he'd been to Max in Kalmar. But, really, now he thought of it, that was only the tip of the iceberg. The fact was, he treated Max as part of the familiar furniture that was always with him. Except when he needed to be alone. And speaking of Kalmar, who knew what Max had got up to when Fulmer had dismissed him outside the conference room. What if he had followed Fulmer, witnessed his meeting with Françoise? Max leaking his secrets? It was possible, but . . .

"How d'you know for a fact it was Max?"

"Because it was me he told, directly."

Fulmer's eyes opened wide. His complexion had gone waxen. "Afterward?"

That smile, more knowing than enigmatic now, but

even more erotic, if that were possible. "Say this for him, the man's got good taste."

Fulmer slumped in his chair. He passed a hand across his brow.

"Betrayal's a bitch, isn't it, Marshall?"

———

"So you've brought me back." He heard nothing in reply; his mind was clearing. "That was the plan all along, why you reached out to me, why you set up the rendezvous in Skyros."

"The rendezvous saved your life," she reminded him gently. "Understand, Keyre despises the Russians. He's at war with them." She watched for a beat, taking the temperature of his reactions. "It's why he asked me to bring you to him."

"I don't believe you."

Steady on, she told herself. *Even the hint of a lie and all will be lost.* "But you do believe me. I know you do."

He thought about this for some time. His sudden bark of a laugh startled her. "Are you telling me that Keyre wants my help?"

She said nothing; there was nothing to say. The situation spoke for itself.

"This is too rich," Bourne said. "Too damn good. Keyre is asking for a favor."

Still, she said nothing. All at once, even knowing how dire the situation with the Russians had become, she felt ashamed at her part in what could only be called an abduction. She knew now what she had known before, but had doggedly pushed away: her position between these two men was destroying her from the inside out. But perhaps that was her fate. She had endured too many indignities, too many insults to her mind and her body to ever be what she would once have been. She was what she had been made into, a product of inhumanity. Like Jason. In fact, precisely like Jason.

Bourne struggled to sit up, and she pressed a pedal that lifted the top third of the bed until he was in a comfortable position. He gave a glance at the IV in his arm, the beeping monitor's eye. "I want to get out of here."

"Not yet."

"I don't care."

He reached to pull out the IV. She said, "You've been unconscious for six days."

That gave him pause, as she knew it would, brought home to him the severity of his wounds.

"You lost a ton of blood," she added.

He let go of the IV needle, lay back against the pillow, but it was clear he wasn't happy about it. "You haven't said another word about Keyre."

"I have nothing left to say."

"I doubt that. What's he want me to do?"

"That's for him to say."

"But you know." It wasn't a question; he knew her too well. Of course she knew; she was being the good soldier, waiting for the general to deliver the marching orders. "Tell him I won't do it."

"You don't know what it is."

"It doesn't matter."

A certain silence threw up its spikes between them. The air they breathed was stretched with tension.

"Listen to me," the Angelmaker said at length.

"Now you're going to tell me he isn't evil."

"Oh, no, Keyre is evil, all right. But the fact is, he's battling a greater evil."

"By selling arms to fight the infidel."

"A case could be made for that, yes."

Bourne shot her a skeptical look. "And how is he fighting the infidel by trading in human trafficking?" He took her wrist; his voice was a raspy whisper. "You and Liis were part of that."

"There is no good side here," she said tersely. "No angels in residence."

"Tell him I want Giza. Tell him to let your daughter go."

She shook her head sadly. "He'll never agree."

"He must if he—"

"No. Don't you understand? He wouldn't let me go. He would never have made that bargain. You forced it. You're in no condition to force anything." She looked away. "Besides, Giza is his daughter, too."

He let go of her wrist. "You shouldn't have brought me here. You know that."

"I had no choice."

"You were only following orders." His voice mocked her.

Her face fell, all pretense gone. "Only one man has the key." Her voice cracked. "How I wish it were otherwise." She turned away abruptly, ensuring he wouldn't see her eyes well up.

"Mala . . ."

"It's no good." She shook her head. "There's no exit for me." She took a breath, turned her head back to him. "You're right. I shouldn't have brought you back."

"Then help me get out of here."

"That won't be necessary," said Keyre, filling the open doorway. So rapt were they in their conversation, neither had heard him open the door. "Nor is it desirable."

He stepped toward them, his eyes burning like coals, and involuntarily, the Angelmaker moved back to stand in the semi-darkness beyond the monitor. Her eyes were blank; her expression revealed nothing. It was as if their intimate conversation had never occurred.

"Look at me, Bourne, not her," Keyre said with silken smoothness. "You're with me, until I say otherwise."

———————

After almost a week, Morgana was growing used to Kalmar—the breakfasts of thick, sun-yellow yogurt, dark bread spread with Kalles kaviar out of a tube, the strong coffee that seemed to burn its way through the lining of her stomach, the ubiquitous muesli, to which Larry London insisted on adding crushed flax and sesame seeds, the open smoked fish sandwiches for lunch. Even the Proviva, a juice drink said to ensure digestive health, which had nauseated her the first day, was now palatable. But the profusion of fresh berries—many of which, like cloudberries, she had never before heard of—took no getting used to at all. She had also become inured to the sonorous bells from the spires of the Kalmar Cathedral and Lutheran churches ringing at all hours. But she never forgave Larry and Françoise for serving her *filmjölk*—the fermented milk Swedes are so fond of—without first warning her.

"The look on your face," Françoise had cried as she and Larry doubled over in laughter. "Priceless!"

Actually, she did forgive them. How could she not? Françoise had saved her from incarceration—and possibly worse—and Larry treated her like an old friend, trusting her completely. In fact, within days of her arrival, the three of them, having swung easily into a routine, were acting as tightly as a family unit. This was particularly gratifying to Morgana, coming from a broken family with a mother and a sister who wanted no part of her.

But of course this was an integral part of the plan Françoise had devised for Marshall Fulmer. Or was it for Gora Maslov? Well, in this case it was for both, though only her brother was aware of it. There was something about working both ends of the block that appealed powerfully to her—a woman brought up with a strong, willful father and brother, who, consciously or not, undercut her at every turn. Their bullying necessitated her building a series of personae, strong as brick-and-mortar edifices, to hide her true identity. This process had begun so early in her life and gone on for so long that she had become lost behind the walls she had erected, until she no longer knew who she really was. Nor did she particularly want to know. This could be viewed as a flaw in her character, perhaps even a weakness. But since no one had yet breached her defenses, certainly not Gora, whose personality dictated that he be attuned to taking advantage of situations rather than people, it was hardly a danger.

Morgana's routine consisted of spending days with Larry London and evenings with Françoise—dinner once or twice with both of them. Larry was smooth without being obvious about it; he knew how to draw her out, to set her at ease. It was a gift, a great one at that.

"You're a photographer," she said the first day they were together. "Why are you interested in cyber-sleuthing?"

"Ah, well," Larry London said. "You have me there."

They were sitting next to each other in what passed for the business center of her hotel, a small windowless room bare apart from task chairs, a fax, and a pair of computer terminals on an unsecured wi-fi so riddled with malware and keystroke loggers Larry wouldn't touch them with a six-foot Cossack. Guests came and went, checking email, logging into their airline accounts, opening themselves up to credit card or identity theft.

"Morgana...Françoise said I could trust you with a secret. Is she right?"

"Françoise and I know each other quite well."

A slow smile crossed his face. "Very well, then." He scooted his task chair closer to hers, looked over his right shoulder, then his left, leaned in and whispered: "My job as a freelance photographer is a cover."

She frowned. "A well-documented one."

"What good would a cover be if it weren't? It was created by the best professionals." Now he drew back, his expression one of sudden doubt.

Morgana leaned toward him to maintain their close proximity. "What is it?"

"I'm not sure this is a good idea."

"Why not? I thought you said you trusted me."

He reflected a moment, then nodded. "You're

right." His voice lowered even further. "Actually, I work for the Company."

Of course she knew that meant the CIA; the putative enemy of the NSA. The two agencies were eternally at odds on how to gather intel.

He allowed her time to digest this bit of information.

"Honestly..." she began.

"Yes?"

"Any American agency antagonistic to the NSA is okay with me."

He laughed softly. "Françoise said you'd say that."

"Did she really."

"Well, something like it, anyway." He opened up his laptop, booted it up, then opened an app that provided him with a military-level shield, a bogus ISP that could not be traced. "Okay," he said, rubbing his hands together. "Let's get the ball rolling."

And that's how, five days ago, Morgana's hunt for the initiative continued. Of course, Morgana was under the impression that she was schooling Larry London in looking for other pieces of the cyber weapon on the dark web, and in a sense that was correct. But it was also correct that he was schooling her, in the sense of getting her used to working with him beside her.

In the evenings, Françoise played the perfect friend—empathetic, solicitous, strong of opinion and the strength to fight adversity.

"We can't expect to succeed," she said over their late supper in a small, ramshackle seafood house near the water, "until we've failed at least once." She extracted a bit of pink langoustine flesh with the tines of her tiny fork. "It's a cliché, I know, but in my experience it's true enough."

"It's happened to you?" Morgana cleared away a piece of shell to get at more of her langoustine's delicious meat. "Failure, I mean."

Françoise laughed shortly. "More than once." Playing Morgana's friend wasn't difficult. For one thing, they had been friends for years, having met in Paris, at the Musée D'Orsay, admiring Édouard Manet's *Le Déjeuner sur l'Herbe*, and, after discussing the painting in the most positive terms, spending the next forty minutes strolling through the museum. Thereafter, they repaired to lunch, where, over salads niçoise and a bottle of a commendable Sémillon, she had presented herself as a business advisor to the rich and famous. At the end of four hours together, they had struck up a lasting friendship. For another, Françoise genuinely liked Morgana. She was smart and quick; Françoise found her naïveté charming. That Françoise was at some point able to use that naïveté to her advantage was an unexpected bonus. If she felt any remorse at using her friends, it was pushed to the sidelines, where it languished unnoticed in the shadows.

"Give me an example," Morgana said.

Françoise considered for a moment, tapping her lips ruminatively with a forefinger. "*Bien,* well, to be honest, I failed as a sister. My brother is a shit." All true. "But as the better person I should have found a way to maintain a relationship with him." Like hell. Also, a lie. But she was considering Morgana's sister, who had cut Morgana off because Morgana did not want to revisit the pain her parents' bitter divorce had caused her. "He, well, you know, he made life impossible for me, so..." Her hand lightly fluttered. "Pffft!"

"I'm sorry."

Françoise smiled. "Don't be. I'm not."

Morgana, abandoning her langoustine for the moment, leaned forward. "You said that you had more than one failure."

"Yes, well, but I'd rather not—"

"Oh, come on. You know all my secrets."

"Not *all* your secrets, surely."

Morgana reached out, squeezed Françoise's hand. "Besides, what are friends for?"

Françoise gave a little chortle. "Since you put it that way." She took a breath. "I made a mistake with Larry."

"Larry London?"

"The very same." Françoise put down her fork. "When we met I fucked up. I came on like an army tank, but that was the wrong approach. It took me six months to mend that particular fence. But the point is I learned, from both the failures. You can't use the same strategy with everyone. Assessing the playing field before deciding on how to act is essential."

"That sounds so cold, so clinical." Morgana's eyes narrowed. "Is that what you did with me?"

"What, no. Oh, my God, Ana, no." Ana and Franny were their secret names for each other, never to be used when there were others around. "I was speaking of business, not friendship. My God, if I was reduced to doing that with friends—with you, of all people—I'd be on antidepressants."

Morgana, with her hand still on Françoise's, turned her friend's hand over, tapped the blue vein on the delicate flesh of the inside. "I'm glad to hear that."

Françoise's sudden laugh was like the sun breaking

through clouds. "Speaking of dear old Larry, how's your search coming? Is he being helpful?"

"Larry's been a help." Morgana withdrew her hand, set it in her lap, as if embarrassed by its intimate gesture. "But I still don't know where the locus is."

Françoise frowned. "The piece is still online."

"Yes, and another just showed up, but it isn't helping me much. It's like a jigsaw puzzle with no clues."

"Then we've got to redouble our efforts to find it."

"Larry and I already agreed on that. We've split up assignments. While I'm working on decoding the algorithm, he's using his sources worldwide to track the locus."

She smiled. "He's closer than I am. In fact, he's very close, which is good because this algorithm is like nothing I've ever encountered before."

"Yes, but we still have no idea when it's scheduled to be deployed."

Morgana took a breath, let it out slowly. "Actually, we do now. One thing I've been able to decipher is that the new algorithm has a built-in Day Zero trigger."

"What does that mean?"

"Ten days from today, the cyber weapon will be deployed, and the American president's nuclear codes will be vulnerable. Bourne or whoever is directing the team will be able to set off a catastrophic event of unprecedented proportions."

"Armageddon."

Morgana nodded. "And as it stands right now, nothing will be able to stop it."

19

KEYRE, THERE IS no way I'm doing anything for you."

"No hasty decisions, Bourne."

"Nothing hasty about this one."

Keyre smiled like an uncle indulging a willful and ignorant adolescent. The two men were sitting in facing rattan chairs with cushions of a tribal pattern typical of coastal Somalia. Between them was a wooden table carved in the intricate Arabic style. On it was a beaten bronze tray on which sat a large pot of tea, two handleless cups, three small plates, one each of dried dates, hummus, and wedges of unleavened bread. A solid concrete floor, rather than beaten earth, beneath their feet, solid walls, lamps lit by electricity provided by a pair of large generators. The room was a far cry from the soiled tents of his first visit.

The Angelmaker stood at some remove. Beside her was a small table on which was placed a buff-colored folder and an army or marine surplus walkie-talkie. She inhabited a spot precisely between the two men, as if in an effort to appear neutral, which Bourne knew perfectly well was an illusion, tempting though it might be to consider.

"I must have missed the line of tanning heads on my way in," Bourne said now.

Keyre kept his smile in place. "Beheadings are part of the past." He gestured with an open hand. "You should eat. You need to build up your strength."

Bourne ignored him, lifted his head slightly, nostrils dilated. "The air smells fresher, too. Is target practice on headless corpses a thing of the past, too?"

Keyre's smile was stretched now, a veneer that Bourne was determined to crack.

"What we have here now is a business," Keyre said. "We even have a CFO."

"A chief financial officer," Bourne echoed. "What's next, a listing on the stock exchange?"

"A lucrative idea." Keyre reached for a date, held it on the tips of his fingers and thumb. "But I'm afraid it's still imperative we fly under the radar."

Bourne grunted. "I can imagine."

At this point, the Angelmaker stepped forward, slathered a triangle of bread with hummus, handed it to Bourne. He waited a moment before taking it. Their eyes met for a moment before he popped it in his mouth, chewed slowly. Keyre ignored her as she returned to the spot of her vigil.

"So . . . " The date disappeared into Keyre's mouth. He ate it, pit and all. "Time to get down to business."

Bourne stared at him. "We have no business."

"So you say." Keyre's hands, fingers intertwined, lay

in his lap, as if to emphasize his calm. "But the fact is, there is business between us—business you *will* want to discuss."

Leaning forward, Bourne dipped a triangle of bread into the hummus, ate it as slowly as the first, while regarding Keyre with a neutral expression.

Keyre now lifted a hand as if he were carrying a tray. This must have been a signal; the Angelmaker turned, took the folder off the table and placed it in his hand before returning once again to her original position. He left it there, for a long moment, then plucked it off with his other hand. Opening it, he held up an eight-by-ten head shot, the features flattened, indicating it was taken with a long telephoto lens.

"This man is known to you."

It was not a question, and Bourne didn't take it as such. "Is he known to you?"

At last the tiniest crack appeared in Keyre's carefully constructed façade. "Gora." He could not keep the disgust out of his voice.

"Yegor Maslov, known to his friends as Gora. Son of the late Dimitri Maslov, head of the Kazanskaya."

"The fucking Russian mafia, yes. A thorn in both our sides."

"General Karpov took care of Dimitri."

Keyre took another date. "You know Gora has taken his father's place at the summit of the Kazanskaya."

"I do."

Plucking another eight-by-ten from the folder, he handed it over. This one was not a head shot. It showed a young woman from the waist up. She was dark-haired, light-eyed, an intense expression on her face as she turned a three-quarter profile toward the telephoto lens. She was very beautiful, in an aggressive, almost warlike manner.

"How about her?" Keyre said. "Also familiar?"

As Bourne looked from the photo to Keyre, the ghost of a smile could be seen in the Somalian's expression. Bourne did not know the young woman, but he sensed an unpleasant surprise coming.

"No?" Keyre cocked his head. "The woman you can't identify, Bourne, is none other than Alyosha Orlova, Dimitri's illegitimate daughter, Gora's half sister. She refused to take her father's name, or he forbade her. Possibly both. They had a naturally contentious relationship, but it was nothing compared to the one Dimitri had with Alyosha's mother, Ekaterina Orlova."

"So Alyosha, as well as Gora, has come to your attention."

Keyre delivered the briefest of grins. "The Maslov clan holds intense interest for me—as it does for you, Bourne. You see, we do have business to discuss."

"No, we—"

"Business beneficial to both of us."

"Keyre, I cannot imagine how the stars could be aligned to allow that to happen."

"And yet they are aligned in this curious pattern, Bourne. Of this you can be assured."

"Tell me, then."

Keyre nodded. "As you wish." He took back the photo of Alyosha Orlova, ran his fingertips over the glossy surface of her features. "There is something about a man on his knees that stirs my very heart," he began in a softer, more contemplative tone. "It's the white flag, you see. The white flag stinks of fear. I enjoy inhaling its scent, savoring its taste before I put a match to it and set it afire."

Silence in the room. They could all have been deep within the bowels of the Lubyanka prison for all that the outside world made itself known. Bourne's eyes were locked with Keyre's.

"I sense how much you hate me, Bourne. I can feel it on my skin like an army of ants."

"Pleasure comes in such odd packages these days."

Keyre delivered a curious smile. "Two weeks ago, thirteen men knelt not a thousand yards from where we sit. I put a bullet in the head of each of them, one by one, going down the line. Then my men buried them. But they weren't erased; the memory of them lingers like the taste of spoiled food in the mouth.

"That's because these thirteen men were Somalians co-opted by the Russians. And not any Russians, mind you." Now he held up both photos, Gora Maslov in his right hand, Alyosha Orlova in his left hand.

"Why would Gora and Alyosha want to attack you?"

"That's the question, isn't it?" Keyre's eyes gleamed eerily. "And it's made more curious considering I have a highly lucrative business arrangement with Gora."

"He's turned on you."

Keyre rustled the photo in his left hand. "Let's not forget about Alyosha. To do so would be a grave error in judgment."

"Maybe she persuaded him to seek a better deal elsewhere."

"Half right, Bourne. You see, the thirteen didn't set out to attack me. They infiltrated my cadre."

"They were looking for something you have."

"Also half right. Because I don't have what they were sent to fetch. I believe it was Alyosha who persuaded her brother—excuse me, *half brother*—to risk his business arrangement with me to steal this item."

"This item must be highly prized."

"Oh, it is, Bourne. It's so highly prized that everyone who knows of its existence—a handful of people, but that's more than enough to ensure extreme danger, I assure you—wants it. They would do anything and everything to get their hands on it."

Out of the corner of his eye, Bourne saw the Angelmaker stir uneasily. "And what exactly is this item?" he asked.

"I've no idea what it was originally called—possibly its only designation was a letter-number combination. But that's of no import. It's come to be known as the Bourne Initiative."

Bourne gave a start. "What?"

Keyre continued as if he hadn't heard Bourne's interjection. "The name given it by someone high up in a division of the American NSA known as Dreadnaught."

"I've never heard of Dreadnaught."

"Of course you'd say that," Keyre said silkily.

"And I have no idea why an *Initiative*—whatever that might be—would be named after me."

"That's easy enough to answer," the Angelmaker said, stepping forward. "The Initiative was the brainchild of your late friend, General Boris Illyich Karpov."

Keyre's eyes narrowed. "You *were* good friends, weren't you, Bourne. *Close* friends."

"What of it?"

"Karpov willed you his boat."

"Again."

Keyre placed the photos back in the folder. "Did it ever occur to you that the Americans who were sent after you wanted to make sure that your friend's boat was destroyed?"

Bourne sat very still. Frankly, in the crisis of the moment, it hadn't occurred to him. Now he kicked himself for not considering the possibility. "There was nothing on the boat," he said flatly. "I searched it from stem to stern."

"What were you looking for?" Keyre asked.

Bourne shrugged.

"You see, there you have it." Keyre gestured for Bourne to continue eating. He poured him more tea. "You had no idea what you were looking for." He tilted his head. "But I must ask you: Why did you search Karpov's boat in the first place?"

Bourne, eating his hummus, said nothing at all.

Keyre supplied the answer. "Because you knew your friend better than anyone. You suspected he left something for you other than the boat itself." Keyre did not smirk, or even smile. His expression was perfectly serious, as befitted one businessman talking to another. "Your friend was like that, wasn't he?"

"You don't know anything about Boris."

"Enough, Bourne. I know enough."

"Tell me about him, then."

Keyre shook his head. "This is not the correct trajectory of this meeting."

Bourne laughed. "*Meeting*? Interesting choice of words."

Keyre gave him a pained smile, the smallest one Bourne had ever seen. "Back to the Bourne Initiative."

"Which doesn't exist."

"Oh, it exists all right," Keyre said.

"In the minds of very small men."

Keyre lifted a forefinger, shaking it. "You know, Bourne, I never realized you had a sense of humor."

"Frankly, I'm surprised you're able to recognize it."

"The Bourne Initiative." Keyre held up a hand. "Please. It does exist. It's a cyber initiative cooked up by General Karpov. No, don't interrupt. The reason the very small circle of people who know about it either want it or want to destroy it is because it's a cyber weapon capable of penetrating the American government's many firewalls and malware-killers to open up the codes to the country's nuclear arsenal." He sat back with the kind of self-satisfied air that made him insufferable. "What do you think of that, Bourne?"

"I think it's bullshit," Bourne said. "In fact, I know it is." He watched Keyre's self-satisfaction slowly slink away into the shadows at their feet. "Boris would never, under any circumstance, countenance creating such a cyber weapon."

"So everyone is wrong except you."

"That's right."

"I wonder. Would you stake your life on it, Bourne?"

"I would, indeed."

"Well, get ready, because that's precisely what you're going to have to do."

20

AFTER A BRIEF stop at a shop in the Arbat, Savasin's driver drew the Zil to the curb at the address Savasin had given him, a gray, nondescript office building in a gray, nondescript *raion*, as Moscow's districts were called. Ordering the Zil to return in three hours, Savasin exited the car, passed inside the building, which smelled of stale sweat and fear, and called a *bombila*, one of the city's fleet of taxis so run-down they deserved the nickname, bomb.

Twenty minutes later, he was deposited in Kapotnya, twelve miles southeast of the center of Moscow, hard up against the MKAD, the Moscow ring road. Savasin was a native Muscovite. Still and all, there were any number of *raions*—especially the seedier ones, where trash lined the streets, the gutters stank of urine, and where in the brutal winters, people froze to death huddled in shallow doorways and beneath parked cars—he had no clear knowledge of, let alone had visited. Kapotnya was one such *raion*—the worst in Moscow, in fact.

It was a crime- and drug-infested district, overstuffed with migrants best ignored by the government. Twenty-seven thousand souls were crammed into a shit-box of crumbling low-rise brick buildings dating back to the fifties and seventies, overshadowed by a monstrous oil processing plant. Not a metro station nor a municipal bus route dared come anywhere near Kapotnya. As a result, the streets and surrounding roads were clogged around the clock with vehicles spewing diesel particulates into the already oil-polluted atmosphere.

After only twenty seconds in the famously foul air, Savasin started coughing. Another twenty and his eyes began to burn, thirty more and his throat felt raw. Pulling a woolen scarf out of the pocket of his overcoat, he wrapped it around the lower half of his face, as if he were passing through a fire. Not much help, but it was something. In his right hand he carried his loaded Makarov, in his left the bottle of a green liqueur he had purchased in the Arbat. He might have been safer on the streets if he had chosen to wear his military greatcoat with the general's shoulder boards, but that surely would be a mistake at his destination. As for his Makarov, his mood, pressing hard against the border of giddiness, gave way to a pressing desire to fire it. And just like that, as if he'd conjured it out of thin air, an opportunity reared its head four and a half blocks from where the *bombila* had dropped him. Three young toughs hanging out across the street with nothing to do but drink beer, smoke cigarettes, show off their tattoos, and generally act like cartoon versions of Mick Jagger perked up at his approach. They called to him in the nastiest manner possible. *Wait,* he thought. *Let them come to you.* When he ignored them, one of them smashed his beer bottle on the stoop, swinging the jagged-edged remainder menacingly. Another slipped out a switchblade. Spewing a chain of epithets his way, each one more obscene than the last, they crossed the street, slipping between vehicles, heading directly for him. Savasin raised his Makarov and shot the leading tough through the heart. He went down between two cars stalled in the traffic. His mates, giving Savasin looks of shock, pulled at their friend as if he were a slab of meat, hurriedly carting him off without either a word or a backward glance.

Savasin continued on his way as if nothing untoward had occurred. Irresolute in the offices of the Kremlin and Moscow Center, he was by every measure assured on the streets of the city. The simple fact was that he wasn't cut out for bureaucratic work, which he found dull and extraordinarily tedious. He harbored the suspicion that the Sovereign had appointed him to the post of first minister for the sole reason of blocking Konstantin from the post. Konstantin, whose mind, like that of the fictional Mycroft Holmes, was perfectly suited to bureaucratic brilliance, and so considered an ally. The Sovereign had already been down a treacherous road with Boris Karpov, too smart by half; he wasn't going to make the same mistake twice. The Sovereign couldn't care less that Savasin muddled along. In fact, it suited him, since the first minister was neither expected nor allowed to administer any important decisions. Any advice he was foolish enough to offer the Sovereign was duly ignored with a smile of such condescension it set Savasin's teeth on edge. So he stopped, which was the point.

The first minister proceeded on, light of heart and, for the first time in a long while, optimistic about his future. The sky above Kapotnya, what he could make out, anyway, was a sickly, sulfurous yellow. Visibility was low. Neither sun nor cloud could be seen. Fire and black smoke plumed from the multiple stacks of the oil plant. It was like being inside a vast man-made dome, which, in a sense, was true enough.

Everyone he passed had scarves wrapped around their noses and mouths. They scurried past him, shoulders hunched, eyes on the ground. Occasionally car horns blared, as if that would get the traffic moving.

After trekking for fifteen minutes through this mini hell, he came to the street he needed, turned left into what would, in brighter parts of the city, be an alleyway. Here, it was a side street. Concrete buildings in the Brutalist Soviet style shouldered the alley into insignificance. The street stank of garbage and human waste. A dead dog had been kicked to the curb. It lay there stiff as a board, its fur, what was left of it, standing up like porcupine quills.

That's me. A dead dog in the Kremlin gutter, Savasin thought in an unseemly spasm of self-pity. And then in another spasm, this time of glee: *At least, it* was *me.*

No numbers here—he had to count the buildings, fifth on the left, just before the street elbowed to the left. When he pulled the door open, he was attacked by a stench so vile he nearly vomited. He crossed the vestibule as quickly as he was able, then vaulted up the steep staircase. He wished he had had the foresight to bring gloves. The sounds echoing through the stairwell were more suited to a hospital ER or, on the third floor an insane asylum: the unnerving noises of the human mind at the breaking point and beyond.

It was as if as he rose he was really descending into the pit of hell. But at last he came to the fourth and final floor, and it was like stepping from a mountain of trash into a serene garden. By some quirk of the building's acoustics, not a sound traveled up from below. Here, it was quiet, here the air was fresh and clean. This was beyond his ken until he saw that the hallway was filled with a profusion of plants and flowers in huge stone pots, breathing in carbon dioxide, breathing out oxygen. Depending from the entire length of the ceiling was a line of grow lights, artificial suns that bathed the foliage in warmth and energy.

A mountain appeared through the thickets, seemed to be heading in Savasin's direction. He came very fast—so fast, in fact, that he plucked the Makarov out of Savasin's hand before he had a chance to react. Not that he had any intention of shooting someone in here.

"You," the mountain said. He was a massive creature with a chest like a bull, legs like tree trunks, and arms like anacondas. His brow was low, his eyes small, his demeanor intimidating. "You," he repeated.

"Timur Ludmirovich."

"More," the mountain rumbled. He spoke Russian as a peasant would. He definitely wasn't a Muscovite.

"Savasin. Timur Ludmirovich Savasin."

The mountain regarded him, and for that moment Savasin felt as a field mouse must feel as an eagle swoops down on him from on high.

"Stay."

Savasin thought of the dog, dead and stiff in the

gutter, as he watched the creature turn on his heel, disappear through a double door in the center of the hallway—a magnificently turned wooden door banded in iron—visible now through the foliage that was shockingly out of place in this dismal dump. With a start, Savasin noted the eagle bas-relief, wings spread, talons to the fore, in the center of each door. And now it occurred to him that the name Orlova was derived from the Russian word for eagle.

Moments ticked by. Savasin lifted the bottle, reread the label, hoping he'd brought the right gift. Time passed without any sense of whether he would gain the interview he sought or would be turned away by the movable mountain.

Finally, one of the eagle doors opened, and the frame filled with the gargantuan creature. He stared balefully at Savasin out of his raisin eyes. Then he raised a hand. Savasin's Makarov looked like a child's toy in his fist. The mountain gestured with the barrel of Savasin's own handgun, beckoning him on.

Unlike the rest of the dank, murky building, the interior of the apartment was awash in light. His gaze traveled upward to the immense skylight. Two clusters of halogen lamps hung from the ceiling like chandeliers. They were a corrective, their blazing illumination draining the natural light of its sulfurous hue. The apartment had been carved out of the entire top floor. Open doorways led left and right, but the vast space into which the mountain led him was the entire apartment's raison d'être. It was filled with yet more foliage, traveler's palms chief among them. On either side of the large, open room rose a pair of fruit trees, lemon on the right, fig on the left. An old man—apparently a gardener—was busy at the fig tree, pruning and fussing. He ignored the guest completely, as did the mountain, now that Savasin had been granted permission to enter the inner sanctum. In fact, the massive man was in the ungainly process of seating himself on a stoutly reinforced bench in front of a baby grand piano. His massive hands hovered over the keyboard, then struck the first chords of Maurice Ravel's heartbreakingly beautiful "Pavane for a Dead Princess."

Astonished, Savasin stood transfixed as the mountain played the piece with consummate skill and a tenderness impossible to comprehend coming from such a hulking creature.

"I see you've met Cerberus."

At the sound of the smoky voice, Savasin tore himself away from the transfixing scene and turned his attention to the woman who, having stepped from behind a tree, now planted herself before a large artist's easel. She held a brush in one hand, a palette in the other. Beside her was a paint-spattered stepladder whose top was an open case filled with tubes of oil paint and a can of turpentine, the time-tested old-school thinner of oils.

Even in her mid-fifties Ekaterina Orlova was a beautiful woman—pale, oval face, eyes of a blue akin to the deepest ocean, an aggressive nose, and wide lips, which were now turned up in an ironic smile.

"Timur Ludmirovich. Shall I say it's good to see you? Perhaps it is, perhaps it isn't." She turned to regard the half-finished painting of a swimmer half submerged in what?—a pool, the sea? It was impossible to tell. Possibly that was the point. The swimmer was in her element and yet out of sight of land.

"The painting is lovely," Savasin said, partly because he meant it, partly because he could think of nothing else to say. He had come all this way, fended off an attack, risen through the stench of an abattoir, and now what? He had conveniently forgotten how intimidating Ekaterina Orlova was. But perhaps that had been deliberate.

The artist, putting brush to canvas, said, "Tell me, Timur Ludmirovich, why have you come?" She wore a smock that once had been light-blue but now displayed all the colors of the rainbow, and some in between.

Savasin lifted the bottle. "I brought you a present."

She laughed, a guttural, utterly erotic sound that came from deep in her throat. She turned. "Now I know you came to ask a favor."

"Just to talk," Savasin said, a touch too hastily.

That laugh again, making him feel things best not spoken of in the area below his belt. She set her brush in a smeared jar of colorless liquid and set the palette on the top of the stepladder. Then she crossed to the piano, where the mountain had placed Savasin's Makarov. Expertly, she ejected the magazine, checked the number of bullets. Then she sniffed the business end. "Whom did you shoot?"

"No one of import."

She smiled, her bared teeth like knives. "Your situation must be very, very bad for you to brave coming here, Timur Ludmirovich."

"Well, I suppose it is."

"Boris is dead."

Her voice had abruptly turned cold as ice, sending a shiver down his spine. Plus, she still held the Makarov.

"'The center cannot hold. The blood-dimmed tide

is loosed. The best lack all conviction, while the worst are full of passionate intensity.'"

She was quoting Yeats, though Savasin was too ignorant to know it. Never mind, the words sent another, deeper chill through him.

"I'm afraid you're right, Ekaterina."

"You did nothing to save him." Her eyes flashed like warning lights. "You who had the means to stop—"

"No one could have stopped his murder." This he knew beyond a shadow of a doubt. "Not all his bodyguards, not all the FSB in attendance. Not even his best friend, Jason Bourne."

At Bourne's name, Ekaterina relinquished the icy rage with which she had been temporarily gripped. Unbuttoning the smock, she set it and the Makarov aside. She was wearing a pearl-colored silk blouse and black, wide-legged trousers of the same luscious material. Ekaterina had always known how to dress well. "Let me see."

Savasin handed over the bottle of absinthe. Ekaterina, having read the label, said, "How on earth did you get this, Timur Ludmirovich? Not at GUM, I'll warrant." She meant the central department store on Dzerzhinsky Square.

"The same avenue where you buy your clothes. A private source."

She nodded in acceptance. "Come," she said, indicating a curved sofa clad in deep-purple velvet.

As if being directed by telepathy, the mountain ceased his playing, rose, and brought to the table in front of the sofa a pair of cut-glass cordial glasses that looked very old and very expensive. Having completed this task, he returned to the baby grand, taking up the reins of another Ravel piano piece, not nearly as sad as the first.

Savasin watched Ekaterina put the bottle aside, pour out glasses of vodka. The toast and draining of the vodka having been accomplished with the minimum of pomp, Savasin set down his glass and turned to his hostess.

"Ekaterina," he said, "I've come to talk to you about Alyosha, your daughter."

21

THERE FOLLOWED A peculiar silence, the kind found in a graveyard at night. It was broken by a laugh from Keyre, like the trumpet of an elephant. He slapped his knee in mirth; he was grinning from ear to ear.

"You see, my dear Angelmaker, I was right all along. The story put about that the Bourne Initiative is the ultimate cyber weapon is so much smoke. And here before us is the only living human being who can confirm my suspicion. Which he has done."

He leaned forward abruptly, elbows parked on his knobby knees. "Here is my second gift to you, Bourne. I've cleared up—well, one essential matter, anyway— why the Americans and the Russians are hot on your trail."

"Mala could have told me all this back on Skyros," Bourne pointed out.

"True enough." Keyre spread his hands. "But where's the fun in that?" He wagged his forefinger again. "You and I both know that we aren't done with each other; we were fated to meet again. But who could have imagined it would be under circumstances where we're in the star-crossed position to help each other."

Bourne turned to the Angelmaker. "I'd like something more substantial to eat."

She took up the walkie-talkie on the table, spoke into it briefly. No one spoke another word until one of Keyre's people arrived with a tray on which sat a bowl of stew and a round of unleavened bread with which to eat it.

Bourne took the bowl off the tray as it was being set down, sniffed it.

"It's goat, Bourne," Keyre said with a wry smile. "You won't find a morsel of human flesh in there."

As Bourne ripped off a piece of bread, scooped up the stew, and began to eat, Keyre said, "So here, in a nutshell, is what we are dealing with: you and I are both under attack because of something your friend, Karpov, dreamed up. Neither of us know what it is, let alone have possession of it. But we won't have any peace until we find out what the general was up to." He steepled his long, spidery fingers. "I think we agree on that, yes?"

Bourne looked up into Keyre's face, swallowed. "With your far-flung network I would think it should be easy enough for you to find out."

"Normally that would be the case, more or less." Keyre sighed. "But these are not normal times, Bourne. Even I cannot infiltrate an American NSA black site."

Bourne stopped eating, put the bowl aside. "What are you talking about?"

"The gist of it is this: it was General MacQuerrie, the

head of Dreadnaught, who dubbed this mysterious data the Bourne Initiative. He set one of his private people, Morgana Roy, by all accounts a cyber genius, to the task of decoding the data. The problem is we only have MacQuerrie's word for what this data is. Was he telling Roy the truth? We can't ask her because she's disappeared. Was he lying, and, if so, for what reason? No one knows the answer to that but MacQuerrie himself, and he's been arrested, due to a damning server leak disseminated by LeakAGE while you were in dreamland.

"So. It seems to me that we have only one way forward. We have to penetrate the NSA black site where MacQuerrie is being held and interrogate him."

Bourne gave a harsh laugh. "It's you who's in dreamland, Keyre."

Once again, Keyre chose to ignore Bourne's comment. "Only one man on earth can get to MacQuerrie, interrogate him, and get out alive. That's you, Bourne. The chameleon."

"Even I—"

"My people have discovered where he's being held, so part of your job has been done for you." Keyre sat forward. "Bourne, there's no other way out for us; much as you despise me, much as you want to see me dead, you know this to be true."

Bourne did. Much as he hated to admit it, there was a lot to be said for Keyre's plan. He kept his gaze fixed steadily on the Somalian. He did not look at the Angelmaker; did not want to see what she held in her eyes for him. There was nothing he wanted more than to be wherever Sara was, even if it wasn't a sun-splashed beach in Bali or Thailand. He missed her with an ache that penetrated to the very marrow of his bones. But they had realized that becoming attached in that way was a liability, too much danger for them both. In their line of business, love was the ultimate liability. Now that it had happened to them, it was better to live in denial than to allow the perilous truth to overwhelm them. But rationality did not diminish Bourne's ache for her.

But he wasn't with Sara, didn't even know where in the world she was. He was here, the present danger to him was acute, and a solution, though extremely treacherous, had been presented to him.

"Bourne, can you come up with an alternative?" Keyre prompted. When Bourne said nothing, he nodded, continuing, "I and my people will provide transportation and all the support you might need."

"I work alone."

"So I've heard."

Bourne rose, stretched his legs. He had already begun strenuous workouts. "Where is the NSA holding MacQuerrie?"

Keyre rose, studied Bourne for a moment. "Seriously, you won't believe it when I tell you."

———

"My daughter?" Ekaterina had gone very still. "What have you to do with Alyoshka?" She jumped up, her agitation setting Cerberus into motion, like the mechanical creature of a clock about to chime the hour. "Do you have her in custody on some trumped-up charge? That's the Sovereign's way, after all."

Savasin held up his hands, palms outward, both to

placate Ekaterina and to ward off an anticipated blow from Cerberus. "Calm yourself. Nothing of the sort has happened. Your Alyosha is as free as a bird."

Ekaterina made a gesture. Cerberus came to an immediate halt but, Savasin observed with no little trepidation, did not return to his place at the piano. He maintained his position, his baleful glare striking the first minister like a series of hammer blows, causing him to rise off the sensuously comfortable sofa.

"However," Savasin began.

"*However* what?" Ekaterina exploded.

"I'm afraid to inform you that Alyosha has put herself in grave danger."

Ekaterina stared at him for a moment, her anger causing her to tremble.

"Continue," she said when she had collected herself.

He gestured. "Shall we be seated?"

"I'd rather stand," Ekaterina said icily. "So would you."

"Indeed, yes." Oh, how this vexing woman cowed him, he thought in anguish. He wished he were back on the dismal streets of Kapotnya, Makarov in hand, like Gary Cooper in *High Noon,* about to settle old scores.

He spread his hands. "Well, here it is in a nutshell. Alyosha has got herself involved with some high-grade criminals, in an enterprise that—"

"Impossible!" Another explosion.

"My dear Ekaterina, for some unknown reason, your daughter has gone and hooked herself up with her brother."

"Alyoshka has no brother."

"All right, then. Her *half* brother."

Ekaterina's eyes opened wide. "Gora?" An emphatic

shake of her head. "No, you must be mistaken. She and I see eye-to-eye on Gora: we both hate him."

"I assure you I'm not." He dug into his breast pocket. This gesture caused Cerberus to start into motion again until he withdrew his hand, held up the mobile phone so both Ekaterina and her giant minion could see. "I have the proof right here."

"Fuck you." With fists dug into her flaring hips, she said: "Show me."

With the mobile held in front of him, screen first, he activated a video. "We are in Kalmar."

"Where the hell is that?"

"East coast of Sweden. Close to Russia." He watched her face closely as the video showed her Alyosha moving along the docks to lean against a railing and, moments later, being joined by a man.

"Who's that?" Ekaterina said, squinting. "Who is Alyoshka talking with?"

"A man named Larry London," Savasin said. "Although that's a legend. His real name is Nikolay Ivanovich Rozin."

"Never heard of either of them."

"Information is my business. For the past ten years, Nikolay Ivanovich has been out in the cold, as we say in the trade. Deep undercover in the West. But my brother recently named him head of *spetsnaz*."

Ekaterina's indrawn gasp was audible. "What is she doing with him?"

"I'm afraid that's not the worst of it, Ekaterina. Please watch."

Her gaze was fixed to the screen as her daughter took her leave of the false Larry London and stepped down to one of the floating docks where strings of boats were docked on either side. Just before Alyosha stepped aboard a boat near the far end and the video ended, the camera was able to pick out its name, stenciled on the stern.

Ekaterina gave another, deeper gasp. "Yegor Maslov!" She put a hand to her mouth. "*Carbon Neutral*. That's Gora's boat."

"I'm very much afraid it is." Savasin shut down the file. "And there you have it."

Ekaterina, eyes glazed over, sank back down onto the sofa cushion. Cerberus returned to the piano. Taking this as a cue, Savarin perched beside her on the edge, all the while keeping an eye on Cerberus's profile. He had switched from classical to pop, was in the middle of a curious slowed-down rendition of Kate Bush's "Running Up That Hill." As a pianist he had a knack for bringing out the heartache in a melody.

Savasin filled his host's glass, handed it to her. She drank it as if in a trance.

"What are we to do, Timur Ludmirovich? Alyoshka has fallen into the wrong hands."

"First, we must determine how far she has fallen," Savasin said briskly, all business now that he had delivered his hammer blow. "Then we must determine how to extricate her."

He watched Ekaterina's dark-blue eyes turn toward him. "We are at a distinct disadvantage."

"Perhaps," he acknowledged. "But then again perhaps not."

"What are you babbling about?" Ekaterina snapped. She was coming out of her shock with almost superhuman alacrity.

"Don't you see? My brother has appointed a man to be the chief of FSB's special operations who is clandestinely in collusion with the head of the Kazanskaya mafia." He grinned broadly. "The whole thing is—I don't know, what's the right word—delicious!"

"I don't believe that would be *my* word," Ekaterina sniffed. "But I take your point." Then, turning, she addressed the old gardener. "Papa, did you get all this?"

When the old man stood up straight, Savasin could see that he was ex-military. He had steel-gray hair, cropped very short, and eyes of the same color as his daughter's.

"Every word," he said in a surprisingly strong voice. Without being beckoned forward, he crossed the atelier, bringing a wooden, round-topped stool with him, warding off Cerberus, who had leapt up in mid-melody in order to assist Ekaterina's father.

"What a world," he said, as he sat on the stool facing them across the low table. "I hope I die before it gets much worse."

"Papa, shush!" Ekaterina said in mock dismay. Turning to Savasin, she said, "He's always saying things like that. It doesn't mean he means it."

"Hah!" her father interjected, draining Savasin's glass of what was left of the vodka. He made a face. "Vile stuff. I don't know how you drink it."

Ekaterina shook her head with a small smile. Clearly, Savasin thought, she was used to indulging the old man's whims.

"Timur Ludmirovich Savasin, First Minister of the Russian Federation,"—her arm swept out—"may I introduce you to my father, Dima Vladimirovich Orlov."

Orlov sat with straight spine on the backless stool,

crossed his arms over his chicken chest. "Such an exalted figure here in my daughter's humble atelier." He wagged his head from side to side. "The modern world moves in mysterious ways; its wonders to perform."

"I wonder," Savasin said, wanting to regain control of the situation before this dotty old man ran it off the rails, "do you think it wise to paraphrase the Christian Bible to me?"

Orlov regarded him a moment, a small, disconcerting smile playing about his lips. "Mr. First Minister, are you by any chance referring to the following quote: 'God moves in mysterious ways; His wonders to perform; He plants His footsteps in the sea, and rides upon the storm'?"

"Indeed, I am," Savasin said, feeling quite proud of himself.

"The verse is quite beautiful—moving even, is it not?" He cocked his head. "No, but I suppose to a Communist ideologue such as yourself the verse, in mentioning the power of God, is anathema."

"I can recognize the poetry in the Christian Bible as well as anyone," Savasin replied somewhat defensively.

"That's quite a statement, First Minister. Are you certain you want to stand behind it?"

"Why, of course."

"Well, as it happens that quote isn't found anywhere in the Christian Bible, whose poetry you purport to admire. It is from a nineteenth-century hymn written by the English poet and hymnodist, Richard Cowper."

Savasin's hands curled into fists at his side. He dug his fingernails into his palms in order to keep himself calm, cool, and collected. Having been led like a lamb to the slaughter by this curious relic, it wasn't an easy task.

"I'm wondering now," he said slowly and icily, "whether you and your daughter want my help in extricating Alyoshka from—"

"Please don't call her that," Ekaterina said.

"It's not your place," Dima Orlov said.

"My place?" This was too much. "I am first minister. It's my place to—"

"Yes, yes, I know who you are," the old man said testily. "However, I am now of the opinion that you are ignorant of who I am."

There now was a deathly silence in the atelier. Cerberus had stopped playing. Having detached himself from the piano bench, he took up a position within what Savasin considered striking distance from him. Beset on what seemed all sides, he did not like that at all.

Already regretting his decision to come here, he said, "You appear to have me at a disadvantage, Dima Vladimirovich."

"Appear? *Appear!*" Dima exclaimed. "There are no ifs ands or buts about it. Are there, Katya?"

"No, Papa, there aren't." She seemed curious and fascinated at the same time. "Your name rings no bells with the first minister."

"Should it?" Savasin said, equally testily. If not for the looming presence of Cerberus, he might well have stood up and made his exit. Then he thought of the dead dog in the gutter and he remained in place.

"Well, you are the first minister, after all. You are privy to reams and reams of information about the citizens of the Russian Federation, not to mention your enemies.

But not me." Dima was grinning. "But that's all to the good. It means my people have done their job."

"Your people?" What *people* could the old man have? Savasin wondered. In his mind, maybe. He glanced at Ekaterina, but it was like looking at a brick wall. She had nothing for him.

Dima's grin was widening. "Let me tell you what I believe is happening here, First Minister. You didn't come to see Katya to help her with our beloved Alyoshka. You came here to elicit my daughter's help in whatever scheme you have concocted to take your brother, Konstantin, down a couple of pegs." He unwound his arms to wave one hand. "I won't ask you whether I'm right, to give you the opportunity to continue dissembling. The three of us must now face the truth of the matter."

"What truth?" Savasin said, the sharp edge making his voice brittle.

"Patience, Timur Ludmirovich," Ekaterina advised.

But Savasin, having endured one humiliation after another, starting with that creep Cerberus, was in no mood to be patient. He leapt up and, keeping one eye on the moving mountain, pointed at them. "I've had it with you two. An hour from now I'll be back with a cadre of FSB agents. We'll see how clever you are when I start interrogating you in the basement of the Lubyanka."

Ekaterina looked up at him from out of damnably serene eyes. "Calm yourself, Tamerlane."

At the use of the name of the great conqueror for which Timur was interchangeable, Savasin tried to bank his fury.

"Gospodin Tamerlane," Dima said, "I am quite certain that you are familiar with the name Ivan Volkin."

"Of course I am." Savasin was confused by the sudden switch in topic. "He was an *eminence grise*, a kind of consigliere to a number of the *grupperovka* leaders."

Dima nodded. "That's right. Last year, Volkin was killed in Moscow by Jason Bourne."

"That is known to me," Savasin said in a calmer voice. "The American agent provocateur did us all a favor."

"He did what the FSB—even the Sovereign—could not do."

"What's your point?"

Dima lifted a hand. "Please sit down."

Savasin waited the requisite amount of time so as not to give the impression that he was following an order. When he was seated, Dima said, "As it happens, Bourne did me a favor, as well."

Savasin frowned. "How, precisely?"

"Ivan Volkin was a fucking pain in my side."

The curse coming out of the old man's mouth was initially startling, but then it got the first minister to thinking that he had sized up the situation all wrong. Sitting before him wasn't any old dotty man, indulged and put to use by his daughter as a gardener. Dima was the power here, not Ekaterina. Savasin almost slapped himself. Egged on by his superior position, he had been blinded by his hubris.

"Then we have something in common," he said in his most accommodating voice.

"That we do, Tamerlane," Dima said. "More than you know."

22

THE LATE HOUR was growing even later. The low lamplight was even lower. Harry Hornden had not returned. Fulmer sat very still, stewing in his own juices. On the one hand, he wanted to get out of here, find Max, and turn him over to Department of Homeland Security. On the other hand, and to his complete surprise, he felt a keen desire to stay here with Gwyneth. It had been a long time since Fulmer had found himself smitten the way he was with this woman. He was floored. How could his wife and children have so quickly come to seem part of another universe, existing as no more than photos in a drawer in a desk in an office belonging to someone he once might have known?

Gwyneth had her back to him. She was pouring herself another drink. His gaze was fixed on the taut globes of her buttocks, as visible as the arcing crease between them.

"Marshall," she said, "may I ask why you're still here?" She turned around. "After all, you have what you came for."

"What is that you're drinking?" Fulmer said, levering himself off the sofa.

"Absinthe." Gwyneth held up her stemmed cordial glass. The drink was emerald green. "The real thing."

Fulmer had heard vague stories about absinthe but he had felt no particular reason to give them his atten- tion. He watched, fascinated, as Gwen placed a cube of sugar in a slotted spoon, placed the spoon over the glass, and slowly poured a thin stream of water from a chilled carafe over the sugar cube. The result was star- tling; the drink clouded up, turning a pale, icy green.

"It's a liqueur. French," she said, putting the para- phernalia down. "It was brought back here by the black expats who spent time in Paris."

"Well, then I definitely have no interest."

Gwyneth pursed her lips. "Who is it you don't care for? The French or blacks?"

"The French are idiots. The French love themselves. The French think they know everything about every- thing, and yet they can't even run their own country. I hate the French."

"And blacks?"

"The French took them in, didn't they? Accepted them as equals. I told you they were idiots."

"Here, try this." Gwyneth held out the glass. "Maybe this will assuage some of your hatred."

"Nothing's going to do that."

That smile again, the slight curving of those luscious lips. "As long as you're here."

She came and stood in front of him, so close he could feel the heat emanating from her. He had no choice but to inhale her scent.

"What's that perfume you're wearing?"

"Do you like it?"

"I do."

She smiled. "I'm not wearing perfume."

If Fulmer were capable of blushing, which he was not, his neck and cheeks would be aflame. To take his mind off his reaction to her, he took the proffered glass.

"You know, absinthe was made for late-night drinking."

He took a sip, experienced many flavors at once: licorice, a very distinct herbal undertone, and a certain bitterness, as if he had been gnawing on a root.

"What do you think?"

"It isn't terrible." He took another sip.

Gwyneth laughed. "It contains thujone, an essential component of wormwood, as well as a combination of powerful herbs. The mind is cleared, energizing the body, while the alcohol serves as a relaxant. Really, there's nothing else like it."

She regarded him from beneath long lashes. "And as for the French, they know how to have sex."

Fulmer engaged her eyes with his own. "I don't like that Max put his hands on you."

She sipped the absinthe while the glass was still in his hand. "Max paid for that privilege, Marshall. You, on the other hand—"

As he grabbed her around her narrow waist, the cordial glass fell to the carpet, spilling what was left of the absinthe on his shoes. Too wrapped up in closing with her, he scarcely gave it a thought.

As he felt her breasts and the heat between her thighs press against him, something was unlocked inside him, some bestial thing that had long been lurking, pacing back and forth in the deepest shadows of his soul, waiting for its chance to be turned loose.

Now was its time, and it reveled in it.

———

Gwyneth's office might have looked like a salon to Fulmer, but in fact it was kitted out with enough bleeding-edge eavesdropping gear, all cleverly hidden from view, to make it the envy of even TMZ.

And so while Fulmer's interview with Gwyneth morphed from friendly banter to a bit of business, to bantering flirtation, to full-on sex of a massive hard-core variety heretofore hidden deeply inside Fulmer's firmly buttoned-down psyche, all of it, from his foul-mouthed imprecations to his all-too-willing submission to the mistress side of his hostess, was duly recorded in high-fidelity and in living color, as was said by both Gwyneth and Harry Hornden.

Later, Harry would deem it "a sight to behold," and toast Gwyneth for peeling away the layers of tough skin that shielded Fulmer from his inner demon, which now belonged, lock, stock, and barrel, to them. At the time, however, Gwyneth was far too busy goading the Fulmerial demon into more and more outré forms of behavior that were nothing she hadn't experienced before, but would be "Holy shit!" unacceptable to the general public.

———

Within eighteen hours Bourne was airborne, in the belly of one of Keyre's transports. He studied the surpris-

ingly deep dossier on General Arthur MacQuerrie the
Somalian's network had assembled. When he had committed it to memory, he set it aside, put his head back,
and fell into a deep and restorative slumber in which he
dreamed of Sara. They were running along the sand on
Beit Yannai Beach, and the sun was in their eyes. Sara
took an abrupt right turn, crashing into the Mediterranean surf. He was right on her tail.

Diving through a wave, he found her on the other
side and kissed her with a fierceness that drove itself all
the way through his bones.

———

The Angelmaker was similarly in the air, heading for the
same destination. As she stared out the Perspex window,
she reviewed the final conversation she had had with
Keyre before heading to his airfield.

"There's good reason why he likes to work alone,"
she had told Keyre.

His eyes narrowed, and he gave her the look she
knew so well, the one that passed through skin and flesh
and bone to lodge in her brain. "I'm not going to have
a problem with you, am I?"

"What kind of a problem?"

"A Bourne problem." Keyre scrutinized every facet
of her face with the exquisite attention of a jeweler
about to cut a precious stone. "It has not escaped my
notice that you have formed an unhealthy attachment
to him."

"You know where my loyalty lies."

"Yes, Angelmaker," he said, putting heavy emphasis on

each word. "I do." He had rubbed his hands together. "So. To the matter of Bourne's preference to work alone."

"I will shadow him," she responded firmly. Then her face clouded over. "Even into the NSA dark site?"

Keyre smirked. "What d'you think?"

The Angelmaker—or was it Mala?—did not sleep a wink on the flights' long legs to America. Instead, she watched the visions unspool behind her eyes. She saw herself as she might have been had her father not sold her and her sister into slavery. As she might have been had she not been taken into custody by Keyre, and he not initiated her into the exquisite horrors of Yibir, had he not incised his magic formulae upon her back, had he not bled her day after day, working on her to morph the pain he inflicted into a pleasure that ensnared her in its insidious web. Always pulled in two directions, she was on the verge of losing her self in the cauldron of Yibir when Bourne had arrived to extricate both her and Liis. What would she have become? A prima ballerina like Liis? She didn't think so. But something. Something other than what she was now: a puppet of man and magic. She no longer knew what was real, what was Yibir magic, and what was her own fantasy.

23

CROWCROFT, TWENTY-ONE ACRES lying ninety-five miles southeast of the Leesburg Pike, had a long and storied history stretching back hundreds of years. Originally bought by an English shipping magnate to house his son, who had impregnated a woman far below his station, it was turned into a tobacco farm by the wayward son, who, as it turned out, had a better head for business than he did for women. Or for politics, for that matter. Having sided with the South in the Civil War and having agreed to house Johnny Reb during those bloody years, he was, in his elder years, thrown out on his wide bottom. For some years afterward, Crowcroft was kept afloat by remnants of the son's ragtag progeny, but time after time it went bankrupt, preyed upon by northern carpetbaggers out to line their pockets as quickly and as unscrupulously as possible. Near the end of the twentieth century it went into foreclosure for the last time. For some years after that, it sat fallow and forlorn on the books of the local bank that had lent money to the unfortunate owners, who, as it happened, were thrown in prison for drug trafficking. The same isolated location, which was perfect for illegal activities at Crowcroft, served as a detriment to selling it to legitimate businesses. Until the U.S. government came along and took it off the bank's hands for ten cents on the dollar.

For the next eighteen months, Crowcroft remained uninhabited while contractors for the NSA made the required repairs and modifications. These modifications spiraled out from the huge Tara-like great house itself to the various barns, which were remade as barracks for the rotating contingent of federal agents trained to guard the property, and the sheds, which now housed multiple banks of electronic equipment, generators, and back-up generators. The old stone walls that demarked the limits of Crowcroft's fiefdom were reinforced on the inside by concrete muscle over a steel skeleton. A network of CCTV cameras was installed to complement the motion and heat detectors. Bomb-sniffing dogs on chain leashes patrolled the grounds day and night.

Arthur Lee, Crowcroft's manager, was the one holdover from the previous regimes, absent the drug pushers, who had summarily kicked him out. He had been vouched for by the bank and vetted by NSA nerds. For the current regime, he was a necessary but invisible member of the Crowcroft estate. He was a descendant of the shipping magnate's son and the African slave he fell in love with and elevated to live by his side in the great house. Many generations had come and gone since her only son was born. Though she subsequently gave birth to four daughters, only the son survived the war.

Arthur Lee was that man's great-great-grandson. He had been born and raised on Crowcroft, had been witness to the good, the bad, and the very, very ugly, all of which had rolled in, done its damage to the acreage, and then ebbed away. Through it all, Arthur Lee, part English, part Angolan, part Powhatan, and who knew what else thrown into the hopper, abided, standing tall. He thought of himself as a mongrel, half jokingly, half bitter. He was decidedly antisocial, suspicious of everyone, but when it came to the crunch, it was Arthur Lee who set the broken leg of Jimmy Lang after he took a header off his tractor one autumn afternoon.

Bourne had met Jimmy Lang through Lang's ties to the NSA, which were tenuous at best. Lang had a fifty-acre farm that abutted one side of Crowcroft. With his wife ill, his children off in college with no interest in the farming life, and no buyer for his acreage, Lang had had to use his brains to figure out how to make ends meet. What he hit upon was the flock of strangers who had taken possession of Crowcroft. God alone knew what they were doing there, but when Arthur needed his help to keep up Crowcroft's appearance as a working farm, he called on his friend; Lang was only too happy to take the extra money. Whoever these strangers were, they paid damn well.

Bourne had come upon Jimmy when, after he had successfully fulfilled the assignment for which the Bourne identity had been created, he was tasked with figuring out what the NSA was doing with that property so far from their HQ. The Treadstone powers-that-were harbored a pathological hatred of the NSA, and were delighted to take every opportunity to undermine the agency, which was why Bourne was given this particular brief. The Treadstone people were ruthless spyocrats. They were aware of his extraordinary prowess, and they were determined to ride him as hard as they could for as long as they could. But none of them was smart enough or prescient enough to figure he'd find a way to break his psychological shackles and drop off their radar screens.

As for Crowcroft, at first it was assumed the NSA was using it to debrief defectors, and perhaps in the beginning it was. But not when Bourne first began snooping around nine years ago. It was Bourne's practice to come upon a target indirectly, slip through an unexpected interstice, and cut to the heart of the matter. This he did by befriending Jimmy Lang. Of course, the basis of the friendship was related to Bourne's assignment, but the two men genuinely liked each other, and afterward he and Bourne remained friends.

This was why Keyre had said, *"Seriously, you won't believe it when I tell you,"* when Bourne had asked him where the NSA had stashed General MacQuerrie.

How Keyre knew of Bourne's friendship with Jimmy Lang was yet another question about the Somalian for which Bourne needed an answer.

"How long has it been?" Lang asked when Bourne approached him in the field. He had swung off his tractor, stood beside it, wiping his hands on a rag he kept stashed in the back pocket of his old-school overalls.

"That long," Bourne said as he put down the small satchel he was carrying and locked hands with his friend.

Lang, with wide-set eyes, a shock of light-brown

hair, and a jaw like a granite boulder, had a body built for the great outdoors. Bourne supposed that with the right training Jimmy could have been a WWE fighter; he didn't have the disposition, though. He was a hunter the way his daddy and granddaddy were hunters: to put food on the family table. He hated violence and inhumanity, which is why Bourne had told him the first time they met what the NSA was really up to in the remade and remodeled great house.

"What've you been up to?" Jimmy held up his hands, palms outward. "Stupid question. Don't ask, don't tell." He indicated with his head. "Shall we head up to the house? Got a rocking chair with your name on it. Plus, there's a bottle of corn whiskey idling away in the pantry just begging to be drunk."

"As good as that sounds . . ."

"Ah." Lang nodded. "A business call. I should've known. What can I do for you?"

"Crowcroft."

"Again." Lang looked off to his left, toward the thick line of trees that separated his property from the NSA black site. When his gaze swung back, he said, "I got bad news on that score. They dynamited the last of those tunnels, including the one you used to get in last time."

Bourne squinted in the deepening western light that elongated their shadows. "I've got to get in there, Jimmy."

Lang sighed. "Well, I sure don't know a way." He considered for a minute, then snapped his fingers. "But there's someone who just might."

"What's his name?"

"Arthur Lee."

"Crowcroft's manager."

"Right." Lang nodded. "He's a good friend of mine." He slapped his left thigh. "Ever since he fixed the leg I broke."

Bourne reflected for a moment. "You can introduce me. I can say—"

"Now hold on a sec. Art's a peculiar bird. For one thing, he don't like big-city people, especially those like to snooping around his property. For another, he's a fistful of Prickly Petes."

In other circumstances Bourne might have laughed. "There's got to be a way," he said. "Tell me everything you know about him."

———

Arthur Lee squinted gimlet-eyed at Bourne when Jimmy introduced them. Jimmy had invited Art to his house for dinner, not an unusual occurrence; Art, an inveterate loner who didn't even own a TV or a computer, had never refused.

"Who's this?" he said, standing in the open doorway. He had a face like a hobo's shoe—every line a crevice, every protuberance a boulder. Black eyes, glossy and wary as a crow's, scrutinized Bourne as if he were a piece of meat hanging in a butcher shop. "I don't know him." As if Bourne were deaf or invisible.

"Jason's an old friend of mine," Jimmy said easily. "Don't stand on ceremony. Come on in, Art."

Arthur Lee did not make a move to step over the threshold. From one fist dangled a bottle of mountain whiskey. "I think not."

"Oh, come on. I made your favorite—"

"Not a bit of it."

As Jimmy had said, the stubbornness in Arthur Lee stemmed from his background, stubbornness born of generations of fury.

"Arthur thinks of himself as some kinda freak," Jimmy had told Bourne while relating as much of his friend's family history as he knew. *"Well, it's more than that, really. He despises the English lord in him. Y'see, Jason, he's overseer and slave all wrapped up in one self-hating bundle. I sure as hell wouldn't want to be him. But don't judge him too harshly. Deep down, he's got a good heart; trouble is he often has a problem locating it."*

Which was why, just after Jimmy had called to invite his friend over for dinner, Bourne used a pair of small scissors he found in Jimmy's bathroom to open up the stitches in his shoulder. Immediately, he started to bleed. When he had come out, blood seeping through his shirt, Jimmy said, "Damnit all, what the hell did you do?" And then his eyes lit up, and he grinned, tapping the side of his head with his forefinger.

Now, as Arthur Lee backed away, Jimmy said, "Hold on, Art, it's not that I didn't want your company, but...and Jason told me straight out he didn't want any help, but, I mean, just take a look..."

Lee hesitated, still suspicious, took a step back toward them.

"What now?"

"His shoulder. Here, take a look..."

Lee squinted. "Awful lot of blood there."

Jimmy nodded. "See what I mean. The boy's as stubborn as you, not wanting to take any help."

Lee took another step forward, studying the mass of blood soaking through the shirt. Then he glanced up at Bourne. "Son, I do believe you're lucky I'm here."

Then, handing Jimmy the bottle of mountain whiskey, he stepped inside, already taking over.

———

Arthur Lee cocked his head. "What did you say your name was?"

"I didn't," Bourne said.

"It's Jason—" Jimmy began before Bourne cut him off.

"Smith," Bourne said, with a quick glance at Jimmy. "Jason Smith."

They were sitting in the hallway just outside Jimmy's bathroom, where he had pulled up three chairs. Lee, leaning on his elbows after peeling off Bourne's shirt, pursed his thick lips. "That's some wound you've got there, Mr. Smith."

"Why don't you call me Jason."

"Why don't the sun crawl down from the sky." Lee addressed Jimmy without taking his eyes off the wound, rattling off a list of items he'd need. While Jimmy was in the bathroom hunting and gathering, Lee continued in a jaundiced tone. "Someone did a right nice job the first time around." He eyed Bourne. "What happened?"

"I live an active life."

Lee gave a little bark that might have been a laugh. "No city feller, huh?"

"I hate cities," Bourne said truthfully.

"Ach, don't get me started."

Jimmy returned with all the first aid requirements, and Lee set about his work. "Arthur," he said, "Jason is something of a linguist."

"Is that so." Lee concentrated all the harder on cleaning and disinfecting Bourne's wound. "I'll bet he doesn't know how to speak my language," he said, in Powhatan, an eastern Algonquin offshoot.

"I would be honored if you would address me directly, Powtitianna," Bourne replied in the same language.

Arthur Lee stopped what he was doing. With surgical thread and needle in his hands, he looked directly at Bourne. "I am no chieftain. But I do thank you for the honor."

As he began to put the needle to good use, Bourne said, "As far as I can tell, you are around these parts, Arthur."

Lee grunted, but he couldn't keep the smile of pleasure off his face. "Done," he said, after tying off the thread. He had returned to English, mainly because of Jimmy. "Keep your activities to a minimum for the next several days."

"I'm afraid that's not possible."

Arthur Lee sat back on his haunches. "What is it you said you do?"

"I didn't," Bourne replied. Then switching back to Powhatan, "I need the Powtitianna's help."

Arthur Lee, the very essence of stillness, regarded Bourne for several moments. "That's a mighty forward request, Jason." Then he broke out into a smile. "Nevertheless, I do believe I'll take it under advisement."

Bourne was naturally eager to get inside Crowcroft, but in Arthur Lee's world all things presented themselves in their time. There was simply no use in being impatient; the man moved at his own speed. Over generous pours of the excellent mountain whiskey he had brought and the equally excellent meal Jimmy had prepared, Bourne followed Lee's lead, sinking into his deliberate pace.

"Where did you learn to speak Powhatan?" Lee asked, midway through the meal.

"In another life I was a college professor," Bourne said. "Comparative languages was my field. I have an instinctive ability to learn languages, the more obscure the better."

"Well, Powhatan sure is obscure." Lee nodded. "Leastwise, these days."

"It wasn't always like that."

Lee squinted at him. "You know?"

"The history of the indigenous people hereabouts? Yes, sir, indeed I do."

"Well, don't that beat everything." Lee pointed with a leathery forefinger. "The decline and fall of civilization." He almost spat, such was his disdain. "And after the carpetbaggers, the industries, the conglomerates, and the criminals, what are we left with?"

"I divorced myself from all that years ago."

"Betrayal upon betrayal, right?"

Bourne nodded. "As it was with you, it is with me," he said in Powhatan, which, as it happened, was a far more powerful and involving language than English.

They drank coffee laced with more mountain whiskey, and for once there was a silence pregnant with expectation around the table. Bourne said nothing; it was for Arthur Lee to approach the heart of the matter that had brought Bourne here.

Lee laid both forearms on the table, hands open, in the manner of the Powhatan at a parlay among equals. The open hands showed Lee's receptive intent far better than anything he could say.

"How may I be of service to you, Jason?"

No point in beating around the bush now, Bourne thought. "The men who run Crowcroft now have devious intent. They are beyond any border of civilization."

Arthur Lee watched him carefully but made no comment. Did he know about the NSA's doings inside the great house? Bourne wondered. The man gave him no outward clue. On the other hand, he was still listening.

"These people are holding a man against his will," Bourne continued. "I need to get inside Crowcroft to reach him."

"Do you mean to free him?"

Bourne felt the black crow's eyes on him like a weight. Arthur Lee needed an answer, and Bourne knew better than to lie to him about his intent. "No."

"Then why?"

"His mind holds the key to a problem that is otherwise unsolvable."

"This problem," Arthur Lee said, "it is of great importance."

Bourne reverted to Powhatan. "Powtitianna, a great many people are trying to kill me because they believe I have the answer."

One eye closed, the other seeming to increase its power of discernment. "Are you a federal agent?"

"Federal agents are among those trying to kill me."

Arthur Lee poured himself the last of the mountain whiskey while he deliberated. He swallowed the liquor, closed his eyes for an instant, savoring the flavor to its utmost. Then he smacked his lips and, addressing Bourne, said, "I understand your dilemma, Jason. Now you must understand mine.

"Apart from several dark years, I have worked at Crowcroft all my life. In that sense, it is more mine than any owner's—including the current ones. Loyalty is of extreme importance to me—as I believe it is to you—thus you will comprehend me when I tell you that my loyalty lies entirely with Crowcroft."

"We are both men of intent, Powtitianna. You know what transpires in the great house."

"Oh, not only in the great house, Jason. No, indeed."

Bourne glanced out the window. "It's dark now. It's time for me to go. Will you help me gain entrance to Crowcroft, Arthur?"

Lee spread his hands. "Jason, over the course of these hours breaking bread with you, we have become friends." His expression bore a sorrow beyond comprehension. "I know what is done inside the buildings of Crowcroft. Terrible things. Things which should not exist in this world. Things that belong to the time of the Southern slave owners and the Northern carpetbaggers who came after. There was little difference between them: both wanted to exploit us, to make their fortunes off our backs. Today is it any different?" He shook his head. "Which makes it even more painful to tell you that all the tunnels have been rendered impassible; every time I go in and out, every square inch of my car is inspected. Men with specially trained dogs surround the vehicle; I couldn't smuggle in a gram of weed even if I wanted to." He sighed. "There is no conceivable way I can sneak you into Crowcroft. I'm afraid your mission is doomed to failure."

24

THERE CAME A time in everyone's life when the innocence of childhood was punctured and the adult world, with all its hatred, betrayal, and sewage, was revealed. The break was often abrupt, shocking; it was always irrevocable. Such a moment came to Morgana Roy on a mid-morning like any other she had experienced since landing in Kalmar. She had awoken early in her hotel room, a floor below Françoise. It was barely light out. She performed her forty-five minutes of aikido exercises, ordered breakfast, showered, and was dressed in time to usher in the room service girl with her rolling cart.

She ate in silence while she watched the news on TV: one story after another about the increasingly warlike stance of the Russian Federation, its growing belligerence toward the United States. The president had called Russia a "regional power," enraging both the Sovereign and the Kremlin as a whole. The stories frightened and sickened her in equal measure. Her fried eggs and pick-led herring lay in her stomach like lead shot. Switching off the TV, she pushed the cart away. The taste of fish in her mouth nauseated her further. She took a swig of coffee, washing her mouth out with it, spitting it onto her plate before taking another gulp, swallowing it this time.

As she had the day before and the days before that, she met Larry London in the lobby. Together they made the short walk to the building where Larry had his temporary office, riding up to the fifth floor. She wasn't comfortable there. If she were to be honest with herself, the entire fifth floor gave her the creeps. It was deserted when they arrived in the morning, was similarly devoid of life when they exited late in the afternoon or early evening.

The office itself was nothing to look at: bare walls painted battleship gray, wood floors, a minimum of Swedish Modern furniture—desks, a sofa, a pair of chairs, a low table, and two floor lamps, that was it. The space was as anonymous as a doctor's waiting room. In fact, with its spray of magazines on the table, that's precisely what it reminded her of.

Three hours of work trying to decipher the latest bit of code she had found led to nothing at all. After so many days both in D.C. and here of slogging through incomprehensible code, a suspicion had begun to grow that she was trying to put together a jigsaw puzzle with the wrong pieces: nothing fit together, no matter which way she tried to integrate the various bits. If there was a unifying algorithm, she had yet to discover it, which was a first for her. She was hitting her head against a wall so often it had begun to hurt.

Abruptly, she pushed her chair away from the laptop, stalked over to the window, stared down at the anonymous passersby on the anonymous street, while she put her fists just above her buttocks and arched her back, stretching hugely.

London, sensing her distress, said. "Time for a lunch break."

"It's your turn to go get it."

"So it is." He nodded. "What d'you want?"

"Anything so long as it isn't fish."

He laughed easily. "Tall order, but I'm sure I'm up to it." He grabbed his coat. "Back soon."

She didn't bother to answer him. She was in a dark mood. The shock of her sudden incarceration had worn off, leaving behind a dull ache, like a bruise on her psyche. Lately, though, she had realized that she was homesick. She missed D.C., missed her apartment, missed the people she had worked with at Meme LLC. Often now, she found herself wondering what had happened to them. With Mac taken into custody, surely Meme LLC had been disbanded. Where had her team gone? Scattered to the four winds, she supposed, which was a pity; it had been a long and painstaking process finding them, meshing them into a well-oiled machine.

With a spasm of disgust at her self-pity, she turned from the window, went back to her laptop. She sat down and began to work again, but her heart wasn't in it, so she left it behind, went out into the street, walking purposefully until she found a shop selling running clothes. She bought a pair of sneakers, set out on a ten-mile run, five miles out, five back. That was her lunch hour, and reconnecting with her body settled her, damped down her anxiety, made her feel more herself again.

Back in the office, she returned to work, feeling refreshed and optimistic. Surprisingly, Larry hadn't yet returned with lunch. Who knew what he was up to? For all she knew, he was having a matinee somewhere discreet. He seemed just the type.

She frowned, picking up where she'd left off on the latest packet of code. For the next ten or so minutes, she was immersed in trying once again to parse the code, and when, as usual, that didn't work, she tried to fit it into the mosaic of the previous bits she had stored on her laptop. The screen flickered; she paid it no mind—the electricity in foreign countries always seemed dodgy to her. Then it happened again, and it was like a mote in God's eye, a speck that had attached itself to her eyeball and was now making her eye water.

She turned her attention to the flicker, but it was gone. She waited, but it didn't return. But then something odd happened. She had gone looking on the dark web for more bits of the weaponized code, had widened her search, expanding into bands of the dark web she had heretofore not explored. A flicker like the shortest bolt of lightning ran down the edge of her screen. Was that the flicker she had seen just before? Her fingers flew over the keys. This time, inside the dark web, the flicker had left a trace of itself. She followed it back, further and further, deeper and deeper, drawing closer and closer to its origin. Which was how, when it appeared again, she was able to catch it—like trapping lightning in the bottle of her laptop.

It was a bit of code, but totally unrelated to the one

she was working to decipher. At first, it appeared to be a dangling bit of code, but a few minutes of concentrated effort on her part revealed that it was only disguised as such. It was, in fact, a message—or part of one, the fourth part, if she was right and the three previous flickers were from the same source.

After so much time frustrated at not getting anywhere with the Bourne Initiative, she had begun to doubt her abilities. But her furious and brilliant work now in punching through the exceedingly clever electronic disguise renewed her faith in the abilities Mac called extraordinary.

She set about decoding the cipher. The first thing she discovered was that it had an authenticating marker. That meant the message was sent either by a large international conglomerate or a state-sponsored agency. But why had it come here into Larry's office space? It wasn't meant for her. In fact, she would never have seen it had she been working as usual; instead, she'd been on a local screen, trying and failing once again to put her malformed pieces of code into a coherent whole. If the message wasn't for her, then it must be for Larry.

There was a moment, brief though it was, of thinking she should just forget about the whole thing. If it was for Larry, which seemed more and more likely, she had no business reading it. But then that authenticating marker stuck in the corner of her eye, as the flicker had before, and she thought, *I won't read the message; I'll just take a peek at who sent it.* She shrugged. It was most likely from Global Photographics, the organization he freelanced for. But then why had it come in from the dark web; that made no sense.

So she copied the marker, sent it out into the dark web. What came back was this: Unit 309. What the hell was Unit 309? She'd never heard of it. She latched on to the site that had ID'd the marker, which led her to another site, and another, and still another, until she was deeper into the dark web than she'd ever been before—so deep that she began to feel uncomfortable. She'd heard stories of the very bad entities winging their way through this section of cyberspace.

Her line of inquiry at last dumped her onto a site selling all manner of armament—not simply handguns, semiautomatics, and the like. Those were a dime a dozen out here on the cyber frontier. No, this site was delighted to sell you missiles, flame-throwers, guided rocket launchers, tanks, smart bombs—the list went on and on.

And then her screen blacked out for an instant, to be replaced by an overlay that blared in large lettering: PLEASE ENTER YOUR AUTHENTICATION CODE in seven different languages. She didn't have one, so she backed out. Or at least tried to. Something had hold of her—a worm algorithm that was trying to find out her identity. It was a very fast worm, and if she hadn't installed firewalls that she had created that went beyond military grade she would have been a dead duck.

As it was, she was having difficulty staying ahead of the worm. As she worked rapidly and methodically she realized that she had encountered this very worm before while she had headed Meme LLC, and her blood ran cold. It was a Russian military worm, which, now that she had ID'd it definitively, she shut down in short order.

It took her less than ten seconds to remove herself from the dark web entirely. She was sweating through her shirt and her scalp itched. Her heart rate was elevated and her hands trembled slightly.

Unit 309 was an organ of the Russian state. Now that she knew that, she knew where to search to ID it. Less than a minute later, she had her answer: Unit 309 was a cyber-infiltration cadre under the command of *spetsnaz*, a division of the FSB, the state security agency.

Her mind had just registered this terrifying fact when Larry London waltzed through the door with their lunch.

"Guess what," he said jovially. "I brought you a cheeseburger and fries." He set the paper parcels on the table. "A nice little bit of home."

Only his name wasn't Larry London, he didn't just freelance for Global Photographics, and he was no undercover operative of the CIA. Of these things Morgana was now sure. Larry London was a Russian spy, and she had been aiding and abetting him.

Pushing her chair back, she excused herself, hurried down the hall to the ladies' room, where she vomited up the remains of her breakfast, which now seemed as tainted as if it had been a vile combination of a glass of vodka and a bowl of borscht.

———————

"I found him near the edge of my property," Arthur Lee said.

The three guards who had stopped him at the front entrance to Crowcroft were dressed in jeans and checkered shirts. They wore Timberland ankle boots and matching gabardine jackets, which, if Lee didn't know it already, would have given them away as feds. He thought they were morons. Dangerous morons, to be sure, but morons all the same.

"Where?" one of the NSA guards said, peering suspiciously into the interior of Lee's vehicle as if they hadn't all seen him every day for the last three years. The guard was built like a heavyweight boxer.

Lee indicated with his head. "Trunk."

While the lanky guard checked the underside of his vehicle with a mirror at the end of a three-foot handle, the bald guard drew his service weapon, opened the trunk.

"He's not tied up," Baldy said, and Boxer, leaning in Lee's window, repeated the statement as if, he, Lee, were the moron.

"He's hurt," Lee said, keeping it smooth and servile the way they liked it. "Hurt bad."

———

"There is, in fact, one way you can get me into Crowcroft," Bourne had said, an hour before. *"As your prisoner."*

Arthur Lee had shaken his head. *"Absolutely not. I'm not going to abet your suicide."*

"I'm hurt, Arthur. They'll see that as soon as you point it out to them. They'll take me to the infirmary. A doctor will look at me."

"And then they'll start to interrogate you."

"Well," Bourne replied, *"I'm sure they'll want to."*

―――――――

"He was out for a while," Lee said now. "In his shape he couldn't hurt a fly."

"Nevertheless," Boxer said.

Baldy went through a barely conscious Bourne's pockets, grunted disgustedly when he didn't find anything of interest. He whipped a plastic tie from his jacket pocket, manacled Bourne's wrists in front of him. Then he transferred Bourne to the backseat, slid in beside him, while Mirror Man stepped around the other side and climbed into the shotgun position. Boxer gave the all clear signal and Baldy said, "Okay, drive." He pointed. "That way." Just as if Lee were a kid caught with his hand in the cookie jar ten minutes before dinner. But then federal morons like these were known to have the compassion of a weasel.

"Where are we going?" Lee asked in the servile tone honed over decades of practice.

"The infirmary," Baldy said.

Lee suppressed a laugh; at least his heart was lighter.

―――――――

Bourne did not look like Bourne. He hadn't needed to use much of what he had in the satchel he had brought; he was already haggard and thinner by five pounds than when he'd stood at the bow of Boris's boat, contemplating his coming rendezvous with the Angelmaker. But, among many other singular talents, Bourne was a master of disguise. The key was not to overdo it—a dab of makeup here, a prosthetic to change the shape of mouth and jawline, above all an altered gait, which was what most observers looked to first. It was a kind of magic, cues that nudged the observer's keen eye in another direction. It was, when all was said and done, a form of sleight of hand. He hadn't had enough time to dye his hair, but just enough to give himself a military high-and-tight haircut.

"We have him, yeah." Baldy was on his mobile. "No ID anywhere on his person. Military type, mebbe ex." He listened for a moment. "Right...Okay...Got it."

"We're almost at the great house," Bourne heard Lee say.

"Keep going," Baldy said.

"But the entrance to the infirmary is right—"

"Do as you're told, asshole," Baldy ordered. "Left past the big oak up there."

They drove past the great house, stately on the outside, rotting from within. The oak tree rose up quickly, blotting out the sky, then vanished as Lee turned down a rutted cart track.

"This is the way to the firing range." A quaver made Lee's voice seem like he was underwater.

"Park over there," Baldy ordered.

Lee pulled over next to what had once been a horse barn and was now a storage area for his tractors and balers. The sharp odors of grease and oil were suddenly in the air.

"Don't move," Baldy said, as he slid off the seat.

Mirror Man grabbed Bourne and hauled him roughly out of the vehicle.

"Against the wall," Baldy said. "We'll do it military style."

"Old school," Mirror Man said, gripping Bourne tighter. "I like that."

They both laughed.

High overhead, a trio of crows stared down with cocked heads, claws gripping a branch of a maple. As Bourne was slammed against the barn wall, they took off like rockets, cawing indignantly.

Mirror Man, palm pressed against Bourne's chest, put his face so close to Bourne's their noses almost touched. Baldy was directly behind him, his sidearm out, standing at a safe distance.

Mirror Man flicked open a gravity knife, brandished the narrow blade. "We're gonna have fun with you, fucker, whoever the hell you are."

25

A SUDDEN BURST OF rain rattled the windows. Morgana looked up from her lunch. The sky was a dark bruise; the air pressure had plummeted far enough so that even here inside the building she could feel its effects. The room seemed to tilt as the air grew thick, weighing on her like a wool blanket. She felt unmoored, drifting in a limbo from which she could find no clear exit.

"Are you all right?"

London's voice made her start. She glanced down at the cheeseburger out of which she had taken a single bite in the twenty minutes since they had begun to eat. "I'm fine." Her stomach rumbled, but the sight of the burger grease made her want to gag. She put the burger down, wiped her hands on the wad of paper napkins that came with it.

"I want to get back to work."

"But you've scarcely eaten a thing," London pointed out.

"Morning sickness," she said, crossing to her laptop and sitting down in front of it.

London frowned. "You're joking, right?"

"What d'you think?"

"I think you got up on the wrong side of the web today." He came and sat down beside her. "That was a joke." When she didn't respond, he swiveled his chair to face her. "Hey, hey, what's up?"

"Hey, hey, what's up?" Would a Russian say that? she asked herself. And then she realized that if she suddenly started behaving so coldly with him he'd surely get suspicious. She put on her sad face, not so very difficult to do. She sighed. "The truth is, I'm missing D.C." She fluttered one hand. "I mean, I'm stuck here in the middle of nowhere, pretty much going back and forth between the hotel and this dump—no offense. And the only people I see are you and Françoise."

"I understand completely," London said.

What would it sound like if he said that in Russian? she wondered.

"But you've been sequestered, Morgana, for your own good. Things are still unsettled in Washington."

"From what I see on the TV things are unsettled all over—Washington, Moscow, NATO HQ. It sounds to me like the world's going to hell in an out-of-control handcart."

"Which is why Françoise has you here, safe and sound, where you can work undisturbed by outside forces."

Like Unit 309, the FSB, or spetsnaz, she thought sourly. But she put a reluctant smile on her face. "Truthfully, Larry, I need a break. I've been at this day and night for days and days."

"No one knows this better than Françoise," London said. "But, Morgana, we're under a severe time constraint here. You have to solve the mystery of what the Bourne Initiative is and how it's going to be deployed." He gestured with his greasy fingertips. "We're almost out of time, and, honestly, we're in your hands."

"Of course." She nodded, the good little soldier. "Forget what I said."

"That's the girl." He smiled broadly. "There'll be plenty of time afterward, I promise you."

She returned to her work—*her* work. She could feel him next to her, smell his woodsy aftershave. Did it remind him of his dacha outside Moscow? The fir trees and the snow? She shivered inwardly at these thoughts. What was his real name? Now that she knew the truth, "Larry London" was such a ridiculous alias.

He and Françoise read her daily reports; they were always the same. No matter how many bits of the Bourne Initiative she unearthed, none of them fit together. That might be because each new piece was in some small or obscure way different than the last, almost as if the thing was a living organism that kept evolving. And yet the one thing each bit had in common was the zero-day trigger that was now six days away.

What she didn't put in the reports was her growing conviction that the cyber weapon was being assembled by people far smarter than she was. So many hours at this and she was still at square one when it came to defining the category of cyber weapon it might be. Was it an über-worm built to penetrate the firewalls that guarded the nuclear missile codes available only to the president, as Mac believed? Or was it a virus that self-replicated, creating a zombie army of botnets; was it a key logger that clandestinely transmitted a user's keystrokes to a third party? The code was nothing like Stuxnet, nothing like Flame or Wiper. Nor was it in any way akin to BlackEnergy, the latest and greatest weaponized malware program. So, then what the hell was it? Maybe Mac knew, maybe he didn't. In any event, he had now been taken off the board. No one could get to him.

On the other hand, at this moment, Morgana was less interested in reliving her daily frustration with the Bourne Initiative than she was in deciphering the section of coded message she had captured on her laptop before Larry had returned with lunch. While he noshed on her fries as he worked, she was simultaneously running three different programs she herself had created in order to break the cipher and analyze the results.

It was an unsettling project to be working on with London sitting right beside her. Neither could see the other's screen, but still she felt goose bumps come out on her skin as she worked or, rather, watched her programs do their thing.

The encryption Unit 309 used was masterly, but it wasn't up to defending against her programs. Eight minutes after she had sicced them on the enciphered message, she was able to read the words *en clair*, and a full-body panic knifed through her:

PKT4: out of time. She is now in your hands. Use her, then dispose of her. Kay

Bourne kneed Mirror Man hard in the groin. As all the wind rushed out of him, Bourne whipped him around, found the knife blade, used it to slice through the plastic manacle. Mirror Man, recovering, jabbed Bourne in the ribs with his elbow. He saw what Baldy was up to, jerked himself free, putting Bourne in the line of fire as Baldy aimed. Bourne chopped down on the side of Mirror Man's neck, hauled him back in line, jammed his body against his as the bullets meant for him struck Mirror Man instead.

Grabbing the gravity knife as Mirror Man's knees gave way, Bourne flicked his wrist, and the knife shimmered through the air, sunlight winking off its steel. The blade buried itself in Baldy's chest. He staggered, knees buckling, then, recovering, launched himself at Bourne.

He fired once as he came, missed. Then he was too close for a firearm, reversed it, seeking to use the butt as a club. Bourne blocked it with the edge of his hand, then grasped Baldy's arm, pivoted back on his right leg, drawing Baldy in and down. With the back of his neck exposed, Bourne smashed his elbow into the first cervical vertebra. It was the smallest and, therefore, the easiest to fracture. It was also the closest to the skull, its disintegration catastrophic. And so it was with Baldy. He went down and stayed down.

Turning, Bourne saw Arthur Lee, staring at him, slack-jawed, from behind the wheel of his vehicle.

"Get out of here, Arthur," Bourne said, lifting a hand in a loose salute. "Stay away from the great house and everything will be fine."

He heard the engine start up, and Lee's vehicle rumbled away toward his small house near the western edge of the estate. Bourne stripped off his clothes, replaced them with Baldy's, zipping up the jacket to cover the bloodstain on the shirt. He found the electronic ID key card in the back pocket of Baldy's pants. Looking around, he saw only the crows, who had returned to their perch, regarding him with their glassy black eyes as he loped back up the track toward the great house.

———

There was a meeting in progress. Bourne could hear multiple voices bleeding out of the half-open door to the library. Someone was being teleconferenced in from D.C.—DoD or the Pentagon. Bourne could see at a glance that the layout of the first floor hadn't changed since he had last stolen inside.

Once, he had to duck away so as not to be seen by someone passing down the hallway. Reaching the locked door to the back stairs, he fitted Baldy's key card into the reader at the side of the door, pulled it open, and proceeded cautiously down the stone steps.

His previous reconnaissance had revealed the interrogation cells to be in the basement, where, in happier times, before the NSA got hold of it, the wine cellar had been; the air still held a whiff of wine must. In typical NSA fashion, the space had been re-created into a strictly utilitarian area with five "holding rooms"—like all government services, the NSA was hooked on euphemisms—all of which abutted observation chambers outfitted with one-way glass panels inserted into the common walls. Farther along was the "laboratory"—another euphemism for a very nasty section containing three rooms, each one equipped with the paraphernalia necessary for the kinds of articulated interrogation that was now illegal and which high-ranking members of the NSA swore before various Congressional subcommittees they absolutely, unconditionally no longer tolerated.

The NSA psych team assigned to Crowcroft had names for these three rooms: My First Experience, Nothing To See Here, and The Drowning Pool. In the first the uncooperative client, as the prisoners were called, was softened up with grueling sessions of incessant questions, interspersed with periods of unexpected explosions of static, a hundred voices talking over one another, death-metal rock shrieking, sudden bursts of blinding light or total darkness; in the second the client was subjected to sensory deprivation; in the third the waterboarding was the centerpiece, although by no means the only extreme measure available to the interrogator.

It was said that no one survived what was known as The Whole Nine Yards intact. Though that might well be the kind of hyperbole the NSA traded in, it was just as possible it came very near the truth.

Since the door was key-coded, there were no guards at the bottom of the stairs. Bourne did, however, have to be mindful of the psych staff, two members of which he spied on his way to the cells.

A quick recon revealed that General MacQuerrie had been graduated out of My First Experience. He must be in the sensory deprivation tank.

The connection corridor between the first and sec-

ond interrogation chambers was so dimly lit Bourne
had to pause to allow his eyes to adjust to the gloom.
Once he did, he advanced to the closed door ahead of
him and slid the key card through the reader. Opening
the door, he hung back, waiting, looking for any movement of shadows, but there was nothing.

Stepping in, he closed the door behind him. Before
him was a shallow float tank of perfectly calm water. He
knew it would be set at precisely the same temperature as
the client's body temperature. Peering through the dim-
ness into the water, he could just make out the outline
of a figure floating in the center, tethered, unmoving. A
mask was over the general's face, fitted with a breathing
tube. MacQuerrie looked like he'd already lost weight as
a result of the shock tactics in My First Experience.

Shedding Baldy's too-tight shoes and gabardine jacket,
which contained Bourne's sat phone in one pocket and
a thick wad of hundred-dollar bills in the other, Bourne
slipped into the water, untethered the client. His hand
was on the breathing mask, but before he could pull it
off, the overhead lights blazed on, momentarily blinding
him. When he could focus he saw the third guard, built
like a boxer, the one he and Lee had left behind at the
front gate. He held his 9mm sidearm out in front of him,
pointing it at Bourne.

"Ed and Marty are MIA and you've been using Ed's
key card all over the place, you miserable little shit."
When he spoke his voice had a weird dead sound, devoid of echo, due to the state-of-the-art soundproofing
in all three rooms. His forefinger slipped inside the trigger guard, balanced on the trigger itself. "Now you're
gonna pay."

26

"HE MADE A deal with the devil," Dima said.

"Who?" Savasin asked. "Karpov?"

Ekaterina laughed, but her father's hand slicing through the air cut her off.

"No, not Karpov," Dima said with a glint in his eye. "Your brother, Konstantin."

The three of them—four if one counted Cerberus— had repaired to Ekaterina's large kitchen, where they sat around a central table while the moving mountain served them food and drink, silent as usual. The food was excellent and plentiful, the drink Iron Mountain black tea from the hinterlands far from Moscow. It was very strong and very good.

"My brother." Savasin set down a forkful of *karsky shashlik*, marinated in red wine and crushed bay leaves. "Do tell." The tender bits of lamb were bedded on wild rice, surrounded by baked tomatoes, string beans showered with slivered almonds. He steepled his hands. "Continue."

"Konstantin is in bed with Gora Maslov."

"The head of the Kazanskaya? That's mad."

Dima poured himself more tea out of the porcelain samovar. "It's the truth."

"Unlike his father, Gora is a weakling. Why in the world—?"

"Precisely *because* he's a weakling. Konstantin can control him."

"But that's only the tip of the iceberg," Ekaterina interjected.

This time, her father did not silence her.

"This also is true, Timur." Dima sipped, watching Savasin from over the rim of the glass. "You are aware of an agent abroad with the legend Larry London, real name Nikolay Ivanovich Rozin."

"Of course." Savasin nodded. "As I told your daughter."

"Little Niki," Ekaterina said with the ghost of a smile.

Savasin's brows knit together in growing annoyance. "What about him?"

"Has your brother mentioned Niki recently?" Dima asked.

Savasin hesitated a moment, then said, "You know he has. You just heard me tell Ekaterina that he's appointed Rozin as the new head of *spetsnaz*."

Ekaterina glanced at her father, then commenced laughing. She laughed so hard tears came to her eyes.

The first minister, glancing from one to the other, said, "What the hell is so amusing?"

Dima put down his glass. "Tell him, my dear."

Ekaterina wiped her eyes. "Dear, dear Timur. Your brother is about to fuck you well and good. Guess whose payroll little Niki is on?"

Savasin gaped at her, swallowed, and said, "Not Gora's. Tell me he's not working for Gora."

"Oh, but he is," Dima said. "And from what you've just told me, Gora's plans are further advanced than I had thought."

"So." Savasin stared down at his *shashlik* for a moment, trying to orient himself. Strange as it might seem, nothing that Dima or Ekaterina said surprised him all that much. He put nothing past his brother; his ambition, his lust for fame and fortune was unbounded. That's why he had hated Boris Karpov so much. The general had blocked his way in every avenue.

He looked up at Dima and Katya. "The most interesting thing about my brother is this: he fancies himself faster, stronger, and cleverer than he is." Savasin spoke slowly and thoughtfully. "But I now have to say this for General Karpov—he actually was faster, stronger, and cleverer than anyone else, including my brother, possibly even the Sovereign. And, unlike Konstantin, he knew his limits, and he never stepped across that line into the danger zone."

Ekaterina frowned. "We were under the impression that you hated Boris Illyich."

"Ah, well. It seems to me now that my hatred was merely a reflection of Konstantin's. I took on his hatred without really knowing why." Savasin placed his hands flat on either side of his plate. "But now you must tell me what the devil my brother is up to."

Dima lifted a hand, and Cerberus cleared the plates, replaced them with small saucers of sweetmeats before retreating to see to the dirty dishes. It occurred to Savasin that the running water might be deliberate and wondered whether even in the Orlov sanctum sanctorum there loomed the specter of hostile ears, electronic or otherwise. He ought to know if there were, no? But then he realized that he knew absolutely nothing of Konstantin's activities over the last year.

Savasin, in no mood for procrastination, said testily, "What about my brother?"

Dima's face clouded over. "Yes, well, we'll get to that in a moment. First, we must speak of Boris Illyich."

"I admit I've had a hand in erasing him and all he's done from the memory of the Russian Federation."

Dima spread his hands. "Timur, this is the trajectory of Russian history, is it not? Who among us has not had the opportunity to erase that which we do not like or find objectionable."

"But in General Karpov's case—"

"In his case, perhaps it was a necessary evil."

Savasin cocked his head. "How so?"

Dima held a saucer of sugar cookies out to the first minister, who silently declined. "Pity. Cerberus made them. They're really quite excellent." He plucked one, popped it into his mouth. "Circling back, we come to what you yourself said about Boris Illyich—that he never overstepped his limits." He licked powdered sugar off his fingertips, wiped them on a napkin. "Now I will tell you why—well, one of the reasons, anyway. Boris had a *stvol*."

"A weapon," Ekaterina said. "A *secret* weapon."

"Even more than that, First Minister." For the first time Dima smiled. It was almost identical to his daughter's smile—midway between that of a dolphin and the Mona Lisa.

"Boris Illyich had a secret weapon *in plain sight*."

Savasin shook his head. "I don't quite—"

"Bourne," Ekaterina said, leaning forward to put added emphasis on her words. "His best friend, Jason Bourne."

"You mean the general leveraged his friendship with Bourne to get things done he couldn't do himself?"

"No." Dima shook his head. "You misunderstand."

"What do you expect, father," Ekaterina said with open contempt. "He's first minister."

"I think it would behoove us all to be a bit more flexible in our thinking."

It was a clever way to gently admonish his daughter without pointing a finger at her, Savasin thought. Then he realized that Dima must mean him as well.

Dima smiled to soften the rebuke. "Listen, Timur. I knew Boris Illyich better than you. And as for Katya, she knew him better than both of us put together."

"He was a Russian, yes, loyal to Mother Russia," Ekaterina said. She was perched on the edge of her chair, her body so tense it found its way into her voice. "But, at heart, he was a humanist."

"Just as Bourne is a humanist," Dima said. "For them, their friendship transcended both politics and ideology."

"I don't get it," Savasin said truthfully; he felt that he had failed at something vital to what was happening now. "A Russian and an American—both spies. They should have been mortal enemies."

Dima tried not to express his frustration. "First Minister, if nothing else, you must understand this about them: they both hated politicians and ideologues, of every stripe. That's what brought them together; that's what formed the bedrock of their extraordinary friendship."

"Why must I understand this?"

"Konstantin wants everything," Dima said tersely. "He craves the unprecedented power General Karpov wielded over the FSB and the FSB-2. In his hands, that power would be, well, destructive to all of us. I still maintain my ties with the *grupperovka* old guard."

"And the money," Savasin replied. "We mustn't forget the money."

"Your cynicism does you proud, First Minister." Dima's mouth twitched upward in a sardonic smile. "Nevertheless, we are talking about your brother. He has the ambition of a Caesar. He knows the Sovereign will never give him your position, just as he would never have given it to Boris Illyich—far too dangerous, considering the personalities involved. The Sovereign's strategy with your brother is the same one he used with General Karpov—give him his head within a circumscribed area, keeping him happy and controlled at the same time."

"It wasn't working with Boris," Savasin said with a distinctly sour intonation.

"Indeed not." Dima nodded. "Boris Illyich had devised a number of work-arounds, none of which were known to the Sovereign and his minions."

"I see. So my brother is seeking to do the same."

Dima nodded. "But while Boris sought an equilibrium between east and west, Konstantin craves the opposite. Like the Sovereign, he wants to destroy the West—particularly America, whose presidents have time and again insulted him and Mother Russia. He bridles every time Russia is termed a 'regional power' in the

Western press, while the United States is known as the only true 'global power.'"

Savasin ran his hand across his forehead, finding it damp. "So he's going to destroy America."

"That is his goal, undoubtedly."

Savasin shook his head. "But how, specifically? Gathering power clearly isn't enough."

"No, it isn't," Dima said. Perhaps it was the changing light, as the day began to die, but he suddenly looked ten years older.

"The problem is we don't know what Konstantin is planning," Ekaterina said.

"We've tried and failed," Dima added. "What we need now—"

"Father," Ekaterina interrupted, "can we trust him?"

"My dear," he said mildly, "we have trusted him this far." He shrugged. "Besides, he has a personal stake in siding with us now."

Ekaterina took a deep breath, let it out slowly. Then, shooting Savasin a sideways glance, she nodded.

"What we need now," Dima continued, "and by *we* I include you, First Minister, is Bourne. We need him to be the tip of the spear. We need him to be our *stvol*.

"As I said, we have failed. Bourne won't. You, Tamerlane, are the only one who can get to him without your brother finding out and sending us straight into the bowels of the Lubyanka."

"What do you say, First Minister?" Ekaterina regarded him coolly. "As it turns out, you need us as much as we need you."

27

BY THE TIME we get through with you, I fucking guarantee you'll wish you were dead."

Bourne popped the face mask off MacQuerrie. The body began to thrash, and Boxer took his eye off Bourne just long enough for Bourne to grab the coping of the pool with one hand, grasp Boxer's ankle with the other.

He jerked hard just as the gun went off, but Boxer was already on his way into the float tank, and his aim was high. Bourne grabbed Boxer's wrist, twisted so hard he was forced to drop the gun. Boxer bent double, then straightened up, the crown of his head slamming into Bourne's chin. His right hand balled into a fist, buried itself in Bourne's solar plexus, sending Bourne to one knee. The water lapped at his nose.

Disengaging, Boxer groped in the water for the gun, but it was nowhere to be seen. Hadn't it sunk to the bottom of the tank? Bourne blindsided him before he could hope to answer that question. Bourne jabbed him in the ribs, then smashed the edge of his hand into Boxer's rib cage. He heard a satisfying crack, and Boxer grimaced. But he was far from done.

Breaking away, he kicked hard, his heel making hard contact with Bourne's left shoulder. Had the water not slowed the kick Bourne's shoulder would surely have been dislocated. As it was, the burst of pain was followed immediately by a terrible numbness that traveled down Bourne's left arm, leaving a trail of pins and needles.

Taking immediate advantage, Boxer grasped Bourne's head on either side, slammed the back of it against the coping. Again and again. And then his forefinger jabbed at Bourne's eye. It never made it. Struck from behind with the butt of his own 9mm, Boxer fell to one side. Bourne could just make out a blurred shadow of MacQuerrie. He must not have had a lot of strength. He staggered backward in the water, the effort of the one blow having done him in.

Bourne, his head in a muddle, black spots crowding his vision, drove the edge of his hand into the side of Boxer's neck. Boxer's head rocked like a bobble-head. Spinning him, Bourne wrapped one arm around his neck, placed the heel of his other hand just below the ear. Boxer, frantic, struggled mightily, but Bourne kept his grip, gave a sharp twist that broke Boxer's neck.

He lay back then against the coping while Boxer's body floated facedown in the water. Despite the shallowness, the chop was as frenzied as if from a school of feeding sharks. Gaining his equilibrium, Bourne waded past the body to the opposite side, where MacQuerrie sat in the shallow water, trying desperately to hold on to the coping. With the lights on he caught his first look at the client; it wasn't General MacQuerrie.

Bourne, taken aback, said, "What the hell are you doing here?"

"Surprise!" the Angelmaker said weakly.

Bourne, arm around her shoulders, drew her away from the coping. Her face was pale, and there was a curious unfocused aspect to her eyes. "How long have you been under?"

"Long enough for it to make a difference."

"You owe me an explanation," he said. "But not now. We have very little time to get to General MacQuerrie and get out of here before we're discovered."

He pulled her out of the water, sat her on the coping before climbing out himself and snatching two towels from a pile in the corner. She swayed slightly as he dried her off. He'd been subjected to every form of interrogation technique during his Treadstone training. He knew what time in the floatation tank could do. At first you're sure you can hold out, but then in the blink of an eye your nervous system goes numb, and you've slipped away from yourself. It doesn't matter what other kinds of torture you've experienced, sensory deprivation is another animal entirely, one you cannot prepare for. Most methods of interrogation involve dealing with pain in one form or other. Techniques have been developed to handle pain, no matter how intense. They all involve carving out a private space for your consciousness that is inviolate and curling your essence inside that space while whatever is being done to your body goes on.

Sensory deprivation is different inasmuch as there's no pain. Instead, there is a cessation of all feeling. You're alone with yourself, and the lack of outside stimuli starts to distort your thoughts. Under these conditions, a private space is of no use, as your own thoughts make it porous.

This is what had happened to the Angelmaker. Whether her adolescent torture at the hands of Keyre made her more susceptible to sensory deprivation or it was due to a quirk in her personality was at the moment irrelevant: she had succumbed; her mind had detached itself from her body.

"Your clothes," he said with some urgency. "Mala, where are your clothes?"

He took hold of her jaw, pulled her head so that she was looking directly at him. Her eyes looked like those of a junkie—the pupils pinpoints, despite the bright light. They wandered over his face as if tracing a route on a map. But she didn't answer.

"Mala. Mala." He leaned in, pressed his lips to hers. They were cold, trembling slightly, as if being affected by electric currents under her skin.

Jason.

He felt her "speak" his name through vibrations transferred from her mouth to his, and took his lips away from hers. Her eyes focused on him.

"In the locker, there," she whispered hoarsely.

She pointed, and Bourne left her momentarily, though her torso was still rocking a little, as if she were someone who had been at sea a very long time.

He returned with her clothes, helped her into them. Then he toweled off and climbed into his.

"Can you stand?" He had helped her into her trousers while she was sitting down. He extended a hand, but she shoved him away.

"Cut it out."

He stood back, checking the door he had come through every few seconds, while she struggled to stand. He could see that her knees were rubbery, but she was as strong of will as she was of body, and soon enough she was up, stalking back and forth beside the tank, her strength flooding back with each stride.

"Ready?" he said, and when she nodded, he led her to the door that gave out onto the short corridor to The Drowning Pool.

This third room was smaller than the others. On one side, an array of standing heat lamps were lined up like birds with bulbous beaks, all directed at one spot. Filling a sweat- and bloodstained wooden butcher's table directly below them were a series of clamps, graduated from small to large, lines of files, scalpels, and a grouping of what appeared to be dental instruments, gleaming in the light from the ceiling overheads. On the other side, an industrial-size stainless-steel sink stuck out from the wall like the snout of an enormous hog. Beside it, a hose that could be attached to the sink's spigot, a galvanized metal trough, a number of cotton cloths through which the water was poured onto the client's face, and a table on which the client—in this case General MacQuerrie—was strapped.

"He's been the gamut," the Angelmaker said. Her voice was steadier now, sounding more like herself.

"The Whole Nine Yards."

"What?"

"That's how it's known here," Bourne told her. "The Whole Nine Yards."

"Lovely." She frowned. "What state is he in?"

Having stepped beside the table, he bent over it slightly so he could look directly into MacQuerrie's eyes. They were open wide, terror having taken up residence behind them. He was strapped down as if he were a mental patient prone to violent outbursts. Glancing up, Bourne signaled to the Angelmaker to keep guard on the door they had slipped through.

"General?" Bourne raised his voice slightly. "General! Can you hear me?"

MacQuerrie's eyes focused on Bourne, but his lips did not move. They were bluish, as if he was chilled to the bone. He was wearing a sweat-stained undershirt and trousers. His hands and feet were bare, blue-white, utterly still.

"General, I'm not part of the NSA group. I'm not here to hurt you. Do you understand me?"

No response.

Bourne unstrapped him. "Do you understand me, General?"

After a long moment, MacQuerrie's lips moved. "Who?" It was thin, barely a whisper.

"Who am I?"

The general blinked. "Yes."

"Let me put it this way," Bourne said, slowly and carefully. "I'm intimately connected to what you call the Bourne Initiative, though, oddly, I don't know why or how."

The general licked his lips. "They tried to break me."

"What did they want from you?"

"I don't think they know. It's possible they didn't even care." He took a breath, blew it out his nostrils. "I'm a traitor."

"In their eyes."

"In here, that's all that matters." He grimaced as a deep shiver went through him. He coughed deep in his chest. "I would be grateful now to sit up."

Grasping him by one hand, placing his other behind his back, Bourne levered him into a sitting position.

"What's that smell? Never mind, it's me."

"We have very little time," Bourne said. "We've got to get you out of here."

"Not even easily said," the general said. He squinted, seeming in no hurry to go anywhere. "You're not Bourne, are you?"

"I told you as much as I can," Bourne countered. "I need you to tell me what the Bourne Initiative is, really."

MacQuerrie was still squinting at Bourne. His cough rattled his chest; he turned his head, spat blood onto the floor. "I've been under duress for . . . I've lost all track of time. How do I know this isn't all a part of the . . . that I'm not still under duress?"

Bourne stripped off his shirt, showing the general his wounds; the bruises he'd gotten during his fight with Boxer were just blossoming. "I've expended a lot of time and effort—not to mention pain—to get to you, General."

MacQuerrie grunted, nodded. "Point taken." He flicked his hand out, stared at the fingers trembling in midair, closed his eyes for a moment. "The Bourne Initiative is a weaponized cyber program started by

Bourne's—or should I say *your*—good friend, the late General Boris Karpov, of the Russian FSB, to penetrate our defenses and winkle out the president's nuclear codes. Are you seriously telling me you don't know anything about that?"

"More than that, I can tell you categorically that Boris would never be party to such a program."

MacQuerrie lifted one eyebrow. "Really?"

"So either that's not the true nature of the Initiative, or you don't know what you're talking about."

"I *always* know what I'm talking about." He grunted again, but this time he expelled a gout of blood. "Ugh, what the hell?"

Bourne laid the general back down, palpated the areas over his vital organs. MacQuerrie screamed.

"What is it?" the Angelmaker asked. "What's the matter with him?"

"What isn't?" Bourne looked down at MacQuerrie. "No point in sugar-coating it, General. Liver, kidneys. As a result there's massive internal bleeding." He bent lower. "Tell me what you know."

"I don't—"

"You always know what you're talking about, General. You're not a liar, are you?"

"Jason, I hear footsteps," the Angelmaker said from her position by the door.

"Turn on the heat lamps," Bourne ordered.

"What?"

"Just do it, Mala. And take your SIM card out of your mobile."

She switched the heat lamps on, and immediately the temperature in the room increased.

"These things could roast the skin right off you," the Angelmaker said, palming her SIM card.

"What they're there for," the general said with an infinite weariness. He'd taken the Whole Nine Yards and was about to pay the ultimate price.

Bourne's eyes locked with MacQuerrie's. "Spill it. Now."

"I suppose it doesn't matter now. The Initiative is indeed a cyber program—a DDOS malware."

"Okay. We've already experienced a handful of distributed denial-of-service attacks. They've brought the Internet to its knees, like a power grid outage. Malware infects and then directs a huge number of DVRs, security cameras, Internet-connected cars and cameras—anything and everything that is an Internet-of-everything device—to create a worldwide botnet, a cybercreature with one mind, which sends massive amounts of queries to any number of websites, crashing them."

"Right. But this one is as different from the botnets we've seen as VR is from the old Asteroids video game. It will slice right through the correctives like a knife through warm butter."

"What's the target?"

"You know your old friend, Bourne. He wasn't a political animal, not at all. In fact, he hated the Sovereign and all he stood for. No, this malware is meant to crash the sites of the world's biggest banks."

"Money," Bourne breathed.

"Yes, money. Of course money. Transferred out while the sites are frozen through a program piggybacked onto the malware."

It sounded right. Just like Boris. And yet, he had the

sense there was something MacQuerrie wasn't telling him, or, more likely, didn't know. That also would be like Boris. "And you know this how?"

MacQuerrie tried to laugh, but another gout of blood was all he could bring up. Through lips stained red, he said, "Your pal Boris and I were partners."

With a deep-felt groan, he turned on his side. His face was deathly pale. His extremities seemed already devoid of blood. "Beautiful plan, Bourne, magnificent." He hawked up more blood, and something else that was black and viscid. "Problem is...someone hijacked the program, shortly after Boris was killed."

"Who?"

MacQuerrie shook his head once, then grew very still.

"General, who hijacked the malware program?"

"There's a third partner, a friend of Boris's." He gasped. "I never met him."

"Who?" Bourne leaned closer. "Who is he?"

"I went on Boris's word."

"General..."

MacQuerrie's eyes seemed to be dissolving in water; they had lost almost all the luster of the living. "His name is Dima." He gasped again, and the fingers of one hand curled, as if grasping for something unseen. "Dima Vladimirovich Orlov."

Bourne glanced briefly at Mala. "I don't know of him. Do you?"

After a moment, she nodded, her face pale and waxen.

"Problem is..." MacQuerrie gave an animal grunt that brought Bourne's attention back to him. "The trouble is that Dima Orlov is free to use the program to attack anything he wants. Get me, Bourne? Any fucking thing. And there's something else . . ."

"General . . ."

But MacQuerrie was done, and, in any event, the Angelmaker said, "Here they come." She shot Bourne a glance. "I don't know what you're thinking, but we're never making it out of here."

28

I 'M NOT HUNGRY," Morgana said when she met Françoise for dinner. "This evening I'd rather walk."

The storm that had gripped Kalmar earlier had spent itself inland, leaving the sky clear and the air cool and refreshed. It was, in fact, the perfect evening for a long walk. Also, a long talk, which was Morgana's purpose in skipping dinner. She was far too nervous to sit still, let alone to eat a meal. There was a lump in her throat no amount of self-calming could clear. Her biggest worry was how her friend would take the news that she had been taken in, as Morgana herself had been, by the falsely named Larry London. She knew Françoise well enough to understand that she prided herself in her friends—they were, to a person, immaculately curated, trusted, and prized.

For a time, they strolled along the waterfront, until Morgana's nose was so filled with the stench of fish she felt her gorge rising. Everyone she passed looked strange, slightly off-kilter, vaguely sinister, even the two boys who snickered seemed to eye her with evil intent as they kicked a soccer ball around. Shadows appeared to leap out at her from the narrow spaces between buildings. Doorways looked smashed down, windows crooked. The noises of the city, usually soft and gentle compared to D.C. or New York, threatened to overwhelm her.

As she turned them inland, Françoise broke the silence between them. "You look troubled. Is anything the matter? Is it the usual? Are you missing home again?"

"No, it's not the usual, though I am missing home, more than ever." Morgana replied so slowly it seemed every word was being pulled out of her.

Françoise took her hand. "Then what is it?" She halted them, so they could face each other. "Come on, you know you can tell me anything, right?"

"Right," Morgana said, though without much conviction.

Françoise smiled. "So come on, then. Let's hear it. I mean, how bad can it be?"

"Maybe you shouldn't ask that," Morgana said with a brittle laugh that ended abruptly. She stared into her friend's eyes. "I've found out something about Larry."

"What? He's fucking around, yes? While he should be working. It's okay, Larry's kind of ADHD, he's on and off everything all the time. It doesn't mean—"

"Stop," Morgana said, jerking her hand away. "Just stop, okay?"

Françoise nodded, frowning deeply. "Okay. What then? I'm listening."

"Françoise, Larry London isn't Larry London."

A look of disbelief crossed Françoise's face. She laughed and shook her head. "What? I'm not following."

"Larry London isn't his real name."

Françoise's eyebrows rose. "No? What is it, then?"

"That's just it. I don't know."

"Then how—?"

"He's a Russian spy."

Françoise's laughter rang out. "Oh, come on! That's ridiculous. Our Larry?"

"He isn't *our* anything, Françoise. He's not at all what he makes himself out to be."

"Really?" Françoise's tone turned skeptical. "Okay, then, show me the proof."

Now it all spilled out: the Internet flash-carrier band that had delivered a four-packet message to Larry—"or whoever the hell his real name is"—the fourth packet Morgana had managed to translate. She took a sheet of paper from her handbag, unfolded it carefully, handed it to her friend. Françoise scanned a hard copy of the message, reading it over and over. Then Morgana pointed to the line at the top in very small print that showed the message came from Unit 309 of *spetsnaz*.

"I don't know about you," Morgana concluded, "but I had to look up that word: *spetsnaz*. It's the 'special action' division of the Russian state police." She shuddered. "I've been marked, Françoise—as have you, I surmise."

Françoise found a stoop and sat down heavily, her eyes glued to the message fragment. "Calm down," she said, as if by rote.

"Calm down?" Morgana's hands flailed the air.

"Françoise, this whole thing...I mean, my God, I'm working for the fucking Russians."

"Wow, I..." Françoise ran a hand through her hair. "Okay, well, let's think this through."

Morgana bent over her. "Hey, there's nothing to think through. I'm already guilty of treason. I want out, Françoise. Now. Tonight. Get me the fuck out of Dodge."

"And leave me here to deal with this clusterfuck myself?" Françoise looked up. "Thank you very much."

"That's not what I—"

"Well, that's what I meant when I said let's think this through. Give me that much credit at least. I mean, I'm as shocked as you are. More, really. I've known Larry a long time. Christ, what a nightmare. What was he hoping to get from me?"

"Besides me, you mean?"

"We met years ago. He couldn't have known—"

"What? We were already friends," Morgana said. "D'you honestly think your meeting was accidental? D'you really think you weren't vetted in every detail of your life—including your friends, associates and clients—before he made contact?"

"Oh, my God." Françoise put a hand over her mouth.

"I know, right?"

"How could I have been so blind?" Françoise crumpled the sheet of paper in her fist. "I should've seen..."

"How could you?" Morgana sat down beside her friend, enfolded her hand, and Françoise began to cry. "No one could have seen it. It was just a fluke—a lucky break—that I stumbled on that fragment."

"Morgana, what would I have done without you?" She wiped her eyes. "We've got to sort this out."

"What? No. This guy's a professional spy. Françoise, he's been ordered to kill me."

"Not until you're done decoding the cyber weapon."

Morgana reared back. "What the hell are you saying?"

Françoise looked down.

"What is it?"

Heaving a sigh, Françoise's eyes met hers. "I can't just cut and run. Larry knows too much about me. I have to figure out a way to—"

Morgana's eyes opened wide. "A way to what?"

Françoise shuddered. "You know."

Morgana uttered an incredulous bark. "Are you for real?"

Françoise's eyes were imploring. "Morgana, I can't do it on my own."

"You must be out of your mind."

"I wish I were, I really do." She squeezed Morgana's hand tight. "But I'm not." Her expression was intense. "Please, Morgana. Help me. Please, please, please."

"Jesus God."

Morgana weighed her intense desire to get as far away from Larry London as she could, as quickly as she could, against her obligation to her friend. It was Françoise who got her out of the NSA's clutches; without her, she would still be in a locked room somewhere in D.C. Françoise had saved her life. She owed her friend big time for that.

"All right," she said at length. She had committed herself, though not without a deep sense of misgiving. "Let's see what we can come up with."

29

"QUICKLY, NOW!" Bourne gestured. "Your mobile. Drop it under the heat lamps."

A smile of understanding lit up her face. She dug the phone out, set it down in the center of the circles of heat, drawing her hand back quickly.

"I never liked that phone much, anyway," she said as she followed Bourne out of The Drowning Pool, through the door opposite the one through which they had entered.

Behind them, the lithium-ion battery that powered Mala's mobile heated up to an intolerable level, and, just as three NSA techs rushed into The Drowning Pool, it exploded in their faces.

Alarms went off all over the place. They sprinted down corridors, the Angelmaker following Bourne's every step. His eidetic memory had imprinted every nook and cranny of the great house. They hid in a utility closet as armed men rushed past on their way to the emergency in The

Drowning Pool; they gingerly climbed an old, disused staircase with several rotten treads to gain the main floor; they escaped the confines of the house, not through any of the four doors on the main floor that led outside, which were doubtless being guarded, but by jumping out a second-floor window that overlooked a huge oak tree, down which they climbed.

They made their way past the huge tree, left down the dirt track. Bourne made sure they skirted the site of the shootings, hurrying them along through copses of oak and poplar, until they were in sight of Arthur Lee's small stone house.

Lee was waiting for them in his old rattletrap of a truck.

"Once I heard the commotion, I knew you'd either be coming through the woods or you'd be dead. One way or t'other the day had gone in another direction." He pointed. "Who's this lovely lady?"

"A friend," the Angelmaker said. "That's all you need to know."

"Sassy critter, ain'tcha?" Lee grinned. "My name's Arthur, but you, missy, can call me Artie."

"Arthur," Bourne cut in.

"Right." Lee hooked a thumb over his shoulder. "Under the tarp back there, situate yourselves between the bales of hay."

When Bourne hesitated, he added, "They check coming in, not going out."

"But with the alarms going off—"

"There's a fire now in the great house, but I'm guessing you know that already." Lee winked. "You just get covered up and leave the rest to me."

They climbed in the back, made themselves as comfortable as possible, being squeezed between bales, pulled the tarp over themselves, tied it down to hooks in the sides of the truck bed.

No sooner had they done that, then, with a protesting shriek of gears the truck rocked away from Lee's house, heading for one of the gates. Soon enough, it was clear that he was making for the eastern gate on the other side of the property, an excellent choice, since it was the one farthest away from the growing mayhem.

By the time they reached the gate, the wail of fire engines could be heard, and the guards, distracted by the noises, addressed Lee only long enough to ask him what was going on. It seemed as if everyone near the great house was too busy to contact them.

"Grease fire, far's I can tell," Lee said easily. "But, y'know, I'm not allowed inside the great house, so it's anyone's guess."

One of the guards grunted. "I'd fucking let you in," he muttered under his breath.

The other said, "Going for your usual evening hay run, Arthur?"

"To the Sizemore farm. That's about the size of it."

The gates opened, and he drove through, out into the darkling countryside. The sun had set, splashing vivid colors across the western sky. Crows wheeled overhead, then made for their nests in faraway trees. A dog barked, then was still. Rabbits were at play in the fields, their heads coming up, their bodies freezing as the truck trundled past.

When they were far enough away from ground zero, Lee tooted his horn; it was a funny sound, like something you'd hear at a circus or a sideshow. Bourne and the Angelmaker scrambled out from under the fluttering tarp. Lee stopped just long enough for them to join him in the cab.

"Where to, missy?" he asked with a crooked smile.

"It's his show," she said, indicating Bourne.

Lee's head bobbed up and down. "Know that already; just bein' polite."

"I appreciate that," the Angelmaker said. "More than you know."

Seeming satisfied with the direction of the conversation, Lee put the truck in gear, and they continued their rumbling journey due east, away from Crowcroft.

"Second star to the left," Bourne said, "then straight on till morning."

"Shouldn't that be 'to the right'?" Lee said.

"Only if we're going to Never, Never Land," Bourne replied.

For a time, they rattled on in companionable silence. Bourne could tell Mala was depleted; she needed rest, but he had questions he needed to put to her.

"I assume you followed me all the way from Somalia," he said.

"That's right." She had her head back, resting on the seat.

"Keyre's orders."

"Right again."

"How the hell did you manage to get into Crowcroft?"

"I didn't." Her eyes snapped open, but they seemed to be looking at something only she could see. "I was stupid. I made a mistake. I underestimated—"

"And they caught you."

"After a fashion."

"After a fashion?"

She smirked. "I got inside, didn't I?"

But at what cost? Bourne wondered, but said nothing, letting a brief pause mark the end of any further discussion of Mala's presence.

"What do you know about this third partner, Dima Orlov?"

"Not much. He's a shadowy figure flitting about the Moscow underworld. I never met him; no one I know has. He's like a ghost." She screwed up her face. "I heard once that he and General Karpov were childhood friends, they had a falling out as adolescents, but you know how deep the bonds run between childhood friends in Russia. The story goes they patched things up in adulthood."

Bourne wracked his memory, trying to recall if Boris had ever mentioned Dima Orlov. But his memory was unreliable, and for the ten-thousandth time he cursed it. His eyes were closing; the motion of the truck, the low rumble of its engine, was making him drowsy. All the adrenaline had drained out of him. He was almost as depleted as Mala looked. It felt so good to see the open road ahead of them, the trees a blur of green, to hear the whistle of the wind through the open windows, feel the air on his skin. Just, for once, to relax.

But in Bourne's world that was a kind of joke. For someone who slept with one eye open, the concept of relaxation scarcely existed, and when, like now, that rare sensation crept over him, it usually had the life span of a mayfly. And, sure enough, this moment would be no exception.

The roaring of big honking motorcycles coming up behind them dissolved the instant's peace like a pin in a balloon. There were four of them—German-style spiked helmets, grinning skulls emblazoned on the backs of scarred black leather vests, fringes and long, stringy hair fluttering like wounded birds. They rode new Harley V-Rod Muscle bikes, the most powerful in the line.

They came up two on each side, muscled arms shining, as well oiled as their machines. They moved in and out, coming just close enough to rattle Arthur Lee. Lee, who had seen just about every atrocity man could perpetrate on another, didn't seem to be the type to rattle easily. But these big guys were armed with handguns. Two had sawed-off shotguns slung diagonally across their backs. One, on the passenger's side, had his pistol cradled in his lap.

One of the four horsemen of the new apocalypse veered toward Arthur Lee. Before Arthur had a chance to zip up his window, the biker brandished a hunting knife with a thick serrated blade.

"Hey, you!" he shouted. "You, boy!" He swung the blade in a shallow arc. It whistled through the air over the moaning of the wind and came within inches of Lee's cheek. "Hey, boy, I have some boots for you to shine! I have some grits to push into your pussy face!" He swung again, Lee cringed away, and the truck careened out of its lane.

The leader laughed. "Careful, boy! Didn't your master teach you how to drive?" Holding his knife high, he swung in again, this time with the blade pointed directly at Lee's carotid artery. Lee turned the wheel over hard, toward the two bikers on the other side.

Bourne had had enough. He was prepared for Lee's sharp swerve to the right. Swinging his door open, he leapt at the biker brandishing the handgun, knocking him clean off the saddle. The biker hit the ground hard, shoulder first, then his head. His helmet flew off and, as he rolled, the side of his head struck a stone outcropping.

Grabbing control of the Harley, Bourne made a screaming U-turn, came at the second biker on his side. He was aiming his big Colt .45 at the spot right between Bourne's eyes. An instant before he squeezed the trigger, Bourne dropped down below the level of the handlebars. The bullet whanged over his head, and he kicked out with his left boot, delivering a hard enough blow to the V-Rod to send it veering off the road. He followed it as the biker struggled to regain control. To do that he had to holster his Colt. Bourne, executing another 180, rushed at the Harley from behind. He struck the biker in the kidney, and the biker winced; Bourne snatched the .45 out of its holster and shot the biker in the back, shattering his spine. The out of control V-Rod roared to a spectacular crash against the guardrail, its gas tank splitting open. Flames sprang up, engulfing the leather saddle and the man sitting astride it, followed by a blinding flash and a red ball of confusion.

Bourne revved the Harley, taking off after the truck and the remaining two bikers. Some distance behind him, a cloud of dust was rising rapidly, and he wondered whether guards from Crowcroft had finally gotten their act together and come after them.

Even so, first things first.

One of the remaining bikers had slipped his sawed-

off out of his quiverlike sheath, was aiming it into
the truck's interior while the leader came roaring back
down the road directly at Bourne. A pair of legs shot
out of the truck's open window, scissored around the
biker's arm. The shotgun went off, tearing a hole in
the truck's fender right above the gas tank. Some of
the buckshot must have penetrated the tank because the
truck began to leak gas like a sieve. Meanwhile, The
Angelmaker, having consolidated her grip on the biker,
drew him off his saddle with the astonishing strength
of her thighs. As she brought his face close to her,
she slammed her knuckles into his windpipe, crushing
the vital cricoid cartilage. She released her viselike grip
and the biker slammed against the curve of the truck's
fender on his hard tumble to the tarmac.

That left the leader. Instead of aiming his shotgun
at Bourne, he swung it behind him. He was staring
at Bourne, a big, fat grin on his bearded face as he
squeezed off a shot right into the heart of the truck's
gas tank. Sparks flew, what was left of the ruined cap
blew off, and flames shot from the open mouth. It was
only a matter of time before the fire spread to the cabin,
or worse, the truck exploded.

As the leader had correctly anticipated, Bourne
swung around him, making for the truck, which was
yawing back and forth in ever widening arcs. Inside the
cab he glimpsed the Angelmaker struggling to regain
control from Arthur Lee. He hoped she was grinding
the gears into neutral in preparation for turning off the
ignition. She knew they had to get out of the cab before
it became an inferno, trapping them inside.

Just as Bourne passed the leader's bike, he felt a flash

of agony in the side of his head. The biker had thrown his sawed-off at Bourne, striking a direct blow. Black spots danced in front of Bourne's eyes; his hands went slack on the handlebars. One foot slipped off the rest, and he swayed, close to taking a fall.

The leader was coming at him, his Colt out and at the ready. He was close enough for the kill shot, but he was a careful man. Closer still, and even with the erratic motion of the Harleys, he couldn't miss. His forefinger, tightened on the trigger, began to squeeze, and then with a deafening roar his head exploded, drenching Bourne in brains and bone. The driverless V-Rod wobbled, then jumped the road, struck the top of the guardrail, flipped like a pinwheel going over.

Bourne didn't get to see the end result. He heard it, though, a great booming, a grinding of hot metal and scorched tires. Then out of the chaos, Jimmy Lang's vehicle appeared beside him. A strong arm grabbed him, settling him back on the saddle.

"You didn't think I was going to let you have all the fun," Jimmy said, grinning.

"Arthur's truck," Bourne said, still slightly disoriented.

"Not to worry," Jimmy said. "They're both out."

At that moment, Arthur Lee's truck went up like a screaming, rageful fireball.

Part Three
Dima

30

IT WAS AN ill-omened day in her life when Françoise was obliged to seek out her brother unannounced. She spent a fruitless but necessary twenty minutes surveilling the area in and around the marina, making certain it was clean. She was sure Gora's people had already done this, but years in the field had ingrained certain routines so deeply she performed them even when logic dictated they were redundant. Fieldwork had proved time and again that logic had little to do with being captured and either killed or put under articulated interrogation.

So it was that forty-five minutes after dawn on the morning after Morgana's dramatic revelation concerning Larry London, she found herself progressing down toward her brother's boat, which lay peacefully at anchor just as it had been when he had summoned her some days ago.

The wind plucked rigging like the strings on a double bass, tap-tap-tapping them against masts. Clouds scudded by overhead, and the new day's sunlight slanted in, warming the back of her neck. There was something jolly and at the same time peaceful about a marina—boats rocking gently in their slips, people going about their deck work with a particular serenity. No one hurried, no one ran, no one shouted. Often, as now, it was all but deserted. And yet the marina remained alive, moving to the pulse of the tide.

Two of Gora's men stood guard at the head of the metal gangway. One, who was new and therefore didn't know her, barred her way. But the other, Sigi, was an old hand, and he waved her aboard. She found Gora below, in the galley, in a silk robe. He was frying eggs and the kind of bacon you could only purchase in America. An aromatic waft of coffee came to her, making her mouth water.

A young blond woman, naked to the waist, was seated at the built-in table, a sheet twisted around her loins. She turned, startled at Françoise's abrupt appearance, but she made no attempt to hide her nakedness.

"Who's she?" she asked in Swedish-accented English.

"Get dressed," Gora said to her, turning the strips of bacon. "And get out of here."

The blonde pouted. "What about the breakfast you promised me?"

Gora threw a fistful of bills on the table, and said, "Go on. Beat it."

When she reached for them, he swept them onto the floor.

Françoise took a step toward the woman. "Gora, there's no need—"

"Keep still," he said in Russian.

The blonde, trembling, crouched to gather them up.

Brother and sister confronted each other warily. Not a word was exchanged until the woman hastily dressed, hopping on one high heel while trying desperately to slip on the other, and crossed the cabin. She shot Françoise a glare as full of hatred as it was of jealousy before flouncing out onto the deck, where Sigi took her in hand.

"Breakfast?" Gora said then, as if the woman had never existed. "It's one hundred percent American."

"So I see."

"Go ahead, sis. Pour yourself some coffee." He eyed her. "You look like you need it."

He lifted the bacon strips out of their own fat, laid them carefully on a sheet of paper towel; about some things he was meticulous. When she had a mug in her hands and had taken the first sip, he said, "I assume it's important."

"Urgent, more like."

His eyebrows rose like a pair of ravens lifting off a tree branch. Using a spatula, he transferred the fried eggs, two at a time, onto plates. Then he meted out the bacon in identical portions. Crossing to the table, which was already laid with two places, he set down the plates. No toast; he hated toast.

They both sat at the same time, facing each other, and began to eat with the same quick motions, as if they were identical twins.

After he had finished precisely half his breakfast, he looked up at her. "Tell me."

So she did. She told him everything that Morgana had related regarding the messages from Unit 309 to

Larry London, or, as they knew him, Nikolay Ivanovich Rozin. "Now she knows Niki is a Russian spy. Now she knows she's been working for the Russians, and she's terrified. I had to talk her down from fleeing the country immediately." She tried unsuccessfully to interpret Gora's flat gaze. "How could *spetsnaz* be so careless?"

"*Spetsnaz*," her brother said, "and specifically Unit 309, have no knowledge of this girl you've brought to us."

"Morgana's a fucking cyber genius," Françoise spit out. "She's going to save you—"

"Maybe she is," he said, chewing on a bit of bacon. "Maybe she isn't." Grease lacquered his full lips. There was a spot of it on his chin. He picked up his last strip of bacon. "The point is, we are now saddled with a liability."

Françoise reacted instantly. "Oh, no. You're not going to harm a hair on her head."

"Alyoshka, did I say anything about doing her harm?"

"You said she's a liability."

Gora shook his head. "No, Alyoshka. I said we are saddled with a liability. My exact words." He looked over at her plate. "Finished?"

She made a contemptuous gesture. "Go ahead."

Picking up her plate, he set it down on top of his own. Then he drove the tines of his fork into the last remaining egg. The yolk ran every which way across the plate; he mopped it up with two of her bacon strips, cramming them in his mouth. He chewed reflectively for what seemed a long while. Times like these, he disgusted her. She wondered how it could be that they shared any amount of DNA. But she waited for him to continue; there was no use prodding him.

"What about you?" he said at length.

She shook her head, not following. "What about me?"

"She knows Niki is a Russian spy. You introduced her to Niki. You and Niki are friends. Does she suspect—?"

"Absolutely not."

"How can you be sure?"

"If she suspected me, Gora, she would have booked the first flight out of here. Instead, she came to me. She thinks Niki gulled me as well as her. We're friends; she trusts me."

"You'd better be right." He pushed aside both plates and gave her the cool, appraising look she hated. "Did it ever occur to you that she's been working you?"

"What? No. Not for a minute. I know her too well."

"None of us know anyone else. Isn't that the first lesson we learn in the field?"

She said nothing, folded her arms across her chest.

"Wait a minute." Gora struck his forehead with the heel of his hand. "How was I so stupid? How did I not see it?"

"See what?"

"You and this woman, this Morgana Roy." He rose from the table and stepped toward her, torso inclined aggressively. "You really *are* friends. You care about her."

"Don't be ridiculous." A ball of ice had formed in the pit of her stomach.

Her brother's eyes were gleaming darkly. "I know your secret now, Alyoshka. The one you would never tell me. You've made the mistake all novice field agents are trained to avoid."

"You're babbling, Gora." But she felt a kind of panic rising up inside her.

"You've become involved with your mark."

She shook her head, a weak response, to be sure.

"You've come to see her as a *person*, you *care* about her well-being." He clucked his tongue against the roof of his mouth. "How you've weakened yourself. Sis." He raised a forefinger. "We shall have to do something about that. Otherwise..."

The cotton ball of panic had reached the back of her throat, and she almost gagged. "Otherwise what?" she managed to get out.

"Otherwise, you'll be of no use to me."

She felt the silence between them like a straitjacket. She found herself in a place she did not like, with no exit.

Gora tapped his lips with a finger, a quick pattern, like a silent song's beat. "Here's what we'll do." The glimmer of his smile turned her bones cold. "You'll get your *friend* to do it herself."

"Do what herself?"

"Don't be dense, Alyoshka. You'll get her to dispose of our liability."

"Who? Niki?" She was aghast. "He's the head of *spetsnaz* now, for God's sake. You're crazy."

Gora grinned. "Crazy like a Russian bear. Konstantin appointing him was simply a power play aimed at his brother. I know that. You know that. Every-fucking-body knows that. Just as they know that it's far too dangerous for the head of *spetsnaz* to be in the field." He shrugged. "Konstantin violated the rules of the game. When his chess piece gets taken off the board he only has himself to blame. We weaken Konstantin, we're free of blame, and we clear the field for you to slip into Niki's old position, make his contacts yours." He chuckled. "That is, *ours*."

"Huh. And how exactly am I to do that? I doubt Morgana's ever even held a gun."

"All the better," her brother said. "Niki will never suspect her until she pulls the trigger, and by then it'll be too late."

"You didn't answer my question."

Gora cleared the dishes, stacking them in the small stainless-steel sink. "Simple," he said, "you'll put her in a situation where she has no other option."

Just like me, Françoise thought in despair.

———

Everybody knows that in the field the best-laid plans are sometimes undone by the simplest of human quirks which, no matter how one tries, cannot be anticipated. Everybody knows no plan is airtight. Everybody knows it can all go sideways, but the plans are made nevertheless because in the field the dice are rolled and the chances are taken. There is no other way.

And so, what everybody knows, everybody conveniently forgets.

One of these unforeseen human quirks had occurred the previous night, when Morgana told Françoise what she had learned about Larry London. When they parted ways, both women to their hotel rooms, Morgana could not sleep. After switching off the light, tossing and turning on a roiling sea of anxiety, she relit her bedside lamp. When reading didn't help, she got out of bed, dressed, and stood by the window, looking out at the street below, just as she had as a kid when high fevers made sleep impossible. Watching the wind in the willows, the play of moonlight on the brushlike branches, soothed her more effectively than a cold compress across her brow. In this urban setting, the streetlights, the occasional passing car, the lamps blinking in mysterious conversation along the marina wharf, did the same. And she stood there, her mind starting to relax as the night staggered to its end and light returned to the world.

A short time later, she spotted Françoise hurrying out of the hotel. She crossed the street, heading toward the marina. Curious where her friend might be going at this ungodly hour, she slipped out of her room, ran down the stairs and out the front door, following in Françoise's urgent footsteps.

She ducked behind the corner of a building as Françoise turned to look over her shoulder. For upward of twenty minutes Françoise appeared to do nothing but survey the area. Why then had she been in such a hurry? Morgana wondered. She hesitated, awash in guilt. What was she doing, following a friend, the woman who had moved heaven and earth to free her from the clutches of the NSA? And yet, she found her feet moving forward, as if of their own volition. *Curiosity killed the cat,* she thought. But it created a terribly strong impulse, one that wouldn't be denied.

At length, she saw Françoise heading along one of the wooden walkways. Boats rocked gently in their slips, rigging snapped, far off a buoy clanged. All soft sounds. Morgana, still partially in hiding, observed that Françoise stopped in front of the slip where a boat named *Carbon Neutral* was tied up. Two burly, rough-looking men with Slavic faces guarded the gangway. One of them barred her way, but the other appeared to know her, for he beckoned to her.

Françoise stepped aboard with the alacrity and confidence that could only come from having been on *Carbon Neutral* before. What in the world could she be up to? Something stirred inside her, a cool, slithery thing that raised questions along with its head.

Moments later, she saw the guard who had recognized Françoise escorting a young blond woman off the boat. Her hair was uncombed, her makeup smeared. Her ultra-short skirt and her ultra-high heels marked her out as a prostitute. With a little cry, she ripped her arm away from the guard's grip, turned her back on him, strode unsteadily away. Morgana marked her drunken progress along the walkway, and when she was almost at the end, where the wooden wharf met the concrete dock, Morgana decided on a course of action.

She waited until the blonde was out of sight of the two men guarding *Carbon Neutral*, then started on her trajectory. As she neared the blonde she increased her speed until, glancing fearfully over her shoulder, she ran right into her.

"Oh, my God, I'm so sorry," she said as she helped the blonde back onto her feet.

"Shit's sake! What's the matter with you, anyway?" the blonde all but snarled. "Idiot! Why don't you look where you're going?"

Morgana put on an apologetic face. "Well, I would have, except for the man who was trying to grab me."

As Morgana had calculated, this little tidbit immediately reversed the blonde's demeanor. "What?"

"It happened back there." Morgana gestured vaguely toward the streets. "I was on my way home after, you know, a long night with..." She cleared her throat. "A guy I met in a bar. I was drunk, not thinking clearly. I was almost at my hotel when this guy grabbed me. When he started to pull me into an alley I kicked him in the balls and ran like hell."

The blonde nodded, captured her unruly hair, which the sea breeze kept blowing into her face, deftly twisted it into a knot at the top of her head. "I know exactly how you feel." She unbuttoned her shirt halfway down so Morgana could see the deep bruise darkening between her breasts. "Something of the kind happened to me this morning."

Morgana squeezed her shoulder in sympathy. "I'd say what we both need is some strong coffee and a good breakfast. What d'you say?" She held out her hand. "My name's Morgana."

The blonde took her hand briefly but energetically. "Natalie," she said. "And, I don't know about you, but I'd love a jigger or two of liquor in my coffee."

———

Down by the marina, soldiers appeared in full camo, helmets, carrying submachine guns across their chests. They were members of the Skaraborg Armored Regiment and an odd sight indeed. Morgana asked Natalie about them, but she had no idea why they might be deployed.

The two women sat across from each other in a small, dark café near the water. It smelled of stale beer and staler sweat, but it was the only place open at this hour. Morgana did not want to take Natalie to her hotel restaurant for fear of running into either Larry or Françoise.

The door kept opening, fishermen coming in straight off their boats, reeking of the sea, scales making tiny rainbows on their slickers as they caught the light. Usually, the banter between the men was lighthearted and inevitably salty, punctuated with raucous laughter. But this morning, as if echoing Morgana's mood, the atmosphere was tight with tension. What banter began petered out quickly and morosely.

"His name is Gora, that much I know for sure," Natalie said. "And he's Russian. I know a little. He spoke to his guards in Russian."

Russian, Morgana thought. *Dear God.*

The smoked fish and thin triangles of dark bread Morgana had ordered were already half gone. The stink of fish no longer bothered her; she was adjusting to her new life.

Natalie stirred enormous amounts of sugar into her black coffee, the café's only substitute for liquor. "And the woman was Russian, too."

Morgana felt the muscles in her shoulders and neck tense. Her head came up like a pointer scenting prey. "What woman?"

Natalie made a face. "A woman came in while Gora was fixing us breakfast. Very beautiful. Gora's demeanor changed as soon as she appeared. He stiffened, became an iceman. He had no more use for me. He began to trash-talk me. Then he kicked me out."

These details rushed past Morgana like a runaway

freight train. "You said the woman was Russian. How do you know that?"

"Gora spoke to her in Russian."

"But—"

"Morgana, I know enough Russian to understand. He spoke to her as one intimate to another, nothing formal about it."

Morgana's throbbing heart was already sinking in her breast, but just to make sure, she said, "Can you describe this woman?"

Natalie had a keen eye, that much was clear after only fifteen seconds. But even if she hadn't, Morgana would have recognized Françoise from the description. Of course it was Françoise. Morgana had been watching; no other woman had gone anywhere near *Carbon Neutral*.

She needed not to think about Françoise for a moment, give herself a little time to recover from the stunned reverberations this revelation had caused deep inside her. She turned her attention to the subdued conversations around them. She still had only a bare-bones understanding of Swedish, so she asked Natalie to listen in and translate for her.

After several minutes of concentration, with her expression seemingly darkening each second, Natalie said: "Now I understand the military presence. The MSB— that's the Civil Contingency Agency—has ordered local governments countrywide to establish operations centers in underground bunkers, maintain a network of emergency sirens, and to coordinate with Swedish Armed Forces." She stared at Morgana. "We're being asked to prepare for a conflict with Russia."

Morgana's thoughts were in total disarray. She had hoped that taking her mind off her own problem would help settle her, get her over the shock. But now this. But whereas Natalie had to consider the bigger picture, she needed to concentrate on her own situation first, which was precisely this: Larry London wasn't Larry London. Françoise Sevigne wasn't Françoise Sevigne. How could she be so blind, why hadn't she seen that the moment Larry was exposed Françoise was suspect as well? The answer was clear enough: emotion. She liked Françoise. A lot. They had been friends for some time, shared intimate moments. They had laughed together, shopped together; they'd even, on occasion, shared clothes. *Good Christ,* she thought. *What have I gotten myself into?*

Natalie put down her coffee cup, placed her hand over Morgana's. "Your face has lost all color. Is everything all right?"

"I'm perfectly fine." Morgana smiled like the porcelain doll she'd adored as a child. "Never better."

31

THE TV, SET to CNN, was muted. Nevertheless, the scroll at the bottom told the breaking story of Russian military forces moving toward the borders of Estonia, Latvia, Belarus—with which the current Kremlin regime had an economic accord but no formal alliance—and already pushing farther into Ukraine. This in addition to the troops and war matériel inside Syria. Despite the Russian Sovereign's claims that all maneuvers were simply part of war games, all this bellicose activity was sending NATO into a frenzy, especially since the new American president seemed indifferent to the threat. Events that had been long simmering appeared to be coming to a head.

Mala turned away from her contemplation of the news. "Whatever the Bourne Initiative is, do you think it could be tied in to the Sovereign's far more aggressive stance?"

"I think it's highly likely, which is why we've no time to waste in getting to Dima. According to General

MacQuerrie, Dima Orlov took advantage of the chaos following Boris's murder to hijack the cyber weapon." Bourne wasn't looking at the screen, but nor was he looking at her.

"You're angry with me," Mala said.

"I didn't say anything to that effect."

"You didn't have to."

"I don't know how you can do the bidding of a man who tortured you," Bourne said. "I don't know how you can keep doing his bidding when I saved you from him."

They were lying on a bed in a chain hotel room on the fringes of Dulles International Airport. Bourne had called his old friend, Deron. After sending him photos of Mala and himself, they were awaiting Deron's messenger with new passports. Bourne still had his prosthetics; he had cut Mala's hair and she had dyed it jet-black. They had checked into the hotel under the names Arnold and Mary Winstead, the same names that would be on the new passports; Bourne had paid cash, in advance.

The color scheme was ocher and brown, the room in dire need of refurbishing. Lights from the control tower periodically swept through the window, passing across the opposite wall. It was a depressing place, though both had been in far worse. For the moment, though, it was home.

"You took me away from him," she said softly. "But you didn't save me from him."

He reached around her, felt along the lines of the ritual scars on her back. "The incantation will only work if you believe in it."

Her eyes, lit with an inner fire, searched his face. "I do believe in it, Jason."

"Why?"

"I have no choice."

"There's always a choice. You still have free will."

She seemed to sink into herself, to ruminate deeply on the problem. As she did so, her countenance darkened. Rain spat against the window.

"You have no idea what I have, what I don't have."

"Then tell me."

She smiled, sadly, wistfully, ruefully. No one else he'd ever encountered could encompass so many emotions with a simple curl of the lips.

"No," Bourne said. "You're going to have to do better than that."

"Then you'll have to do better." She reached for him. "This is to be our lingua franca now, the currency with which we do business."

He held her at bay, shook his head. "Mala, don't."

She tossed her head. "Why not? I've dreamed of this moment, why should I not have it?"

"Why? Because I don't want it."

"It's the one thing you've withheld from me. And I want it."

He got up off the bed, moved away from her. He did not want her to touch him. "What you want is wrong, Mala. You must know that."

"I don't care," she raged.

"I know that." He said it calmly, softly, as if gentling her.

Abruptly, she turned away from him, but not before he saw that she was silently weeping.

————

Four Harleys by the side of the road, a man and a woman to ride two of them.

Hours ago, they had said good-bye to Arthur Lee and Jimmy Lang. Arthur had wanted to accompany them all the way back to D.C., but Bourne had reminded him that, considering the carnage, the best thing for both of them was to return to their respective homes as quickly as possible and resume their normal lives as if nothing had happened. Jimmy had concurred, and in the end, Arthur had conceded the point.

Bourne's next objective was to get himself and Mala into Russia as swiftly and efficiently as possible, while keeping so far under the radar they wouldn't be picked up by any clandestine organization; he was still acutely aware that both the Americans and the Russians were hunting him.

Keyre's transport plane was awaiting him, refueled and maintenanced, but the pilot and crew had orders to bring Bourne back to Somalia, so using it was out of the question. Bourne did not want Keyre to know where they were going, and while he couldn't be with Mala 24/7 to ensure she wouldn't contact the Somali magus herself, at least he'd had her destroy her mobile.

So while Arthur and Jimmy took the license tags off Arthur's truck, then climbed into Jimmy's vehicle, Bourne and Mala had taken possession of two of the motorcycles, the pairs setting off in opposite directions. On the way, Bourne had called Deron with his requests. Still in rural Virginia, he had withdrawn money from one of his many accounts under assumed names in banks throughout the world. They shopped for new clothes, and while Bourne purchased a pair of scissors,

Mala chose the black hair dye color. Around three in the afternoon, he'd checked them into the chain hotel.

Bourne would buy their tickets as soon as he received their passports. The first leg was to Frankfurt. After a ninety-minute layover they would be booked on a two-hour, forty-minute Lufthansa flight into St. Petersburg. Even with their false identities, Bourne did not want to risk entering Russia through Moscow, where surveillance was always uncompromising. So they would take a train from St. Petersburg to Moscow. It was a long trip, but it couldn't be helped.

Their flight out didn't leave until after ten p.m.; there was time to kill, so to speak. They had a bite to eat and then, exhausted, they went up to their room and, sprawled side by side on the bed, slept like the dead.

———

The rain continued to beat against the window, the lights from the airport control tower flickered in and out of the room like a serpent's tongue. Someone in an adjacent room turned on the TV, a punch line followed by canned laughter seeping through the thin walls. Bourne, awake but unmoving for some time, slammed his fist against the wall, and the sounds ceased.

All at once in this shabby hotel room on the edge of everything, he felt his isolation, something he had lived with and grown used to, as keenly as a knife blade to his throat. He missed Sara more than he had missed anyone for a very long time. Once again, he wondered where she was, hated that he was unable to contact her while she was on assignment for Mossad. He understood as no one else the need for absolute security in the field, but that didn't—couldn't—stop his desire to be with her, to feel her body warm against his.

The phone ringing broke the train wreck of his thoughts, and he snatched the receiver off the console. It was the front desk.

"Yes."

"This is Carolyn, Mr. Winstead. A messenger is here from Tiffany's, sir. He insists on delivering his package to you in person."

"Send him up, Carolyn." *A messenger from Tiffany's* was the code phrase he and Deron had decided on. "Thank you."

"My pleasure, sir."

He woke Mala, the Angelmaker. It was time to go.

———

"We've found a passenger manifest listing," Ellison said into his mobile. "It's one of the names Bourne's been using since his Treadstone days. Paid cash, as expected." He grunted. "The twist is this time it's a mister and missus."

"You're all in place?" Marshall Fulmer said.

"At Dulles International, yes, sir," Ellison replied. "The team is deployed."

"Excellent," Fulmer said. "I'm on my way."

Dirk Ellison put away his mobile, signaled to his team to take their places. He glanced at his watch: 9:45. The international flight that Bourne and his female companion were booked on was scheduled to depart at 10:45; it would begin boarding in fifteen. There was no way Bourne and the woman were getting on that plane. Personally, he thought the woman might very well be that Mossad agent Bourne had been seen with, but, really, it didn't matter to him. Fulmer had been quite explicit: Bourne was the target; nothing else mattered.

Ellison watched the passengers at the gate in the departures lounge with his trained eagle eye—two young people of indeterminate gender sharing everything, a Coke, a burger, and whatever racket that passed for music those people listened to; an elderly threesome of yakking women, gray hair aflutter, hyped up for their first trip abroad; a couple with their three kids, reminding Ellison of the vast hole where his personal life began and ended.

But, hey, he was CIA through and through; second generation, in fact. His father was twice decorated in one of those so very desired secret ceremonies inside HQ that Ellison himself had yet to be invited to. But once he captured Jason Bourne, that would change in a heartbeat. He'd make his father proud of him. As a dedicated CIA agent, he hated taking orders from anyone other than his boss, or *his* boss, but times were changing; cross-agency missions, though despised by all the various mandarins, were now becoming more numerous. He didn't like it, but having made his case to his superior, he knew unequivocally that he had no say in the matter.

However, he had plenty of say in this matter right here, right now, and he was bound and determined to make the most of it. That's why, when he spied the couple coming down from the first class lounge, heading toward the gate as the door opened and the flight was called, he and his team closed in on them from all sides, trapping them in a move from which there was no escape.

32

MUCH TO HIS chagrin, Fulmer was obliged to take Harry Hornden, the freelance journo he had climbed into bed with, on his trip to the airport. Like it or not, Hornden was now a de facto part of Fulmer's entourage, sitting in the place of honor, beside Fulmer. Fulmer's nostrils flared. Was it his imagination or was there a whiff of sulfur coming off the web scribe

Fulmer sighed, working his butt into the backseat of his custom Cadillac Escalade in a fruitless attempt to make himself more comfortable. Time was when journalism was a profession to be proud of. He recalled the era when the CBS News of Douglas Edwards and Walter Cronkite was the crown jewel of Bill Paley's so-called Tiffany Network. The news division was an advertising loss leader, but so widely respected and prize-winning it was worth it. No more. In this day and age, networks could no longer afford loss leaders. Plus, the advent of Rupert Murdoch's brand of shock-value news upended that American applecart forever.

Now, Fulmer thought sourly, the so-called news was a joke, made up of people like Harry Hornden, who had opinions in the place of a journalistic background. And he wasn't even among the worst of them. But they all inhabited their own ring of hell, pulling breaking stories out of their butt holes.

"Marsh," Hornden said now.

Fulmer hated when anyone called him "Marsh," let alone this shmuck, so he grunted by way of reply. Anyway, his mind was elsewhere, already at Dulles, seeing Bourne in a small, windowless room with cuffs on his wrists and ankles. What a story that would be, and, like it or not, Hornden was the perfect journo to break it.

"So there are two men walking down the street," Hornden continued with a certain gleam in his eye. "It's the week before Christmas, bells are ringing, carols coming from outdoor speakers, the scent of free-cut pine trees in the air. One man says to the other, 'I sure don't like this talk of racism all of a sudden.' 'Me, neither,' says the second guy. 'You're not a racist, are you?' the first guy asks. 'Hell, no,' second one says. 'You?' 'Not a bit of it.' "Good,' the second guy says, 'Let's go get drunk.' 'Capital idea,' the first one says, 'and we can catch us a faggot and roast his chestnuts over an open fire!' "

Hornden laughed so hard tears came to his eyes. At some point, he became aware that Fulmer wasn't joining in his merriment. Wiping his eyes, he nudged Fulmer. "What? You think you're too pure to get a laugh out of that joke?"

"It's not funny. It's not even a joke." Fulmer was

straining to look past the building traffic choking the off ramp to Dulles. "Can it now, Hornden. As soon as we get to the airport I've serious business to transact."

Leaning forward, he tapped the new head of his security detail, sitting up front, on the shoulder. Max, his betrayer, had been arraigned and was now sitting in a federal facility, awaiting interrogation. "Louis, please get on the horn and find out what the fuck is going on. I can't afford to be late."

"Already on it, sir." Louis had his mobile to one ear. Now he spoke into it so softly no one could hear what he was saying.

Temporarily mollified, but still on edge, Fulmer sat back in the seat.

"So," Hornden said, "you're as pure as the driven snow. No warts on you, right?"

Fulmer hardly heard him. Whatever Louis had done was working. The traffic was breaking up, and they were pushing their way forward. He caught glimpses of the gleaming shell of the international departure terminal's exterior now.

"Marsh, you're not listening to me." Hornden's voice had turned plaintive, reaching up the scale to unbecoming heights.

Fulmer brushed his words away as he would a bothersome fly. "I told you to can it and I meant it."

"You're choice, Marsh. I mean, you're running the show, right?"

"Right as shit," Fulmer said distractedly.

"But then of course you'll miss out on all the fun."

Fulmer's brow furrowed as he glanced over. "What fun? What are you babbling on about, man?"

Hornden had extracted his mobile from his coat pocket. It was one of those oversize jobbies that people obsessed with selfies were so fond of, Fulmer observed with distaste.

"Well, *this*, for instance." On the screen of the journo's mobile was a photo of Fulmer *in flagrante delicto*. Fulmer was nude, his flabby buttocks high in the air between Gwyneth's widely spread legs. Fulmer's reddened face was visible in the mirrored tabletop, and, to make matters even worse, the lovely and lubricious Gwyneth was grinning lewdly at the camera.

"Where...where did you get that?" Fulmer said stupidly. His mind seemed to have frozen solid, encased in a block of ice.

"This still frame is only the icing," Hornden said with a malicious grin. "Take a gander at the cake, Marsh. I've titled it '*Corpus Delicti*,' or 'Caught in the Act.'" And then the video began to play, the whole sordid sexual encounter from smoldering beginning to mortifying end.

———

"How did you do it?" the Angelmaker said, comfortably ensconced in her first class seat.

Bourne was looking out the Perspex window at the passing clouds far below. "Do what?"

"Get us out of the country without a hitch?"

When he turned to her, his smile was lacquer thin. He could not see her the same way, not anymore. "I created a diversion."

She frowned. "What kind of a diversion?"

"I bought two tickets to Istanbul in the name of one

of my old Treadstone aliases and his wife. That sent up red flags in all the right quarters, I have no doubt. That flight was leaving twenty minutes after ours."

She laughed. "Brilliant."

Over their indifferent meal, he said, "Tell me what else you know about Dima Orlov."

She frowned at the piece of unidentifiable meat speared on the tines of her fork. "It isn't much."

"Nevertheless. Everything you know."

The atmosphere between them had subtly altered, as if a breeze from the east had cleared away a cloudbank that had lingered far too long in one place. He heard everything she said through this clear lens. He was no longer obliged to scrutinize every move and expression she made; he already knew what lay beneath her tough reptilian armor.

"Everything I know," she said reflectively while she chewed her bit of meat.

"Your information is all third-hand, I take it."

"No. Not at all. I was friends with Dima's daughter, Katya."

"Past tense."

"Well, yes." She put down her fork; she hadn't eaten much. "Once, we were close—close as mother and daughter. But like many mothers and daughters we had a falling out."

"About what?"

She laughed softly, bitterly. "She accused me of using her to get close to her father."

"How far off the mark was she?"

"Huh. That's the pity of it," the Angelmaker said. "She wasn't off at all."

"You felt nothing for her."

It wasn't a question; she didn't take it as such. "Well, you know me." She gave him a glancing sideways look. "Nice woman, though. Smart, strong-willed. And yet she was inextricably tied to her father."

"Why did you want to get close to Dima Orlov?"

"Keyre sent me. He wanted to do a deal with Dima."

Bourne waited a moment for everything to sink in. "You do realize the irony of that situation."

Another lightning sideways glance. "You mean the 'inextricably tied' bit."

The flight attendant rolled her cart parallel to their seats, took their trays, asked if they wanted dessert, coffee, or perhaps an after-dinner drink. The Angelmaker wanted a brandy; Bourne wanted nothing more than to hear the end of the story.

After the brandy was poured and they were alone again, Bourne said, "It seems to me that in some ways Katya is an older version of yourself."

"I can see how you'd make that mistake." The Angelmaker took a sip of her brandy, set it down on her tray-table. Bourne had already stowed away his.

"Clarify it for me, then."

"Mmm." The Angelmaker bit her lower lip. "Well, for one thing Katya loves her father. For another, she loves him maybe a little too much."

"And you?"

"You're joking, right? You've met my father."

"And your mother?" Bourne asked. "In all the time I've known you, neither you nor your sister ever mentioned her."

There ensued a long silence. The Angelmaker sipped

her brandy. The plane began to shudder and the FASTEN SEAT BELTS lights flashed, but they were already buckled up. The turbulence grew worse, and she held onto her glass to keep it from tumbling over.

"My mother. You want to know about my mother?" She knocked back the rest of her brandy, looked around for the flight attendant to get a refill, but they were all sitting down because of the turbulence. "Okay, for the record, she taught me how to say 'Fuck you.'"

"But you were just a little girl."

"There you go, then."

The turbulence departed as quickly as it had arrived. The lights had been lowered, seats had been reclined to the horizontal, mattresses placed, along with quilts covering the passengers. A few read or watched a film, but most were taking advantage of the seat turned bed.

"One sentence can't be the sum and substance of your mother," Bourne said.

"Why are you so interested?" she said sharply.

"I can't remember mine."

She was staring at the blank TV screen ahead of her. "Did it ever occur to you that's a blessing?"

"Not for a moment."

Without another word the Angelmaker unbuckled herself and strode back toward the toilets.

It was several seconds before Bourne realized she had taken her brandy glass with her. Why would she do that? The glass was empty. She could simply be returning it to one of the crew, or . . .

Unbuckling, he followed her down the aisle. She opened the accordion door to the right-hand toilet; she was still gripping the glass. He launched himself along the aisle, at the last minute plucking a fork off a food tray the attendant had yet to clear.

Jamming it into the door, he stopped it from closing completely, kept the Angelmaker from sliding the lock all the way across.

"What are you doing?" he said softly, leaning against the door.

As an answer, he heard the sound of the glass shattering. Any moment now the blood would be spurting out of the opened vein in her wrist.

"Stop it, Mala. Stop it."

Using the tines of the fork as a lever, he worked at prying open the door. He could tell that she had thrown her full weight against him.

"I've no other choice." Her voice was dull, mechanical, as if in her mind she was already dead.

Then, in the sliver of open space, he saw her lift a shard of glass out of the sink, turn it inward. The pale skin of the inside of her wrist rested just below it.

The tines of the fork snapped off.

33

F OR MARSHALL FULMER, a day he'd anticipated being filled like a piñata with all kinds of bright, shiny toys, chief among them having Jason Bourne finally, *finally* taken into custody, had been, in a painful heartbeat, stood on its head, turned 180 degrees toward the dark side.

First, Hornden shows him the hard evidence of his dalliance with a madam, then even before he has a chance to digest that clusterfuck, that idiot Ellison calls to tell him that, no, the couple he took into custody weren't Bourne and his companion, after all, but a couple about to set off on their twentieth-anniversary celebration, of all things! And now where was Bourne—who, Fulmer knew, worked alone? No one knew, certainly not Ellison or any of his crew. Had Bourne even been at Dulles at all?

And Fulmer wouldn't even be thinking of all the ways he could crucify Ellison had it not been for the fact that, considering what Hornden had on him, a major coup like capturing Jason Bourne would have almost made up for him quite stupidly falling into a honey trap.

Running a shaking hand across his face, he told the driver to return to the office. But Hornden said, "Hold on."

He gave the journo a withering look. "What? Why?"

"We need to go to the VIP airstrip." Hornden pointed. "It's that way."

"Fuck you," was all Fulmer could manage, but there was no force, no venom behind it. He sat back in the seat. All the air, all the exhilaration of the now-distant morning had gone out of him.

"Sir?"

He became aware of the driver looking at him in the rearview mirror. "What?" He waved a hand as if the matter were of no import to him. "Oh, do as Mr. Hornden suggests."

Beside him Hornden chuckled. "'*Suggests,*'" he repeated under his breath.

Fulmer considered asking Hornden what they were going to do at the VIP airstrip, but he didn't want to give him the satisfaction. With Hornden, these small, petty victories were all that were left him. Pathetic.

With Fulmer's credentials they passed through the manned gates. Hornden told the driver to pull over to the left and park.

"Okay," he said, opening the rear door, "let's take a walk."

In the darkness of near midnight, the overbright lights on the tarmac elongated their shadows eastward. A light breeze ruffled Fulmer's hair, but Hornden's stayed in place, as if it had been plasticized. Ahead of them, a private aircraft with Dutch insignia crouched, its door open wide in welcome, a rolling staircase set in front of it.

"After you," Hornden said when they reached the foot of the stairs.

No more "Marsh," Fulmer noted. For some reason, this gave him a sense of foreboding.

Stepping into the interior, he saw that it had been retrofitted, seats pulled out, replaced with lounges, desks, flatbed seats, and the like. There seemed to be only one person on the plane; where the crew was he had no idea. The man was slim, tall, saturnine, dark-eyed. Fulmer had seen enough bespoke Savile Row suits and John Lobb shoes to recognize them on the figure who came around from behind a desk and strode toward him with his hand extended.

"Mr. Marshall Fulmer, I have wanted to speak with you for some time, ever since you were a senior senator, in fact." He spoke with a decided Russian accent. "But to be perfectly frank, this meeting was some while in the making."

Fulmer's foreboding ratcheted up to a nauseating level as he took the man's cool, dry hand. *The honey trap?* he asked himself.

"And you are?"

"Oh, pardon me." He gave a little bow from the waist that Fulmer took to be ironic. "Konstantin Ludmirovich Savasin, *Federal'naya sluzhba bezopasnosti Rossiyskoy Federatsii.*" Translation: Federal Security Service, Russian Federation—the successor to the KGB.

Blood drained from Fulmer's face. He felt the floor slipping away from him. As bad as it had been before, he knew that his day had just fallen into the abyss. Now that he was confronted with the head of the FSB, he had no idea how deep the abyss went.

Freeing his hand from Konstantin's grip, he pivoted toward Hornden. "Are you kidding me? You're a Russian agent?"

The journo grinned. "The fun never stops today, does it, Marsh."

Fulmer sank into a seat, head in his hands. "Jesus Christ."

Konstantin gripped his shoulder. "Not to worry, old boy. We won't be asking too much of you."

"Jesus Christ," Fulmer moaned.

"Marshall—may I call you Marshall? Marshall, look at me." Konstantin sighed in a theatrical manner. "Come, come, stand up and take your medicine like a man."

Still in shock, Fulmer slapped his thighs and stood up. His eyes were red-rimmed and there was a tic battering one eyelid as he looked Konstantin in the face.

"You work for me now, Marshall."

Fulmer moaned like a child in pain.

"Please, look on the bright side."

Fulmer's brows knit together. "The bright side?"

"Yes, of course. You are national security advisor for a very different kind of president of the United States."

It was only then that the full import of his situation hit him, and, doubling over, he vomited onto the pile carpet of the aisle.

With a look of distaste, Konstantin stepped back in order to keep his John Lobb shoes pristine. He snapped his fingers. "Mr. Hornden, please be kind enough to inform the crew. Their presence is required immediately to clean up the mess the national security advisor has made."

"At once," Hornden said crisply, pulling out his mobile.

"In the meantime." Konstantin hooked his fingers inside Fulmer's collar, hauling him to his feet. "There is a front cabin. Let us repair there so that we may get on with the business at hand."

Fulmer trudged on feet made leaden by terror and shame. He was in the midst of a nightmare, he kept telling himself. At any moment he would awaken in his bed, the morning sun would be shining, the birds calling to one another.

Sadly, but predictably, that never happened. This *was* a nightmare, but a waking one. And so, without quite knowing how he got there, he found himself sitting opposite the saturnine man in his elegant suit and expensive shoes who just happened to be the head of Russia's most feared security agency.

On the narrow table between them sat a slim notebook computer, a bottle of vodka, its surface already coated in frost, a bucket of ice, and two old-fashioned glasses. Without a word, Konstantin used a pair of silver tongs to transfer ice cubes from the bucket to the glasses, then poured them each three fingers of vodka. He lifted his glass in toast.

"Nasdarovje." He cocked his head. "No? To a long and fruitful association. Still, no?" He shrugged. "Well, then, to your health, Marshall." He clinked the rim of his glass against the one still sitting on the table, for Fulmer had not as yet touched his. He drank, then set his glass down.

"Take a sip, Marshall. This vodka is good—the best. It'll calm your nerves, I guarantee it." When Fulmer still made no move to touch the glass, Konstantin said, "As you wish. Now, down to business. What I want from you is simple. Well, we want to start out easy, don't we? Your orders will get more complicated over time."

Konstantin went at the vodka again. "You're to tell the president and your Pentagon comrades that what you call the Bourne Initiative is nothing more than Russian disinformation."

"But it isn't."

"Of course it isn't, Marshall. Let's not start being naïve this late in the game."

Mention of the Initiative served to focus him. Fulmer's mind was starting to thaw, to come unstuck from the deep freeze into which it had been hurled and held by the day's back-to-back shitstorms—the video evidence of his dalliance; the knowledge that he had done it with...how could he have had such strong feelings for a madam; losing Bourne; and now this...

"Then..."

"This is the start of what you will do for me, Marshall—disseminate disinformation that will give us a leg up on foreign affairs, on alliances with other nations, with negotiations on currently thorny topics with your government."

He lifted up a slim briefcase, snapped it open, laid a file with official Russian Federation, FSB, and, most tellingly, *spetsnaz* stamps on its cover. He laid his hand over the file. "In here are documents—*genuine* documents—from Unit 309, our cyber hacking and disinformation group, backing up your assertion that there is, in fact, no such thing as the Bourne Initiative under that designation or any other."

He pushed the file over. Fulmer didn't even look at it. "No."

"No?" Konstantin reared back. "What do you mean 'no'? Those photos, that video will ruin you personally and professionally."

Fulmer reached for the glass, tipped it to his lips, then decided against it, set the glass down with the vodka untouched. He needed his mind perfectly clear, not clouded by Russian vodka. Now that he had his wits about him again, his feet on the floor, as it were, he could see a path out of the abyss into which he had been cast. In fact, there was no abyss; it was a figment of the shock that had gripped him.

Pushing the glass away, Fulmer looked up at Konstantin. "No, they won't. Not in this new era. I give it up to Jesus, and all will be well. Oh, some feathers will be ruffled, mainly my wife's, but she'll get over it. As for my new job, just look at the president—he gets away with anything and everything. The American public is different now; it gets its news from social media, it can and will forgive just about anything. Arrogance and repentance in equal measure is a formula they swallow hook, line, and sinker."

He took up the frosty bottle, refilled Konstantin's glass while leaving his own glass still untouched. "So come, *gospodin*, and let us come to—how to put it best?—a more equitable arrangement."

"Boldly played, Marshall. Were I in your position— naturally, I wouldn't be—but if I were, I imagine I'd do the same."

Fulmer looked smug.

Konstantin extracted a manila envelope from his briefcase, slid it across the table.

Fulmer's brows furrowed. "What's this?"

"Open it, Marshall."

Now everything was flipped; Savasin calling Fulmer by his Christian name was grating on him. He hesitated a moment, then snatched the envelope, turned it over, and opened it. Inside, he found a series of eight-by-ten photos. With a trembling hand, he spread them out. A ball of ice formed in the pit of his stomach. He was staring incredulously at a series of photos identical to the ones Hornden had shown him on his mobile device. Except for one terrifying difference: in these, he was making love to a young girl. Black as coal, and clearly under age.

"Tell me, Marshall, I assume you've heard of *kompromat*," Konstantin said in a voice turned silky. "It's an old KGB trick," he went on without waiting for an answer. "We used to hire prostitutes—swallows, we called them—to seduce our targets in honey traps. But, as you have so eloquently pointed out, that methodology is old hat; it's a broken wheel. Times change and so does methodology. We've updated *kompromat*, just as we've updated the KGB to the FSB."

"A devil by any name," Fulmer managed in a hoarse voice.

Konstantin laughed. His fingertip tapped the photos, one after the other. "Be it ever so humble, Marshall. This is your new home. And I—I am your new master. Your control, in the jargon of espiocrats."

He continued to tap the photos. "Would you care to

take these with you, Marshall? A clear and present reminder of your *adjusted situation*. No? All right then." He gathered the photos up, slid them back into the envelope, which he deposited in his briefcase.

"Now, I told you that we had updated *kompromat*. I've just shown you one way. Here's another. You are very important to our plans, long term as well as short term. We required an unbreakable lock for you, and Alyosha Orlova provided it."

"What? Who?"

"You know her as Françoise Sevigne." A slow smile spread across Konstantin's face. "You've received some very bad advice lately, Marshall." Opening the laptop, Konstantin brought it out of sleep, pressed several keys, then swiveled it around so Fulmer could see the screen. "Very bad, indeed."

Fulmer was looking at the web site of Fellingham, Bodeys, the company to which Françoise had suggested he move his business. Which he had done forthwith.

He shrugged. "So?"

"So, *this*." Reaching around, Konstantin pressed a key that brought up a list of Fellingham, Bodeys' clients. Among them were the worst of the worst: Robert Mugabe; Viktor Bout, the former world's number one arms trader, now in jail; three heads of the most powerful Mexican and Colombian drug cartels; two ISIS commanders; the Somalian Keyre, who took over after Bout was caught. The list of malefactors, criminals, and terrorists, though short, was as bitter and hard to take as a spoonful of castor oil. "These are very bad people, evil people that your money is keeping company with. Who knows what deals Fellingham, Bodeys is devising for their clients—you included, Marshall. And if you don't comply, we'll send this list and the details of your ill-gotten gains to Justin Farreng and LeakAGE. We'll do to you what you did to General MacQuerrie, and you know what happened to him."

Fulmer stared at the screen, transfixed by the ramifications of the ingenious trap the Russians had devised for him. The realization suddenly swept through him that the honey trap was merely a way to gain his attention while the real trap closed around him. Good God, Françoise was a Russian spy. Through his disgust and humiliation he felt a vague sense of admiration that they had found him deserving of such meticulous attention and planning.

Konstantin, who seemed to be following Fulmer's thought process via his changing expressions, now said: "You will take the Unit 309 file and run with it, Marshall, convincing the administration to forget all about the Bourne Initiative, giving us time to find out just what the hell that sonuvabitch General Karpov had in mind."

"Why?"

Konstantin's voice was hard as iron. "Because I told you to." Then his tone softened a bit. "But just this once, since you're new to the game, I'll tell you. You're going to help us discredit and destabilize elements within your government and clandestine agencies."

Fulmer went bone-white, as if his flesh had melted away, leaving only his skull. "I can't—I won't do that."

"Oh, you most certainly will." Konstantin smiled with his teeth. "You see, Marshall, you are completely compromised. You have no choice. No choice at all." He raised his eyebrows. "Don't look so downcast, Marshall. We know you harbor great ambitions. Am I on target? Bull's-eye, I'd say. We can and will help you with that, Marshall. In four years you want to run for president. Capital idea, say I! We can imagine nothing better for you. We're patient, you see, very patient. We can wait while you consolidate your power base—with our help, of course. And once you win the nomination, if you continue to play by our rules, we'll win you the election. Triumphant, you will be swept into office like a conquering Caesar. What joy, no?"

He drank more vodka. "In the meantime, there's another service you will do me. And this one is as urgent as the first. Perhaps more so. What I want from you are the Treadstone files on Jason Bourne."

At Bourne's name, Fulmer shook his head. "Impossible. All the Treadstone files were incinerated, as dictated by protocol."

Konstantin sighed. "Marshall, the files weren't destroyed. You know it and I know it. They were ferreted away from prying eyes." He took another sip of the chilled vodka. "You don't know what you're missing." He shrugged again. "Ah, well. Onward. Find the files, copy them, and send them to me via Mr. Hornden." He leaned forward, tapped Fulmer on the knee. "*All* the files. I want to know everything there is to know about Bourne's training, what he was subjected to, how well he stood up under interrogation techniques."

Fulmer shook his head. "Why?"

"Because when I know what he resisted, I'll be able to find that one, single method that will break him."

Finally, Fulmer had something to laugh at.

Konstantin cocked his head. "You find this funny?"

"I do." Fulmer could not stop laughing. He seemed to have lost all control of his emotions, just as he had lost control of his life, which was now in the hands of the enemy. "Do you know how many years it's been we've been trying to catch that bastard, only to have him slip through our fingers time and time again?"

"Just today, as well. So?"

"So what good will the files do you when he can't be caught?"

Konstantin finished off his vodka. "Oh, he can be caught, Marshall, I assure you."

Fulmer shot him a sideways glance; the fog that was blurring his brain anew began to lift once more. "Really?"

"There were three partners in the cyber Initiative. Two of them are dead. The one who is left is named Dima. Dima Vladimirovich Orlov. It just so happens that I have a mole inside Dima's organization. I know that's where Bourne must be headed. To Dima. To find out about the Initiative set up by his friend, that sonuvabitch Karpov."

Konstantin stood. "And when he arrives, you will have already handed over the Treadstone files. I will know how to deal with Jason Bourne, and I will accomplish what has eluded everyone else who has tried and failed to find and trap him."

"Why do you want Bourne, anyway? What's he to you?"

Konstantin peered down at Fulmer as if from Olympian heights. "Just get me the files, Marshall, and all will be well with you, your reputation, and your illegally amassed fortune."

34

"CAN I HELP you, sir? Is there something wrong?" The flight attendant, well trained to keep any negative emotion off her face, smiled her plastic smile. "Something I can do for you, sir?" She pointed. "This toilet is free, if you—"

Bourne robed himself in his blandest smile. Move along. *Nothing to see here.* "It's all good, thank you. My wife's a bit indisposed. She needs a bit of help. I know exactly what to do."

"Are you sure, sir? We have—"

"Absolutely sure." His smile brightened. "Happens from time to time." He shrugged. "What can you do."

She nodded, then turned away, returning to the galley area where she and the other first class attendants were chatting, their rest period having begun.

"Mala . . ." Bourne jammed his fingertips around the edge of the door, hauled it open.

"Get in here," she said.

He stepped in, closed the door behind him. Then he took the shard of glass out of her hand—she hadn't yet punctured herself—and dropped it back into the sink.

"What d'you think you're doing?"

She stared at him, her eyes large and questing. "My mother called me Anjelica. I always hated that name—Mala. It was the name my father insisted on, my official name. My mother called me Anjelica," she repeated, more softly now, her voice barely above a whisper. "In secret, when we were alone together. Before, when I was born, she tried to argue with my father, but he beat her for that, too."

He beat her for that, too. There was no point in asking her to elaborate; that sentence said it all.

"Mala—"

"No, don't." She crossed her arms under her breasts. "You have no idea how much I despise myself." She held up a hand to forestall any comment. "Listen to me now." She was trembling slightly, her eyes enlarged with incipient tears. "I have no daughter. Giza doesn't exist. As with all his girls, Keyre was sure to keep me from getting pregnant; the process would spoil our appearance, we would be less than perfect, and that would necessitate us being thrown in the trash, like a piece of rotten meat."

She took a deep, shuddering breath, let it out. "The child—Giza—was his idea. He said I should use the imprisoned daughter card if you started to doubt me. It would, he said, bind you to me in a new and different way."

She produced a rueful smile, tentative and, if he could believe anything about her anymore, frightened. "So, you see, my father was right. I've earned my name—a malediction, a curse."

For a time, Bourne said nothing. Then he gestured at the sink. "Was this fake as well?"

"I . . . I don't know. Maybe . . . maybe if you hadn't broken in I would have. What is left of me? I no longer have substance. I no longer have the ability to make choices. And now . . . now I wonder whether I ever had it."

Grabbing a couple of paper towels, Bourne moistened them, then scooped up the glass fragments, pushed them down into the waste disposal hopper. He ran the water repeatedly until all the glitter had washed down the drain.

"We need to get back to our seats," he said.

"I can't."

"You can," he said, "and you will." He turned her to him. "You have a life to live, Anjelica. A long one."

At the sound of the name her mother had called her, her lips formed a tentative smile. "That sounds good coming from you." The smile never reached her eyes. "Not that you'll believe me. I know I've used up all my credibility with you."

"Come on," he said, reaching for the door. "Someone has to believe in you."

Reaching out, she held his movement in abeyance. "Not you, Jason. Anyone but you."

He glanced down at her hand and she snatched it away.

"Don't you see? I'm like a scorpion. No matter what I say, no matter which way I twist or turn, in the end I'll sting. It's my nature."

"I'll keep that in mind." He opened the accordion door, pressing them up against each other in the process. She flinched away, as if stung or burned, but in the end she followed him back to their seats. As with, it seemed to her, everything else in her life, she had no choice.

———

"Come on now, smarten up, Morgana. You have no choice."

Morgana regarded Françoise with a look of vague bewilderment, which was now calculated, rather than blindly innocent.

"Go with the flow," Soraya had said. And: *"You'll think I've thrown you to the dogs."* She thought that part was behind her, but now she was further along in her brief, burrowing deeper down, and the dogs—the real dogs of war—were heading toward her with teeth bared.

"Why don't you do it, then?"

"It's you he's after. I need to stay out of it."

They were at breakfast the next day, Françoise knocking on her door at daybreak, the sky still in the process of throwing off the veil of night. Hours before Larry London would wake and come to her with room service breakfast, as was his habit. In a rickety café habituated by local fishermen coming in with their catch or on their way out onto the choppy gray water. The stench of fish, both fresh and smoked, was only partially watered down by the fug of cigarette smoke.

"Or seem to stay out of it," Françoise added, as she poured another packet of sugar into her coffee, stirred in cream.

It was all Morgana could do to keep her gorge down. Her breakfast lay before her. It was no more appetizing now than when it had been brought out of the kitchen.

"I'm not saying...I mean, there must be another way out."

"There isn't. You know there isn't." Françoise's voice was clipped, her tone hard, the better to emphasize the finality of her words.

"Okay, well." Morgana's gaze slipped sideways as the door opened to admit a couple more fishermen in their thick rubber slickers and high, gum-soled boots. The fish stink grew stronger than Morgana thought possible. "I'm not saying I'll do it, but what's your plan."

"It's simple," Françoise said, "like all the best plans. The less moving parts the better."

Morgana could agree with that. She nodded. "Fire away." She winced at her choice of words.

"The plan takes advantage of Larry's weakness."

"What weakness?"

"Women. Or hadn't you noticed?"

"It's hard to miss," Morgana said. "I just didn't see it as a weakness."

"Neither does Larry. That's the best part. It's hiding in plain sight."

Françoise took some coffee, made a face, then set the cup down in its saucer. The café was packed and noisy, which is why she'd chosen it for their early-morning rendezvous.

"Larry's always wanted to bed me despite my bad treatment of him back when. I haven't let him, of course, but the key thing here is I haven't cut him off at the knees either. So..."

"So what? You're going to seduce him? How does that help us?"

"Do you know how to handle a handgun?"

"Not really, no," Morgana lied. The moment she discovered that Françoise was a Russian spy, she had quit telling her the truth about anything. The tricky part was to act natural, not to give her former friend the slightest hint of the change in their relationship. She had enough to worry about with Larry ordered to kill her without being afraid Françoise might beat him to it.

Lions to the left of me, lions to the right. Here I am, stuck in the middle with you. She sang this to herself to take the edge off the fear and loathing, the claustrophobic sensation of being trapped.

Françoise tossed her head. "Doesn't matter. You'll be so close to Larry you couldn't miss if you tried."

Morgana's stomach gave a lurch, her heart rate increasing. "What are you talking about?"

"Just this." Françoise leaned over the table, lowering her voice, though in the good-natured din there was no need. "Tonight I'm going to let Larry seduce me. I'll pretend to get a bit drunk. Then I'll lean over the table, like I am now. Only tonight my shirt buttons will be open enough for him to see the tops of my breasts. That's all the invitation he'll need, believe me."

Morgana had trouble breathing, as if the air around her had turned gelid, as if she were submerged beneath a dark and ominous sea. "And then?" She could scarcely get the words out.

"And then you'll come out of the closet with the handgun I will provide and kill him."

"What?"

"One shot to the back of his head." She cocked her hand like a gun. "Blam!"

"That's crazy. Forget it."

"Don't worry, Morgana, I'll make sure he's on top. His back will be toward you." Françoise smiled winningly. "He won't know what hit him, I guarantee it."

Through the smeared windows the sun was burning off the last of the early morning's gray mist.

"Honesty is inefficient," Mala said.

"In our world, at the edge of civilization."

"No, I mean anytime, anywhere. Honesty reveals too much, leaving you feeling defeated."

They were back in their seats. Bourne had drifted off a bit, but it was the kind of surface sleep he'd learned at Treadstone. He made sure he was sensing Mala; if she had left her seat again he would have been right behind her. She had ordered a vodka with plenty of ice, drinking it slowly, methodically, in the way people do when they're determined to get drunk. Bourne wasn't about to let that happen; he'd cut her off before she got halfway there. But he didn't stop her now, sensing that she needed the fortification to tell him whatever it was that was burning its way through her mind.

It was a time of loss for Bourne. Boris was dead, Sara was who knew where, in whatever kind of dangerous situation, and he was sure he was losing Mala, though in what way he could not yet discern. But then what had been their connection? Maybe it had been spun of spider's-web silk, apt to be broken at a moment's notice, or with a wrong turn. Perhaps their connection was an illusion; she wasn't like any other woman he had met or would likely meet. Like the Sphinx in the desert outside

Cairo she was a complete enigma. And, quite possibly, therein lay her allure.

Mala stirred beside him, the ice cubes tinkling against the glass as she took another sip. She held the vodka in her mouth a moment, savoring its icy bite before swallowing it.

"Having said that, I'm going to tell you a story. It will be up to you to decide whether or not it's true." She took another sip, settled back in her seat. "For some time after my convalescence, after you left, I had no idea what I was going to do with my life. You had so kindly and generously put my sister into ballet school, and she took to it like a duck to water; her life path was set. But me...?" She shrugged. "I know you believe that I contacted Keyre, that he has some magical or psychic hold over me. I suppose that would have made a good tale, but it's not true. I felt nothing toward him—not hate, not fear, not attraction—nothing at all.

"I needed to get away from the family you put me with. They were nice enough and very helpful to me, but in that house, late at night, or even in the early morning over breakfast, the stench of burning flesh would come to me. I'd have to push my chair back, run to the bathroom and vomit. As if that could rid me of the smell. It couldn't, of course it couldn't. That stench will be with me until the moment of my death."

She pressed the call button, and when the attendant arrived, she shook her empty glass to ask for another. She remained silent until the second vodka arrived and she'd taken several slow and deliberate sips, moving further along the road to getting drunk. Bourne watched her like a hawk.

"So I had to leave," Mala continued as if there had been no interruption. "I missed my mother; I had to find her—it was a kind of fever. I went home to Estonia. I spent six weeks looking for her, but there was no sign of her. It was as if the earth had swallowed her whole. Words are inadequate to express my despair. I was an orphan. Worse, I didn't know whether my mother was alive or dead.

"I wandered, then, to Prague, don't ask me why, then Rome, and ended up in Paris. I was grieving, and more importantly, considering how my life turned out, I was angry—angry at my father for selling us out, at my mother for not stopping him, even Liis, for having a life I did not, could not have."

She pursed her lips, her eyes heavy-lidded, as if these memories still weighed mightily on her. "Paris in the springtime, with the horse chestnuts in bloom and the couples young and old holding hands and kissing as they strolled along the banks of the Seine. What was there for me in Paris, you may ask? I had remembered that my mother spoke to me about Paris when I was little; she even taught me some French. I looked for her there, too, but, of course, it was impossible, like looking for a needle in a haystack. Then, one afternoon in the Tuileries, while I sat on one of those green metal chairs, feeling the sun on my face, I met Françoise. She stepped, rather rudely, between me and the sun, to get my attention, I suppose.

"It was clear from the first moment of our meeting that afternoon, and confirmed soon after as we sat at a café, drinking espressos, that she had meant to meet me. Someone had told her about me, and I imagine you can guess who that someone was.

"As soon as you had placed me with that family and left, Keyre began monitoring me, my movements from city to city, and he had sent Françoise after me. She'd just missed me in Rome, but, despite the lovers all around me, I was comfortable enough in Paris, feeling closer to my mother, hearing French spoken, to give her the chance to catch up.

"Of course, she didn't tell me this right away. She had a way about her—ingratiating without being in the least condescending. Gradually, as we spent more time together, I formed the impression that her background, like mine, was something she wished to forget. That formed a bond, you see. That it was a false bond was something I learned much later, after she had indoctrinated me into her way of life, had trained me. She became my mentor and me her willing acolyte. Under her tutelage, I began to make money—lots of it. I became a go-between, taking a rake-off from both sides. That the deals were shady, that the principals were on the wrong side of the law—often as far on the wrong side as you could get—was of no interest to me. The money was. I was addicted." Her smile was rueful. "You see, Keyre's Yibir magic worked on me, after all."

She was drinking faster now, as if her impending inebriation could save her from herself. Almost finished with her second vodka, she was about to hit the call button like a hospital patient in pain who keeps giving herself intravenous doses of morphine, when Bourne stopped her.

"Go on," he said softly. "Where did it all go wrong?"

Mala closed her eyes for a moment. "I suppose you could say that it all went wrong the moment Françoise came between me and the soothing warmth of the

Parisian sunlight. But I know that's not what you meant." She took a breath, stared into the cubes in her glass. "What happened was this: I discovered that Françoise was not what she appeared to be—no, that's not quite right. She was precisely what she appeared to be. On the surface. But underneath, down where it counted, she was someone else. She wasn't French as she purported to be; she was Russian. Her name wasn't Françoise Sevigne, it was Alyosha Orlova."

The name sent a lightning bolt through Bourne. "She isn't, by any chance, related to Dima Vladimirovich Orlov, the man we're going to see, is she?"

Mala nodded. "His granddaughter."

"And Katya, the older woman you were once friends with, is Alyosha's mother."

Mala nodded. Bourne sat very still, thinking that this woman was like an onion—the more layers you peeled away, the more intense the experience.

"Alyosha has been long lost to Orlov; she's the black swan of the family."

Bourne shifted in his seat, as if his mind, working at light speed, made it impossible for his body to remain still. A skein was forming, but he had yet to make out its final shape.

"And that's when you found out that she was working for Keyre."

"Yes and no," Mala said. She seemed calmer now, as if, having broken, the storm or the fever that had gripped her had become a shadow of its former self. "Yes, she was working for Keyre, but at the same time she was working for the Russians. To be more specific, her half brother, Gora Maslov."

Revelation after revelation; strand after strand working itself into a pattern. "So she's the black swan for a good reason. She's the illegitimate daughter of Katya Orlov and Dimitri Maslov. And she's more loyal to the Maslovs?"

"She grew up with the Maslovs but never took the name. I doubt Alyosha knows the meaning of loyalty." Mala glanced at him. "And, yes, I'm fully aware of the irony of that." She ran a hand through her hair. "I should tell you something about Keyre and Gora Maslov: they've been doing business together."

"Gora is Keyre's Russian arms supplier."

"Correct. Until a week ago, that is. Suspecting that Keyre was skimming profits, Gora sent a team in to infiltrate Keyre's cadre. Keyre found out and executed them all. Alyosha was the facilitator linking them, but now that they're the bitterest of enemies, they no longer require her services. I don't know where Alyosha is or what she's up to."

———

Crouched in the clothes closet in Françoise's hotel room, Morgana lay the compact 9mm Beretta Nano across her thigh. According to plan, Françoise had left the door ajar so Morgana could see a sliver of the bed, but more importantly hear how the plan was progressing and when to emerge.

Morgana had to hand it to the bitch—she'd come up with an excellent plan. As she had said, very few moving parts. The question was whether everything would go according to the plan; there was no trust left inside Morgana when it came to Françoise. She had snapped on latex gloves, had already checked the ammo in the Beretta's magazine to make sure she wouldn't be firing blanks. But what if both Françoise and Larry London were waiting for her to emerge to shoot her to death? But why wait for her to emerge? Which is why she tensed when she heard voices, the door swinging open. Françoise's high laugh. Only now it occurred to her that she was a sitting duck. If they were going to kill her it would be now; stuck in the darkness, amid Françoise's scent and her clothes, there was no escape for her. She lifted the spare pillow she had been clutching, stupidly using it as a shield. Of course it wouldn't stop a bullet, but the gesture was automatic, a very human response to imminent danger.

A line of sweat popped out at her hairline, and the back of her neck felt hot, as if she had come down with a sudden fever. She licked her lips; her mouth was dry, with an unpleasant taste she identified as bile. At any moment she was afraid she might piss herself.

"No you don't," Françoise was saying. "There isn't a man in the world capable of that!"

"Why don't we find out?" Larry's voice was in a deeper register, furred with sexual desire. A good sign; at least the bitch had told the truth about seducing him.

Another high laugh from Françoise, followed by a squeal of delight as the two of them passed through the narrow view afforded Morgana. The bedsprings reacted as the pair launched themselves onto it.

Several moments passed while Morgana heard the rustle and slither of clothes being stripped off, then an excited "Oh!" from Françoise and an answering "Mmmm" from Larry.

The sounds of lovemaking, so much a part of the experience for the participants, vacillated between frightening and ludicrous when heard by an outsider, like Morgana, who cringed as the pace increased.

When she heard Françoise cry out, "Oh, please!" which was their agreed-upon signal, she pushed the closet door open and slowly stood up. As Françoise had promised, Larry was on top, humping away in that animalistic manner endemic to certain men for whom their own pleasure was paramount.

She crossed the pile carpet, silent as a cat, carefully stepping over strewn clothes or sidestepping them altogether. Close up, the grunts and groans seemed even more absurd, the rising and falling of Larry's body, the hard thrust of his pelvis seeming to her a kind of violence that made her shudder.

She was almost close enough now, and she lifted the Beretta, her right arm straight, her left hand clutching the pillow. As she advanced, she felt her heart rate exceeding normal levels. To counteract it, she slowed her breathing. While she had extensive training with guns, she had never killed or even shot at a human being. Now, at the last minute, she felt as if her resolve might fail her. True, she had seen with her own eyes that Larry London had orders from Russia's *spetsnaz* to terminate her, but still the taking of a life, even in self-defense, was no small matter. It was not an act to take easily, or without regret. But she also knew that regret was a shooter's worst enemy—her father had told her as much the first time he had taken her deer hunting and she had missed the clear shot. *"You hesitated,"* he'd said. *"Your hesitation was a manifestation of remorse. You weren't sure you wanted to kill that buck. Morgana, you cannot fire your weapon unless you're sure. When you pull the trigger your mind must be clear, your intent certain. Otherwise you may as well put your weapon away."*

And so now, the Beretta a hand's-span away from the back of Larry London's head, she put aside her qualms, she refused remorse, kicked it into the metaphorical gutter. Leaning forward from the waist, she pressed the muzzle of the Beretta into the pillow, then lowered the pillow against her target's head—for that was how she thought of him now: no name, simply her target.

Nearing orgasm, her target didn't even notice the slight pressure. Taking a breath, she let it out slowly and evenly. Then, with clear eye and mind, she squeezed the trigger.

Larry London's head and, in fact, his entire frame rocketed downward, then rose again like a fish to the hook. There was surprisingly little blood, but a lot of feathers floating like a halo around London's head and shoulders. Morgana felt numb, as chilled as if she had just climbed out of a meat locker. For a moment, she remained still as a statue while her mind caught up with the actions of her body.

Françoise, struggling to shove London's body off her, fixed one eye on Morgana.

"Give me a hand," she said, her voice muffled.

Rage roiled Morgana's gut. As if that rage was a key opening a door, a way out, vivid, intense, and, yes, inevitable, revealed itself to her—the path—the only path—to invert her intolerable situation and escape the lions' den.

"Dammit, Morgana, are you listening to me?"

Morgana blinked. "Yes. Of course."

Elbowing her target's head to one side, she pressed the smoking pillow down onto Françoise's face and pulled the trigger of the Beretta not once, not twice, but three times.

"There." Her voice was a guttural whisper as she placed the 9mm in Larry London's right hand. She stood up straight and tall.

It would be natural to assume that she was observing the scene as if from a distance, outside herself, as if someone else had pulled the trigger four times. She was feeling none of those things. In fact, Morgana had never felt so vibrant, so alive, so in control. Every color throbbed with an intensity new and astonishing to her, the lamplight so brilliant it might have been able to cut glass. She felt the blood rushing through her arteries and veins as if it were a river, wide and deep, and almost intolerably beautiful. She felt her heart so intimately she might have been holding it in her hands.

She had passed beyond the veil, entered a life others never even dreamed of. She'd been blooded; she understood completely that she could never go back, even if she wished to. She was happy here in this new world, exhilarated, exalted. She felt herself initiated, anointed; she was now wreathed in shadows, her work hidden from the world at large. A child of the night.

Good God, she thought, *I've taken to this new life like a fledgling to the air.*

"There you go."

She surely was talking as much to herself now as to Françoise.

35

"IF YOU GO from Moscow to Budapest,'" Bourne said, "'you think you are in Paris.'"

Mala laughed. "Who said that?"

"György Ligeti," Bourne replied, "the Hungarian composer of modern classical music."

Mala stared out the window as the Sapsan bullet train, taking them from St. Petersburg to Moscow, sped at 155 miles per hour across what looked like a frozen landscape. But then the Russian landscape tended to look frozen even in summer.

"He was right."

They had deplaned in St. Petersburg, passing through immigration without incident, which was a relief. Transferring to the Glavny train station was likewise easy enough. However, the only seats available on the Sapsan were in a private conference cabin; they were the most expensive tickets, especially in the current Russian economy, which was no doubt why they had remained unsold. Bourne had snapped them up, again paying cash. In less than four hours the Sapsan, the Russian word for peregrine falcon, would pull into Moscow's Leningradsky Station. They had had time to buy themselves midweight sheepskin jackets for protection against the chill of late afternoons and evenings.

He was going to continue their conversation, but she had fallen asleep, just like that, from one moment to the next. For her, sleep was a blessing, he understood that, and he closed his eyes. But for him sleep was impossible now. He rose, left his seat vacant, stepped out of the compartment, and went along the aisle to the next car, needing to get away from the reverberations of her memories, which were making him claustrophobic.

He found himself in the first class car, filled mostly with businessmen hunched over their laptops and a smattering of American tourists, staring blankly out at the blurred landscape or reading their guidebooks, prepping for their days and nights in Russia's capital.

He was about halfway down the car when he was brought up short as the door at the far end swung open and a man came through. There is a look to FSB agents that goes beyond cheap suits and grim expressions. It's their thousand-yard stare, the look they give you that makes it clear they think you're little people, that your life is virtually worthless, that they already have you in custody.

Without a second thought, Bourne turned around, only to find a second FSB agent coming toward him from the way he had come. This one opened his coat slightly, revealing his Arsenal Strizh, a full 9mm Parabellum pistol, the successor to the storied Makarov. Whatever he saw in Bourne's eyes caused him to shake his head. His hand swept out, indicating the other passengers in the car. At that moment, Bourne felt the presence of the first agent, the taller and thinner one. The muzzle of his Strizh, hidden by the wings of his open greatcoat, pressed against the base of Bourne's spine.

The stubbier one jerked his head, said, "Let's go," in a Russian accent that told Bourne he came from St. Petersburg.

With Stubby in the lead, they marched Bourne back to the conference cabin.

"Open it and step in," Stubby said. "Just as if nothing's happened."

"Nothing *has* happened," Bourne said, and received a hard poke in the back with the Strizh's muzzle.

"*Svóloch'!*" *Dick!* the agent said from behind.

"*Zatknís'!*" *Shut up!* snapped Stubby, clearly the senior partner.

Bourne opened the door and entered the compartment. Mala was still fast asleep, her torso slumped, her head turned away from the door. The agents stepped in on Bourne's heels.

"Don't wake her," Bourne said.

The taller agent snickered, as if to say he couldn't care less about the woman. "We weren't told about her." He could not keep the salacious tone out of his voice as he eyed Mala.

"Stay away from her," Stubby said in no uncertain terms.

The tall agent tore his gaze from Mala to look at Stubby. He opened his mouth, as if about to say something, but at the last moment apparently decided against it, bit his lip instead.

"I'm going to get him," Stubby said. "Don't do anything stupid."

Taller snickered again. When Stubby was gone, he waved the Strizh in Mala's general direction. "What's her story?"

"What's yours?" Bourne said.

He swung the pistol toward Bourne's knees. "Don't make me, shithead."

He sidled around so as to keep his eye on Bourne while he approached Mala. "She a good fuck?"

"Better than your mother."

Taller's neck and face went beet red. When the color reached his hairline, he touched Mala's foot tentatively with one of his steel-toed shoes.

"I told you not to wake her," Bourne said.

"Who gives a fuck what you say!" Taller drew back his foot and kicked Mala's ankle hard.

Before he knew what was happening, she had swiveled her hips, cocked her left leg and lashed out with a mighty kick to his solar plexus.

Taller made a guttural sound like an animal going to the slaughter. Bourne caught him around the neck, swung him into the table.

"Ack!" Taller exclaimed, even while he jammed his elbow into Bourne's side.

Mala grabbed the pistol out of his grip, but the men were so tightly wound together she couldn't aim properly.

"Don't!" Bourne shouted. "The shot will only bring more FSB."

Then he was too busy dealing with Taller, who had managed to reverse their positions. Now he slammed

Bourne against the compartment wall, jammed the heel of his hand under Bourne's chin, pushing upward. Then, using all his weight, he body-slammed Bourne against the wall, over and over. Mala, reversing the pistol, brought the butt down on the back of his head, but he seemed unfazed.

Bourne brought his hands in, used his thumbs to dig into the bundles of nerves just below and behind Taller's ears. That the FSB agent felt. Grabbing him by the front of his jacket, Bourne turned him, rammed his head against the window with such force the glass shattered. Still, Taller wouldn't give up. His hands sought Bourne's neck, his red-rimmed eyes blazed with fury, but when Bourne pressed down on him, the jagged shards of glass punctured the back of his neck. One of them severed the third cervical vertebra from the fourth, and Taller was done. His hands dropped away and all the fire vanished from his eyes as his body went slack.

Before Bourne and Mala had a chance to exchange a word, the compartment door opened and Stubby entered, his right arm holding his Strizh straight out in front of him. Before he had a chance to take in the scene, Mala had stepped forward, wrapped one arm around his, and broke it at the elbow.

Stubby gave a yelp, dropped to his knees. Bourne stepped toward him and Mala aimed Taller's pistol at whoever came through the door next.

"That's enough," First Minister Timur Savasin said. He brushed past Stubby without giving him so much as a glance.

"Is it," Mala said rhetorically. She kept the Strizh aimed at Savasin's head. "I don't think so."

Savasin raised his hands, open palms toward them. "I come in peace," he said.

"That's a sick joke," Mala said, indicating the two agents.

"You certainly did a number on them." He was looking at Bourne, seeking to engage him directly, rather than through his companion, whose identity was a mystery to him. "I apologize for any inconvenience their, um, overzealousness caused you."

"As you can see, the inconvenience was all theirs."

Savasin shrugged. "They're replaceable, I assure you."

"So it goes in the Russian Federation," Mala said.

"Mr. Bourne, since I have no dominion in this compartment, would you be so kind as to ask your companion to lower her gun. This conversation will be somewhat more difficult with a Strizh pointed at my head."

"In a moment, perhaps," Bourne said. "I want to know what the hell this is all about."

"I confess it's a long story," Savasin said.

"I'll bet," Mala said, ignoring Bourne's silent signal to desist.

"Tell me who you are," Bourne said.

"You know very well who I am."

"Even if I do, I want to hear it from your own lips."

"Timur Ludmirovich Savasin, First Minister, Russian Federation."

Bourne crossed to the sofa, sat down on it. "For days now this woman and I have been hunted by *spetsnaz*. On whose orders? Yours?"

"That was a mistake."

"Really?" Mala said. "Jason, let me put a bullet in this lying bastard's brain."

"She'll do it, Timur Ludmirovich," Bourne said. "Killing is like breathing to her."

Savasin licked his lips. "Who is she, Mr. Bourne?"

"The Angelmaker," Mala said.

Savasin started. "I thought the Angelmaker was a bit of fiction, a fairy tale made up by certain people to frighten their competitors."

"If killing them was frightening them," Mala said, "then that's what they did."

Savasin stared at Bourne. "She is who she says she is?"

"Take it to the bank, Timur." He gestured to Mala. "Let's have it."

Without taking her eyes off Savasin, she came to Bourne, handed over the pistol, which Bourne aimed at the first minister. "See if he's carrying—and take his mobile as well."

Savasin closed his eyes for a moment as she put her hands on him. His right hand trembled a bit.

"No weapons," she said, stepping away. "Got his mobile, though. Only the one." She came and sat beside Bourne on the sofa.

"What about Stubby there?" Bourne said.

Savasin looked bewildered "Who?"

"Your man with the broken arm. Looks to me like he's in real pain." He looked at Savasin. "I assume you have more men aboard."

The first minister nodded. Taking the mobile from Mala, Bourne said, "Tell me how to contact them. Let's have them clean up this mess."

———

Ten minutes later, when, save for the broken window and some smeared bloodstains on the floor, a sense of order had been restored to the conference cabin, and the door had been closed and locked against further intrusion, Bourne said, "You said you had a long story to tell." He glanced at his watch. "We get into Moscow in just over an hour. You had better hope you can tell it in that time."

"All right." Savasin nodded. "May I sit down?"

"I think it best that you remain standing." Bourne still had the pistol pointed at him. "Begin, Timur Ludmirovich. Tick-tock."

———

At the same time Bourne, the Angelmaker, and Timur Savasin were hurtling from St. Petersburg to Moscow, Savasin's brother, Konstantin, was on his swift jet winging its way home. He spent the first part of the nine-hour and twenty-five-minute flight reading the Treadstone material Marshall Fulmer had kindly provided. He read the Bourne file three times straight through, then he went back to check certain paragraphs, using a pen with red ink to highlight a number of words and phrases he wished to keep uppermost in his mind.

After a light meal, washed down with a glass of icy vodka, he set the files aside, thumbed the buttons on his seat, lifting his legs and reclining him back. Folding his hands across his belly, he closed his eyes and allowed his mind to traverse the file, to linger over those paragraphs and, especially, the words and phrases he had highlighted in red.

In this fashion he drifted off, and when, an hour later, he awakened, he had his answer. He had identified the weak spot in Bourne's armor. He knew how to drill down to the core of him.

36

I DON'T EVEN know their real names."

"Alyosha Orlova and Nikolay Rozin," Soraya Moore said over the secure line that was a part of the government jet she had sent to pick up her agent in the field and bring her out of the cold. "You did a stellar job, Morgana."

The jet was parked at the airport in Kalmar, where Morgana had boarded it as it was being refueled. The interior was an odd design: only four seats, front and aft. In between, a series of what looked to be storage lockers.

"Have you been back to the hotel?" Soraya asked.

"No. I slept at a friend's."

Soraya's voice became wary. "What friend?"

"Her name's Natalie Soringen."

"I'll have her checked out," Soraya said. She sounded more than a bit annoyed but seemed to put that aside when she said, "You will have no problem at your old hotel."

"I'd assume the place would be swarming, following the murder-suicide."

"I fixed it with Stockholm. There'll be an inquiry, but that will be window dressing. And, best of all, the identities of the deceased will be suppressed."

"I'm impressed. How did you manage that bit of magic?"

"That's why I get the comfy chair." Soraya laughed. "I pointed out to the Swedish powers-that-be that not only were the victims Russian nationals, but they were spies. No one in the Swedish government wants a diplomatic run-in with the Kremlin."

"Let sleeping lions lie."

"That's one way to put it, I suppose."

After a moment's silence, Morgana said, "I don't want to go home."

"What's that? But your brief is done—a more thorough success than I could have imagined. I was tasked with bringing down Alyosha Orlova—Françoise Sevigne, as you knew her. I chose you not only because you were a field neophyte but because Françoise had befriended you. She trusted you; you were one of her scam targets. An important one, I might add."

Morgana was taken aback. "Why didn't you tell me who she really was?"

"I think you can answer that yourself."

Morgana considered a minute. "You wanted all my responses to be genuine. You didn't want to give her a hint anything was amiss."

"Sometimes," Soraya said, "keeping your agent in the field in the dark is the best course of action."

Morgana knew she was right, knew that she had

done the right thing, but still she was stung. Soraya had used her, just as Françoise had. But soon enough she realized that the two motivations were light years apart.

"Okay. I understand," Morgana said, "but the reason I got suspicious was I saw Alyosha board a boat docked at the marina here. It's Gora Maslov's boat."

Silence on the line. Finally: "What are you saying, Morgana?" in a measured, cautious tone.

"I want to go after Gora Maslov."

"Wait a minute! You can't just—"

"Look, Alyosha was working for Maslov, that much seems true. I want to know what they were up to."

"But—"

"Don't you?"

"Perhaps. But, with your brief completed, my primary objective now is to get you home safe and sound. I've already subjected you to enough danger."

Soraya Moore was a pro, seasoned at that. She possessed the control's hard, pragmatic line of thought. But she also had something else, Morgana thought, something that drew her to Soraya, that made her want to work for her. It struck her at their first interview, when Soraya put out the first recruitment feelers. She had a heart, and a heart was something very dear to Morgana. She thought she loved Soraya, even though she knew perfectly well you should never love your boss—or, in this case, your control. But then why not? she wondered. Wasn't loyalty at a premium in the world of spies? Something to be held close, something precious.

"I'm the one in the field, Soraya," she said now. "I think I'm better—"

"Stop right there. Morgana, listen to me. I threw you to the lions, it's true. But this was a special circumstance. I had no one else."

"Thanks very much!"

"You misunderstand. I had full confidence in you and what you're capable of. But the truth is you lack training. I can't allow you to remain in the field."

"As you know I'm an ace at all firearms. What you don't know is that my father—"

"A former SEAL. I've read his jacket. He was quite a fine one, brilliant, really."

Now Morgana loved Soraya even more. "Yes. He trained me himself." Another bit of silence. She could almost hear Soraya thinking, recalculating, recalibrating the conversation. "Plus, really, when you think about it, my job at Meme LLC was to solve puzzles—the most difficult puzzles, I might add, puzzles that stumped others in my area of expertise. I find that the field is no different; it's a matter of solving puzzles."

"No, it's very different, Morgana. In the field you're constantly in harm's way."

"I find I like that." This time the silence was tense and brittle. She was about to say, *I'm staying, no matter what you say,* but she felt the wrongness of it. Her mouth could lead her down a bad path with a bad ending. Instead, she said: "But I'll come home." Hearing her father's voice in one ear, she waited a beat before adding, "If that's what you think is best."

Silence. Then: "You're a very clever girl."

"Thank you."

"I took a lot of chances with your brief. What if your friend Françoise didn't come through with her promise?

I would have pulled you out of custody. You were never in any real danger as long as you were here in D.C."

"But once I came here, to Kalmar, I was in the real lions' den." Now was the time, she thought, to push it. "What you must understand is that I've become one of them now—a lion. Like my father."

"I appreciate the confidence you've gained, but I fear you're overreaching. You'll be going up against Gora Maslov, a hardened *grupperovka* boss. He'll eat you for breakfast."

"I don't think so," Morgana said, a thrill down her spine: she had won. "I have a way in."

"And what might that be?"

"The point is both Fran—Alyosha and Rozin were deeply interested in the Bourne Initiative, the code for which, I should add, I've not been able to crack. And now I don't think I or anyone outside the Russian team that General Karpov hand-picked to design it will."

"That's of no importance now," Soraya said. "The Bourne Initiative is nothing more than noise, Russian disinformation."

"What? It most certainly is not. The Initiative is real. I've been working on fragments of it and—"

"Getting nowhere, right?"

"Yes, but—"

"All meant for us to chase our tails like idiots. I got this directly from Marshall Fulmer, the new national security advisor, and he ought to know."

"I don't know where he's getting his intel from, Soraya, but I'm telling you it's bogus."

"An intercept of the Russian Unit 309. I've seen the pages, Morgana. They're authentic."

"They're authentic, all right. Authentic disinformation," Morgana said forcefully. "I know those code fragments are real beyond any shadow of a doubt. Do you know how? I found a legitimate zero-day trigger embedded in every one of the fragments I pulled out of the dark net. That's the only thing I was able to decode, but it's vital."

Another silence on the line, longer this time, the tension ratcheted up a couple of notches. "I'm listening. Continue."

"I'm damn good at my job. Don't you think I'd be able to spot fake code, no matter how well put together? No, the Bourne Initiative is real, and it's a ticking time bomb with an unknown target."

"Okay. Let's say you're right. I can't go to the higher-ups and tell them that based on what you've said. Fulmer will swat me down like a gnat. I just got this position; until I prove myself I've got to watch my p's and q's. I can't rock the boat."

"Then don't tell anyone. We'll act together."

"The two of us won't be enough."

"Working alone is essential in this instance."

"So you've said. You sound like the one person I believe can help us without physically interfering with whatever you have in mind with Gora. And he knows Gora. Though he knew his father even better. In fact, he was involved with General Karpov in killing Dimitri Maslov."

"Who are we talking about?"

"Jason Bourne."

Morgana looked around, as if they had just now entered top-secret territory. The interior of the plane was still and serene, no one in her vicinity to overhear her end of the conversation. She returned her attention to Soraya half a world away. "I don't understand."

"Remember a few years back when Bourne was accused of trying to assassinate the former president, and it turned out he'd saved him instead?"

"Sure."

"That was because of me—Sonya and I, who were being held captive."

Morgana gave a gasp. "When your husband was killed."

A small hesitation. "Yes."

"I'm so sorry, Soraya. All over again so sorry."

"Thank you. But to get back to Bourne, he and I go way back. We were in the field together."

"So you're former colleagues."

"More than that. Let's just say I know him more than well."

"Huh!"

Soraya laughed, dry and rough as sand. "Well put."

"I've been wanting to speak with him ever since Mac sent me the first fragment of Initiative code. If anyone knows about the Initiative it's got to be Bourne." Morgana's excitement was ramping up. "You know how to get in touch with him?"

"No, but I know someone who does. A man right here in D.C. by the name of Deron."

"Do you have Deron's number? I'll call him the moment we hang up."

"Deron won't talk to you, let alone tell you how to get in touch with Bourne," Soraya said. "No, Deron knows me. I'll call him."

"I'll sit tight, then."

"Back to the Initiative itself. You don't know what it's meant to do?"

"No."

"Do you know when the zero-day trigger is set for?"

"Yes. Forty hours from now." Morgana took a breath. "Another reason why I need to stay here."

"Bourne may not know this. He needs to."

"Yes."

"Now tell me what you have in mind." Soraya's voice was sharp and clear, which told Morgana a great deal about her. Unlike the other mandarins who ran various clandestine services whom she had met or had to deal with, Soraya was flexible. As a former field agent, she knew that you were sometimes required, or forced, to pivot on a dime in order to react to or take advantage of the changing situation in the field.

Morgana had had all night to think about a plan and Natalie to talk it over with. She knew she couldn't get to Gora Maslov on her own. "Maslov must be involved in the Bourne Initiative. That's why Alyosha went to see him. Why else would he be here in this Swedish backwater at the same time as Alyosha and Nikolay, with them presumably helping me break the code? And if I'm right and they are all in it together, then he is our chance to get to the Initiative before its inner clock detonates."

Silence on the line, just the hollowness, the faint arrhythmic clicking of the security programs that shielded their conversation from electronic spying.

"All of this tracks," Soraya said. "The bits of mysterious code you've pulled off the dark web could be enticements—coming attractions, you might say. In that event, the Bourne Initiative is going to be auctioned off to the highest bidder, imminently."

"And I believe Gora will be one of the bidders. Now you can see why physical backup is the last thing I need. The more of our people here, the better the chance of Gora becoming suspicious."

"Lord, what have I unleashed in you?"

"The law of unintended consequences, that's what," Morgana said. "And it's not your doing. Sooner or later I think this was bound to happen."

"I think it's my good luck, then." The sound of what might be Soraya shuffling papers. "You'll need some form of backup, Morgana."

"I've got you. You're all I need."

Soraya laughed. "You're really a piece of work."

"It's the only way I know how to be now. And for better or for worse, I have you to thank for that."

Soraya sighed. "Hold on." Several moments passed with only the hollowness and the electronic clicking. When she returned, she said, "Give me three hours. I'll have a secured Bluetooth earwig and a pair of earrings couriered to you from our Stockholm office."

"Earrings?"

Soraya laughed again. "The transmitter for the earwig is in one of them. Don't lose it."

"There are a couple of other things I need, stat."

"Name them." Morgana did. "You'll have them." Then Soraya's tone altered. "And, Morgana?"

"Yes?"

"I won't forget this."

"Is that good or bad?" Morgana asked, but Soraya Moore had already disconnected.

———————

"I am to use Dima Orlov's name with you, Mr. Bourne."

Bourne sat forward. "Why?"

"He and I are working together."

The Angelmaker laughed. "Dima Orlov working with the first minister?" She shook her head. "I don't think so."   •

"I'm not here as first minister," Savasin said. "I did not seek out Dima as first minister, but as the brother of Konstantin, who has plans to capture you, Mr. Bourne. Capture you, torture you, then kill you."

"Many have tried," Bourne said.

"Konstantin is a snake. He's ruthless and devious. He lives to create diabolical traps. I beg you not to underestimate him."

"More people have died underestimating their enemy than I care to count." Bourne waved the Strizh back and forth. "I wouldn't concern myself with that."

"But I do, Mr. Bourne. Very much so. Your safety, your knowledge is critical, Dima believes, to finding the codes for the Initiative, for keeping them out of the hands of maniacs like Konstantin."

"Of course my help is critical," Bourne said. "According to General MacQuerrie, Dima Orlov is the one who stole the Initiative right after Boris was murdered."

"What? But that's impossible."

"Why?" Bourne said. "Why is it impossible, Timur?"

"Katya said that he and General Karpov were good friends."

"Maybe that's true," Bourne said, "but the Angelmaker here knows that Boris's death set the two remaining partners against each other. You see, Boris was the peacemaker. Both Dima and MacQuerrie trusted him, but it seems they didn't trust each other. Now only Dima is left, and Dima has the Initiative."

"Then why did he rope me in?" Savasin shook his head. "What does he need me for?"

"Did he contact you, Timur?"

"No. I went to him."

"Why would you do that?" Bourne asked.

"Because my brother . . ." Savasin's voice trailed off as his thoughts transferred onto another track.

"Konstantin, yes. Dima needs you as protection against the threat your brother presents to him. Konstantin is a threat to you; that's how he roped you in."

"And you," Savasin said. "Why did he send me to find you?"

"Friends close," Bourne said. "Enemies closer."

Bourne lowered the pistol, set it down between him and Mala. He gestured. "Take a pew, Timur. It's true-confession time."

———

And so for the first time in his life, including when he was a little boy, Timur Savasin sat down and spoke honestly. He could not remember when he had learned to lie about everything—the moment, or time, was too distant for him to dredge up. But he knew the habit was formed as a response to Konstantin, a kind of protection from the malefic entity his parents had given life to.

And in talking honestly he experienced an enormous sense of relief, as of a terrible weight being lifted from his shoulders, as if his brother had consigned him to the role of Atlas, the weight of the world crushing him every waking moment, from which he had finally freed himself.

"The ironic thing," he said, after he had recounted his meeting with Dima and Katya in great detail, "is after having spent so many years hating and fearing Boris Karpov, I now feel as if I'm moving into his orbit. Konstantin covets General Karpov's position and power, and I know I must do everything in my power to stop him. Karpov was a humanist, Dima and Katya have opened my eyes to that. And now I am eager for the opportunity to understand his friendship with you, Mr. Bourne. Perhaps that is the one good thing that will come out of the dire straits we all find ourselves in, sparked by General Karpov's cyber Initiative, which has come to be known by both the Americans and us as the Bourne Initiative.

"Dima and Katya believe that you are the key to retrieving the codes. They are convinced that Karpov must have left some clue for you that will lead you to it, because it's clear to me that none of the original three partners, two of whom are dead, know what happened to it."

"If, as MacQuerrie believed, Dima hijacked the Initiative, then there is something—some key element—missing from it, and they think I have it," Bourne said.

"Do you?"

"No," Bourne said. "Boris left me his boat, which was sunk by the Americans. That's it."

"Well, that's disappointing."

"When it comes to Boris, people have gotten everything wrong. He would never have created a cyber weapon aimed at the United States. Knowing Boris as I did, I never believed that bit of fiction. What was his aim, then? MacQuerrie said that the code was meant to freeze the security systems of the largest international banks, allowing the three of them access to all the banks' accounts. MacQuerrie believed they were on the cusp of pulling off an electronic theft of unprecedented proportions."

Savasin's eyes narrowed. "I am no novice in reading between the lines, Mr. Bourne. There is something about General MacQuerrie's explanation that doesn't ring true to you."

"Not exactly," Bourne replied. "My sense is this. Boris loved money as much as the next person, more maybe. But he wasn't about to steal from anyone and everyone; that simply went against his grain. So what then? First, I believe Boris was getting ready to leave Russia. He had just gotten married; he had no other family left alive. When he left Russia on his honeymoon, he couldn't be pressured to return. He and his wife weren't coming back.

"So if we accept this scenario, which I do, where was Boris going to get his drop-dead money? He was well off, but not an oligarch by any means; he was unbribable. No, the cyber Initiative was meant to allow him to pick and choose, to take from the terrorist leaders and criminals who were housing their money in those banks whose coffers would be open to him. That plan is Boris Karpov to a T."

"Then he was murdered."

"Which set off a power struggle between the two remaining partners," the Angelmaker said.

"During which someone made off with the codes," Bourne continued. "He or she has them and now means to auction them off to the highest bidder, someone who doesn't have Boris's sense of morality."

Savasin raked his fingers through his hair. "They've created a very deep pit, indeed."

"Add another 'very,'" Bourne said. "MacQuerrie told me that while Boris meant the codes to freeze banks' security software, the Initiative could be directed at the deepest secrets of a sovereign nation."

"Like the United States."

"Or the Russian Federation."

"The stars are aligning." Savasin smiled. "You see, Mr. Bourne, you and I are moving toward the kind of détente you shared with General Karpov for many years."

Mala grunted in clear derision.

"I think it's safe to say," Bourne said, "that we're nowhere close to a détente, Timur."

Savasin nodded, keeping his expression neutral. "As you wish. But now I must tell you something, and from what you've told me the truth of it is unclear. Dima said that there is a timer set into the Initiative."

"A timer?"

"Yes. A zero-day trigger, he called it."

Both Bourne and Mala knew what a zero-day trigger was.

"Did he tell you when the exploit will activate?"

Savasin shook his head. "He claimed not to know. But he also said that the day was close. Very close."

Mala looked from Bourne to Savasin and back again. "There are two things Dima can do with the Initiative if he can retrieve the codes. He can use it for himself, or he can set up an international auction. Can you imagine how much such a cyber weapon would fetch on the clandestine network that terrorist leaders, demagogues, and heads of state of evil intent inhabit?" Her gaze returned to Savasin. "That group would include your Sovereign, First Minister, you know that, right?"

"It would also include my brother," Savasin replied. "He's doing everything in his power to get his hands on the Initiative." Savasin leaned forward, elbows on knees. "To do so, I guarantee that he's going to cross any and all lines he feels he needs to. Sooner or later, Konstantin always gets what he wants."

37

I'M ONLY DOING this for the money." Natalie, the young woman Morgana had spoken to after she had debarked from Gora's boat, swept her blond hair behind her ear. "I have a toddler. She was at my aunt's the night you slept over."

"Spare me," Morgana told her bluntly. "You want your revenge on Gora Maslov. You wouldn't have agreed to meet me otherwise."

They were in Kalmar City Park, standing at the apex of a small but beautiful wooden bridge painted a bright Dutch blue. Below them, in the water of the pond it spanned, water spiders skated across the surface, and now and again, a fish would rise, its mouth agape to scoop up unwary insects flying too low.

Natalie stirred uneasily beside Morgana. "Okay, but there's only so much punishment and humiliation I'm willing to take."

"Think of your toddler at home," Morgana said with

evident cynicism. "Do you have an ailing mother, as well?"

Fire erupted behind Natalie's eyes, then just as quickly was extinguished. Her laugh was deep-throated and genuine. "Christ, I can't get away with anything with you."

"Better not to try," Morgana said, her tone lightened considerably by an intimation of friendship. How quickly she had learned from Françoise. It was still difficult to think of her as Alyosha Orlova.

"I like you, Morgana. You're not like other girls I've met."

"I don't believe in playing by the rules," Morgana said, "because they're all made by men."

"Men like Gora." Now Natalie could not keep the bitterness out of her voice. "Corrupt men. Evil men."

The afternoon was waning, the light richer, deeper, the shadows lengthening, so that the children who skipped along the bridge behind them broke out in laughter, running after each other's shadow, as if they could actually be caught. *To be a child again!* Morgana thought. She thought of Peter Pan, whose shadow Wendy had to stitch on him so that he would have one just like everyone else. She felt a bit like Peter Pan now, skimming, like the water spiders, over the atmosphere of Kalmar, seeing the park, the neighboring castle, all the way down to the marina, where Gora's boat basked in the late-day sunlight like a monstrous beast waiting to tear her limb from limb.

"Time to go," Morgana said softly. "He was pleased to hear from you, yes?"

"Insofar as Gora can be pleased, yes, I suppose so. I told him I wanted more money."

"That I'm sure he could understand. And when you told him you might be able to bring a friend this time?"

"He laughed." Natalie spat into the water, scattering the spiders, who must be thinking, What gods are these? "He laughs like a fucking hyena."

They had been through all this before, of course, but Morgana's plan was so acutely calibrated it paid to repeat every step of it multiple times. Plus, it calmed her—like a well-worn prayer before bedtime.

Natalie took Morgana shopping for a dress shorter than any Morgana had ever tried on, let alone worn, heels far higher than any she had ever tried on, let alone worn, and the right pieces of paste jewelry—a bracelet and a necklace just a touch longer than a choker.

"Men like a jewel nestled in the hollow of your throat," Natalie told her. "It reminds them of where their tongue will be in the middle of the night."

When she saw Morgana dressed for the evening with Gora, she said, "You look like ten thousand bucks."

"You mean like a slut."

Natalie shrugged. "Like everything, it's a matter of perspective. I think you're hot; so will Gora."

Morgana lifted the hem of the dress to reveal the small pistol in its chamois holder strapped high up on her inner thigh.

Natalie winked. "Now for the *pièce de résistance*. Makeup!"

The same two goons Morgana had seen when she had spied on Françoise stepping aboard Gora's boat were still at their posts, eyeing everyone who came within fifty paces with undisguised suspicion.

Natalie swallowed the pill Morgana had given her. "This had better work," she muttered under her breath as they strutted down the wooden planks.

"Maybe they won't pat us down," Morgana said, out of the corner of her mouth.

"Right. I think this is nuts, but for the money you're paying me you're the boss."

It was dark; the sun had set more than an hour ago, and lights sparkled along the pier. The water around Gora's boat danced in reflections of the cabin and deck lamps. The sky was a milky gray, the undersides of clouds pale as fish bellies. The goons recognized Natalie, but the one who had hustled her off days ago gave no indication he recalled the incident.

They gestured, and Natalie stood very still. They checked her evening bag, though it was clearly too small to hold a weapon of any serious danger. As they patted Natalie down, quickly and expertly, they flashed glimpses of their Strizh pistols in snug shoulder holsters. Natalie was clean. Then they turned their attention to Morgana. She spread her legs a little, as if she were bracing herself against the rocking of a small boat.

They found the pistol, of course, and grabbing her by the arm, hustled her onto the deck and into the main salon, Natalie just behind.

One of the goons held up the pistol. "Look what we found," he said in guttural Russian.

"On which one?" Gora said. He had been sprawled on one of a pair of sofas, but now he sprang up. Perhaps deliberately, he was flanked by a pair of marble busts of

Roman caesars set on black columns. He wore a cream-colored silk shirt, lightweight slacks, and huaraches. He glared at Natalie. "Is this some kind of payback?"

"It was on the other one," the goon said, handing over the pistol to his boss. "The new girl."

"That so?" Gora turned his attention to Morgana. "What's your name?" he said, switching to English.

"Lana."

He was standing right in front of her now, close enough for her to smell his scent, part cologne, part sweat.

It was emblematic of how he viewed her that he did not ask for her last name; either he didn't care or he assumed she would lie. "Do you know who I am, Lana?"

"I don't care who you are," Morgana said, "as long as I get paid at the end of the session."

"The *session*," Gora said mockingly. "How professional are we?" With his dark brows knit together, his tone hardened as he brandished the pistol. "What the fuck d'you think you're doing, bringing a weapon like this onto my boat?"

"Having a little fun." Morgana's heart was pounding so hard it was giving her a headache.

"Fun?" Gora echoed. "Okay, bitch, I'll show you some fun." He aimed the pistol at Natalie's forehead. His eyes never left Morgana's. "Shall I pull the trigger?"

The point was not to bat even an eyelid. "Go ahead."

"Blow your friend's brains out."

"If that's your pleasure."

A flicker of hesitation passed across Gora's face, like a fleeting shadow, and was gone. His expression hardened like clay in the sun. "If you mean to play chicken with me, you've made a serious mistake." He pulled the trigger.

A spray of water hit Natalie square between the eyes.

The goons looked stunned, Natalie blew water out of her nostrils, and Gora stood still as a statue, while Morgana laughed and laughed until tears came to her eyes. By that time, Gora was laughing, too.

"Jesus Christ," he said. "Jesus Christ." Then, waving a hand: "Someone fetch her a towel."

He handed back the gun, grips first, and watched Morgana tuck it away in its holster, all the while giving him a good look at her creamy thighs and the tip of the shadowed triangle above.

"Natalie, I've underestimated you," he said as Natalie patted her face with the towel she had been given. "You really know how to choose your friends." He still hadn't taken his eyes from Morgana. His gaze roamed over her body in the way of ancient Roman slave traders; he did everything but look inside her mouth at her teeth and gums.

"You know, Lana," he said, "I can see your nipples through the fabric of your dress."

Like all women, Morgana had been subjected to the male gaze, but never like this. It was like being undressed and eviscerated. She had been reduced to a piece of raw meat ready to be devoured, without even a single thought as to its effect on her. In that one moment, Gora had stripped her of her humanity. It hurt—it hurt more than she could have imagined, like a knife slash, the first brick in the wall of domination. She wondered how Natalie managed it without curling up like a flower deprived of the elements it needs to survive and thrive.

"Perhaps it's the trick of the light."

A wicked smile sprouted on Gora's face like a noxious weed. "Right."

Natalie had been completely forgotten. She was old news, used goods, her value greatly diminished. Gora was homing in on the new girl: virgin territory, so to speak.

"Why don't you lift up your skirt again," Gora said. "I'd like to see that pistol wrapped around your thigh."

"You're the man," Morgana replied. "Why don't you do the heavy lifting?"

Gora laughed and reached for the hem of her dress. Morgana stepped back a pace. He came after her, faster this time. As his fingers were about to touch the hem, she swatted them away.

Gora stopped then, looking at her as if through a different lens. "You're not like the others, are you?"

"I am who I am," Morgana said neutrally. "Nothing more, nothing less."

"That's for me to decide."

He held out his hand, and when Morgana took it she felt as if she had put her head between the open jaws of a crocodile. Her skin began to crawl.

Morgana could sense Natalie's jealous gaze, mouth partly open, pearl teeth visible, but she had no idea what she was really thinking. She just prayed to whatever dark gods ruled her new shadowed world that Natalie wouldn't lose her composure, that she would follow Morgana's plan to the letter.

She allowed him to draw her down the wood-paneled corridor, past doorways to the formal dining area, the study he used as an office, several guest cabins.

The master suite was enormous, as plush and well appointed as any five-star hotel suite. It was all polished wood and brass fittings. A crystal chandelier hung from the center of the ceiling, and oriental lamps on hand-carved tables that were built into the wall haloed everything in an intimate glow. The king-size bed was covered in Frette linens, the love seat and two club chairs were covered in moiré silk. The teak deck was covered in an antique Isfahan carpet that quite possibly belonged in a museum. On the walls hung a Marilyn painting by Warhol and an early-career one by Jeff Koons, of the provocateur-artist himself entwined lustfully with his former wife, the former Italian porn star, Cicciolina. It was meant to be erotic, but in Morgana's opinion was just plain crass, which is how she found pretty much all of Koons's work to be. However, the Warhol's garish primary colors and Koons's even more garish subject matter clearly mirrored Gora's idea of setting the mood for a night of Russian debauchery.

Morgana glanced around. No books, not even a bad erotic novel. *Why am I not surprised?* she thought. At last, her gaze alighted on Gora Maslov. Natalie had said that in whatever he does Gora tries too hard, and she was right. This was even reflected in his clothing, which was meant to seem casual, but like the bedroom itself, was a self-conscious attempt at aping the hip-hop mogul of current American culture. It was all she could do not to laugh. But, having absorbed the intel on the Maslovs Soraya had sent with the courier, she knew there was nothing amusing about the family's history of murder, extortion, intimidation, and criminal enterprise. Dimitri, Gora's father, was especially impressive, until he was gunned down in a barber shop, 1930s Chicago gangster style, by Boris Karpov.

It seemed to her now, regarding Gora's vainglorious pose, that the son was suffering under an inferiority complex, trying and failing to live up to his father's image. This was not a good sign. People like Gora tended to be nasty, volatile, aggressive, sometimes violent, beneath their calm, smiling exterior. She needed to be especially careful not to make a false step. This setup could go south in the space of a heartbeat. She took off her heels.

When he grabbed her, Morgana said, "I have to pee."

"He likes to watch me pee," Natalie had told her.

Gora pointed to an open doorway behind her: the bathroom glowing like a jewel box. She turned, headed toward it, acutely aware of him following a pace behind.

When she crossed over the threshold, he said, "Don't you want to close the door?"

"Not especially." She did not bother to put down the seat; instead she turned back toward him, hiked up her dress, and slowly bent her knees. With her legs on either side of the porcelain bowl and her eyes steady on him, she canted she hips slightly forward.

His gaze burned into her. His mouth was half open. She could see a stirring beneath the zipper of his trousers.

"Ready?" she said. "Tell me when."

A little animal noise exploded from the back of Gora's throat.

A high-pitched scream, a loud crash, and the excited voices of the goons raised in explosive Russian curses put an immediate damper on Gora Maslov's erotic fantasy. With a guttural curse of his own, he ran out of the bedroom, down the corridor.

What he confronted was Natalie on the carpet, beside a pool of stinking vomit and the broken shards of one of the busts of Caesar. The other bust—of Augustus, as it happened—looked down upon this plebian mess with true caesarian disinterest.

"What the fuck happened?" Gora shouted.

"I dunno, boss," Goon Number One said.

"She clutched her stomach, staggered, knocked the head off its pedestal, and was sick," Goon Number Two continued.

"Then she collapsed," Goon Number One concluded.

"Is she alive, dead, or in between?" Gora asked.

"Dunno," they both said at once.

"We haven't checked," said Goon Number Two.

"Well, for fuck's sake, do!" Gora shouted. Whatever had sprouted in his trousers had suddenly turned inward like a frightened turtle.

Meanwhile, according to plan, Morgana had moved swiftly and silently on little bare feet down the corridor to Gora's study. She knew she had very little time. She was looking for some proof that linked Gora to the impending auction of the Bourne Initiative, but what form that might take she had no idea.

"Even if you don't think you have time, take in the whole scene," her father had taught her. *"Nine out of ten times whatever you're looking for will get caught in the corner of your eye."*

And so it was. Desk, task chair, laptop, mobile phone and sat phone lying side by side, neat as soldiers on guard duty. The laptop was off, the mobile was guarded by a fingerprint reader, the sat phone had no numbers stored in it. Not a scrap of paper on the desktop, and the drawers contained nothing of value. But a blotch of yellow stuck in the corner of her eye: a Post-it note stuck to the left-side bezel of the laptop's screen. It was curious how many people did that with their most important reminders. So insecure, and yet, like incriminating emails and texts, done all the time.

Moving around behind the desk, she leaned over, took a close look at what was written in the little yellow square: an international phone number and the word *Keyre*. A name? A place? She didn't know. Just below, another international number, this one without a name or a place. Using the mnemonic her father had taught her, she memorized the numbers, figuring they must be extremely important if Gora hadn't stored them in either phone.

"She isn't dead," Goon Number One said as he crouched beside Natalie in the salon.

"Well, that's something," Gora said distractedly. In his mind's eye he was seeing the image of Morgana, her dress raised, her knees bent, her white thighs exposed, asking him, *Tell me when.* The frightened turtle had vanished, replaced by a snake, slowly stirring. "Get the cleaning materials," he barked at Goon Number Two. "Clean up this mess, then get back to your usual post on the dock. At this late stage I don't want anyone nosing around."

As Goon Number One lifted Natalie's head and shoulders off the carpet, she gave a tiny moan. Her eyelids fluttered.

"Clean her up, too, then get her to bed in one of the guest suites," Gora ordered. "And for fuck's sake get that stink out of here."

Goon Number One wiped Natalie's mouth with the still-damp towel from her water pistol experience, then lifted her in his arms, following his boss down the corridor toward the guest cabins.

"Make sure you get her out of those soiled clothes," Morgana heard Gora say over his shoulder to Goon Number One. "Wash off all the muck. There'll be something for her to wear in one of the closets."

Morgana was standing in the corridor outside the master suite when Gora saw her.

"What's happened?" she said.

"Nothing. Your friend got sick, that's all."

Morgana's brow furrowed. "How sick?"

"I told you, it's nothing."

Gora reached for her, eager to return to the image in his mind's eyes, but Morgana flew past him, running down the corridor.

"Wait!" Gora cried, and then, seeing that she wasn't listening, "Fuck all." He headed after her.

Morgana entered the room where Goon Number One had laid Natalie on the bed. He was cleaning the muck off the front of her dress, copping a feel of her breasts whenever he had the chance.

Crossing to where Natalie lay, Morgana swatted the goon's hands away. "Get out of here. I'll take care of her."

The goon stood up, looked over at his boss. Gora gestured with his head, and the goon obediently stepped back.

"Nat," Morgana said, bending over the bed. "Nat, what happened?"

Natalie stared up at Morgana, mouthed, *I'm going to kill you.*

Morgana gave her a grin only she could see, before trying to turn her over. Natalie moaned as if she were in great distress. Morgana made a show of putting her ear to Natalie's chest. "Something's wrong, her breathing's labored," she announced in a voice bordering on hysteria. "She might have inhaled some vomit. If her lungs are filling with liquid we'll need to get her to a hospital or she'll suffocate."

"No," Gora said, taking a step toward them. "No hospital."

"All right then. Do you have a pair of large scissors?" she asked over her shoulder.

"What for?" Gora said.

"The zipper is in back. I can't turn her over, she's in too much pain," Morgana replied. "I'll need to cut off her dress to give her some relief."

Gora again gestured with his head, and the goon stepped out of the cabin. Morgana could hear his footsteps receding down the corridor. The idea was to get Gora so agitated that he'd fixate on Natalie, giving Morgana room to execute the last, and most delicate, part of the plan.

Moments later, Goon Number One returned with a pair of kitchen scissors, which he handed to Morgana. "Stay here," she said. "I need your help. Hold her dress away from her so I won't cut her."

Again, the goon glanced at Gora, who nodded, almost wearily. He was done with being the Good Samaritan. All he wanted now was his alone time with Morgana, her dress rucked, her thighs exposed to his avid gaze.

As the goon bent over, pulling Natalie's dress away

from her chest, he could not help taking a look down her bodice. That was when Morgana buried the scissor blades into his left side. The goon grabbed her by the throat, callused fingers digging in, trying to rip it out. She struck him hard right above the left kidney with the edge of her hand. He winced, his eyes bloodshot, and she used his own momentum against him, bringing his side back toward her, twisting the scissors in the wound.

Blood spurted, the goon convulsed, and Gora started, unable to see what had happened. Natalie grabbed the goon's Strizh and, when Morgana cast the goon's body aside, pointed it at Gora.

Morgana turned back to Maslov. "Now, Gora, it's time for you to answer some ques—" But she saw Natalie's finger tighten on the trigger, and cried out: "No, no, no!"

She lunged for Natalie's hand, but it was too late. Natalie squeezed the trigger once, twice, three times, just as Morgana had done with Niki, the false Larry London. Gora, eyes open wide, grabbed his chest, staggering back, falling to his knees. His fingers convulsed, trying vainly to stanch the blood pouring out of him. He was staring at Natalie, his mouth, leaking blood, working soundlessly.

"Fuck you, fucker," Natalie spat as he fell over onto his face. She remained rigid, her right arm like a tree branch, in her mind still the weapon aiming at where Gora Maslov had stood a moment ago.

Morgana snatched the Strizh out of Natalie's now compliant hand. As Goon Number Two rushed in, pistol at the ready, having been drawn by the gunfire, she shot him neatly through the heart.

"Dammit, Nat. I told you no deviations."

"I didn't deviate," Natalie said, rolling off the bed. "I meant to kill him from the first." She eyed Morgana. "Why d'you think I agreed to your plan? Just for the money?" Hiking up her skirt, she pulled down her panties, revealing a part of her she'd kept hidden from Morgana: a garden of bruises, deep and dark as secrets. "What's money without revenge?"

38

JASON BOURNE RECEIVED the first call as the Sapsan bullet train was nearing Leningradsky Station in Moscow.

"Hello, Jason, it's your old friend Soraya."

Bourne was standing between Mala and Savasin, so he stepped away down the corridor.

"Soraya, it's really you?"

"It is."

"Where are you?"

"Back in the saddle."

"D.C.? Doing what?"

"Stepping back into the old pond. Now I've been asked to take over Dreadnaught."

"And you said yes."

"I missed the life, Jason. Too much."

"And Sonya."

"Thriving." A pause. "Where are you?"

"Russia. Moscow, to be exact."

"I'm going to give a new operative of mine this number."

"I wish you wouldn't."

"Morgana has been on the Initiative now for over a week. She's a very special person, and she has firsthand intel you need to hear."

"Why don't you relay—"

"You need to hear it from her, complete with her inflections. Take her opinions seriously, will you?" Before he had a chance to answer, she said, "When this is over, come see me in D.C. I guarantee you safe passage."

"No one can do that, Soraya. Not even you."

"Then I'll come to you."

The second call came as they were pulling into the station, readying themselves to disembark.

"Bourne."

"I have very little time, Morgana."

"None of us do." Morgana's voice buzzed in his ear like an insistent fly. "The Initiative contains a zero-day trigger."

"I know."

"Do you also know that there's exactly twenty hours before the Initiative is deployed?" Silence. "I didn't think so." She took a breath. "I still don't know what it's going to be deployed against, but I will tell you that Gora Maslov was involved up to his eyeballs."

Bourne caught the past tense. "Was?"

"He's dead, Bourne."

"You're sure?"

She barked a laugh. "I was there. His half sister, Alyosha Orlova, is dead as well."

"You've been busy."

She took another breath. "Two international phone numbers on a Post-it I found on Gora's boat might be everything you need."

"Tell me."

She recited the first number. "There's a name or a place written after it: Keyre."

"A name. A Somali arms dealer—he filled the vacuum when the authorities caught up to Victor Bout."

"That bad."

"Worse, if that's possible." The train had stopped, passengers were disembarking, dragging their luggage. The ones with briefcases were on their mobiles, talking without seeing. "And the second number?"

"No name." She read off the string of numbers; Bourne memorized them. "That it?"

"One more thing." He heard her breathing down the line and knew she was working herself up to what was most difficult for her. "Alyosha and Nikolay Rozin were also involved in the Initiative, in a way I can't yet work out, except that Alyosha's father was Dimitri Maslov."

Bourne was stepping onto the platform while talking to Morgana. His mind was working overtime, but at the same time his eyes were quartering the platform and, indeed, the entire expanse of the station in his field of vision. He did this unconsciously, as a matter of course, every detail caught in the web of his gaze.

"Soraya was right about you," he said. "Let's keep in touch."

With that he folded away his sat phone. Mala and Savasin were in front of him, the first minister's people grouped at the end of the platform, waiting for them.

The remaining two guards who had been on the train with him were busy off-loading the corpses of the two who had been killed during the journey.

The crowd of debarking passengers had thinned, a majority of them shying away from the huddled group of FSB operatives with their long coats and grim faces. The grayness of Moscow hung like a pall over the tracks, and the atmosphere was considerably chillier and sharper, as if the station's HVAC system were pumping out blasts of air imported from Siberia.

Echoes of voices and shoe soles on concrete were dying away like embers losing their inner glow. Steps ahead of him, Mala was taking her time digging a verbal knife between Savasin's ribs. Four repairmen on an electric cart, laden with substantial toolboxes, plus a well-secured rectangle of tempered glass, passed them by, stopped outside the first class car, then clambered in with the slab of glass. Clearly, they had been alerted by the crew to the damaged window and carpet in the conference cabin.

Farther along, at the mouth of the vast station hall, the FSB gang shifted on their feet. Bourne, who had completed his inventory of passenger faces, turned his full attention toward Savasin's greeting committee. His penetrating gaze moved from one face to another, and what he saw gave him pause. One would think that they'd been looking around as he had, the better to pick up any potential threats to the first minister. Such was not the case, however. All of them—Bourne counted seven—were staring fixedly at Savasin.

Bourne checked their surroundings. They were almost at the head of the bullet train, which was on their right. To the left, across the platform, the next track was empty. Two other platforms and three tracks extended further in that direction.

Hurrying to catch up with Timur and Mala, Bourne kept his eyes on the FSB men, who had begun to stir in the manner of bees when their hive is invaded by a human hand. A sudden dull flash of metal, and Bourne had caught Mala by the collar, was swinging her around and down onto the platform. The guns were out now, and he pointed to the gap between the Sapsan and the platform. As Mala wriggled herself into the gap, vanishing beneath the train, the first spray of bullets peppered the side of the train nearest Savasin. Whatever passengers remained ran for cover, and the pair of security guards attracted to the gunshots took one look at the perpetrators and, without a word, melted back into the interior of the station.

Grabbing the first minister, Bourne dragged him down to a prone position, slithered into the gap, hauling Timur into it after him. Behind them, the bristling hive was in motion, as coordinated as bees in flight. Four agents raced down to the front of the Sapsan, while the other three peeled off to patrol the platform on the other side of the train. Two men slid down into the gap, following Bourne, while the remaining two paced along the platform, eyes focused on the gap between the Sapsan and the platform for the slightest sign of movement.

Below the gap, where the Sapsan's narrow undercarriage dwelled, the space widened out, black as pitch, but with room to both hide and maneuver.

Bourne, shadowed and all but invisible, struck the

first of the FSB men on the side of the neck, a blow so devastating that the man dropped his Strizh from nerveless fingers. Bourne grabbed him and drew the man into the shadows with him. The second agent made his appearance in the narrow space. When, gun drawn, he crouched down to check out the shadowed area, Bourne shoved his comrade at him. As Bourne had anticipated, the second man shot first and asked questions after. He put a bullet through his comrade's chest before Bourne, emerging from the darkness, grabbed him by the front of his coat and slammed the heel of his hand into the man's nose. Blood fountained; the man reared back right into Mala's grip. Wrapping her arm around his neck, she twisted hard with her other hand, breaking the man's neck.

"It looks like there was a coup in your absence, Timur," Bourne said as he and Mala armed themselves with the fallen men's weapons.

"My brother," Savasin said with active distaste.

"Going after the first minister," Mala said. "That takes brass stones."

Bourne waved them to silence as he got down on his stomach. They followed suit, and the three of them made their wriggling way between the rails, where there was enough clearance for their prone bodies but not much more. Bourne went as fast as he could, knowing that the gunshot would bring the others converging on the spot the explosion came from.

In fact, he was counting on this. There were five remaining FSB agents. Having all of them in a group was much more to his liking than having them spread out over the station. Having worked their way halfway down the Sapsan, he tapped Savasin on the shoulder, mouthed for him to stay where he was. Then he signed to Mala, who snaked her way to their left, toward the platform on the far side of the train.

Bourne himself rolled to his right, moving toward the gap between the train and the platform. On the verge of being able to get to his feet, he paused, watching for moving shadows, listening for hushed conversations, or even single voices.

When, after five minutes of the only form of surveillance available to him, he discerned that at least the spot he had chosen was clear, he picked his way forward into the gap. Again, he paused to listen; again he heard nothing but the normal noises attributable to engines, steel wheels, sighing hydraulics, and, every once in a while, the conversation of the repairmen coming through the broken window in the conference cabin.

Working his way backward, he headed for the front of the train.

39

IVAN WAS NEARING the end of the line. He'd been working on trains more or less his whole adult life—actually even before that. His father had worked on the trains in Moscow, though of course he'd never even dreamed of anything like the Sapsan. But the Sapsan had been Ivan's baby from the moment it had rolled into the yard at Leningradsky Station. He'd had to spend a week in a stuffy glass box of a classroom where he was taught every aspect of the Sapsan's workings, then another week working hands-on in the yard. That was how he came to love the Sapsan, and he thought of his father every time his gnarled hands touched the sleek outer shell or the even sleeker innards.

Unfortunately, Ivan thought as he surveyed the destruction of his most luxurious conference cabin, he was saddled with a trio of near-idiots. They were young, it was true, but they were also lazy, un-teachable, and almost always high on some illegal substance that Ivan refused to acknowledge, let alone identify.

It was not always thus, he thought with an inward sigh. When he came up through the ranks the young-sters were enthusiastic, eager to learn an honorable trade. No more. Nowadays, the young ones were in-fected by modern-day culture. Clubbing, whoring, and hanging out drinking, smoking, and making mischief were their off-hours avocations. Useless carbuncles on the ass of decent society, that's what they were, Ivan thought sourly as he directed Fool Number One to scrub out the carpet with a solution he had concocted to take out vomit and bloodstains from the special car-pet in first class without affecting the color.

He ordered Fool Number Two to vacuum up the shards of glass from the blown-out window. Luckily, there weren't many of them, as the blow had come from the inside, but those that were there were bloody, and they all donned thick rubber gloves to protect them-selves. Fool Number Three was in charge of making sure the pane of glass didn't strike any hard surface or topple over. Nevertheless, as Ivan picked his way over to the blown-out window he kept an eagle eye on Fool Number Three, the youngest, rawest, and highest of the trio.

Possibly that was why he didn't sense the Angel-maker until she was in his face. She grabbed the front of his uniform, pulled him hard against the chrome frame of the window, and put a forefinger across her lips in the universal sign for silence. Then she grinned at him, though all his terrified mind registered was her bared teeth. He had the irrational thought—though consider-ing what was going on in the world today it was hardly impossible—that she was going to tear into his throat with those sharp, white teeth.

Instead, she drew him to one side while a man with the watchful, steely eyes of someone who saw and understood everything at first glance climbed in through the open space where the window had been. It was a long window; there was plenty of space. When the man looked at Ivan, Ivan's guts turned to water, and he felt an urgent need to piss. Then the man smiled at him, not in the feral way the woman had, but rather it was the smile of a comrade, an old hand with whom you could share a cold vodka and a cigarette at the end of a long day. He asked the woman to let go in perfect, fluid, Moscow-inflected Russian. He looked Russian, too. Ivan relaxed somewhat.

As for the three Fools, only the youngest one, mouth gaping open, noted the man's appearance. The other two were too occupied in trying to attend to their duties to notice, let alone care.

"What's your name?" the man said.

"Ivan Ivanovich," Ivan said, blinking like an owl in sunlight.

"Well, Ivan Ivanovich, my name is Fyodor Ilianovich," Bourne said, using a legend he'd employed before in Moscow. "I'm very pleased to meet you."

Ivan stared at him as if mesmerized. He did not know what to say. He suddenly longed for a glass of strong tea, or better yet, a vodka. Even a cigarette would do, he thought, but none of these amenities were on offer.

Bourne turned, and so did Ivan, gaping at two more figures clambering through the opening. One was the woman with the feral smile. The other was a figure out of the newspapers and state TV. Ivan goggled. It couldn't be!

And yet Fyodor Ilianovich confirmed his tentative identification. "May I introduce Timur Ludmirovich Savasin, First Minister of the Russian Federation. First Minister, this is Ivan Ivanovich, an upright citizen, and I trust a patriot, of the Russian Federation."

If I didn't see it with my own eyes, Ivan thought, *I wouldn't believe it. What on earth is the First Minister doing climbing through the window of my carriage?*

"Of course, of course!" Ivan said, coming out of his brief stasis. It was totally lost on him that no one bothered to introduce the woman with the feral smile. In point of fact, he was relieved. "Of course a patriot, First Minister."

"Ivan Ivanovich, it is an honor to meet a true patriot of Mother Russia such as yourself," Savasin said in his most formal voice.

Ivan all but passed out. To his utter chagrin, he was sweating profusely. "The honor is all mine, First Minister, I assure you."

Savasin smiled. "I—we—need your help."

"Anything, First Minister," Ivan said. "I am entirely at your service."

———

And so it was that Ivan Ivanovich, nearing the end of the line, experienced the greatest day of his life—notwithstanding it being an experience he swore never to tell anyone, not even his wife and three sons. Twenty minutes after they had crawled through his window he was leading the first minister, Fyodor, and the woman with the feral smile out of the first class carriage and into the electric cart. All of them were wearing train yard workman's uniforms and caps, stripped off Fools One, Two, and Three, who had been bound and gagged virtually naked, and thrust into the bathroom, under his benign and—he had to admit it!—amused gaze. Ivan locked them in himself with his master key that opened every door on every train and in the train yard itself. After thirty years on the job, he had amassed any number of privileges.

One of the trio, he could not tell which, but he imagined it to be the woman with the feral smile, glanced behind them, where five men in trench coats, holding pistols in their hands, frowning deeply like old men at a comrade's funeral, stood on the platform, discussing God alone knew what. Ivan did not want to know, just as he did not want to know the nature of the first minister's current difficulty. His heart was filled with the opportunity—call it a gift!—he had been given to do his duty as a citizen and—his chest swelled with pride at the thought—as a patriot. He had never in his life felt more Russian, not when he had gotten married, not during the occasions of the births of his three sons, nor the wedding of the eldest. These were all beautiful moments in a man's life, to be sure, but they were shared by almost every man. But this moment, this one was special. It was unique in his life—shared with no other. Only Ivan Ivanovich. And he would remember it and bask in its glory until his last dying breath.

"Come see me when this is all over," Savasin told the old man as he let them off on the far side of the train yard, a place so vast the station itself was barely a smudge on the near horizon. Ivan Ivanovich smiled shyly, brushed some soot off the first minister's lapel, and gave them a military salute. And that was how Bourne, Savasin, and the Angelmaker left him.

They made their way through a gap in the cyclone fence the old man had pointed out to them. Daylight was dying, the last glimmers of sun sparking off the tops of Moscow's tallest buildings, turning them to molten gold. A strong north wind had sprung up, sending the temperatures plummeting by at least ten degrees. Scattered clouds rushed by overhead, except for a gathering in the west, like birds seeking out the last rays of the sun before Moscow slipped into darkness.

Across a narrow service road a municipal parking lot spread out like an old lady with too much weight. And like that old lady, the tarmac was cracked and pockmarked by time and harsh weather.

It took them some time to find a car they could break into. Muscovites still maintained the habit of taking their steering wheels with them when they parked, to ensure their vehicles would still be there when they returned. But at last Bourne found one intact, broke in, and hot-wired the starter. Savasin climbed into the passenger's seat and, without a word of protest, the Angelmaker occupied the backseat. It was the first minister who knew Dima's new address and the best route to get them there unnoticed. They did not speak about the incident at Leningradsky Station. Savasin was sunk in gloom. Bourne felt it best not to disturb him, and the

Angelmaker, uncharacteristically, refrained from mocking Savasin's humiliation. Seeing with their own eyes how his own FSB had been turned against him, acting on orders from an older brother who, though in an inferior post, somehow wielded more power than he did, seemed punishment enough.

40

ONLY TWO DEAD?" Konstantin's glance bounced off the pair of corpses lying on the Sapsan platform of Leningradsky Station and up to the remaining five men. "Bourne must be losing his touch."

"Two dead is an unacceptable number, sir," Viktor, the leader of the *spetsnaz* squad, said. "These are my people."

Konstantin's eyes glittered, and his voice crackled with harsh energy. "No, Captain, you and everyone else in the FSB are *my* people. Never forget that."

Viktor stared stoically at Konstantin, perhaps in silent rebuke, perhaps not. Konstantin elided over it; the captain and all these men were beneath his notice. So far as he was concerned every member of *spetsnaz* was cannon fodder. On the front line, in enemy territory, theirs not to reason why.

Besides, Konstantin had more important matters to attend to than standing around with the little people. Turning his back on the captain and what was left of his detail, he said, "Scrape the remains off the platform, Captain. The sooner the better. The Sapsan's next departure has been delayed far too long as it is."

"*And fuck you too,* sir," Viktor muttered under his breath as he watched Konstantin blur into the haze of the station.

———

"We're being followed," the Angelmaker said, half turned so she could look out the rear window.

"For about a mile now," Bourne replied.

"Well?" Her voice was like a newly sharpened stick. "What do you propose to do about it?"

This barbed exchanged brought Savasin out of his self-imposed exile from the real world.

"Nothing."

"Why the hell not?" the Angelmaker said.

Bourne smiled. "Patience."

They were still on the Outer Ring Road, more than five miles from the address Savasin had given Bourne. With a jolt, the first minister looked around, their location snapping into place. "Bourne, we're nowhere near the exit we need to get to Dima's."

"That's the point," Bourne said, as he swung off the Outer Ring Road. He sped down the off ramp and onto the tangle of city streets.

"They're still on us," the Angelmaker reported.

Bourne said nothing, concentrating on the road ahead. He was looking for an anomaly: a detour, a construction site, an abandoned warehouse. Instead, he found a trestle train crossing.

"Hang on," he said tightly, as he turned the wheel hard to the right. The car rattled down the tracks.

Savasin's eyes opened wide, his mouth hung open in stupefaction. "I don't think this is a good idea."

"Nobody asked you, your highness," the Angelmaker snapped.

When Mala had started to call the first minister "your highness" Bourne had not a clue. Perhaps when they had been walking and talking together on the platform in Leningradsky Station.

The car behind them had turned onto the road that paralleled the tracks. Bourne could see its shadow flickering between the pine trees. Night had fallen, as suddenly as if an immense cloak had been thrown over the city. Lights burned, but dimly, as they were on the far outskirts where factories, power stations, and slums huddled against one another as if in an attempt to keep warm. The air was filled with soot and oil particulates; the pines were black with it. And then the moon, made hazy by the thickened atmosphere, lost its shape, vanishing altogether in the gathering clouds. It began to snow, a gray shower in the twin beams of the headlights, reminding Bourne of the photos he'd been shown during Treadstone training of the houses surrounding Auschwitz and Buchenwald half obscured by the pall of gray ash pluming from the tall brick chimneys of the crematoriums.

Bourne increased his speed, even as the snow began to come down first in veils and then in sheets, inflicting multiple compressions on visibility. It was no longer possible, for instance, to be sure they were still being paralleled by the following vehicle. Then, all at once, a

powerful spotlight pierced the snow and the pine needles. It swung back and forth like a maddened eye,
before picking them out. It flickered, its dazzling light
dancing off the side of their car, then leaving them in
utter darkness for long moments at a time.

Savasin appeared mesmerized by the blinding light.

"How did they pick up our trail?" the Angelmaker
asked.

Bourne was too busy at the moment to give either
of them attention. He was fully concentrated on the
dimly glowing ball of light that hovered four feet above
the tracks. It grew brighter as it rushed toward them.
And then, as the Angelmaker cranked down her window, over the howling of the gusting wind they heard
the distinct *clickety-clack* of the oncoming train, felt the
strong push of the air it drove before it.

"Bourne, what the hell are you doing?" Savasin shouted
in clear distress. "You're going to get us all killed!"

Leaning forward, the Angelmaker clamped down on
Savasin's shoulders, said, "Shut up, your highness. Let
him do what he does best."

The train was almost upon them now. The engineer
must have seen them, finally, because he let out a blast
on his air horn, and then, seeing that the car ahead
wasn't turning, sounded the horn again and again,
until the searchlight from the car running parallel to
them swung to illuminate the train so the occupants
could see what was coming.

This was the moment Bourne had been awaiting. He
turned the wheel hard over left. For a heart-stopping instant the car stalled as the tires hit the left-side rail. Then
he gunned the engine and the car, bouncing upward,

ran over the rail, and they were off the track, crunching down over the narrow cinder bed, still in danger of being clipped by the front of the train, which was so close now it loomed over their heads like a fire-breathing demon, a solid wall of flashing steel and grinding wheels.

Then they were in the woods, jouncing between spindly pines, churning the gray snow to slush, the almost bald tires slipping and sliding until Bourne guided them beyond the far tree line, onto a country track that eventually led them to paved road. Fifteen minutes later, they arrived at a crossroad with signs enough to orient Savasin.

"That way," he said, pointing to their right.

Instead of heading in that direction, Bourne pulled over onto the verge, though there was no traffic visible in either direction. He got out, leaned into the Angelmaker's open window, and said, "Your turn."

She dutifully got out, went around to slide behind the wheel. Bourne opened the front passenger's door, told Savasin to get in the back. Then he took his place beside the Angelmaker.

"Now," he said to Savasin, "direct us to the closest metro station that will get us nearest to Dima's place."

"The Kapotnya Oblast has no nearby metro stop," Savasin said. "No municipal buses, either."

"Just get us closest you can then," Bourne said.

Savasin considered a minute, then said to the Angelmaker, "Go left." And then, as if to himself, "We're just inside the Outer Ring Road, eastern Moscow. We need to travel south, but not too far."

He directed them to the Domodedovskaya metro station.

"This is where you and I get off, Timur." Bourne turned to the Angelmaker. "Considering how far we've been followed, it will be more secure if we split up. Take the car. Change it for another, if you deem it wise. You know Dima's address. Meet us there."

The Angelmaker nodded. "Take care of yourself. And do me a favor, keep his highness in line." With that, she was off, a thick cloud of exhaust trailing after her.

Bourne led Savasin down the steps. The Domodedovskaya station was Brutalist modern. It had none of the opulent charm of the metro stations in and around the Inner Ring Road, where a magical mystery tour of old czarist Russia, post–World War II exuberance, lit by bulbous chandeliers, awaited the gawking tourist.

They took the metro in a leisurely northeasterly direction, emerging in the Alma-Atkinskaya station, in the Brateyvo District, across the Moskva River from Kapotnya. The Alma-Atkinskaya station was even more modern, having an almost space-age look. But that was to be expected from the newest of Moscow's outlier stations.

Out in the gray night, the snow continued to fall, blurring the ranks of identical gray modern residential high-rises, and haloing the light from the occasional sodium light that wasn't smashed.

Bourne saw the car first—a black Zil, with a long snout and blacked-out windows. They shot first—two men pointing pistols through zipped-down windows. Pulling Savasin down behind the bulk of the station's entrance that emerged from underground like a boil spoiling to be lanced, Bourne squeezed off three shots, two of which hit their mark. The hostile fire ceased as quickly as it had begun. The driver put the Zil in gear but made the mistake of flooring the accelerator. The Zil began to skid sideways on the thin coating of ice concealed by the snow. That error in judgment allowed Bourne to fire three times at the driver's side of the windshield; the third trigger pull told him the magazine was empty. The Zil screamed as if it felt pain, and Bourne was running hard toward the car, Savasin fast on his heels. The Zil, driverless, was still making tight circles when Bourne wrenched open the driver's door and hauled the dead man out. One bullet had struck his chest, the other his head.

Launching himself forward, Bourne gained control of the car, stopped it long enough for Savasin to scramble in beside him. Bourne went through the clothes of the two shooters, looking for identification, found none. The two men exchanged clothes with the dead shooters. Blood spatters aside, the new outfits suited them better. Plus, the overcoats made them instantly warmer.

Abandoning the Strizh on the backseat, Bourne grabbed the shooter's pistol. Then he turned to Savasin, who had turned up his collar against the rising wind.

"Shit," Bourne said.

Savasin, knotting his tie, said, "What is it?"

"The Angelmaker asked how they were able to follow us." Bourne picked up the train worker's coat that the first minister had been wearing, pulled out a pin with a gleaming head from the underside of the collar.

"What the hell is that?" Savasin asked, alarmed.

"A miniature GPS tracker," Bourne said. Dropping the pin, he ground it beneath the heel of his shoe.

"That fucking Ivan Ivanovich," Savasin said.

"It looks as if your brother has been one step ahead of us."

"But how the hell would he know we'd run into Ivan Ivanovich?"

"He didn't," Bourne said. "But thinking ahead like a chess master, Ivan Ivanovich was just one of his plans. If we escaped his men—which we did—we'd seek out someone who could help us, someone in uniform who could lead us to other uniforms we could put on. The shattered window was his good fortune. The men in uniforms were more or less right in front of us."

A string of Russian curses exploded from Savasin's mouth. Then he said: "He'll pay for this."

"Forget Konstantin for the moment." Bourne checked his watch. "We need to get to Dima as quickly as possible."

Savasin pointed to the section of the Outer Ring Road. "Head north. Good thing I know all the short-cuts in Kapotnya."

If Morgana was right, they had sixteen hours until the zero-day trigger of the Bourne Initiative was engaged.

41

SORAYA, CONNECTED TO Morgana via her wireless earwig, made all the arrangements. A car was waiting for Morgana and Natalie. However, Natalie asked to be let off before the car got to the airfield where the Dreadnaught jet was standing by.

"But you can't stay here," Morgana said. "It's far too dangerous. You've been seen boarding Gora's boat multiple times. The police are going to be looking for you."

"I can't leave my son, Morgana."

"Then that wasn't a line."

Natalie smiled. "No. I'm not going anywhere without Karl." She squeezed Morgana's arm. "Don't look so alarmed. This is my country. I know how to get around. I know how to evade the police." She laughed. "I've been doing it almost all my life."

"This is different," Morgana said. "You know it is. Three people dead, my God. I'll take you and Karl back to the States with me."

"So I can do what, exactly?" Natalie shook her head. "Thanks, but no thanks. Sweden's my home. I'm not leaving."

With her hand on the door handle, she turned back. "Morgana, I know I fucked up." Her brows knit together. "Why aren't you angry with me?"

"I know what Gora did to you, how far he pushed you, how he humiliated you."

Natalie bowed her head. "Thank you." And she was out the door, walking down the street before Morgana had a chance to say anything more.

———

As it turned out, it was just as well Natalie didn't want to come back to D.C. with her. Inside the Dreadnaught plane, as it was readying to take off, Soraya's voice buzzed in her ear. "Sat phone. Now."

"Change of plans," Soraya said when Morgana had dialed in on the sat phone. "I hope you're not homesick, because you're not coming back to Washington, at least not right away. Things are still too hot and everything is happening so fast now I haven't had a chance to smooth the way for your return."

The plane had taxied to the head of the runway. The engines were revving up.

"Where are you sending me?" Morgana asked as she strapped herself in.

The plane hurtled down the runway and lifted off. With a hum of hydraulics, the wheels retracted.

"Somalia," Soraya said. "I want you to keep an eye on the arms dealer, Keyre, whose mobile number you found on Gora's boat. There's been an awful lot of chatter sur-rounding him all of a sudden. The storage lockers are filled with a wide range of arms and electronic listening devices; use anything you need. I want to know what's going on."

"Will do."

"And, Morgana. Keep your distance, at all costs. I can't overemphasize the danger this man represents."

"I hear you."

"I mean it," Soraya said before signing off. "Keyre's a fucking nightmare."

———

The filthy air enveloped them, soot fell from the sky and turned the snow black before it hit the ground, cinders crunched under their soles, and evil-smelling eruptions belched from the immense smokestacks of hapless Kapot-nya. As Bourne and Savasin picked their way along the sidewalks, the sky was so low it was impossible to tell whether it was composed of clouds or smoke. The sun-less afternoon had slid unnoticed into turbulent twilight. Street lights—those that worked—cast a dim and fitful il-lumination on the sulphurous atmosphere.

Vehicles crawled slowly forward, then stopped for long minutes. The hellacious traffic had forced them to abandon the Zil. The sidewalks were bloated with people making their way home. Old men sat on icy stoops with their heads in their hands, exhausted simply by breathing. Teenagers zigzagged through the crowds, picking pockets or selling the latest iterations of cheap and dangerous drugs. No music, no car horns tonight, only small noises that constituted a deathly silence.

Bourne let Savasin lead the way. He was torn between needing to get to Dima as soon as possible and his instinct to continually scan the immediate vicinity for Konstantin's people, although how Savasin's brother could know where they were now that he had crushed the life out of the GPS, he could not imagine. Still, several times he guided the first minister into a doorway to observe the pedestrians coming up from behind them. He found nothing suspicious, and each time they continued their journey, hurrying now, shouldering their way through the crowds, stepping into the gutter when their way was blocked by knots of people too dense to push through without drawing attention to themselves.

"Next block," Savasin announced. "Ekaterina, Dima's daughter, gave me instructions on how to approach and enter the building." He pointed to their left, and they turned a corner. "It has a back entrance, of course, but there's also a side entrance, a small door, painted green, that the concierge uses on occasion. This way."

The side street, too narrow for vehicles of any sort, was nearly deserted, and they picked up their pace. It was faced by blank brick walls, nearly black from the soot and the dismal weather.

Bourne saw the green door coming up on their right. It was, indeed, narrow, hidden by shadows, so that it was easy to miss. Savasin stepped up to it, turned the crusty handle. Nothing happened; the door remained closed.

"Ekaterina didn't give you a key?"

Savasin shook his head. "She said it would be open."

Moving the first minister aside, Bourne examined the door. It was made of metal, much dented and as beaten up as a boxer. Here and there slashes of red could be seen, vestiges of an earlier coat of paint. An old lock was rusted into uselessness. Putting his shoulder to the door, he slammed into it once, twice, and with a soft shriek it gave grudging way. It was a poor fit for the frame, the bottom flange scraping the concrete floor of the gloomy hallway within.

Here, Bourne held them up. They stood, silent, deep in the shadows, while he accustomed himself to the cluster of small sounds—the boiler, water running through the pipes, floorboards creaking, the wind whistling through cracks in the windowpanes. It was like listening to a living thing. The building breathing in its own particular rhythm. Then a baby crying, a violin playing a soft, sad melody, a burst of laughter, quickly throttled. Footsteps on the stairs disappearing behind the sound of a closing door. Now no one on the stairs.

"Top floor," Savasin whispered as they emerged from the service area, reaching the vestibule.

Bourne did not bother to turn on the thirty-second light to illuminate their way. Instead, he indicated to Savasin to follow his lead in slipping off his shoes. Carrying them in one hand, they ascended to the first floor, where Bourne kept them still as he listened. The baby had stopped crying, but the violin was scraping away, occasionally hitting sour notes that made Savasin wince.

Bourne held them again on the landing to the third floor. The violin was louder now, obviously coming from one of the third-floor apartments. The melody, such as it was, had started all over again from the beginning, note for note the same as before.

Halfway up to the top floor, Bourne halted them again. He wished he were alone; he did not like dragging Savasin around with him, but he'd needed him to get to Dima Orlov. Now, not so much.

He began again to ascend, but when the first minister began to follow him, he put an arm out. "Wait here," he whispered.

"After coming all this way, after everything Konstantin has thrown at me to stop me, there's no way I'll be left standing on the threshold."

Bourne studied him for a moment. The young violinist hit the same sour note. "You have the Strizh you took from the gunman?"

"Sure." Savasin nodded, slipping it out to show Bourne. "But why would I need it? We're in the one place in all of Moscow safe from my brother."

Bourne said nothing, climbing up the last of the stairs, the first minister on his heels. Savasin had told him to expect the presence of the mountain-size protector named Cerberus and, as they reached the final landing with its riot of thick foliage, its magnificently turned wooden doors banded in iron and sporting the eagle bas-relief in the center of each door, wings spread, talons to the fore, Bourne saw that he hadn't exaggerated. Cerberus was the largest human being he had ever come across. The guard dog's raisin eyes regarded Savasin, lit up dully with recognition, then turned his attention on Bourne. He grunted.

"Hold that thought," Bourne said. Taking out his sat phone, he dialed the second number Morgana had dictated to him over the phone, the one she found along with the one for Keyre's mobile, the one without attribution.

He had noted that the number had a Russian prefix, as well as one of the very new Moscow exchanges created due to the proliferation of mobile phones. They heard a phone ring behind the decorative doors—a very distinctive melody, Ravel's "Pavane for a Dead Princess."

"I know that melody," Savasin said before it cut out abruptly. "It's Dima's favorite."

"No, it isn't," Bourne said, hearing the voice at the other end of the line say, *"Gora?"*

Bourne waved to Cerberus, who opened the doors, allowing them entrance to the Orlovs' vast atelier-apartment.

"I told you not to use this number unless—" Ekaterina broke off as she and Dima watched in shock as Bourne strode toward them, his sat phone against his cheek.

"Not Gora," he said with a millimeter-thin smile. "Gora's dead, Ekaterina." He pointed the Strizh at her heart. "This is the end of the line—for you, your father, for the auction, for the Bourne Initiative."

He heard Savasin's warning shout at the same time the immense blur came hurtling toward him.

How can someone so big move so fast? he wondered. Cerberus slammed into him, sending him tumbling across the floor. As his right shoulder struck the wooden boards, the Strizh flew out of his hand, skittering just out of reach. No matter, the mountain was upon him, battering him with fists as big and destructive as medieval maces. Bourne felt his left side go numb with the pounding he was taking. He tried to get to his knees, but Cerberus slapped him with the back of his hand. Bourne recoiled, and to the sound of splintering wood, he crashed into the stack of frames waiting to be assembled.

Giving him no respite, Cerberus closed in. Bourne got in three or four quick blows, which, astoundingly, appeared to have no effect whatsoever. Cerberus was bent over him, his raisin eyes filled with red rage: Bourne had threatened his mistress. Dimly, Bourne could make out Ekaterina calling her guard dog off, but he was beyond hearing, beyond anything but the simple principle of destruction.

His massive hand closed around Bourne's neck, squeezing so hard Bourne thought his eyeballs would pop out of his head. His breathing was labored, his heart was racing too fast; black spots appeared before his eyes, clouding his vision. His left side was still numb, useless. All he had was his right hand and, even as his world closed in to a pulsing red spot and his lungs strained for oxygen that wasn't coming, it scrabbled at his side, found a length of frame and, with the mitered end upward, with his last reserves of strength, drove it through Cerberus's throat, severing his spinal cord at the spot between the second and third cervical vertebrae.

All the air seemed to come out of Cerberus along with his blood. He deflated like a balloon stuck with a vandal's knifepoint.

Bourne rolled him off and scrambled to his feet as best he could. His training allowed him to go into *prana*, using long, slow breaths to reoxygenate his system. Not that it mattered. The violin melody from downstairs was gone. In the ensuing silence Konstantin Savasin appeared seemingly out of nowhere, surrounded by two of his men, trench-coated and armed with short-barreled Uzis. One of them had disarmed the first minister who, with his arms behind his back, looked white as a sheet.

"Taste." Konstantin, suave, slim, and saturnine, sauntered toward Bourne. "There's no accounting for it." He turned to his brother. "When you lie down with dogs, dear brother, you're sure to get fleas."

Responding to a hand signal, his other man came toward Bourne, the muzzle of the Uzi pointed at his midsection.

"Keep still," Konstantin admonished, seeing Bourne's muscles tense. "The thing will cut you in half in about three seconds." He shrugged. "Besides, from the look of you, I doubt you have much fight left in you."

At that, his man slammed the metal butt of his Uzi into Bourne's chin, and Bourne went down like a sack of cement. The last he knew a booted foot was closing in on the side of his head.

Then the silence of a vast and unfathomable night.

42

WHEN BOURNE AWOKE it was to see Ekaterina Orlova's face hovering over him like a full moon in all its glory.

"Usually," she said, in her smoky voice, "it's the last person to speak who's the mole. Isn't that the way it works in your world, *gospodin* Bourne?" She nodded. "But here, in *my* world, I'm the first to speak with you. I, the mole. The one who's made the alliances my father was too old or too hidebound to make himself. He couldn't see how much the world had changed, how much faster it was going to change. Like all old people, he's not a fan of change."

Her smile was like that of a badger—territorial and belligerent. And like a badger she had small, sharp teeth. She eased herself down onto a straight-backed chair, and Bourne realized he was similarly seated, save that his wrists were tied behind his back, his ankles strapped to the front chair legs. It was a metal chair, very heavy, which he discovered when he tried to rock it back and forth without success.

"I had a choice, you see—between the two brothers. Once Boris was gone, my father's power crumbled into so much sand. We could not stand alone; he did not understand that." She shrugged. "Who knows? Maybe he didn't choose to understand. His fire is banked low; most days he's content to cozy up to his plants and his painting. Pasture work, if you catch my drift. So I chose the stronger of the brothers. Konstantin has plans and, with the Somali's help, the wherewithal to implement them. Plans poor Timur Ludmirovich could not even comprehend." She pursed her lips. "He tries, poor dear, but, well, we both know his elevator's not going too high."

Her laugh sent shivers down Bourne's spine, not that Bourne could feel them. The numbness on his left side had spread to his spine—not a good sign.

"Actually, much as I liked Boris, his death was an unexpected blessing. We were slated to make a great deal of money when the cyber weapon he'd had made shut down the ten targeted banks worldwide. Now, however, there is far more money to be made by going to auction. Including us, there are fifteen entities—individuals, governments, rogue military entities, industrial conglomerates—drooling to get their hands on it."

He was split in two now. Part of him was listening carefully to every word Ekaterina said while the other part was working on repairing whatever the hell Cerberus had done to him.

"One of those is, of course, Konstantin. He wants the Bourne Initiative so that he can present it to the Sovereign, thereby cementing his power in the Federation for a very long time." She wrinkled her nose, leaned close enough for him to smell her stale breath. "The fly in the ointment, and where I come in, is that Konstantin and the Somali, Keyre, are at war. Konstantin was stupid enough to have underestimated Keyre, delivering a shipment of Kalashnikovs of which some were defective. He claimed innocence, of course, but Keyre didn't believe him. Then, several weeks ago, Konstantin blundered again. Responding to actionable intel that it was Keyre who had taken the Initiative and was trying to short-circuit the auction, he had Gora send a cadre of men into the Somali's camp to steal the Initiative. Big mistake. Keyre caught them and beheaded them all. He sent the heads back to Konstantin packaged in dry ice via DHL."

Having been partially revived by his inner self, the outer self bestirred, albeit creakily. "So Konstantin had become a liability."

"In the medium term," Ekaterina confirmed. "But as for now, he still serves an important purpose." She reached out, drew her fingertips along Bourne's cheek. "One piece is still missing: whatever it is Boris left you regarding the Initiative. We all think the coding is complete, but we can't be sure until you tell us."

"Why don't you ask the coders?"

"Why don't I? That would be so simple." Ekaterina rested her elbows on her knees. "Unfortunately, life's never simple. The fact is I don't know what group of hackers Boris dug up on the dark web and paid to build this cyber weapon, and neither does anyone else." She pointed a finger at him. "That leaves you."

"I can't tell you anything," Bourne said between thickened lips. "Boris didn't leave me anything."

"Liar!" She was in his face now. "He left you his boat. You were on it. You must have searched it, don't tell me you didn't."

"Of course I did, but if he left anything for me I didn't find it."

The disconcerting smile again, more teeth showing this time. "Sorry, *gospodin*, but no one believes you."

"It's the truth, whether you believe it or not."

"I don't. None of us does. Which is where Konstantin comes in." She rose. "I'll leave you to his not-so-tender mercies." The smile turned crooked, like the expression on a jack-o'-lantern. "Are you familiar with the fizzy drink trick? You will be soon enough."

Her laugh drifted after her as she left the room and closed the door. It was only then that Bourne realized that he was in a small, windowless room off to one side of the atelier. The door was reinforced metal and had a peephole at eye height. He barely had time to register these details before Konstantin and one of his men entered. The man was carrying a funnel and a case of thirty-two-ounce bottles of soda. He put the case down by the left side of Bourne's chair, then stood at attention. He held the funnel as if it were his Uzi: it had a long, curved snout.

"Wicked-looking thing, isn't it?" Konstantin said. "I don't really like to use it. Court of last resort. But that's where you find yourself, Bourne. And time is rapidly running out."

He sat down in the chair Ekaterina had vacated, a buff-colored folder on his lap. "I'm not going to ask you nicely the way Katya did because I know you won't answer. So we'll just start the process further along the line."

"I know this trick," Bourne said. "It won't work."

"Oh, I know," he said, grinning like a jackal. "But one has to have a bit of fun now and then." He picked up the folder, waved it in front of Bourne's face. "In any case, I've read your file."

"What file?"

"Your Treadstone file, *gospodin* Bourne." Konstantin fluttered the folder like a fan. "I know every bit of your training."

"You're lying. All Treadstone files are buried so deep—"

Opening the folder, Konstantin read out several lines to verify his claim, then he closed it with a slap of his palm. "One has to have friends in high places." He shrugged. "Otherwise what's the point."

He gestured with his head. "Vlad."

Vlad took a rubberized bung out of his pocket. It was an obscene shade of pink. He pried open Bourne's jaws and crammed it into Bourne's mouth, even as Bourne shook his head violently from side to side. The moment the rubber came in contact with his saliva it expanded, filling his mouth so completely he had only his nose to breathe through.

Vlad inserted the end of the funnel into Bourne's left nostril, pushing it down through his sinuses. Bending, he drew up a bottle of soda from the case, unscrewed its top.

"Here we go, Bourne," Konstantin said. "We're dropping you into the Marianas Trench. Be sure to let me know how you like it."

Vlad tipped the bottle, poured the carbonated water into the funnel. That was hellish enough, when the carbon dioxide hit the back of Bourne's throat and burned its way down his esophagus and into his stomach, but Vlad kept pouring.

Bourne jerked and twisted. His insides felt as if they were being fried and then turned inside out. His head felt as if it were about to explode. All this was experienced by the outer part of him, while the inner part, the one that had been busy limiting the damage Cerberus had done to him, worked assiduously to bring feeling back first into his spine and then to his left side. He had been trained well. The only way to survive articulated interrogation was to wall off a part of your mind so securely that nothing could breach its defenses. That accomplished, one form of torture was pretty much like the next, or the one before it, for that matter. Whatever agonizing indignities were perpetrated on the body, that part of the mind remained safe, keeping you sane in the face of a thousand dark paths to insanity.

Bourne's body gagged, got hold of itself, gagged again. The other Bourne, the inner one, stared up at the ceiling, turning it into blue sky with birds wheeling freely. And Vlad kept pouring, and Bourne kept gagging so vociferously that once the bung bulged out of his mouth before Vlad rapped it back in with his knuckled fist. More fizzy water, more agony. Bourne's eyes watered; the whites turned red. He was drenched in sweat, and the muscles in his extremities trembled uncontrollably. And still, Bourne's gaze never wavered from the birds high above. As they breathed, he breathed. As they lived, he lived. They spoke to him, soothed him, circling, circling...

43

UNTIL FROM FAR away he heard Konstantin say: "Enough."

And then, "Unplug him, Vlad. Bring him back to the surface."

When Bourne came to, Timur Savasin was standing in front of him. He had no memory of vomiting up an entire bottle of soda, but the evidence was all around him. The floor, his shoes and socks, the bottoms of his pants legs were sopping wet.

Konstantin clucked his tongue. "Look at you, Bourne. Back from the dead, yes, but looking the worse for wear. Did you enjoy your little vacation?"

It was then that Bourne saw Konstantin had a gun pressed against the side of his brother's head. "So now to the finale," he said. "Or, rather, I should say the starting line." He tilted his head. "Your Treadstone file revealed your one weak spot, Bourne. You're a humanist. You actually care about human lives." He pursed his lips. "Which makes you some kind of conundrum I'm at a loss to explain." He shrugged. "Well, I suppose some mysteries aren't meant to be solved. No matter. The point here is that if you don't tell me what Boris Karpov left you, I'm going to blow my brother's brains all over your face. How's that for a succinct message?"

"Okay, let's have a talk," Bourne said through the cotton of his swollen lips. "There's no reason to kill your brother."

"Oh, there are any number of reasons, Bourne, but at the moment I have no time to enumerate them. The auction is almost upon us." He removed the gun from the side of his brother's head. "Go ahead. Tell me what Karpov left you regarding the workings of the cyber weapon."

Of course, Bourne had nothing. He was playing for time in order to keep Timur alive. He was about to open his mouth, to tell Konstantin some nonsense that, knowing Boris's MO as well as he did, would make some sense, when the sound of a gunshot hammered them from the other side of the door.

Konstantin started. "Go see what the fuck is happening out there," he told Vlad.

But before Vlad could get to the door, two more shots exploded. Then nothing. No one inside the room moved. The harsh noise of their breathing was the only sound. Then, a knock on the door, not urgent but relaxed, as if a neighbor had come to ask for a cup of sugar.

Konstantin gestured silently for Vlad to see who it was. Obediently, Vlad put his eye to the peephole, only to be hurled backward by the bullet that, having shattered the glass of the peephole, penetrated his eye and lodged itself in his brain. As he slammed against the rear wall, Timur took advantage of the shock to wrestle the handgun out of his brother's hand. Konstantin punched him full in the face, and he staggered back. With a snarl of fury Konstantin launched himself after him, grabbing his gun hand, lifting it above their heads.

A fifth gunshot shattered the door's lock, and the Angelmaker stepped inside the room.

"Jesus Christ," she said, seeing Bourne, "what the hell did they do to you?"

Bourne gave her a lopsided grin. "Not enough." He gestured with his head at the two antagonists. Konstantin and Timur were locked in a death grip, neither one giving any quarter.

"Now that's what I call sibling rivalry."

"Get me out of here," he said.

"In a minute." The Angelmaker appeared fascinated by the two brothers locking horns.

"They'll kill each other," Bourne said.

"That's what I'm counting on."

"Mala. Cut me loose."

"You'll stop them."

"I will."

"They're like a pair of Siamese fighting fish."

"Mala!"

She shrugged and, with a knife, cut through his bonds front and back.

Konstantin drove his fist into his brother's solar plexus, doubling him over, and tried to wrest the gun from Timur. Bourne raised himself off the chair, got halfway to where the brothers were struggling, went down on one knee. He waved the Angelmaker back, rose of his own accord, closed with the two brothers. He wrenched the gun out of their shared grip. Reversing it, he smashed the butt into Konstantin's face, shattering cheekbone and eye socket. Konstantin moaned, sank to his knees. Bourne dropped him with a massive blow to his right ear. He lay unmoving.

"Christ, that was close," Timur said, the relief clear on his face. Then, as Bourne grabbed his arms, "Wait, what are you doing?"

Bourne pushed him into the chair he had occupied.

"Now that's better." Grinning, the Angelmaker bound his wrists and ankles.

"What is this?" Timur said. "I led you here, I gave you my trust, now you tie me up?"

"I've no intention of letting you get your hands on the Initiative," Bourne told him.

"I'll kill you for this!" he shouted. "Both of you!"

Bourne turned the gun on him. "Think hard, First Minister. Do you really want to threaten us?"

"He did kill your brother," the Angelmaker pointed out.

"Now your path is clear," Bourne said. "I suggest you make the most of it." Before Timur could reply, he stuffed the rubber bung into his mouth.

"Someone's sure to come by," Bourne said.

"Sooner or later," the Angelmaker added. "And if not?" She shrugged.

As they crossed the room, Bourne swept up the folder that contained his Treadstone file, slid it inside his shirt.

"What was that?" the Angelmaker asked.

Bourne had questions of his own. "What about Dima and Ekaterina?"

"What about them," she said tersely.

"Dead or alive?"

"Do you really care?"

"Ekaterina told me she was running the auction."

"That's what she said, on the point of death," the Angelmaker said with distaste. "It was a surprise. My money was on Dima. She told me that he was the one who made contact with Konstantin."

Bourne reacted. "Then who has the Initiative?"

"Ekaterina wouldn't have kept it here," the Angelmaker said. "Too insecure."

"That leaves Keyre."

"It always comes back to him, doesn't it?"

Bourne stood at the open doorway. He was never so happy to get out of anywhere. At that moment, the Angelmaker turned back to the curled body of Konstantin Savasin. She leaned over. "You dead yet? Well, just to make sure . . ." Flexing her right knee, she stamped down hard on his neck.

The sound of vertebrae cracking was not a pleasant one. Except, possibly, to her.

44

OMALIA. THE HORN of Africa. A gleaming citadel on the oceanic edge of a poverty-stricken, burnt-out landscape. Before, there had been nothing but fishermen and the maimed remnants of constant war, until hunters of another sort, led by the Yibir magus, Keyre, arrived. Pitching their tents, they set about creating a port, first of all, and then the warehouses to house the bounty brought in by Mexican and Colombian cartel drug money. Then the warlords of African and Mideast nations got wind and wanted to join the party. After them traipsed the Russian *grupperovka*, oligarchs, and elite Kremlin *siloviki*, the Eastern European mafiosi, the deeply corrupt politicos and greedy merchant bankers from Western Europe and, last and best of all, all manner of quick-buck merchants, including a smattering of crafty espiocrats from the United States. And like everything the United States stuck its snout into, the sky then became the limit—for Keyre and everyone else enjoying the fruits of his illegitimate labors. Now there was peace. Keyre's peace. Now there was prosperity. Keyre's prosperity. Now the war was exported all over the world. The killing, carpet-bombing, gassing continued, only not here in Keyre's haven.

Bourne and the Angelmaker arrived very early in the morning. Bourne had slept the whole way. Under the names Arnold and Mary Winstead, the fictitious couple whose passports Deron had had made for them before leaving D.C., they had taken a commercial flight from Moscow to Istanbul. Before leaving Russia, Bourne had phoned Abdul Aziz, a longtime friend and importer-exporter with connections all over the Middle East and Africa.

Zizzy, as he was known to his friends and family, was more than happy to accommodate Bourne's requests. In Istanbul, they had transferred to the private airstrip reserved for VIPs and visiting dignitaries, where Zizzy had one of his company's jets standing by, along with a doctor and nurse to treat Bourne. When he heard that Bourne was injured, it was all Bourne could do to keep Zizzy from getting on the plane himself. But he did meet his friend and female companion at the private airstrip to see for himself that his friend wasn't on death's door. "Because," he said, his usually sunny face an aggrieved mask, "then, my friend, I would have no choice but to take you straightaway to my home where both the doctor and my wife would nurse you back to health."

By the time Zizzy's plane touched down in Somalia, Bourne had been treated, filled with fluids of various sorts, shot full of antibiotics, and, with a shot of morphine, sent off to slumberland while doctor and nurse worked to patch him up.

A salmon-pink slash heralded the rising of the sun. Having danced across the Arabian Sea from the southern tip of Kerala Province in India, a warm on-shore breeze ruffled their hair. Apart from a low bank to the west, the sky was almost cloudless. The sun was going to be merciless.

A jeep, battered and dusty but with a full tank of gas, was waiting for them, courtesy of one of Zizzy's trading partners in Mogadishu. It took them just over an hour to reach the area. That left no more than two hours to get to Keyre and somehow stop the Bourne Initiative's zero-day trigger from self-actualizing.

The perimeter of the citadel had expanded even since the last time they had been here. Cranes and earthmoving machinery were hard at work among the pyramids of sunbaked bricks, sandstone, sacks of dry concrete, and various tile roofing materials.

They were stopped at the main gates. As the Angelmaker negotiated with the guards, Bourne caught a glimmer in the corner of his eye, a quick shard of light from the rising sun glancing off a metallic or glass surface. He might have thought nothing of it, but it was out past the perimeter of the cyclone fencing and the Uzi-toting guards who patrolled ceaselessly, day and night. He might have mentioned this to the Angelmaker, but he didn't. Instead, as they passed through the perimeter into the citadel itself, he said, "Keyre has done nothing but lie to me. He told me that the Maslovs were the ones he was doing business with."

"They are."

"But he also told me that Gora and Alyosha sent the thirteen men to infiltrate this village. In fact, it was Konstantin Savasin who sent the men. It was Konstantin he was at war with."

"Who told you that?"

"Ekaterina Orlova."

"And you believe her?"

"She had no reason to lie."

"And Keyre does."

"It's a way of life with him."

They passed supply depots with doors open as men on forklifts filled them with barrels of oil and other liquids used in construction and demolition. They passed immense generators housed in concrete structures, open-topped for venting, food halls, barracks, even a parade ground of earth pounded flat, with a flag flying from a forty-foot pole in the center and, where in more peaceful settings decorative fountains might be, four anti-aircraft weapons at the corners. Keyre's quarters were, of course, in the center of the compound.

To her credit, the Angelmaker made no attempt at refutation, so Bourne continued. "Keyre also lied about not knowing anything about the Bourne Initiative. He knows almost everything about it, since he's running the auction."

"Again Ekaterina."

"Yes."

"She was quite the chatty Kathy with you, wasn't she?"

Bourne gave her a grim smile. "She was trying to recruit me."

"She was the easy way."

He nodded. "And Konstantin was the hard way."

"You survived both."

"With your help."

"Then bravo to both of us." She turned off the ignition. "I don't think Keyre was lying to you about one thing: he doesn't know how real this thing he's about to auction off is. If it's the real deal or a bust."

"He'd run an auction without knowing the real value of the item?"

The Angelmaker barked a short, unpleasant laugh. "For the right amount of money Keyre would sell anything to anyone."

They arrived at the center of the citadel: a two-story building larger than any of the other residential structures, even though its sole occupant was Keyre. He required a good bit of room—for his offices, his library, his study, and, of course, the laboratory—the place, originally in a humble tent, where he had worked on Mala and would have on Liis if Bourne hadn't violently intervened.

Bourne was concentrated on the coming confrontation with Keyre and, to some extent, on the enigmatic woman about to get out from behind the jeep's steering wheel. But at the back of his mind hovered the sun-bright glimmer out beyond the citadel's perimeter.

Inside, Keyre stood, arms folded across his chest, in a large, round room Bourne had not seen before, so modern Bourne couldn't believe it existed in the bleak, war-scarred countryside of Somalia. Clad in pure white marble, it must have cost a fortune to build. A high, domed ceiled was pierced by an oculus through which sunlight moved during the course of the day. The room was centrally located. There were four doors, mirroring the placement of the four anti-aircraft guns around the parade ground. Through one open door, Bourne could see a table that looked suspiciously like the one he had seen in the tent where Keyre had worked on Mala years ago. Another, a solid mahogany door slightly ajar, led to a vast bedroom suite. The third was fully open, revealing a modern kitchen of white tile and stainless-steel appliances, gleaming beneath overhead lights. The fourth door was closed. It was made of metal, like that of a bank vault. Arrayed around the walls were flat-panel screens, showing various points around the perimeter of the compound. Below them were banks of terminals.

Keyre welcomed them like conquering heroes. Naturally, he was overjoyed when Bourne told him the good news. "So it's for real!" He rubbed his hands together. "And even better, some of the Russian participants are out of the picture. I haven't heard from either Gora or Alyosha."

"You won't be hearing from Ekaterina, either." Bourne turned to the Angelmaker. "But then I'm thinking you already know this."

"Yes," Keyre acknowledged. "The Angelmaker told me that Ekaterina and her father are out of the picture completely."

Bourne returned his attention to Keyre. "She shot them dead. Which, I'm assuming, was why you insisted she come along with me. You knew the path you set me on would lead to Ekaterina and Dima."

Keyre raised a forefinger. "Knew, no. But I suspected as much. For some time now, my lines of communication with the Russians have been somewhat, how shall I put it, sketchy."

"Which was why you needed me. You knew my close knowledge of Moscow and its people in certain circles."

"Like Karpov."

"Like Karpov," Bourne acknowledged. "But I was right about Boris. He himself would never have conceived of such a cyber weapon as you described to me. It was meant instead to enrich him and his two partners. But after his death the Initiative was hijacked, its purpose redirected." Bourne stared at Keyre. "Who could have done that, do you imagine?"

"If I'm to be honest, Bourne, I thought it was Konstantin."

"The Russian *silovik* who ordered thirteen Somalis turned by *spetsnaz* to steal it from you?" Bourne shook his head. "I don't think so."

Keyre cocked his head and, without missing a beat, said, "Did you ask him?"

"I was too busy killing him." Bourne flexed his hands at his sides. "So, let's count the people who *didn't* hijack the Initiative: Konstantin, his brother Timur, Dima Orlov, Ekaterina Orlova. I knew Gora Maslov—"

"I'd heard he was shot to death by one of his whores."

"Gora was too stupid to think of it," Bourne went on. "And as for Alyosha, she's dead, too."

Keyre raised his eyebrows. "Really? Now that *is* a surprise."

Bourne refused to be sidetracked. "So that leaves who exactly, Keyre? You. Only you. You hijacked the Initiative. You've had it all the time. You just wanted me—and Mala—to avenge the insult the Russians—particularly Konstantin—visited on you."

Keyre blew a contemplative puff of breath between his lips. "A fanciful tale, Bourne." He gestured with the flat of his hand. "But just for the fun of it, let's assume everything you've told me is true. What now?" His eyes sparked. "Will you attempt to wrest the Initiative away from me? Will you try to stop the auction?" He was almost laughing.

"You're hoping for that," Bourne said.

Keyre nodded. "Indeed I am."

"Actually, those aren't the first things on my mind," Bourne said. "The Initiative has a zero-day trigger."

Keyre's eyes narrowed. His smile was gone now. "What do you mean?"

"Remember Morgana Roy, the cybersecurity expert you mentioned who worked for General MacQuerrie? When she told me that there's a trigger built into the Initiative's root code it got me to thinking. Why would Boris want such a thing? I mean, if he was going to sell it—which I know he wasn't—or if he was going to use it as a cyber weapon—which I know he wasn't—a zero-day trigger would make no sense. In either case, it wouldn't be needed. In fact, it would become a detriment. An unnecessary race against time. But if he had it designed to take down the cyber-infrastructure of international banks, a zero-day trigger is logical. Boris must have known that the banks initiate a certain number of the largest international transfers in bulk at a certain time each week. That's when the theft on an unimaginable scale would take place."

"So that's what it was created for. Thievery." Keyre laughed. "That Karpov. I've got to hand it to him. Brilliant man. But, you know, so am I. Yes, I hijacked the

Initiative. And I also redesigned it. It wasn't too difficult if, as I did, you had the entire coding. So. First, I set up the auction idea. But then the Sovereign contacted me. He wanted the Initiative because he had something big cooking. Something very big indeed. He offered me money, lots and lots of money. But he also offered me something even more valuable than money. Can you guess?" Keyre's eyes danced merrily. "He offered me and my shipments safe passage in the ports beyond even my reach." He shrugged. "It was an offer I couldn't refuse, especially when he added that he wanted me to rid him of"—Keyre snapped his fingers—"what word did he use? Oh, yes. He wanted me to rid him of several 'unstable' individuals. You see, your friend Karpov's betrayal of him hit home. The Sovereign no longer trusted anyone around him. He wanted them gone."

"Including Konstantin."

"Yes."

"Which suited you perfectly."

"It did."

"So you sent the Angelmaker to bring me to you."

"Well. Yes. But first through neutral intermediaries I had your whereabouts transmitted to the Russians and Americans."

"We could have been killed," Bourne pointed out.

"No, no, Bourne. I had too much faith in you. And in the Angelmaker. I knew she'd bring you to me."

"So no auction."

"A ruse. I kept it going for cover."

Bourne frowned. "Cover for what?" He checked his watch. "The zero-day trigger will activate in twenty-three minutes."

"Ah, well, that. I'm sure you've heard the news stories about the Russians massing along the borders of the Baltic States. Well, instead of shutting down the banks, as Karpov planned, the Initiative will freeze NATO's communications and defense infrastructure. Once that happens, the Russians will cross the borders into Latvia, Estonia, Lithuania. Then it will be Sweden and Finland's turn. By the time NATO figures out a way around the Initiative, the Russian putsch will be a fait accompli."

"Keyre, you can't do this. Even for you—"

"But my dear Bourne. It's already done. At least it will be in, what, nineteen minutes."

And, as it turned out, Bourne was right in having the glimmer stuck in his consciousness like a splinter, because at that moment twin explosions rocked the camp as the generators blew, plunging the citadel into an electrical and electronic abyss.

———

Center. Breathe. *"Timing is everything,"* her father, the angel on her shoulder, said in her ear. Aim. Squeeze the trigger. *Ka-boom!*

Chaos.

But before that . . . Morgana had staked out Keyre's citadel for some hours, familiarized herself with the daytime and nighttime peregrinations of the guards, as well as their shift changes. She lay on her belly, peering through the powerful eyepieces of the military-grade field glasses she'd found on the plane and stuffed into a backpack, along with everything else she thought she'd need, and finally she saw the Angelmaker exit a jeep. In this one instant, remembering Mac's recitation of her kills in just the past five years, ending with *"She's a menace,"* her decision was made for her.

She watched as the Angelmaker entered Keyre's building with Jason Bourne. Her blood was running hot, and she had wanted to fire then and there, but the timing was off. With no way to ensure that all the guards would be pulled off of their posts, she needed to wait until they were in the right positions. She had already calculated how long it would take her to reach the area of cyclone fence she had targeted, and she factored this in.

When the time was right, *Ka-boom!*

And amid the chaos she scooped up her backpack and ran. She was through the fence, the wire-cutters left behind, and inside Keyre's citadel without attracting any attention. The twin explosions had caused more chaos than she had anticipated.

She ran toward her target.

Last lap, she thought. *Do or die.*

She was on her way.

45

WHAT DID YOU DO?" Keyre growled.

Bourne spread his hands.

"He didn't do anything," the Angelmaker said. "I was with him the whole time."

"Maybe you were, maybe you weren't." Keyre glared at her. "Maybe the two of you cooked this up together.

"I'm not blind." In a blur, he reached out, grabbed the Angelmaker's upper arm, brought her to him. "I see the way you look at him. I know how you feel about him."

Bourne, who knew how dangerous she could be, was appalled at the slackness in her the moment Keyre touched her. Her eyes grew soft and dreamy, her head tilted back slightly, exposing the pale flesh of her throat, as if to a lover. She bent backward, as if about to swoon. Bourne had never seen her like this, and it frightened him. It looked to him as if in Keyre's grip she had lost all control.

He lunged at her, trying to wrest her from the Somali, but she wouldn't help him work her loose.

Keyre bared his teeth, the lips drawing back, exposing black gums, in an atavistic expression, revealing all the history and power of the Yibir. "Don't you get it yet, Bourne? Look, look. She doesn't want to come."

He was right, but that didn't stop Bourne from chopping down on Keyre's wrist. As his hand dropped away, Bourne wrapped an arm around the Angelmaker's waist and dragged her away. She fought him.

"I hate you, I hate you, I hate you!" she cried, in eerie echo of the first time he had come to save her. It was as if they had all stepped back in time, as if the present was replaying the past in perfect synchronicity: Keyre laughing, Mala squirming and shouting, and him doing his best to contain the anger and panic of her younger self. In this unstable state, he half expected her to call out for him to find Liis and save her.

Perhaps to forestall her, he whispered into her ear: "You told me you had a daughter, that Keyre was holding her hostage. What else have you lied to me about?"

"That's what I do. I lie," she said, pointedly not answering him. "I warned you about my scorpion nature."

He had no answer for her. With a sickening lurch, he saw no path through the thorny forest of her inscrutable nature. She was drawn to Keyre like a flame, she always would be. He kept trying to save her, but only she could save herself from the Yibir mesmerism, and he honestly didn't know whether she possessed the inner strength.

Time seemed to slip away from him. He saw Keyre coming toward him, he felt Mala's breath against his cheek, the heaving of her body, the flailing of her limbs, as if she had lost her coordination. He saw Keyre's fist coming toward him, he saw the gleaming Damascus blade held in it, but they seemed to have no meaning for him. Not until the razor-sharp edge sliced into the meat of the arm he held around Mala.

With a shock, fire rode up his arm. His shoulder felt like it had been dislocated. As if from a great distance, he saw it drop away from Mala, he felt the blood as if it were someone else's blood. He became aware of Mala yanking the gun from him, saw her take a staggering step back, her arms held out straight in front of her, both hands wrapped around the weapon's grips. Strangely, Keyre didn't continue his attack, but stood his ground three paces from Bourne, as if rooted to the spot. Blood dripped from the tip of the knife, which was now pointed at the floor. Dimly, Bourne wondered whether the blade was coated with a drug that was now in his system.

"You see how it is now, Bourne," the Yibir magus said. "It won't be me who doles out justice, it will be the Angelmaker."

"Mala," Bourne heard himself say. "Her name is Mala."

"I'm afraid not, Bourne," Keyre said, a note of genuine pity in his voice that pierced Bourne more deeply than if Keyre's knife had found his heart. "Mala died a long time ago." He pointed toward his laboratory. "She died, upon the same table that sits now in the middle of that room. All my paraphernalia is the same, in fact, it's in the exact same spot the old tent occupied. Just the surroundings have changed."

His expression was enigmatic; it was as if he had sunk

inside himself, as if that essential part was hidden from Bourne, maybe from Mala as well.

"Mala is dead, Bourne. You've never accepted that fact. Mala died and in her place I created the creature you see before you: the Angelmaker." He inclined his head toward her. "It will be the Angelmaker who will dispense justice to you."

Mala had swung the gun in his direction. Her expression was as unreadable as was Keyre's. Her eyes seemed to be looking inward, or perhaps through him. What was she, in fact, seeing? What Keyre wanted her to see? If so, Bourne knew he was finished. One thing Konstantin had been right about. He'd read Bourne's Treadstone file, and he had gleaned the essential information. Bourne could not kill Mala, perhaps not even at the point of death. Part of him loved the part of her he still believed to be alive, despite Keyre's contention otherwise.

"Kill him," Keyre said. "Kill him now."

And then from out of the depths of Bourne's unconscious came the one last try to save them both. "Anjelica," he said to Mala. "Your mother called you Anjelica. I'm calling you Anjelica, because that's who you are. Anjelica didn't die here years ago. She's here now. She is you."

Mala blinked.

"Anjelica."

A small smile, perhaps of recognition, lit her face. Her lips parted as if to reply to him, and then she pitched forward onto her face, felled by a gunshot that had come from directly behind her. Locked as they were in their own world of fatal consequences, neither Bourne nor Keyre had heard Morgana's stealthy entrance into the building. And until the gunshot, Mala had blocked Keyre's view of her.

Both he and Bourne shouted at the same time, in shock and grief, perhaps, but the sounds, like those of an animal, were indecipherable. As they went at each other, Bourne felt a rage, pure and powerful, rise up within him. Now she was gone. Bourne knew she was gone without having to kneel beside her, check her pulse, or listen for her breath. She lay as she had fallen, deathly still, nothing more than a husk now, and perhaps, at last, at peace.

Bourne soon found that there was no good way to fight Keyre. He was as slippery as an eel, seemingly as immune to the blows Bourne rained on him as if he were made of stone. As for Morgana, she was trying her best to get a clear shot at Keyre, without success. Meanwhile, Keyre's returned blows were taking their toll on Bourne. In his weakened state, he knew he couldn't hold out for very long. He needed to end the struggle quickly or face defeat and death.

With lightning speed he went through his options, none of which seemed to him to give him much of a chance. But there was one, though the riskiest of the bunch, which might see him through. With the next strike from Keyre, he doubled over, moaning in pain. Taking the bait, Keyre doubled down on his attack, which built to such a frenzy that he completely disregarded his defense.

That was where Bourne got him. From his knees, Bourne drove a fist upward and, with the Somali bent over him, his knuckle struck Keyre squarely in the sternum, shattering it. In shock, Keyre seemed to freeze for a moment. And in the moment, Bourne acted. Rising from his penitent's position, he buried his fist in Keyre's side. Ribs went, at least two, possibly three, stove in by the power of the blow. The third strike caught Keyre's left kidney. The fourth and fifth, as well.

Bourne grabbed a handful of the Somali's hair, dripping sweat, and, using the massed tips of his fingers, drove the shards of Keyre's sternum inward, into his organs. Blood poured out of Keyre's mouth, his eyes turned upward, as if beseeching his unknown Yibir gods for a surcease that did not come. Bourne was in no mood for mercy. Taking Keyre's head in his hands, he slammed his face into his raised knee.

Keyre dropped like a stone and lay in a widening pool of his own blood.

At the sound of pounding boot soles, Bourne turned to see a pair of guards run into the room. Morgana shot them both before they could fire. Bourne and Morgana's eyes locked again, and a strange mixed message passed between them. She had killed Anjelica, but then the Angelmaker had been about to kill him. It was her nature, as she had told him. The nature of the scorpion. He nodded to her, and she nodded back.

He looked down at Mala's body, the surprised expression on her face. Her eyes were as blank as those of the Sphinx. What had she thought at the end? he wondered. He thought of her tortured life, both when she was with Keyre and after. He had never left her; he'd been a poison in her blood that no amount of figurative transfusions could defeat.

In the end, despite all of his help, Keyre had owned her, body and soul.

"Bourne!" Morgana cried.

The sharpness of her voice broke the spell, and he told her how Keyre had altered the Initiative to shut down NATO to accommodate the Russian Sovereign.

"That's it then," she said in despair. "Even if we were to somehow get through to someone high up in NATO, even if the person would believe us, it would be too late."

"But there must be a way," Bourne said. "Boris wouldn't have had the Initiative constructed without a fail-safe. A key. A way to shut down the zero-day trigger in case of emergency."

She looked up, a gleam of hope in her eyes. "If he left it with anyone, he left it with you. He must have. You two were thick as thieves; you were the only one he trusted. You must have it."

"Everyone seems to think I do," Bourne said. "But I don't."

"All right then. But to have even the remotest chance I have to get a look at the completed code."

He nodded. "This way."

Bourne led her to the only metal door in the room. Fireproof. "I'll bet anything what we need is behind here."

It occurred to her then that the complete code had been her holy grail from the moment she had been given her slightly hysterical orders from Mac. She had hit a wall and had decided to take a different route altogether; the route her father would have had her take. But all the while, like an itch she couldn't scratch, her failure at piecing together the Initiative never left her mind. It had increased in stature, like a myth, like fabled El Dorado. Now she fairly shook at the thought of actually seeing the finished code.

"We have less than ten minutes to find the Initiative and to somehow defeat the zero-day trigger, and, look, there's no lock." She could not keep the despair out of her voice. "There's not even a handle." She pointed. "Just this rectangle affixed to the surface."

"It must be the locking mechanism."

"But there's no keypad. How—?"

Bourne touched the plate. His fingertip made an impression, just as it would on a haptic mobile phone or laptop screen.

"Good God," Morgana said. "How can we possibly know what to input? There are no numbers, no letters, nothing but a blank screen."

"Quiet," Bourne said. "I'm thinking,"

"Well, think quickly," she said. "We're at seven minutes and counting."

The trick was to put himself in Keyre's mind. A horrible thing to have to attempt, but it had to be done. He turned back to look at his corpse. What would the Yibir have used to gain entrance, something no one else could possibly know? How could he know? How could anyone know? His gaze drifted inevitably to Mala. So many names, so many identities.

Without warning, he was thrown back to their night on Skyros, the blackness, the turbulence of the storm, how he had traced the runes on her back, committing them to memory, even as she turned away, as if she were ashamed of them. He froze.

The runes.

Tentatively, he touched the screen again, and then ever more authoritatively began to trace out the shape of the scars on Mala's back.

"What the hell are you doing?" Morgana said, but it was clear that she was fascinated.

"Keyre was a Yibir magus." Bourne was halfway through now. "He scarred Mala—the Angelmaker—with these runes." He was done. He held his breath.

The door clicked open, and they rushed through. They found themselves in a dimly lit room, windowless and claustrophobic. Apparently it had its own generator, because all the electronics were working. On a semicircular table was a powerful desktop surrounded by two laptops. Four screens showed different areas of the citadel and the port. It was clear from them that the explosions had morphed into fires that had spread to the neighboring buildings. As they watched, transfixed, a warehouse of war matériel went up in a ball of fire and black smoke. Keyre's men were swarming all over that section of the compound in a frantic effort to keep the rest of the stored weapons and ammo from going up and destroying the entire village.

The laptops were open but their screens were dark. Perhaps they were waiting patiently for the auction that would now never come. The desktop screen was on and active.

"It's the Initiative!" Morgana cried. "I recognize the bits of it I've tried and failed to decipher."

"But you discovered the zero-day trigger," Bourne said.

Setting her backpack down, she perched on the mesh task chair. "Yes. That much I was able to decode." She turned to him. "D'you really think there is a fail-safe?"

"Knowing Boris, I do. He was meticulous about such things. He made sure he accounted for every contingency." He stared at the screen, his mind racing. "It would be logical if the fail-safe was in the same bit as the zero-day trigger, wouldn't it?"

Morgana's fingers were racing across the keyboard. "It would. But then why didn't I see it before this?"

Bourne glanced at his watch. "Three minutes left."

Morgana, half bent over the keyboard, her fingers a blur, kept combing through the code of the cyber weapon. "Honestly, I'd need hours, if not days to find it. Unless, of course, someone knew the key code."

"I've told everyone under the sun I don't have it. Boris didn't leave me anything."

"Nothing?" Morgana lifted her fingers from the keyboard, rocked back and forth in despair. "Ninety seconds. I'll never be able to stop it."

"Well, his yacht, but that's at the bottom of the Mediterranean now. You can be sure that I searched it thoroughly before it was sunk."

She picked her head up. "What was the name of the boat?"

"What? Why?"

"You said he left you the boat." She turned to him. "What if the boat is the key?"

Bourne's heart started to race. "*Nym*," he said. "Boris's boat was named *Nym*."

As she turned back to the keyboard, he spelled it out for her.

"N-Y-M," she repeated back as if to herself. "Fifty-three seconds. Here goes."

She typed in the letters. Nothing happened.

"Shit," she said.

"What is it?"

"I must have entered the key in the wrong place." Her fingers frantically worked the keyboard, and then—

Everything stopped.

"There," Morgana said.

The screen went dark.

"Got you, you sonuvabitch."

———

For Morgana that was the end of her second successful brief for Soraya Moore. But for Bourne, there was one more thing left to do. Much as he wanted to, he couldn't carry Mala's body out of the citadel, even amid such chaos, so he did the next best thing.

In Keyre's laboratory, he stared at the table with its old bloodstains, now almost black as pitch. How much pain and suffering had this table seen—not only Mala's, but all the young girls who had come before her.

Searching through the magus's supplies he came upon a can of flammable liquid. What he had done with it, how he had applied it judiciously to his "girls" Bourne could not—and would not—imagine.

Standing in the doorway, even with her phone against her cheek, briefing Soraya, bringing her up to date in hushed tones, assuring her she had made a copy of the code and then destroyed the fail-safe-locked original, Morgana sensed his great sorrow. She did not pretend to understand his relationship with the Angelmaker, nor why he could feel anything for her at all. But it wasn't her place to understand, and she did not judge him.

She watched silently as he doused the table with the liquid, then ran a thin line of it across the lab's floor to where the Angelmaker's body lay. There were a number of devices that created a flame in the lab, but Bourne deliberately chose the most primitive of them—long wooden matches.

Scraping the head of one along the side of the box, he watched the flame flare up. He wished he were the kind of person who believed in God; he wished he knew a prayer.

He composed his own. "Good-bye, Anjelica," he whispered. "You will be remembered."

Then he threw the match onto the center of the glistening table.

About the Author

ROBERT LUDLUM was the author of twenty-seven novels, each one a *New York Times* bestseller. There are more than 225 million of his books in print, and they have been translated into thirty-two languages. He is the author of *The Scarlatti Inheritance*, *The Chancellor Manuscript*, and the Jason Bourne series—*The Bourne Identity*, *The Bourne Supremacy*, and *The Bourne Ultimatum*—among others. Mr. Ludlum passed away in March 2001. To learn more, you can visit Robert-Ludlum.com.

ERIC VAN LUSTBADER is the author of numerous bestselling novels including *First Daughter*, *Beloved Enemy*, *The Ninja*, and the international bestsellers featuring Jason Bourne: *The Bourne Legacy*, *The Bourne Betrayal*, *The Bourne Sanction*, *The Bourne Deception*, *The Bourne Objective*, *The Bourne Dominion*, *The Bourne Imperative*, *The Bourne Retribution*, and *The Bourne Ascendancy*. For more information, you can visit EricVanLustbader.com. You can also follow him on Facebook and Twitter.

If you enjoy Robert Ludlum's Jason Bourne series, don't miss his Paul Janson thrillers!

To prevent a war in Asia—one that could quickly spread to the rest of the world—Paul Janson and Jessica Kincaid must learn the truth behind a young woman's murder . . .

Robert Ludlum's™

THE JANSON EQUATION

Written by Douglas Corleone

Please turn this page for an excerpt.

Joint Base Pearl Harbor — Hickam
Adjacent to Honolulu, Hawaii

Ten minutes after the Embraer Legacy 650 touched down at Hickam Field on the island of Oahu, Paul Janson stepped onto the warm tarmac and was immediately greeted by Lawrence Hammond, the senator's chief of staff.

"Thank you for coming," Hammond said.

As the men shook hands, Janson breathed deeply of the fresh tropical air and savored the gentle touch of the Hawaiian sun on his face. After six months under Shanghai's polluted sky, smog as thick as tissue paper had become Janson's new normal. Only now, as he inhaled freely, did he fully realize the extent to which he'd spent the past half year breathing poison.

Behind his Wayfarers, Janson closed his eyes for a moment and listened. Although Hickam buzzed with the typical sounds of an operational airfield, Janson instantly relished the relative tranquility. Vividly, he imagined the coastal white sand beaches and azure blue waters awaiting him and Jessie just beyond the confines of the US Air Force base.

Hammond, a tall man with slicked-back hair the color of straw, directed Janson to an idling olive green jeep driven by a private first class who couldn't possibly have been old enough to legally drink. As Janson belted himself into the passenger seat, Hammond leaned forward and said, "Air Force One landed on this runway not too long ago."

"Is that right?" Janson said as the jeep pulled away from the jet.

Hammond mistook Janson's politeness for genuine interest. "This past Christmas, as a matter of fact. The First Family vacations on the windward side of the island, in the small beach town of Kailua."

The three remained silent for the rest of the ten-minute drive. Janson's original plan upon leaving Shanghai had been to land at nearby Honolulu International, where he'd meet Jessie and be driven to Waikiki for an evening of dinner and drinks and a steamy night at the iconic Pink Palace before boarding a puddle jumper to Maui the next day. But a phone call Janson received thirty thousand miles above the Pacific changed all that.

Janson had been resting in his cabin, on the verge of sleep, when his lone flight attendant, Kayla, buzzed him over the intercom and announced that he had a call from the mainland.

"It's a US senator," Kayla said. "I thought you might want to take it."

"Which senator?" Janson asked groggily. He knew only a handful personally and liked even fewer.

"Senator James Wyckoff," she said. "Of North Carolina."

Wyckoff was neither one of the handful Janson knew personally nor one of the few that he liked. But before Janson could ask her to take a callback number, Kayla told him that Wyckoff had been referred by his current client, Jeremy Beck, CEO of Edgerton-Gertz.

Grudgingly, Janson decided to take the call.

As the jeep pulled into the parking lot of a small administrative building, Janson turned to Hammond and said, "The senator beat me here?"

The flight from Shanghai was just over nine hours and Janson had already been in the air two hours when Wyckoff phoned. From DC, even under the best conditions, it was nearly a ten-hour flight to Honolulu, and Janson was fairly sure there was snow and ice on the ground in Washington this time of year.

"The senator actually called you from California," Hammond said. "He'd been holding a fund-raiser at Exchange in downtown Los Angeles when he received the news about his son."

Janson didn't say anything else. He stepped out of the jeep and followed Hammond and the private first class to the building. The baby-faced PFC used a key to open the door then stepped aside as Janson and Hammond entered. The dissonant rumble of an ancient air conditioner emanated from overhead vents, and the sun's natural light was instantly replaced by the harsh glow of buzzing fluorescent bulbs.

Hammond ushered Janson down a bleak hallway of marred linoleum into a spacious yet utilitarian office in the rear of the building, then quietly excused himself, saying, "Senator Wyckoff will be right with you."

Two minutes later a toilet flushed and the senator himself stepped out of a back room with his hand already extended.

"Paul Janson, I presume."

"A pleasure, Senator."

Janson removed his Wayfarers and took the proffered seat in front of the room's lone streaked and dented metal desk, while Senator Wyckoff situated himself on the opposite side, crossing his right leg over his left before taking a deep breath and launching into the facts.

"As I said over the phone, Mr. Janson, the details of my son's disappearance are still sketchy. What we do know is that Gregory's girlfriend of three years, a beautiful young lady named Lynell Yi, was found murdered in the *hanok* she and Gregory were staying at in central Seoul yesterday morning. She'd evidently been strangled."

The senator appeared roughly fifty years old, well groomed, and dressed in an expensive, tailored suit, but the bags under his eyes told the story of someone who'd lived through hell over the past twenty-four hours.

"The Seoul Metropolitan Police," Wyckoff continued, "have named Gregory their primary suspect in Lynell's death, which, if you knew my son, you'd know is preposterous. But of course my wife and I are concerned. Gregory's just a teenager. We don't know whether he's been kidnapped or is on the run because he's frightened. Being falsely accused of murder in a foreign country must be terrifying. Even though South Korea is our ally, it'll take time to get things sorted out through the proper channels." The senator leaned forward, planting his elbows on the desk. "I'd like for you to travel to Seoul and find him. That's our first priority. Second, and nearly as important, I'd like you to conduct an independent investigation into Lynell's murder. Now may be our only opportunity. I'm a former trial lawyer, and I can tell you from experience that evidence disappears fast. Witnesses vanish. Memories become fuzzy. If we don't clear Gregory's name in the next ninety-six hours, we may never be able to do so."

Janson held up his hand. "Let me stop you right there, Senator. I sympathize with you, I do. I'm very sorry that your family is going through this. And I hope that your son turns up unharmed sooner rather than later. I'm sure you're right. I'm sure he's being wrongly accused, and I'm sincerely hopeful that you can prove it and bring him home to grieve for his girlfriend. *But* I'm afraid that I can't help you with this. I'm not a private investigator."

"I'm not suggesting you are. But this is no ordinary investigation."

"Please, Senator, let me continue. I'm here as a courtesy to my client Jeremy Beck. But as I attempted to tell you over the phone, this simply isn't something I can take on." Janson reached into his jacket pocket and unfolded a piece of paper. "While I was in the air, I took the liberty of contacting a few old friends, and I have the names and telephone numbers of a handful of top-notch private investigators in Seoul. They know the city inside and out, and they can obtain information directly from the police without having to navigate through miles of red tape. According to my contacts, these men and women are the best investigators in all of South Korea."

Wyckoff accepted the piece of paper and set it down on the desk without looking at it. He narrowed his eyes, confirming Janson's initial impression that the senator wasn't a man who was told no very often. And that he seldom accepted the word for an answer.

"Mr. Janson, do you have children?"

As Wyckoff said it there was a firm knock on the door. The senator pushed himself out of his chair and trudged toward the sound.

Meanwhile, Janson frowned. He didn't like to be asked personal questions. Not by clients and not by prospective clients. Certainly not after he'd already declined to take the job. And this was no innocuous question. It was a subject that burned Janson deep in his stomach. No, he did not have children. He did not have a family—only the memory of one. Only the stabbing recollection of a pregnant wife and the dashed dreams of their unborn child, their future obliterated by a terrorist's bomb. They'd perished almost a decade ago, yet it still felt like yesterday.

From behind, Janson heard Hammond's sonorous voice followed by a far softer one and the unmistakable sound of a woman's sobs.

"Mr. Janson," the senator said, "I'd like you to meet my wife, Alicia. Gregory's mother."

Janson stood and turned toward the couple as Hammond stepped out, closing the door gently behind him.

Alicia Wyckoff stood before Janson visibly trembling, her eyes wet with mascara tears. She appeared to be a few years younger than her husband, but her handling of the present crisis threatened to make her look his age in no time flat.

"Thank you so much for coming," she said, ignoring Janson's hand and instead gripping him in an awkward hug. He felt the warmth of her tears through his shirt, her long nails burrowing into his upper back.

If Janson were slightly more cynical, he'd have thought her entry had been meticulously timed in advance.

Wyckoff brushed some papers aside and sat on the front edge of the desk. "I know your professional history," he said to Janson. "As soon as Jeremy gave me your name I contacted State and obtained a complete dossier. While a good many parts of the document were redacted, what I *was* able to read was very impressive. You are uniquely qualified for this job, Mr. Janson." He paused for effect. "Please, don't turn us away."

"Turn us away?" Alicia Wyckoff interjected. "What are you talking about?" She turned to Janson. "Are you seriously considering refusing to help us?"

Janson remained standing. "As I told your husband a few moments ago, I'm simply not the person you need."

"But you *are*." She spun toward her husband. "Haven't you *told* him?"

Wyckoff shook his head.

"Told me what?"

Janson couldn't imagine a scenario that might possibly change his mind. He'd just left Asia behind. He needed some downtime. Jessica needed some downtime. In the past couple years they'd taken on one mission after another, almost without pause. Following two successive missions off the coast of Africa, Janson and

Kincaid had promised themselves a break. But when Jeremy Beck called about the perpetual cyber-espionage being perpetrated by the Chinese government, Janson became intrigued. This was what his post–Cons Ops life was all about: changing the world, one mission at a time.

Wyckoff pushed off the desk and sighed deeply, as though he'd been hoping he wouldn't have to divulge what he was about to. At least not until *after* Janson had accepted the case.

"We don't think Lynell's murder was a crime of passion or a random killing," Wyckoff said. "And we don't think the Seoul Metropolitan Police came to suspect our son by themselves; we think they were deliberately led there."

Janson watched the senator's eyes and said, "By whom?"

Wyckoff pursed his lips. He looked as if he were about to sign a deal for his soul. Or something of even greater importance to a successful US politician. "What I say next stays between us, Mr. Janson."

"Of course."

The senator placed his hands on his hips and exhaled. "We think Gregory was framed by your former employer."

Janson hesitated. "I'm not sure I understand."

"The victim, Lynell Yi, my son's girlfriend, is—*was*, I should say—a Korean-English translator. She'd been working on sensitive talks in the Korean demilitarized zone. Talks between the North and the South and other interested parties, namely the United States and China. We think she overheard something she shouldn't have.

We think she shared it with our son, and that they were both subsequently targeted by someone in the US government. Or to be more specific, someone in the US State Department."

"And you think this murder was carried out by Consular Operations?" Janson said.

Wyckoff bowed his head. "The murder and the subsequent frame—all of it is just too neat. Our son is not stupid. If he *were* somehow involved in Lynell's murder—an utter impossibility in and of itself—he would not have left behind a glaring trail of evidence pointing directly at him."

"In a crime of passion," Janson said, "by definition, the killer isn't thinking or acting rationally. His intellect would have little to do with what occurred during or immediately after the event."

"Granted," Wyckoff said. "But according to the information released by the Seoul police, this killer would have had plenty of time to clean up after himself."

"Or time to get a running head start," Janson countered.

Wyckoff ignored him. "Lynell's body wasn't found until morning. She was discovered by a maid. There wasn't even a 'Do Not Disturb' sign on the door. Whoever killed Lynell *wanted* her body to be found quickly. *Wanted* it to look like a crime of passion."

Janson said nothing. He knew Wyckoff's alternative theory was based solely on a parent's wishful thinking. But what else could a father do under the circumstances? What would Janson himself be doing if the accused was *his* teenage son?

"Tell me, Paul," Wyckoff said, dispensing with the

formalities, "do you *honestly* believe that powers within the US government aren't capable of something like this?"

Janson could say no such thing. He *knew* what his government was capable of. He'd carried out operations not so different from the one Wyckoff was describing. And he would be spending the rest of his life atoning for them.

"Before I became a US senator," Wyckoff continued, "I was a Charlotte trial lawyer. I specialized in mass torts. Made my fortune suing pharmaceutical companies for manufacturing and selling dangerous drugs that had been preapproved by the FDA. I made tens of millions of dollars, and I would be willing to part with all of it if you would agree to take this case. Name your fee, Paul, and it's yours."

For something as involved as this, Janson could easily ask for seven or eight million dollars. And it would all go to the Phoenix Foundation. A payday this size could help dozens of former covert government operators take their lives back.

And Janson had to admit he liked the idea of looking closely at his former employer.

And if by some stretch of the imagination the US State Department was indeed involved in framing the son of a prominent US senator for murder, the government's ultimate objective would likely have widespread repercussions for the entire region, if not the world.

"I have one condition," Janson finally said.

"Name it."

"If I find your son and uncover the truth, you'll have to promise to accept it, regardless of what that truth is.

Even if it ultimately leads to your son's conviction for murder."

Wyckoff glanced at his wife, who bowed her head. He turned back to Janson and said, "You have our word."

Dosan Park
Sinsa-dong, Gangnam-gu, Seoul

As the brutal cold burrowed deep into her bones, Jessica Kincaid couldn't shake the feeling that she was being followed. She lowered her head against the gusting wind and stole another glance over her left shoulder but saw no one.

You're being paranoid. You're the one doing the following.

Across the way, Ambassador Young's chief aide entered an upscale Korean restaurant named Jung Sikdang. Kincaid cursed under her breath. She couldn't very well walk into the restaurant; Jonathan would recognize her right away. And she sure as hell didn't want to wait around outside in the bitter cold for an hour while Jonathan enjoyed his evening meal. *Damn.* She'd been so sure he was heading straight to his apartment, where Kincaid could knock on the door and hopefully corner him alone. But no. An hour of surveillance, wasted.

After leaving the US Embassy, Kincaid had headed north to the Sophia Guesthouse in Sogyeok-dong. It was her first time visiting a traditional *hanok* and she was instantly charmed. Fewer than a dozen rooms surrounded a spartan courtyard with a simple garden and young trees that stood completely bare in solidarity with the season.

Rather than poke around uninvited, she went straight to the proprietors, a husband and wife of indistinguishable age. Both spoke fluent English. Although wary at first, they gradually opened up to Kincaid once she agreed to join them for afternoon tea.

Seated on low, comfortable cushions, Kincaid asked the couple whether they had ever seen Lynell Yi or Gregory Wyckoff before their recent visit. Neither of them had. Nor had they personally overheard the loud argument that was alleged to have taken place the night of the murder. The guests who *had* overheard the argument—a young Korean couple from Busan—had already checked out. Kincaid had seen their home addresses listed in the police file Janson had obtained on the plane, so she moved on.

After tea, Kincaid asked if she might have a look around, and the couple readily acquiesced. As they walked through the courtyard toward the room where Lynell Yi's body was found, the husband launched into a semicomposed rant about the disappearance of the *hanok* in South Korean culture. The one-story homes crafted entirely of wood, he said, were victims of the South's "obsession with modernization." As he pointed out the craftsmanship of the clay-tiled roof, he noticed Kincaid's chattering teeth and explained that the rooms were well insulated with mud and straw, and heated by a system called *ondol,* which lay beneath the floor.

The wife took a key from her pocket and opened the

door to number 9, the room in which Wyckoff and Yi had stayed. It was located in the newer section of the *hanok*. Kincaid was surprised to find that the two-day-old crime scene was already immaculate. There was no yellow police tape, no blood or footprints or any other evidence to be seen. According to the husband, a team had rushed in and cleaned the place up and down the moment the police indicated they were finished. Kincaid made a mental note to check whether this was normal procedure in the Republic of Korea.

The room itself was cozy, about half the size of a one-car garage. But it was also elegant in an understated way. There were no beds or chairs, just traditional mats, a pair of locked trunks, and a small color television set you probably couldn't purchase in stores anymore. She'd seen the room in evidence photos, but the pictures didn't do the place justice.

Kincaid walked to the window, which was made of a thin translucent paper that allowed in natural light. She placed her hand on one of the speckled walls and thought that if she gave it a solid punch, her fist would land in the next room. So much for proving that fellow guests couldn't possibly have overheard an argument between the victim and the accused. But what truly puzzled her was that the police noted no signs of a struggle. Given the size of the room, that seemed all but impossible, especially considering the fact that Lynell Yi had apparently been the victim of manual strangulation.

"Tourists from the West still love to stay in *hanok*," the husband said, collapsing her thoughts. "They do not come to Seoul to stay in a high-rise they can see in New York City or London."

Kincaid nodded. She understood his passion, and unlike Janson, she could certainly understand why the young lovers might have slipped away from their modern apartment nearby to experience an amorous night in a traditional Korean home. Maybe she was just more romantic than Paul—or maybe Paul had previously been inside a *hanok* and had been reminded of the six-by-four-foot cage he'd been kept in during the eighteen months he spent as a prisoner of the Taliban in Afghanistan. That would certainly be reason enough for him to dismiss the *hanok* as a desirable place to stay. Either way, Kincaid didn't think Janson's theory that the young couple had been on the run held much water.

———

Following her visit to the Sophia Guesthouse, Kincaid waited in line for a dish of spicy chili beef then headed south back to the US Embassy. By then it was nearing five o'clock Korean time, and she was hoping to catch Jonathan exiting the embassy after calling it a day. Jonathan was probably in his mid- to late twenties, not a teenager but certainly closer to Lynell Yi in age than most people employed at the embassy. And when Kincaid asked if there was anyone in the office who knew Lynell Yi well, the ambassador's glance toward the doorway made her suspect that Jonathan might hold some of the answers to questions she had about Yi's job, maybe even her relationship with Gregory Wyckoff.

Jonathan exited the embassy at a quarter after five and walked to the subway station at Chongyak. There he took the 1 line, and Kincaid hopped into the subway car trailing his. He got off just two stops later and boarded the 3. On the 3 train, he seemed to settle in for a lengthy ride. And lengthy it was; he didn't step off the train again until they were south of the Han River in Gangnam-gu, the district made famous—or infamous—by that obnoxious pop song Kincaid heard over and over at clubs around the world.

Sweet Jesus. Now that she'd thought about it, she couldn't get the damned song out of her head.

Kincaid continued to watch the restaurant. As she held her arms across her chest against the cold, she experienced that feeling again. That odd sensation that while she was watching Jonathan, she too was being watched. *But by whom?*

She searched the faces of the few people on the street braving the freezing weather. She eyed a group of teenagers huddled at the far corner of the park. She counted four males and two females, all probably under the age of eighteen. An unlikely bunch of spies, to say the least.

To her left, she spotted a vagrant hunched over on a park bench.

A vagrant? In these temperatures? How could he possibly survive the night?

The sun was dipping low behind the mountain; dark was falling fast. If she didn't identify her stalker soon, it would be all but impossible. She reached into her pocket for her phone to call Janson but then thought better of it. She'd already informed him that she'd followed Jonathan to the restaurant. She could handle this on her own.

She turned away from the restaurant, retreating back into the park. The group of teens paid her no attention.

The vagrant didn't stir. Two males were walking fast straight toward her, but as they approached she noted they were holding hands, exposing their fingers to the cold. In this weather, that was true love.

A minute later she moved past the couple, deeper into the park. She stole another look over her shoulder. Had any of the people she'd seen earlier followed her? None that she could tell. But she felt a pair of eyes on her nevertheless.

Kincaid quickened her pace as her pulse sped up and her head filled with images of men in fedoras and dark trench coats, with handguns hanging at their sides.

In the center of the park, she spun around and spotted movement in a copse of trees. An animal? No. Unless a grizzly bear escaped from the Seoul Zoo, this creature was too large to be anything but a human being.

She continued moving forward as though she'd seen nothing. But she heard a rustle and was suddenly sure that whoever was following her knew he'd been made. Which meant that he was probably a professional.

With no one else in sight and the cover of dusk protecting him, her attacker finally made his move and launched himself out of the shadows.

Kincaid didn't hesitate, didn't bother looking back, just took off in a sprint across the park in the direction of the river. Over the shrieking gusts of wind she heard her pursuer make contact with bushes and low tree branches as he cut a parallel course north toward the Han, attempting to overtake her.

But Kincaid was fast. Fastest in her class at Quantico, where her professional life began. In the time since she'd left Virginia to join the FBI's National Security Division, she'd put on a few years but not a single extra pound. And her world hadn't paused since she'd been stolen away by the State Department after catching the eyes of some spooks from Consular Operations.

It was times like this when brimming with confidence counted, and that was a trait she'd had in spades all the way back to her childhood in Red Creek, Kentucky. She'd taken that confidence with her when she'd boarded a Greyhound bus, leaving her daddy behind for the first time in her life. And over the years that confidence had been refined, first by the Bureau, then by Cons Ops, and most recently by Paul Janson.

She charged through a row of bushes and found herself back on a street. She paused a moment to catch her breath, which was billowing in large white puffs before her eyes. Through the mist she eyed a taxi, and her arm shot up almost instinctively.

The orange taxi slowed and pulled to the curb and Kincaid opened the door and dove into the backseat, shouting, "Go, go, *go*."

As the taxi peeled away Kincaid raised her head just in time to see a tall Korean man breaking through the bushes, stopping on a dime, then raising his arms with a gun in his hands. She watched him take aim and nervously waited for the sound of a gunshot, the shattering of window glass, the buzz of a bullet as it streaked by within inches of her face.

Mercifully, the assassin never fired.

Praise for *The Unquiet Dead*

"Impressive . . . Throughout Getty and Khattak's solid and comprehensive investigation, Khan's talents are evident. This first in what may become a series is a many-faceted gem. It's a sound police procedural, a somber study of loss and redemption and, most of all, a grim effort to make sure that crimes against humanity are not forgotten." —*The Washington Post*

"Beautiful and powerful." —*Publishers Weekly* (starred review)

"Khan has brought every ounce of her intellect and professional experience in working with Muslim refugees to this affecting debut. Her use of certain mystery conventions echoes the masters . . . Yet for all of the echoes of the greats, Khan is a refreshing original, and *The Unquiet Dead* blazes what one hopes will be a new path guided by the author's keen understanding of the intersection of faith and core Muslim values, complex human nature, and evil done by seemingly ordinary people. It is these qualities that make this a debut to remember and one that even those who eschew the genre will devour in one breathtaking sitting." —*Los Angeles Times*

"A spectacular debut. Khan has written a heartbreaking book that stays with you long after you've put it down."
—Reza Aslan, #1 *New York Times* bestselling author of *Zealot*

"Ausma Zehanat Khan's gripping first novel tackles questions of identity, culture, revenge, and war horrors in a strong police procedural. . . . Khan illustrates her powerful storytelling through her well-sculpted characters. . . . An intelligent plot and graceful writing make *The Unquiet Dead* an outstanding debut that is not easily forgotten." —Associated Press

"Flashbacks to the Bosnian War and glimpses into the personal tragedies of Khattak and Getty make this debut . . . even more compelling and hauntingly powerful . . . Anyone looking for an intensely memorable mystery should put this book at the top of their list."   —*Library Journal* (starred review, Debut of the Month)

"Evocative, surprising, and important. With its mesmerizingly personal voice, each lyrical sentence reveals another suspenseful layer of this complex and heartbreaking mystery. Harrowing and disturbing, its delicate strength creates tension on every page."
—Hank Phillippi Ryan; Anthony, Agatha, Macavity, and Mary Higgins Clark Award–winning author of *The Other Woman*

"This is Canadian-born Khan's first novel and what a debut it is! . . . Khan knows her subject, knows her hometown, and knows how to keep the suspense building. This is a writer to watch."
—*The Globe and Mail* (Canada)

"Exceptional . . . Khan's novel is self-assured and sobering, suspenseful and smart."   —*Milwaukee Journal Sentinel*

"Gripping."   —*The Denver Post*

"Khan's stunning debut is a poignant, elegantly written mystery laced with complex characters."   —*Kirkus Reviews*

"It would be enough that Ausma Zehanat Khan's *The Unquiet Dead* gives us an intriguing new detective team in Esa Khattak and Sgt. Rachel Getty. But it does far more than that. Khan creates an engrossing story that allows her to sift through the emotional rubble of real-world tragedy. In the end, it isn't just gripping. It's devastating."
—Steve Hockensmith, Edgar Award–nominated author of *Holmes on the Range*

Ausma Zehanat Khan

The
Unquiet
Dead

MINOTAUR BOOKS · NEW YORK

THE UNQUIET DEAD. Copyright © 2014 by Ausma Zehanat Khan. All rights reserved. Printed in the United States of America. For information, address St. Martin's Press, 175 Fifth Avenue, New York, N.Y. 10010.

www.minotaurbooks.com

The Library of Congress has cataloged the hardcover edition as follows:

Khan, Ausma Zehanat.
  The unquiet dead / Ausma Zehanat Khan. — First edition.
    p. cm.
  ISBN 978-1-250-05511-8 (hardcover)
  ISBN 978-1-4668-5831-2 (e-book)
  1. Murder—Investigation—Fiction.   2. Murder victims—Fiction.   I. Title.
  PS3611.H335U58 2015
  813'.6—dc23

2014032396

ISBN 978-1-250-05518-7 (trade paperback)

Our books may be purchased in bulk for promotional, educational, or business use. Please contact your local bookseller or the Macmillan Corporate and Premium Sales Department at (800) 221-7945, extension 5442, or by e-mail at MacmillanSpecialMarkets@macmillan.com.

First Minotaur Books Paperback Edition: December 2015

D 10 9 8 7 6

For my parents,
Dr. Zehanat Ali Khan
and
Mrs. Nasima Khan,
whose love and shining example
are everything

Let justice be done lest the world perish.

—HEGEL

1.

I will never worship what you worship.
Nor will you worship what I worship.
To you, your religion—to me, mine.

Esa Khattak turned his head to the right, offering the universal sa-
laam at the conclusion of the evening prayer. He was seated with his
legs folded beneath him on a prayer rug woven by his ancestors from
Peshawar. The worn red and gold strands were comforting; his fingers sought them out when he pressed his forehead to the floor. A
moment later, his eyes traced them as his cupped palms offered the
final supplication.

The Maghrib prayer was for Khattak a time of consolation where
along with prayers for Muhammad, he asked for mercy upon his
wife and forgiveness for the accident that had caused her death. A
nightly ritual of grief relieved by the possibility of hope, it stretched
across that most resonant band of time: twilight. The dying sun
muted his thoughts, much as it subdued the colors of the *ja-namaz*
beneath him. It was the discipline of the ritual that brought him
comfort, the reason he rarely missed it. Unless he was on duty—as
he was tonight, when the phone call from Tom Paley disturbed his
concentration.

He no longer possessed the hot-blooded certainties of youth that
a prayer missed or delayed would bring about a concomitant judgment of sin. Time had taught him to view his faith through the prism

of compassion: when ritual was sacrificed in pursuit of the very values it was meant to inspire, there could be no judgment, no sin.

He took the phone call from Tom Paley midway through the prayer and finished up in its aftermath. Tom, the most respected historian at Canada's Department of Justice, would not have disturbed him on an evening when Khattak could just as easily have been off-roster unless the situation was urgent.

CPS, the Community Policing Section that Khattak headed, was still fragile, barely a year into its existence. The ambit was deliberately vague because CPS was a fig leaf for the most problematic community relations issue of all—Islam. A steady shift to the right in Canadian politics, coupled with the spectacular bungling of the Maher Arar terrorism case in 2002, had birthed a generation of activist lawyers who pushed back vigorously against what they called tainted multiculturalism. Maher Arar's saga of extraordinary rendition and torture had mobilized them, making front-page news for months and costing the federal government millions in compensation when Arar had been cleared of all links to terrorism. A hastily concocted Community Policing Section had been the federal government's response, and who better than Esa Khattak to head it? A second-generation Canadian Muslim, his career had seen him transition seamlessly from Toronto's homicide squad to national counterintelligence work at INSET, one of the Integrated National Security Enforcement Teams. CPS called on both skill sets. Khattak was a rising star with an inbuilt understanding of the city of Toronto's shifting demographic landscape. At CPS, he was asked to lend his expertise to sensitive police investigations throughout the country at the request of senior investigating officers from any branch of government.

The job had been offered to Khattak as a promotion, his acceptance of it touted as a public relations victory. Khattak had taken it because of the freedom it represented: the chance to appoint his own team, and as with INSET, the opportunity to work with partners at all levels of government to bring nuance and consideration to increasingly complex cases.

And for other reasons he had never offered up for public scrutiny.

His mandate was couched in generic terms: sensitivity training for police services, community support, and an alternative viewpoint in cases involving minorities, particularly Muslim minorities. Both he and his superiors understood the unspoken rationale behind the choice of a decorated INSET officer to head up CPS. If Khattak performed well, then greater glory to the city, province, and nation. If he ran into barriers from within the community as he pursued his coreligionists, no one could accuse the CPS of bias. Everyone's hands were clean.

It didn't matter to Khattak that this was how he had been lured into the job by his former superintendent, Robert Palmer. He loved police work. It suited an analytical nature tempered by a long-simmering hunger for justice. And if he was being used, as indisputably he was, he was also prepared to enact his own vision for CPS.

What flame-fanning bigots across the border would doubtlessly call community pandering, a fig-leaf jihad. Take anything a Muslim touched, add the word jihad to it, and immediately you produced something ugly and divisive.

But Tom wasn't one of these. Chief historian at the Department of Justice, he was a gifted academic whose fatherly demeanor masked a passion for the truth as sharp and relentless as Khattak's own.

He had called to ask Khattak to investigate the death of a Scarborough man named Christopher Drayton. There was no reason that CPS should have an interest in the man's death. He had fallen from a section of the Scarborough Bluffs known as the Cathedral. His death had been swift and certain with no evidence of outside interference.

Khattak had pointed this out to his friend in measured tones, and Tom had let him. When he'd finished, Tom gave him the real reason for his call and the reason it encroached upon Khattak's jurisdiction.

Khattak heard the worry and fear beneath Tom Paley's words.

And into the remnants of Khattak's prayer intruded a series of recollections from his youth. Of news reports, hurriedly organized meetings and volunteer drives, followed too slowly by action. He saw himself as a young man joining others in a circle around the flame at Parliament Hill. He absorbed the thick, despairing heat of that summer into his skin. His dark hair flattened against his head; he felt in that moment his own impotence.

He listened to Tom's labored explanation, not liking the hitch in his friend's breath. When Tom came to the nature of his request, Khattak agreed. But his words were slow, weighted by the years that had passed since that summer. Still, he would do as asked.

"Don't go alone," Tom said. "You'll need to look objective."

Khattak took no offense at the phrasing. He knew the unspoken truth as well as Tom did.

Because you can't be.

"I'll take Rachel." He had told Tom about his partner, Rachel Getty, before.

"You know her well enough to trust her?"

"She's the best officer I've ever worked with."

"She's young."

"Not so young that she doesn't understand our work. And I find her perspective helps me."

He meant it. But even as he said it he knew that he would work with Rachel as he had done in the past. Withholding a part of the truth, of himself, until he could see the world through the clear, discerning eyes that watched him with such trust.

He knew he could turn to his childhood friend, Nathan Clare, for background on Drayton. Nate lived on the Bluffs and would understand why he'd agreed to Tom's request. Nate would understand as well the toll compliance would take. But Khattak's bond with Nate had long since been severed. It was a mistake to think Nate still knew him at all.

He'd meant the last words of his prayer to be a blessing asked for his family, in a space he tried to keep for himself, exchanging solitude for solace. Lately, he'd come to accept that there was no separate peace. His work, and the harshness of the choices he had made, bled into everything.

He rose from his prayer rug to find that dusk had given way to dark. He thought of the tiny documents library in Ottawa with its overflowing shelves. He'd spent most of that long-ago summer there, collecting evidence.

And he remembered other words, other blessings to be sought with a premonition of ruin.

They are going to burn us all.

2.

I keep wondering, where have all the good friends gone?

Rachel took her own car to the Bluffs. A couple of times when she and Zach were young, their father had taken them to Bluffer's Park for picnics. She remembered the suppressed pleasure in Don Getty's eyes as his son dragged him to the marina to watch the boats. Even then, the park had been filled with immigrants. Children scrambling unsupervised, shrieking with pleasure. She'd been an afterthought, but her Da had taken time over Zach.

She got out of the car, scuffing her runners against the dirt in the road. She had driven around the crescent slowly so as not to miss the house called Winterglass, an imaginative name for the three-story structure settled at the edge of the Bluffs, as much a part of its surroundings as the trees that framed the park or the wind that had worn down the stone over time.

The first and second stories were separated by a horizontal band of stonework that wrapped around the house. Above the white doors, a pediment supported a recessed arch. On either side of the arch, chimneys flanked an elegant arrangement of windows.

On the east side of the house, a balcony set on white columns floated above a ground-floor terrace. The long, curved drive was edged by maple trees, the small garden before the house embroidered by a gathering of roses. A single ornament rested within its diamond-shaped border: a chipped stone eagle balanced on a plinth.

A weathered house and a thing of beauty, its name subtly inscribed on the plinth.

Khattak hadn't given any reason for meeting at this house. He'd provided a short summary on Christopher Drayton, but unless she missed her guess, Drayton's house was at the opposite end of the circle. She'd already called Declan Byrne, her junior team member, for background on Drayton. As far as Dec could tell her, a man had gone for a stroll at night and fallen to his death. An ordinary man leading an ordinary life.

The only drama she could squeeze out of this was the possibility of suicide. Yet the coroner's report had ruled it an accident.

So why was CPS being asked to dig around Drayton, and why had her boss asked her to meet at Winterglass?

Restless, she kicked at her front tire just as Khattak's BMW pulled up behind her.

"Bit upscale, isn't it, sir?" she said by way of greeting. She meant the house, not the car. Her envious appraisal of his car had been documented on previous excursions.

"Hello, Rachel."

It was too dark out to read his expression. He sounded withdrawn. Fatigued, maybe, though it hadn't dampened his good looks.

And he wasn't gotten up in one of his closely tailored suits. He was wearing black trousers and a dark, fitted shirt. No tie, no cuff links, grappling a string of beads in his right hand. When they stepped under the house's porch light she saw the beads were green agate. He was fingering them in a nervous gesture unusual for him.

"This isn't Drayton's house, sir."

"No. This is Winterglass."

Which sounded like he expected the name to mean something to her.

Biting back the temptation to remind him she could read, she countered, "Never heard of it. Did Drayton use to live here?"

She heard Khattak's quick intake of breath, saw the string tighten around his fingers. He turned to face her and, as always before his direct attention, she squirmed a little.

"This is the home of Nathan Clare. I haven't been here in some time."

"Nathan Clare? *The* Nathan Clare? The writer?"

She was babbling. Everyone knew the internationally acclaimed author. His last book, *Apologia*, had outsold all his previous works combined. He had made a name for himself intervening in national debates on multiculturalism. Every few years his essays would be collected together and published in a volume, cementing his credentials as a somewhat reclusive public intellectual.

She'd heard him on the radio and had liked his voice and his dry sense of humor. She had meant to purchase the book selection he'd endorsed, but time had gotten away from her. That, and her job. She wasn't on duty tonight, but CPS hours were irregular, and she worked at being someone Khattak could rely on.

She felt a little awed at the thought of meeting Clare. Then she grasped what Khattak had just said.

"You've been here before, sir? You know Mr. Clare?"

He rang the doorbell.

"Yes. Drayton lives nearby. I thought that Nathan might know him."

Now she remembered that the writer was also the son of Loveland Clare, a diplomat in the Stephen Lewis tradition, a fact she correlated to the spike in her nervousness.

When the door opened, they were greeted by a tall man with a slim, straight nose and a delicate face and jaw. His straw-colored hair was worn long in the front, obscuring his gold-rimmed glasses: he was the perfect example of Rachel's idea of an English gentleman. He was even wearing a tweed jacket. Well-fitted, she observed, and though Khattak was tall, this man had an inch or two over him.

"Esa?" He sounded shocked.

Rachel's eyes widened. Khattak hadn't called to set up the visit?

"May we come in?"

The man in the doorway stepped back, his attention occupied by Khattak, who offered no identification, Rachel trailing behind them. They were led through an entrance hall with a sculptured staircase to a double-height room that defied her every expectation of grandeur. Or was it grand? At least fifty feet across, something about the room managed to suggest warmth. Its floor was a bleached pine, offsetting furnishings in delicate green and the most elaborate Chinese carpet Rachel had ever seen. Velvet sofas anchored the carpet across from a wall of glass that must have given the house its name. Situated on a curve of the Bluffs, the wall overlooked white cliffs and black water extending over a limitless distance.

She didn't know where to look first. The blue and white porcelain that shimmered on the room's tables? The painted white chandeliers suspended between a set of peacock chairs? Or the classical architecture of pilasters and arches that ran the perimeter of the room to support a gallery on the second level? Under a set of casement windows, a grand piano with a raised lid occupied an antechamber that led outside, sheet music scattered across its bench. A silk banner was flung over a nearby chair.

Gawking, she turned back to hear herself being introduced.

"Sergeant Rachel Getty, my partner at Community Policing."

Nathan Clare took her hand. She was surprised at the strength of his grip: there was something romantic, almost effeminate, about the elegant bones of his hand. She took a green-and-white-striped chair at his invitation, ducking his assessment of her, knowing the picture she presented to the world. Boxy, square-shouldered, round-cheeked, indifferently dressed.

When Nathan smiled at her, she said awkwardly, "You must like music. You don't have any photographs on your piano."

She'd seen plenty of soap operas where a Steinway served mainly as a repository for antique picture frames.

"Nate believes pianos are for playing."

The "Nate" caught Rachel by surprise. Both the nickname and the comment implied familiarity, making her wonder how well her boss knew Nathan Clare and whether that had been a sneer in his cultured voice.

Nathan sat back on the green sofa, watching Khattak string the beads together around his wrist.

"I haven't seen that in a while. Does it help while you're working?" There was a hint of challenge in his manner.

Sitting next to Khattak, Rachel was able to see the string of beads more clearly. Every now and again, the agate stones were sectioned off by a little marker, dividing the string into segments. It was a rosary or—what was the word Khattak had taught her?

A tasbih, the Muslim equivalent.

She realized that Nathan was watching her. He had swept the hair from his forehead, and now she could see the hazel eyes behind his glasses, intent but also kind.

"We've come about your neighbor, Christopher Drayton. I was hoping you might have known him."

"Everyone in the neighborhood did. He was well regarded here, generous with his time. People were shocked to hear of his fall, myself included, but I suppose no one was quite as distraught as Melanie. Melanie Blessant, his girlfriend."

"You knew him well, then."

"As well as I know all my neighbors, I'd say. He was an educated man, he enjoyed books, art. He'd been here for dinner several times to discuss various projects he was interested in with mutual friends. On some of the same nights you were invited. He was funding a small museum—something that would interest you. I can give you a list of the guests, if you'd like." He rummaged in a small drawer and handed the paper to Rachel.

Khattak brushed it aside.

"Did he often walk by the Bluffs?"

"I believe so, but the people who live here are well versed in the dangers of erosion. It's easy to lose your footing out there."

"Had you ever seen him from these windows?"

"You know these windows don't face the path, Esa."

There was a note of chiding in Nathan's voice that took Rachel aback. The tenor of the whole conversation seemed strange to her, the room imbued with an inexplicable anxiety. The tasbih was taut around Khattak's hand; Nathan Clare's posture was stiff. That both men knew the source of it was clear: it was Rachel who was in the dark.

Nathan turned to her.

"Do you like the house?"

She couldn't help being caught by the cloudy expanse of lake beyond the windows. Waterfront views were not to be had off the dim streets of Etobicoke, where she lived.

"It's stunning. From the outside, I thought it might be a little pompous, but it isn't."

She bit her lip. Sometimes she was too honest and in this case probably naïve as well. There were thousands of dollars worth of antiques within the room, pieces she could neither name nor identify, yet all possessed of a consonance that pleased the eye. Things to live with rather than admire. The careless sprawl of music suggested as much.

"You can play the piano if you'd like," he said, following her gaze.

Rachel couldn't play. Though Don Getty had done well for himself in life, the arts weren't a luxury he'd encouraged his children to indulge in. It was her mother's old recordings she had listened to when her father was out of the house, the needle scratching over Chopin's nocturnes, her mother's favorite composer. Part of her mother's life before she'd married Don Getty, as inaccessible to Rachel as her mother's thoughts.

Rachel made her way to the piano, called there by a secret longing. The banner casually placed on the chair beside it looked like a miniature flag, a blue Superman shield imposed upon its green background, the initials *CK* appliquéd at one corner.

The two men followed in her wake like an entourage, Drayton forgotten.

Khattak reached around her and took the banner.

"You still have it," he said.

He deposited the tasbih in his pocket, his hands relaxing.

"It was a pledge, Esa. You know that."

Khattak's gaze switched to the fireplace, taking in the blank space above the lip of white marble.

"The portrait's gone."

"It was more than time."

A rectangular space between the white and blue chinoiserie was less faded than the rest of the wall. Something had been there, and again she was the outsider, in the dark as to why they were here at all when they should have been at Drayton's house, searching for indications of homicide.

"I'm sorry, Mr. Clare. How do you and the inspector know each other?"

Nathan smiled at her and she blinked. The smile transformed her notion of the introverted writer into something much more visceral. A more than ordinarily attractive male, with glints of light turning his straw-colored hair gold.

"Didn't Esa tell you? We were at school together. We're old Seatonians." And when she still looked blank, he clarified, "Upper Canada College."

Openmouthed, the piano forgotten, she turned to Khattak.

"You went *to school* with Nathan Clare, the writer?"

"He wasn't 'Nathan Clare, the writer' then. And we've come about Christopher Drayton, not my unsavory past."

Nathan grinned at him, the first unforced gesture she'd seen from either man.

"It was unsavory, wasn't it? At least, all the good parts."

Her eyes lit up at the teasing. Here was someone who might deflate the always unruffled, ever-so-proper Inspector Khattak. She wanted to delve deeper into the mystery of this hidden friend, megawatt writer or not, who must be awash in particularly useful inside information. Despite their rocky start when she'd first joined CPS, she'd come to admire Esa Khattak and to value his opinion. She just wasn't

sure that she understood him as well as she'd like to. And if Nathan
Clare could help her with that, she wouldn't object.

But the mood died in an instant as Khattak answered, "Most of
the bad parts as well, I'm afraid. I'm sorry to have bothered you. We
should go."

"Sir—"

There were at least a dozen questions she could think of that they
hadn't asked Nathan Clare—at least he could clarify the list he'd
given them, why he'd had it to hand, and why it even mattered.

"Now, Rachel."

She scurried along behind him, swallowing a grimace. Whatever
brief connection she had felt to the author, Khattak was her boss.
Her boss who ignored the question Nathan called after him.

"Did you ever read *Apologia*, Esa?"

And that wasn't a question he seemed ready to answer.

3.

He was a modest and reasonable man.

They left their cars where they were. It was a silent ten-minute walk from the far end of the circle to Drayton's address. There was no cordon of police tape around the house, a large home typical of those built on small lots when fifty-year-old bungalows were scraped down to make way for new luxury models. The exterior was stuccoed in white, a color Drayton must have repainted yearly, because the outside bore no traces of wear.

She wasn't sure what they were looking for, wasn't sure why a name like Christopher Drayton would pop up on the CPS radar. On the face of it, it didn't seem like a minority-sensitive situation. All she knew was that her boss was doing a favor for a friend on his own time, and he had asked her along to the party.

"Figure the girlfriend did it, sir?"

"What?"

"Melanie Blessant. The one Clare mentioned. Maybe followed him out after dark, pushed him over the edge."

They were meandering their way through the well-proportioned living spaces, a family room and salon that mirrored each other in dimension, furnished with expensive if generic taste. Everything was in order, well tended, as if death had not visited this house.

Her question was meant as a gentle reminder that nothing about this assignment appeared to fall within their purview.

They had reached the kitchen at the back of the house: dark

cabinets, earth-colored stone, stainless-steel appliances, a desk where the mail was tidily sorted. She thumbed through it. Credit card statements, utility bills, a landscaping service, the usual. Adjacent to the kitchen was the study, a glimpse through its French doors disclosing bookcases and a wide desk. She tried the handle. The doors were locked.

Khattak produced the keys.

"Local police were asked to leave this room locked so we could take a look for ourselves. Take some photographs, will you?"

Rachel pondered this. Drayton's body had been found two days ago. Why had Justice moved so swiftly to secure this particular scene when the body had been found at the base of Cathedral Bluffs?

She had her answer when the doors spread wide to reveal a room twice the size of any other on the main floor. She unearthed her camera and set to work.

The chair from the desk was situated in the center of the room, facing windows that looked out upon the garden. It was an old-fashioned oxblood leather chair without casters, but that wasn't what had captured Rachel's attention. Nor was it the reason Khattak stood still beside her.

On the floor in front of the chair lay a 9-millimeter pistol, pointed away at the windows.

"Uh, sir . . ."

"I see it."

"What's it still doing here? Has it been printed?"

"There are only Drayton's prints on the gun. It isn't loaded. The forensic team was asked to leave the room once it had finished, so we could take a look."

Rachel knelt down for a closer look. She knew it was a 9-millimeter, but the make was unfamiliar. There was a black star inside the circle on the plastic grip. Something else caught her eye on the floor not far from the gun. It was a resinous puddle the size of a quarter plate. She scraped it lightly, her nails raising a white line on the puddle as the flaky residue came off beneath her fingertips.

"Candle wax," she breathed. She rose to her feet, perplexed. "Sir."

She described a semicircle with her index finger.

"There's several of them."

She counted the puddles under her breath.

"Someone's tried the door as well."

He showed her the scratch marks around the keyhole.

"But they couldn't get in or they would have cleaned this mess up?" Rachel hazarded. "What does any of it mean? Drayton didn't die here. The gun hasn't been fired, his injuries were consistent with a fall." She looked around.

"There aren't any candles in the study, sir."

"Rachel."

Khattak was at the desk, trying the drawers. One was locked.

"Maybe he kept the gun there."

Her guess proved correct. The wide drawer yielded to Khattak's key. Inside, a kerchief was folded to one side, boxes of ammunition were stacked on the other.

"What did Drayton do?" she asked slowly. There was no permit in the drawer. It didn't make sense that a retired man in his sixties would need a small army's worth of firepower.

"He was a businessman."

"What kind of business, drugs?"

Khattak shrugged, not meeting her eyes.

That was Rachel's first clue. Khattak was never evasive with her. When he withheld information, he told her the reason for withholding it. His leadership at CPS had been characterized by a spirit of inclusion. He wore his authority more lightly than any other police officer Rachel had ever worked with. He was certainly nothing like the old bull Don Getty, thirty-five years in the police service, the last fifteen as superintendent, and God help you if you got under his skin or in his way. As Rachel, being his daughter, was prone to do.

Khattak was the polar opposite of Don Getty's bluster. Urbane, soft-spoken, respectful, decisive. The only thing he had in common with her Da was his insight into human behavior. And he'd been candid about his shortcomings as well, something Don Getty could never be. With the great Don Getty, one didn't participate or contribute ideas. One merely bowed and scraped like the rest of his sycophants. *Yes, Chief. No, Chief. Of course you have it right, Chief.*

Khattak allowed her to tell him when he got it wrong. He *asked* her to tell him. Just as he had told her to do during their first case in Waverley, when she'd thrown his affair with Laine Stoicheva in his face, using the well-known sexual harassment claim Laine had brought against him like a machine-gun attack. His composure hadn't altered. He'd taken her aside and in simple, blunt phrases told her the truth about Laine.

There'd been no need to share the truth with Rachel: she was no threat to him. Rachel had fallen as far as she could go before Khattak had brought her into CPS. She'd thought it a consolation prize of sorts, won for her by her father's influence when no one else was prepared to take her on.

But Don Getty had had nothing to do with it. Esa Khattak had asked for her. He had chosen her specially.

We're not just two birds wounded by the same stone, Rachel. Your evaluations were phenomenal.

They had been. It was the claim she had brought against her former boss, Inspector MacInerney, that had seen her fall as swiftly as she had risen. The claim that had died for lack of evidence when his other victims had stayed quiet to salvage their careers.

And just like that, she was a pariah in the service.

You know what it's like to be judged, Rachel. You know in your bones what it's like to shatter the truth against a wall of disbelief.

Khattak had been cleared of all charges brought by his former partner, Laine Stoicheva. He hadn't gone into details, Rachel hadn't asked. It was enough to know they had this in common. His confidence earned her trust. She didn't always agree with him, but she'd learned to respect him. She didn't want to take a step back.

His catlike eyes were watching her. She could tell he knew what she was thinking.

"What's up then, sir? You know more about this than you're telling me."

Blunt as ever. Direct and to the point. It was the thing about her she knew Khattak valued most. And she couldn't change her spots if she tried.

The handsome face that looked back at her in the dimmed light of the study was troubled. And not about the case, she thought, or noncase, as it were. It was something deeper. His fingers were working the beads again.

"Tell me what you see," he said.

She nodded, trying to ignore the stale, slightly smoky scent in the room. This was often how they began.

"No photograph of Drayton yet, but here we are in a house that looks and feels expensive, probably about right for a retired businessman. It's a little large for a man on his own, at least four bedrooms, I'm guessing. It's well kept, somewhat impersonal, suggesting he might have had a touch of OCD and maybe not much personality. There's no art anywhere on this floor, just a map above the desk. He keeps a gun in a locked drawer with plenty of ammo, but on the night of his death the gun is found on the floor in this room, although it hasn't been fired. And there's several puddles of what looks like candle wax on the floor without any sign of candles. Maybe they're in the garbage. Maybe he took them with him on his walk and dumped them over the Bluffs."

She ran over the summary in her mind.

"I haven't seen that make before," she added. "Nine millimeter is my guess. We'll have to look more thoroughly to see if there's a license anywhere. Has it been identified?"

"Not yet."

"I admit it's odd, but there's no sign of a struggle here, nothing in the coroner's report to indicate that he was restrained or dragged or pushed over the cliff with unusual force. But, if he was taken by surprise, I don't know that we'd see any evidence of that. He was probably sitting here looking out at his garden before he went for his walk and lost his way. So I ask you again, sir, what's going on?"

Khattak hesitated, then he picked up a set of picture frames that rested on the desk, handing one to Rachel.

"There's Drayton for you. Possibly with his girlfriend. I don't know who this is."

Primming her lips at the evasion, Rachel studied the first photograph. It had been taken in broad daylight in Drayton's garden. A stocky man with a head of white hair and a square jaw had his arm around a beautiful woman who came to his shoulder. She was petite and curvy. Rachel squinted at it. Maybe not beautiful, with those bloated lips and that hyperinflated chest. She looked like a Barbie doll, her clothes straining over a nipped-in waist and the flare of her hips. Her loosely curled hair was an unlikely shade of platinum blond. It tumbled over her chest in a style suited to a much younger woman. Like Drayton, she wore sunglasses.

The other photo was of two teenage girls in tank tops and shorts. They looked alike with their clever heart-shaped faces, a smattering of freckles, and long, straight, toffee-colored hair. The younger one was smiling at the camera.

"His daughters? An estranged former family?"

Khattak shook his head.

"I haven't answered your question, I know. There's a reason for that. I'd like to see what conclusions you draw without the weight of prior knowledge."

Weight was a peculiar choice of word, Rachel thought. Maybe that was the reason that Khattak looked almost haggard. Or spoke to her so formally.

She gave him back the photographs, marched over to the bookshelves she hadn't inspected yet.

"But eventually you'll tell me. It's not exactly a thrill to work in the dark."

"The light's no better, believe me."

As Khattak worked through the other drawers, she turned her attention to Drayton's library. Nathan Clare had said he was an educated man. The books reflected that. An educated businessman with a more than passing interest in languages. Italian, Russian, Albanian, German. He also had a complete set of the works of Nathan Clare. Several volumes of essays and at least a dozen novels. All except *Apologia*. The rest of the selection was unremarkable, available at any bookstore display. Some new fiction, some books on health, a little political humor, and a set of gardening books. Plus the classics, with new hardbound covers.

On the last shelf she found a curious assortment of teen fiction interspersed with atlases and books on medieval history. A navy wool jacket hung on a peg beside the shelf. Absently, she checked the pockets.

The outer pockets were empty. The inner pockets held a pen and Drayton's wallet. She went through this. Driver's license, check. Credit cards, check. Gym membership, check. The discount cards of various retail chains. The billfold contained a modest amount of cash and a folded piece of paper. She withdrew it, frowning at what she read.

"Sir. Here's something."

She handed the paper to Khattak. Its edges were torn at the top and at the bottom, leaving no more than half a page. Even that was more than enough for the single sentence typed at its center.

Is this waiting more desperate than the shooting?

"Something's been torn away. There must have been more to it. It explains the gun, doesn't it? Maybe an indication of suicidal ideation?"

Khattak didn't answer, so Rachel went on.

"Of course, we could ask why he typed it. There's a computer and printer on his desk but suicide notes are usually handwritten, unless there's some kind of manifesto attached."

"Was there anything else?"

"I haven't been through these cupboards yet." She pointed to the cabinets at the base of the bookshelves. "His taste in reading is pretty bland. What about the desk?"

"Paperwork, mostly. Bills, mortgage information, insurance policies. I'll read those in a moment. There's a folder here on the museum Nate mentioned. I haven't gone through it yet."

She went back to work. Most of the cupboards were empty. Some contained computer gadgets, speakers, printer cables, and the like. There were no photo albums, no congratulatory cards on retirement, no evidence of the business Drayton had run. Midway through, though, she found what she was looking for. The central bookcase was anchored to the wall because its cabinet contained a safe. Not a high-tech safe but the standard kind available at Walmart, weighing in at several hundred pounds with a digital lock. To open it, they'd need to call in a team member or unearth the combination among Drayton's papers.

"This is where he should have kept the gun."

Khattak joined her at the safe, hunching down.

"Perhaps he needed the safe for something more important than the gun."

"Like what? A will? A fortune in black-market diamonds? The guns that go with that ammo?"

"We need that combination if we're to find out."

"It might be in his papers. It's probably not anything as obvious as his birth date."

Khattak was studying the digital display.

"It's five digits."

"I'll keep looking."

There was a filing cabinet beside the printer. It was jammed tight, but most of it was old tax returns on a business Drayton had run. A profitable parking lot he had owned downtown. No evidence of drugs or guns or anything else out of the ordinary. Nothing that would necessitate the deadly black weapon on the floor. She yanked the lower drawer forward. It was caught on a file that had slid in over the others. When she pulled it out, the papers inside spilled through her fingers.

"Sir."

The pages were identical to one she had found in Drayton's wallet. The tops and bottoms torn away, a few chopped-off sentences in the center of each page.

She read through them slowly.

This is a cat-and-mouse game. Now it's your turn to play it.

What was it you told me? You survive or you disappear. Somehow you managed both.

As you took everything from me, you asked if I was afraid.

How could I not be afraid?

Do you hear as we did the starved wolves howling in the night?

Do you feel as if you'd never been alive?

Can you right all the wrongs of the past? Because I tell you that the sky is too high and the ground is too hard.

Something about the words frightened Rachel. Alone each sentence meant nothing. Together they ran like a kind of damaged poetry.

She looked up to find Khattak's face had changed, his weariness shed for animation. The randomness of the words meant something to him.

"This doesn't read like a suicide note, sir. Maybe a confession. And what's missing here? Why are the pages torn?"

He already knew, she could tell.

"He didn't write these himself," she went on. "Someone was sending them to him. That's what's missing from each page. The salutation and the signature. Someone was threatening him."

"I don't think these are threats."

"Then what?"

"Reminders. If someone did send these pages to Drayton, it's because they wanted to remind him of something."

"And you already know what that something is," she concluded, exasperated. "I'm not much help to you like this, sir. Wouldn't it be easier on both of us if you just told me what you know?"

Khattak set the pages down on the desk, sizing her up.

"There's nothing concrete for me to tell you. I'm relying on your clearheadedness. You have a knack for digging things up that most people would leave alone."

Rachel rubbed a hand over her lank, dark hair. How many times did she have to remind herself not to wear a ponytail at night? It did nothing for glamour and it gave her a headache.

"Right now the only knack I have is for some fresh air and my bed. Call it a night, sir?"

He handed her the pages.

"Take these with you. Something might come to you."

"What about you?"

"I'm going to see if I can find the combination to that safe. And if not, we'll call someone in."

He didn't want any of this to be true. He didn't want the words on the pages to have the meaning that Tom Paley's phone call suggested to him.

The sky too high, the ground too hard.

He ran the name Tom had given him over his tongue, hating the way it sounded, hating the rise and fall of its syllables.

Would the past not serve them better left in the past? Its muted face buried, its gravestones a world away? Things he wished he hadn't seen, people who rose like ghosts in his mind. And always that music—its trenchant melody, insistent, unrelenting: there was something here once. *We* were something.

He heard his wife's voice raised in reproach.

We owe the living the truth. It's the only coin of justice left to offer.

Samina had always been braver than he, able to see things as they were, able to shoulder her way forward to difficult truths.

This truth wasn't difficult.

It was devastating.

That was what he hadn't been able to bring himself to tell Rachel Getty, despite the trust in her dark eyes.

He knew, of course, why he had gone to see Nate. Throughout his life, every one of his sins had been confessed to Nate. The only letters he had written, the only stories he had told, had been to Nate. If he'd said to Nate, "I think Christopher Drayton was murdered and here's why," Nate would have understood him instantly. There would have been no need for further explanation.

Esa and Nate. Clare and Khattak. Seaton's diabolical duo.

He'd seen the pleasure in Nate's eyes at the door, the hope. The hope that Esa had finally let go of the anger and judgment that had characterized the last two years of their friendship. The banner should have made it easy, the absence of Laine's portrait even more so.

He told himself he was a compassionate man, not one to judge lest he be judged. As Nate had once judged him, staring across the divide as if he'd never seen him before.

So he'd wanted to tell Nate about Drayton, wanted to seek his help, except that one moment was always with him. Nate turning away when nothing could have hurt Khattak worse than Nate's defection.

His wife's death was still the emptiest part of him. His deep-rooted faith and the seven years that had passed since had made it bearable— but if he was honest with himself, it was the presence of Nate, always beside him, that had enabled him to see the way forward again. It had given him a means of putting his tragedy into perspective: he wasn't alone to suffer. Others had suffered and would suffer far more than he ever had. With hardship would come ease. *Lo, with hardship comes ease.*

Lately, there had only been hardship.

He knew what he sought from Nate, as much as he knew why Rachel had become a friend. A friend he would protect and shield in any situation even as he kept a part of himself from her. But who besides Tom Paley could he discuss Drayton with? Tom, who wanted the knowledge less than Esa did.

That Drayton was a man risen from hell.

4.

Father, take care of my children, look after my children.

"I've learned a little more about the museum," Khattak said.

"How long were you at Drayton's house last night?"

"Enough to discover two important things. One, the will's not at hand, but there are two insurance policies that name Melanie Blessant as the beneficiary. And two, Drayton was preparing to a make a major donation to a local arts project called the Andalusia Museum."

"How major?"

"At least a hundred thousand dollars worth, maybe more."

Today Rachel was in Khattak's car, cautioned to leave her breakfast sandwich in her handbag until she could remove herself from its immaculate environs. Her stomach rumbled but they both ignored it. Khattak had gotten used to her habit of eating on the fly.

"Pickup game this morning?"

It was Rachel's most common excuse for missing breakfast. She was a forward on a women's hockey team and her schedule was erratic.

"We lost four to one. Looks like I'm not getting in enough practice." She smirked at him. "Who's David Newhall and why are we meeting him?"

"One of the neighbors from the list Nate gave us. Someone who might shed some light on Drayton and the museum. He's listed as a director on the project. He works at the university up here. Have you been here before?"

"No, thank God. I was at the downtown campus. I heard they used this place as a stand-in for a nuclear bomb shelter on *War of the Worlds*."

As they pulled up the long drive to the Scarborough campus, Rachel could see why. The new signage wasn't fooling anybody. It was still just a series of concrete blocks.

"I think they call this brutalism," Khattak offered.

"It's brutal, all right."

They made their way to the administrative offices where significant reconstruction was under way. From the outside dark and dour, inside it was all glass walls and newly minted light. The corridors were thronged by students lining up to arrange for their photo ID. A pert Asian receptionist waved them through the line to a small inner office.

"Mr. Newhall's expecting you."

So that was one phone call Khattak was prepared to make.

Inside, they were greeted by a man of middle height with a wedge-shaped face, cropped black hair, and close-set eyes behind square frames. His speech was clipped and he spoke with pronounced impatience.

"How may I help you, Inspector?"

Rachel, he ignored. She sat back in the chair he had offered, fascinated by the thick, dark eyebrows that bristled when he spoke, an outlet for the nervous energy he exuded.

"As I mentioned on the phone, we were hoping for some background on Christopher Drayton. I understand he was a friend."

Newhall didn't answer right away. On the desk before him was a plentiful amount of paperwork, cordoned off into separate piles. He ran nail-bitten fingers along the edges of these, his gaze moving between Rachel and Khattak. She was struck by an impression of guardedness.

"I knew him in passing. We live in the same general area but I doubt I knew him better than any other of my neighbors."

"Nathan Clare told us you were working together on a museum project."

Newhall stopped drumming his fingers on his desk. "I'm afraid Nathan is mistaken. Chris Drayton had nothing to do with it."

"He was planning to make a sizable donation. We found a list of museum directors among his papers with your name on it."

Newhall adjusted his glasses. His scowl took in Rachel as well. "I thought Chris fell from the Bluffs. A simple accident."

"As far as we know, that's correct. We're merely following up. As a director, you must have some idea why Chris would be interested in supporting your project."

He laid a slight stress on Drayton's name. Newhall dismissed it.

"He was a latecomer to the museum. He wanted something to stamp his name on. He had a passing interest in Spanish history, he must have decided it would do."

"A hundred thousand dollars suggests more than a passing interest to me. In his papers, the museum is called the Christopher Drayton Andalusia Museum."

For some reason, this information rendered Newhall motionless, his nervous energy concentrated. When he spoke, his tone was thoughtful. "He had a certain grandiosity about him," he admitted, "but nothing about the museum is for sale. Mink would never allow it."

Rachel straightened in her seat with interest, brushing an imaginary crumb from her rust-colored jacket. She'd been out of uniform for a while now but hadn't done much to supplement the track suits that made up most of her wardrobe. The jacket was an exception. She wanted to reflect well on Khattak, who was never at a loss in this department.

"Who's Mink?" she asked.

"I'm sorry, I meant Mink Norman. She's the director of the project, the sole reason it exists. I'm surprised her name wasn't on your list."

Rachel couldn't decide if Newhall was pointing them to someone else because he had something to hide or because he was genuinely attempting to be helpful.

"I'm not sure I understand what the museum has to do with Chris's death," Newhall added.

"At the moment, we're simply getting a sense of the people Drayton knew. Nathan Clare mentioned he'd invited you both to the same dinner."

"Did he also happen to mention that as far as social events go, it was a disaster? The great man pontificating about his largesse to anyone who would listen? He used his wallet to shunt aside people who'd put in two years' work on the house. He even had that ghastly Melanie Blessant work her dubious magic on a few of the directors. We heard him out, but that was as far as it went."

"I'm sorry, what house is this? I thought we were talking about a museum."

Before he could answer Rachel's question, the receptionist knocked at his door. "Your first appointment is here," she mouthed through the glass.

Newhall jumped to his feet like a spring unbound. Khattak and Rachel followed suit, Rachel trying to place his flattened manner of speech.

"One moment, Mr. Newhall. What *about* the house? And what is it you do at the university?"

He patted the files on his desk, a look of quiet pride on his face. "I'm an administrator. I work with the student body on bursaries and scholarship applications. As for the house, if you've been to see Clare you must have seen it—it's on the same circle. The museum *is* the house. Its name is Ringsong, which I might point out is the only name we ever considered for it."

"May we have your home address, sir?" They had it already from Nathan Clare's list, she just wanted to see if he would give it to them.

Newhall raised his eyebrows but didn't demur. He lived on Lyme Regis.

Rachel was familiar with it. It cut across both Scarborough Heights and Cathedral Bluffs. It was also within walking distance of Drayton's house.

"We may stop by sometime," she told him.

Again there was that fractional pause that made Rachel think of a fox warily skirting a trap. She knew death brought out hitherto unsuspected depths in people, but this was something else.

"Come by any time you like. I'm glad to help on any matter related to Chris. I didn't appreciate his attempts to railroad us, but for all that, he was a kind man."

There was no sorrow on his face as he spoke, nor as he ushered them from his office.

"Works with people, does he?" she muttered under her breath.

"We'll talk in the car," Khattak said easily, as if he'd gotten everything he wanted from Newhall. And maybe he had. He had a head full of information as to why they were meandering after Drayton in the first place. They hadn't seen his body. Their search of his home had been cursory. No background information had been pulled beyond the commonplace. And there'd been nothing the least bit interesting about the man except the fact that he'd had money to burn and, apparently, an inexplicable desire to turn patron of the arts in the golden years of his life. And he gardened. If something about this was making Khattak anxious, she'd have loved to know what it was.

She hoped the trust they'd established during their case in Waverley wasn't a chimera. She valued it. She wanted it again, because it had been a long time since anyone had trusted her and she'd felt the same in return. She was looking for the equalizer.

Rachel lowered her window. It was a crisp fall day outside, with a coruscation of wind that arranged the air in rippling phrases. The broken spindles of leaves were assembled in piles along the sidewalks as they drove.

"What now?" she asked Khattak.

He made a show of consulting his wristwatch, one of the few men she knew who still wore one in the days of the iPhone.

"We should visit Melanie Blessant, if only to rule her out. She seems to have loomed large in Drayton's life. And if possible, I'd like to view this museum."

Rule her out of what? Rachel wondered. A fall from the cliff? But she knew the cherished maxim of "follow the woman, follow the money" as well as Khattak did.

They had an accidental death, they had a woman who benefited from it, and they had a great deal of money in play. Or at least, they would, once a will turned up.

"What about the safe? We could get Paul or Dec on it. Paul, most likely."

Paul Gaffney was the tech expert on their team, a viable choice. Khattak's agenda didn't seem to suggest any hurry to unlock the safe, however.

As if in answer to her thoughts, he said, "Let's give it a day or so before we start using up resources. We may find there's nothing here after all. A man fell to his death, that's it."

From the tone of his voice, that was what he was hoping for. A short, simple solution that was anything except what was rattling around in his thoughts.

His face was paler than usual today, the line of his mouth tightly held, his movements edgy. Something was weighing on him like an anvil. And it was either Drayton or Nathan Clare.

"What did you think of Newhall?"

She waited for him to brake at the crosswalk ahead, which he did at the last minute. An elderly woman in a pair of green flannel pants glared at them over her shoulder as she sped through the crosswalk.

"He seemed cagey, I thought," she went on, without waiting for his answer. "Also a bit intense. A little quick to take offense."

"He didn't like Drayton, but if he's comfortable with us coming by his house, he must have some notion of public duty."

Rachel pondered this. She hadn't found Newhall remotely attractive, yet there was something compelling about his lean-limbed energy.

"He did a fair bit of finger-pointing. Gave us two other names to go for."

Khattak looked at her briefly. "There may be no fingers to point. It could be he thinks there's nothing to hide."

"We didn't ask him much about Drayton himself," she observed.

"I think Ms. Blessant will be able to tell us what we wish to know."

"The grieving widow?"

"She isn't a widow, and for all we know, she may not be grieving."

"The insurance policies speak for themselves. So might the will. A hundred thousand dollars that doesn't go to some frou-frou museum might end up lining her pockets instead."

Khattak grinned. "Newhall said they weren't going to take the money."

"I'm thinking given Drayton's Barbie doll taste in women, maybe Newhall's real beef is that Drayton didn't waste much time on him. He may have focused a little more on the lady with the strange name. Mink something. Maybe she had plans for the museum that Newhall didn't know about. Maybe the blessed Blessant wanted to put a stop to that."

Khattak looked at her, his cat-eyes shrewd. "So you're no longer proceeding on the accident theory."

"Murder, murder everywhere," she replied airily. She could smell the freshness of the lake in the air. They had arrived at Ayre Point, a street that was bordered on one side by a park, its shade trees spread wide in stately indifference. Bluffs, park, forest, and lake made it splendor to splendor without the people and their crumbling homes.

Ayre Point consisted of a succession of 1970s-style houses: bricked-up bungalows with low roofs and small front yards, vans and pickup trucks serving as one wing of a crowded assembly. Rachel smoothed down her slacks, tweaked the lapels of her jacket. Remembering last night, she'd abandoned her ponytail, content to brush her sleek hair down her shoulders. Nothing could be done with it, and not for lack of trying. It was like Asian hair minus the silky gloss. She'd secured her side part with one of her mother's gold hair slides, a fact that made her self-conscious when she thought of her no-nonsense hockey team. She shrugged it off. Melanie Blessant wasn't going to bother about her. Not once she got a look at Khattak, who epitomized the female holy grail of tall, dark, and handsome, if you subtracted a certain ascetic quality.

Nobody likes a preacher boy. She chuckled to herself. Whether he was saint or sinner, she didn't know. His private life was difficult to read. What was far more explicit was the reaction of every woman who came within his radius. Although why she was so sensitive to it was a quality she preferred not to examine in herself.

Melanie Blessant's house was at the corner, its green roof steeply sloped over an exterior of dust-colored brick. Cement slabs piled on top of each other provided access to a front door. Telephone wires and a giant fir tree blocked any view afforded by the bay window that fronted the street. Maples covered the rest of the space.

Straddling a pair of lawn chairs on the neatly mown front yard were two teenage girls. They were sipping lemonade, dressed in the teen uniform of blue jeans and jerseys. One was listening to her iPod. The other was reading a book.

Rachel checked her watch. They should have been in school.

Khattak showed his identification, greeted them politely, and asked for the woman he assumed was their mother.

"Mad Mel's not here right now," the older girl informed them, setting aside her book.

Rachel took a closer look at them. These were the girls from the photograph on Drayton's desk, so much alike in appearance that they had to be sisters. They were tawny-haired and bright-eyed, with the clean young limbs of saplings. The younger girl removed her earphones, her face as clear as the cup of a lily rising on its stem.

"Don't call Mum that, Hadley," she scolded without heat. The face she turned to the older girl bore the kind of warmth that Rachel had long since ceased to expect of siblings. The girl tugged her sister up from her lawn chair and extended her hand in a mimicry of adult courtesy. Khattak shook it gravely.

"I'm Cassidy Blessant and this is my sister, Hadley. Our mum won't be home until later this afternoon."

"Would you happen to know where she went?"

"She's in her natural habitat," Hadley drawled. "Getting closer to Chris in death than he'd ever let her in life."

"Hadley!" The younger girl's face fell. Spoonfuls of light that leaked through the trees splashed across her clear complexion.

Hadley shrugged. "It's true. You may not like it, God knows I don't, but that is in fact what our dear, devoted mother is doing. Going through Christopher's things as we speak, hoping to dig up one final, pricey bauble."

"You're referring to Christopher Drayton, the man who fell to his death from the Bluffs?" Khattak asked the question gently.

Cassidy's face clouded in response. "Mum's really upset about it. They were in love. They were going to get married and we were all going to live in Christopher's house."

Her childlike manner of expressing herself coupled with the wistfulness in her voice made Rachel appreciate that she *was* a child. At most, a very young thirteen.

"Bull." Hadley contradicted her without compunction. "Chris didn't want that crazy wedding and I never had any intention of leaving Dad. If Mel had ever shacked up with him, I'd have gone to Dad in a flash."

Cassidy bit her lip. "Chris was really good to us, Hadley. You said you loved your Italian lessons with him. He was nice to us. We had our own rooms whenever we stayed over."

"Did it ever occur to you that he wanted something in return? Like Mel at his beck and call? She wouldn't have been much use to him if she'd had to come home to us every night. And if she abandoned us, as she obviously wanted to, there'd be no reason left for us not to go to Dad."

"I don't want to go to Dad. I loved it with Mum and Chris."

Her lip trembled and Rachel felt a pang of compunction. They had let the dialogue between the sisters play out because it was more revealing than anything they could have asked, but Cassidy was too young to face up to Hadley's brutal truths. If, in fact, any of it was the truth.

"Where is your father?" she asked, curious.

"Our parents are divorced," Hadley said bluntly. "We're the prize they fight over to make each other miserable. Or at least, Mel makes our dad miserable, since he's the one who actually cares about us. Mel only wanted custody for one reason. She keeps us for the money. My dad has a lot of it."

Her attention switched beyond them to a boy on the other side of the street. She shook her head at him. It was a small movement that Rachel caught. She was warning him off. The boy didn't appear to notice. He was dressed with considerable panache in slim-fitting jeans that tapered down to his ankles and a loose shirt with its sleeves rolled up to the elbows. Beneath the long-sleeved shirt was a blue Dr. Who T-shirt that bore the legend, *Time Travel, It's Easier by Blue Box*. The hair that fell forward across his brow had been styled with close attention. He crossed the street toward them, and once he brushed past her, Rachel caught the unmistakable tang of marijuana on his clothes.

"These are cops," Hadley said, her voice fierce. "They're looking for Mel."

The boy ignored her, genially tugging at Cassidy's red-gold hair. "What's up, Goldilocks? You look like someone's stolen your porridge."

She responded at once, her face lighting up. "Hadley's being mean about Mum. Make her stop, Riv."

Rachel liked his aura of emo-chic, but she really hoped that the name he presented to the world wasn't some hippie-go-lucky version of River.

It was a hope dashed. He extended his hand, looking up at her from under his sideswept bangs, through meltingly long eyelashes. "Marco River," he said. "Most people call me Riv."

He really did belong in a boy band, Rachel thought, suppressing a grin. "That's a great name," she said. His smile in response was good-natured.

"My parents call me Marco, of course. So does Mink—but you know how it goes with the kids." He shrugged one arm over Hadley's shoulders, the other over Cassidy's. Both girls seemed to relax in his presence.

Rachel couldn't decide if she was more disarmed by his candid blue eyes or his casual charm.

"Hadley's my girlfriend but Cassie's my best girl," he went on.

Apparently, smoking pot made one loquacious.

"Mink Norman?" Khattak asked. "Do you know her?"

The sharpness of the question didn't faze him.

"Sure. We all do. Hadley and Cass have summer jobs at the museum, and Mink lets me hang around if I'm useful." He grinned at the girls. "Which as anyone will tell you, I am."

"I imagine so." Even saying it, Rachel felt a hundred years old. This good-looking boy, like all men of varying sizes, ages, and temperaments, had probably dismissed her already, but he was somehow managing to be generous with his charm. His easy smile encompassed her along with the girls.

She waited to see if there was anything else Khattak chose to ask.

"The Andalusia Museum," he said. "The same one Christopher Drayton took such an interest in." He made it a statement, the kind he often used as a fishing line.

"Ringsong," Hadley corrected sharply. "It's named after the great Andalusian poetic tradition, a blending of cultures and faiths, the holy and the vernacular."

"She writes the descriptions for the exhibits," River said drily. "That's why she talks like that."

Rachel couldn't resist. She smiled back at him, liking his sense of humor. It was a cheerful teasing absent of mockery. Hadley poked him in the ribs.

"Is that all you wanted to know?" she asked Khattak. "Do you need to know where Chris's house is?"

"We've been there, thank you. I apologize if we've disturbed you."

"Wait," she said. "Why are you looking for Mel? Why did you want to know about Chris? He was nice to everyone," she added, reluctantly.

Cassidy reached out and squeezed her sister's hand. "He really was nice," she confided. "It's too bad for Mum. He made her so happy."

Hadley might have said otherwise, Rachel thought, but she was not as abrasive a sibling as she'd seemed at first. Or perhaps the boy mellowed her. She opened her mouth, only to shut it without saying anything.

Khattak was careful with his answer. "These are routine inquiries into an accidental death, to make sure we haven't missed anything."

Not careful enough. Riv's fingers tightened on each girl's shoulder.

"Like what?" he asked. "What could you have missed?"

"Depression, financial concerns, health worries. At this stage, we simply don't know."

Hadley and Riv exchanged a quick glance.

"Cass," Hadley said. "Go into the house."

"Why? I want to hear too."

Hadley signaled the boy with a subtle movement of her eyebrows. "Take her in, Riv. I'll fill you in later."

She wouldn't, Rachel guessed, but Riv obeyed her at once. So he possessed the charm while this possibly no more than fifteen-year-old girl held the actual authority. Hadley waited to hear the door close and then she rounded on them.

"Are you talking about suicide? Do you think Chris killed himself?"

"I'm not sure we should discuss this any further without your mother present."

"Forget my mother. You'll get more sense out of me than you'll ever get from her. The only thing she can concentrate on is whether Chris left her anything and which of her little black dresses she should wear to his funeral. Now, I want to know. Did Chris kill himself?"

"Why would you think that?" Khattak countered.

Hadley tossed her long hair back over her shoulders. "Well, why would you be here if something wasn't wrong? Why would you even care?" Her expression altered, lost its edge. "Look," she said in a rush, "I didn't mean any of that other stuff. It's not Chris's fault that I wanted to live with my dad. He's my dad and I love him. Chris knew that. I'm sure he understood. It's just—he didn't want that big wedding Mel was always on about, so he couldn't have thought that Dad would just allow us to move in. Do you think Chris thought it might still happen?"

She was looking for reassurance, for some kind of expiation. If she had resisted Drayton's parental overtures and Drayton in turn had come to view his future as grimly unmarked by the things he wanted most, there might well have been some connection between Hadley's fears and Drayton's stark reality.

"Did you notice anything different about him these last few weeks?" Rachel asked, neither confirming nor denying Hadley's suspicions.

Hadley stilled. She was standing close enough to them that Rachel could tally the freckles on the bridge of her nose and spy out the gold flecks in her intelligent brown eyes. Unlike Marco River, no whiff of marijuana rose from her clothing.

"He was a bit more serious, maybe," she offered, then added swiftly, "I don't know why. He spent more time in his garden. He was really happy with the landscaping Aldo and Harry had done at the back."

Rachel considered this. A man improving his property, whether for the sake of its value or for his own creature comfort, hardly seemed the kind of man to contemplate a spine-crushing end to his existence.

And what explained the gun and the absence of candles?

"Did the power ever go out at his house?"

Hadley looked blank, as well she might.

Rachel hastened to clarify her question.

"Did he use a lot of candles during the evening?"

Because if he had, that might explain one mystery, although it didn't account for the gun.

Hadley grimaced as an unpalatable thought surfaced. "Maybe he and Mel did? I mean, I think he tried to be discreet around Cass and me," she said, weighing her words. "But he wasn't perfect."

Meaning, Rachel translated, that this more than on-the-ball teenager had quickly deduced that her mother was having sex with her tutor.

Khattak cut across her thoughts.

"Why Italian lessons instead of other languages?"

"Oh, that. He was fluent in Italian because of the businesses he'd owned in Italy. He said we could pick what we wanted to learn. I would have chosen Spanish, but he didn't speak Spanish. I couldn't see the point of German or Russian, and Cass has always wanted to go to Italy. For the fashion," she tacked on, fondly.

Khattak's face tightened with sudden knowledge. Rachel began to feel irritated. She didn't mind that the boss wanted her to look at the scene with fresh eyes and come to her own conclusions. What she minded was that she had no context for filtering the information that was coming through in dribbles from the people who had known Drayton.

Was the business in Italy significant? Did Drayton's fluency in Russian matter? Did the books on Albania suggest a financial interest in trans-European organized crime? What about the unfamiliar 9-millimeter gun? How could she make any of these deductions if she didn't have the faintest idea of what they were investigating? The dark halls of her imagination were pretty unlikely to conjure the truth from smoke.

She sighed.

"Who are Harry and Aldo?" she asked for want of anything more to the point.

Hadley gave her the quintessential teenage shrug, embodying all things from indifference to disgust. She was rubbing her shoes in the spongy grass, which when Rachel did it was a sure sign of boredom.

"Gardeners. They have a local landscaping business that's doing pretty well. They did the gardens at Winterglass and at the museum. They take on plenty of individual jobs like Chris's house as well."

More connections to Drayton. They'd been on Nathan Clare's list, she remembered. Not on the guest list for his dinner parties, but mentioned tangentially. The Osmond brothers, like the singing group. Maybe they were Mormons too.

She wanted to scuff her own shoes.

"I guess we'll head over to Mr. Drayton's house then. Does your mum have a key?"

"Not to everything," her daughter said, with no small measure of satisfaction. "Just the front door. She's been dying to get into his office, but I guess despite their amazing mystical connection, Chris still had his secrets."

The bitter words stabbed at the air like fingers of lightning. They left her looking after them with her thin arms crossed over her chest, her eyes like bronze metalwork, unblinking and inscrutable.

5.

*I took my mother's head into my hands and I kissed her.
I never felt anything so cold before . . .*

In the car, he didn't wait for Rachel to ask. "I know nothing of Drayton's past or any businesses he might have run. I've only suspicion, Rachel. I'm not even sure I'd call it that."

"What would you call it, then?"

"Dread."

Rachel accepted this without knowing why. Maybe it was the hunted look in his eyes.

The day was warming up, a languid sleeve of blue draping the air with heat. As she did most days when the outdoor ice rinks were closed due to warmer than average temperatures, Rachel cursed mightily at global warming. She hadn't spent a lifetime recycling to suffer these miniature blows.

"You've known Nathan Clare for years," she said after a while. "Haven't you ever seen this house or museum or whatever you want to call it?"

"Ringsong? I haven't. It must be newly built. We'll go there after this stop."

This stop was Drayton's house, with its burnished aisles of flowers, the autumn grass rising vast and green, a backdrop to roses with gleaming thorns and orange-shouldered lilies that shifted against bright filaments of air.

The Osmond brothers knew what they were doing. And the back

of the house, where the windows of Drayton's study broached the glassy expanse of lake, must have been even more peaceful. A place of dreams. A place to lose oneself in a solitude of light. A whimsical thought. One to be expected from a student of literature though not necessarily from a hockey-playing policewoman.

"I'll meet you in a moment," Khattak said. "I'd like to see what the landscapers have done around the house."

More secrets. Or a chance to size up Melanie Blessant on her own. She could take it either way.

She let herself into the house. They were too late to prevent Melanie from tinkering with the lock on the den again, but Rachel doubted she'd gained access. Drayton had fortified his study well. She was right: she found the woman mixing herself a drink in Drayton's kitchen.

"Ms. Blessant?" Rachel held up her ID. "I'm Sergeant Rachel Getty. Hadley told me you were here."

Melanie Blessant snorted, choking on her drink. From the bleary-eyed look of her, it wasn't her first.

"Of course she did, the little rat. Anything to screw me over."

Not the first words Rachel expected from a woman as lushly upholstered as Melanie Blessant. The photograph had given her some indication and Newhall's description of her dubious magic had confirmed it, but in the flesh the woman was something else.

She'd want to be thought of as enchantingly helpless. What else, with those pillowy lips and the white-blond hair that set off china-doll eyes? Not to mention the ridiculously high heels and deep-necked zebra print that hugged her curves. It was an excess of everything. Divine effusion in the form of expensive European scent. Shiny teeth, tiny bejeweled hands, perfectly set hair. Ropes of gold and diamonds blazed between her breasts, dangled from her ears and smothered her delicate wrists. Her makeup was subdued but still eye-catching: blue eyes rimmed with smoky liner, lips emphasized by semi-nude gloss, bronzer defining nature-defying cheekbones. Altogether too much woman, too much perfume, too much everything. Rachel's back ached at the thought of lugging around the other woman's double-barreled weight.

"I've come about the death of Mr. Drayton. I'll have to ask you for your key to his house."

Melanie set her glass down unsteadily on the quartz countertop. Her flawless complexion hardened into a mask.

"I'm not giving you anything until I've seen his will. This was supposed to be *my* house. We were supposed to be married. Then the damn fool had to go and get himself killed."

"Killed?" Rachel echoed.

Melanie waved her glass at the other woman.

"He fell, didn't he? He fell and he didn't even think about what that would do to me." She yanked the bottle on the counter closer to her, possibly a plum brandy, and a potent one from the look of things.

"I'm very sorry for your loss, Ms. Blessant."

"My loss?" Melanie snorted. "Forget my loss. What about that wedding he promised me? What about the money?"

With some effort, Rachel kept her expression impassive. Had Christopher Drayton really wanted to marry this woman? Granted, her breasts were enormous, but was that the only thing that counted with men anymore? How had he missed her mercenary nature? Or maybe he hadn't cared. Maybe a man in his late sixties was looking for nothing more than ready comfort or the sexual indulgence he had long since thought himself past.

Somehow that didn't figure with her notion of the Italian lessons. He hadn't only wanted Melanie. He'd cared for the girls as well.

Khattak tapped at the patio window. Rachel moved to let him in. She nodded at Melanie Blessant, hunched over Drayton's breakfast bar.

"Ms. Blessant, this is Inspector Khattak of Community Policing. He has some questions for you about Mr. Drayton."

The woman ignored her, pouring herself another drink. And then she stopped cold when she saw Khattak's face reflected in the mirror that hung on the far wall of the breakfast nook. Without speaking, she performed a series of subtle motions: arranging the expression on her face, running a quick tongue over her lips, drawing in her breath to boost her décolletage, sucking in her waist. Straightening her back, she turned on her stool and extended a limp hand.

"Ms. Blessant," he offered, as Rachel had, "I'm so sorry for your loss. I understand you and Mr. Drayton were very close."

"Melanie, please," she breathed. Rachel watched, amazed, as Melanie's blue eyes filled with tears. "It's been terrible," she whispered. "I don't know how I'll manage without my sweet Chrissie."

She glanced up at Khattak from beneath a thick fringe of lashes before continuing, "He was everything to me and my girls. My poor, sweet girls. They're absolutely devastated."

Rachel choked back a snort of disgust. Check one for the ingenuous glamour-puss. Check two for the doting mother. Her performance went some distance toward explaining Hadley's naked hostility.

Melanie shifted onto her feet, putting an unsteady hand on Khattak's shoulder. Her fingers tested the flesh beneath his shirt. Even with her heels, she reached no higher than his collarbone, a fact she clearly delighted in.

"How can I help you, Inspector? I'd do anything for Chrissie."

With a swift look at her shoes and a perfectly straight face, Khattak asked, "Shall we walk in the garden? It's a beautiful day for it."

The shoes meant that Melanie would have no choice but to avail herself of the Inspector's strong arm. A sardonic grin on her face that Khattak ignored, Rachel followed them into the garden.

She listened absently as he asked the routine questions about Drayton's state of mind, the unexpectedness of his death. Melanie clung to his arm, her fingers gripping like talons. She was adamant in her denial of any suggestion of suicide. Not her Chrissie. Not when he had so much to live for. The wedding. The girls. The family they would become. He'd already prepared the house for them, both girls had their own rooms. And he'd given her a free hand in redecorating the master, paying the extravagant bills without batting an eyelash or asking her to account for any of it. If his little Mel was happy, Chrissie was happy.

She'd been planning a gala reception at the Royal York. She had a wedding planner on retainer, one of those artsy downtown photographers booked to do the pictures, florists, caterers, wedding announcements—they'd been so busy these past few weeks. Her Vera Wang gown was hanging in Chrissie's closet, along with the accompanying bridesmaids' gowns he'd simply insisted on buying for Hadley and Cassidy. It doesn't have to be Vera for them, she'd assured him. That was spoiling them too much, but Chrissie wouldn't hear of it.

"What's good enough for my Mel is good enough for her girls."

She produced a sob on cue, turning her face into Khattak's shoulder. No tears now, Rachel noted with a wry twist to her mouth.

"Hadley said Mr. Drayton was against an elaborate wedding," Rachel interjected helpfully. Well, pseudohelpfully, anyway.

She caught the look of malice Melanie shot her from the shelter of Khattak's shoulder.

"I was excited, can you blame me? I might have gone a little overboard. Chrissie was the type to prefer something smaller, like in his garden. He'd crown me with lilies, he said. He was romantic like that." This time a genuine sob escaped her throat. She stared at Rachel defiantly, attempting to disown it. "That didn't mean he wasn't going to do what I wanted. Chrissie always did what I wanted. Besides, he knew I wouldn't move in with the girls until the wedding had taken place. I didn't want *Dennis* accusing me of negligence." She spat the name of her ex-husband at them.

A negligence of the heart, perhaps.

Rachel glanced around the garden. Its vivid spires balanced against the scroll of waves that rolled and unrolled to a distant rhythm. It would have been a lovely place for a wedding, intimacy rendered sacred in these groves. In Melanie's place, she would have agreed to it. Except she could never see herself in Melanie's place. When she thought about what the future might hold, she saw only her work.

Instead of the promise of love and companionship, there was the constant presence of loss. And work was the one thing that could make her forget, the one place she could do something that mattered, that healed. Even if Melanie didn't seem in need of healing.

Rachel did some quick calculations in her head. Landscaping, the Royal York, Vera Wang—it added up.

"Perhaps Mr. Drayton had some financial troubles. A wedding in his garden would have reduced the expense considerably."

"No," Melanie said petulantly. "He just didn't like fuss. He didn't even want to sit for our wedding photos."

She patted down her dress, admiring herself, inviting them to admire her also, bathed in the glow of autumn light.

She pouted, an action that made Rachel think of an inquisitive puffer fish with its same moist oval of a mouth.

"I guess I don't blame him. Chrissie was nearly thirty years older than me. Maybe he didn't want everyone noticing."

A possibility, Rachel conceded. Perhaps the contrast of so much plush flesh barely bounded by her clothes had made Drayton feel his years. The years that may have hinted at future inadequacies.

"Was Mr. Drayton in a rush to be married?"

Melanie released Khattak's arm and gave Rachel a purely woman-to-woman look. "He wasn't missing out on anything, if that's what you're asking."

It hadn't been, but it was as good a lead as any. "Was it you who was eager to get married, then?"

Everything about the woman suggested haste. With her ex-husband no longer on a leash, maybe it had been a straightforward exchange of sex for security. The woman had a libido; the way she was eyeing Khattak was ample evidence of that.

Melanie swept her arm wide, knocking petals from several of the roses as she did.

"If you think this is about Audrina, let me assure you it isn't. I'm the only woman Chrissie cared about. The only one he wanted to marry, and he was in no danger of changing his mind."

"Who's Audrina?"

Khattak was busy admiring the fruit of the Osmond brothers' labor, so Rachel kept at it. One conversational thread was often as good as another.

Melanie's pouting lips snapped tight, but the massive injections of collagen she had endured meant they couldn't look anything but sultry.

"Some tart he picked up somewhere. I never met her, she was never at the house. Sometimes when Chrissie couldn't sleep, I'd hear him talking about her, but if I asked him in the morning, he'd say it was nothing. Some silly crush from his past. There were no texts from her, no phone calls."

Khattak turned back to them, his fingers absently handling the peach-colored petals of a rose known as Joseph's Coat.

"Your fiancé wasn't sleeping well?"

Melanie renewed her pout, this time attempting a sexier twist on it. "Not for my lack of trying, Inspector. A woman does what she can." She brought a platinum lock of her hair to her lips and twirled it. Rachel smothered a laugh. This was the Scarborough version of Marilyn Monroe's *Niagara*. "I told Chrissie not to worry about it, but I guess he couldn't get those letters off his mind."

"What letters, Ms. Blessant?"

"Melanie, please." She pressed Khattak's outstretched hand, removing the rose from his grasp. "Oh, every now and again Chrissie would find these letters on his doorstep. Typed letters, stupid ones. They never made any sense to me."

As Khattak's interest sharpened, Melanie blossomed before Rachel's eyes.

"Mr. Drayton showed them to you? How were they addressed?"

Her thick-coated eyelashes flickered. "The envelopes weren't addressed and Chrissie didn't exactly show me the letters. I'd find pieces of them in his desk drawer from time to time."

The same things that Rachel and Khattak already knew.

"Once, I found them shoved into an atlas like he was trying to keep them from me. My Chrissie never liked me to worry." Nor would any man, her tone implied. Her raison d'être in life was to be cosseted. "It was total nonsense, anyway. What does it even mean, 'I think it would be better if none of us had survived'? Why would anyone say that?"

She didn't seem to care about the answer.

"Can you tell us anything else about the letters?" There was a stiffness in Khattak's voice that Rachel couldn't place.

"I wish I could, Inspector, but Chrissie agreed with me. He said they were nonsense and he should probably burn them." She tilted her blond head to one side, her china blue eyes widening in sudden awareness. "But he always dreamt about Audrina on those nights when he got one. Maybe the little slut was sending them to him."

Rachel made a note of the name. Could the candles have been for the purpose of burning the letters? If so, why had she found so many remnants in Drayton's file cabinet? The puddles of resin had consisted only of candle wax, not residues of ash.

She signaled Khattak. She was finding Melanie Blessant both vulgar and tedious. She wanted to get to the museum.

"I wonder, Melanie, would you have the combination to your fiancé's safe? Or access to any of his papers?"

Melanie shook her head, her platinum locks bouncing, displeased at this reminder of her limited prerogatives in Drayton's life. "I need to know about his will. Chrissie said he would take care of me. He *promised* he would. I know he wouldn't leave me all alone in the world."

The subtraction of Hadley and Cassidy from her life didn't surprise Rachel at all, but Khattak's response was kind.

"For the time being, we'll have to ask you for your key and that you stay away from this house until we've completed our inquiries. You should know, however, that you are designated as the beneficiary in Mr. Drayton's life insurance policies. Regarding his will, if you know his lawyer's name, you should contact him. He'll be able to guide you further."

Melanie's impossible heels saw her sway into Khattak's chest.

"Thank you, Inspector, thank you! You don't know how worried I've been. Does the policy say—?"

"One hundred thousand dollars each. There are two of them. But they won't be settled until we've ascertained that Mr. Drayton's death was no more than an accident."

Melanie stared at them shrewdly, her whole mood brightening.

"Chrissie didn't kill himself. He had no reason to. I'll swear that to anyone who asks."

She had the confidence of a woman who knew that the objections of any rational male could be softened by a comprehensive glance at her cleavage.

She turned in her key without protest, a spring in her step as she let herself out of the garden.

6.

Do you still believe that we die
only the first death
and never receive any requital?

"I want to look for that atlas, Rachel."

"I'd like to get to that museum before it closes, sir. And shouldn't we get something to eat?" The breakfast sandwich being a faded memory at this point, leaving her purse redolent of egg whites, cheese, and sausage.

"After this, I promise."

Rachel screwed up her face in concentration. Only one section of Drayton's bookshelves held any atlases—the same one that contained the teen fiction she now ascribed to Hadley and Cassidy. They were heavy books. She took them out one at a time, shifting them to the surface of Drayton's desk. Khattak shook them out. No letters fell loose, none were concealed between the endpapers or slipped inside their covers.

"No luck, sir," she concluded.

She was in the act of setting the final one back when she saw that Drayton had folded down the corner of a particular page. She opened the atlas to study the borders of the country mapped on its pages. It wasn't Russia or Albania.

In a quick flash of intuition she connected the name of the woman Melanie had called a little slut. Audrina. Shortened, it was a five letter word. A word dark-penciled on the map.

She left the atlas open on the desk to make her way to the safe, adrenaline juicing her veins. The glimmer of an idea was taking root in her mind.

"What is it?"

She pointed Khattak to the atlas.

"I think I might be able to figure out the combination."

If it was as simple as a substitution code. Numbers for a name Drayton hadn't been able to get out of his mind, a name that kept him up at night. A preliminary attempt taught her that a straightforward substitution wouldn't fit the five-digit display. Using paper from Drayton's desk, she tried another tack. If she divided the alphabet in half and assigned the numbers one through thirteen, only one combination would spell the name she had found on the map. She punched in the numbers 45911 and the digital display lit up. As she pulled the small lever forward, she heard a click. The safe opened without resistance.

Drayton hadn't been mumbling the name of another woman in his sleep.

He'd said *Drina*, not Audrina. The name on the map was also the code.

Dozens of letters cascaded from the safe into her lap. She shifted through them, catching odd phrases here and there.

Yellow ants, your days are numbered.

Bend down, drink the water by the kerb like dogs.

Take the town. Comb the streets house by house.

Make them shoot each other. Then kill the rest.

They took my son. They shot him before my eyes.

I'm thirsty, so thirsty.

How sorry I am to die here so thirsty.

A terrible sense of dread pressed against Rachel's heart. Her stomach dropped, her palms went damp. She knew what she was looking at, but she wanted to hear it confirmed. She needed Khattak to admit what he long must have known.

The letters were never meant for Christopher Drayton.

They identified another man altogether.

Her voice raspy in her throat, she skewered Khattak with a look.

"Who the *hell* is Dražen Krstić?"

7.

Under a big pear tree there was a heap of between ten and twelve bodies. It was difficult to count them because they were covered over with earth, but heads and hands were sticking out of the little mound.

There's never any joy.

Khattak's phone rang, a temporary reprieve from questions he could no longer ignore. He didn't believe the truth would set him free. The truth in this case was a trap. One he had willingly entered, on the word of an old friend. Because friendship was more than a source of comfort, or a place of belonging. It was a responsibility. One that Nate had failed. He wouldn't fail Tom in turn.

That's not the only reason, Esa, you know that. You're not detached, pretend as you must. This is about identity. Yours. And his.

The phone call corroborated his fears. He'd told Rachel not to use up resources, not to widen the circle, but he'd sent a picture of the gun to Gaffney. And now Gaff had told him what some still resistant part of himself didn't want to know.

"Bring those with you. You said you were hungry," he said to Rachel.

"Sir—"

It wasn't an evasion. He had never meant to keep her in the dark this long.

"I'll answer your questions while we eat."

And Rachel, ever loyal when she should have been screaming at him, bagged the evidence without a word and followed him to the car.

Evidence? What evidence? A man fell to his death.

If he kept repeating it to himself, it might prove true.

He chose a restaurant near the marina, familiar to him through colleagues at 43 Division. And through Nate. He and Nate had eaten here all the time. The food was good, the views abundant.

His salad arrived swiftly along with Rachel's grilled chicken sandwich.

She tossed the bag of letters beside his plate.

"Talk," she said.

Glad of the excuse not to meet her eyes, he turned his attention to the bag. A disjointed phrase slipped toward his salad.

Not one of our leaders remain. No one returned from Omarska.

Rachel was already putting pieces together.

"Who called you from Justice, sir? Who asked you to find out if Christopher Drayton really fell from the Bluffs?"

His salad tasted dry in his mouth. This was Rachel. This was going to be a nightmare for every branch of government involved, but Rachel he trusted. She had more than proven her loyalty in Waverley, but it wasn't loyalty alone that had shown him her real worth. Rachel had a dogged commitment to the truth that outstripped her pride and ambition alike.

"Tom Paley," he said at last. "He's a friend." There was no point delaying the truth further. "He's also the Chief War Crimes Historian at Justice."

Rachel's mouth fell open, disclosing an impressive amount of chewed-up chicken.

She was bound to know Paley's name. Every now and again, his Nazi-hunting endeavors surfaced in the press.

She swallowed with difficulty, setting down her sandwich so she could count off her fingers. "The map Drayton marked. It was of

Yugoslavia. The code to the safe—it was Drina, like the river on the eastern border."

"Like the Drina Corps," Khattak amended. "Like the gun. It's a Tokarev variant, the M70 model. Standard issue for the Yugoslav National Army—or the JNA, as it was known."

"What are you saying, sir? That Drayton owned a Yugoslav army weapon? Where would he have gotten it?"

"Not Drayton." Khattak looked at her steadily. "Dražen Krstić."

She stared back unblinking.

"Lieutenant Colonel Dražen Krstić was the Chief of Security of the Drina Corps of the VRS in 1995. He was General Radislav Krstić's direct subordinate. He was a superior officer to the security organs of the Drina Corps brigades. He also had a unique relationship with the Military Police and the 10th Sabotage Detachment of the Main Staff."

"Hold up," Rachel said. "I'm lost. Main staff of what?"

"The VRS." He folded his hands to cover the letters. "The Bosnian Serb Army."

There was a deadly little pause. It had never bothered Rachel that Khattak was a decade older than she, but she could see now that it had its disadvantages. He spoke of a war he had witnessed, whereas she had been a child during the dissolution of Yugoslavia.

Memories of news coverage began to filter through. The secession of a republic known as Bosnia Herzegovina. A UN force on the ground. Shrill politicians. Hand-wringing. Yes, there had been plenty of hand-wringing.

"Did you say 1995?" she whispered. He nodded, his expression not quite impassive.

"And the Drina Corps's area of responsibility?"

"It was Srebrenica."

Srebrenica.

Now the dread had meaning.

So too the letters.

"And Drayton?"

"Tom thinks Drayton may have been Dražen Krstić."

The notorious war criminal at large. One of the chief perpetrators of the executions at Srebrenica, where eight thousand Muslim boys and men had been murdered near the endpoint of a war that had seen Yugoslavia dissolve into flames. Eight thousand dead in less than a week.

Their hands tied, their bodies smashed, bulldozed into mass graves in an attempt to obscure the war's greatest slaughter. An act commonly described as Europe's greatest atrocity since the Second World War.

Overlooking the rape, terror, and destruction that had characterized the three long years before the culmination of so much death.

Khattak could never hear the word *Serb* without thinking of its dark twin, Srebrenica.

And he could not think of Srebrenica without remembering his younger self, a self whose ideals and vocation were nearly lost to him now. The younger self that had participated in a student network against genocide, brave or foolish enough to accompany a humanitarian aid shipment to the once exquisite city of Sarajevo.

On Tuesday there will be no bread in Sarajevo.

He heard the cellist's melody again: mournful, insistent, accusing. It had sounded as a requiem in the streets of Sarajevo.

You failed us.

And then you watched us die.

The shipments had been no more than a bandage. Inadequate, deficient, robbed at airports and checkpoints by the same guns that had wiped the history of Bosnia from the map. The theft of United Nations fuel had supplied tanks and convoy lines, enabling the war to continue unto a world without end.

Memory itself erased.

A fig leaf in the end, for stone-faced passivity in the face of mass murder and the camps created for the purpose of torture and rape. The names indelibly stamped in memory: Omarksa, Manjača, Trnopolje, Keraterm.

It wasn't passivity that had defeated the Muslims of Bosnia. He thought now that such merciless slaughter could never have been possible without the international community's intervention. Forestalling air strikes. Appeasing the architects of the war while military units with names like the White Eagles and Drina Wolves pillaged and burned. Equivocating over "warring factions," eager to accept the fiction that a people under threat of extinction had fired mortars upon their own marketplaces to generate international sympathy or to provoke military action.

Action that couldn't be provoked, no matter the horrors on the ground.

Until Srebrenica.

Srebrenica that crystallized a truth acknowledged far too late.

The obliteration of Bosnia had been a slaughter, not a war.

Enabled by an arms embargo that had left its victims helpless in the face of VRS tanks, guns, propaganda, and hate.

The tragedy of Srebrenica will haunt our history forever.

Just as it haunted Khattak. Too many dead, too little done for the innocent. He still believed in a community, an *ummah*; in his best moments, he saw himself as a guardian. If he failed to discover the truth about Drayton, would he still be able to think of himself that way?

It had never been a question of ethics because nothing his work required of him had been in conflict with the truth. His counterterrorism work had been a requirement of faith, not an abjuration.

During its three-year siege, Srebrenica had known terror enough for eight thousand lifetimes.

He read the letter he had covered with his hand.

Lt. Colonel Dražen Krstić,

It took some persuasion to convince my Serb neighbor with whom I had lived my whole life that I was suddenly his enemy and that I was to be killed. And yet you managed it.

"Unless someone identifies him as Krstić, how can we really know?"

"Is that why you left me in the dark? You hoped it wasn't going to be Krstić?"

"There's a fairly significant Bosnian community on both sides of the border. How do you think it will play that a war criminal managed to acquire Canadian citizenship?"

"Does that matter?" Rachel pushed back. "If Drayton was Krstić, isn't it far more important we confirm that he's dead?"

"It will matter like hell to the Bosnians. They've a mosque not far from where you live, Rachel. And it's largely a refugee community."

Rachel pulled the bag of letters back toward herself, smoothing the plastic with her fingers.

"Sir," she said, carefully. "Did Tom Paley ask you to look into this for the purpose of covering it up? Because the biggest storm this will unleash will be at CIC."

Canadian Immigration and Citizenship. If they had granted Drayton his papers.

"Justice will take its share of opprobrium too. No, Rachel, that's not it. If they wanted it left alone, Tom could have left it alone. He didn't need to call me. He wouldn't want this on his conscience, and no one at CIC would have wanted Drayton in the country. He might have come across the border with forged papers, we'll find out eventually. What matters is that someone knew who Drayton was. Someone was sending him these letters. And then Drayton died."

"A fall," Rachel countered, playing devil's advocate.

"A fall," he echoed, a tightness in his chest. "Was it a fall? If this was Dražen Krstić, there are thousands of people who'd want to see him dead."

"Wouldn't they rather have justice? See him exposed and paraded in front of the press before he's locked up for good? That's what I would want."

Muslims, you yellow ants, your days are numbered.

Khattak couldn't be quite as confident.

A flush rose in his face, the moment of confession upon him. "They tried, Rachel. That's why Tom called me. For nearly two years, he's been receiving letters about Drayton. Anonymous letters. Someone's been asking him to investigate. Persistently. Tom meant to do it, he always meant to. Time got away from him."

"And now Drayton is dead."

"It's not all on Tom. In seventeen years, very few of these men have been apprehended, even fewer convicted. In the towns and cities of Bosnia, victims see the men who abused them walking free every day. Profiting from their crimes while the crimes they perpetrated can never be undone. Rapists. Sadists. Torturers. Thugs. And the missing—"

He ran out of words.

Rachel tried to understand. She'd read enough of history to appreciate the destruction of Yugoslavia for what it was. A bloodbath. Overseen by an intractable, perhaps even complicit, United Nations. As a police officer, she didn't have an ounce of Gandhian blood in her. She scorned those who genuflected at the temple of nonviolence, their voices ringing with praise of the defenseless victims of butchery while they sat on their hands when the gods of carnage came calling.

And she'd followed a bit of the general's war crimes trial.

General Ratko Mladić, commander of the Bosnian Serb Army, in the dock at the Hague's International Criminal Tribunal for the former Yugoslavia.

Charged with crimes so monumental they had required the formation of a separate court to hear them.

Genocide. Complicity in genocide. Crimes against humanity. Violation of the laws of war. Deportation. Murder. Extermination.

Seventeen years the survivors of Srebrenica had waited to see Ratko Mladić account for his actions.

On the day he had faced them in court, Mladić had drawn his finger across his throat.

In a recorded statement of guilt, VRS officer Momir Nikolić had confessed little more than: "I am aware that I cannot bring back the dead."

Whatever hatred these men had spewed had consumed them, unable to recognize the civilization they had destroyed.

There was never a place called Bosnia.

We deny the existence of a camp called Omarska.

We deplore this time of war and hatred.

We are working for peace, peace is what we want.

All were sentences glimpsed from the letters.

"What was the letter writer doing, sir? What does it all mean? Was Drayton being threatened? "

Neither one of them had finished their lunch. Rachel had been starving. Now her stomach was unsettled, protesting any thought of food.

Khattak raised his hands, as she had sometimes seen him do in prayer, and brushed them over his face.

"God knows." He said it seriously. "Perhaps reminding him of his crimes. Perhaps documenting them." He turned the bag over, sifting through more of the letters. "It's not as if these are threats." Through the plastic, his fingers measured first one line, then the next. "It's testimony, Rachel. These letters are testimony."

"From what? War crimes trials? You said yourself, there haven't been many."

"Not just the trials. These read like statements of witness. To the war itself. Perhaps reminding Drayton of what he and his confederates so pitilessly wished to obliterate."

A place of belonging for all of its people.

"Muslims weren't the only victims of that war," Rachel said, a trace of worry in her voice. She'd come to believe in Khattak's utter impartiality.

"No," he agreed. "But they were the only victims of Srebrenica. The only people of Bosnia under threat of extermination."

He pushed one of the letters at her.

The mosque in Foča burned for days. They danced the kolo *over its embers.*

"Foča?" she asked.

There was an expression on Khattak's face that she'd never thought to see. Haggard, haunted, almost without hope.

"A town in southeastern Bosnia. After the war, it was renamed Srbinje. The destruction of the Aladza was the least of its tragedies." He hesitated. "You could find out more from the witness testimony at the trial of Dragan Zelenović. There are a few others who have been tried for crimes at Foča as well. It's not—easy reading."

Rachel swallowed.

"So this is not just about what Krstić did at Srebrenica."

"There's been a tendency for history to cling to Srebrenica like a touchstone while ignoring the crimes that transpired before." He shook his head, his dark hair disarranging itself across his brow. "Srebrenica wasn't the beginning. It was the end."

He seemed to be taking a largely forgotten conflict much too personally, which worried Rachel.

"You're not Bosnian, sir." Her attempt at subtlety. "You seem rather—invested."

Khattak smiled. He always smiled when she expected him to take offense, something that continually caught her off guard. Not to mention the smile itself. Disconcerting at the best of times.

"You're not a Muslim girl. And yet, you were rather invested yourself in the death of Miraj Siddiqui."

Their last case and the first time she and Khattak had worked together to solve a murder. Miraj Siddiqui had been a young woman from a small Ontario township. They had caught the case because her death had been flagged as an honor killing.

It was a fair point. How to respond?

"I'm just saying—look, your background is South Asian."

"Pakistani," he added helpfully. "Don't beat around the bush."

She glared at him. "That didn't require security clearance, did it, sir? It's just—you seem to know an awful lot about this. You seem to *care* an awful lot about this."

"Empathy," he said easily. "The reason we work so well together. You have it in spades."

"I was a kid when Yugoslavia fell apart. I had no reason to know or care anything about it."

At once he became serious. "If it had fallen apart, I don't know that I would have cared much either. But it was severed, Rachel. By gangsters on the ground and cowards at the Security Council."

"That's exactly what I'm talking about. Who carries that kind of conviction around in their heads?"

"I wasn't a child then." He ate the last few bites of his salad. "Let's talk about this more later. We should be getting to the museum."

Prevarication.

She was the queen of prevarication, so she had no trouble recognizing it.

If Christopher Drayton was really Dražen Krstić—a man who had butchered Muslims in their thousands—that might be a reason to call upon the head of Community Policing, especially if that head was also an old friend.

Her gut told her there was more to it—more about Khattak that she didn't know, which was no surprise. She hadn't known about Laine Stoicheva until he'd taken the time to tell her. She definitely hadn't known about Nathan Clare or she would have read all of his books by now. Especially the one he'd mentioned to her boss—*Apologia*. She made a mental note to hunt it down. She was pretty sure there was something more here—something about the war that was more personal to him.

Khattak rarely shied from the truth. In her working experience with him, what he asked for was time to ascertain the nature of the truth. He was cautious, thorough, and eventually, the truth came to light.

Her own skills in this department were of no little assistance. She made connections quickly, leaps of intuition that were somehow in her blood. She liked to pound ahead wherever they took her, and Khattak usually let her.

This time he asked for patience.

She wanted to see the museum as well. Spanish history wasn't her strong suit, but she'd always wanted to visit Barcelona. Each fresh winter that rolled by, she cursed herself for not having purchased a ticket. Maybe this year.

She'd rather think of Spain than of Krstić, but her bloodhound instincts were up.

What would a man like Dražen Krstić have wanted with a museum on the history of Moorish Spain?

8.

All my life I will have thoughts of that and feel the pain that I felt then and still feel. That will never go away.

It was Tuesday night. It had taken them all day in the blistering heat to walk the four kilometers to Cinkara. It was no uglier than any of the other buildings. It had the same pockmarked face and shattered windows of all the concrete blocks. They had made munitions here once. Maybe, maybe there would be weapons of some kind, a gun she could hold. Maybe there would be food or clean water. One thing she knew was that there would be people. The road was full of them, everyone hungry, everyone frightened, everyone hot.

One of the girls in her class had fainted at the roadside. She wanted to stop and comfort Edina, but her sister wouldn't let her. Her sister kept her slippery hand locked tight within her own, bruising it with her hold, and marched her forward, talking to no one, listening to no one. It was only the two of them now. They had already seen their brothers to the woods. Four boys, ranging in age from thirteen to twenty-one.

"We will meet you in Tuzla," Nesib said. "Look for us in Tuzla. And when you get to the base, look for our neighbors, they will help you. Look for Mrs. Obranovic. She will make sure you are safe."

None of this had been said to her. Nesib, the handsomest and oldest of her brothers, had given his instructions to her older sister.

"And listen," he'd said. "Stay in the middle of the crowd. Keep your faces turned away. Don't go near any of the soldiers. Do you hear me? Always look away from them."

Her sister had nodded. Then Nesib tried to push the last of their food into her sister's hands. She pushed it back, spreading her hands wide, refusing to take it. Her stomach was crying but she knew it was right what her sister had done. Their laughing, joking, beloved Nesib was losing his teeth. He was the skinniest of them all because he gave his share to whichever of them cried the most or complained the loudest. Only her sister was good enough not to take Nesib's food, though she was hungry too.

Her sister was right. It was a very long march to Tuzla.

Her brothers would need the food in the woods.

She thought that maybe Nesib was so worried that he might not even remember to say good-bye to her. But he had kissed her and kissed her, squeezing her tight, before saying to her sister, "Don't let go of her hand."

Her sister had nodded, solemn as an oath-taker.

"All the way to Potočari, don't let go of her hand. If the soldiers come, you run into the woods."

And then he had pulled at her sister's braid and kissed them both again.

"Allah keep you, my little sisters. Allah is wise and protects us all."

He read the Fatiha over their heads, then he took their brothers and left. None of them looked back.

Her sister had obeyed Nesib as if it was the most important thing in the world, the most important lesson she could learn. She had kept them marching despite her complaints. She had cried, begged, even thrown a tantrum, but her sister wouldn't stop.

She held her hand in a death grip.

If they died on their way to Potočari, she would still feel that grip.

Cinkara was even hotter and more crowded than the road had been.

She hated it. She hated that Nesib had left them and that everyone was crying and angry and frightened. They made her frightened too.

Her sister kept pushing and pushing, dragging her by the hand, through the crush of bodies until they got to the center.

And every now and again, her sister, whose head kept turning from side to side, would call out, "Mrs. Obranovic? Mrs. Obranovic, are you here?"

They found a concrete wall to lean against. There had been so much heat this July that even the concrete was warm against her bare arms.

She was so hot and thirsty she thought she might fall to the ground like Edina.

And then, her sister let go of her hand and darted into the crowd.

Stunned, she sat back, too frightened and thirsty to move. She couldn't even call after her. Everyone had left her. Their parents had died two months ago in the shelling. Now Nesib and her sister were gone. She was alone. She wasn't going to make it.

She began to cry, but it had been so long since she'd had any water to drink that the tears wouldn't come. For some reason this made her angry.

She cursed Nesib, she cursed her parents, and loudest of all, she cursed her sister.

And then she remembered that smiling, hungry, skinny Nesib didn't like it when she cursed. She recited his prayer instead.

"Allah will keep us, Allah will protect us. Allah will keep us, Allah will protect us. Allah will keep us, Allah will protect us. Allah keep Nesib, keep Nermin, keep Jusuf, keep Adem, keep my sister."

"She is a good one, this little girl. Look how she says her prayers."

It was Mrs. Obranovic!

Her face broke into a smile of unrestrained joy as she found her sister behind the bulk of their neighbor. Her sister hadn't left her alone in the world. She hadn't broken her promise to Nesib by letting go of her hand. She'd seen Mrs. Obranovic and dashed into the crowd!

And now they were both with her.

Mrs. Obranovic studied their hungry faces and reached into the basket she carried on her shoulder. She had a plastic carton of water. She twisted off the lid, giving each of them a little to drink. Then she reached back into the bag and produced a half loaf of bread. She gave all this to them with a little bit of yoghurt.

"It's gone bad, I think, in this heat, but take it anyway. You girls need it."

She couldn't help herself. She kissed Mrs. Obranovic's hands.

Such a wonderful woman. So blessedly, blessedly kind!

The noise and heat and crush around them faded. She relaxed against the concrete wall, happier than she'd been in weeks. As if in harmony with her moment of contentment, the people around her quieted from their terror. Everyone went thankfully still.

Dutch soldiers in their UNPROFOR gear and blue helmets were approaching through the crowd.

Her stomach full, her thirst a little quenched, she smiled at them and waved her hand.

9.

I addressed one of the wingborn singers,
who was sad at heart and aquiver.

"For what do you lament so plaintively" I asked,
And it answered, "For an age that is gone, forever."

Now that she was standing before it, Rachel couldn't believe they had missed this house upon their former visit to Nathan Clare. It was four doors from Winterglass and roughly double the size, albeit entirely different in style. A style unseen in the climate of southern Ontario, let alone at the edge of an eroding series of cliffs.

The Andalusia Museum wasn't just a museum: it was a house drawn from the rural architecture of southern Spain, where internal spaces expanded outward in a marriage of gardens and stone. In Scarborough, it was impractical at best, foolish at worst.

From the street the house fronted, Rachel could see the lake through a row of French doors and recessed windows. The loveliest part of it was the shining coil of light that illuminated the courtyard within.

She marveled at it. The grace of modeled plaster played against slurried brickwork and roofs of red clay. A portico and forecourt beckoned beneath the rusticated arch that crowned a flight of terracotta stairs. Under the sconces on the cast-stone surround, the name Ringsong was outlined in tiny bronze and blue mosaic tiles.

Ringsong.

Something to do with Andalusian love poetry, she recalled.

It didn't belong on this street, yet she had difficulty imagining it anywhere else. It was too rich, too alluring, too beautifully imagined. It made her think of constellations in a southern sky unfolding against the velvet of night or the sweet taste of nectar in a miniature golden cup.

All it required in addition was an encampment of glossy-necked peacocks. There was plenty of space for them to wander in the tiered garden that surrounded the house, plantings she was fairly certain wouldn't survive the winter.

The house was filling her head with fantastical thoughts.

To dispel the magic, she pressed the doorbell, Khattak silent at her side.

For someone who'd been agitating about their visit to the museum, he had little to say. She shot him a glance. His face was meditative, absorbed. She could tell he was impressed.

A woman close to Rachel's age, in her late twenties or early thirties, answered the door. She wasn't the coal-eyed, caramel-skinned beauty Rachel's imagination had conjured up to go with the house, a woman of Spanish warmth and languid bones, another stereotype dashed.

If anything, the woman's grave young face made her think of the soft-spoken Jane Austen scholar whose course she had taken as an undergraduate. Dreamy-eyed, a little withdrawn, but there the comparison faltered. The woman who answered the door had a guarded, subtle face with eyes the pale blue of Waterford china. Her sheaf of hair was the color of wheat, neatly captured at the base of her neck. She was narrow-shouldered with wristbones that hinted at a painful fragility. Dressed in a white silk blouse and tailored gray trousers, she was mildly attractive, though too self-possessed for true beauty.

Pale-hearted, Rachel thought in another flight of fancy.

Before they could introduce themselves, Marco River appeared at her shoulder.

"Well met," he said. "These are those cops, Mink. The ones I was telling you about."

So much for the element of surprise. And what kind of kid said "Well met"?

Khattak made polite introductions with more than a touch of warmth in his voice. As Mink led them inward through the forecourt, Rachel wondered if it was the woman or the house that attracted him. They passed under an arch inlaid with a narrow river of Moorish tiles and then through a space Candice Olson would have described as a flex room. It was a space between spaces, inviting them deeper into the house, yet Rachel could have lingered in it for hours. The antique Moroccan carpet that warmed the floor, the assembly of indoor palms potted in sand-colored stoneware, books and pamphlets on Andalusian history—all of these demanded time and care.

She changed her mind in the forecourt, where curtains of wind brushed against her face, carrying the scent of grape myrtle, jacaranda, and chorisia from the courtyard through a wood-planked door. Small pedestals with glass cases were arranged in a circle in the forecourt, each with a manuscript page on display and an accompanying beautifully lettered description of the exhibit.

Was this Hadley's work?

Three sides of the house opened onto a courtyard planted with flowers, olive trees, citrus, and palms. A massive hearth dominated one end, fortifying a large alfresco seating area. Cassidy Blessant was curled up in one of the armchairs, her long legs tucked beneath her as she paged through a magazine.

Rachel expected it to be *Seventeen* or some teen gossip rag; she was surprised to discover a calendar with photographs of Arabian thoroughbreds.

"This is a resting place," Mink informed them. "To give people time to reflect on what they've learned in a space that's purely Andalusian."

"Outwardly impassive, preserving the artistry of its craftsmen for the interior."

Mink nodded at Khattak, pleased. "Like the Alhambra," she agreed, "with its Court of Lions." They exchanged the glance of intimates who spoke an exclusive language.

Mink led them through the courtyard to the great room, the first room that conformed to Rachel's notion of what a museum should be. Exhibits were arranged on white marble pedestals and in bow-front cabinets, each with the same hand-lettered descriptions. Carved beams and a progression of clerestory windows subdued the immense space; tall glass lanterns were hung at regular intervals between the beams. The room was a spectacular contrast of dark timber against pale stonework. Three pairs of French doors opened to the courtyard, dressing the room in a canopy of light. The entire effect was effortless.

Rachel loved it. From his arrested expression, she could tell Khattak felt the same.

"I hope you don't mind if we keep working while we talk. We're due to open in October and we're a bit behind."

The "we" included Marco River, who was now ensconced with Hadley at a huge wood table in the center of the room. They were seated on high-backed stools, bent over a table piled high with any number of disparate objects, manuscripts, and books. Hadley was using the fine nib of a calligrapher's pen on cream notecards that matched the milky tones of the room. Riv leafed through a dictionary, presumably assisting with vocabulary. His knee was touching Hadley's, who ignored it.

"Why Andalusia, Ms. Norman?" Rachel asked.

"Won't you call me Mink?" She invited them to the table to inspect her collection, sliding onto a stool across from Hadley and Riv.

"That's an unusual name."

"My sister is Sable," Mink said drily. "Our mother had two passions in life: fashion and theater. She respected the animal rights movement but deplored the need to give up her precious furs. So she took her revenge with typical drama—by naming us after them."

Rachel smirked. "No siblings named Otter and Ermine?"

There was the briefest hesitation before Mink laughed. "None. Now, how may I help you?"

Khattak was quick to step in. Rachel had the uneasy feeling that he was more than a little interested in their hostess.

Great. He'd been the one man she'd met who she thought could resist blondes.

"I would love to know more about the museum."

"It's a passion project," she said simply. "I'm a librarian. I've studied languages and history. There's no place that speaks to me more than the civilization of Andalusia. Cordoba, Granada, Seville, Toledo—it was a sparkling moment in our collective history." She was dismantling an ornate picture frame as she spoke, intricate gold decoration incised on black steel.

"Moments that come rarely and are soon extinguished," said Khattak, something indefinable in his voice.

She paused in her work. "I don't know that I would call seven hundred years of Moorish influence on Spain 'soon.' All history is eventually extinguished, but its monuments may well endure. Like the Alhambra. Or this one."

She placed the photograph intended for the steel frame before him on the table. Forgotten, Rachel peered over his shoulder.

It was an exquisite Spanish building with a cascade of horseshoe arches in white.

"A mosque," Rachel said.

"A synagogue," Mink corrected. "Actually, this is Sinagoga de Santa Maria la Blanca, or Saint Mary the White, a structure that seems extraordinary to us now, though it was perfectly appropriate to its time." Her fingers brushed Khattak's at the edge of the photograph. "It was built by Mudejar architects for the Jewish community of Toledo, at their request." She placed a special emphasis on the last words. The smile that edged her lips was wistful. "Muslims," she elaborated for Rachel's benefit. "Moorish architects designing a Jewish place of worship on Christian soil. Can you imagine such a sharing of religious space today?"

Khattak had once prayed at the Dome of the Rock next to a Syriac Christian, a fact he was willing to discuss, if not advertise.

"I think they did it on *Little Mosque on the Prairie*." Not Rachel's most brilliant offering, but true as far as it went.

"Saskatchewan—the new Andalusia."

Mink said it gently enough, but Rachel caught the undertone of mockery. Khattak was slow to remove his hand, she noted.

"Where do the exhibits come from?" he asked Mink.

"I've been collecting little bits of history ever since I can remember. Nothing very valuable—most of it is just a translation of poetry and religious manuscripts, which, thanks to Hadley, we've prettified. The forecourt exhibits are a series of ring songs, a tradition that began with the Andalusian Arabs who had a genius for assimilating cultures and ideas. Arabic was the lingua franca of Andalusia—admired, almost venerated for its great poetry and expressiveness, not feared and despised as it is today. The ring song rejuvenated Europe's indigenous tongues, gave voice to feelings and ideas that Latin couldn't begin to grapple with. The ring songs from our exhibit are from Arabic, Hebrew, and Romance. It's a remarkable synthesis. Andalusia was a remarkable synthesis."

She would have made a great teacher. Her passion for her subject, her ability to slice through centuries of history to the shimmering idea at the heart of it, would inspire the museum's visitors: it was more captivating than her remarkable endeavor.

But it was a humble project as far as museums went. Scattered objects. More description than representation. For the life of her, Rachel couldn't see why Christopher Drayton would have been prepared to make such a major donation. Just to put his name on a wall or a plaque? If David Newhall's thinking was illustrative of the museum's directors' position, they hadn't wanted his money. Yet a hundred thousand dollars might have purchased more than a few trinkets or seen to the upkeep of this fabulous house.

Where had the funding for the museum come from? Surely not from a librarian's salary. And did she live here? Had she been prepared to turn down Drayton's offer? Rachel's list of questions was growing longer.

"So what happened to Andalusia?"

"Fanaticism, fundamentalism of all kinds. Petty-minded rivalries from within, ignorance and fear from without. The Inquisition. The Reconquista. Before you knew it, Iberia's Jews and Muslims had vanished into history. We think of it commonly as a case of Christians expelling or forcibly converting the peoples of the peninsula. In fact, there were all kinds of alliances between the communities and they changed frequently. It wasn't Christians who burned the Great Library of Cordoba." Mink looked pained at the mention of it, as if it were a loss that had occurred only yesterday. "It was Berbers riding an orthodox tide that swept the Muslim world."

Book-burnings. Those inveterate moments in history when knowledge and the transmission of it was the most dangerous currency of all.

"What they were striking at—as did the Inquisition centuries later—was a culture of enlightenment. Knowledge shared, refined, debated, and ultimately transformed. Ideas, books, histories could come from any source, and the Umayyad rulers of Spain had instantaneous access to everything created and translated in the staggering knowledge-production factories of Baghdad. Knowledge was priceless, whether religious or secular, indigenous or foreign. The prince of Cordoba housed countless scribes, editors, and bookbinders in his palace." Her smile was reminiscent, her blue eyes alight. "They say in Cordoba books were prized more greatly than beautiful women or jewels. In Andalusia, the mark of a city's greatness rested on the caliber of its libraries and the quality of its scholars. That's what we're trying to re-create here, in some small part. That wonderful spirit of inclusion and mutual learning. The Library of Cordoba held over four hundred thousand volumes, with a catalogue librarians only dream of."

Which was an interesting history lesson, and Rachel could see that the librarian was moved by it, but it still didn't explain Christopher Drayton's interest.

Or maybe it did. Khattak, who as far as Rachel knew had no particular attachment to Moorish Spain, was listening to Mink with the fervent attention of the masses in Saint Peter's Square on Easter

Sunday. Maybe this idea of a vivid, elastic pluralism gave spark to magic. The kind of magic that opened wallets and turned serious men into dreamers. Or maybe it wasn't Andalusia at all, but the woman herself.

"What was Christopher Drayton's interest in the museum? We've learned that he was to make a significant financial contribution to it."

Mink took a moment to slip the photograph of the synagogue into the steel frame she had prepared. When she looked up at Rachel, her face was composed.

"Chris was a neighbor and a friend." She lowered her voice. "I think he was a little lonely and the idea of the museum was something that intrigued him. People who know nothing of Spain beyond Madrid and Barcelona are often captivated by their first venture into its Moorish past. By what the wonderful writer Maria Menochal has called palaces of memory."

Rachel scowled. Was this a second dig the quiet librarian had aimed at her? Or was Rachel just being sensitive because she'd imagined herself on a sunny Mediterranean beach?

Her answer was overloud. "How could he be lonely with a bosom companion like Melanie Blessant?" She was quite pleased with the emphasis she'd laid on the word *bosom*. Until she saw Hadley and Riv's heads come up.

Mink shrugged, her face tight, searching for other work at the table to occupy her hands. They fell upon a small book of poetry, its author Arab, its title *The Neck-Ring of the Dove*. Fascinated by it, Khattak took it from her.

Her voice lowered further, she said directly to Khattak, "There are other needs men have beyond what Melanie offered. Understanding. Communication. A certain sympathy of thought."

Khattak held her gaze without comment.

Rachel scratched at her neck. Her boss was being decidedly unhelpful during this interview, neither asking his own questions nor following up hers. Mink Norman was clever, but she was also ordinary to a fault: where was the distraction?

"Are you saying you possessed this sympathy with Mr. Drayton? Was that why he planned to make such a large donation?" Rachel asked.

"We never intended to be too ambitious with Ringsong. We hadn't expected the kind of budget that would permit us to purchase manuscripts and so on. I'm not a curator of objets d'art. I'm a librarian. I wanted to tell the story of a civilization of the word. A civilization in love with language and learning. "

"Would Mr. Drayton's money help with that or not? One of your directors, David Newhall, said that it came with a steep price tag. You'd have to rename the entire project after Drayton."

Mink stiffened, bracing her hands on the table. Hadley and Riv looked up again, sensing that the mood had changed.

"We hadn't decided about the donation. As far as I knew, there were no strings attached. We'd already named the house, and the house is a public trust. We built it with a great deal of grant assistance."

"We?"

"The Andalusia Society. We've over two thousand members."

"Do you live here?"

"The house has a set of private rooms. That's part of my arrangement as librarian. Should I leave the job, naturally I'd leave the house."

There was a thrust and counterthrust to her conversation with Rachel, a suppressed antagonism, as if she recognized in Rachel a cunning, obstructive enemy. There was something wary about Mink Norman, some powerful emotion tamped down beneath a calm exterior.

"If, as you say, there were no strings attached, why the hesitation? Surely the money would come in handy."

"I have no fund-raising agenda," she replied with dignity. "There's a process by which new members are vetted. The same is true of donations. Christopher did wish to help us, but we had to weigh this against his request to come on board as a director."

"So there *were* strings attached."

It was the obvious conclusion. Drayton wanted more than the indulgence of a passing interest in a history entirely unrelated to himself. He wanted a role in directing the museum itself.

Rachel looked through the windows to the courtyard. Maybe it wasn't the museum he'd had an interest in. He'd chosen to live in an unprepossessing home on a pretty street with magnificent views. Maybe what he wanted was the house.

If Mink were no longer librarian, maybe a man of his independent means could talk his way into some form of guardianship.

House, kids, adulation, and Melanie.

The perfect life.

She changed tack.

"Did you see Mr. Drayton on the Bluffs on the night of his death?"

"No." She answered exactly as Nathan Clare had. "You can't see the path to the Bluffs from these windows."

But was it true? Rachel would have to get out there and walk it to discover just what could be seen of the museum and Winterglass from the Bluffs.

If everyone had liked Chris Drayton and no one had seen him on the night of his death, what did his death really signify? And yet, she couldn't shake the feeling that Mink was holding something back. Perhaps an affair with Drayton. Was she the reason he'd dragged his feet about Melanie's plans for an over-the-top wedding? Hadley and Riv were whispering to each other across the long table, the boy's hand caressing the girl's neck, another gesture Hadley ignored. She was watching the three of them with canny, glittering eyes.

The conversation was at a dead end. Unless Khattak had something to offer, Rachel couldn't think of anything else to add that seemed remotely connected to Drayton's death. Unless she simply came out and stated: *"Do you have any reason to suspect that Christopher Drayton was a Bosnian Serb war criminal?"*

She was tempted, but she didn't want to tip her hand too soon. It was hardly something Drayton would have advertised if he were

Dražen Krstić. And that was another thing—what rational reason could a man accused of exterminating Muslims and eradicating Bosnian history have for his attraction to the Andalusia museum? Weren't the two ideas fundamentally opposed? One a civilization of pluralism and tolerance, the other a culture of hate?

If she'd understood Mink's little lecture properly, the Andalusians had created something beautiful out of their divergent identities. In the hands of the Bosnian Serb Army, difference—whether Muslim, Catholic, or Jew—had meant destruction and death.

There were no personal items in the museum area of the house that could offer further insight into the character of Mink Norman and her association with Christopher Drayton. Rachel tried anyway.

"You mentioned your sister, Ms. Norman. Where is Sable now?"

Mink smiled with genuine warmth at the mention of her sister.

"The music you see everywhere? It's Sable's. She studies piano at the Mozarteum University of Salzburg. She'll be home again for Christmas break."

One sister a librarian, one sister a musician. An educated family. Rachel envied their opportunities.

"Your parents?"

"It's just the two of us, I'm afraid."

Another field of inquiry dried up. The only sensible thing to do was to begin a comprehensive investigation into Drayton's real identity. Without that information, there was little point to harassing those Drayton had known passingly or well.

The music reminded her of Winterglass and Nathan Clare. She mentioned him to Mink, watching her guarded face.

"Come on," Riv said from his side of the table, his dictionary abandoned, one hand on Hadley's knee. "Everyone from here to Timbuktu knows Nathan. He's amazing. And he gives the best parties."

"That's all right, Marco. And yes, it's true. Nathan loves the piano. He's quite proficient. He often loans us music."

On the other side of the courtyard was a colonnade of arches through which Rachel glimpsed fountains that seemed to drop through the air to the lake. She very much wanted to explore further but could think of no reason to stay.

"Shall we go then, sir?"

Khattak caught her glance, moved away from the table. "I'd like to take a closer look at the exhibits. You've been up early, call it a night."

Rachel cleared her throat. Had the museum and its proprietor so bewitched him that he'd forgotten? "You're my ride, sir. I'll need a lift to the subway at least."

He straightened quickly. "Of course. Then I'll return later, if I may."

The words were said somewhere in the vicinity of Mink's burnished hair. Her blue eyes encompassed Khattak, acknowledged a private communication.

In the car, Rachel said, "A blonde, sir? Really?" And left it at that.

10.

*Easily predictable events have been proceeding inexorably
in the cruelest, most atrocious fashion.*

For more than a week now, Rachel had been asked to do nothing
further on the Drayton investigation. She'd resumed her regular
workload with Dec and Gaffney, saying little about the previous
week's excursions, wondering when Khattak would show up at their
downtown office again. She had a few ideas about what they should
do next and found Khattak's silence troubling. Had he ruled out the
idea that Drayton was Dražen Krstić? If so, based on what evidence?
Or had he found something that cemented his certainties? Was he
even now reporting to his friend at Justice? He'd told her to keep
the letters, and she'd spent her evenings digging into the history
of the Bosnian war, trying to find out more about Krstić.

Initially, she'd thought that the letters spoke from the perspective
of a survivor of the war with a very specific axe to grind, but Khattak
had been right. The letters weren't just about the massacre at Srebrenica. They were far more wide-ranging, as if the letter writer was
making a darker point, outlined in blood.

Sarajevo, did you hear my warning?

The sun on your face looks like blood on the morning.

She hadn't been able to trace either the letters or the source of
those words. The only prints on the letters had been Drayton's. The
words she had just read were conceivably from a translated poem or
song. And Sarajevo wasn't the only name she had found in the letters.

There were others, all of them, apart from Srebrenica, unfamiliar to her. Gorazde, Bihac, Tuzla, Zepa.

She'd looked them up. All six cities had been UN-designated "safe areas," under United Nations protection. All six had come under siege, repeated bombardment, the destruction of religious and cultural monuments, and the recurrent targeting of water, electricity, and food supplies.

The letter writer encompassed it all.

Today a funeral procession was shelled.

Charred bodies lie along the street.

The whole city is without water.

Srebrenica, like Sarajevo, had suffered a three-year siege. In Srebrenica, civilians kept alive by a trickle of UN aid ultimately became victims of genocide. In less than twenty-four hours, safe area Srebrenica had been depopulated of its Muslim inhabitants: women and small children forcibly evacuated under the eyes of the Dutch battalion stationed there, men and boys murdered in their thousands.

Nearby Zepa escaped the massacres but suffered the same depopulation.

All at the hands of the logistically efficient killing machine known as the VRS or Bosnian Serb Army, supplied materially and in all the other ways that mattered by the reconstituted Yugoslav National Army.

We will not reward the aggressor with the carve-up of Bosnia, redrawn along ethnically purified lines.

And yet they had.

Many of the post-1995 online commentators on Bosnia used the satiric term *unsafe area Srebrenica*. Rachel couldn't fault them. It was a compelling history lesson: how quickly the violent ideals of ultra-nationalism led to hate, how quickly hate to blood. If Drayton had been Dražen Krstić, his hands were bloodier than most.

The letter writer wanted to remind him of this. More than anything, he or she intended to disrupt the idyllic latter stage of life

Drayton had constructed for himself: peaceful home, lovely garden, voluptuous fiancée, made-to-order family.

Had there been a ring on Melanie Blessant's finger? Rachel couldn't remember.

Another line of inquiry to follow up. There was the will to consider, the insurance policies—if Drayton hadn't yet made a bequest to Ringsong, it was possible that his will left everything to Melanie. If Melanie had known as much and if the wedding was slow to proceed—if Mink Norman was somehow seducing Drayton's wealth to fund what she had called a passion project—Drayton's death might have nothing to do with the identity of Dražen Krstić at all.

The letters may have been intended merely as torment, the need of a clever and isolated individual to maintain control over Drayton.

She made a list of things to check out: the disposition of the will, whether the wedding had been confirmed, Drayton's relationship with Mink Norman, the identity of the letter writer.

She was ready to chase down all possible leads as to Drayton's true identity, including a visit to view the body: she was waiting for Khattak's call.

She glanced up from her desk to the glass doors of his office. Still empty. She could see his bookshelves on the wall, nearly all police business except for a few personal selections, one of which was *Apologia*. Would he notice if she borrowed it?

She slipped into his office and helped herself to the book. Its black and white cover held an undertone of midnight blue. It featured a wrought-iron bench shaded by a tree in a desolate garden. Singularly uninformative.

She flipped through the first few pages until she found the dedication.

To EK, whose friendship I valued too little, too late.

Her intuition had been right. There were deep waters to traverse between Esa Khattak and Nathan Clare. She slipped the book into her bag, closed the lights, and made for home.

11.

*All my joys and my happiness up to then have been replaced
by pain and sorrow for my son . . .*

She walked up the porch steps to their dark two-story in Etobicoke.
She noticed, as she always did, that the stairs needed sweeping and
that the paint on the porch was peeling badly. Her Da was retired
from the service, but he spent most of his time in front of the television, often cursing at it. In the evenings, he went to the local pub
where he traded the same war stories that had been doing the rounds
for the last thirty years. He was a heavy drinker. His drinking had
defined her whole childhood: it had made a victim of her mother
and driven her brother, Zachary, to the streets while still a teenager.

Zach had been fifteen the last time Rachel had seen him.

Ray and Zach, they'd been to each other during those good days.
Ray-Ray, she'd been when Zach was little. A seven-year age difference had separated them, but Zach had been the light of her
world, the baby she'd done her best to raise. Her father's rages and
her mother's efforts at making herself disappear had been successful. There'd only been Rachel for Zach. And that less and less, as
Rachel put herself through school.

She and Zach had shared the same dream. She'd get an education
and a job, and she'd make a home for herself and Zach. A home away
from the paralytic rages of Don Getty and the helpless murmurings
of Lillian, his wife. No matter how much she longed for closeness
with her mother.

But as Zach had shot up and filled out, it had been harder and harder for him to wait. He'd fought back against their Da, usurping Rachel's role as his protector. Her Da had been prepared to use his hands on his boy. Rachel, he'd never touched. She'd been the one to calm him down, usually with a dose of sharp-tongued humor.

When Rachel was the protector, Zach had gone untouched.

When Zach stood up for himself, everything had changed.

She'd called the cops round a couple of times, but the men who'd come by had been friends of Don Getty, friends who knew his wife, and when asked by them if everything was all right, Lillian had flapped her hands at her sides and apologized for calling them out. No one had mentioned Rachel.

As a child, she had judged her mother for it and held her accountable. As a police officer with years of training behind her, she knew no one was more to blame for the turmoil in their home than Don Getty.

"You better watch it, Da," Rachel had said. "You'd better not touch Zach again."

"He's just a boy," her mother had felt brave enough to add.

"He's got a man's fists. If he uses them, he'll get what a man's got coming."

In some twisted way, had Zach been proud of that? His father finally acknowledging him? Rachel didn't know. All she knew was that the decision had hardened inside herself. All over the city there were families like hers, kids like her and Zach who needed help and were scared to end up at Child Protective Services. The cops were supposed to help kids like her and Zach. They weren't supposed to look the other way when one of their own used his fists on his kid.

She wasn't going to be that kind of cop. She was going to be the kind that stood in the way of the fists, the kind who took on a guy twice her size, soaked in alcoholic rage, the kind who beat him down, cuffed him, and offloaded him into her car. The kind who talked to vulnerable women who couldn't protect themselves and kept the promises they made to help them.

She'd told all this to Zach, but he hadn't understood.

"You want to be like Da?" he'd raged at her, already a foot taller than she was, betrayal in his copper-brown eyes.

"I want to be the exact opposite. I want to do good things with my life, Zach. I want to help kids, if I can. Kids like you and me."

Two days later, Zach was gone.

She'd seen the blame in her mother's eyes every day after that. What they'd had wasn't perfect, but it had been a family. The best kind of family her mother could manage under the pressure of her husband's outbursts. That's what Rachel's actions had destroyed. She and her brother living together under their parents' roof. A roof that provided little in the way of shelter for her mother or her brother, but she'd promised she'd never leave as long as Zach lived there. Rachel pitied Lillian, but she hadn't been able to understand the chains that bound her parents together. It was no kind of life for them. It had been no kind of life for Zach. And when Zach had left, Lillian Getty hadn't shared Rachel's introspection or her inner struggle. She'd blamed her daughter for the absence of her son.

I didn't make him leave, Mum. It was Da's belt and your silence that chased our precious boy away.

Zach hadn't lived in this house in seven years, which raised the question as to why Rachel was still there, living under the same roof, drinking the same poison night after night.

She hadn't stopped searching for her baby brother and she never would.

One day Zach would turn up.

And she'd be here when he did. Waiting for him to forgive her. Waiting for him to love her again, the one person in the world who did.

She bypassed her parents in the living room. Her Da was in for the night, his glazed eyes watching *World's Worst Police Chases*. Her mother sat quietly in a corner, carefully folding down magazine pages to avoid any telltale rustle. Neither greeted her.

She took the narrow wood stairs to her bedroom, set down her bag, hooked her jacket over the back of a chair. There was no game tonight, and she was too tired to play if there had been. With dragging movements, she turned her computer on.

She'd given the Drayton case less than half her attention, pushed Khattak much less than she normally would have, for a single, pressing reason. She'd turned up a lead on Zach.

After all this time, she'd been looking in the wrong place. Halfway houses, homeless shelters, rehab centers, addiction programs. All the things she'd imagined could happen to a boy fending for himself on the streets. She had a friend in every division in the city and she'd called in a lot of favors. Zach's image was on posters and flyers she'd circulated year after year.

She'd tried bus stations, train stations, other metropolitan areas. Zach's friends, his school, everyone who'd ever met him. Even the cops who'd come to the house.

There'd been nothing. Just seven years of silence.

And a folder of e-mails to a long-defunct address that he'd stopped accessing seven years ago.

How would a kid on the streets get e-mail, after all?

And now this hit, from a friend in North York who had a daughter in the arts program up there. A student exhibit at a gallery inside the university.

Her friend had sent her the list of five exhibitors, five students in the Bachelor of Fine Arts program.

Four of them meant nothing to her.

The fifth was Zachary Getty.

It was maybe her brother, maybe not. She'd chased down leads like this before, only to end up with nothing, coming home to her mother's silent, reproachful eyes.

Because Lillian knew.

She knew why Rachel had joined the service. She knew why

Rachel's temper had quickly derailed her career—she knew where that temper came from, and what fostered Rachel's constant need to prove herself.

She hadn't said, *"Sweetheart, it's all right. What happened with Zach wasn't your fault. We miss him too. We're searching too."*

They hadn't searched.

Zach dead or Zach alive was all the same to them.

All they needed was each other and their mutual dysfunction.

Lillian Getty had certainly never said to her, *"Forgive yourself, Rachel."*

Was it because her mother couldn't forgive her? Was that why she withheld her grace and her guidance? Was it the reason for her silence? The conversations that tapered off, the half starts, the eyes haunted by secret knowledge?

What had happened to Lillian Getty?

Had Don Getty happened?

Had there never been any more to her mother than martyred sighs and silent compliance? Had it become Lillian's choice in the end?

Rachel remembered another woman altogether. A woman with a bright spark in her eyes when Rachel had rescued a broken-winged bird on their porch, or played her mother's records. A woman whose loving hands had stroked Rachel's hair when she had cried herself to sleep at night, after her father had turned on Zach again. A woman, who despite Don Getty's strictures, had packed little treats in their lunch, along with notes that reminded them of her love.

She wished she had kept even one of those notes from her childhood, as a means of holding on to the woman she had once fiercely loved—instead of the enemy she had made with her decision to follow in Don Getty's footsteps.

It didn't matter. None of it mattered. Zach dead or alive, hurt or harmed, lost and confused—none of it seemed to matter to Rachel's parents.

It mattered only to her.

She had a name and a place and a time. And it was three nights to the exhibition.

She wasn't about to share any of that with Don or Lillian Getty.

12.

Whoever was on the list to be killed would be killed.

Friday morning Khattak called her. He gave her directions to the Bosnian community's mosque, which wasn't far from her home at the corner of Birmingham and Sixth. It was too early for the Friday prayer, so she found a spot in the parking lot close to the main entrance, a freshly painted white door. The word *Dzamija* was inscribed above the door, the Bosnian spelling of the Arabic word for congregation or community, a fact Rachel had learned during her training at CPS.

The gray building indicated its character with a modest spire of minaret and a phalanx of long, narrow windows topped off by tiny arches. Sunlight warmed the stone; on its grounds the maples were a soft, crushed gold.

Rachel found the women's entrance and left her shoes in a caddy near the door. She proceeded inward by intervals: through a narrow aisle, a tidy library and the outer chamber of the women's prayer space. At the threshold to the main hall, she met Khattak.

The week had not worn well on him. His dark hair was disheveled, the crow's feet at the corners of his eyes were more pronounced, there was even a hint of shadow about his jaw. Instead of his usual sleek splendor, he was dressed in a loose-fitting white kurta and tapered cotton trousers. His green tasbih was wound about his wrist.

"What are we doing here, sir?" was her greeting. "I thought Drayton was a dead end by now."

Khattak shook his head.

"I've been asked to tread carefully so I've done a little digging, called in some help. And I have a couple of visits lined up for us today. You've had the letters printed. Did you find anything?"

"Someone was careful. Only Drayton's prints are on them."

"Did you learn anything else?"

"Very little." She'd elaborate later if he wished, though she imagined there were only so many ways she could tell Khattak he was right. He must be tired of hearing it.

"If this is as sensitive as you're suggesting, this might not be the best place for us to be." She cocked her head at the members of the Bosnian community milling about.

"We've a meeting with Imam Muharrem. I was hoping he might know something about Krstić." He lowered his voice as he said the name. "I've brought a photograph of Drayton."

Rachel didn't ask where he'd obtained it. She'd gotten used to the element of mystery peculiar to her boss. She knew he'd tell her everything she needed to know eventually.

They found the imam at the *mihrab* in the main hall. He was dusting the prayer niche in the wall behind him, a selection of Qur'ans reposing on the lectern before the *minbar*, where he would stand to give the afternoon sermon.

He set down his duster and embraced Khattak, kissing him on each cheek, then holding on to his hands in a prolonged handclasp as he studied him.

"Inspector Esa," he proclaimed. "I am very glad to have the chance to meet you, Asaf has told me so much about you. And this is your colleague, Sergeant Rachel." His bright blue eyes beamed at Rachel. "It's a pleasure to welcome you here."

Asaf, she'd gleaned from Khattak earlier, was the regular imam who gave the services at this location. Imam Muharrem was a visitor from Banja Luka in Bosnia, whose presence allowed his overburdened host to take some time off with his family.

Rachel liked the look of him. He was excessively tall, clad in long, white robes that she thought of as Turkish, with a clean-shaven face and a warmth of manner that enhanced his natural authority. His English was lightly accented, his movements calm and deliberate.

Nothing about multiculturalism antagonized Rachel. She liked all kinds of food, clothing, cultural customs, and music. The one thing that held her aloof was a fear of offending through ignorance.

She apologized for her uncovered hair, but the imam waved the apology aside.

"You were good enough to remove your shoes. It is an honor for us when any guest chooses to visit the *Dzamija*."

"I didn't realize the imam was responsible for maintenance here." She nodded at the duster, one eyebrow aloft.

His answering smile was immediate.

"There is no work of God's too minimal for His caretaker. But let me take you into my office and give you some tea."

He swept them along the hall to an office at one end of an adjacent corridor. It was a well-proportioned space made smaller by rookeries of books gathered up in piles. On top of these, letters in several different languages were stacked at random. Dictionaries, travel guides, and Arabic-language Qur'ans filled up a bookcase behind the imam's desk, a tidy space anointed with a desk lamp, clock, and laptop computer. The impression of mild chaos was balanced by the neatly organized bulletin boards that ran the length of one wall.

He poured them small cups of lightly scented tea from a samovar arranged precariously close to his printer. Glass-green light filtered through the open windows, framed by the yellow branches of maples. They could hear birdsong from the trees.

It was an environment of great charm, and Rachel relaxed into her seat.

"Now, tell me why you have come and what it is I may help you with."

Enjoying the tea that tasted of green apples, Rachel let Khattak present his information.

A close-up photo of Drayton was passed across the desk. "Do you recognize this man, Imam Muharrem?"

In one of his deliberate gestures, the imam steepled his fingers under his chin and bent close to study the photograph. "He isn't a member of our congregation, not that I recognize—but I am still a newcomer here."

"What part of Bosnia and Herzegovina are you from?"

"As so many of us are, I am a refugee and a wanderer." The answer wasn't a circumvention, for he went on to add, "Most recently, I have been conducting historical research in Banja Luka."

A shadow crossed Khattak's face. The sun settled at the window's edge.

"Could I ask you to be more specific? What type of research?"

"You know Banja Luka?"

A slight nod from Khattak.

"We are trying to document what remains of our heritage—the heritage of the Muslims of our sorrowful country. A study was done on the mosques of Banja Luka." He smiled at Rachel, his teeth white and even. "I was a scholar at Ferhadija, the Ferhad Pasha mosque complex. A jewel of our Ottoman past, modest perhaps in scale, but certainly our finest example of sixteenth-century architecture." He brooded over the photograph. "Of course, all the mosques of Banja Luka were destroyed, not just Ferhadija. Let me show you."

He set down his glass of tea and turned to the bookshelf behind his desk. There he searched for a few moments before finding the one he wanted and opening it to a centerfold that displayed two photographs side by side. One was a photograph taken in 1941 of the Ferhadija complex. The second was a flattened area of grass where what remained was the merest outline of the mosque's foundation.

"Razed to the ground in 1993." He fingered the photograph. "That was the last time I stood under the doomed shadow of its minaret. Even then Banja Luka was not safe."

"You were a refugee in Banja Luka?"

"I am from Brčko," he said simply. "I ended up in Manjača."

Names that meant something to Khattak, if not to Rachel. The imam was quick to seize on it. "You *know* Bosnia," he said. "I should have known the name Esa signified a connection."

Not from her CPS training but from Khattak himself, Rachel had learned that Muslim names could transcend sects, ethnicities, communities, and nations. The name Esa could be found in the Arab world, the Indian subcontinent, the villages of Turkey and Persia, or further east in Malaysia and China. It simply meant Jesus.

"I've been to Sarajevo," Khattak answered. "During the war." He took the imam's book and leafed through its pages, one at a time.

"You were *mujahid*?" The imam's question was reverent, a tone Rachel had never formerly associated with the word.

Now Khattak smiled, his hands open on the book that documented the ravaged history of a people. "I was a student," he corrected. "A humanitarian aid worker alongside other students concerned about the siege of Sarajevo."

Imam Muharrem shifted in his seat. Rachel had the impression that Khattak's words were not entirely welcome.

Rachel thought of his words: *I am from Brčko. I ended up in Manjača.*

Hesitating, she said, "I don't know the names of those cities you mentioned, sir."

"Brčko is my home town. It has the misfortune to lie on the Serbian border to the north. Manjača was a camp the Serbs ran on the mountain. First, it was where they held Bosnian Croats. Later, it was mainly us they detained."

"Prisoners of war?"

A curious expression crossed the imam's face: part memory, part judgment.

"It was where they sent many of the people of Banja Luka. All the educated people. The community leaders they hadn't killed outright. The teachers, the doctors, the businessmen, religious leaders—myself. It was a place of unrelenting misery." Under his breath, he recited a prolonged prayer. She caught the word *rahem*—mercy. "I should not speak of it, because then I would speak not only of Banja Luka and Brčko but also of Prijedor and Foča. Of the terrible places where the Serbs ran their rape camps." He took the book back from Khattak and closed it with a snap. "I have counseled too many of our sisters. I do not wish to relive their suffering."

Rachel swallowed. She was a police officer with seven years in the service, but there were entire areas of war crimes testimony she had deliberately avoided in her research.

She was unfamiliar with the names Imam Muharrem had recited. Since Khattak remained silent, she offered, "I thought the great tragedy of the Bosnian war was Srebrenica."

The imam flinched as if she had knifed him in the ribs. "Each of us is the citizen of a fallen city. The killing in Brčko took place three years before the Serbs overran safe area Srebrenica."

Three years. He said it with exactly the same note of bitterness that permeated Rachel's research. She wanted to know more, yet felt she had no right to ask. After all these years, did anyone have the right to send survivors of the war plunging into the pitiless void of memory?

"We've no right to encroach on your privacy, Imam. I've wanted to understand a little better, that's all."

Imam Muharrem held her gaze across the desk. Something in her face must have reassured him.

"If we do not speak of it, it does not mean we do not dream. Survivors are quiet because they are haunted, because they still cannot entirely accept what happened. Yes, there was a method to the madness of their killing, but what was the reason for it? In Brčko, they loaded refrigerated trucks with bodies and dumped them off at the *kafilerija* to be burned in the furnace. In two months, they killed three thousand people. They slit their throats, drained their bodies, and dumped them into the river. Or they killed people with three bullets, the Chetnik salute, and then robbed the dead. They mutilated the bodies and raped the women in front of their husbands, parents, and children." He went quiet for several moments before adding, "Luka-Brčko also had a torture room. I will not tell you what happened there."

He turned his head to the side, light settling softly on his shoulders. "I was in Banja Luka when they took my family. I thought I would carry the guilt of that forever. Until the day I was sent to Manjača, where my friends were murdered before my eyes. I was the only imam to survive. They asked me to care for their families, and I have tried to do the best that I can."

He spread his hands wide as if what he had done was no more than his duty, when he had just conjured up an unfathomable horror. Her face, like Khattak's, was abnormally pale.

"I don't think you came here to hear this," he said, when neither of them said anything further. Condolences were out of the question. She hoped Khattak would know how to proceed.

"I've troubled you with painful memories of the war, Imam Muharrem," Khattak said at last, sharing Rachel's struggle for words.

The imam's hands were steady as he decanted more tea for them. They took a minute to sip it, its soothing fragrance a balm on the air.

Imam Muharrem's lids lowered over his eyes.

"It wasn't a war, my dear Inspector Esa. What happened in my country was simply a slaughter."

He managed a smile. Rachel admired his ability to do it.

"Didn't our president say, after all, 'Sleep peacefully. There will be no war'?"

"A terrible naïveté," Khattak countered.

"It was the Bosnian spirit. We'd lived together so long, intermarried so deeply, spoke the same language. We imagined ourselves a people of the most enlightened pluralism. The Orthodox and Catholic churches, the synagogues—they were part of us. And thirty thousand Serbs resisted the siege of Sarajevo by our sides. Across all these boundaries the fascists insisted upon between us, we kept our belief in the spirit of our nation." He set down his glass again. "And we paid for it."

"And if I told you that one of the men responsible for these crimes was at large here in this city, what would you say?"

The imam's eyes shot to his. He straightened in his seat. "Is that why you have come? Such a man should be denounced. He must be brought to justice at once."

"He's met his justice. He fell—or was helped—to his death."

"That is not justice. We need these people to answer for their crimes. Whom do you speak of, Inspector Esa? What is this about?"

Khattak showed him the photograph of Drayton again. "Are you certain you do not recognize this man?"

Now the imam tried harder, studying the photo with greater care. From his desk drawer, he removed a magnifying glass and scrutinized it further.

"Could this be Krstić? A commander of the Drina Corps? The international forces said they were never able to capture him. How do you know this is him?"

"That's why we came to you. We don't know. We know this man as Christopher Drayton. Ten days ago, Drayton fell to his death."

The imam's fingers tensed around his glass. "I wasn't in Srebrenica, so I wouldn't have seen Krstić personally. But some of our congregants are refugees from the enclave. Shall I ask them? The Drina Corps commanders mixed with the people at Potočari. Someone will have seen him. Someone will know."

Khattak contemplated this option. Rachel knew he would rule it out.

"Will you give me a little time, Imam Muharrem? I have a few other leads that may confirm Drayton's identity. I would prefer to be certain before this news becomes public to the Bosnian community. And I have something else to show you, something you may be able to help us with."

"You would not plan to keep the truth from us?" The imam's gaze was searching.

"We would not have come to you were we not committed to finding the truth."

Imam Muharrem pressed a hand against Khattak's cheek then let it fall.

"Then show me."

On cue, Rachel removed the letters from her bag. She removed their covering and passed them to the imam.

"These are letters that were hand-delivered to Drayton, as far as we can tell. Can you tell us anything about them—maybe help us to understand them?"

"These are typed," he said in surprise. "In English. It is not my best language. Let me find my glasses."

He produced them from the same desk drawer that held the magnifying glass. One at a time, he shuffled the letters between his fingers. He read several phrases aloud, phrases Rachel had been unable to trace.

I have just been informed that the besieged city of Jajce has fallen to the aggressor.

Massive air attacks continue in Bosnia today. We cannot defend ourselves yet no one is coming to our aid.

For having uttered a wrong word, people are taken away or killed.

The camps remain open.

The enemy ring around the city is being strengthened with fresh troops.

For the past three days, Serb forces have been conducting a fierce offensive against the town of Bihac.

Today Serb forces shelled the city of Tuzla. While writing this letter, the city centre is under heavy mortar attack.

The famous National Library has been set on fire and is still burning.

He came to a halt, his breathing heavy and removed his glasses. He looked at them both curiously. His long, well-shaped hand rested on a letter that contained a single sentence.

On Tuesday, there will be no bread in Sarajevo.

"You do not know what this is?" Their silence answered him. He studied the letters again. "These are statements made by our government before the United Nations Security Council. Our country was burning while they insisted on negotiating their imaginary peace, deaf and blind to the scope of the evil confronting them."

Khattak jerked in his chair.

"Ah. You do not like that I use this word, Inspector Esa? Yet in your work as in mine, you must see its face, you must know that evil exists in the world."

He showed them another letter as he laid the Qur'an by his glasses.

Defend us or let us defend ourselves. You have no right to deprive us of both.

"That was our president, doing his best to rescue us. Somehow, it reminds me of the Divine teaching."

He held up a translated verse of the Qur'an.

If Allah helps you, none can ever overcome you; but if He should forsake you, who is there after Him that can help you? In Allah, then, let the believers put their trust.

"To hold on to our trust in the aftermath of such evil has been the hardest test of faith one can face."

Uncomfortable with the turn the conversation had taken, Rachel cleared her throat. "What about the rest of the letters, sir? Are they government statements? Some of them don't appear as if they are."

"I cannot be certain. They sound to me like fragments of testimony from those who survived. If these letters were sent to the man from the photograph, does this not prove he was Dražen Krstić?"

"It's a strong indication," Khattak said, "but it isn't conclusive. We need more."

At his signal, Rachel gathered up the letters and returned them to her bag.

"There is one thing," said the imam. "A sister who is part of the mosque community relayed a story from her mother. She saw Krstić at the gates of Potočari. She said he was more fanatical than most."

"Meaning?"

"If this man you've come about is Dražen Krstić, there will be a tattoo on his hand. It was common among the paramilitaries, but Krstić had it also."

He sketched it for them on a piece of paper tucked into his Qur'an.

Four letters that resembled the Cyrillic *s* written as a *c* filled in the spaces above and below a Serbian cross. Beneath it, the imam had transliterated a phrase.

Samo sloga Srbina spasava.

"Only solidarity saves the Serbs," Khattak translated.

"You know of it."

"As you said, Imam, it was common to the paramilitaries."

"A man named Christopher Drayton would never mark himself this way. If you find it on his hand, he will be Dražen Krstić."

13.

*No one knows what will come tomorrow
and no one knows in what land he will die.*

Rachel pulled in at the morgue and flashed her ID. She was expected. This was the second meeting Khattak had promised for the afternoon, a viewing of Drayton's body. He'd stayed behind at the mosque to attend the Friday prayer. He'd more than fulfilled his CPS mandate if the imam who regularly presided over services was a friend.

The first time Rachel had seen Khattak pray, she'd been embarrassed for them both. Religion figured very little in her life, though she supposed she was a lapsed Catholic. But Khattak was comfortable in his faith, pragmatic: he made so little of it that her feeling of discomfiture vanished. He didn't preach and she didn't listen, a good enough partnership.

She understood the imam's feelings. God had never helped her with her search for Zach, and she wasn't willing to falter her way back to trust. But then again, perhaps God would surprise her.

Witness the body she was studying on the table. A better-looking man than she'd expected, with a face more youthful than his years indicated. There was bruising about his forehead, yet nothing about his expression indicated terror or pain, nor even the mild surprise she had come across with other bodies that she tried not to think of as corpses.

Lash was the Urdu word Khattak had taught her for corpse.

It seemed right: each dead face she studied was like a whiplash across her consciousness.

She reached for Drayton's right hand and turned it over.

The thumb and forefinger were heavily callused.

From a gun grip? she wondered. What had these hands done? Were they responsible for deeds so dark that Drayton had chosen his fall from the cliff?

And then her questions were put to rest. She found the tattoo, the cross divided by Cyrillic letters.

Only solidarity saves the Serbs.

She waited for the Friday prayer to end, and then she called Khattak to tell him what she'd found.

"I need something else from you," he said.

Startled, Rachel wrote down what it was.

14.

Somewhere life withers, somewhere it begins.

The blue rain sank against the mullioned windows of the pub. The temperature had dropped. It was a good night to be indoors, drinking warm ale that nourished the throat as it spread its warmth to his toes.

"You're nervous," his sister said.

"I am," Nathan admitted. "I didn't expect Esa to say yes. I'm not sure I know what to say to him."

"I still can't believe I missed him at the house."

They turned together to wait for the pub's door to open, each of them cherishing different hopes for this reunion. Nate, an end to the two-year severance of a friendship that had meant everything to him. Audrey, the return of the security she hadn't known since the death of her parents. Nate was to blame for where the three of them had ended up, yet Audrey couldn't hold it against him, couldn't hold anything against the brother who had raised her in the absence of their parents and kept her safe.

There was a fire in the grate, a warm bubble of conversation from patrons divesting themselves of steaming raincoats, and a faint light that anchored it all. The door inched open, bringing Nate to his feet. He'd brought Audrey with him as a buffer in the hopes that the sight of her would melt Esa's reserve. Esa had never been able to withstand her.

Instead, the door disclosed a rain-soaked Rachel Getty, her dark hair plastered to her head, her mascara describing inky configurations about her wind-reddened cheeks. He held back a smile; she looked so lost and disconsolate. Esa needed his own buffer, it would seem, but at least he'd agreed to come.

He went forward, grasped Rachel's hand, and dragged her back to meet Audrey. He was unprepared for the strength and smoothness of her grip. His hand tingled as he let hers go, watching as she and Audrey sized each other up. Was there something between Rachel and Esa? Would she view Audrey as a potential rival? He didn't think so, not for all the diligently recorded "sirs" that peppered her conversation. But there was a warmth there, a trust. Observing others was the habit of a lifetime, and Esa he knew as well as he knew himself.

Esa liked Rachel Getty. Very much. So he was prepared to do the same.

The door opened again, and this time it was his friend.

Khattak's eyes searched the pub for Rachel. When he found her, he visibly relaxed. It made it easier for him to come forward and grasp Nathan's hand. Not what he would have done in the past, but maybe Nate was getting too old for that thunderous back clap anyway. He would take what he could get—a friend who tentatively ventured the customs of friendship again.

And then Esa saw Audrey, who flung herself at his neck.

When he saw the broad smile that chased the last trace of diffidence from his friend's face, Nathan found himself smiling as well.

Rachel's eyes widened at the sight of the small, gold whirlwind that launched itself without ceremony at her boss.

Who was she? Nathan Clare's sister, fair enough, but what was she to Khattak that she could wrap herself so confidently about him and he—instead of starching up and shaking her off—draped one arm over her slender shoulders?

She was everything that a strong, square-built, hockey-playing female police officer most definitely was not. Pretty, petite, girlishly feminine without being cloying. Chic, expensively dressed even for a night at the pub, her russet scarf and body-hugging dress a perfect complement to her figure and coloring. Instead of the babyish tones her squeal of delight had seemed to indicate were at hand, her voice was low-pitched and sweet.

Rachel hated her on sight.

She was wet and disheveled and afraid that she stank of the morgue. Between her lumbering awkwardness and the other woman's easy grace, no greater contrast was possible.

"There's absolutely nothing you can say to make up for your total and utter neglect," Audrey scolded Khattak. "Two years? Two years without a word and everything I've learned has had to come through Ruksh? Is this because of that hijab thing?" Her quick sputter of laughter was as appealing as everything else about her. "Because I thought we were past that."

Rachel studied the trio, bemused. Nathan and his sister, the masculine and feminine poles of all that was privileged and charming, with the same fine-boned faces and golden grace; Khattak, leanly exotic and entirely at home in the company of his friends.

What was she bringing to the party? Why had he insisted on her presence with that note of entreaty in his voice? She'd said yes because she owed him, and if she was honest with herself, because she didn't want to spend another night of turmoil speculating about the possibility that she might have found her brother. She didn't take her honesty far enough to admit that she drew comfort just from Khattak's presence.

She sipped at her lukewarm Molson Canadian, letting the warmth of the others' conversation wash over her. She was tired. The search for Zach had been long and filled with disappointments, the imam's stories not easily set aside. The day's revelations chipped away at her. Even on a dead hand, the Serb tattoo menaced her.

In death, Drayton's face was unrevealing. Could this have been the man to send so many innocents to their deaths?

There *was* no art to the mind's construction in the face. She couldn't tell. There was no way to know what kind of mind or soul had breathed beneath that invariably brittle arrangement of bones.

Khattak's interaction with Nathan Clare was stilted, but Audrey's presence seemed specially designed to dilute the uneasiness. Maybe she'd been invited for the same reason as Audrey: to preserve a barrier between the two men.

"We're ignoring Rachel," Audrey said, laughing. "That's really rather odious of you two. First you drag her out here after a long day's work and then you don't even ask if her drink needs topping up."

"I'm fine," Rachel said quickly. "I'm driving home in the rain, so this is my limit."

"And where is home?" Audrey persisted. "Surely you can't mean to drive across town at this hour. There's traffic closures everywhere, it will be a nightmare." Her voice was genuinely friendly, genuinely interested—genuinely everything that was affable and good-natured if Rachel had had the patience for it.

"All part of the job." Her eyes met Khattak's. "I should be going now, sir."

"Sir?" Audrey hooted. "How long have you two worked together, did you say? Ruksh says Esa always calls you Rachel."

Rachel didn't know who Ruksh was. She fought down the swift bubble of pleasure that her name was ever mentioned in any context outside of work.

Suddenly abashed, Audrey must have realized how she sounded. "I'm sorry, Rachel, I didn't mean to presume. I know what police work can be like."

How? Rachel wondered.

"First, let me tell you some of the things that *Inspector* Khattak may be too tight-lipped to divulge. Esa has a sister my age—we grew up together. Her name is Rukshanda. Naturally, as the much younger sisters of two devastating men, we developed a *tendresse* for each other's brothers. We grew out of it, of course."

Her face was aglow with laughter in the soft light of the fire.

"Though not before I attempted a religious conversion and started to wear a headscarf. Unfortunately, my lack of flowing tresses made me no more attractive to what I then determined was quite a dim-witted federal investigator." She made a moue of distress, inviting the others to laugh. "Ruksh was equally foolish about Nate, which was the only thing that prevented me from retreating to the attic to die of mortification. I'm sure Esa kept all my love poems, though. Unless Samina disposed of them?"

A swift glance at Rachel's confusion and she added, "Samina, Esa's wife. I hope you don't mind me telling Rachel, Esa. She's your partner, after all."

Khattak held up his hand. "Yes, Rachel's *my* partner, sprite." He turned to her, his face grave. "I should have mentioned her before. We were married very young, and then some years later, my wife was killed in an accident."

"I'm very sorry, sir." She didn't know what else to say, taken aback by the information. There was more than pain in his face. There was guilt. Was it the reason he'd never shared this with her before? Or was it simply that he was more unguarded around his friends?

"She was the loveliest person, Rachel," Nathan said. "You would have liked her very much."

Despite herself, she felt touched. This was a gathering of old friends—she was the outsider. Yet everyone was taking so much trouble over her. She knew it could only have been because of the way Khattak had spoken of her. She felt valued, respected, a feeling she rarely experienced at home. The only thing Don Getty had taught her was how to be tough. Kindness she had learned from Zach, and in rare stolen moments from her mother.

When she overlooked her outsider status, she realized the story Audrey had confided was actually quite funny.

"Er . . . how old were you during this headscarf incident?"

Audrey seized her hand in delighted response.

"You won't blackmail me with that, will you, Rachel? It really was too dreadful—here I was convinced that anointing myself with new religious credentials would make me irresistible to my very first deathly crush—" She took a moment to squeeze Khattak's hand. "And instead he looked at me as if I'd grown another head. Too, too devastating. If it wasn't for Ruksh, I'm convinced I'd have thrown myself into the lake, painfully itchy headscarf and all."

Rachel's sudden smile was unguarded. She looked up to find Nathan's attention upon her. "Wearing the scarf is an art, I'm told."

He responded in kind. "The art Audrey favors most is drama. It's there in everything she does, even her choice of profession."

"You're an actor?" Rachel asked.

There was another delighted spurt of laughter.

"Nate loves to tease. No, I run a small NGO working with women. I went to university and then I didn't know what to do with myself. I couldn't possibly live up to Nathan's prestige but I thought, here's something I can do. I embroil him in it constantly but I secretly think he uses it as material for his books."

"Then he's overdue," Rachel said, feeling her way. "It's been some time since *Apologia* was published. Have you been working on something new?"

It was an innocuous question. There was no reason why it should have sent the conversation crashing to the ground. She looked from one face to another, puzzled. Khattak's gaze found the window. Audrey bit her lip. Nathan cleared his throat, searching for words.

"I've—not been writing much lately. It seems I can't find anything else to say."

It was clear that he addressed these words to Khattak. They were met with silence.

"Writer's block?" Rachel ventured, though common sense told her to drop the subject. "It's sort of an occupational hazard, isn't it?"

"Like drunken domestics for police officers," he agreed.

Rachel stiffened. His guileless eyes—lovely eyes, really, flecked with bits of bronze and green—indicated it was a random hit.

"All in a day's work," she repeated.

"I hear you're investigating Chris Drayton's fall." It was meant by Audrey as a change of subject. Khattak took it as such.

"There are some leads we're following up," he said to Nate. "Some unresolved questions as to background and finances. I've been wondering about that dinner you mentioned—the one you arranged for Drayton to speak about the museum."

"I've seen your car at Mink's house a few times this week. So it's the museum that interests you."

This was news to Rachel. Khattak hadn't mentioned it to her, and she wondered why. He was often reticent at the beginning of an investigation but seldom secretive.

"She's an interesting woman," he said without emphasis.

Nate stared across the table at him, a sudden glint of discovery in his eyes.

"Fascinating is how I would put it. If she's with a potential donor for less than half an hour, she doesn't leave empty-handed."

"You set up the dinner specifically for the museum, then."

"Not exactly. It was Chris who asked me to arrange it. He was adamant about getting on the board of the museum. He thought of it as a prestige project, something that a man at his stage of life should attach himself to. He was willing to pay his way in. Mink was somewhat resistant to the idea, so Chris thought a dinner might soften her up."

"I'd have thought she'd welcome an influx of money," said Rachel. "The upkeep on that place can't be cheap."

"It's not. The house is worth upwards of a million dollars. Most of the exhibits were already in Mink's possession, but if she wanted to expand, Drayton's investment certainly wouldn't have hurt. And from his perspective, gaining a reputation as patron of the arts was essential to his sense of himself."

"How long has Ringsong been here? Inspector Khattak said he hadn't seen it before. In the past, I mean. Whenever you saw each other last."

She stumbled over the words, aware that she'd inadvertently trespassed.

Nate rescued her. "It's been about two years. A year to build and a year for Mink to get the museum on its feet. It's due to open very soon, so I know this phase of things is critical."

"Do you expect it to open on time?" Rachel asked. Probably Khattak had asked Mink the same questions. She still wanted to hear. "Would there be any reason for Drayton's death to delay it?"

"I can't think of any. Mink is very capable. I've never known her to run overbudget or behind schedule."

"And did you make a contribution, sir?"

"Please. At least call me Nathan. Or Nate if you like, all my friends do. It was Andalusia," he said with a fond glance at Khattak. "The golden age. How could I not?"

"You sound as though you and Ms. Norman are quite close."

It was a question pertinent to the investigation. Somehow it came out sounding as if Rachel were jealous. She found herself blushing. Khattak, too, appeared oddly interested in the answer.

Nathan's glance traveled between them, a suspicion of mirth in it.

"I wouldn't say I've spent as much time at Ringsong in one week as Esa has but yes, we're friends. I find the project mesmerizing: Mink's passion for it is contagious. And it's been good for the girls too—Hadley and Cass. It's saved them from being used as ammunition between their parents and it's given them a sense of purpose. Mink knows how to make people feel valued. It's certainly given Marco more freedom to hang about."

"Riv," Audrey corrected.

"I refuse to call a seventeen-year-old boy Riv when he has a perfectly acceptable first name."

Audrey punched him good-naturedly in the arm. She opened her mouth to respond when the door to the pub gave way, divulging a new group of patrons. Her face froze in an expression of dismay. In a swift gesture under the table, she pressed her brother's hand.

Rachel swiveled in her seat. The new arrivals were a group of cops, mostly in uniform. They laughed and talked easily, stopping at the bar to give their order. In their midst was an extraordinarily beautiful woman whose dazzling features and wickedly curved body drew the eye of every man in the room. She was dramatically dark-eyed and dark-lashed, raindrops clinging to her hair and gliding down the silky skin of her cheek. She wore a skin-tight dress made of some metallic material that gathered the light inward and clung to every curve. With a sexy pout, she bent before the fire to warm her hands.

It was like a bomb had gone off, sucking all the air from the room.

Conversations were suddenly louder, her companions jostled each other to get close to her. Her smile beguiled: her movements were sinfully lithe as she touched one man's cheek, ruffled another's hair, squeezed the elbow of a third.

Was Rachel imagining it or were there sparks of electricity in the waves of her jet-black hair?

The woman looked over and caught them watching her. She checked mid-movement, disentangled herself from her companions, and made her way to their table, where she dismissed Rachel and Audrey without a second glance.

"Look who's here!" Of course her voice would be low and throaty. She leaned over the table, enveloping them in the musk of her perfume. Her smile glittered between the heavy wings of her hair.

"Nathan, darling! More devastating than ever!"

She turned the other way, saw Khattak, widened her black eyes fractionally and sailed on. "The old gang, together again. How perfectly wonderful! You've brought along a plaything, I see." Her sleek white hand pointed at Rachel, the dark eyes sweeping over her and away. "Not up to your usual standard, Esa." She dragged the name out, catching her tongue between her teeth. "I hope you boys aren't fighting over her the way you fought over me."

Her laugh was a sexy growl in her throat. She accompanied it with a pivot of her hip, thrusting her décolletage at Nate. "Have you missed me? You never have me anymore." She brought her hand to her lush mouth, miming dismay. "I meant, you never have me over anymore. Surely my portrait doesn't warm your bed?"

Rachel choked on the heady scent that clung to the woman, just able to discern the contempt on Audrey's face through the cloud of fragrance around her.

"You're drunk, Laine," Nathan said with disgust. "Go back to your friends."

"I thought I was among friends," she purred in return. "Don't you remember how to be friendly, darling? Don't you remember lying on your back and begging me not to stop? Or was that you?" Whiplash quick, she turned to Esa. "Men! So easily interchangeable, so easy to forget." Before Esa could object, she leaned down and kissed him full on the lips. "There! I *thought* I remembered you. As decadent as ever."

Khattak got to his feet, politely shouldered Rachel aside.

"If this performance is for my benefit, I'll put an end to it by leaving. Rachel, I'll call you tomorrow. Thank you for coming out."

"Rachel?" Laine crowed. "As gloriously humdrum as the rest of you! Audrey darling, don't tell me you've become so petty that you haven't thought to give Little Miss Dreary the makeover she's gasping for. She'll need it to stoke that libido, am I right?" She stood chest-to-chest with Khattak.

"Shut up, Laine," he said brutally. He signaled one of the men behind her shoulder, offloading Laine into his arms. "Your friend is drunk. Kindly take her with you."

"I'm not drunk, sexy," she called over her shoulder, as she was guided to the fire. "I miss you, Esa, I miss your bed."

Khattak muttered an imprecation under his breath and an apology aloud to Rachel.

"Why did you ask her here?" he said to Nathan. "You've learned nothing, have you?"

Nate scrambled to his feet. "Esa, wait—I didn't call her. This was an accident, you have to believe me."

"Like you believed me?" He didn't wait for an answer.

———

Defeated, Nate sank back into his seat. "Goddamn her."

"Who *was* that?" Rachel breathed. The woman had descended on them like a tornado, leaving just as much destruction in her wake.

"That was Laine Stoicheva, total and utter bitch," Audrey said. "Pay no attention to anything she says. She lives for trouble. Eats and drinks it too, I think."

Laine Stoicheva. The last partner Khattak had worked with before Rachel herself. She'd heard the stories. Heard the truth from Khattak himself, yet the woman in person was like an undefused bomb. She oozed sex. And as Rachel could see from the lapdog expression of every man around them, she wasn't accustomed to rejection.

Khattak's account of Laine Stoicheva's demotion had included no mention of Nathan Clare. Laine had divided her attention between both men.

"I should get home," Rachel said to the others. "It's a long drive."

"I didn't know she'd be here," Nate said to his sister. "How could I have known?"

"He'll calm down. He'll realize that's the case."

"He won't," Nate said bitterly. "That's only the second time in two years that he's spoken to me."

Rachel looked from brother to sister, feeling decidedly *de trop*. She murmured a good night and slipped away to her car, caught by an icy blast of rain.

It was a relief to breathe the rain-drenched air, to feel its spiraling wetness against her cheeks. She slid into the driver's side and started the engine.

It choked.

She tried again, her eyes searching for Khattak's BMW.

It was gone. Why did the man have to appear and disappear so quickly? She'd have sworn he was a magician. She let loose a fluent string of curses. Now, she'd have to call in a tow truck for a boost, and she'd still be sitting here when Laine Stoicheva and the Clares eventually found their way to the lot. They'd see her because she'd been stupid enough to park near the door with plenty of lighting.

Rain had been her only worry then. Balanced against potential humiliation, it seemed a small price to pay.

She scrabbled in her purse for her phone. Maybe her Da would come.

She choked back a laugh. Not tonight or any night. Her Da wasn't in the business of rescuing damsels in distress. Just like with Zach. Dead or alive, it was the same thing. Why worry about Rachel driving home at midnight? She was a police officer, not a teenage girl. Except that when she'd been a teenage girl, no one had worried either.

Keep the boat afloat. Keep everything the same. Nobody speak. Everyone survives.

There was sharp knock at her window.

She rolled it down: Nathan Clare stood there, dripping with rain. Like her, he hadn't had the sense to bring an umbrella. "Let me give you a lift."

"I can't leave my car here overnight."

"You can. I'll settle it so that it's ready for you in the morning. Now, where can I drop you?"

"What about Audrey?" she asked him, not seeing his sister.

"She's met a friend who will drop her. Get your things while I call."

Common sense told her to refuse. Her personal sense of awkwardness insisted on it.

But there was Nathan Clare, soaking wet and miserable, not budging from her window as he made his calls.

"You'll catch cold," she said ungraciously. "Let me get my bag from the trunk."

The thought of someone else driving through the city to Etobicoke in the rain imbued her with bliss. Not having to worry about her car or fix the problem herself—well, this was the first time someone had stepped in for her. The first time anyone had seemed anxious about her feelings.

The scene in the pub had been insulting and confusing, but Rachel was used to both. What she wasn't used to was the generous offer of help and comfort. She found herself stretching out her legs in the luxurious interior of an Aston Martin, watching traffic lights swing past rain-darkened streets in long green streaks.

Nate glanced over at her, his hands tight on the steering wheel. "I think I owe you an explanation."

"Honestly, you don't. Inspector Khattak told me about the charges Laine manufactured against him, I'd just never met her. I can see why she was a problem."

"That's all he told you?"

"That's all that mattered to our job. He doesn't owe me anything else."

Nate brushed his gold hair to one side. His fingers came away damp. "I wonder why you think that, Rachel. Esa speaks very highly of you to Ruksh. It sounds to me as though he considers you a friend."

Rachel flushed with embarrassment at the thought of herself as the subject of such personal discussion. The suggestion that Khattak might share the quiet regard she felt for him was unsettling. She cleared her throat. "He's also my boss. And I want to do well with him."

"I think you have done. Audrey tells me as much. He has a strong sense of what's right."

And though she hadn't wanted to be drawn into this conversation, Rachel asked, "Then why haven't you spoken in two years?"

Nate kept his attention firmly on the road. "It doesn't mean he's not stubborn. He's stubborn and judgmental as hell. If he thinks his trust has been betrayed, there's no convincing him otherwise. When he brought you to Winterglass, I thought he might be thawing. He wouldn't have brought you, I thought, if he didn't want me to meet you. To let him know what I thought of this woman who figures so largely in his life."

Rachel flushed red. "I'm not—we're not—we work together. We came here because of Christopher Drayton."

"I think that was an excuse for Esa to reach out. You must have seen that he's asked me hardly anything about Drayton. Or Mink, for that matter. When Esa is interested in a woman, he tends to go quiet."

Rachel wanted to ask if there had been many—there had to be something behind the reputation he sustained at work, even if she hadn't seen it herself—but it didn't seem appropriate. And she wondered if Nate was right. Had Khattak wanted to reach out to a friend he had somehow lost along the way? Had he needed her presence as a shield? All the things they should have been doing to confirm Drayton's identity had been delayed. He hadn't called her for a week, and then only to visit an imam unconnected with the case.

"Were you both in love with her?"

Drayton, she cursed herself. *You should be asking about Drayton.*

"No." His sudden awkwardness appealed to Rachel, if only because she identified with it so thoroughly. "Audrey said she would tell you, but she tends to dramatize things. The truth is theatrical enough."

"Two friends fighting over a woman who plays them off against each other?"

A faint color rose in Nathan's face, softening its incipient lines. "I—these are good guesses but they're off the mark. Esa was never interested in Laine. She was his colleague at INSET. She may not seem like it, but she has an excellent brain and a knack for intelligence work. It was a good partnership, but she wanted more, which was something I didn't know. He should have told me about the trouble she was causing him, but he's somewhat conservative in these matters. I suppose he thought he was being gentlemanly. I'd come by several times to meet Esa after work, and I noticed Laine." He shrugged helplessly. "Who wouldn't? What stunned me was that a woman like that noticed *me.* She was interested in me. She didn't have to try all that hard. One look at her and I was besotted." He smiled at the old-fashioned word. "I planned to marry her, and then she brought her claim against Esa."

"That must have been the end of things," Rachel said, in as neutral a tone as she could manage.

"You would think so. You would think I'd know Esa better than anyone—or that I'd learned to trust him in thirty years." He glanced over at her. "Laine was an obsession with me. I couldn't think or sleep for wanting her. I would have done anything she asked. In the end, I did."

"I don't understand." From the wretched expression on his face, she had the feeling that she didn't really want to know.

"Laine asked me to testify on her behalf at a closed hearing. Against Esa. And I did. That's why he hasn't seen me in two years. That's why I wrote *Apologia*."

Rachel clasped her hands together. Her fingers felt numb.

"He was cleared," she said weakly. "And you never married Laine. He must have forgiven you."

"When he brought you to meet me, I hoped as much. He tried to warn me once, but when I wouldn't hear it, he didn't say another word against her. In your case, there's no reticence. When he brought you to Winterglass, I knew something had changed. And then Laine tonight—let's just say, she destroys everything she touches."

Rachel considered this in silence. She barely knew Nathan Clare, really only knew him through the veneer of his public persona as writer and commentator, yet she felt that she owed him whatever she could bring to bear. Perhaps that was kindness. "It can't be as bad as you're imagining. He came tonight. By the morning, he'll know that Laine's being there wasn't your fault. He just needs time to think."

"That's the most dangerous time, when he's thinking." His smile was brief. "Read *Apologia*. Then you'll know what I did."

On the day of the hearing, Nate had been the last to leave the room. He had shaken Laine's touch from his body but why, *why* had Esa not told him? He had the answer a moment later, agonizing in all it revealed of himself: he shouldn't have had to.

They had known each other since they were seven years old. They had weathered every storm, shared every confidence, loved each other's families, loved each other.

Known each other.

And Laine Stoicheva had detonated a grenade within the stronghold of their friendship.

Esa had left without a word, without a glance. That had been two years ago, and even *Apologia* had made no difference.

On the night he'd driven to Esa's house to stumble through whatever apology he could try to make to rescue the only friendship that mattered in his life, Esa had said simply, "I thought if there was anyone in the world who would know what I'm capable of, it would be you. It can never be the same now."

"*Rahem*," Nate had dredged out of nowhere. The plea to recognize the Islamic concept of life-giving mercy. He knew there were a lot of things Esa could have said in response—don't you dare drag faith into this now when you've betrayed it so utterly—but what he said with a look of regret was, "I could never wish you ill, Nate."

And the door had closed.

On thirty years of friendship, it had closed.

It hadn't opened again, even when he'd written his dedication: *To EK, whose friendship I valued too little, too late.*

15.

While the Serb soldier was dragging my son away, I heard his voice for the last time. And he turned around and then he told me, "Mummy please, can you get that bag for me? Could you please get it for me?"

With no word from Khattak and no clear direction on what to pursue next, Rachel's instincts told her to revisit Melanie Blessant. She had called Khattak and been unable to reach him. She had tried the Blessant house with the same result. And the days until Zach's exhibit were passing, not in suspended animation, but with a concentrated intensity, every hope and whisper magnified until her head began to ache from the pressure of her thoughts.

It was a relief to knock on Melanie Blessant's door, despite her awareness that as poorly tended as the house was, it was still more presentable than her own. A wan light seeped through the canopy of maples that bordered the walk, a reflection of the diminishing day, a reminder that as swiftly as time passed, it offered no reprieve from her restlessness. She didn't know if that long-anticipated moment of reunion with her brother was a source of creeping dread or solace.

No one answered the doorbell or her more insistent knock. Whatever she had tried to make of it, this was a dead end, a lost afternoon. There were no games on the schedule, no extra time she wanted to spend at home with her parents, no diligent partner to be found pursuing his own leads. She returned to her car and rolled the windows down, drumming her fingers on the steering wheel. It was one of those rare afternoons free of the rain that had made the fall so miserable, and yet her expectations made her wretched.

The sound of a car pulling up interrupted her thoughts. A luxury vehicle slowed in front of her Neon to park in Melanie's driveway, flattening the weeds that sprang from cracks in the stone. Rachel recognized the passengers as Hadley and Cassidy Blessant. The man who stepped out to open Cassidy's door resembled them so closely, he could only be their father.

"I'm sorry girls. I think it's better if I don't come in."

There were signs of tension in his otherwise pleasant face as he squeezed his daughter's hand.

"Daddy, you promised!"

From where she was parked, Rachel could hear the longing in Cassidy's voice, could hear them all, an unforeseen opportunity.

"Don't be a baby, Cass." Hadley unbuckled her seat belt, her manner brisk. "You know what'll happen if Mel has to deal with him."

She grabbed her bag and took a moment to glare at her sister in the backseat. "Come on, get out." The smile she turned on her father was unexpected. So expressive of warmth and trust and utterly unlike the front she had presented to Rachel and Khattak earlier.

"You know we love you, Dad. Don't believe anything the Grand Narcissist tries to tell you."

One of her nicknames for her mother, Rachel guessed, more in keeping with what she'd perceived as the girl's sardonic nature. Her father tried to hold back a smile and failed.

"I wish I didn't have to leave you here. I thought this would all be over once your mother married Drayton."

"What would be over, Dad?"

Hadley answered her sister, her voice tart and impatient. "The child support. The spousal support. The never-ending demands. The custody battle, Cass. Mel didn't want us once she had Chris. We could have gone back to Dad once and for all."

"Chris wanted us," Cassidy protested. "He made room for us. He said it was our home."

"I want you more, honey. Your home will always be with me."

Dennis Blessant sighed and Rachel could well imagine his thoughts. He was a handsome, well-dressed man whose careless appeal had suffered more than the usual depredations of middle age. His sandy hair was graying, and there was an air of general fatigue about him that she attributed to the divorce, along with the custody battle— although she marveled at the thought of a man for whom responsibility and family meant everything. A man who chose the company of his daughters. To Dennis Blessant, fatherhood was a source of ceaseless fulfillment—not an affliction, which was all Rachel knew of the matter.

If Drayton had indeed been planning to marry Dennis Blessant's ex-wife, Dennis's freedom had been close at hand. Any financial strain caused by Melanie's tactics also would have ended. Rachel puzzled over the custody decision: How had Melanie done it? Had her plea for her children been sincere and well-reasoned? Or had her exaggerated femininity done more to sway the family court judge than any show of saccharine devotion? Leaving Dennis Blessant and his daughters shattered and undone.

They seemed in no hurry to leave their father, leaning against his car, warming their legs against the hood.

"Is that boy still hanging around you, Had?"

Hadley grinned. "Marco, Dad. And yes, he is. I'll bring him with us next time, if that's cool."

"Bring him," Dennis said, his hands relaxed in his pockets. "Just make sure he knows I carry a gun."

Both girls laughed, and again Rachel wondered at Dennis Blessant. He looked at his girls as if they were the only things that mattered in the universe; moon, sun, and stars combined in one celestial profusion.

And then Melanie Blessant descended on them from a considerably less elevated plane, the screen door slamming shut behind her.

"Your time is up, Dennis," she said, weaving her way toward them. "You're not allowed to overstay, so I want you gone right now."

Whatever the very real loathing on Dennis Blessant's face gave away, he responded mildly enough. "All right, girls. I'll see you next weekend, then."

"*Not* next weekend, Dennis," Melanie contradicted sharply. "It's every other weekend, as you very well know. Don't try to mess with the custody arrangement or I'll have you back in court by the morning. *And* I'll be making a motion for the adjustment of child support."

"Still torn up over Drayton, I see."

He would have been wiser to resist, thought Rachel. Those were words to light the tinderbox of Melanie's temper.

"Mel," Hadley interrupted before her mother could go off. "Cass and I are at a museum dinner next weekend. Dad's taking us there and picking us up. We'll be back on Sunday, we talked about this."

Melanie fiddled with the string of her midriff-baring tank top. The temperature was starting to cool off, a fact that didn't appear to have registered on her decision to reveal nearly as much flesh as her outfit concealed. Sugary pink lip gloss and a skin-tight pair of cutoffs completed her ensemble.

How grateful their father must be that his daughters had chosen not to emulate their mother's style of dress.

"I'm sick to death of that museum," Melanie said. "That used-up librarian wanted Chrissie's money and she invented that museum to get it. I knew what she was from the moment I met her."

Hadley made no effort to hide her contempt. "I'm sure she knows what you are too."

"Don't you dare take that tone with me, Hadley! I knew why she was sniffing after Chrissie, but her pathetic little plan failed. He didn't leave her a dime. Everything comes to me." Her face beamed with gratification. "I'm the only beneficiary of Chris's life insurance policies."

"I'm very glad to hear that," Dennis answered. "It should make all the difference to your spousal support."

"You bastard," she hissed at him. Then she rounded on the girls.

"You're not going to any party and if he tries to take you, I'll call the police, don't you think I won't!"

Hadley shoved her sister toward the house. "Get inside, Cass. You don't need to hear this." She turned on her mother. "I'd have thought you'd prefer us to go with Dad than Riv. Your choice, either way."

"I knew this was about that boy!"

"Yes," Hadley drawled. "That same boy you slobber over every time he comes by. Could your top be any lower, Mel? Or your shorts any tighter?"

"You're just jealous of what I have. And really, who could blame you?"

Dennis's "Don't you talk to my daughter that way" overlapped Hadley's "Isn't that a case of the pot calling the kettle black, Mel dear?"

And then Melanie slapped her.

Dennis grabbed her wrist.

The entire family was oblivious to Rachel across the street in her car. She knew she should intervene, just as she knew that intervention would cut short the family's revelations. She hesitated, her hand on the door handle.

"Don't, Dad. Once the will is read and those policies are paid out, she'll clear out of our lives for good. And if she takes you to court, ask the judge what happened to the money you gave her for our laptops."

He was torn, Rachel realized. He didn't want his daughter to talk about her mother this way. Especially when everything she said was true.

Spittle gathered in the corners of Melanie's mouth. "It was never about the money with me and Chrissie," she spat at them. "I loved him! I loved him and she can't stand that because no one will ever love her the way that Chrissie loved me."

"I hope not," Hadley said, her face deadly serious. "I wouldn't want a man who called me a whore every time he climaxed."

Melanie gaped at her, thunderstruck.

"What? You didn't think we heard you those nights you made us stay over? And obviously you liked it or why else would you put up with it? I have a hell of a lot more self-respect than that."

Melanie's nails bit into Hadley's arm.

"I want you out of my house right now!"

Hadley stood her ground, picking off her mother's fingers one by one. "Can't," she said without humor. "Custody arrangement, remember? How else will you get your money?" She stepped between her parents, urging her father back into his car. "You'd better go, Dad. Cass and I have a shift at Ringsong anyway. We'll see you again on Friday."

She turned to her mother, her tone derisive. "And I don't think you're going to be a problem, are you, Mel? Otherwise, I might have to tell Dad the real reason Chris wanted us to move in with him. In case you thought I didn't know."

She kissed her father calmly and walked to the door to talk to her sister.

Only Rachel noticed that her hands were shaking at her sides.

16.

The National Library of Sarajevo is burning.

*A radio broadcast instructed Muslims to put white ribbons
around their arms, go outside, form columns and head
towards the main square.*

He was in love, he decided, with the house. It wasn't a museum to
him. It was a place of restful beauty, a space that his layered identities could lay claim to as home. He waited for Mink in the second
courtyard reached through a colonnade of Andalusian arches, its
tiled fountain at play beneath a stately turret. The white stripe of the
Bluffs broke off from the darkness, the lake a gleaming shadow beneath them. Stars and sky stretched above, a timeless motif on an
illimitable canvas.

The green coins of Andalusia extolled the courtyard's virtues.

He sat still and calm between the palms and orange trees, waiting
for the woman whose presence breathed life into all.

When she came, it was as if she detached herself from shadow,
bringing with her a pale and rarefied light. After a moment of fancy,
he realized she held a candle between her hands. She placed it on the
table beside him, sliding easily onto his lounger, tucking her delicate
feet beneath her. It had been like this between them from the start:
a hushed and glowing intimacy, where if he wished, he could reach
out and unclasp the golden knot of her hair or lay his hand upon
hers, upheaval in so simple a gesture.

"Esa," she said. "You've been enchanted by Andalusia."

"Or by the woman who breathed it into being."

She brushed his words aside. "Look what I've brought you." She placed a dish of fresh dates in his hand.

He knew he should rise, find another seat, place some distance between them, but Mink was as sweetly scented as her garden. It was its own magic, that and the soft words that painted for him a distant civilization, a time of grace and elegance, a grand achievement.

The Library of Cordoba.

Of course a librarian would cherish such a memory.

"Paper was the beginning of it all. From Baghdad it was shipped to all the capitals of Islam. It was a competition of knowledge—who could build the grandest library, fill it with the most books—who would read and translate and comment. They were experts at classification. Such a catalogue they had—the thought of it makes me envious."

"Those words transformed the world."

"Think how little we know of such marvels. How little we appreciate those moments of history where differences were glories yet to be discovered, synthesizing a greater creation. This tribalism we worship now is an ugly thing."

"Tribalism?" he questioned.

"Patriotism, nationalism," she said impatiently. "Call it what you wish. Mine the only flag, mine the only way. All else is inferior, trample it underfoot. Despise it, detest it."

"We've come some distance since then," he suggested. He wasn't sure that he wanted to talk. He was here because of Christopher Drayton, but he thought that what he wanted was for Mink to sit at her table, quietly intent, turning the pages of her manuscripts in her hands. And he would do no more than absorb the luxuries of Andalusia and watch.

"Have we?" she asked him. Her hands did what he had longed to do, unraveling the gold coil of hair, letting it slip down to caress her shoulders as gently as a folio of wind. "You're an adherent of Islam, yes, Esa? Your name," she said, with the curve of a smile. "It declares it for you. So, what of the Ground Zero mosque?"

"A volatile situation."

"Indeed. And what of Murfreesboro, Tennessee? And all the other places where your people are unwelcome. Welcome to live, just. But not to worship or declare their way of faith."

"There's fear and ignorance everywhere. It's not exclusively practiced against Muslims. Look at Rwanda. Or Nazi Germany. Or the barriers Hispanic immigrants face."

"Or the Inquisition," she finished. "The culture of power versus the power of culture. One side consistently loses."

"We've a kind of Andalusia in this country," he teased, hoping to lighten her mood.

"Yes," she said seriously. "That's very true, but less true I think across the border. Inquisitions, pogroms, genocides—those are endpoints. Demonizing, fear, the passing of laws of exclusion, the burning of libraries—these are beginnings. Historians are vigilant as to beginnings. Too often we fail."

"I wouldn't have thought that was their calling," he said. "I imagine them lost in ancient worlds like the palace of the Alhambra or Madinat az-Zahra."

"It's dangerous to be so comfortable—to live in the past alone."

"Isn't that what museums are? Halls of the past?"

"Reminders," she said, reaching for a date from his hand. "Of things that could be, if we dared to dream a little differently. If we opened ourselves up."

"You've made this very personal." He gestured at the great room beyond the colonnade.

"I suppose I like to imagine this time of Muslim princes whose Jewish viziers conducted dialogues with Christian monarchs, reliant upon one another, influenced by one another, respecting one another. The Convivencia. In love with language, learning—what shouldn't I admire?"

He laid his hand on hers.

"Shall we talk about Drayton?" he said gently. "I would like to understand his attraction to the museum."

"You've just praised it yourself. Why wouldn't Christopher have felt the same? He was an educated man."

Khattak hesitated. He'd been coming to the museum for more than a week, finding excuses to stop by and linger beneath the palms, attracted by something he couldn't name. His heritage was neither Arab nor Hispanic, yet he laid claim to the intertwined identities of the civilization of Islam.

He should have asked much more about Drayton. And yet somehow, in her presence, all other thoughts eluded him. There was the material of who she was and the hope of what he still wished to discover. A feeling he hadn't known since the loss of his wife.

Her pale blue gaze challenged him. He cleared his throat and spoke. "Is it possible that Christopher Drayton wasn't who you thought he was?"

"What do you mean? Not a friend or advocate?"

"That." He lowered his voice so that Hadley and Cassidy, at work in the great room, wouldn't overhear. "But more than that. Did you ever have reason to suspect that Drayton might have another identity?"

Her hand smoothed over a palm leaf. "Is that why you're investigating his death?" She thought a moment. "Was he a bigamist?"

"Nothing like that. You've no reason to doubt he was who he said he was? A man who'd made money from businesses he owned in Italy and was prepared to spend it on the museum?"

"I didn't know about Italy," she said slowly. "I thought he was a man with a somewhat forceful personality who was searching for a way to put his mark on the world."

"Wouldn't such a man have had his own ideas?"

Mink pleated her hands against the bark of the palm.

"That's very common," she said. "There are dreamers and there are donors. Once they've given their money, they tend to reshape the dream in their own image. In Christopher's case, it was certainly about ego. Does that help?"

It was interesting, he thought, yet not quite the answer he expected.

"There's something you're not telling me," she said. "Is it a question of trust?"

"No, absolutely not." The connection between them was a tenuous one. He had no wish to risk it. "Does the name Dražen Krstić mean anything to you?"

"I feel that it should." She moved away from the seating area to stand by the turquoise tiles of the fountain. The sound of falling water murmured at them. "I can't quite place it."

"Did Drayton have an accent of any kind?"

"No," she said, startled. "His voice was rough, perhaps a little gravelly. I thought it was another sign of a man wishing to impress others with his consequence. Are you saying his real name was Dražen Krstić? That he was putting on some kind of act? Why would he do that?"

"Often when people take on new identities, they try and retain some trace of the old. The names Christopher Drayton and Dražen Krstić resemble each other."

She smiled. "Insomuch as Hebrew ring songs resemble Arabic ones. Who was Dražen Krstić? Does it really matter if Christopher wanted to leave something in his past behind?"

He didn't answer this. "Did you notice anything unusual about him? Any markings? Did he speak any other languages?"

Each time he asked Mink a question, she undertook some small action before she answered it. Now, she dipped her fingers into the upper tier of the fountain, interrupting its minor cascades. In another witness, he would have seen it as subterfuge.

"He spoke many languages. He was teaching Hadley and Cassidy Italian. As to the others, perhaps French, German? He did have a mark on one hand, a cross I believe. But then many people are attached to symbols of their religion."

She glanced pointedly at the tasbih on Khattak's wrist, a gesture that struck at him, collapsing his fluid identities inward like a lightning strike: one a symbol of thousands of the unquiet dead, the other the mark of their murderers.

"I'm sorry, Esa," she said quickly. "What have I said? I don't understand."

"It's nothing." He tried a smile and held out his tasbih. "In its proper context, it embodies grace. I know without the logo, the cross does as well."

He should tell her. There was nothing he should keep from this woman who cherished the complexities of Muslim Spain.

"Logo?"

"Entwined with the cross on his hand. The four *s* symbol: literally, it's translated as 'Only concord saves a Serb.'"

"But that's a twelfth-century motto, attributed to the Orthodox church."

"It has a much more contemporary significance."

She straightened from the fountain abruptly. "Krstić?" she repeated. "I do know that name."

"He was a commander of the Drina Corps in 1995. You're much too young to remember. As Chief of Security, Dražen Krstić was one of the men who orchestrated the Srebrenica massacre."

She froze. "Are you saying that *Christopher Drayton* was that man?"

"The tattoo is suggestive. And he was receiving letters addressed to Dražen Krstić."

He studied her closely.

The soft curve of her lower lip trembled. She touched a hand to the back of her neck. "What possible interest could a man like Krstić have had in Ringsong? It doesn't make sense."

Khattak had thought about this long and hard. "If Drayton was Krstić, there may be two possibilities. First, he had built a new life for himself in a nation where we're so intermixed that difference ceases to matter or points of contestation are immensely civil. Perhaps he saw

his contribution to the Andalusia project as a means of atonement."
He watched the play of emotions across Mink's face. "You don't
think so. There is a second possibility, though I find it difficult to
contemplate."

"Tell me," she whispered.

"He wanted you to change the name of Ringsong to the Christopher Drayton Andalusia Museum. He wanted a seat on your board
of directors. And you've told me that donors often wish for greater
say in how their money is spent—in fact, they 'reshape the dream.'
So I've asked myself, what is the history of Moorish Spain most
known for today? Its palaces? Its libraries?" He shook his head. Nothing about the preservation of memory fit with his knowledge of the
ideology of Dražen Krstić.

But Mink, alert and lovely, was with him. "The Reconquista," she
said simply. "The Moor's last sigh."

"Seven hundred years of the Moorish occupation of Spain
brought to an end by the Spanish Reconquest. Expulsions. Forcible
conversions. The implosion of a people's blended history of centuries of coexistence. And always the burning of books. Even memory
erased."

Shaken, she said, "He often talked about the Reconquest. He did
seem preoccupied more with the end of the period than its achievements."

"The culture of power versus the power of culture," he quoted.
"One side always loses."

"I may have viewed the past as a loss, but Christopher saw the
expulsion that accompanied the Reconquest as a triumph. And yet,
I still can't believe that explains his interest."

"Then why were you so reluctant to take his money?"

Somehow, some part of Mink must have known that this was not
a man to support a multiethnic, multilingual ideal. Her lips flattened
in recognition of it.

"I must ask you not to speak of this to anyone," Khattak said. "If

Drayton *was* Krstić, we have a problem of some magnitude on our hands."

Mink looked at him sharply. "Are you here about his identity or are you here because of his death?"

He couldn't stop himself from saying it. "At this moment, I'm here because of you."

It was a risk, a venture, spoken to a woman neither of his faith or culture, a line he had not been able to envision himself crossing. In time, he had thought, there would be a woman as dear and familiar to him as his beloved Samina.

He had noticed Laine Stoicheva. No man could be blind to that formidable sex appeal or powerful charisma. But she had touched no part of him the way his wife had. She was electricity without accord, a magnetism that was all outward. Her thoughts, her heart, were brittle, broken. She had wrung Nate dry. Such a woman could not attract him.

Here in this silent, prayerful space, he'd found something that had been missing in all the long years without the wife he'd adored. He'd found Mink and he wanted her. It was that simple.

When he'd solved the riddle of Dražen Krstić, he would leave behind the killing fields of Bosnia for the contradictions and glories of this Andalusian idyll.

"I need to think this over," she said. "Please leave now, Esa."

His face fell. He shouldn't rush her. They had known each other a week, no more. "I'm sorry. If you think of anything else, please call me."

He'd been dismissed. He should go.

"Esa." Her low voice halted him. "You know you can come back any time you'd like. This—" She gestured at the catalogue that awaited her in the great room. "All of it needs time."

He accepted that, releasing himself from the perfume of Andalusia. At the door he looked back at her, small and sheltered beneath the palms, her thoughts preoccupied by his revelation. He raised a hand in farewell and she smiled.

He moved quietly through the forecourt, so quietly that he had come upon Hadley and Riv in one of its shadowy corners without giving away his presence. Riv was holding her by the forearms, his expression pleading.

"You have to tell him," he said urgently.

"Why?" Hadley's voice was clipped and cold.

"Look, if you're worried about Mel—"

"I'm not. She's the last person I worry about. Ever."

"Then if she's not holding you back, what gives, Had? Why won't you tell?"

The girl's stiff posture unexpectedly crumpled and Riv folded her into his arms. The teenagers clutched at each other as Khattak moved closer, still hidden in the shadows.

"It's too hard," Hadley whispered. "Everything we've done these past six months has been too hard. Keeping Cass safe. Keeping him away. But it's done now."

Riv's hands clamped down on her shoulders.

"You should tell your dad, Hadley. He'd understand. He wouldn't want you to cover for him. And he might have seen something— after the fight."

Hadley swallowed and stepped back. "What fight? I don't know what you're talking about."

"What? Of course you do. The night Chris fell."

"No. No, I don't."

She had seen him, Khattak realized. Her hands were digging into Riv's forearms, warning him off.

Khattak stepped forward.

"Did you want to talk to me?" he asked gravely.

Riv's skin turned white under the pressure of Hadley's fingers.

"No," she managed on a gasp. "I'm—no. We're fine, aren't we, Riv?"

"Fine," he agreed, but Khattak read shame in the body angled away from his.

He studied their guarded faces. "If you know anything about the

night Christopher Drayton fell, I hope you understand how important it is that you tell us. We're here to listen and to help. Please
believe that."

But he could see the doubt in Hadley's eyes, the underlying panic.
Whatever she had debated telling him was locked away again,
sealed off by an undeclared darkness. It wasn't something he could
demand from her. He would have to wait. And while he was waiting, he would puzzle through Drayton's connection to Ringsong.

"Thanks," she whispered.

"Peace be with you," he said, and meant it.

17.

I don't have a photograph of my child when he was small . . .
I want to apologize for crying because you cannot compare
this with what has happened but this is also something that is
important to many people.

The art gallery was housed inside a university building so ugly it seemed like a contradiction in terms. She and Zach would have laughed over it in better times.

"Ray," he would have said. "Where did they find this architect? In the big-box department at Walmart's?"

After Ringsong and Winterglass, it seemed like a monstrosity: a long, narrow concrete block with ridges of additional concrete arranged at the entrance like a façade. It, too, could have served as a bomb shelter.

The building sat between two other much more decorous arrangements of steel and glass, and the gallery was really a passageway for students in transit between them. There was a fast-food stand in its midst, so she guessed this was an example of art designed as part of a living space. She wasn't impressed. Near the potato chips was a panel of red paintings, delineated by a series of screaming white faces superimposed on each other.

Further down the hall, a second artist had created sculpture from leftover scraps in the recycling bins. The word *recycled* screamed across the bellies of his tortured iron figures. Someone else had bravely attempted a representational field of lilies. Two slender individuals in their twenties dismissed it as derivative.

Discouraged, she muscled her way through the winding coil of students to the exhibit at the end. She had dressed to blend in, wearing jeans and a T-shirt, and when she saw the artist, she was glad that she had. He wore a black shirt and black jeans. Otherwise, he was her twin. Square-shouldered, lanky and tall, with shaggy dark hair worn long over his collar and with deep-set eyes, the color of Rachel's own.

It was Zach.

For a moment she couldn't absorb it. The boy had grown into a man, but it was Zach. Her baby brother, Zach.

He was dwarfed on both sides by vertical cityscapes painted in shades of gray, blue, and black. Rachel could see at once that these paintings were different. The buildings crowded together, meeting each other at their pinnacles, suffocating the street dwellers below. They spoke of exclusion and hunger and want, loneliness and isolation.

It was Zachary's work, improved a thousandfold, bespeaking the maturity of a boy who had been on his own for the past seven years.

She waited until a group of admiring young girls had walked away, then touched his sleeve. The smile of welcome on his rugged features died on his lips as he recognized her. The things she had planned to say choked in her throat. She waited for him to speak.

"What are you doing here, Ray? Why have you come?"

The words were clipped, his manner frozen.

"What I am doing here?" She faltered. "What are *you* doing here? Do you have any idea how long I've been searching for you?"

"Not very good at police work then, are you? Or maybe you weren't really trying."

She stepped back as if she'd been slapped. "*Zach!*" she cried. "How can you say that? Do you know how hard I've tried to find you? Do you know what you've put me through, put us all through?"

Her brother's eyes stared through her. "It's always about you, isn't it, Ray? Well, maybe you didn't give me enough credit. Maybe you were looking in rehab clinics when you should have been trying the local schools."

"I'm sorry." She fixed her gaze on the cityscape behind him to prevent herself from crying. "I tried everything I could think of. You made it so hard. There was never the slightest trace of you."

He shouldered past her to an easel where brochures of his work were arranged. He sorted through them, but she knew it was a delaying tactic, so she reached for his hand.

He wheeled around to face her. "This is one part of my life that no one named Getty has touched or ruined. I'd like to keep it that way."

"I'm not here to ruin it, Zach. Jesus, you're my brother. I care about what happens to you. I needed to know if you were dead or alive. I needed answers."

"And you thought I'd be strung out on drugs, didn't you? You'd made something of yourself, but there was no chance that I would."

"Jesus, Zach! You were fifteen. You may not know what happens to kids on the street but I'm under no illusions."

"That's right." He scowled at her. "You're out of uniform, I see. Does that mean you quit? Because I never could understand why the sister I looked up to more than anyone would want to follow in the footsteps of the man who beat me bloody."

"Zach, please." She took his hand again. "Look, can you take a break? Can we just sit somewhere and have a drink?"

"You look like you need it, Ray." He shrugged but he didn't resist. "Whatever."

They found a spot at the cafeteria where Zach could oversee his display from a distance. She bought them both Cherry Cokes.

She tried to think calmly, act calmly. "You've done really well for yourself. Is this exhibit part of a program here?"

"What you really mean is am I a registered student? Surprise, surprise. I'm a fine arts major. It's amazing what you can do with a student loan."

Something he had chosen, despite Don Getty's attempts to beat it out of him.

"That's wonderful, Zach, so wonderful. I'm proud of you. Your work is really good."

His eyes softened at this but his tone remained confrontational. "What would you know about it?"

Rachel jerked a hand at the series in red. "I know those are garbage. So are those." She waved at the sculptures. "But your stuff is good. You get something from it."

He shrugged again, sinking lower into his seat, the gesture instantly reminding her of a teenage Zach bent over his homework at the kitchen table.

"I would have helped you, Zach. At any time, if you'd come to me."

He slurped at his Coke. "How could you have? You'd left for your training."

"I thought it would help me find you. Honestly."

She patted her brother on the arm, hardly able to believe that this was Zach Getty, alive and well, sitting across from her, noisily drinking a Coke.

"Why are you still at the house, Ray?"

She wanted to cry. Didn't he know? Didn't he know the only reason in the world she would continue to share a roof with Don and Lillian Getty? "It was the only place I knew you might come back to."

"But I never did." There was a suspicion of moisture about his eyes.

"No, you never did."

A silence built between them as she tried to think what to say next. "So tell me a little about yourself, what your plans are."

His shoulders relaxed. Instead of meeting her gaze, he kept his attention on the visitors at his exhibit, assessing their level of interest.

"I can't stay here long, Ray."

"Please, Zach."

He folded his straw in two, inserted it through the tab on his can, spraying himself a little in the process. "I live on campus. I'm a year from graduating. Then I head to Vienna for the summer to study the Viennese painters."

She thought of Mink Norman's sister. "Have you ever heard of the Mozarteum?"

Zach looked at her. "Sure. It's in Salzburg. Different city. Why?"

"It came up during an investigation I'm on."

"So you're still in the police. No uniform though."

"I got promoted. I work at Community Policing now."

"That minorities crap?"

"At least Da hates it. That's a plus."

Zach grinned at her and she caught her breath. It *was* Zach, it wasn't a mirage or her own hopes materialized into delusion. A cautious little ball of hope began to unspool itself in her heart. "Would it be all right if I asked how you got here? How you managed?"

He didn't flare up. If anything, his expression was pensive. "It wasn't easy. I stayed with my friends, at first. Then I moved around a lot. I fast-tracked through school because I knew I could get loans for university and move out on my own."

Rachel's heart seized up at the thought of it: so much danger, so much risk. Anything could have happened to him. "Weren't you scared?"

His level gaze said a lot about the man he was growing into. "I was a lot more scared at home. And I was sick of feeling that way."

Which made Rachel think of their mother. "Seven years is a long time to go without any contact, Zach. I don't— I wouldn't have expected you to want to have anything to do with Da, but what about Mum? You can't let her keep suffering, wondering what happened to you. I mean, I'll tell her, but at least you should make a phone call."

Zach looked at her so oddly that her heart constricted. He would bark at her, telling her she had no right to dictate his decisions when she'd done nothing to help him in the past seven years.

"You've lived at home this whole time?" he said.

She nodded. "I told you. I wasn't going to leave if there was a chance you might come back."

"You were punishing yourself," he concluded. "And now you're lost in that house. You never found your way out. I don't understand why she did that to you."

Rachel's stomach lurched. She had a sick feeling that something bad was coming.

"I wasn't punishing myself." But she had been. She knew it. She just didn't know how Zach had seen it so quickly, so clearly. Maybe it was because he knew her better than anyone. "I hoped one day you might remember what it was like. Not with you and Da or even with Mum. I mean with you and me."

Zach's eyes were wet. He stood up and brushed off his jeans with brisk movements. "Someone's screwing with you, Ray. When I figured out what I wanted to do with my life, I called Mum. She's been giving me cash since I started my program. She knows where I am because I call her once a week. On a cell phone that she bought me. I've gotta go."

There was no bombshell he could have delivered that would have shattered Rachel more.

It simply wasn't possible.

In the desperate years of her search—years of turmoil and misery that nothing could set in balance—Lillian Getty could not possibly have known where her son was. Don Getty managed all her money. She didn't have a dime of her own to give to Zach. Silent, timid Lillian didn't have the wherewithal to find or arrange a cell phone for Zach.

She'd stayed quiet and grieving in the corner of her living room without a word of consolation or hope for Rachel.

Because she hadn't known where Zach was.

No. It wasn't possible.

Rachel trudged after Zach, elbowing her way through students and teachers alike.

"Zach," she called. "That can't be true."

He stopped cold. She cowered inwardly, expecting his rage. But when he saw her ashen face, her pained incomprehension, he did something astonishing. He gathered her in his arms, shoving his face down into her shoulder.

She didn't know if he was crying or she was.

"I'm sorry, Ray. I shouldn't have told you like that. She told me that she told you. She said you didn't want to see me again. I could hear you in the background sometimes. She said you refused to take the phone from her."

And it was clear that her brother still didn't know what to believe.

No, no, no, no, no!

Pain sliced through her heart, exploded in her brain.

What kind of woman would do such a thing to her children? Divide them from each other and kill the memory of the only love and security they had known?

Lillian Getty—pale and timorous on her chair, reading her magazines.

Knowing that Rachel wouldn't leave as long as she held out any hope for Zach. Knowing that her dread for Zach had leached the happiness out of any small moment of personal achievement. Knowing that all Rachel cared about in the world was her baby brother Zach.

Why had she done this?

Don Getty used his fists and only his fists.

Lillian had ripped out her heart.

She gasped out her pain into Zach's ear, her fingers clutching his neck like those of a drowning swimmer.

All this time Zach had been safe and Lillian had known, while Rachel shouldered her burden of terror and guilt.

"Ray-Ray." He murmured her childhood nickname. "Come back another time. We can't talk about this now." He drew away from her, hastily wiping his eyes.

"What if I lose you again?"

"You won't. Here." He drew a napkin from his pocket and scrawled his number and address on it in blue ink that smeared as he wrote. She took it with shaking fingers.

"Take this," she said, fumbling her business card from her bag. "You can find me at this number anytime."

She touched her brother's face, his hair, her fingers trying to memorize the man she saw before her now. She reached around him for one of his brochures and tucked it into her bag.

"I have money now, Zach. I'm working. I could help you. We could find a place together, make some changes—"

He cut her off. "I can't think about any of that now, Ray. I have my own life here. I'm being graded on my exhibit, I have to focus."

She nodded helplessly. "But you'll call me?"

"I'll call you."

"If you need anything—"

"I'm okay, Ray. Try to believe that."

She smoothed her trembling hands over her face, tried to get her thoughts in order. "Don't say anything to Mum, Zach. Don't tell her that we saw each other."

Because if she could make Zach disappear once—

"No," he agreed. "You either."

She nodded again, knowing he wanted her gone but loath to leave. "Could I have one, Zach? One of your paintings to keep at work?"

He studied her card. "I'll send it to you. Now, please go."

She hugged him once more, aware that even though he was sending her away, insisting that she leave, he was bruising her shoulders with the fierceness of his grip.

They looked at each other uncertainly, their faces mirroring the same pain.

And then she forced herself to turn away and leave her brother behind.

There would be a reckoning of all she had learned. And when it was done, she would walk away without looking back.

18.

Simply, they left no witnesses behind.

The next morning, she called Nate. She'd stayed at the office overnight reading *Apologia*. She wasn't ready to face her mother. Instead, she'd gotten her skates out of her locker, found an indoor rink, and raced around its perimeter for an hour. Spent, she'd ordered pizza and hurtled through Nathan's last book. She'd been bleary-eyed and exhausted, taking her mind off her troubles by focusing on Nate's. She understood what the book was now, the meaning of the dedication. It was Nate nakedly displaying his longing for forgiveness.

He was just as screwed up as she was.

That was why she had called him. That, and for a tour of the Bluffs.

He was waiting for her at the trailhead. She greeted him with a wave.

"Have you ever noticed," she said as an opening, "that everything about you matches your hair?"

Nate blinked at her. He was wearing a tweed jacket the color of autumn leaves and narrow slacks in the same shade of amber as his eyes. On his feet were the sensible shoes Rachel had proposed for a walk along the Bluffs.

She grinned, getting out of the car. "It's like a palette—the country gentleman's catalogue for fall. Do you have a valet?"

"I have Audrey," he said drily. "She hasn't gotten out of the habit of thinking of me as her personal dress-up doll."

"She has an eye for things," Rachel said. She felt safe in her compliment because it was directed at his sister. From the corner of her eye, she could feel the intensity of his regard.

"Shall we walk?"

He was guiding her down the path Drayton would have walked the night he fell to his death. The lake unfolded before them like a bolt of blue silk, a tangy breeze fresh against their faces. Rachel was glad she had opted for her ponytail and running shoes. The ground was uneven beneath her feet, covered with a sparse, thready grass that gave way in places. She could hear the rumpled murmur of water against the shore. The Bluffs rose in an illumination of chalk-white cliffs before them, the path winding its way above the headland.

Rachel found the spot marked with yellow police cones without much difficulty, Nate trudging along behind her. Sixty-five feet below them, the detritus of the lake had scrubbed the shoreline clean.

She looked around.

It had rained often during the past ten nights. There were no tracks on the ground, no broken tree limbs, no indication of any kind of a struggle. She looked inland. The walk had taken them fifteen minutes. She could make out the barest outline of Nate's house. Ringsong receded even further into the distance.

If anyone had seen a figure walking on the Bluffs that night, there would have been no way of identifying the man as Christopher Drayton. If he'd been pushed to his death, someone would have had to have been following him closely. And why would he have stood there so obediently, making it easy for the person who wished him harm? Unless the relationship between Drayton and his pursuer had been one of trust—if it had been Melanie Blessant, for example.

If it had been anyone at all, she reminded herself. As Khattak was fond of saying: *a man fell to his death.*

She stood beside Nathan companionably, their hands shoved in their pockets, their faces reddened by the walk. She could taste the lake on her lips.

"Rachel," Nate said after a time. "Why would anyone push Chris to his death? Or why would he commit suicide? There must be something more to the matter here, and it's obvious you think it has something to do with the museum."

She would tell him, she decided. This mucking about in the dark was pointless. It was getting them nowhere. "The chief got a call from a friend at Justice, from the War Crimes division. There's some suspicion that Christopher Drayton was actually an alias. We think his real name was Dražen Krstić."

Nate stared at her, perplexed. "Dražen Krstić?"

"An indicted Serb war criminal. One of the logisticians of the massacre at Srebrenica."

"*That's* why they asked Esa to dig around?" He lost a little of his color. "They think that Chris was Krstić? That's simply not possible."

"Why not?"

She was curious as to how Drayton had submerged his true identity so thoroughly.

"His English was perfect, for one thing."

"He spoke several languages fluently. Why not English?"

"No. He was a patient man, immensely kind and vigorous. He had an appetite for life. He loved teaching kids. He loved beautiful things. He threw himself into the museum—my God, the museum!"

Rachel waited. She was finding this most instructive.

"A man like Dražen Krstić would have had absolutely no interest in the Andalusia project. It would be antithetical to his sense of himself—to the ideology that fueled the Bosnian war."

"You know something about it, then." She filed away the troubling contradiction of the museum for later consideration.

"Of course I do. When Esa went to Sarajevo with his student group, I was the one he wrote to about the siege."

"You didn't go with him?"

"I couldn't. My father was a diplomat. It would have embarrassed him. I did what I could to help Esa from this end."

Rachel tried to remember her student years. She'd been hungry to learn, but her risk-taking had taken another form.

The cops turned their backs on us, Ray. How could you want to be one of them?

I don't, Zach. I won't be anything like them, you can trust me.

She hadn't begun to come to terms with the knowledge that she no longer needed to carry the burden of guilt and dread that had defined her life for the past seven years. She didn't know if she felt lighter or merely empty. She wondered what Drayton had thought, venturing too close to the traitorous edge of the Bluffs. Had he jumped? Had the ghosts of Srebrenica haunted his peace too fully? Was his support for Ringsong meant to be an absolution? Had he accepted the things the letter writer had said about him?

I would like to appeal to you Mr. Krstić, whether there is any hope for at least that little child that they snatched away from me, because I keep dreaming about him. I dream of him bringing flowers and saying, "Mother, I've come." I hug him and say, "Where have you been, my son?" And he says, "I've been in Vlasenica all this time." So I beg you, if Mr. Krstić knows anything about it, about him surviving somewhere . . .

Were there tears in her eyes, or was it mist from the lake that spread below them?

If she had received such a letter—a mother begging for the where-abouts of her missing son, one body among the thousands in Srebren-ica's mass graves—she knew she would have found herself standing at the edge of a precipice, praying for the ghosts to leave her in peace.

But the man whose hands and brain had overseen so much death—how would such a man be moved by a letter? By a mother's agonized plea?

"Drayton was receiving letters addressed to Dražen Krstić. Letters that knew what he had done."

"Blackmail?" Nate asked, threading his fingers through the swoop of his straw-gold hair.

"Reminders, the boss said. I think they're accusations. We took them to an imam at the Bosnian mosque and had him look at them. There was an arms embargo, it appears."

"Yes," Nate said. "It made my father furious, I remember. The matériel of the Yugoslav army remained in the possession of Greater Serbia while the Bosnian territorial units were disarmed in preparation for the war. The international arms embargo prevented any hope of self-defense. My father observed that it was the first time the United Nations had actually supervised a genocide."

"Too harsh a condemnation, surely."

"'*The tragedy of Srebrenica will haunt our history forever,*'" he quoted, his voice soft.

"Where's that from?"

"The UN report published after the war. My father used to wonder if the war could have continued quite as long or reached such a violent conclusion without the role that the UN played. Do the letters speak of it?"

Defend us or let us defend ourselves. You have no right to deprive us of both.

She supposed they did.

"I just can't believe it of Chris. It would have been too great a charade. The thing he loved best was time in his garden. You could find him there in the evenings, chatting with his lilies. People who create such beauty can't possibly possess such ugliness within them."

Of course they could. People were full of contradictions, bewildering even unto themselves.

She'd seen her Da at the marina with Zach, his face alive with joy. And she'd seen her Da take his belt off and beat Zach bloody with it. And when she'd worked the Miraj Siddiqui case with Khattak, she'd seen sides of the human mind she hoped never to see again. Death and loss and betrayal, wound up in each other.

There was a fragile thread of connection between herself and Nathan Clare. He'd opened himself to her within days of knowing her. He'd directed her to *Apologia*. She wondered if she could say anything to him.

"Isn't that what you thought of Laine Stoicheva?"

His head whipped round toward her, his gold eyes like flinty coins. And then he smiled. "Yes, you're quite right. I should know better as a writer. I'm either observing contradictions or inventing them. It's just that Chris was—too normal, too human. And then, why the museum?"

Rain began to spatter lightly over their heads. They turned back.

"Maybe it was a form of atonement."

Nate neither agreed nor disagreed. He struggled to twist his thoughts around this idea of a dual identity. He fell into step with Rachel, conscious of the solidness of her beside him, the fixed, dependable nature of her movements. She moved quietly, without fuss, her ponytail bouncing behind her.

"You'll need to keep this information to yourself, though I wondered: do you think any of the people that you know, perhaps someone you invited as a guest to one of your parties—could one of them have been the letter writer?"

Nate considered this, his steps careful and sure on the precarious surface of the Bluffs.

"I honestly can't imagine so. Perhaps if I went back over my guest lists, something might stand out. Have you studied photographs of Dražen Krstić?"

Rachel glanced at him sideways. "Yes. I've looked at everything I could find. We're a bit restricted as to resources because the boss is keeping things quiet for now. The pictures I've seen are some fifteen years old. If it's the same man, he's greatly changed. Heavier. Older. We found a gun at his house. A JNA army pistol."

"A gun? Chris didn't own a gun. He abhorred them."

"Krstić didn't. They were second nature to him."

Her phone rang. The call was from Khattak. She listened, then turned to Nate. "I've got to go. There's been a break-in at Drayton's. If you could just try to remember if there's anything at all about Drayton that seemed strange or would suggest he had something to hide, that would be helpful."

"I could come with you."

"It's more important that we establish a break in Drayton's cover.

He must have slipped up somewhere if he was Dražen Krstić. Think about it and let me know."

That wasn't the reason she had asked him to show her the path through the Bluffs. And she didn't think it was the reason he wanted to accompany her now. In fact, she knew why.

With his writer's instinct, or whatever it was, he'd recognized a fellow screw-up.

19.

How is it possible that a human being could do something like this, could destroy everything, could kill so many people? Just imagine this youngest boy I had, those little hands of his, how could they be dead? I imagine those hands picking strawberries, reading books, going to school, going on excursions. Every morning I cover my eyes not to look at other children going to school and husbands going to work, holding hands.

Allah knew why this was happening. Only Allah knew. Only Allah could say why He had reached down His divine hand and touched them with the mark of the believers—the mark that cursed them. They had lost everyone else. His father, the brave ammunition courier, killed on the road to Tuzla. His grandfathers deceased from starvation. His uncles, cousins, brothers, and friends—some had stayed in the woods. Some had been executed inside the white house in Srebrenica. Some had been shot point-blank not far from the base at Potočari. Some had been beaten by axes and truncheons, or had their throats slit in the night, during the long wait for deliverance. Some were on trucks and buses that had materialized swiftly from nowhere and just as swiftly disappeared to unknown destinations. He had seen them take the boys from the line that separated the men and women. He knew they would take him, a skinny fourteen, just as they would take Hakija, at ten years old, the baby of their family. They would not say, "These are children, leave them." They would say, "These are prisoners. We will exchange them."

But there would be no exchange.

If they could take the baby that was crying from want in the unmerciful heat and shoot him in the head, why would they leave Hakija and himself? They would not. They would call them out as Turks, as balija. *They would say, "Fuck your Muslim mothers." They would make them sing Chetnik songs.*

Then they would tie their hands behind their backs, drive them away to a school or warehouse as they had done to others at Vuk Karadžić, and murder them all. They would lie there dead, forgotten, the last men of their family. Their mother would never find their bones. In time, she would forget the shape of their faces.

The Chetniks were coming.

There were rumors of more than just the Drina Wolves.

Someone had seen Arkan and his Tigers.

He kissed his mother, three times, four, and on the last kiss, he jerked Hakija's hand away from hers and whispered fiercely, "They are going to kill us. I will take him to the woods. I will find you again at Tuzla."

His mother had wept, pleaded, begged to take Hakija with her on the bus to Tuzla until she had seen just ahead of her in the line, Mestafa wrenched from his mother's struggling grasp.

"We need to question him," the Chetnik said. "He must be screened for war crimes."

Mestafa, Hakija's classmate, was eleven.

She let them go. Pressed her last bit of bread into their hands.

"Take this, my Avdi, my prince, the last hope of our family. Come back to me in Tuzla, Allah keep you safe, Allah bless and protect your road."

They melted away from the line, dodging the Chetniks, dodging the Dutch who were helping them. He saw that not every boy or man had been lucky enough to kiss his mother or wife or daughter farewell. Already, they looked like skeletons to him. He didn't want to be one of them. He would find his cousins in the woods, find a way to reach the column that had broken out for Tuzla. If he was crafty and careful—and how else had he stayed alive all this time—he and his brother would cross the divide into the free territory where they would be welcomed like heroes. There was food and water in Tuzla. His father's men were in Tuzla. His mother, Allah keep and protect her from the animals, would be there waiting. And this nightmare would be over.

He tucked Hakija's hand into his own, placed his other finger on his little brother's lips.

"No matter what they promise us, we don't talk now," he warned him.

Haki had always trusted him. He kissed his mother sweetly and left the line without protest.

Not knowing then that they would be hunted like animals with just as little chance of survival.

Before, there had been other words. A possibility of hope, of survival. He had heard it on the radio. They would send the airplanes. They would all be saved. The former meaning of all good things would be restored. Green fields no longer a killing ground where men he had known all his life collected their ammunition for this purpose. Animals peacefully at pasture, food fresh and plentiful, water sweet as nectar. And all of it a lie.

They were milling around in circles in the heat.

No one knew the way.

No one had a weapon.

They were trapped on all sides.

"Come down from the hills," the Chetniks said. "We will give you a ride. We will give you water. Why do you suffer for no reason?"

There was nothing to do, no one to ask. They hadn't found any member of their family. They didn't see any of their neighbors. It was just this writhing, dislocated circle of men. Boys, too. Others like himself and Hakija, their eyes desperately searching the faces of their elders. Should they go down? Should they surrender? A man had tried to run and been shot. Lazily. Easily. By a soldier adjusting his rifle on his shoulder.

What should he do?

What was the safest thing to do with Hakija?

"This one is just a boy," a soldier said. "Bring him down from the hill. Give him some water."

In that moment, he decided. Hakija needed water. He needed water. For now, they would come down off the hill near Konjević Polje with all the others. There would be another chance for escape and he would seize it. Later.

A soldier gave Hakija water from his canteen while he clung to his brother's hand.

He looked the Chetnik in the eye, polite and determined.

"Don't separate us," he said. "He is only ten."

"No," the Chetnik said. "I won't separate you."

When Hakija was finished, he received his share from the canteen. He sipped quickly, mightily, knowing that next time he might not be so lucky. In that moment, he saw a halo around the Chetnik's head. He saw that his eyes were kind, his hands gentle. He thanked him for his goodness.

"Stay on the bus with your brother," the soldier told him. "Keep hold of his hand."

They were shepherded to the bus like lost sheep. His hands were clammy from the heat; so were Hakija's. Still, they held on. The bus was as hot and crowded as the trek had been. But it was a mercy to be able to sit. He thanked Allah, he praised His glorious names. There was nothing else to do but sit and wonder and be afraid. Without showing he was afraid to his brother.

The drive was short and Hakija slept until they arrived at Kravica where the bus pulled up in front of a warehouse. In the field outside the warehouse, there were hundreds—or was it thousands?—of men. They were sitting on the ground with their hands behind their heads. Resting, their faces were just like his. Stoic. Bewildered. Terrified. They knew what was coming but they didn't absolutely know. They hoped, just a little, that the sun would rise without blood. They begged for water. He wished now he had not been so selfish with the canteen. He should have asked his brothers. He should have asked the thin, petrified men all around him, "Uncle, will you take a sip?"

He had thought only of himself and Hakija.

The engine died. The door opened and the Chetniks began to argue.

The driver wanted the men to get off.

The soldiers who guarded the warehouse refused. "We already have too many here. Take them somewhere else."

From the warehouse he could hear screams. Cries of desperation.

Not the warehouse, then. It would be hard to escape with Haki from the warehouse.

Allah show us a way, he whispered. Allah deliver us from evil.

There was noise all around them. More buses, some trucks. More people. More prisoners. There were too many. It was a convoy now. An officer came with orders. Their bus driver shrugged. He started up the engine again.

For so long, there had been no fuel in Srebrenica. Here, in moments, so many trucks, so many buses. The convoy began to travel again. He pushed Hakija's head down and craned his neck out the window. They were leaving Kravica behind, but where would they be taken next? Where would the road end? Would there be food or water when they got off the bus?

He didn't think so.

Those quiet men in the field told him otherwise. Their pleas for water had been ignored. In the woods, some of the men had drunk their own urine. If necessary, if they got to that point, he and Haki would do the same. He would have to wait and see.

The fields rolled by, the green fields of his country. He felt as if his stomach was being wrenched from him, but it wasn't a physical feeling. It was in his mind. The mind that schemed and planned and thought of survival. The mind that had seen the bodies of the men hunted down in the woods.

Where was the bus going? When would it stop?

He read the signs for Bratunac.

He knew what was in Bratunac. He didn't want the bus to stop in Bratunac.

It stopped at the school: Vuk Karadžić. The site of the massacre three years ago.

He would not tell Hakija.

Even Hakija knew about Vuk Karadžić and the killing.

He didn't need to know that his brother had made the deadliest decision of their lives, to come down from the hills in the hopes of getting water.

He put his hands over Hakija's ears. Haki knew the sound of screaming and gunfire as well as he did. In the school there was death.

Please, he prayed. Let it be like the warehouse. Let it be full. Let them say there is no room for us.

Abruptly, the convoy came to a halt. A Chetnik rapped on the door.

Don't open it. Almighty Allah, Lord of all that is good, please don't open it.

The driver slid the doors wide, admitting his friend.

"Don't let them off the bus," the Chetnik said. "There's no room. We're not finished in there."

Praise Allah, praise Allah.

He wouldn't think about what the words meant, what it meant to be finished. He would only think about opportunities. Opportunities to escape with Hakija at his side.

The driver shut the door but still he could hear the screams from the school. Wasn't it wrong to kill people inside a children's school? They had done it three years ago, they were doing it now. What about the day when the children came back and needed a place for their classes? What would they do then? Unless they already knew that no one was coming back.

It was true, but he didn't want to admit it. Everywhere they had stopped, he had seen the faces of dead men.

The convoy came to its final stop.

And he understood that they would spend this night at the execution site, but with the infinite mercy of Allah's grace and favor, he prayed they would not be taken off the bus.

Hakija would sleep but he would stay awake, alert to the sound of Chetnik boots, Chetnik guns. He would watch and see what he could learn. He would think of his mother, waiting for them in Tuzla.

And as he listened to the sounds of his people dying all around him, he would try with all his might not to break down and cry.

20.

All wounds will be healed but not this one.

Rachel took over from the local police with minimal fuss. The person who'd broken into Drayton's house was Melanie Blessant. The local landscapers, the Osmond brothers, were the ones who had called the police. They waited in the garden while Melanie arranged herself in a confrontational posture on the hood of Rachel's car.

"We asked you not to return to the house, Ms. Blessant," she said. There was a hint of exasperation in her voice. "What were you looking for?"

"It's my home, too. I lived there with Chris. You can't keep me out of it."

"As of this moment, we don't know what your legal standing is. Mr. Drayton may have had heirs. He may have debts with regard to the house: a mortgage, liens. These are things we need to clear up before we can ascertain the extent of your rights. And of course, a will would greatly help."

Melanie batted her baffled blue eyes at Rachel. She was dressed in leopard-skin leggings so tight they were in danger of splitting across her rear as she twisted from side to side on Rachel's car. With that and the ample cleavage spilling from a leopard-print bra showcased inside a white hoodie, the entire effect dazzled.

"Wasn't it in the safe?"

"Have you ever seen it there, Ms. Blessant? Did Mr. Drayton tell you that he kept it in the safe?"

"Not exactly, but where else would it be? I didn't see it anywhere else in the house."

Her tone was martyred. Evidently, the police were to blame for her misfortune.

"If he had a will, Mr. Drayton most likely kept it at his lawyer's office. We'll have that information very soon, I'm sure. And in the meantime, do you have the combination of Mr. Drayton's safe? Have you ever removed anything from it?"

Melanie Blessant slid off the car with the practiced movement of a pole dancer at a strip club. She dusted one hand over her der-riere, her gaze taking in the Osmonds. She produced a sexy little smirk. As she raised her hand to brush a lock of hair from her face, Rachel caught sight of the ring on her finger—bold, bright, and blinding.

"Chrissie liked his privacy. I didn't mess about in his stuff. He wouldn't have liked it."

Before his death, Rachel thought. Afterward, she wouldn't have been as fussy.

"Did you ever see any of the papers he kept in his safe? Apart from the letters we've already discussed?"

Melanie pretended to think, slipping one foot out of its sandal and rubbing it luxuriously against the back of her calf. Aldo and Harry Osmond watched her, fascinated. She was like a human Bar-bie doll, but it didn't mean she was any less intriguing. Surely that wasn't glitter she had dusted between her breasts? It matched the dangly earrings she wore. Nate should have inserted Melanie into one of his books.

"I don't think there was anything else. I mean, I wouldn't know." She patted her hair complacently.

He lost his temper with you, Rachel translated.

"You told us before that you'd read some of the letters. What did you make of them?"

"You expect me to remember that nonsense?" She turned on Ra-chel like a shrew. "Why would I, if Chrissie warned me off?"

"Just on the off chance."

Rachel waited her out, knowing an audience would be irresistible to a woman like Melanie.

"Things about maps and rivers, not my cup of tea, I can tell you. Directions, I think?" She made it a question. "And a whole lotta names, too strange for normal people to understand." A look of comprehension dawned over her face like a long-delayed sunrise. "I mean, the strangest thing is that the letters weren't for Chrissie at all. Some idiot just kept leaving them for him. Telling him to take the death road."

Now this was something.

"The death road?"

"That's what I said." Melanie tapped her nails against the side mirror on Rachel's car. "That's exactly what I said. It doesn't make sense. What kind of map talks about a death road or death march?" Her eyes became fatuous and wide. "Unless? Was it Las Vegas, do you think? Maybe Death Valley?"

Rachel sighed. There would be no elucidation here. Still. There was something about the safe. Something not entirely forthright.

Watching Melanie Blessant flounce her way across the street to her dark sedan, the headache that had subsided over her morning walk with Nathan returned to Rachel in full force. She squinted against a watery sun, thinking. Her gaze came to rest on the Osmonds. Why had they been here to call the police? She introduced herself, advancing into the garden.

They were two brothers in their early thirties with square faces that tapered down to narrow chins and eyes the color of steel bolts, sometimes blue, sometimes green, depending on the light. Scrawny, with the thick-skinned hands of gardeners. They wore dirt-stained T-shirts under their coveralls, and Harry, the younger of the two, shaded his face with a wide-brimmed hat. Aldo, the elder brother, fielded Rachel's questions, his eyes wary.

"You've heard about Mr. Drayton's death?"

Aldo nodded. He placed one hand on his brother's shoulder and held it there, his knuckles white against his sunburnt skin.

"Yet, you're still coming round."

"We owe Mr. Drayton two more treatments." His voice had a sliding pitch Rachel found unusual. "We worked well together on his garden. We wouldn't want to neglect it now."

"How long had your arrangement with Mr. Drayton been in place?"

"Two years? A little more? He liked our work very much."

She switched her attention to Harry.

"What did the work involve?"

Aldo reached over to adjust the brim of Harry's hat, pulling it low over his face. Rachel noticed the creeping system of lines about his eyes and mouth as he did so. For a young man, he had a gaunt, watchful quality.

"My brother doesn't talk much." He placed a hand to his head in a speaking gesture. "He has some difficulties."

As discreetly as she could, Rachel peered under the hat. In the first instance, she had missed the childlike nature of Harry Osmond's expression, the obvious befuddlement. Now she saw that his blue-green eyes were uncomprehending, the hand that clutched at his brother anxious and unsure.

"I'm sorry," she said. "Did you plant these flowers?" She indicated the border of sprawling lilies. "They're very pretty."

Harry's grip on his brother's wrist eased slightly. "Lilies," he said with careful accuracy. "My favorites. My favorites, Al, right?"

"Yes, Harry. Harry likes all the flowers. He likes their colors and their scent."

"No," Harry contradicted, his mouth set in a stubborn line. "Lilies. Lilies are my favorite."

Aldo rubbed his hand over Harry's shoulder, a patient, familiar gesture. "Yes, Harry. Lilies are your favorite. There are some at Winterglass too," he told Rachel. "But not at Ringsong." A trace of amusement colored his expression. "Miss Norman had very specific ideas about the garden and the courtyards. I told her the plants wouldn't survive the winter, so she's planning to transfer them to a green-house."

"It should be a warm winter," Rachel said. "Getting warmer every year."

"Not warm enough. Not for orange trees. They need special pre-cautions. Now, miss, if you don't mind, we weren't quite finished when we saw the broken window."

With a typical lack of nuance, Melanie Blessant had broken the small oblong window beside the front door to let herself into Dray-ton's house.

"You're going along to the back?" she asked them. "I'd like to see the back."

In grudging silence, the Osmonds led her to the back of the house. Here, Rachel stopped to take stock. The garden exploded in a pro-fusion of herbaceous borders, roses and lilies—hundreds of plants and flowers that she hadn't a hope of recognizing. Peonies? Chrysanthe-mums? Ranks of color, blooms piled high as snowbanks, scent and texture and astonishing variety. The garden gave the house its charac-ter, its charm. Drayton had placed comfortable loungers at intervals beneath the shade trees. She leaned against one, watching the broth-ers at work.

Harry's job was to spray fertilizer on the grass, a simple enough task. Aldo crouched onto his haunches to prune deadheads and trim back the hedges, supplying the appropriate tools from the pockets of his coverall. They were silent as they worked, ignoring Rachel.

She moved closer.

"When was the last time you and your brother saw Mr. Drayton?"

Aldo rose from his knees in a smooth motion, balanced against the handle of his garden shears. He looked from Harry to Rachel, a vigilance in the act that puzzled Rachel.

"Three days, maybe four, before we heard about his fall. He'd asked us to come and consult on new plantings."

"Both of you?"

Again that wary glance across the yard at Harry.

"Yes."

Her instincts told her to separate the two. "Perhaps Harry would like to show me the new plantings." She strolled over to the far end of the garden, her pace easy, her manner relaxed. Aldo followed at once.

"We didn't put anything in. We just discussed his ideas. Look, miss." He gripped her wrist with surprising strength. "Harry can be unpredictable. I can answer anything you want to ask."

Rachel detached Aldo's grip without difficulty.

"Is that so, Harry?" She smiled at him, her voice gentle. "Did you like Mr. Drayton? Chris?"

"He was nice to me," Harry said. Then he frowned. "He wasn't always nice, was he, Al?"

"He doesn't know what he's saying. He was nice, Harry, remember? He let you plant the lilies."

"He was nice," Harry agreed, pushing up the brim of his hat. "He let me plant the lilies. Orange lilies. Yellow."

"When wasn't he nice, Harry? Can you tell me?" And then as Aldo moved to intervene, "Mr. Osmond, would you wait beside the loungers?"

"You have no right to question my brother." His voice became rough, irregular. "He doesn't understand you."

Rachel placed both hands on her hips and faced Aldo Osmond squarely.

"Do you have something to hide, Mr. Osmond? Does Harry? Do I need to take you both in?"

"We have nothing to hide. I just don't want my brother to become upset."

"You have nothing to worry about, sir. I have a lot of experience in these matters."

Aldo didn't back away. "He's my brother. It's my job to watch out for him."

"You can listen to everything I have to say. Just wait over there, please."

"I'll stand here. I won't interrupt."

"See that you don't. Harry, will you show me where you planted the lilies?"

Harry turned off his sprayer. He motioned Rachel to the very edge of the garden, where the lilies rose and fell in orange rows. Harry's hand caressed their delicate heads.

"These are the pretty ones."

He led her further down the path. With every step, she was conscious of the livid rage Aldo aimed at her back.

"Do you like these lilies?" Harry asked her.

"I do. Very much. Did Chris like them too?"

"He liked the orange ones. He didn't like the others. He yelled at me. He said I did wrong. The wrong ones."

"Show me."

"It's nothing," Aldo denied. "It was nothing."

"Mr. Osmond, you said you wouldn't interrupt. I'd like to see them, Harry. Will you show me?"

Harry took her to the far side of the garden. Planted in a bed that circled a maple tree was a covey of yellow flowers, their buttery heads bowed on their stalks.

"He didn't like these? But they're so pretty."

Harry shifted from one foot to the other.

"He yelled at me, right, Al? He said it was my fault. But I didn't plant these. I didn't, did I, Al?" He jumped from foot to foot, his voice rising.

Aldo joined them, his shoulders slumped in defeat.

"You've upset him now." He reached for his brother's hand and stroked his own callused palm over it. "It wasn't your fault, Harry. You didn't plant these." The lines in his face hardened as he scowled at Rachel. "I don't know why Mr. Drayton didn't like them. It's not a good place to plant, in the shade of a large tree, but we wouldn't have made such a mistake. He asked us about it and I showed him the landscaping plan we had sketched together. No plantings under his maple. Harry doesn't know how to read people. He thought Mr. Drayton was angry at him."

"Did he yell at him?"

"He wasn't the kind of man to yell at anyone. Especially not Harry. He seemed more disturbed than angry but he didn't explain why."

"Did he ask you to uproot them?"

"No." Aldo sounded puzzled. "He asked us to leave them. He said he needed to think about them. Maybe he didn't like yellow."

"He didn't like yellow," Harry echoed.

Rachel nodded at them.

"I appreciate your help, Mr. Osmond. And I apologize if I upset Harry. It was nice to meet you, Harry. Thank you for showing me your work."

As she made her way back to her car, she heard Harry protest.

"I didn't plant them. That wasn't my work."

Rachel met Khattak at his office and waited for him to finish his phone call. He was speaking to a contact at Immigration, but from his scowl he wasn't getting the answers he wanted. She cast a furtive glance at his bookcase. Would he notice that his pristine copy of *Apologia* was missing? She turned her attention back to him as he ended his call.

"What did you find out?"

Rachel straightened her spine.

"It was Melanie Blessant who broke in. She said she was looking for Drayton's will. Apparently, she's not content to wait to hear from his lawyer. Is there a will, sir?" She hadn't overlooked Khattak's absence from the investigation. Nor did she know what leads he was working on his own.

"There is." He slipped his phone inside his pocket. "The lawyer's name is Charles Brining. We have an appointment with him in the morning. He wasn't prepared to speak on the phone about the terms of the will. You sound as if you didn't find Ms. Blessant all that convincing."

"I'm not entirely sure it's the will she's looking for. She's just *so* stupid," she added, thoughtfully. "I can't quite believe it's real. She saw other papers in the safe, though she'll tell you that she didn't snoop around in 'Chrissie's' things. The amazing part is that she didn't get why Chrissie received so many letters that weren't even addressed to him. Maps and rivers and such."

"The Drina," Khattak confirmed at once. "And the Drina Corps."

"There was more. Something we didn't find in the papers we took from his study. She talked about a death road." She resisted the temptation to roll her eyes. "She thought it meant a trip to Las Vegas."

"The road of death," he echoed.

"You know what it is."

"It's what survivors call the escape route to Tuzla. The men who managed to break out of Srebrenica. Many were killed or captured along the road, to be executed later. Some reported chemical weapon use."

"I didn't know that."

Khattak checked his watch but it was a deflection, not a sign of impatience.

"It came out in a Human Rights Watch report a few years after the fall of Srebrenica. They couldn't definitively substantiate the witness testimony, so they called for a wider investigation. The Yugoslav Army was known to have developed delivery systems for a chemical agent called BZ."

"Christ." Rachel no longer bothered to curse under her breath. "Are you telling me those weapons were used?"

"I suspect as much, but I can't say with certainty. Survivors said the mortars caused a strange smoke to spread out around them. Some of the men exposed to it experienced hallucinations. They turned on their friends or killed themselves. The physical evidence of chemical weapons use remains elusive, however. Does Ms. Blessant know something about this? Should I talk to her?"

"She'd like nothing better, I'm sure. I can't be certain what Melanie knew. What I do think is that if she did know something—if there was something in that safe that penetrated through what passes for her brain—she simply didn't care about it. Whatever she knew, it didn't change her plans. She wanted to marry Drayton desperately. And she wanted to give him a ready-made family."

"We should be asking ourselves what the girls' father thought of that. It's a fairly steep price tag, giving up your girls to a fugitive accused of war crimes."

"If he knew."

"Someone knew. I wonder if it was Melanie Blessant."

"She's not going to tell us, sir."

"There may be a more roundabout way. Her daughter Hadley strikes me as being quite observant." He recounted what he had learned at the museum, but Rachel was shaking her head.

"She's a minor. We can't question her without a parent present."

"Then let's ask Ms. Blessant. Let's see how far her motherly concern extends. Perhaps she'll be satisfied if Mink Norman is present." His voice caressed the name and Rachel scowled.

"Do you think that's wise, sir? We can't have interested third parties contaminating a line of inquiry."

"There's no reason to think of Ms. Norman as an interested party."

Rachel's eyes searched his face. "Isn't there, sir? Surely, we can't know who the interested parties are yet. At least until we've discovered the identity of the letter writer. Can you say with certainty it wasn't Mink Norman?"

He didn't concede her point, but he didn't sidestep it either. "I know there's more to these letters than we've understood. We need to go back to the Bosnian community. It's time we started asking questions there."

"I thought we were supposed to keep this quiet. Surely we're not going to treat Bosnians as suspects when we haven't had the nerve to come clean about Drayton."

"I'm saying we should pursue both avenues, Rachel. You've had a good instinct about Melanie Blessant that I'd like to follow up. We need to talk to the parents and, failing that, to their daughters."

"And while you're managing our community policing mandate, what will I be doing?"

Khattak didn't hesitate. "Read the letters more closely. Something may strike you."

"You're seeing Melanie on your own?"

"I think it's the likeliest chance of success."

He was right, of course. Melanie would be eloquent under the spell of his attraction. And if this bothered Rachel, she told herself it was for professional reasons.

To Khattak she said, "And if it isn't?"

"Then I'm willing to bet that she doesn't much care if we interview her daughters."

"And what if the girls aren't there?"

"Then they're likely at Ringsong."

They'd come to an impasse. Rachel thought about objecting again but left it. "Be careful, sir. We're working in the dark here. We don't know anything about anyone."

"I think you'll find once you've gotten to know her that there's nothing to fear from Ms. Norman."

"Is that what you call her?" Rachel asked, curious.

"You don't trust easily, do you Rachel?"

"I wouldn't have thought that was a useful quality in a police officer." She hesitated. "I'm just wary of provocative women, sir."

Khattak's gaze made a slow inventory of the shelves in his office before coming to rest on Rachel's face. "Is that a comment on my personal behavior?"

Nervous sweat soaked Rachel in an instant. "Of course not." She had never, ever wanted to traverse this ground with Khattak. He knew the entire history of her sordid entanglement with MacInerney and hadn't once ventured a personal remark. Her voice stayed trapped in her throat.

"We don't share much about our personal lives, do we?"

There was a rueful note in his voice. She swallowed on a ball of fear.

"That's all right though, isn't it?"

She did not want to talk about Don Getty. Not with Khattak.

Not with anyone. If this was an overture of friendship, she'd do her best to deflect it at once.

"But something's been worrying you, hasn't it?" he went on. "Outside of this case."

Oh God. How to answer him?

"The specter of a war criminal walking our streets is more than enough to worry me, sir. I hope I've given this case my full attention."

She studied her fingernails. She'd find time for a manicure if she could just walk out of this office now. When he didn't speak, she forced herself to look at him.

He seemed more than a little uncomfortable himself. "Rachel. This is supposed to be a position of leadership. If you ever wish to speak with me about anything, I can assure you it won't leave this office."

Oh God, she thought again. Did he know about Zach? Had he noticed her lack of focus, her mind constantly wandering to her brother? Was that what this was about?

Tears flooded her eyes and she began fumbling needlessly through her bag. "I'd best get on these letters, sir. Thank you, though."

Without meeting his eyes, she made her way out of his office to her desk.

Only later would it occur to her that his unexpected compassion had skillfully diverted her from the subject of Mink Norman. And that she'd forgotten to mention the lilies.

21.

I apologize to the victims and to their shadows. I will be
happy if this contributes to reconciliation in Bosnia, if
neighbors can again shake hands, if our children can again
play games together, and if they have the right to a chance.

Despite his desire to return to Ringsong, Khattak returned to the Blessant house, where he found Melanie and her daughters at home. He had debated pushing Hadley harder the other night, but now he realized the conversation would be better served away from the museum and Mink's subtle influence. He might have been reluctant to acknowledge Rachel's warning, but he couldn't discount it altogether.

Rain pelted his cheeks as Melanie let him in on her way out. She'd granted his request for an interview with the girls without hesitation. If she knew anything more about Drayton's will or his papers, she refused to discuss it, her mind preoccupied.

"Talk to them all you want," she said. "Just don't let that boy in, because I'm not running a whorehouse here."

He winced at her manner of indicating concern and watched her go, hips swinging, heels slapping against wet concrete, an umbrella sheltering her crown of blond curls.

"She's headed to the pub," Hadley said, coming to meet him at the door. Her skin was paler than usual, but otherwise she seemed composed. "We're in here."

He followed Hadley to the dining table where Cassidy was seated in front of a polished paper cutter. She was absorbed in the task of measuring cardstock. As he entered the small room, she spared him a shy smile.

He could see why the girls preferred to work in the great room at the museum. The interior of their home was small, cramped, and shabbily kept, old furniture crowded together, yellow wallpaper peeling from the walls in long, damp folds. Whatever money their father had given his ex-wife, it hadn't been spent on this house. The girls were identically dressed in faded jeans and blouses that had seen better days. He caught Hadley's eyes on him, knew she had understood the judgment in his face, and hastened to cover it.

"You're not at Ringsong today."

"Mink's busy tonight. What can I help you with?"

Hadley came to stand in front of Cassidy's chair, blocking his view of her sister, a gesture that made him feel inexplicably sad. Why did it seem to him that this fierce young girl faced the world alone, bearing the weight of intolerable burdens? Or was she alone? Marco River melted into the room like quicksilver, toweling off his dark hair. It was obvious he hadn't used the front door.

"Sorry I'm late. I had to wait for the tiger to leave."

A kinder way of referring to Melanie than Hadley's "Mad Mel." For Cassidy's sake, he thought. It couldn't go on. Whatever secrets they shared between them, he would have to find a way to them move forward.

"Your mother gave me permission to ask you a few questions."

"That's because she's an idiot," Hadley said without blinking.

"You and your mother aren't close?"

She made a quick, precise movement with her hands, directing him away from the table to the adjoining living room. They took seats at the far end in front of the bay window.

"I want to hear," Cassidy protested.

"No you don't. Sit with her, Riv."

The boy obeyed, his eyes gentle on Cassidy's upturned face.

In the living room Hadley turned her full attention on Khattak. "I can't stand her, and the feeling is mutual."

"I'm sorry to hear that."

"Why? I've got one good parent which is better than a lot of kids." She flicked a hand at Riv. "Riv's parents are potheads who got him hooked." She narrowed her eyes at Khattak. "I'll deny that if you try to make anything of it."

Khattak nodded gravely, careful not to look over at Marco. "That doesn't interest me at present. I was wondering how well your father knew Christopher Drayton."

He had been expecting panic, but there was anger in the set of her face, anger and something more. Bleakness.

"Mad Mel was planning to marry him, so Dad had to get to know him a little."

"What were his feelings about the marriage?"

"He was ecstatic." Hadley's voice was dry. "Mel's had him on a very tight leash since the divorce. Chris marrying Mel meant freedom for all of us."

"How so?"

"Dad wouldn't have to pay out the monstrous spousal support that keeps Mel afloat. She's never had to work for anything. And even if she did, minimum wage wouldn't pay for her surgeries." She pinned Khattak with a steely gaze. "Do you think she's beautiful?"

"I'm sure many men would think so."

"They'd be idiots. There's nothing real about Mad Mel—either inside or outside."

Her contempt was undercut by the pain beneath her words.

"Do you think that's what men like?" she went on. "All that plastic tarting-up? So you can't tell what's real or not, just that there's a lot of it?"

She gave her own slender frame an unsparing glance. She was still young enough to need approval, to wonder if she suffered from the comparison to her lavishly endowed mother.

Khattak answered with care. "Without taking anything away from your mother, I think it's safe to say that most men have a more discerning palate. Less can be more." He thought of Mink's elegant hands sliding over her manuscripts.

"You really think so?"

"I think Marco would agree with me. He hasn't taken his eyes off you since he entered the room."

The boy flashed him a grin from the dining table.

"He's probably worried that you're grilling me."

Khattak smiled the smile of a man who'd once stood in an adolescent's besotted shoes. "That's not worry I see in his face."

She heard the humor in his voice and blushed. His words must have been some comfort, because she pushed her shoulders back and raised her head to meet his gaze. "Dad was actually very grateful to Chris. He was taking a huge problem off Dad's hands, and we would have been free to move in with our father after that, so no more extortionate child support either."

She placed a heavy emphasis on the word *extortionate*. It must have been her father's word. It made Khattak think of the letters. He'd get to those in a moment.

"I understood that you were to live with Christopher Drayton after the wedding took place. You have rooms at his house, your mother said."

"No." Hadley's voice flattened. "We were never going to live there. Not in this lifetime or any other. The wedding was the end of the road for us."

"Didn't you like Mr. Drayton?"

"We have a perfectly good father of our own, so why would we settle for a substitute? Why would I want to be around Mel a minute longer than I need to? She makes no secret of the fact that we'd just be in the way."

And yet, she couldn't entirely hide the note of longing in her voice. No matter how harshly she spoke of her mother, there were better memories buried beneath her pain.

"She mentioned that Christopher Drayton wanted a family."

"Did she?" Hadley said without inflection. "What he wanted and what I want are two very different things."

"What about Cassidy?"

He caught the flare of panic on Hadley's face.

"No," she said, a grim anger in her voice. "Cass goes where I go."

"Unless she decides otherwise."

He said it to get to the root of her alarm.

"Cass feels the same way about things as I do," Hadley muttered.

But did she? What did this forthright, clever girl fear so much that she balked at telling him the truth? Because something in her manner spoke eloquently of deception.

"Tell me about the fight."

Instantly, she went still and quiet. She shook her head, freckles standing out against her pallor.

"I can't. I don't—"

"Hadley." He leaned forward, his tone confiding. "This is not your burden to carry. You don't need to protect Christopher Drayton or anyone else."

He'd said the wrong thing. He'd only reminded her of what she thought she had to lose by speaking.

"There's nothing. I don't know anything."

He tried another tack.

"Did you ever see any unusual letters in Drayton's possession? Did your mother ever talk about them?"

The change of subject afforded her no relief. If she held herself any more closely, her bones would snap.

"Letters? No, not letters."

"Something else then? A will perhaps? Papers to do with the museum?"

"No, nothing." She was lying. And the more she elaborated, the more evident it became. "We only went there to study Italian. I wouldn't say we were friends."

Khattak cast about. "Was he a good teacher?"

"He was all right." She bit her lip. "The only reason Mel wanted us to have those lessons was so that she could work on Chris. Flirt with him, get him interested. I guess it worked."

She should have said, "Obviously, it worked." That's what the bitterness in her voice conveyed, a bitterness he couldn't place. Her phrasing told him that there was something else going on entirely.

He raised his voice slightly. "Did you go to these lessons, Marco? With a name like yours, you must have been interested in Italian yourself."

"Sometimes. If Hadley couldn't go and Cass had a lesson, I'd go."

"Why was that?"

A frozen silence stretched between Hadley and Riv. It was broken by Hadley's sharp intake of breath. "Cass likes company. She's younger than she seems. That's why she's not prepared to let go of Mad Mel just yet."

Every piece of information directed him back to Melanie Blessant and away from Christopher Drayton. At some cost to Hadley, he realized.

"I thought you said Cassidy was ready to move with you to your father's."

She faltered for a moment but hit back hard with, "I said *after* Chris and Mel got married. What sense does it make to live in a stranger's house when we have a beautiful home of our own? Cass and I weren't about to be split up for the sake of Mel's libido."

It was a bold performance, but the hint of uncertainty that under-scored the last word rendered it false. There was something dark under Hadley Blessant's collected surface, something else beneath the stony front she tried to project.

She was a girl in trouble.

And with a man like Dražen Krstić, he feared what that trouble might be.

He turned his attention to Cassidy, whose head was diligently bent over her work.

Hadley came to her feet with startling force. "I don't think I want to answer any more of your questions, Inspector. And if you want to talk to Cassidy, you'll have to ask my dad."

"I have your mother's permission." He made the observation only to test her response.

"You need to ask the parent who actually cares about our welfare, and that would be my father. Now, please—leave us alone. We have work to do if we're going to meet the deadline for the opening." Her shrill voice rang through the room, causing Cassidy to turn their way, bewildered.

"I appreciate your honesty," he said, his tone mild. "I didn't mean for my questions to upset you. I just want you to know—" He came to his feet as well. "If you ever need help, you can talk to me or Rachel at any time."

He hoped she would believe him.

"Why are you so interested in Chris's death? It's not because you think he fell, is it?"

And just like that, his moment was before him. A moment when he could open his investigation up a little, trading truth for truth, offering honesty in exchange for a reluctantly given confidence, proving himself worthy of a teenage girl's trust.

Yet the cataclysmic secret of Drayton's identity could not be released at will: not without consulting Tom Paley, not without mapping out the implications for the Department of Justice, Immigration, and most of all, for the Bosnian community.

The ugliness of Dražen Krstić's life darkened the space between them. Hadley caught his hesitation, but he went on regardless.

"We don't think Drayton was who he claimed to be. We fear there was another side to him altogether. It's possible that whatever secrets he kept may have led to his death. But I think you already know this."

"The Bluffs are treacherous. People often think they're safe when they're not." She whispered the words through lips so dry they were stretched taut against her gums.

"We've considered that possibility as well."

"Good—I mean, good."

She didn't say anything else, although Khattak gave her time. It wasn't working. Nothing he'd said had convinced her to trust him. She was much too frightened. Not of someone but for someone.

"What did your father and Drayton argue about?" he asked at last.

Hadley raised one arm in front of her body as if to ward off his question. Tears spattered her freckled skin. Throat working, she opened her mouth to speak. And then fainted dead away.

22.

Mr. Stakić is here. He's a physician just like I am, and he made decisions concerning the camps. He knew that we were there. He knew that his colleague Jusuf Pasic, who was facing retirement, had been taken to Omarska and killed there. He knew about dozens of doctors, physicians being taken to Omarska and killed. Why? These people were the Muslim intelligentsia and they meant something. Is there an answer to all of this?

Charles Brining's office was located in one of the gleaming glass towers that stood opposite the Scarborough Town Center. As they traveled through the air-conditioned chill of its lobby and elevator, Rachel cast a surreptitious glance at her boss.

Was it her imagination or was Khattak's smooth front unraveling a little? The knot on his tie lacked its usual exactness. The pen inside his shirt pocket had leaked ink, leaving a small blue teardrop at its corner. His manner was abstracted, his forehead creased as if he was fighting off a headache. Which only made sense, after his disastrous interview with Hadley Blessant. He'd given her the barest of details, admitting candidly to his failure. And his sense of shame.

She hoped their time with Drayton's lawyer would be more profitable. To that end, she'd made more of an effort than usual with her dress code. On the whole, she detested lawyers, although every now and again, she came across one who made her forget their unmitigated unhelpfulness when she'd tried to emancipate herself and

Zachary from Don Getty's control. Charles Brining wasn't one of them. He was a twig-thin, nervous man in his sixties with the bespectacled face of an absentminded owl and the irritating habit of clearing his throat before each utterance.

He met them in his firm's conference room, a space that aimed at the glamour of the high-powered conglomerates on Bay Street. The seedy, well-thumbed magazines gave the lie to a shining mahogany conference table and the floor-to-ceiling windows that looked out upon ramps to the 401.

His discreet assessment of the duo from CPS took in Rachel's crumpled Banana Republic suit in an unflattering shade of taupe and the ink stain on Khattak's otherwise pristine shirt.

"I've considered the will, as you've asked," he said as an opener. He had the querulous voice of an elderly woman unable to follow the bidding at her bridge game. "It's quite straightforward. With the exception of a single bequest, he leaves his fortune in its entirety to a Mrs. Melanie Blessant. The house and the chattel are left to the same—ah—lady."

Rachel pounced. "You've met her, then."

Brining blinked at her through his spectacles. "Yes, ah—yes. Mr. Drayton brought her with him once."

"Did he discuss the disposition of the will with her?"

"I advised him not to do so."

Rachel and Khattak exchanged a glance.

"Why was that?"

"General prudence." Brining cleared his throat, his pronounced Adam's apple bobbing up and down as he spoke. "The lady has a somewhat—grasping demeanor."

Rachel grinned. "Did she ask you about the will?"

"She spent her time in our lounge, refurbishing her nail polish. She did—ah, drop in to ask a question or two, but naturally, I was not at liberty to speak of Mr. Drayton's confidential matters."

"Naturally," Rachel agreed. "You mentioned another bequest."

Brining worried the tip of his tongue against his lips, a motion that caused the tuft of white hair on his head to shiver slightly. "Yes. Of a charitable nature in that it was a bequest to a registered non-profit. Informally, I believe it's known as Ringsong. The name on record is the Andalusia Museum Project. The fund was to be administered by the museum's board of directors."

"When you say 'fund,' how much money are we talking?"

Brining looked abashed, as if the mention of actual hard numbers was an indecency. "My dear Sergeant Getty, the man had done quite well out of his business. Even with all that's owed in taxes and death duties, he was quite comfortably able to bequeath the museum a quarter of a million dollars."

"*What?*" Rachel hissed. "You've got to be kidding."

"I assure you I am not."

"But why would he want to give so much money to such a small project?"

"It was quite a passion project of his. He wanted to leave a legacy, and the Reconquest of Spain from the Moors was a legacy he respected very much. It seemed somehow personal to him. Is that helpful to you?"

"It confirms certain theories," Khattak said, echoing the lawyer's noncommittal manner.

"Then perhaps I should add that the amount available to Mrs. Blessant is substantially more."

"How much more?"

"Something in the nature of two million."

Rachel's shock was evident.

"Just what type of business was he in?"

"He operated a parking lot in the city that was remarkably lucrative. And of course, he brought savings with him from his businesses in Italy."

Rachel's knees knocked together. The thought of Melanie Blessant in possession of so much ill-gained fortune made her feel nauseated.

"Do you know the nature of those businesses?"

"Import-export, I believe. Christopher didn't discuss the specifics with me."

"You were on a first-name basis?"

Brining bristled. "It's atypical, I assure you. We were of a similar age, with similar interests. He was a hospitable man: we socialized occasionally."

Rachel rushed to soothe him. "Of course. You say you had similar interests. Might I ask what those were?"

Brining's smile was unexpected. It disclosed a series of irregular, closely corralled teeth with a gap at the center.

"I'm quite fond of vacationing in Italy. The food is divine. And we both enjoy a tinker in our gardens. Peaceable hobbies."

"Indeed." Khattak cut in. "What would happen to Mr. Drayton's bequests, if it became public knowledge that Christopher Drayton was not in fact his true identity?"

The unexpectedly charming smile disappeared. "I'm afraid I don't quite follow."

"If Christopher Drayton was an assumed identity rather than a real one."

A shrewd flash of intuition lit up Brining's eyes. "Is that the nature of your interest in this matter?"

"Yes."

"I suppose it would depend. If the identity was a legal identity, as per a perfectly justifiable legal name change, it would have no impact at all. If he'd never formally registered a change of name, there would be issues, certainly, but none that might not be overcome with careful and thorough paperwork."

Careful and thorough paperwork were Charles Brining's holy grail, Rachel deduced at once.

"That's not the issue, is it, Inspector?" Brining's rheumy gaze darted between the two detectives. "If Mr. Drayton were some type of fugitive or if the funds themselves were to be of suspect provenance— illegally gotten gains," he elucidated for Rachel's benefit, "then naturally, the bequests would be held up until Christopher's legal right to the funds could be determined. If any of his assets were found to be the gains of criminal enterprise, they would be seized by the jurisdiction most concerned with the crime." He lowered his voice. "Does this pertain to organized crime?"

"We don't have that information yet, although we are in the process of acquiring it. Would you be able to do something for us, sir?"

"That—ah—depends." Ever cautious, the lawyer waited for clarification.

"Would you notify the beneficiaries of their bequests but also warn them that the actual dispensation of funds will be held up until our investigation is concluded?"

"That was within my ambit, regardless. I shall do so immediately."

"And if they press you for additional information—"

"Naturally, I shall say nothing, as I know nothing," he responded with a twinkle in his eye.

"You're very good."

Brining dismissed this. "I must say, however, Inspector—"

"Yes?"

"I cannot imagine Christopher Drayton to have been anyone other than who he claimed to be. A generous man whose greatest pleasure was his garden, with perhaps a weakness for improbable women."

Rachel grinned at the word. It was a brief yet perfectly calculated description of Melanie Blessant's pneumatically enhanced attractions.

"You say improbable, sir. Why so?"

"She presented herself as—what's the common vernacular? Ah yes. No more than a trophy for Christopher's arm. A somewhat artificial woman with a voracious eye for Christopher's credit cards. He didn't seem to mind that." Brining's white tuft trembled as he nodded at Rachel. "Yet I had the distinct impression she knew everything there was to know about Christopher, down to his last cent." His manner became grave. "If Christopher Drayton was indeed an assumed identity, I have very little doubt that Mrs. Blessant knew the truth of it."

———

"Let me make a call, Rachel."

Rachel cooled her heels by the car, noting anew the sprawling ugliness of the shopping mall across from them. In the last two decades, its big-box stores had multiplied exponentially, robbing the façade of any appeal.

Khattak made no effort to screen his call from her hearing. He made a polite but firm request to be put through to Tom Paley at Justice. Some moments passed before the call was connected.

"Tom? It's Esa here. I think I have confirmation."

Rachel listened without pretense as Khattak described the letters and the gun in Drayton's study, his own suspicions, and lastly, Drayton's tattoo.

"You'll need to trace the money. It's the fastest route to the truth." He listened for a moment. "I can't confirm it through DNA unless you or the ICTY have a sample on file. Do you have that?" Another pause. "I didn't think so. Listen, Tom, we should talk in person. I'll come to Ottawa tomorrow. We need to discuss exposure."

Rachel scowled. Just what in hell did he mean by that?

As if he'd heard her thoughts—or just read the anger on her face—he went on, "It's time you notified Immigration, more than time. And I've a duty here with regard to the Bosnian community. You can't possibly expect this to remain quiet much longer."

Another long silence, and this time it was Khattak who looked angry. "Who told you about Imam Muharrem? I see. Then let me say this, the Bosnian mosque was our first, best lead in terms of confirming identity. The imam has offered to put us in touch with survivors who were at Potočari when Krstić was there. Survivors who won't have forgotten what he looks like or who he is. I'm well aware of that, Tom. And yes, I'll be discreet."

He snapped his phone shut. "They'll trace the money. It's what they should have done from the first."

"What about Immigration?"

"Yes, that's the question, isn't it?" He stared up at the glass tower to Brining's office. "There was no legal name change, that's one thing

I can tell you. However Krstić got here, it was as Christopher Drayton."

"You've been widening the net," Rachel said. "Why didn't you tell me?"

"If this blows up, as I've every reason to believe it will, I don't want you caught in the crossfire. They'll come after me. I need to make sure you stay above it so we can salvage any justice that's possible from this mess."

"That sounds personal, sir."

"If you'd been through a single day that Sarajevo was under siege, you might find it personal as well. It won't compromise my judgment."

Wouldn't it? He hadn't mentioned the bequest to Mink.

"Sir, what about the museum?"

"What about it?"

"A quarter of a million dollars. That's quite a motive. Money left as a bequest is entirely different from a donor's gift. It comes without strings attached."

"If Drayton is Dražen Krstić, I've every confidence that Ms. Norman will refuse the gift."

"Have you?" Rachel bit her lip. "If the money's dirty, there's no gift to leave. But Mink Norman wouldn't have known that."

Comprehension flared in Khattak's eyes. "Suppose Melanie Blessant did know. Suppose she understood the letters she snooped through all too well. Maybe she did have the combination to the safe and she got rid of anything that definitely pointed to Krstić. Knowing that it might be an obstacle to his fortune."

Rachel wondered if he could hear himself—the thin and paltry hope.

"There's a number of problems with that, sir." She chose her words carefully. "If she married Drayton, she was getting everything anyway. And from all accounts, not to mention the blinding piece of statuary on her finger, they *were* to be married."

"She might have preferred the money without the man. There was a considerable age difference. And Drayton wanted her daughters to move in as well, whereas Hadley's given me to understand that the last thing her mother wanted was to allow the girls anywhere near her love nest."

"All right. Then if she had the combination to the safe, why would she leave the letters behind? If she wanted to obscure Drayton's true identity, surely she wouldn't leave behind dozens of letters that address him as Dražen Krstić and accuse him of heinous crimes."

"That part might have been true. She might not have understood the letters." He met Rachel's gaze and caught himself. "No, you're right. It doesn't add up. She's a calculating woman, not a clever one. She may have seen the letters and the will—Brining said that Drayton retained his own copy, by the way. She may have known what Drayton was and simply not cared about anything except her own security. She wouldn't necessarily have understood that the letters posed a threat to her inheritance under the will, but Rachel—all this presupposes that Dražen Krstić was more likely to have been helped to his death by a mercenary woman than by the person who sent him the letters."

Rachel mulled this over, chewing at the end of her ponytail.

"You're saying that the likeliest answer—"

"Is that he was killed by a survivor of the massacre he perpetrated."

"A man fell to his death from the Bluffs," she mused.

"It can't be a coincidence. I just don't see it."

"Nor I," she agreed. "And Melanie's the type to prefer to have a man around, doting on her every whim. Maybe she didn't know about the will, despite what Charles Brining said. Maybe Drayton alive was her only guarantee of security."

"How long had Drayton been receiving the letters?"

Rachel spit out her hair. "Why? What does that matter?"

"We have to ask ourselves: why now? If the letters had been arriving for some time—months, even years, what precipitated Drayton's fall at this time? Was there a precipitating event? That's what we need to know."

"He's only lived on the Bluffs for two years, we know that much."

"Assuming that he'd been receiving the letters for the whole of that time, what does that tell us?"

"I'm not sure." An idea began to form in her mind as the significance of the dates stamped itself into her awareness

"Sir, there were two precipitating events, if you think about it." She knew he would only accept the first. She offered them both anyway. "One, the wedding was on the horizon. Drayton was about to marry Melanie Blessant, transferring himself and his money into her hands."

"Go on."

"Two, the museum's about to open. He wanted in. The board may have wanted his money, but they had no intention of renaming the project in his honor. Or of allowing him a greater say in directing the museum."

"Melanie marries Drayton, she gets the money. Drayton dies, Melanie gets the money. In one scenario, Dennis Blessant is off the hook but has to wrangle over his girls. In the other, Melanie no longer wants the girls."

"You're thinking the *father* is a likelier suspect?" Why wasn't he looking at the museum?

"I'm not saying that." His tone was patient. "I'm simply running through all possibilities. I've no doubt at all that Drayton was Dražen Krstić. There are multiple scenarios here, but we can't ignore the letters. Whoever wrote them had a motive strong enough to have seen to Drayton's death." Rachel hesitated before she said softly, "I'm glad you see that, sir, because there's something else."

When he raised his eyebrows at her, she told him about the lilies.

23.

*Verily God will not change the condition of a people
until they change what is in themselves.*

This driving around in the middle of the day was tiring, but at least
the city traffic wasn't terrible. They were back at Drayton's garden.
Khattak stood under the maple tree. The heads of the yellow lilies
sagged toward him on their stalks. He brushed them lightly with
his fingertips.

"I know what these are. Do you have your camera?"

She produced a small digital camera from her blazer pocket. He
snapped several photos.

"If Drayton was as upset as the Osmonds claim, there's an excellent
reason for it."

"He didn't like yellow?"

"This is the Bosnian lily, a native plant. It was a symbol on Bosnia's
flag at the time of its independence from Yugoslavia. The coat of arms
that bore the original fleur-de-lis is a much older symbol. It represents
the arms of the Kotromanić family, who ruled Bosnia during the
fourteenth and fifteenth centuries."

"So someone planted these to upset Drayton. To remind him of
the war."

"And his role in it. Did the Osmonds say when the flowers first
appeared?"

"No. Drayton thought Harry had planted them, but Aldo showed him the sketch for the landscape design. He said they'd never plant lilies in such deep shade."

"Drayton believed them?"

"That's what they said. Plus, they consulted with Drayton over every plant in the garden. They'd hardly throw in something as a surprise."

"You said the younger brother suffers from mental illness. Violent?"

"I don't know. Aldo Osmond was definitely not receptive to the idea of me questioning him. Harry's easily upset, but he seemed harmless to me."

"So what do we have? The letters, the lilies, the tattoo, the gun."

"He's Krstić," Rachel said. "I don't doubt it either."

"We need to pay another visit to the *Dzamija*."

"You're planning to tell the imam?"

"I'm hoping there's something more he can tell us."

"You don't expect him to stay quiet, do you."

It wasn't a question. It was an observation that troubled Khattak at a personal level.

"I don't know that I could in his shoes. After what he's been through. Dražen Krstić, here? Living a peaceful, successful life? I don't know that I could stomach it."

"He's a spiritual man."

"He watched his friends and mentors murdered in Manjača. I don't know how spiritual anyone feels after such a thing."

"I don't know what faith has to say in answer to that," she said, after a moment.

"I've struggled with it, but I don't either."

She decided to forego any mention of lunch, caught by Khattak's somber mood. They drove to the mosque in silence, through back roads that bypassed the traffic building on the highways. She palmed a Mars bar from her bag and made quick work of it.

"I've another if you want," she mumbled around a mouthful of chocolate.

"I need to feed you better. Or at least let you take a lunch break once in a while."

"That place at the marina was good."

"This is your neighborhood. What's here?"

"Popeye's Chicken? Spadina Garden? What are you in the mood for?"

"Those are a little out of the way. I have to drive to Ottawa tonight."

An awkward silence fell. Rachel wasn't slow to understand the reason for it. "If I lived on my own, I'd invite you over and whip something up for us." It wasn't that she couldn't cook. She just didn't like to.

"I'd like to meet your father one day."

That was Khattak. Clear and direct to a fault. He'd seen her discomfort, pinpointed its source, and spoken to its root. She cleared her throat, her skin suddenly clammy.

"It might not be the experience you're hoping for, sir."

"I don't think it will be as bad as you fear, Rachel. I've worked with some obdurate individuals at INSET."

She choked on her last bite of chocolate. "You know a little about my da, then."

He slid the car into an empty spot in the mosque's parking lot and gave her a friendly glance.

"Don Getty's reputation precedes him everywhere. He's enormously popular."

Except in his own home, she thought. Aloud she said, "That's good to know. Maybe another time, then. We're here now."

But there would never be another time. She would make sure of it.

This time they were directed to the slightly shaggy lawn behind the mosque where Imam Muharrem strolled back and forth beneath an avenue of mulberries. He was dressed more casually today, a thin white sweater adding warmth to his robes.

A group of children scampered over the lawn in search of a soccer ball, their ages ranging from five to fifteen. Their playful laughter filled the air, as a particularly determined little girl kicked at the older boys' knees. Rachel smiled. Any girl who fought the odds, convinced that she could win, reminded her of herself.

Although the imam's welcome was warm, a wariness darkened his eyes. "You are back, my friends. With news I hope."

Khattak ran through the information they had gathered so far, giving the imam time to absorb it. His gaze brooded over the children at play, following the progress of the soccer ball.

"He has the tattoo?"

"He has it, but I caution you that it was a common symbol among the paramilitaries."

"Krstić was not a paramilitary. He was Chief of Security of the Drina Corps. He was General Radislav Krstić's direct subordinate. You know what they say about Lieutenant Colonel Krstić, don't you?"

"I'm afraid I don't," Khattak said.

"I've spoken with some of the survivors since your last visit. I've asked about this man. They told me the same thing: Krstić was everywhere during the murders. He arranged the logistics, he oversaw the executions."

Khattak waited. "Yes, I'm sorry. I did know that."

"Then perhaps you will tell me what you are waiting for. There should be an announcement to the community, to the country. There must be an accounting of what Krstić was doing in this country. How he arrived here."

"I promise you that all those things will be arranged once Krstić's identity is confirmed. We cannot confirm it through physical evidence—we simply don't have any. We're following his paper trail, his money. I can assure you of one thing, though: he did not come into this country as Dražen Krstić. He was already Christopher Drayton when he arrived here."

The imam came to a halt near the shaded entrance to the back of the mosque. A few of the older children had opted out of their game to watch him. He waved them off with a faded smile.

"He fooled your government, this means."

"I think he fooled a lot of people, sir." Rachel tugged on the lapels of her blazer. "I doubt that anyone who knew him then would recognize him now."

"Should we not test this? We can arrange for people who saw him in Srebrenica to identify him. Not just from our neighborhood but from many cities in America: St. Louis, Chicago, Des Moines. We can set this matter to rest."

Khattak hesitated, his movements ill at ease. "I'm afraid that wouldn't settle it, sir. Given the amount of time that's elapsed. They would say that memory alone cannot be trusted."

The imam's lips tightened. "And when memory is all we have? They took everything else. Our papers, our homes, our cities, our loved ones. They even robbed the dead of their teeth."

His words made Rachel think of a line she had read in the letters. *They stripped us of everything. There was no kindness, no decency.*

She wondered what Khattak could possibly say to alleviate the other man's anger.

"You insult us, Inspector. The truth is terrible enough. We have no reason to manufacture lies about the horrors my people suffered."

"I know that, believe me I do. I'm not saying that identification wouldn't help. I'm saying we must follow every possible lead until we are certain of Krstić's identity beyond a doubt. Wouldn't you prefer it that way?"

The little girl kicked the ball straight at the imam. He caught it with a deft movement and tossed it back to her, his face grave.

"It would give many people peace to know that Krstić is dead."

"For that peace to be real, they would need to know that Drayton really was Krstić. All I'm asking you for is a little more time. I'm heading to the Department of Justice this afternoon. I should be able to tell you much more once I've had that meeting."

Imam Muharrem studied him.

"So you will be the truth-bearer, Inspector Esa. You will tell your masters what they do not wish to hear, insist to them on the truth of what you've learned. And they will say to you, Inspector, 'How can you trust the memory of these Bosnians? A people too weak to save themselves. We owe them nothing. Let us preserve our silence.'"

"Imam Muharrem—"

"Can you deny it? Was Srebrenica not the worst hour of so many Western governments?"

"The Canadian battalion wasn't in Srebrenica in 1995, sir. And while they were there, they lived on combat rations as an act of solidarity with your people." Rachel had done her research but she didn't know what made her say this; perhaps a flicker of deep-seated shame.

The imam took her up on it. "The Canadian battalion was evacuated at the insistence of your government. Unlike my people, who could not be evacuated and were left behind to be murdered. I'm afraid a ration of two beers a day is not my definition of solidarity, Sergeant. We experienced the same pressures as your commander in Srebrenica, but we did not share his relief from it." He shook his head. "Canbat or Dutchbat, it would have made no difference. The outcome would have been the same. What does it matter to the mothers of Srebrenica if entire governments resign? Will that bring back the dead?"

"Sir—"

"You do what you must, Inspector. I will do the same." He saw their expressions and added, "I do not mean that as a threat. I will wait to see what your government does. I think this will make you unpopular, Inspector Esa. If you expose your government, you may not reach the heights you were otherwise destined for. Your Community Policing may fail before it has a chance to begin."

Khattak slid his hands into his trouser pockets, the gesture unforced. "Please let me worry about that, Imam Muharrem. We cannot possibly fail you twice."

It was a kind thing to say, Rachel supposed, words that reassured the imam but did nothing to dispel her own anxiety. She couldn't quash the feeling that Khattak was far more invested in the outcome of this case than he was prepared to concede. If he'd been brave enough to join a student humanitarian mission, his conscience should be clear. Why did he bear the burdens of Bosnia so personally?

She admitted she didn't know what a person who subscribed to the same faith might feel. The bonds of religious solidarity? A call to action? A sense of failure? Guilt? Shame? How far did the bonds of this dimension of identity extend? What did faith demand in this instance? Maybe Khattak's recollections of a city under siege were what drove him repeatedly to the golden idyll of Andalusia, to Mink Norman and her museum.

Her steps heavy, she trudged behind Khattak through the narrow passageway that led to the mosque's front door. Both sides of the hall were lined with group photographs that depicted community activities. Cookouts, picnics, basketball tournaments, children's races. A few were the solemnly arranged groups of board members and clerical advisory committees, identified by name but not by date. One of these dominated the others in a massive black frame cropped by a velvet mat. Six men in poses of varying seriousness were gathered before the mosque's *mihrab*. One was a man she recognized.

She tugged at Khattak's jacket.

"Sir," she said. "Isn't that David Newhall?"

24.

We heard it on the radio. They will send the airplanes now.
They will save us now.

They were pushing and pounding him from every direction, asking questions he couldn't answer. He didn't have time to take stock of their desperation when the same feeling was oozing from his pores.

It was hot. God of the heavens and earth, it was hot. His neck and hands were slippery with sweat, the shirt he hadn't changed in three days was soaked through. He reeked like a wild animal and he was hungry. There wasn't a scrap of food within three square miles, not a drop of water to spare.

The sky had shriveled, hanging over them like a judgment, corrosive and dull.

The whole place was a rathole.

He didn't care about any of that. All he cared about in a rapidly shrinking world was four irrefutable realities. His mother, father, brother, and brother.

Was it twenty thousand people or thirty?

It felt like every person he had ever met in his life was here, every grandmother who had touched his hair, every girl he had flirted with in high school, every officer who had rotated in and out of this open jail. Yet each face had changed, condensed into a pair of terrified eyes and desiccated lips.

Everyone was carrying something, everyone was searching for someone. He couldn't help.

Even if he found someone he could use his translation skills on, there was nothing to say.

Today he had only one message to communicate, and he would sound it out over and over again, even if he had to wend his way through every last corridor of this concrete maze, breaking every window the mortars hadn't exploded. Even if he had to crawl over every single body jammed behind the gates that obliterated the name of the battalion stationed there.

He would find the major, take his gun and kill him if he had to.

Today, there was only one truth, one order that mattered. One thought that hammered him through the stench, the cries, the incremental terror.

His family was not leaving this base.

He heard a stranger's moan. "I'm not going to any safe place. The Serbs are going to take me."

From every direction he heard similar cries.

Noise. Chaos. Terror. Misery. Four words that now made up his world.

They had closed the gate. They had sealed the hole in the fence. What did the Dutch know that he didn't? There were some five or six thousand people inside the base, but how many more had been left outside? Fifteen thousand? Twenty? Where would those people go? What would they do when the enemy came?

He knew what the gate was. It was a dividing line between those who would live and those who would die. Inside the base was life. Outside, death.

He shoved his family forward. His mother complained and he pushed her harder. They had to get away from the gate. They had to push their way inside as far as the soldiers would let them. If he had to step on other people, if he had to crawl over their bodies he would. You didn't manage three and a half years without running water, electricity, or a steady supply of food just to give it all up at the end. He was valuable. He wasn't going anywhere. And neither was his family.

He expected bad things to happen. He had always expected them: the first shot fired in the war, the first mortar launched at Sarajevo, the first village burned and looted in the east, corpses piled high beside the rubble of the mosque.

Bad things had happened. Worse things were coming. The base was the only safety there was.

The Dutch were the only protection they had, the thin blue-helmeted line between survival and mass murder. He didn't care about the graffiti that marked their compound, adding insult to injury. He didn't care about the lies they had told him up to this very moment. He didn't care about anything except what their blue and white flag represented.

Safety. Survival. The chance to weather the siege for just another day.

He wouldn't think about the faces on the other side of the gate. He wouldn't think about the panic or the hopelessness in their eyes.

Noise. Chaos. Terror. Misery.

That was all there was. That's what he wouldn't think about.

He realized they'd reached the endpoint, his small desk just outside the major's office. He gave the chair to his mother and placed his youngest brother on the desk. Ahmo was a small, wiry thirteen. Malnourished and terrified but trying to hide it.

They were getting to the place where no one could hide anything anymore.

His father and his other brother, Mesha, paced nervously at the door. He knew they wanted cigarettes. He wanted one himself, the way he wanted other things. Water from the tap. A phone call to his girlfriend. An acre full of livestock.

Bread and circuses.

Nothing mattered except survival.

Mother, father, Ahmo and Mesha.

That was it.

The major came. He looked harried and angry. Preoccupied with his orders. Whatever he'd been expecting, it hadn't been this onslaught of refugees. Thirty thousand people at Potočari. Thousands and thousands outside the gate.

He could feel the sweat on his skin, taste the panic on his tongue.

"We waited all night," he said. "Where are the planes? The safe area is under attack. Srebrenica will fall."

The major ignored him, as he'd known he would. He was searching his office for something that didn't take him long to find. A megaphone. He handed it to Damir, his eyes skirting over his family.

"What's this for? What do you expect me to do?"

"We pay you to translate. So translate."

"We waited all night. Where are the planes?"

The major was sweating too, he saw.

"Tell the people they must leave the base. Tell them now, Damir. This is UN property."

"UN property?" *He spat out the words.* "Do you think we care if this is UN property? Do you understand what's waiting on the other side of the gate?"

"Tell them. They must leave in groups of five. They must leave now. We can't have the Serbs see them as provocation."

"Provocation? They see us as fodder. They see bodies, dead bodies. Fields and fields full of them. Are you crazy?" *he demanded.* "This base is the only thing keeping these people alive."

His voice ratcheted out of control. He could hear himself raving like a madman, spittle flying from his lips. The major backed away in distaste.

"Don't make me call my men, Damir. Tell the people to leave the base at once. Five at a time. Everyone must go."

"Now you want to call them? Now? Why don't you tell your men to guard the gate? Why don't you tell them to help the people come in? Why did you seal the fence?"

"Procedure."

Damir threw away the megaphone. "Your procedure will see us dead and buried in the ground. No, not in the ground. They'll shoot us where we stand and leave our bodies to rot. Have you seen what's happening at the gate? Have you?"

The major avoided his eyes. "If you won't translate, you have no purpose here."

"I work for you!" *Damir screamed.* "I've worked for you through this whole bloody mess, translating your lies, making your lives easier. You expect me to tell my people to march out the gate to their deaths? They're *separating the men and women at the gate. They've taken the men. Do you know what that means?"*

"They are screening for war crimes, that's all. There will be a prisoner exchange."

"Are you mad? Demented? Didn't you hear Mladić? He said we would have blood up to our knees. What do you think they're doing with the men? And not just the men but the boys? What do you think, Major? How many lies will you tell us?"

The major grabbed the megaphone and forced it back into his hand. *"If you won't translate my instructions, someone else will. But you'll have to leave. You're all going."* He pointed at Damir's father. *"He can stay. Your father is a negotiator. He can stay with you on the base. Everyone else must go."*

He now knew that terror had a color. A red as bright and immersive as blood. *"What about my mother? What about my brothers? If they go to the gate, they're as good as dead."*

"Everyone must go. No one has permission to stay on the base."

"They're not going. I won't let you take them."

There was no door that protected his small workspace. If there had been, he would have barricaded his family inside.

His father could see what was happening. And Mesha. He was nineteen. He didn't speak English but he could see what was coming, plain as day.

"Tell your family what I've told you." The major's voice was implacable.

All these months of indecision, and now at last the major had found his resolve.

"What is it? What's happening?"

He started to cry. There was nowhere else for his panic to go but tears. And when he started, Ahmo did as well. Huge, gulping sobs.

"You can stay, Father," he managed. *"He says you can stay but no one else."*

Mesha swore at him.

His father and mother stared at him without answer.

"They are making everyone leave the base. All of us. Except for the negotiators." He gestured at his father. *"And those who work here."*

"Negotiators—what a joke. We never had any power to negotiate. What are we negotiating? The manner of our death?"

At his brother's words, his mother began to cry.

His father pointed behind him. "I won't stay without Ahmo and Mesha. I won't let the Chetniks take them."

He turned to find that from among the crowded corridors of the base, the major had summoned three of his soldiers and three of the military observers, weapons at the ready.

"What in hell are you doing?"

"Your family will show the others. Tell them to leave."

Mesha rolled forward on his feet. Damir blocked him with an arm across his chest.

"Listen to me, Major, please! Don't make them go out there. Let them stay with me on the base! They won't take up any room. They don't need any rations. I won't tell anyone. Just let them stay. Let them stay, I beg you." His tears rained thick and fast, blurring his glasses.

"I've said your father can stay."

"He won't stay without my brothers," he shouted. "Can't you see what you're doing?"

"That's his choice. He doesn't have to stay if he doesn't want to. But General Mladić knows who he is."

"I know that! Do you think I don't know that? Please, Major!" His voice tore in his throat. He saw the decision in their faces, the inexorable reality. There was no weakening of the major's voice.

"Please, Major, just my brothers. Just Ahmo and Mesha. Don't send them to the gate. You know what's waiting on the other side of the gate."

The major turned away, nodding at his men. Damir latched on to his arm with desperate strength.

"Stop begging these bastards for me! I don't need you to beg for my life," Mesha said.

He swore at his brother over his shoulder. "Please, Major. This is all the family I have. I beg you, let them stay."

"Take them out."

The soldiers began to shepherd his family through the crowd.

He followed along, desperate, hysterical.

"Please. Just Ahmo then, just Ahmo. He's only a boy. He's only thirteen."

"Don't worry," one of the observers said to him. "They're not separating children."

"They are. Please. I know they are. Please. Leave Ahmo. Let Ahmo stay. I beg you. I'll give you anything. I'll do anything. I'll tell all these people to go. Just leave Ahmo."

They marched ahead without answering. His family trailed between them, a tiny rivulet dwarfed by mountains.

His father stopped for a moment, turned back.

"Please, Father, stay," he whispered. "Stay with me."

"I cannot leave your brothers. I must protect them from our enemies. You stay, Damir. You stay and look for us when you can. Look for us in Tuzla."

He saw death in his father's eyes. There would be no Tuzla.

For the thousands of men on the other side of the gate, there would be no Tuzla.

He knew at last what he must do.

"Wait!" He hurried along beside them, elbowing the same people he had treated so shamefully in his rush to reach safety. "If they won't let you stay, I'm coming with you. We'll go together."

His father's eyes were kind, so kind.

"You stay here, Damir. You'll be safe and I will know you are safe. Stay."

"I'm coming."

He'd known this day would come.

Cities falling, villages burning. Rape. Torture. Madness. Death.

This last day in Srebrenica had been inevitable from the beginning.

His right hand grasped Ahmo's. His arm brushed Mesha's.

Whatever happened, he would be with them. The last faces he saw would be theirs.

Three years in frantic pursuit of survival would end here.

Mesha took his arm.

"You are not coming."

"I am not staying."

"You are staying on the base," his brother screamed into his face. "You are staying because you can stay, that's the end to it!"

"I won't!" he screamed back.

"You will. You are."

He shoved Mesha aside. Mesha grabbed him by the neck and punched him in the face.

He fell back, stunned.

"Mesha!"

"You stay," his brother sobbed. "I will take care of Ahmo and our parents. You stay because you can stay." Mesha pulled him close, wrapped his arms about his neck, kissed his cheeks. He felt the hot wet slide of his brother's tears. "You live," he told Damir. "You live and you remember."

The soldiers pressed them forward.

He watched their silhouettes recede into the crush.

He looked down to find the megaphone in his hand.

25.

30 Dutch = 30,000 Muslims.

Khattak met Tom Paley at Café Morala on Bank Street. He'd wanted
to meet at Justice, but Tom had sidestepped him. Instead, he'd suggested a place away from his colleagues at War Crimes, this café
with its bohemian vibe and sinful Mayan hot chocolate. The proprietor's homemade black bean panini was legendary.

Khattak wasn't in the mood to eat. He ordered a strong cup of
coffee and waited for Tom in the café's sunny interior. His friend,
when he came, looked as disquieted as Khattak felt. He ordered the
panini from the menu and a small bag of alfajor Argentino cookies
to go with his hot chocolate.

"Everything here's homemade. You should try the cookies. They're
out of this world."

Khattak studied his friend's face. He'd always thought of Tom as
a comfortable man, energetic but running to fat, with a shiny pink
skull and an absentminded manner that fooled no one. His knowledge of his field was encyclopedic, his reputation international.

"We've a mess here, Tom. I hope you've found something."

"Immigration status." Tom bit deeply into his panini, its melted
cheese scouring his chin. He dabbed at it with his napkin. "He came
as an investor with the requisite funds tied up for a five-year period.
He landed as an Italian citizen with documents to suggest he was
the son of ex-pat Americans who made their home there."

"What do we know about the documents?"

"We've requested them. Immigration does its own check, as you know. Police clearances, provenance of funds. He ran textile factories in Italy to substantial profit. Based on his records, they thought the money was clean. We'll need to dig deeper now. The fact that they didn't means the passport forgery must have been first rate."

"He's had seventeen years to learn a new trade," Khattak said bitterly. "Easy enough to erase traces of a past life. What brought him here, I wonder?"

"Too many old associates in Italy, most likely. Too many people apt to recognize him or come calling for a share of the company's profits."

"Krstić wasn't the kind of man most people would dare to blackmail."

"The Drina Corps and the paramilitaries aren't what you'd call most people. Blackmail would be nothing to them. Krstić worked hard. He was a success. Most people don't and aren't, but they're happy to hitch a ride on someone else's coattails."

"This is all speculation on your part."

"True."

"He may have had personal reasons for moving to Canada."

"He hasn't been here long. Three years. Two at the present address, buried away at the edge of Scarborough. We haven't been able to trace any personal connections."

"Scarborough's not that remote. He's been keeping company with Nathan Clare. Although—" Khattak paused as he sifted through the facts he'd learned about Drayton's plans to marry Melanie Blessant. "His fiancée did point out that he was loath to sit for a well-known photographer. He may consciously have been attempting to shelter his new identity. Where was he for the first year?"

"Manitoba. What about this museum you've told me of? Wouldn't that raise his profile?"

Khattak sampled one of the cookies. It melted into his coffee, changing its flavor.

"It would have. If people were to associate a much older, much heavier man by the name of Christopher Drayton with a fugitive named Dražen Krstić. His contacts at the museum would have been limited to the intelligentsia."

"Then why not the wedding photos?"

"Maybe he was more afraid of local publicity. Krstić must have known there's a fairly significant Bosnian community in the city. He may have viewed a portrait in the wedding section of the paper as a danger to himself. Tom, I have to ask this. Why did you ignore the letters you were sent about Krstić?"

Tom finished his sandwich and turned his attention to the trio of teenage girls that spilled through the café's door into its warm interior. They jostled each other for seats, draping their handbags over wooden chairs before lining up in front of the chalkboard menu. They were pretty and lively; for a moment, everyone in the café stopped to watch them make their selections.

Tom sighed. "You know how this kind of work is, Esa. You've been in intelligence. You collect so much information, it takes time to sort through it all. We're understaffed, underbudgeted—I can't keep up with my correspondence. This didn't ring any bells. Typed letters in the mail. No prints, no DNA. No reason to think it was anything more than someone trying to work through their personal pain by casting about for answers. The letters were accusations, nothing more. There were no photographs, no proof. In time, I would have asked someone to do a little digging. The last letter made it a bit more urgent. It said that Krstić was dead."

"So you called me."

"I called you." Tom lingered over his chocolate-soaked cookies. "Because I could call you. Because your unit exists, and I couldn't think of anyone more closely connected who would know what to do with the information. And because that last letter worried me."

"Why?"

"It said: 'Krstić is dead. Everything is finished. I don't need you anymore.' And then the letters stopped. In my experience, when someone has a pathology, that doesn't happen. It made me wonder."

"You must have wondered before that."

Again, Tom sighed. "What do you want me to say? Sometimes we miss things. Can you say with certainty that Drayton is Krstić?"

"Come on, Tom. The tattoo and the gun make it certain. And you'll have used facial recognition on the photograph I had the morgue send you."

"Esa, this will be a terrible embarrassment for the government. For me, more than anyone." His evasion answered Khattak more effectively than an open admission would have. "Immigration at least did their due diligence. They only have so many resources."

"And the investment of half a million dollars may have dampened their enthusiasm for a more rigorous examination of Drayton's credentials."

"I don't think so, Esa. They've sent me everything they have. They didn't miss a single step. Drayton went to a lot of trouble to cover up his tracks."

Khattak wished he could feel more for his friend. He had other worries, other priorities. The teenage girls had taken the table beside them and chatted to each other noisily. He lowered his voice.

"Make the same arguments that Immigration will. Your resources were limited. The letter writer offered no proof, not even a photograph. If your letters are anything like ours, it was difficult to pinpoint the source of the writer's information. You can't be held accountable for that, Tom. What will matter is how swiftly you resolved things upon learning of Drayton's death. You called me right away. Based upon my findings, you've made major strides investigating Drayton's background. You've matched the photo. You know Drayton is Krstić."

Tom looked over at the table of girls wistfully.

"Yes. It is Krstić. And we'll have to announce it, and there could be hearings. Someone's job on the line. Maybe mine."

"Never yours, Tom. Not with your reputation. And frankly, shouldn't we be more concerned about the Bosnian community?"

Tom studied him as if seeing Khattak for the first time. "That is your remit," he agreed.

"My God, Tom! There's a limit to objectivity. Krstić was ubiquitous at the execution sites. He's knee-deep in blood."

"I'm not denying that, Esa. And I'm not asking you to do anything you shouldn't. All I need is a heads-up. If you're worried about the Bosnians, isn't it best that we coordinate our response? Or is something else bothering you?"

Khattak looked over at the table beside them in time to see the girl with long, blond braids widen her eyes at him.

"The letter writer worries me," Khattak said. "*Krstić is dead. I don't need you anymore.* Why? Because the letter writer killed him when the government wouldn't act?"

"Christ, are you laying that at my door?"

"Of course not. If he was killed by one of his victims, we have a much bigger problem on our hands. A trial, a scandal, the evacuation of Canbat revisited. All of that and more."

"There's something you're not telling me."

"Drayton wanted to get on the board of the museum, Ringsong. His presence was strongly objected to by one of the directors, a neighbor of Drayton's. I interviewed him during the course of the investigation. His name is David Newhall."

"So?"

"I was at the Bosnian mosque in Etobicoke yesterday. My sergeant found David Newhall's photo hanging there."

"What? Why?"

"Because his real name is Damir Hasanović."

The girls beside them forgotten, Tom stared at him, aghast. *"Damir Hasanović?"* he whispered.

"Exactly," Khattak said. "The translator at the UN base in Potočari. Dutchbat gave him refuge on the base. That's why he survived the Srebrenica massacre."

"It can't be."

"If you check with your friends at Immigration, I think you'll find he came here as a refugee."

The blond girl brushed her leg against his. She apologized brightly. He ignored it.

"That's not all. I think Newhall is the man who sent the letters to you and to Drayton."

"And Drayton is dead."

"Which means Dražen Krstić is dead."

"Damn," Tom muttered. "Goddamn it all."

"I think that sums it up."

"You need to interview him again."

"I plan to. Rachel's looking into his background. With CPS resources."

The two men weighed each other.

"But you'll let me know whatever you find."

"I won't forget that you asked me to investigate, Tom. Of course, I owe you that. I've a long drive back tonight. I'll call you with any news."

"It was good of you to do this for me."

Khattak's answering smile was brief. "I think you know I did it for myself."

26.

It was a crime committed against every single one of us.

Rachel was surprised to find her parents sitting together in the family room, a program on the television that her mother particularly favored. Her father wasn't napping, nor was there a beer on the coffee table in front of him.

"Hey, Da," she said, tossing her keys on the console in the tiny dark foyer. Winterglass, this was not.

"Where've you been then, girl?" he said in response.

She debated telling him. Sometimes hearing about Khattak made her father ballistic: he still thought of her boss as a politically correct, affirmative-action appointee to a unit whose purpose he'd once described as barefaced boot-licking. Once or twice, they'd been able to discuss the finer points of an investigation without it ending in tears or slammed doors or a shattered beer mug or two.

She brushed off her weariness and came to sit beside Don Getty. One part of her mind observed her mother's leery glance.

"Mostly up in Scarborough. Trying to figure out if some guy fell from the Bluffs or was pushed."

"The Bluffs, eh. You go by the marina?"

"I did, Da."

Her father was still a handsome man with bullet-gray eyes and a head full of thick white hair that stood on end when brushed. His jowls and neck were thicker because of the drinking, but his bearing was otherwise compact and upright. She had noticed more and more of late that his eyes were more likely to be alert than blurred by booze.

"Rachel," her mother intervened softly. "You shouldn't talk about the marina. You know how your Da is."

She hadn't mentioned the marina. Her father had. She wondered what had made her mother say it with that gently martyred air of hers.

The years had not worn well on Lillian Getty. Her wardrobe rotated through a series of faded-print dresses with full skirts and fitted tops. Occasionally, her lips would be smeared with a coral shade of lipstick that emphasized their thinness. Her dark eyes and lifeless hair were the same as Rachel's own. In Lillian's case, a permanent treatment had transformed it into a gauzy cloud about her head.

"Da likes the marina," she said to her mother. "He always has. He used to take me and Zach all the time."

She rarely mentioned her brother. She still hadn't told either of her parents that she'd found him. Over the past few days, she'd brought up his name in one innocuous context or another to test their reaction. For the most part, her father had ignored her. Her mother, however, had darted anxious glances at her, opening her mouth to speak before changing her mind.

"I did, girl, you remember that?"

Rachel patted her father's hand, another rare gesture.

"'Course. You taught Zach everything there was to know about boats. Sorry the water wasn't my natural element."

"Seasick. That's what you were. But you were a fine swimmer, Rach. Built like one of those East German girls."

She didn't bother to correct him. In his day, there had been an East Germany, and Don Getty hated to acknowledge change.

"Thanks, Da. It's helped me with hockey too."

"Strong shoulders. Nothing wrong with that. Don't let any man tell you otherwise."

"You know our Rachel doesn't date, Don."

It was another subtle put-down. A contradiction for its own sake, intended to annoy her father with little thought to Rachel's feelings. She'd never noticed this about her mother before. But then she'd been blind to her mother's seven-year secret.

"I would if the right guy asked me, Mum. I've met someone, actually."

Her father grinned at her. He wasn't used to her defiance of her mother. He was taking his own small pleasure in it. Christ, but her parents were messed up.

"Good-looker? Cop? Got some heft on him?"

"Be realistic, dear. Rachel has to take what she can get."

She'd been making it up, some hazy thought of Nate in her mind, but now she felt furious. What kind of mother said something like that to her daughter? In that moment, the meek and mild Lillian Getty reminded her of Melanie Blessant.

"I don't, actually, Mum. He's great-looking. And tough, Da. And smart as hell."

"You sure he's real?" Her father slapped her knee with a laugh. It was the big, blustery laugh she remembered from scarce moments during her childhood. It made her smile.

"I've pinched myself, I can tell you." She eased out of her blazer, folded it across her knees. "It's not serious. We've only just met. I'll let you know how it goes."

"How about some dinner then for our girl?" He narrowed his eyes at his wife. "You've been sitting there for hours doing nothing but turning pages."

Lillian coughed. "I did try to be quiet, dear. For Rachel? I don't think . . . I didn't make enough. She's usually not home."

Rachel was used to this. She lived under her parents' roof but was otherwise completely self-reliant. She took most of her meals on her way to or from a pickup game. She could see her father was getting angry. Best to defuse the situation at once.

"It's good, Da. I've got a game to get ready for and then I'll grab a bite. You know you can't load up on carbs right before a game."

"I know you would if you had a choice." He glared at his wife who held up her hands in dismay. Helpless, useless Lillian Getty. Or had that always been Rachel's own delusion? Had she missed the steely core that had allowed her mother to shield the only relationship whose loss she still grieved?

"Honestly, I'm okay. Thank you, though."

"You don't need to thank your father for watching out for you," Lillian snapped.

Rachel raised her eyebrows. What was this little game of her mother's? She had seen Lillian through the lens of helpless anger for so long that she'd assumed her mother possessed no agency of her own. She was Don Getty's passive foil, her moods conditioned by her husband's rage.

This wasn't the same woman, with her careful jabs and her sly taunts at Rachel.

This was a woman fully equipped to keep a devastating secret, playing some twisted game of revenge against her husband with no regard for the fact of Rachel's loneliness and guilt.

Was she nothing to either of them? Had Zach been everything?

Her mouth turned down. It was enough to know she had caused her mother's pain. It was too much to accept that her mother might wish to hurt her in turn.

Maybe the only way forward was to talk about Zach—to bring her brother out in the open.

"There's something I've been meaning to tell you, Da, about Zach."

"Rachel!" Her mother's voice shook the small room. "I've told you again and again not to upset your father."

It was true. It was the constant refrain of their childhood.

Children, hush. You're disturbing your father.

She must have had reasons that Rachel hadn't known, and still didn't know to this day.

Don Getty scowled at his wife but he stayed in his seat. "Let the girl talk. She's got something on her mind. You've been looking for the boy, I know. I've seen the posters."

Rachel swallowed. It was a day of sea changes, she thought. Before this moment, her father hadn't mentioned Zach in seven years.

"You've found him then."

Tears pricked at her eyes, muffled her throat.

"I didn't know you knew. That I'd been looking, I mean."

"Ah, girl. I'm not much use as a father but I know when my girl's upset. I know why, too."

It was the drink, she realized. Without the veil of alcohol between them, she could see her father as clearly and acutely as he was seeing her.

"Tell me then, Rach."

"She has nothing to tell. It's nothing but foolishness."

The television blared commercials in the background. She heard the anxiety ring clear as a bell in her mother's voice. And made the decision to continue.

"I've been looking and I found him. He's a student at university. A friend of mine recognized his name."

"University."

"Yes." Rachel gave him a tremulous smile. "He's a year from graduating, Da. He's studying art. He'll be going to Europe soon." She held her breath for the last part, afraid of his reaction.

Her mother stood up, her hands shaking. "You're lying," she breathed.

Rachel turned on her.

"You know I'm not, Mum. You *know* I'm not."

Her father disregarded this. His breath came out of his strongly built body in a collapsing whoosh of air. His shoulders sagged. He reached for the remote to shut off the sound from the television.

"He's well, then? My boy's well? He's happy?"

It was the last reaction she'd expected from him.

"Yeah," she said. "He's doing really well. He's not in any trouble or anything. He's really smart. He's standing on his own feet."

Her father turned his face away from her. She could see that his throat was working, choking on words.

"I'd tell you more if I could, I've only just seen him. I don't know very much. Shall I tell you if I see him again?"

Without speaking, he nodded his head.

She stood up, not knowing what else to say, and met her mother's gaze. All the fuzziness and weakness of will she'd associated with her mother evaporated under that gaze. What she saw was a woman, wretched and determined. For a moment, she couldn't speak.

Nothing made sense.

No one made sense.

She grasped at her game like a lifeline. "I'd better go up and change."

Her father brushed a hand over his eyes. He straightened his shoulders and turned the television back on. "You get ready, girl. I'll take you. It's been a while since I've seen you play. Left wing, aren't you?"

"That's right, Da. Are you sure?"

"Sure as sure."

As she turned to the stairs, she caught sight of her mother's reflection in the mirror above the console.

She mouthed six words at Rachel, each as clear as daylight.

You don't know what you've done.

Shocked, Rachel flew up the stairs to her room.

27.

When I close my eyes, I don't see the men.

In fourteen days, Srebrenica will be gone.

Rachel parked in the driveway of the blue and white house at the corner of Sloley Road and Lyme Regis. It was a plain two-story with a double garage, its shutters painted periwinkle blue, its white siding crisp and fresh. The maple that bordered the sidewalk was still aglow with autumn loveliness. The lawn was covered with unraked leaves.

A wreath hung above the letter slot on a plain blue door.

She paced the sidewalk waiting for Khattak. Dec and Gaffney had compiled a first run of background information on David Newhall for her; the house on Lyme Regis belonged to him.

She considered its geography off Cathedral Bluffs. Here was another neighbor of Drayton's. A neighbor of Winterglass and Ringsong. The house was a little further back from the escarpment. A neighborhood or two away from Melanie Blessant. A small stage for the actors of this drama. Significant? She couldn't tell.

David Newhall was a legal name change, unlike Christopher Drayton's alias.

She understood now that Newhall's clipped manner of speaking had been an attempt to mask his accent. He'd come to Canada just after the fall of Srebrenica, legally, as a Convention refugee. He'd changed his name two years ago. Around the same time he'd moved into this neighborhood. Before that, he'd lived alone in a small apartment not far from the mosque.

If their last visit with Imam Muharrem hadn't ended on such bad terms, she would have sat him down for a lengthy discussion on the true identity of David Newhall.

Masks, she thought. First Drayton, then Newhall.

It struck her that in the short time since she'd met Nathan Clare, whom she viewed as a touchstone, she'd been the audience to a pantomime. Players moving together and apart in a complex orchestration.

That was one thing she'd learned from studying Damir Hasanović's file.

Newhall was the one who'd sent the letters.

She gave a slight wave as Khattak pulled up on the driveway beside her. They'd talked on the phone in the morning. She'd given her report on Newhall, he'd told her what Justice had found. Justice had a statement prepared. They were holding off on the announcement until Khattak's investigation turned up a result.

Time was definitely not on their side.

If Drayton had been pushed, she hardly expected Newhall to own up to it.

If he *had* assisted Drayton to his death, sent the letters, planted the lilies, she couldn't say she blamed him. Newhall's account of survival was harrowing, his losses inestimable.

When the Serbs took Srebrenica, they wiped from the earth three generations of men.

She envisioned grandfathers, grandchildren. Rows upon rows of exiguous green coffins, wept over by the wretched. The resting place of the men of Srebrenica.

The unquiet dead and those who mourned them.

How had she become one of them?

Her Da had always said of her that her problem wasn't that she thought too much. Her problem was that she felt too much.

As well as she could, she understood Newhall's anger, his terse dismissal. He'd not only had something to hide—he'd had to suppress his tragedy in its entirety.

The young boys were crying out for their parents, the fathers for their sons. But there was no help.

She understood the letters with perfect clarity now, the chronicle of the fate of Newhall's family. Zach had been resurrected after seven pitiless years. Newhall held no such hope.

"This doesn't feel right, sir."

"I know, Rachel, but we need to see this through."

He moved to the door and rang the bell, his elongated shadow falling across the lawn. Rachel's steps crunched over the leaves.

When Newhall opened the door, she had the same impression of jittery energy as before. He ushered them into a parlor with the jumpy movements of a cat, nervy and quick-jawed. The room was simply furnished with a white chesterfield and a pair of suede armchairs placed beneath two windows. Late-afternoon light threw shadows upon a worn Turkish rug with a geometric pattern. Newhall took a seat in the corner that left him in darkness. He didn't offer refreshments.

He focused on Rachel.

"Have you learned anything?"

This time she caught it. The hint of a foreign pattern of speech: she would have guessed it as Russian.

"We've learned a great deal, sir. We know who you are, for example."

He straightened in his seat. Beyond his shoulder, she glimpsed a dining table piled high with stacks of file folders.

"What do you mean? I've told you who I am."

"Your name is Damir Hasanović, isn't it?"

"If you look at my driver's license, you will see my name is David Newhall."

"You're denying it, then?"

"There is nothing to deny. It was a perfectly legal name change."

He leaned forward and placed his hands on his knees, composed and at ease.

He'd been waiting for this moment, she realized. Anticipating the confrontation.

Khattak spoke. "Mr. Hasanović, you changed your name to Newhall two years ago. Why?"

"It was a fad. It seemed to be going around."

Rachel sucked in a breath. "Then you knew about Drayton."

"Christopher Drayton, Dražen Krstić. I knew the moment I first laid eyes on him. So?"

"When was that, sir?"

"At Clare's house. Two years ago. Before I moved here."

"And why did you move here?"

He shrugged. "I like the Bluffs. I like to walk along the escarpment." He threw down the words like a challenge.

"Did you ever confront Mr. Drayton with your knowledge?"

"I did not. Next question."

"Why not?"

"I thought there were other avenues. As a Canadian, I imagined I might have some recourse to justice." He stressed the last word.

"You sent the letters to War Crimes," Rachel concluded.

"Yes. Nothing came of it."

"Yet you never accused Drayton directly."

"I did not wish to precipitate his flight."

"He might have fled if he'd known who you were."

He flashed them a wolf's smile, his teeth small and dangerous. "It was one of the wonders of Potočari. Thousands of people desperate for security. How could Krstić notice them all the way we noticed him? He had no reason to know me. We'd never met."

"But you knew him."

"Wouldn't you like to ask me how?"

Rachel cleared her throat. "Will you confirm that he was in fact Dražen Krstić?"

Newhall laughed. "Does my confirmation matter? Have you not seen the tattoo on his hand? Are you asking me if Krstić was there? In Srebrenica, at Potočari? Is that what you want to know?"

She looked at Khattak. He motioned her on.

"Was he?"

"Ah. You are asking me how I recognized him. Was it from his Chetnik tattoo? His military haircut? His thick, squat neck? Was he there when they ordered my mother and father from the base at Potočari? Did he give the order to shoot my brother Mesha? Was he there when they took Ahmo away for questioning? Was it he who guaranteed our safety if our weapons were surrendered? Was it Krstić who promised a prisoner exchange?" He stared into the distance. "They gave us no prisoners, just bones. But not Ahmo's bones. Not Ahmo. No one can tell me where his bones lie."

"Mr. Newhall—"

"Call me Damir, dear Sergeant. It must be confusing for you. Christopher, Krstić. David, Damir. I think on the whole I prefer my Bosnian name. They've erased everything else. But you haven't come about that, have you? You want to know how I recognized this man who lived here so safely, so sweetly undetected. Was he there at the base, is that right? Do I recognize him from the gate? Or is it from the execution sites that I remember him? Was he at the famous white house for the torture and beatings? Or was he with the bulldozers they brought in to cart away the corpses? Or at the factory during the night, smoking and laughing when they took away the girls for the evening rapes? Did I recognize him? Yes, I knew his face. I will never forget his face. What does any of it matter now? Didn't he fall from the cliffs? After his successful retirement in this safest of havens?"

How could we know that the little towns would fall and we would run out of these sacred havens?

Without a doubt, Newhall was the letter writer. She couldn't think what to say, so she left it to Khattak to ask, "Did he, Damir? Did Dražen Krstić fall to his death? Or did you help him?"

"I would not help him to anything." His contempt was obvious. He'd said his piece. The energy drained out of him. He leaned back in his chair, his hands limp upon his lap. Rachel noticed a photograph on the table beside the lamp.

She gestured at it. "May I?" Newhall flicked the switch. He handed her the photograph.

An elderly couple sat on a sofa surrounded by their painfully thin sons. The father wore the kind of cap she'd seen Khattak wear at prayer. A kerchief was knotted over the woman's faded hair. The boys were watchful, hollow-eyed.

"My brothers. The last photograph. The last I have of anything. The bones of my parents were identified in 2010. I went home for the fifteenth anniversary of the massacre to organize their funeral prayers. You could see the green coffins for miles, it seemed. The earth was thick with them."

He said it without blinking. His eyes were dry.

"Of Mesha and Ahmo, I have only this photograph. Their bones are cold. Where were they murdered? How were they killed? Where do they lie? This photograph cannot answer me. Beside my father and mother, their graves are waiting. Do you think Krstić knew? Do you think he could have told me?"

Is there any hope for at least that little child they snatched away from me, because I keep dreaming about him?

Why was she crying when Damir Hasanović wasn't?

"Did you ask him?"

He seemed surprised at her tears.

"He wouldn't have known. He gave orders, he supervised execution sites. He wouldn't have known a single one of our faces. *Balija* were all the same to him."

She palmed her face with her hand, deeply embarrassed. "You wrote him letters," she said. "In your letters, did you ask him?"

All the men of our family were killed. I can read you the list of their names.

I realized then that nothing good was in store for us in Potočari.

"What letters?"

"You sent letters to Dražen Krstić. Dozens of them. And you planted the Bosnian lily in his garden to remind him."

"Ah. His garden. His small, safe haven." When Newhall smiled his knife-blade smile, she felt her blood run cold. "Do you think a man with his finger on a trigger that killed thousands of Bosnians needed a reminder? Did he feel haunted? I doubt it, Sergeant."

"You've admitted you sent letters to the Department of Justice."

"Justice." He rolled the word over his tongue. "How swiftly such a word loses its meaning."

"Look, sir. I know you've spent nearly twenty years trying to get justice for your people. I know you've testified in case after case at the Tribunal. We know about your work with the Mothers of Srebrenica. You've brought lawsuits against the Dutch government. How could you throw that away for one man? Especially a man like Dražen Krstić."

"*Your* government was never going to see justice done. You preached peacekeeping at us while practicing cowardice. We remember your secret pact to evacuate your battalion from Srebrenica by stealth, leaving my people defenseless. It was your representative, Mr. Mac-Kenzie, whose claims about 'ancient ethnic hatreds' satisfied so many. Let the savages fight it out. Except they wouldn't let us fight. They tied our hands and left us to die."

"I'm not sure what you mean, sir."

"The arms embargo," he said wearily. "What else would I mean?" A brief hint of calculation appeared on his face. "Or is it possible you think I meant something else? The day of the fall. The day that dawned without the airstrikes the UN had promised when the Serbs rolled their tanks into 'safe area' Srebrenica. The day the killing began."

Where are the planes? When will they strike?

What further proof did she need?

"You sent the letters to Krstić."

"Did I? Can you prove such a thing?"

"Are you denying it? Everything you've told us comes straight from those letters."

"Does it? Do the letters mention Ahmo and Mesha? Do they tell you that Ahmo was only thirteen years old?"

"Well, no—but everything else."

Hasanović shrugged. "As far as I'm aware, Christopher Drayton fell from the Bluffs, a dangerous place to walk at the best of times. I can't help you with anything else."

"You moved here two years ago, is that correct?" Khattak interjected.

"Yes. As I said, I like this neighborhood."

"Just after Drayton moved here," Khattak noted. "Why did you leave the Bosnian community? You were heavily involved with the mosque in the past."

Hasanović paused. "There's no law I'm aware of that requires Bosnians to live in ethnic ghettos or religious cantons. At least, not in this country."

"Please answer the question."

Hasanović sized him up, his hooded eyes sharp. "My community has rebuilt. They've found a place for themselves—a way to struggle back to some form of happiness. I have nothing to rebuild."

"Where were you on the night that Drayton fell?"

"At a meeting about the museum. At Ringsong. Anyone will tell you."

"Why did you change your name? Was it to hide your identity from Dražen Krstić until you could find an opportunity for vengeance?"

Hasanović stood up and took the photograph of his family back from Rachel. "Do you think my life's work has been about vengeance? That I feed myself on the same delusions as the fascists?" Misery twisted his mouth. "I changed my name so I could forget who I am. For some, memories are a homeland, a palace. For me they are a prison—a graveyard." He touched his fingers to his youngest brother's face, his dark gaze turned inward. "It's my curse not to forget." His face crumpled. "Will you go? Please just go."

They left him in the shadows, the photograph clutched in his hands.

Rachel's hands shook as she let herself into her car. Khattak paused by her window.

"Was he telling the truth?" She looked up, but Khattak's face was in the shadows. "He never confronted Drayton? He never told him who he was?"

"The man I know Hasanović to be would not stand idly by if he learned a war criminal was living down the street from him. The name change suggests he was biding his time, hiding from Krstić."

"He denies sending the letters."

"I'm not sure that I believe him."

"What about the lilies?"

"He didn't deny that."

"He called the garden a haven. It wasn't his only use of the word."

"He was mocking us. The same way he kept saying 'safe area Sre-brenica.' One of six safe havens."

"Christ."

"Indeed. We can't talk here. And we should talk to Nate about what we've learned."

She perked up at once. She wanted to see Nate again, to see if that nebulous connection she'd imagined between them was anything more than wishful thinking on her part. She glanced sideways at Khattak, assuming a neutral expression. He wanted to say something to her, she could tell. And then her hopes were dashed as Khattak took a call, his shoulders tensed against the news. From two blocks away, she heard the sirens.

"Change of plans," he said. "There's been an incident with Melanie Blessant."

28.

Any rape is monstrously unacceptable but what is happening
at this very moment in these rape and death camps is even
more horrific.

Two cars were parked on the road outside the Blessant house. One
belonged to Dennis Blessant. The other was a police cruiser. Khattak
went over to talk to their colleagues. Melanie stood just outside the
front door that hung askew in its frame, her arms crossed over her
overflowing chest.

Dennis Blessant and the girls waited by his car with Marco River.
There were scratch marks on the man's face, but he wasn't in handcuffs. Hadley stood in an unconscious imitation of her mother's posture, wrinkling the rose-colored dress she wore. Her hair was pinned
up. Cassidy was similarly attired in blue. Both girls looked lovely.

"What's going on?"

"You're cops? Why do we need more cops?" Dennis Blessant asked
them.

"We're here on another matter. We're investigating the death of
Christopher Drayton." She took note of Hadley's pallor, of Cassidy
biting her knuckles. "You're Dennis Blessant?"

"I try not to acknowledge it on days like these."

"Your wife called the cops on you? Did you get physical with
her?"

"Good God, no." He hesitated. "Just with the house."

"I called them," Hadley said. "He came to pick us up and give us a ride to our dinner. Mad Mel lost control of herself. She attacked him. I called them so we could get on with our night."

"Hadley," Cassidy whimpered. Tears slid down her face, leaving a trail through the powder she'd applied. "Don't say too much."

Hadley bent down to adjust the strap on a high-heeled shoe. "I'm not letting people think Dad's a wife-abuser. That's exactly what Mad Mel wants."

"Mum, Hadley. Mum."

The gentle correction softened her older sister. She signaled to Riv. He put his arm around Cassidy's shoulder and led her across the street.

"Christ. She does this every time I come to get the girls."

"You share custody, Mr. Blessant?"

His laughter was harsh. "I try to share it. She'd suffocate my girls if she could." He said it loudly enough for his ex-wife to hear. Raging, she flew across the lawn at him. Khattak intercepted her, receiving the full impact of her overblown frontage.

"Inspector," she bleated. "You have to help me—Dennis was threatening me."

"God, Mel. More lies? I've warned you to be careful about Dad. You need to stop the lies."

The woman would have jumped on Hadley if Khattak's grip had let her.

"You have to believe me, Inspector. He hates me and he hated Chrissie. They fought, did you know that? The night that Chrissie fell. Maybe Dennis pushed him just to get at me. Because he knew Chrissie loved me and wanted to take care of me like he couldn't."

Khattak released her. "Is that true, sir?"

Hadley looked between her father and mother, her face ashen.

"Of course it's not true! That man was saving my life. He was taking this witch off my hands. No more alimony. No more child support."

"I knew it!" Melanie shouted. "I knew this whole 'I love my girls' thing was a lie! You wanted Chrissie to take them over. You wanted them off your hands!"

A tearing sob escaped Hadley's throat. She shoved past her mother into the house.

"You useless bitch. You don't know anything. I argued with Drayton because he wouldn't agree to marry you unless I gave you full custody of Hadley and Cass. I told him that would never happen. I begged him to marry you anyway."

"You're lying!" she shrieked. If she could have bulldozed her way past Khattak, Blessant would have been on the ground, shielding himself from the fury of her nails. "The only thing Chrissie *wanted* was to marry me! You wouldn't let him. You wanted to keep me in this rathole forever."

Dennis wiped a hand over his face, agog. "You're a lunatic. Do you hear yourself? I went down on my knees and thanked God the day you met Drayton. You couldn't marry him fast enough for me."

"You followed him." She was howling at him now. "You followed him to the Bluffs and you shoved him over. Maybe you did it because you wanted me to be miserable. Maybe you did it to show you can still control me. Or maybe you did it because you knew Chrissie was a thousand times the father you are. You knew he'd get the girls if I pushed for it."

Just as Rachel stepped forward to intervene, Hadley rocketed out of the front door and threw herself between her parents. She held a large envelope in her hands that she waved at them.

"Your goddamned lies." She swore at her mother. "I warned you, Mel. Don't say I didn't warn you." She upended the contents of the envelope over the lawn. "There's your Chrissie. There's the bastard you wanted to marry. And you're the one who knew about his will. You're the one who followed him. If anyone pushed him, you did."

"No!" Cassidy's wail reverberated across the street.

"I'm sorry, Cass, I'm sorry. But it's true, it's all true."

Rachel stared at the contents of the envelope with horror, Dennis

Blessant slack-jawed beside her. Hadley had scattered documents and photographs across the lawn between her parents. Rachel slipped on her gloves and knelt on the grass to collect them.

Some of it was pornography. The most depraved and violent pornography she'd come across: terrified women tied up, threatened and debased by knives and guns and other implements of torture. Cross-cutting these were Polaroids. Close-ups of Hadley and Cassidy in their beds at Krstić's house, sleeping. He had drawn their covers aside and photographed their legs, their breasts. There were photographs of Hadley and Cassidy coming out of the shower, their hair wet, their towels slipping.

Bile rose in her stomach.

"Sir," she said to Khattak. Blessant tried to take the photographs from her. She blocked him.

"I'm sorry, sir, these are evidence."

"My girls," he whispered. "My girls. Hadley, did he—?"

"No," she said quickly. "My God, no, Dad. I never would have let him. I never left him alone with Cassie for a second. But Mel was willing to. She couldn't see what was right in front of her face." Her voice dripped with contempt.

Rachel felt sick. A fifteen-year-old girl was talking about her mother.

"What do you mean?"

"I knew what kind of a man he was when he called my mother a whore every night," Hadley said with disgust. "'Shut up, you stupid whore. Take it, you filthy whore.' And still she kept pushing him for a wedding date."

"He loved me," Melanie said blankly. "He loved me and I loved him. I don't care what they say he did. He didn't do it."

Hadley grabbed her by the shoulders and screamed into her face. "He was a war criminal, Mother! *Christopher Dražen Krstić!* He killed people. He raped them. Didn't you ever ask yourself why he wanted us at his house? Didn't you ever wonder why he insisted you get sole custody? Didn't you see the pictures?" Her face was soaked with tears. She wiped her nose with the sleeve of her dress.

"No," Melanie whispered. "It's not what you're saying. He was a family man. You're making this all up."

With a swift movement, Rachel blocked Dennis Blessant's sudden lunge.

"Why won't you believe me?" Hadley released her grip on her mother's arms and turned away. "You're my mother. Why would I lie to you?"

Melanie hesitated. "You don't want me to be happy." But her voice lacked conviction. She made a tentative gesture to reach for her daughter, then dropped her hands. "It's just a misunderstanding," she said. "You misunderstood him."

"I didn't, Mum." She hadn't used this name for her mother in years, Rachel was sure. "Honestly, Mum—I didn't." She sank down onto the grass, crying.

Rachel couldn't bear it.

"Sir," she said again.

Khattak motioned the officers from the scout car over. "Take them in," he said of the Blessants. "To separate rooms. We'll meet you there." He looked at Rachel. The color had left his skin, a green tinge beneath its surface. "We'll need someone to stay with the girls."

Rachel swallowed her nausea. This was the last moment in the world to rely upon Mink Norman. She watched him make his call, rose from her knees, and awkwardly gathered Hadley into her arms. Hadley didn't resist. After a moment, she rested her head on Rachel's shoulder.

Riv brought Cassidy back from across the street and all three of them hugged each other.

Hadley gripped Rachel's wrist. She motioned at her sister. "Don't let her see," she mouthed.

Rachel shoved the envelope under her blazer.

Khattak patted Marco River's arm.

"Audrey Clare is coming," he said quietly. "She'll take you to Winterglass. Stay there, won't you?"

Riv stared at him, man-to-man. "I won't leave until you say it's okay."

He took Rachel aside. "We'll need to get someone from Crisis Response up there, but for now Audrey will be able to handle things. What she does with her NGO is mainly social work."

He could still surprise her.

"And what about us, sir?"

"Was the will among those documents?"

"Yes."

"Then let's begin with Ms. Blessant."

29.

We saw them rape the hadji's daughter—one after the other, they raped her. The hadji had to watch too. When they were done, they rammed a knife into his throat.

Khattak didn't want to talk to this woman. He loathed her. Charles Brining had been right. There was nothing about Chris Drayton's past that Melanie hadn't known. She just hadn't cared.

He thought of Hadley and Cassidy, their luxurious youth and innocence. Their devotion to their father. He rued a system that left them under the negligent care of a woman like Melanie. The photographs sickened him. They weren't something Drayton had purchased off the Internet and hoarded like a treasure. They were personal, intimate. Photographs Drayton had either taken himself or had his subordinates take for him. The women were Bosnian. The photographs were from rape camps.

Khattak had had them copied and dusted for prints. Tomorrow he would send them to Tom Paley with an urgent request that they be forwarded to the tribunal at the Hague. For the twenty thousand rapes that had been reported during the war, much less than the actual number that had taken place, fewer than forty men had been sentenced—less than a handful of these at the international tribunal. Perhaps the photographs would bring other men to justice. After that, he fervently prayed they would be destroyed.

"You knew the code to Drayton's safe?"

He was as far across the room from Melanie as possible. Rachel sat opposite her at the small table in the room. Melanie didn't bother with deception.

"Yes. I watched him open it once."

"You took the envelope from the safe? That's how you knew about the will?"

"I didn't take it. I just happened to see it in there once. I had a look."

"So you knew he was leaving everything to you."

"So what?" She sniffed. "I loved Chrissie. I wanted to marry him. He was no good to me dead."

"I think you'll find that's true, given his real identity. His policies will be void, his assets frozen until their provenance is determined."

"Come again?" All pretense of kittenish helplessness dropped from her manner at this threat to her windfall.

"His money. It's likely not his to leave. The bequests from his will won't be paid out. Tell me, Ms. Blessant. If you didn't take the envelope from the safe, how did Hadley come to have it?"

Melanie's face reflected her indecision about Hadley's revelations. "She just told you. She was spying on us. That's probably how she figured out the code."

"Her prints weren't on the safe."

This time her answer came quickly. "I like to keep it clean in there."

"Did you see what else was in the envelope?" Rachel asked. "The photographs, the letters to Dražen Krstić?"

Melanie arranged her breasts on the table like two giant lumps of unbaked bread. Rachel backed away. Melanie's façade was beginning to splinter: there were cracks at the line of her jaw, cords that stood out against her neck, white lines in her suntanned cleavage. The faintest blur of mascara discolored the pits beneath her eyes.

"I told you, it was just the one time. I had a quick look."

Rachel very much doubted that that had been Melanie's only incursion into Drayton's privacy.

"You saw the photographs," she insisted.

"What of it?"

Rachel wanted to smack her self-satisfied face. "What of it? Ms. Blessant, those were photographs of your daughters in various states of undress."

"No," she denied immediately. "He loved them. They're just pictures of the girls asleep."

Khattak jerked forward. "Do you really believe that? After everything your daughter just said to you?"

"Oh honey," the woman said. "You don't think it's possible Hadley was looking for a little attention? Because her father doesn't give her enough?"

And Rachel saw how the woman had already orchestrated an alternate scenario in her mind—one that renewed her vendetta against her husband at the expense of Hadley's need for solace and support. That fleeting moment when Melanie Blessant had truly seen her daughter had already passed.

"You can't honestly believe your daughters weren't at risk."

Melanie stared at her, gritty-eyed. "He was a good man. His interest in them was harmless."

Rachel nearly choked. The woman's need to believe in Drayton's single-minded adoration of her had made her blind to everything else.

"Did you find the other photographs harmless as well? Considering their connection to Dražen Krstić?"

She shrugged, the movement rippling through her breasts like an underwater wave. "What man doesn't hold on to a little pornography? Why would I care about that? And who the hell was Dražen whatever to me? No one."

"Not quite," Rachel said. "He was an indicted war criminal, a fugitive from justice. That wasn't pornography you were looking at. It was evidence of his crimes."

"Don't kid yourself, honey. It was women tied up. Or don't you know that most men are into a little kink?"

Rachel wanted to slap her. "You evidently did. Weren't you worried about your daughters in view of the 'kink' your boyfriend was into?"

"Fiancé," she corrected automatically. Her gaze stroked over her sumptuous figure in the mirror behind Khattak's head. "Why would I worry? I could handle anything he wanted."

In a clinical voice, Khattak asked, "You didn't feel a responsibility to protect Hadley and Cassidy from his appetites?"

"I've told you before. The only one Chrissie wanted was me. Hadley's never had that kind of attention from a man—you can't blame her for feeling a little jealous."

It was obvious that she believed this. Rachel didn't know if that increased or lessened her disgust. In her own twisted way, was this how Melanie found common ground with her daughter? Because nothing they were saying about Dražen Krstić was getting through to her.

"Ms. Blessant, did you see your husband follow Mr. Drayton to the Bluffs the night that he fell?"

"I heard the fight. I was with Chrissie that night."

"But not when he went to his walk."

"He asked me to leave. He said his mood was off after Dennis. He wanted to be alone."

"So you didn't see your ex-husband follow him."

"No. But I know he did. He won't rest until he's ruined everything for me."

"You're referring to his desire for custody."

"Yes."

"Then you did know that you and your daughters were a package deal for Drayton."

"You're turning it into something it wasn't. We both knew he'd make a better father for them than Dennis."

Khattak left it. "Did you light candles that night before your ex-husband arrived?"

"Are you crazy? In this heat?"

"It's been raining off and on for the past two weeks."

"Even if it was, it was sweltering."

"You didn't mention any of this to us before."

"You didn't ask. Say," she said, lively with a new thought. "This would be news, wouldn't it? Big news? Who Chrissie really was? The kind of news the papers pay big money for? If they're going to freeze Chrissie's assets, I mean."

She had already forgotten her daughter's anguish.

Revolted, Rachel opened her mouth to speak. Khattak swiftly forestalled her.

He leaned down toward the table, faced Melanie head-on. "Ms. Blessant, I find you appalling."

And when that came up in the inevitable complaint against CPS, Rachel would swear on her life that Khattak had never said it.

"Shall we drive you back to your car, Mr. Blessant?"

"Call me Dennis. You're not keeping me here?"

"We only brought you here to spare your daughters any further unpleasantness."

Dennis barked out a laugh. "That's one word for it, I suppose. My ex doesn't exactly scream maternal devotion from the rafters."

"If you were so poorly matched, why did you marry her?" Rachel asked.

"For the same reason men do most stupid things. She has a great body. I thought that was enough. I had money. She thought that was enough."

He followed them to Khattak's car, settling into the backseat. "I was supposed to take my girls to a dinner tonight. I doubt they're in any shape for it now."

"They're up at Mr. Clare's house. You can ask them, if you like."

He'd been about to leave off his seat belt, then thought better of it. "Cops, right? Look—Mel wasn't always as bad as she is now. She was good to the girls, at first. She treated them like little dolls. When we split up, she took it pretty hard. I would have said that half of what she says and does to the girls is to punish me. It isn't about them. They're her daughters. At some level, she loves them."

Rachel picked on his choice of words. "Would have said?"

"The photographs, Christ, the photographs. What the hell was he? Some kind of pedophile?"

"We don't know. We don't know how deep his perversions ran. He was a sadist, without doubt."

"So Hadley wasn't kidding. He really did call her mother a whore." He sat up straight. "Did he hurt my girls? Did the bastard touch them?"

"We don't know, sir. This is the first we've heard of any of this."

"But you were at our house. Looking into him and Mel. What did Hadley mean when she called him a war criminal?"

Rachel eyed him uneasily. "We're not at liberty to discuss that, sir. It's best if you just focus on your girls for the present."

They pulled up beside his car.

"Mr. Blessant, would you hold up a moment?" Khattak said. "Your ex-wife said that you argued with Drayton on the night of his death. On what subject?"

Dennis fumbled for his car keys. It had been easier to talk to the woman. She looked tough, but her manner was kind. He didn't trust Khattak's courteous detachment.

"Like Mel said. About the girls. He tried to convince me to give Mel full custody." He shuddered. "Thank God I said no. It would always have been no. I'd been counting the days until Drayton took Mel off my hands. I knew the girls would choose to come to me then. Hadley always wanted to, she just wouldn't leave Cassie behind. Thank God," he said again. "Thank God she was watching out for my baby. What the hell was Mel thinking? If she knew about Drayton, how could she have ever let him near the girls?"

Rachel was still wondering the same thing. "I think Ms. Blessant was so focused on getting Drayton to marry her that she didn't pay attention to anything else. What we don't know is why. Was her spousal support insufficient?"

Dennis gave his bark of laughter again. "Mel has expensive tastes. She runs through her monthly allotment in a couple of days. Then she spends the money that's meant for the girls. She always wants more.

I gave her money to buy the girls new laptops for school, clothes, other supplies. Mel burned through it all. Since then, I've given Had the money directly. It turned her mother against her, but Hadley's tough." He said the last sentence uncertainly, his voice trailing into silence.

From the shock that made his face sag, she knew he was thinking about the night's revelations. About Hadley and Riv working to shield Cassidy. About Hadley making horrific discoveries and having to contend with them on her own.

"Ms. Blessant knew about Drayton's will. Did you, sir?" Khattak's face gave nothing away. It expressed no more than a mild interest in his answer.

Dennis tried to think. "I didn't. I would never have asked him such a personal question and Mel had no reason to tell me." He flapped large white hands at them. "You have to believe me. I didn't know about any of this. Drayton was worth a hell of a lot more to me alive than dead."

"What about the custody issue?"

"I never thought he was serious. I thought he was trying to make things easier for Mel, trying to show everyone what a nice guy he was. He *was* a nice guy. He was always agreeable. The custody issue was the first sticking point, but I thought we'd both cool off and talk things through sensibly. I wasn't worried. I was relying on Hadley to convince Cass that her home was with me. That the three of us belonged together."

Both parents had relied on Hadley's common sense and toughness altogether too much, Rachel thought. But one was a man who loved his daughters, the other a woman who balked at seeing reality for what it was.

"Where did you go after the argument with Mr. Drayton?"

"I drove home. I was angry, I had to get out of there." Then he realized what he'd said. "Not like that. I'd been so certain that everything was about to turn around and the news that it wasn't came as a bit of a shock. I needed time to think out a strategy."

"Where was Ms. Blessant while the two of you were arguing?"

Dennis grimaced in disgust. "Upstairs. Preparing her boudoir, as she calls it. Making herself available to Drayton."

"And the girls?"

"At home. Christ! I can't believe I let them stay over there. Anything could have happened to them."

"It didn't, Mr. Blessant. It's likely that Drayton was waiting for the marriage and your wife's permanent move to his house. He wouldn't have wanted to risk jeopardizing his access to the girls."

She had meant it be comforting. She could see from his face that it wasn't.

Khattak's phone rang. He murmured something into it and waited.

"The girls can stay with the Clares tonight, if you'd like."

"No." Dennis made a visible effort to pull himself together. "They're my daughters, I'm responsible for them. They'll need me. Especially after tonight."

Khattak spoke into the phone again and shut off the call.

"Audrey Clare is a social worker. I'd ask her advice, discreetly, on what tack to take with the girls. I'm sure you'll find her some help to you. We can also arrange for a social worker to come to your house, if you prefer."

Dennis stopped his frantic hunt for his car keys. He could see that they genuinely meant to be helpful. In these few minutes with him, they'd expressed more concern for Hadley and Cassidy's welfare than Mel had done since their divorce. The realization hit him like a sucker punch.

"I appreciate it," he said, quieted.

"We'll need to talk to your daughters at some point, sir."

"Fine. When they're ready. And in my presence, is that clear?"

Rachel liked him a little more. "Of course, sir."

They watched him drive away.

"What now, sir?" she asked. "Nice work with Mad Mel, by the way. Appalling isn't the word I'd have used, though."

A hint of humor appeared on Khattak's face. "I know. That's why I said it. Before you could say something else."

"We could charge her with child endangerment."

"Think of what that would do to the girls," he advised. "All we need is the threat of action. If she persists in denying Blessant custody of their daughters, we can threaten her with criminal charges. She may not have believed that Drayton was a predator, but she should at least have come forward with what she did know."

"That's blackmail, sir."

"I doubt she'll fight us. She has other worries to focus on now. Like how she'll manage without Drayton's money."

"What about the spousal support? Blessant said she's bleeding him dry."

"I'm afraid there's nothing we can do about that. The law will have to run its course."

"Do you still want to talk to Nate?" The casualness of her inquiry earned her a sharp glance from Khattak.

"Yes. And while I do that, you can go through the photographs."

She couldn't hide her disappointment.

"Bring them with you," he said. "Nate knew Drayton. He might see something we wouldn't."

It was a threadbare excuse, a barely masked attempt to include her, or perhaps he still needed her as a safeguard against Nate's attempts to reconcile the past, but it didn't matter. Rachel was happy to accept any excuse at all.

30.

Mina was crying the most. She said, "We are not girls anymore. Our lives are over."

It was only afterward that she would remember that the women had begun screaming as the soldiers took hold of their arms. They wrested her bruised hand from Mrs. Obranovic's grasp, shoving her neighbor aside. She saw now that though they wore the uniforms of the Dutch, they were Chetniks.

In moments, they had collected her sister Selmira and herself, along with an older girl in her twenties. The older girl was crying, terrible deep sobs where she couldn't catch her breath. Her sister held her hand as though she would never let go, but she could feel her perspiration. Selmira was frightened.

"Let us go," she said. "We're children. Let us go. Show us you are honorable."

She couldn't repeat the word the Chetnik said in response. It was the bad word, the word they called the Muslim women and girls, girls like herself and Selmira.

They were taken to another building where it was dark. Someone had thrown a filthy mattress on the floor. There were people around, but they were trying not to look. She swallowed. One of the Chetniks had left the hall to call another man. The ones who stayed behind grabbed the older girl and threw her onto the mattress.

"Let's start with this one," they said.

Selmira began to scream. She had never heard her sister scream before. It was loud, high-pitched, terrifying. She started to cry.

The Chetniks stopped. They left the third girl on the mattress and came to grab her sister. One of them slapped Selmira across the face. She kept on screaming.

"Should we start with you?"

"Run!" Selmira screamed at her. "Run! Get out of here, go!"

She had promised Nesib she would listen to whatever Selmira told her. She ran for the door, straight into another soldier, this one in the Bosnian Serb uniform. He grabbed her by the arms and dragged her into the room with the mattress.

"Nole," Selmira called, sobbing with relief. "Nole, you have to help us."

She looked up. It was Nole, Nesib's best friend. The one who stole food for them. The one who had come to tell her brothers to head for the woods.

The Chetniks swore at Nole, who had recognized her and let go of her arms.

"They're not going anywhere," the one who had slapped Selmira said. "They're ours. The general said to enjoy ourselves."

Nole pretended to think about this. She could tell he was pretending because one of his hands pressed softly against her neck.

"The Colonel is calling for volunteers to load the trucks. It's chaos out there."

She held her breath. Maybe the Chetniks would believe him.

"Afterward," the Chetnik said. "They won't miss us for ten minutes."

"We'll get in trouble," Nole said. "Leave them here. They're not going anywhere."

The man who had slapped Selmira yanked her head back by pulling at her scarf.

"You're trying to protect your little slut. The little slut who knows you."

"I'm trying not to get called out by Krstić. I've said they'll still be here. We have all night."

"Liar," said a third man. "They've finished loading the trucks for the night. We're free until the morning."

Nole shuffled his feet, thinking.

The man holding Selmira ripped her blouse at the neck.

"I've waited a long time for this," he said. "You do what you want."

The Chetniks returned to the girl on the mattress, who had never stopped crying. Nole couldn't stop them.

Selmira began to unbutton her blouse. "Friends," she said. "My sister is a baby. She's only ten years old. You're men, you don't want her. Let the little one go and I won't fight you."

Nole moved decisively. He shoved her away from Selmira and shouldered her to the door. No one moved to stop him. The girl on the mattress was choking, her legs in the air.

Nole hissed in her ear. "Get back to the base and hide. Don't stop for anyone. Hide. Be clever. I'll get your sister."

This time she didn't stop to wave. She looked at her sister surrounded by Chetniks and ran through the door for her life.

31.

It is inconceivable for me all of this that is happening to us.
Is life so unpredictable and brutal? I remember how this time
last year we were rejoicing over building a house, and now
see where we are. I feel as if I'd never been alive. I try to
fight it by remembering everything that was beautiful with
you and the children and all those I love.

They found Nate in a bright room that led off the kitchen at Winterglass. Its views were of gardens, not the water. In the sinking light, the trees looked like skeletons of themselves, brushed with sweeps of pink and bronze.

Nathan called it his morning room. An embroidered English sofa with matching chairs was set before a raised bronze table. The floor was a blond wood patterned with blue diamonds, a color reflected in a set of French mirrors on either side of a modest fireplace.

"When will you come with Ruksh?" Nate asked Khattak. "Not that Rachel isn't welcome."

"Not while we're on a case," he answered. "Another time, perhaps."

As Rachel took her seat across from a floor-to-ceiling canvas that featured a frolicking spaniel, she took note of Nathan's pleased reaction. A thaw was setting in.

"You're having difficulties?" Nate asked. "I can tell from your face."

"We're learning difficult things," Khattak said carefully. "We know that Drayton wasn't the only one living under an alias. So was David Newhall."

"Newhall?" Nate tilted his head up to the ceiling, lost in contemplation of its whimsical cornices. "Why on earth would he need an alias?"

"Do you remember a man named Damir Hasanović? The translator for the UN at their base in Potočari?"

"I remember. He testified before the international tribunal."

"He's been living here as your neighbor. You've entertained him in your home."

"Damir Hasanović?"

"David Newhall." Before Nate could object, Khattak asked, "Is it possible?"

Nate thought about this. Twilight softened the lines at the corners of his hazel eyes. From his pocket, he took a Waterman pen that he tapped against the table.

"It seems ridiculous to have been so blind. First Chris, now David. I thought of these men as my friends."

Rachel wanted to tell him she thought the friendship was sincere, but how would she know? Maybe they had each used Nate for their own ends or as a means of getting to each other.

"Hasanović was one of Dražen Krstić's victims. He lost his family to the Srebrenica massacre. I think he moved here to keep an eye on Drayton. He says he met him at your house and recognized him at once."

"It's true. Mink asked me to invite him as a board member of the museum. That was a little over two years ago. He met Chris that night."

"And moved here when?"

"A week later? Maybe two?"

"He was stalking Drayton," Rachel said. "Once he'd seen him, he had to make sure Drayton didn't disappear."

"And he changed his name so Chris wouldn't know." Nate slapped a hand on the table, making them jump. "The letters. David wrote the letters?"

"He didn't admit it, but it's the obvious conclusion."

"Are you saying David had something to do with Chris's fall? That he planned for his death?"

"He says not. He also told us he loves to walk along the Bluffs."

"And you think—what? This can't have been coincidence?"

Khattak looked at his friend. His enthusiasm didn't mean that he viewed Drayton's death as an intellectual puzzle dependent on the cleverness of a solution. Nate well understood the human cost, the toll in blood and agony—who better? His warmth and interest expressed his desire to reach out, to offer Khattak his support.

He hadn't been to Winterglass in two years. Nate's openness, his close attention to Rachel, were meant to bridge that distance. Khattak couldn't fault him. He no longer had the appetite to shoot Nate down and watch him suffer.

He knew that Damir Hasanović would have given anything for another moment with his brothers.

He would give anything now to know where Ahmo and Mesha lay buried.

Perhaps he had tried, despite what he'd told them. Tried to wring a last confession from Krstić, a man who knew neither weakness nor remorse. And in that reckless moment of anger, he'd shoved the older man from the cliff, sending him to his death, just as Krstić had condemned so many others.

"It's not coincidence," he said to Nate. "He moved here because he wanted to bring Krstić to justice. He notified the Department of Justice as soon as he recognized him. When his letter-writing campaign proved fruitless, he could have turned to the media. He must have feared that with the first hint of exposure, Krstić would slip away and would never have to account for his crimes. Newhall—Hasanović—would never learn where his brothers lie buried."

"Then you do think he killed him."

"I think he wrote the letters. I think he planted the lilies in Drayton's garden. I don't know if fate intervened and Drayton fell before he could see his plan through, or whether Drayton's fall *was* his plan. We'll check his movements, of course, but that's bound to be inconclusive."

"Like everything else about this case," Rachel said glumly.

"Will CPS be making an announcement about Krstić?"

"With the Department of Justice. Once we've given them an answer about Krstić's death."

"What if there is no answer?"

Khattak's fatigue was evident. "I don't know."

Nate had known him long enough to know what he was really saying. "You don't want David to have done this."

"I wouldn't blame him. Who would? But no. That's not what the people of Bosnia deserve."

Rachel was more prosaic. "Say you do everything by the book and a man like Krstić still walks free. How could we expect Newhall to take that quietly?"

It wasn't an argument for vigilantism. It was Rachel's habit of getting inside the skin of a case, the skin of another's pain.

It was what Khattak most respected about her.

"It's not who Damir Hasanović is. I don't want his life's work to be reduced to Krstić's death."

As he said it, Khattak knew it came down to the same thing it had always been about. Identity. His. Theirs. The victims of genocide.

And what had been different? Only religion.

In Sarajevo, twenty years ago, people had refused to believe in the war at first.

Different? What do you mean, we are different? We are the same people. We speak the same language, share the same culture. We marry each other, we celebrate Christmas. How are we different?

The greatest general of a Sarajevo under siege had been a Bosnian Serb.

We are one people, the Bosnians.

Until the fascists had killed the enlightenment, burned the countryside, sundered the nation.

Those who hadn't believed in the war had died anyway.

Acts committed with intent to destroy, in whole or in part, a national, ethnical, racial, or religious group, as such: killing members of the group, causing serious bodily or mental harm to members of the group, deliberately inflicting on the group conditions of life calculated to bring about its physical destruction.

Yes, yes, and yes.

He had felt it then, as a student in a besieged city. He felt it now again: the hot flare of rage and futility in his stomach.

Was this what they were? The new Jews of Europe with Bosnia a slaughterhouse whose bloody imprint had faded in memory?

Everywhere the radical right was rising: Sweden, France, Belgium, Denmark, Holland. While a steady stream of vitriol drifted north of the U.S. border.

The war had begun with a program of hate and the steady administration of incendiary propaganda.

You Muslim women, you Bule, *we'll show you.*

You will see, you Muslims. I will draw a cross on your back. You will all be baptized.

We will burn you alive.

And in fourteen days, Srebrenica will be gone.

Damir Hasanović was a man admired and respected the world over, a man whose only mission had been justice. A man who'd sacrificed everything to that end.

For his reputation to be torn down at this last when Dražen Krstić had known nearly two decades of prosperity was something Khattak couldn't bear. It was something he wouldn't do.

One part of him knew that no matter the provocation, Hasanović couldn't have caused Krstić's death. But from a hollow place within himself, the place where identity folded back upon itself to reveal rawer, more vulnerable layers, he acknowledged a more insidious truth—the part that wished he had done it himself.

Rachel waited for Khattak to speak, unable to dispel her sense of disquiet. Little things were tugging at the edge of her awareness. Things she had seen or heard yet failed to understand. Maybe it was the night she'd spent reading about Ratko Mladić. Maybe it was the eerie watchfulness of her mother or the newfound sobriety of her father. Maybe it was Zach's continued absence from their lives.

She was missing something—brittle, intangible, and just on the edge of discovery.

She lined up the photographs she had taken from Hadley across the bronze table. She included everything they had collected during their first visit to Drayton's house. Personal papers, the holdings of his filing cabinet. The letters she had read that haunted her like the poetry of the damned. The things the imam had interpreted for them.

Nate came to look over her shoulder.

"You need a cup of coffee," he said. "And then I can help you tackle this."

"I need three."

She was grateful for his support, for his kind eyes and steady hands, or maybe grateful wasn't the word. She chose not to question her strange kinship with Nathan Clare. He was the part of Esa Khattak that opened up to her, sharing himself as an equal. She didn't complain about her relationship with Khattak, she knew they were an excellent team, just as she knew there was something of himself he held back.

Which was fine with her, because there was plenty she was holding back herself.

Khattak stirred from his reverie, shifted the papers on the table. His long fingers pushed a folded sheet of paper toward her.

"What's this? I don't remember seeing it before."

Rachel flattened it out on the table's smooth surface. "Piano music? I found it in Drayton's house. Maybe Nate or Mink gave it to him."

Nate appeared behind her shoulder with a tray of coffee.

"No," he said thoughtfully. "Chris didn't play, as far as I know. And I don't think it is piano music." Rachel studied the minute notations on the five-line staff as Nate set down his tray.

"You're saying this isn't music? It's some kind of code? Something someone sent him?" It reminded her of a spy novel she'd read.

"No, it's music. It's just not arranged for the piano. Look at this. It's written in treble clef. The piano accompaniment below it links two staves: treble and bass."

"What is it then?"

"An arrangement for the violin. I can play the melody for you if you like."

"I don't know that it matters," said Khattak. "Did he play the violin?"

"No. If he were a musician, he'd likely have offered music lessons instead of languages."

Rachel's interest sharpened. "So why did he have it, then?" She'd gotten it from the back of his filing cabinet, crammed in with the first batch of letters she'd found. "It could have been sent to him like the letters. Maybe it means something."

"Shall I play it and see?"

They followed Nate into the great room.

"This will be a bit rough."

It wasn't. He transposed the notes easily, his foot on one of the pedals. It was slow, insignificant. Until it became relentless, urgent. Thick with heartache. A layered anguish inhabiting the room, swelling out from the piano to the upper gallery. Nate's fingers lingered over the keys. The music built to its intolerable climax.

Just imagine this youngest boy I had, those little hands of his . . .

Mummy, I've come. At last I've come.

Where have you been, my son?

I waited for you to come through the woods. Each passing day was an agony. Until there was no hope left that you would come.

I never believed that people could do this.

Her heart was breaking. The music was breaking it.

"Stop," Khattak said.

Nate lifted his hands, placed them in his lap. His face paled at the expression on Khattak's face. "You recognize it."

"Did you give it to Drayton?"

"No. It sounds familiar but I can't place it."

There was a sickness beneath Khattak's skin. "The Adagio attributed to Albinoni. Vedran Smailović played it on his cello in the streets of Sarajevo."

For citizens of a fallen city.

"Do you think Drayton knew what it was?"

"I think a man like Krstić would have made a point of finding out."

"You were right then, sir. It wasn't just about Srebrenica."

"Perhaps there's some symbolism here," said Nate. "Srebrenica was the final movement of the war."

His words hung on the air with the closing notes of the music.

Rachel forced herself to take up the photographs again. It was too much. All of it was too much, the letters, the music, the silenced voices of the missing and dead. Something in the case had to break.

"What are these?" Nate asked, his voice hushed. "A specialized form of pornography?"

"They're from the war. These women may be dead, for all we know."

"I think this one *is* dead. This isn't a photograph, is it? It looks like a color photocopy." He pointed to a grainy image on a faded page. The figure in it was clothed. The body hung from a tree. Dark gold hair framed the face. The pink scarf that spilled down its neck had been used to hang the body.

"These others are prints, this one isn't. Why?"

"It's not from his collection." Khattak's voice was harsh.

Rachel hadn't noticed the photograph before, the disturbing image buried by others even more graphic.

"This is just a girl," she said. Images revolved in her mind. "A girl like Hadley or Cassidy. Look at the way the paper is folded. It was sent to him, like the letters. They murdered women as well?"

"Ten thousand women died in the war. I'd guess the girl in this picture hanged herself."

They looked at each other grimly.

"Someone wanted him to know this. David Newhall?"

"It may have been his cousin or his niece. Perhaps a friend."

Rachel shook her head. This was something else. Something out of place, like the music, the gun, the residue of the candles. A connection she wasn't seeing.

"Drayton had a gun," she said slowly. "He was threatened with exposure. Someone sent him the letters, the picture, the sheet music. The Bosnian lily was planted in his garden. Doesn't it seem like momentum was building against him? He wanted Hadley and Cassidy, but Dennis Blessant stood in his way. He was pressured on all sides: Melanie, Dennis, the letters. He took a walk along the Bluffs at night, the same night he had the argument with Dennis, yet he didn't take the gun. Why not? Why did he leave the gun on the floor surrounded by puddles of wax?"

"Maybe someone took his gun and forced him to go on that walk," Nate suggested.

"His are the only prints on the gun. He left it behind on purpose. I just can't figure out why."

"If Chris really was pushed, someone must have followed him on his walk. Dennis Blessant?"

"Whoever followed him would have had to wait until Melanie returned to her own house. They'd have to wait until Dennis drove away. Neither Melanie or Dennis reported any cars or noise on the street. As far as we know, there were no silent watchers in the undergrowth."

"Melanie's too self-involved to have thought about the presence of others. Dennis was probably distracted by the argument."

"And Drayton's house is secluded from the rest of the street. So there could have been someone there." She balled up her fists in disgust. "Again, that leaves us with nothing conclusive. Just the same old question of the gun. Did Drayton fall, or didn't he? I doubt we'll ever know." She faced her boss squarely. "So where do we go from here, sir?"

"Perhaps we need to widen our net. Find other suspects."

"No one has a greater motive than David Newhall. His parents, his brothers. Can we really afford to take his testimony at his word?"

"Hasanović worked for fifteen years to identify his parents' bones. What does that say about his patience? This isn't the end he wanted for Dražen Krstić. You won't convince me of it."

Rachel was afraid to dispute it. It was the first time she'd heard Khattak speak with such emotion. He wasn't a man who dealt in ultimate truths; as she did, he traversed the underground cities of doubt and discrepancy where human frailty revealed itself in layer upon layer of incongruity. She owed it to him to try, regardless.

"Maybe he didn't see it as murder. If I were standing in Newhall's shoes, Drayton's fall would look a lot like justice to me."

Khattak's face closed down. If he couldn't convince Rachel, what hope was there? She was only arguing what everyone would think once Newhall's true name was revealed, as it would be. And just like that, the decades of Hasanović's struggle for justice would be washed away, the tragedy of Bosnia swept aside for the cheap titillation of scandal. Khattak was determined not to let that happen.

"Sir," Rachel said, reading his resistance in the stiffness of his posture, his slightly bent head. "You said we should widen the field. I still think it's possible there's a museum connection here. The average person doesn't walk away from that kind of money."

She flinched from Khattak's look, as cold and remote as if he'd never worked with her, never known her loyalty or perseverance at his side.

"Mink won't take the money—not when she knows where it came

from." His tone suggested an implicit faith in the librarian. He turned away. "I need some air. I was planning to walk over to Ringsong. Maybe there's something more Mink can tell us about Drayton or the girls, something she hasn't thought of yet."

This was worse, Rachel realized. Worse than misunderstanding each other over a war in a place that meant little to most people. It was worse that he couldn't separate his work from his desire to return to the museum like a touchstone.

"We're not done here, sir."

"I am. Finish with Nate if you like."

Rachel knew she couldn't change his mind. "Be careful, sir. Let's not give too much of our case away."

Khattak's gaze disquieted her. "I'm not sure what it is you fear from Mink Norman. Whatever it is, you're wrong."

She'd been slapped down but she had to risk saying it. "Then would you ask her about the meeting on the night of Drayton's fall? Because that's where Newhall claimed he was. At least we should know if that much is true."

Khattak didn't argue. His assent was somehow worse than any rebuttal he could have made.

She drove home, avoiding Nate's sympathy, his assiduous offer of help. Slowly through cantering drifts of rain, past the outline of Newhall's house in the gloom and the van parked in its driveway, straight down the highway until an hour later she was home, her thoughts churning, her stomach aboil. It was how her body coped with anxiety. Or with fear and shame. She hadn't done anything to deserve Khattak's rebuff, yet she yearned for his good opinion. Of her work, nothing more, she insisted to herself.

It would have been companionable somehow to review the photographs with Nate, but not after Khattak's cool dismissal. He'd seen into her. Recognized her weakness and exploited it, making her seem feeble and possessive. She shrugged it off. What did her feelings matter when set against Hadley's or David Newhall's? Or the girl who had hanged herself. Perhaps the answer had been here all along.

She spread the photographs she had taken at Drayton's house across her bed.

The gun that lay on the floor. The puddles of wax. The atlas opened to the Drina River. The papers he'd collected: some stored in the safe, some jammed into his filing cabinet, some taken by Hadley Blessant. The yellow-headed lilies. The Adagio in G Minor.

The music made her think of Zach, although not because he'd had the chance to play any more than she had. In her head, she lumped the arts together. Someone who loved music adored art and vice versa. Look at Nathan Clare. A man of letters whose home was filled with exquisite paintings and objets d'art. Who was willing to fund a museum about a long-ago time in a faraway place. The beauties of Andalusia: literature, history, cultural synthesis. A place of learning and libraries, those palaces of memory. The ring songs of Andalusia, the music of a dazzling civilization.

Music, history, art, and lore.

A long ago time in a faraway place—the golden palaces of memory.

Her fingers arranged the photographs she'd taken at Drayton's house in a circle. The music. The photograph. The lilies. The gun. She peered closer.

And now the coagulum that had clouded her perceptions evaporated into discovery.

I feel as though I'm in a pantomime.

Was it the Blessants? she had wondered. From the beginning, the Blessants had been an occlusion.

The music. The photograph. The lilies. The gun.

It had to be. It could be nothing else.

She was playing a hunch, the kind Khattak would discard without a word, but it didn't matter. She had finally grasped the nature of Christopher Drayton's death. She needed to meet the survivors the imam had told them about.

Once she'd taken care of two small matters.

With gut-churning certainty, she found her phone and dialed her brother. When he'd listened to her request and made his promise to help, she made another call, this time to schedule a meeting with Audrey Clare.

The woman who had been at the periphery of Drayton's murder.

The woman who held the key to the truth.

32.

This was the city's still center, the very essence of Islam: in a
walled courtyard, water, a tree, and the warm geometry of
stone. In the deep blue velvet sky by the minaret hung a
sliver of incandescent silver light: the first moon of spring.

There were things he wanted Mink to say, things he wanted her not
to say.

Was he there as Esa Khattak, director of Community Policing? He
thought not. He thought he was there to listen to the sound of water
murmuring through rooms of stone. He was there to cup his hands
over the sweet globe of her face. He was there to share the hard things
within himself. Things he could not say to Rachel, the language absent between them where words were quietly necessary.

"It's late, Esa," she said, opening the door.

He made excuses, lied to them both. "Something's happened. I
must speak with you about Hadley."

The door gave way. The first fresh sails on his personal ship of joy
began to unfurl. He followed her, heedless of the tension that narrowed her shoulders, shortening the smooth sweep of her neck.

"Esa," she said, drawing the name out over her lips. "Is it wise of
you to come here on your own?"

"I thought we were beyond pretense."

"Aren't you here to ask me questions about your case? About
Christopher Drayton?" She sounded angry.

With an effort, he made himself remember Hadley. This was Andalusia, not a garden of bones. Not the darkling meadows of Srebrenica. "May we sit in the courtyard?"

She'd stopped at the forecourt. He stood close, inhaling the scent of oranges from her hair.

"Ask me what you've come to ask."

He thought for a moment of one of the verses Hadley had lettered for the display.

We see / that things too quickly grown / are swiftly overthrown.

"Did Hadley ever speak to you about Drayton? Did she suggest that she may have been frightened of him?"

"Frightened? Why?"

"That's what I'm asking you."

"Yes. I see that you return here time and again to ask me questions." He studied her face, seeking a clue as to her anger.

"Don't look at me like that. You've come for your work, why else should you come?"

"Mink, I have a duty—"

"I don't care about your duty. Why do you come to Andalusia? What do you want from me?"

He began to feel angry himself. "Isn't it a place of welcome?" He didn't say, as he'd thought so many times, of belonging. "I've come because Hadley is close to you. She was worried about Drayton—I thought you might have known."

"So you've come to taunt me with my imperfect sheltering of my charges. You say Drayton was a fugitive, a *war criminal*, and you accuse me of having left the girls in his path."

"I'm not accusing you of anything. I thought perhaps she may have told you something that would help with our questions about Drayton's death."

"You told me about him, Esa. If I knew something that would have helped you, wouldn't I have said so by now?"

"Not if it was a confidence from a young girl."

"So you expect me to break that confidence."

He stared at her helplessly. Her pale eyes were like moonstones in the delicate light of the forecourt. She wore her hair loose. It fell in soft gold waves that made him want to banish the subject of Hadley altogether. "I thought you'd want to help me. As you did before."

She pursed her lips. The skin around her eyes tightened. "You're pulling me into something ugly. Something that has no place here. Something that defiles this space."

His heart thumped in the silence. Was she right? No matter how virtuous its goal, his work contained within it an unalterable ugliness. Drayton's photographs were visceral proof of that. It was a place Khattak spent his days in, a place his thoughts lived. It would always be so with him. It would always be part of him.

A sense of remoteness closed about his heart. He'd thought more of her than she was, reading into her erudition the same strength and compassion that were second nature to Rachel. Rachel was neither graceful nor poised like this woman. She was blunt, straight as an arrow, and all too human in her personal failings.

Mink was—what was Mink? The illusion of a moment? His heart's long-delayed awakening? He rejected the thought as an unnecessary indulgence.

"I can return in the morning with my sergeant, if you prefer, but I must ask you all the same. Did Hadley Blessant confide in you about Christopher Drayton?"

Her face altered, went soft. "I've made you angry, I'm sorry. I've been so worried about the opening. The girls weren't at the dinner tonight and I didn't know why. They didn't call me so I cut things short, rushed home. And earlier today I received such a distressing call. I'm sorry, Esa," she said again. "These are not your problems. Will you come in?"

She couldn't have said anything more calculated to wipe away his anger. His sense of mistrust faded. He took the hand she held out to him. In moments she was curled up beside him beneath the palm trees' overlapping shade.

"I don't know anything," she went on. "Hadley didn't tell me anything. I wish she had, you've made me worry. What happened tonight?"

Rachel's voice sounded in his head. He discounted it.

"Drayton's interest in the girls was far from fatherly. I thought Hadley might have talked to you about it."

A sharp line formed between her brows. "What do you mean? That he— Was he preying upon the girls? Is that it?"

He held her hand within his own, feeling the rapid beat of her pulse at her wrist. From his touch? He hoped so. "He intended to. The fall interrupted his plan."

"My God. Those poor girls. Why didn't Hadley tell me?"

"She may have feared that her father was involved somehow in Drayton's fall. She may not have wanted to give him a motive."

Mink laced her fingers through his. "That explains why she wouldn't have told you. It doesn't explain why she didn't come to me. You were right. We are close."

"She's a self-contained young woman who's used to managing for herself. With a mother like Melanie Blessant, that's not surprising. Tell me about your call."

"It was nothing. You've more important things to worry about."

She was still caught up in his news about Hadley.

"Tell me."

"A lawyer called me today. He told me about Christopher's will. About the money he left the museum. He also said his assets were frozen."

"Does that pose a problem for Ringsong? Are you in financial difficulty?"

"I would never take his money." Her voice rang with conviction. "Not after what you've told me about him. How would I know where that money came from? It's blood money."

The tightness in Khattak's chest unclenched. He'd expected her to refuse the money, and she had. Why had he expected that this subtle woman whose work celebrated a world both beautiful and fragile would step without a qualm into the dark realm he inhabited?

She went on in a calmer voice, "I doubt there's an art institution in the world that wouldn't benefit from greater patronage, but we've been fortunate in our grants. We planned on a small scale and we're well within reach of our goals."

"I'm glad." He smiled into her hair. The earth was suddenly beautiful; the lush accumulation of blooms hummed with praise through the courtyard. He let the field of silence stretch between them. "Will you send me an invitation to the opening?"

"Are you sure you want to come?"

"I can't think of anything I'd like better."

"Then I will. Esa," she said urgently, "if Chris is all that you say he is, does it matter so much if he fell or was pushed? Isn't the service of his death enough? Can't you leave it alone?"

"What if it was Melanie Blessant, as a shortcut to Drayton's will? Or Dennis Blessant himself, to put an end to any possibility of losing custody of his daughters? Motives wholly unconnected to Drayton's true identity?"

"What if it wasn't?" Her large clear eyes sought out the sliver of moon on the horizon. "What if his crimes came home to his doorstep? Don't his victims deserve some form of redress?"

"I think what we owe his victims is the truth. Whatever it turns out to be."

Mink shook her head. He felt the movement against his chin.

"What is it?"

"I was just thinking how absurd it would be if this man who posed as our friend and benefactor—this dangerous war criminal—buried himself in this corner of the world only to be murdered by the woman he intended to marry."

"It's not the right narrative, is it?"

"So do tyrants meet their end. In these strange, ignominious ways."

"We've no evidence that he didn't fall. We can't place anyone at the scene, we can't prove or disprove anyone's alibi." Abruptly, he remembered Rachel's caution. "I think I'd better go. I still have some work."

And this wasn't the way a man of his convictions should proceed. Not if he wanted from Mink what he'd once had with Samina. However tempting the night, the walled garden, the woman.

"One night you'll stay longer," she said.

His ship of joy set sail, his silent restraint forgotten.

"Ask me again when this is over."

33.

*We saw our sons and husbands off to those woods and never
heard anything about them again.*

Today no man from our family is older than thirty.

It was their last dawn.

He and Hakija had survived the night on the bus to witness a final
dawn. The air in the bus was soft and warm, his brother was still asleep.
The killing had stopped for the night.

He thought of observing Fajr prayer in that moment. He thought of
words his mother had taught him when he was small.

"Say: I seek refuge in the Lord of Daybreak, from the evil of that which
He created. From the evil of the black darkness whenever it descends."

He wouldn't dream of praying now, not with Chetniks all around them.
A prayer was as good as a death warrant. He could think of it, though: the
Sustainer of the Rising Dawn had seen them through to the morning.

The engines roared into life, as Hakija jerked awake. He put his hand
on his brother's neck and cautioned him to silence. Hakija wanted water
but there was no water. If he put his head out the window to ask, a Chetnik
would shoot him.

The bus moved on, heading north. He recognized the valley town of
Zvornik. He knew the fates had been no kinder here. He couldn't afford to
think about Zvornik or Srebrenica or the people left behind at Potočari
when his mission was survival.

The bus turned off the main road and his stomach fell.

If they weren't going to a camp to be exchanged, where were they going? He tried to measure the time by the sun but quickly lost track. He was thirsty. He admitted to himself that he was also terrified. He wasn't alone. Every face on the bus reflected the same fear back to him. The uncles and older boys who might have comforted them could only think of themselves. It made him think of the Day of Judgment when not a single soul would speak up for another.

Was this their judgment, then?

They pulled up in front of a school in the village of Grbavici. He counted the vehicles in the convoy. Five buses, six trucks. As the men were made to disembark, terror rose like a wave through his body, strangling his throat, expiring through his fingertips. The bus meant life. The school, he knew, was the end of the road.

He whispered into Hakija's ear. "They're letting us rest now, don't worry. Just don't say anything out loud. Pay attention to me. I'll tell you when it's time to go."

Soldiers milled all around them. He was careful not to catch anyone's eye. He pushed Hakija before him through the crowd into the gym, where the men were packed in tight. The heat and fear coming off the other men's bodies seared his skin. Clammy and sick, he clung to his little brother.

Chetniks came into the hall, laughing and talking. They passed water around the gym. A wave of energy pulsed through the men who fought for the water. He and Hakija were close to one of the Chetniks. The soldier saw them and pushed a bottle at them. He grabbed it and pulled Hakija into his chest, where he forced half the bottle down his brother's throat. The men around him caught sight of their prize. They shoved Hakija aside and the bottle fell from his grasp to spill on the floor. Like the others, Avdi dove down and licked it from the floor, his dry tongue taking swift swipes like a cat. They shoved at him and pushed him, each fighting for his turn. He heard his brother's high-pitched call. He clambered out from beneath the crush of bodies and fought his way back to Hakija's side.

"Did you drink?" he asked. Hakija nodded. "Me too."

They grinned at each other, two survivors of the ride to Grbavici. He grabbed his brother's hand and moved him through the crowd as close as

he could to the back of the gym. His watchful eyes had realized an oppor-
tunity. Like the other boys, they were shorter than everyone else. They
couldn't be seen from the front.

Then a rustle went through the crowd. Someone whispered, "The gen-
eral."

He craned his neck to see. Around the crush of emaciated men, he saw
the reason for this new wave of fear. It was Mladić himself, slapping his
men on the shoulders, laughing with some, rolling back on his heels.

"We are taking you to a camp," he said.

Avdi didn't believe him. Especially when they picked two men out of the
crowd and told them to blindfold the others as they passed through the door.

The crowd in the gym began to narrow into a river, men pressing them
from all sides as they were taken to the door, blindfolded and led back to
the trucks and the buses. Around them in the gym, men were fainting.
The heat of the day was building.

He tried to fight the tide, Hakija's hand slippery in his, but the crush
was too great. There were too many Chetniks in the building now, corral-
ling them from the back and the front.

When they arrived at the door, he squeezed himself and Hakija through
before the other men could blindfold him. He needed to see. If he didn't see,
he wouldn't know the moment for escape.

"Don't worry," he whispered to his brother. "We've had water, next
we'll have food. Remember? The general gave out chocolate at the gate."

He said it to reassure Haki. To himself, he thought: it was a taste of
sweetness before dying. Some of the children had taken it. He'd known
that no matter how hungry, he must not take anything from the hands of
the executioner.

There was a terrified murmuring on the bus, but like the men themselves,
it was weak and subdued. This time the distance the bus traveled was short.
When Avdi peered through the window, he saw that the Chetniks had
brought them to a field in the raging heat. It was a pretty meadow, a place
where children must have played before death had come to his country.

He knew what was coming. He could see the bodies in the field where
the Chetniks had their guns cocked.

"Are we going to die?" Hakija asked him, almost calm.

"No," he whispered back, fiercely. *"I didn't bring you all this way just to die. You stay by my side. You move when I move. Don't do anything else."*

Rows and rows of men were lined up in the field. He could smell the blood leaching up from the earth. It made him want to vomit. If Hakija hadn't been with him, he would have given himself long-denied permission to faint.

The moment the Chetniks turned their attention to the next load of men to disembark, he grabbed Hakija's hand and squeezed in between two of the rows. They couldn't run, but maybe the first round would miss them.

He waited for the Chetnik commander to give the order.

"Now!" he hissed.

He threw Hakija forward and tugged his body beneath his own. The men behind them fell on top of him just as he landed on the shoes and legs of the man in front of him.

None of the bodies moved. They lay still and quiet: a perfectly arranged series of corpses.

Pinned beneath warm, bleeding bodies, his hand made a furtive search of his brother's torso. No wetness, no wounds. Lord of Daybreak, Lord of the Angels, his maneuver had worked. Haki's face was turned sideways. He could see his tears. He licked them up quickly. There were Chetnik boots behind them. The soldiers were patrolling for survivors.

Blood from the neck of the man who lay on top of him dripped onto his face. Moving his hand a little at a time, he brushed the blood over his brother's spotless face.

"Don't move," he said directly into Hakija's ear. *"Don't breathe."*

His brother obeyed him, eyes closed, body frozen. For a second, he thought Hakija was really dead.

He couldn't think of any prayers so he said his mother's name over and over again in his head. Shots fired all around them. Haki flinched but the bodies around them covered the small movement. Boots receded in the distance.

"Is anyone alive?" a soldier called.

"Please," a man answered weakly. *"I'm alive. Please help me."*

The soldier went over and fired a single shot.

Another group of men was led from the buses to the field. There was another volley of shots, another round of thudding bodies hitting the earth. The scent of the meadow turned sick with decay. And still he listened.

"Please," an old man called, as his turn came to be lined up. "Children, we didn't do anything. Don't do this to us."

He was silenced by a shot.

Someone else begged for his life. Another shot followed.

A man cried and murmured for his daughter.

"Fuck your daughter."

"Better yet, let us fuck her." Another shot.

The other men stayed quiet. They knew it was a game now. Speak and die. Stay silent, die. Move. Die. Lie still. Die. Stay on the bus. Die. Stumble through the field. Die.

Death was the only outcome.

He and Hakija lay facedown in the blood-soaked grass. Underneath their bodies, he held his brother's hand, stroking his palm. The hours passed, the heat of the day building to an excruciating crescendo. They both lost consciousness after a time. When Avdi woke again, it was to feel the ants crawling over his face, his arms, his legs, their tiny incursions unbearable as they delved in the stickiness of blood. He felt them in his mouth. His body itched to scream.

After a time, the sun went down. Now the field was lit by the bulldozers the Chetniks had brought to dig the graves. Newly drunk, they were braying at each other, firing sporadically, shooting at men already dead as a diversion.

He checked his brother's face. Hakija's eyes were closed, there was no sign of life.

He spoke into his ear. "Are you all right?"

Haki's eyelids flickered.

"Good. We have to move soon. Before they come to bury us."

"Everyone is dead," his brother said.

"I know. But we're still alive. Wait for my signal."

It began to rain, a steady, drilling, persistent rain. The soldiers had moved to a distant part of the meadow, firing at random. He turned Hakija's face toward the rain and opened his own mouth. The rain began to wash the ants away. He felt the heaviness of the body that covered his. It was slowly stiffening, turning cold. All this time, he'd been determined not to look. Now he thought maybe he should. Maybe he would be able to tell someone that their brother or father or son hadn't made it. Before their bones disappeared into the earth, he would know what had happened to at least one man among these thousands.

He looked at the corpse's face. It was thin like his own, narrow like his own, hungry like his own. Marked by the madness of terror like his own. He was a boy in his late teens wearing tennis shoes. He would have taken his papers if there were any but none of them had any papers. The Chetniks had stripped every trace of their identity. They would bury their bodies nameless and faceless.

He memorized the face, pondered the young man's shoes.

"You are my brother," he thought of the man whose body he had used as a shield. "I won't ever forget you."

The lights of the bulldozers went dead. The taunting stopped.

Drunk with killing and soaked in brandy, the Chetniks began to withdraw from the field.

He gripped Haki's hand. This was their only chance before they swapped in a new patrol. "Get ready," he said. His legs were numb beneath the weight of bodies, he didn't know if they would work. He didn't know if Haki could walk. But it was walk or die, so they would walk.

He counted to five hundred in his head.

There was no more sound, no more soldiers. Perhaps they'd gone quiet on purpose, waiting to see if any bodies rose from the dead. He'd have to risk it. There'd be no way to crawl free from the bulldozer's pit.

"Now," he said. He freed Hakija from the shelter of his body. He struggled to shove aside the bodies that had toppled over them both. It was hard work. The men were thin but their corpses were fixed in death. At last, he freed them both. Panting, he said to Hakija, "Don't stand up, just crawl. Follow me. If you hear anything, freeze."

Moonlight cut a swath through the field. He traced its path to the woods at the edge. His pace quickened. Every five seconds he looked behind to *make sure that Haki was at his heels. Reassured, he moved on, his hands slippery with sweat and blood.*

Now he didn't look. He couldn't. He felt bodies give way beneath him with odd concavities, he found tiny patches of grass redolent with blood, he thought at one time that he heard a bone snap from the pressure of his body. He blinked salt from his eyes and kept at his task.

It took them thirty minutes to reach the woods. He climbed into the shadows, pulling Haki up behind him. He grabbed his brother close to his chest and hugged him jubilantly, kissing his rain-washed face over and over.

"See? We made it. I told you we would." He ran his hands over Hakija's arms and legs, an action he hadn't dared undertake before. "Are you hurt? Were you shot?"

Hakija shook his head, a ragged smile on his lips.

"Let's find our mother."

But for a moment he didn't move. For a moment, as he hugged his brother close, he looked out over the field they had left behind. A field so full of bodies that he couldn't see the earth. The shadows of the bulldozers hulked over the ground.

In every direction he looked, there was death.

Until this moment, he hadn't cried. For Hakija's sake, he hadn't cried. Now he could do nothing else. Sobs tore through his body. He stifled them by biting his fists. He said the prayers the Chetniks had ground to dust beneath their boots. He asked God to accept his single Fatiha as an offering for all his people. His tears were the only comfort his brothers would know at the place of their dying.

He didn't let Haki look.

As they slipped into the woods toward sanctuary and life, he glimpsed an unearthly vision in the moonlight that hallowed the ground. He was headed for Tuzla down a death road.

The ghosts in the field rose in rank after rank at his shoulder.

34.

I knew all of them who did it. They were my neighbors.

As Rachel drove to the location of Audrey's clinic downtown, rain began to fall, slowing traffic to a crawl. Audrey was coming from an out-of-town appointment, a longer drive than Rachel's, yet she appeared as calm and lovely as on their first meeting. Even the rain had chosen to spare her: her hair was beautifully styled, her makeup tasteful and fresh. They met in the parking lot in front of Audrey's clinic, a humble space whose windows were decorated with posters of hands reaching out to the hands of women around the world. The clinic's name was lettered in white on a cherry-colored backdrop. Unpretentious and welcoming, much like Audrey herself.

"Shall we go inside?" Audrey asked her.

"This won't take long." Rachel withdrew the envelope that held Drayton's papers from under her jacket. "I wanted to learn about your work here. And your clinic."

She liked the fact that Audrey didn't seem to mind the rain, taking the time to consider her question with her laptop case over one shoulder, the keys to her Jaguar cupped in her hand.

"It's called Woman to Woman. We do advocacy work on behalf of victims of violence."

"What kind of violence?"

"Rape victims. Torture. Girls who've been reclaimed from the sex trade. In some rare cases, domestic violence, although there are other organizations for that."

"What kind of background do you need for that?"

"Mostly you need money, if you're truly passionate about it. But if you're asking about my credentials, I've done a master's degree in psychology and another in social work."

Exactly as she'd thought. There were depths to Nathan's sister that were going to prove invaluable. "Do you have a moment? I'd like to show you something related to this case."

Audrey waited as Rachel produced the photograph of the girl who had hanged herself.

"Who is that?" Audrey breathed. "Where did you get it?"

"I'm showing you this in confidence. It was among Drayton's papers. You said you've worked with victims of rape and torture, which means you must have an international clientele."

Audrey nodded. "Refugees, mostly, or women with landed status who are just beginning to open up about the violence they've endured."

"Which parts of the world?"

"Congo. The Sudan. Burma. Rwanda." Her eyes narrowed in realization. "Yes," she said. "Bosnia and Croatia, as well."

"Why might a girl from Srebrenica hang herself? Like the one in this photograph."

Audrey set down her laptop case to study the photograph more closely. "It's impossible to say conclusively. The uncertainty of the war may have been too much for her—a kind of existential dilemma. She may have lost loved ones that day or earlier in the war and felt she couldn't go on without them."

"And what if she was raped?"

"Is that what happened here?"

"I don't know. Would suicide be a likely consequence?"

Audrey spread her hands helplessly. "It's possible, Rachel. Rape was a feature of the war."

"Isn't that true of all wars?"

"As a side effect of chaos, lawlessness—the powerful preying upon the helpless. But in Bosnia, mass rape was a policy of the war, systematically carried out, implicating neighbors, paramilitaries, soldiers. Those who wouldn't participate were threatened, they were told it was a bonding ritual. The policy was to terrorize and humiliate their victims so they would never return to the scene of their degradation, thereby ethnically 'cleansing' entire cities and villages. Any building could be transformed into a rape camp. A school gymnasium, a town hall—in Foča, it was the high school and the Partizan Hall." She twisted her keys between her hands and drew a breath. "I can't begin to tell you. We've helped women from Foča at Woman to Woman." She studied the photograph again. "The men there were drunk on rape. Once you've demonized the Other so thoroughly, it doesn't matter what you do to them. They cease to be human. A woman subjected to that type of brutality might well decide to bring her suffering to an end. I wouldn't rule it out."

"This was a kid," Rachel said. "Maybe fourteen years old."

"That wouldn't matter to the perpetrators. They gang-raped children as a matter of course."

Rachel's stomach heaved. She'd dealt with terrible things in the course of her work but nothing as dark and sinister as this. This man who'd lived among them—a teacher of languages, a lover of gardens, a patron of the arts—he had given these orders, let his men run wild, held none to account. She thought of Hadley and Cassidy. The war had not exhausted his menace.

She considered Audrey with her pixie haircut, her designer jewelry and clothing: a girl raised in wealth and privilege to enjoy a lifetime of the same. Yet she had founded an organization dedicated to helping the vulnerable, when sharing their stories must have been a trauma in itself.

"Why do you do it? This kind of work, I mean. You don't have to, right?"

"Ah, I see." Audrey collected her laptop. "I could live off my brother's wealth or my trust fund, jet-setting about the globe, is that what you mean?" She shrugged. "I'm no saint, Rachel. There are plenty of luxuries I haven't given up." She waved her keys at Rachel.

"My Jag, for example. I suppose you think I'm just another dilettante dabbling in celebrity causes."

Rachel swallowed uncomfortably. Until this graphic conversation, she had to admit the thought had crossed her mind. She cleared her throat. "No. I can't see a dabbler sweating it out in graduate school. It's just— I'm a cop, and I still find this stuff hard. You've had to immerse yourself in misery."

"There's hope as well. The women we work with demonstrate incredible bravery. We learn from them every day, it's hardly a one-way street." She fluffed up her rain-dampened hair with one hand. "It's what our parents taught us, both Nate and me. If you're given a gift, you have a responsibility to put it to use. That's why Nate is so invested in immigration policy and multiculturalism: it's a buttress to the work of our NGO." She smiled impishly. "That and the fact that we grew up with Esa and Ruksh."

Rachel had noticed a common factor about people whose work she admired. They made themselves the smallest part of the equation. As if reading her thoughts, Audrey's smile softened into reflection.

"It was my mother, really. Wherever my father traveled on his adventures, she found a way to reach out to the women, to work with them."

"She sounds remarkable," Rachel said. She wondered what it would have been like to have been raised by such a woman. "You mentioned Foča." She pronounced it gingerly. "Would your organization have assisted anyone from Srebrenica? Would you be able to put me in touch with any of the survivors?"

"I'm afraid not, no. If you'd like to speak with one of the families from Foča, I can ask them. We haven't dealt directly with anyone from Srebrenica."

Audrey reached out and grasped her hand.

"I'm glad you came into our lives, Rachel. I'm glad Esa brought you. Let me know if you need my help with anything else."

Rachel pulled into the mosque's parking lot with more speed than care, her tires screeching. It had taken an hour to fight through traffic, her worst suspicions confirmed by Audrey's revelations. She hustled her way inside through a larger crowd than usual to Imam Muharrem's office, where she banged on the door.

He didn't answer so she tried the knob. The charming room was empty. As she pondered her next move, a man appeared at her elbow. Small, slight, with twinkling eyes, he asked if he could help her. She introduced herself as Esa Khattak's sergeant.

"I'm looking for the imam. Imam Muharrem. He said he could introduce us to some of the survivors from Srebrenica."

The small man's face relaxed. "Muharrem is away at a lecture. He will be back tomorrow. My name is Asaf, perhaps I can help you."

She seized on the name at once. He was the mosque's full-time imam, the man Muharrem had been asked to relieve. "Asaf? Imam Asaf? I think you know my boss."

"I know him well. I would be delighted if I could be of service to any friend of Esa's."

"Would you be able to help me locate some of the survivors? Would any of them be at the mosque today?"

The young imam ushered her into the office. As if sensing her agitation, he went directly to the samovar and poured her a cup of tea.

"Please take a seat, Sergeant, and tell me how I can help you. I can make calls and ask if anyone is available to meet you here. I'm sure you understand that I prefer not to give out numbers until I've learned a little more about your interest. Many of these people have struggled to put the past behind them."

"Imam Muharrem didn't tell you about our previous visit?"

"I've been on holiday." His blue eyes twinkled at her. "I'm sure you understand that those are the moments one chooses to get away from the pressures of work. He may have called me, I regret I didn't answer."

"No, it's all right. Look, to be honest with you, I'm trying to understand a little better about what happened in Srebrenica during the war. It's relevant to a case we're working that involves a man named Damir Hasanović."

"Damir?" The imam sat back in surprise. "I haven't seen him in some time."

"Two years," Rachel said.

"Yes, two years. He was an active member of our congregation, on the board of the mosque and so on. He did a great deal of work with the community and he was very much in demand internationally, as well. I hope he is not in any difficulties."

"I hope not as well. Would you be able to tell me a little more about his work? What kinds of things he did?"

Asaf had a quick, intelligent face enhanced by the gentlest of smiles. He would be good at his chosen vocation, she thought, providing spiritual solace to many.

"He acted as a translator and an advocate. He helped many people come to this country as refugees. He advised our students on access to education. He arranged driver's licenses, housing, he explained the immigration settlement services to them. If anyone had difficulty with any level of government, he acted as their representative until their issues were resolved. He wrote letters to the media, he gave tours of the mosque. He lectured at schools. Most of his time was spent on behalf of the memorial."

"The memorial?" Rachel echoed.

"The genocide memorial in Srebrenica. To recognize the dead by name when names were all we had. It was an international project but we had a devoted group here in our city. It's strange," he mused.

"What is?" She found both his tea and his manner soothing.

"It's not only Damir the community has lost—we still don't know why or where he went. He was invaluable to us."

"Who else?" Rachel prodded.

"The others who worked on the memorial. Survivors like those you wish to meet."

"Survivors of Srebrenica?"

"Yes. Of the killing fields, there are only a handful of men who survived. Damir arranged to bring Avdo and Hakija here."

Rachel stared at him, dumbstruck.

"What is it, my dear?"

"I'm sorry, Imam. What names did you say?"

"Avdo and Hakija. Osmanović. They were to be executed at Grbavici. By some miracle, the boys escaped when the executions were halted for the night. They made it through the woods to the safety of Tuzla."

"Your gardens are beautiful," she mumbled through lips that felt numb.

The imam quirked an eyebrow at the irrelevance of her remark. "I think you need more tea, dear Sergeant."

She handed him her cup without protest. She wouldn't have objected if he'd added a shot of whiskey.

"Yes, that is Avdo and Haki's work. It's good that they came here—thanks to Damir, they were able to build productive lives, even with Haki's condition."

"What condition is that, sir?"

"The boys were buried under a mountain of bodies. That's how they escaped. Avdi had a plan, it seemed. He knew they would end up at an execution site. From the moment he was loaded on a bus, he plotted their escape." Asaf's voice marveled at it. "I don't know how he did it, how he managed. He's very resourceful. Sadly, by the time he found their mother in Tuzla, Haki was catatonic. After that, it was a simple matter for Damir to arrange their evacuation. And Haki's had wonderful, ongoing treatment in the city. It's helped him a great deal, although it's doubtful he will ever fully recover."

"No," Rachel agreed, thinking of Harry Osmond. "I can't imagine what that would be like."

Asaf made a reassuring noise in his throat. "If you are interested, their testimony is available on the Web site of the tribunal. It has been used in several of the Srebrenica convictions."

"And these were the people who worked with Damir Hasanović on the memorial?"

"Tirelessly. Damir tried to bring the Sinanović family as well. The boys were killed in the woods—some have said by chemical weapons. Their bodies have been identified. Selmira, their sister, died on the base."

Rachel was having trouble assimilating the information.

Everything she had imagined was true.

The music, the photograph, the lilies, the gun.

Her voice husky, she asked, "She was killed?"

Asaf's face clouded over. He lifted a Qur'an from the desk and placed both hands over it as if to calm himself.

"I don't know if I should speak of it, dear Sergeant. I'm not sure I have the right."

Rachel wasn't trying to trick him when she said, "We would like to do her justice." She produced the photograph of the girl hanging from her scarf in the darkling woods of Bosnia. "Is this Selmira?"

Asaf's gentle face crumpled.

"I seek refuge in Allah," he whispered. "Where did you get this?" His fingers gripped the Qur'an.

"Tell me about Selmira," she said. "Did they kill her at Potočari?"

He shook his head from side to side. Like Imam Muharrem, he murmured prayers under his breath.

"She was fourteen years old when she took her own life. She was taken by the Chetniks and raped. It was Damir's dearest wish to place her name on the memorial, but the rape of our daughters is something the community struggles with. The shame is a lasting stigma. It was why Selmira hanged herself."

"Shame and horror," Rachel agreed.

It was what Audrey Clare had taught her, well-versed in the trauma endured by rape victims through her work with her organization, the work she had lightly dismissed. Rachel had remembered Nate's description of his sister as a human rights advocate.

The photograph had been her first clue. When she had paired it with the lines of one of the letters, she'd understood.

Keep the good ones over there. Enjoy yourselves.

"You said Damir Hasanović tried to bring the Sinanović family here. What did you mean?"

He poured more tea for them both, his hands trembling on the samovar.

As she listened to his explanation, she irrevocably understood why Khattak had defended Hasanović from the heart.

The music, the photograph, the lilies, the gun. The clues arranged in a circle on Nathan's table. The words that whispered their damning indictment.

On Tuesday, there will be no bread in Sarajevo.

The besieged city of Jajce has fallen to the aggressor.

They are shelling Bihać.

They are shelling Goražde.

They are shelling Tuzla.

They have shelled Srebrenica.

They have killed Avdo Palić, the defender of Žepa.

They assassinated our prime minister while the French troops watched.

Everything around us is on fire and we ourselves are nearly smoldering.

The National Library is burning, it's burning. Will no one save it, save us?

They will burn us all.

They will burn us all.

Rachel left the sanctuary of the mosque and stood outside, breathing deeply. The thunderheads massed on the horizon echoed her own turmoil. The words meant something. They were chosen for a reason. They directed Drayton to a revelation, an accusation.

A revelation she feared. Especially because Khattak was nowhere to be found.

The rain that had been so mild during her interview with Audrey picked up, muffling the sound of her phone ringing. She hoped it was Nate, the one person who could reach Esa.

The number was unfamiliar. Three rings later, she registered it as Zach's. When she answered the phone, the first thing she said was, "Zach, I love you. Not for a moment have I stopped. Whatever this is with Mum, we'll figure it out together, I promise. You won't have to choose. Just—don't stay missing from my life."

Her brother made the awkward humming noise that substituted for tears with him. He mumbled under his breath.

"What was that?"

He said it again, this time more clearly. Rachel heard him out: his confession of love, his apology in turn, his promise not to disappear again. She told him about the missing and the dead, what it did to your heart and your sanity never to know. The emptiness, the terrible black hole of the pain and dread that consumed you. He whispered and cried and apologized all at the same time.

Then he gave her the information she'd asked him to check and as she listened, her breath blew out in a blasphemous whistle. "Holy saints of Heaven and Hell."

Everything she'd feared had come true.

The dead are not alone.

When Khattak still didn't answer, she called Nate.

"I can't find Esa." His name slipped past her lips of its own accord. "Is he with you?"

"No, I'm sorry, but he isn't. You sound worried."

Instead of using her earpiece, she was cradling her phone against her shoulder while the hard rain drilled her windshield.

"It's not like him not to answer his phone. He doesn't do that."

"Unless he's at Ringsong," Nate concluded. "Shall I find him?"

A rush of gratitude for his offer swelled up in Rachel's heart. It wasn't just the book he'd written; the roots of his friendship, once offered, ran deep.

"Yes. And get him out of there, if you can."

"I think you might be blowing things out of proportion."

"Trust me, I'm not. Please, Nate, go now."

She let the phone fall into her lap and turned on her siren.

Nate found them in the flex room between the portico and forecourt. Mink was wearing a white smock over jeans and a T-shirt, a carpet vacuum beside her on the floor, a duster tucked into the pocket of her smock. A large clear jug filled with water suggested she'd been watering the plants. She'd been chatting with Esa but her smile for Nate was unambiguous.

"How lovely to see you. It's been much too long."

From the look on his face, Esa didn't agree.

"You've had my books to keep you company," Nate said.

Many of the books on Moorish history were from the collection at Winterglass.

"They were a donation, please don't forget." Mink's delight in the words was obvious, just as it was obvious that her reaction brought Esa no pleasure. Nate frowned. He was unsettled by the tension Esa's body language communicated. Surely Esa didn't think that he was interested in Mink when he'd paid such unequivocal attention to Rachel.

"You've made wonderful progress since my last visit," he said to Mink.

She grasped him by the elbow. "This is nothing. Esa knows, he's seen the great room. We've taken a more amateur approach to things, though I doubt anyone would judge Hadley's efforts as less than superb. I like the idea that we've done things with our own hands, like the craftspeople who bound books and built mosques of such immaculate beauty."

"Still living in the past, I see," Nate said.

She smiled, though for a moment her fingers bit into his elbow. "A historian's natural provenance, I'm afraid. Esa, are you coming?"

He followed them to a great room ablaze with light.

"I've just refurbished the lanterns," she said. "I wanted to see what the effect would be on the exhibits."

Her worktable was gone. In its place, she'd added numerous display cases and pedestals, some with modulated lights arranged above them to illuminate well-chosen treasures. Previously, where there had been photographs and manuscript pages, Mink had added woven carpet fragments, an ivory casket and a game box, stone capitals inscribed with Arabic calligraphy, a geometric panel from the Alhambra, glazed earthenware bowls, and swords beside their scabbards: artefacts that ranged from the tenth century to the fifteenth.

The pride of the collection was six folios from a blue and gold

Qur'anic manuscript dated to the late fourteenth century. She hovered over the display.

"It's on loan," she said. "Just for the opening. They've installed their own alarm system, so don't get too close."

"It's breathtaking."

On a single manuscript page on vellum, Esa painstakingly identified the Verse of the Throne. The majesty of it made him swallow. Nate read his emotion and tried to distract Mink with his passable recollection of Rachel's questions.

"I can't believe you pulled all this together in two years."

"I had to call in a lot of favors."

"Those regular meetings must have helped as well. Directors, donors. They need constant assuaging."

Mink laughed, arresting Esa's attention. "An excellent description. It will be worth it in the end."

"I hope Chris's death hasn't cast a cloud."

Her eyes widened. "Does he know?" she asked Esa.

He nodded in response.

"It did at first. Chris was—if not a friend, at least someone I could interest in Ringsong. But now that I've learned who he was, although it sounds callous, I've no reason to miss him."

"It isn't callous," Esa reassured her. Nate watched his friend take Mink's hand in his own. The luminous warmth of her smile encouraged the gesture. No wonder Rachel was worried.

"Was there a meeting on the night that Chris fell? I think David mentioned it to me."

"Yes," she agreed, without looking away from Esa. "We did meet. David and I and some of the other directors. They wanted a progress report. We hadn't gotten this far then, so I missed my chance to impress them. However, we do have another meeting at the end of the week. It should put everyone's fears to rest."

Nate pounced on the word. "Fears?"

"The usual, I'm sure," Esa answered for her. "Deadlines, budget—will the museum open at the time and on the scale promised."

"You've either been reading my mind or my literature," Mink teased.

"How long have you known David?" Nate could see his questions were unwelcome, at least by Esa, but he kept them up.

"Two years? A little more? Ever since we began work on the project."

He ambled through the room, trying to think of ways to attract Esa's attention, distracted by the exhibits. He enjoyed the great room in Ringsong nearly as much as the same space in his own house. The dark timber, the white stonework, the clerestory windows: they were a concert of loveliness.

Mink had kept personal touches away from the house's main floor. Presumably, she kept her personal effects and furniture in her own rooms. As he drifted from manuscript to manuscript, he realized he knew little of her beyond their shared passion for the finer things in life—music, art, books. She had appeared in his life at the moment he'd lost Esa, filling in the space Esa had occupied with their common history and interests. With Mink, he'd found a link to Esa through Andalusia. He'd known from the first what the museum would mean, the resonances Esa would find within it.

A place where pluralism thrived, where languages and lives intermingled.

He'd known Esa thought of Bosnia as a second Andalusia, with its Ottoman mosques and the library that housed the histories of its peoples. What he hadn't guessed was how largely Mink figured in Esa's thoughts. He'd assumed his friend would find a woman like Samina in time, a woman of his own faith and culture, whose view of the world harmonized with his friend's.

There was nothing to fear from the gentle entanglement of Mink Norman, and yet Nate was uneasy. Community policing was the most unforgiving of mandates: Esa needed his objectivity. If there was a connection between the museum and Drayton's death, he needed to isolate it. He wandered back to them, well aware that his presence was an intrusion. Their heads were bent over the Qur'anic folio, dark and gold together.

"Do you know Albinoni's Adagio?" he asked idly.

Mink didn't look up. Her hand rested on Esa's. "I'm sorry?"

"It's a piece of music. Esa knows it. Perhaps if you don't, Sable might?"

"If it's well known, I'm sure she does. She may even have played it. It's been kind of you to loan her your music."

"I'm looking forward to hearing her play. After I meet her, of course."

"You'll have to throw one of your parties."

He gazed about the room, a thought striking him. "Where do you keep the piano?"

"In our private quarters. The board didn't want responsibility for it."

"The sound would be lovely down here, drifting out to the court-yard, vanishing over the water."

"You have the writer's gift of evoking a mood." Her laughter en-compassed both men. "It would be exquisite, I agree, but one can't have everything. I've been fortunate enough to realize a dream—I'm more than content."

"You've a lot to be proud of here. I doubt anyone else could have accomplished as much in just two years."

"As I said, my friends have been good to me." She looked from one man to the other. "Is anything the matter? Is this something other than a friendly visit?"

Nate waited for Esa to say something, anything. When he didn't, Nate sighed heavily and shoved his hands into his trouser pockets. "I should get back. I'm sorry if I intruded." To Esa he said, "Walk me out, would you? I've a message for you."

They had developed their own code of silent signals during their misspent youth. Esa couldn't miss what he was asking.

"I'll just be a moment," he said to Mink.

Uneasy, Nate felt the weight of Mink's stare on the back of his neck

He waited until they had reached the terra-cotta steps to grab Esa's arm. "Come with me," he said. "You shouldn't stay here alone."

"What are you accusing me of?" Esa's eyes were hard green stones.

"Nothing, you fool. Rachel called me. She said to get you out of here. You need to take a step back."

"I need to step back?" He shook off Nate's hand. "You've been involved with the museum for two years—"

"Yes, two years!"

"—and it's taken you until my arrival to realize that Mink's a captivating woman."

"I'm not interested in her!"

"The hell you aren't. You've been hanging all over her."

"I was asking Rachel's questions, questions you were supposed to ask. Did you listen to her answers?" He lowered his voice with an effort. Even now she might be standing by the portico.

"I saw the way she smiled at you."

"She doesn't give a damn about me. It's you she's interested in, and either way it doesn't matter. There's something wrong with the museum, something about the meetings or David Newhall—I don't know what it is, just something. Can't you feel it?"

"I deal in facts, not suppositions."

"Well, what do the facts tell you?" Nate asked desperately. "Chris moved here two years ago. David came two years ago. And the first I heard of the museum was two years ago."

He faced Esa's wrath without flinching.

"What in God's name are you talking about? The museum has nothing to do with Drayton. Newhall told us he was at the museum on the night of Drayton's fall and he was. Along with other members of the board."

"Which members? Ask her to tell you." He could handle Esa's contempt, if he could just get him to look at the truth.

"What's your theory, then?" Esa challenged. "That Mink is covering for David Newhall? Why would she? You asked a question, she answered it. You wanted to know about the music, she told you."

"And you believed her?"

"Are you saying you don't? You used to have more faith in the women you claimed to love."

And there it was. The indictment he had waited for all this time.

Brutal, bitter, the words hung in the air between them. Then Esa thought better of it. "Nate—"

"No. I'm glad you finally said that. I was a fool over Laine, I admit it. Everything I believed about her was wrong. Everything I did was wrong. But if you're angry, it shouldn't be over this. Mink is a friend, that's all. It's not me who stands in your way, it's Rachel."

Nate blinked rapidly as he descended the steps. "There was a time when you didn't assume the worst about me, Esa. I was your friend. That's all I'm trying to be."

36.

I cannot find words for what happened there.

Rachel found Nate pacing the gardens behind his house. He looked wet and cold and very much alone.

"Where is he?" she demanded. "Wasn't he at Ringsong?"

"He's still there now. He wanted me gone."

"Christ. We need to get over there right away."

They had raised their voices over the wind, a wind so fierce and sudden that it picked apart Rachel's ponytail, sending dark strands whipping about her face.

Nate shrugged. "Not me. I've told you, he doesn't want me around." He shivered as the wind began to howl.

Rachel was too full of urgency to feel the cold. "Grab your jacket, you're coming with me."

She had the unique ability to override his better judgment, her voice sounding in his ear all the way to the cloakroom and back again to the drive. He shouldered his way into the jacket he reserved for walks along the escarpment. A steely rain slanted against the horizon, the lake beyond arranged in little thrusts of chaos against the shadowy outline of the shore, the white bone of the Bluffs at a treacherous distance.

As her voice carried on, his pace sped up. He came to an abrupt halt at the museum. "That's Aldo's van, the one they use for land-scaping. It wasn't here earlier."

"I've seen it before. Last night outside David Newhall's house."

She sprinted up the terra-cotta stairs and jammed her finger on the doorbell. When there was no answer, she moved through the portico and forecourt to the great room. The only person in it was Hadley Blessant. She was taking photographs of the exhibits through the powerful lens of a camera.

"Where's Inspector Khattak?"

"He's not here," said Hadley, a slight frown sketched between her brows. "Is something the matter?"

"Do you know where he is?" Rachel couldn't conceal the anxiety in her voice. Hadley lowered the lens of her camera.

"They went for a walk on the Bluffs."

"In this weather?"

"I told them. It's not a good idea to walk the Bluffs in the dark. Mink said she needed the air and your inspector wouldn't let her go alone."

"Damn chivalrous fool," Nate muttered under his breath.

"Does this have anything to do with my father?"

Rachel spared a moment from her own worries to address the girl's concern. "No, Hadley, nothing at all. Don't worry about your dad, he'll be fine."

She didn't thank Rachel, but as she shifted her weight from one foot to the other, Hadley offered, "Do you want me to come help you look? There's a flashlight in the flex room."

"I'll find it, thanks." Rachel's gaze searched the room and the courtyard beyond, the windows lashed by rain. "Why is Aldo's van parked out front?"

"They were here. Mink called them a little while ago but she decided not to wait for them, so I told them she took the path along the Bluffs. If the van's still there, they probably went after her."

Rachel's voice climbed an octave. "His brother was with him?"

"And their friend. Mr. Newhall. They meet about the museum every now and again. The Osmonds come to look in on the gardens."

"Thanks." She grabbed Nate by the elbow. "Let's go."

They made their way outside, the rain driving against their faces in little spikes. Rachel began to run, Nate at her heels. Within five minutes, she'd turned her ankle.

"This is crazy," Nate said. "There's nothing to be afraid of. What you've told me simply doesn't make sense."

"You needed to read more as a kid" was her answer. She hobbled along behind him, blinded by rain, the flashlight skipping ahead down the muddy, rain-soaked path. Lightning pulsed against the sky, the Bluffs outlined like the hollows of a skull. The tumbling waves of the lake roared into the silence.

"There!" Nate pointed ahead in the distance, where shadows were grouped against an outcropping of white clay. Three men stood huddled together, shouting against the wind. A man and a woman were balanced in each other's arms at the very edge of the cliff.

Rachel tried to resolve the picture in her mind, dashing water from her eyes. Once she understood what it was, she raced past Nate down the path, her ankle forgotten. Nate tracked her, his feet slipping in the mud.

"Esa," he called. "What in God's name are you doing?"

The group at the edge froze in position. Rachel skidded to a halt in front of Mink Norman.

"Come back," she heard Esa say. "We'll walk here another time."

The three shadows against the rock loomed larger as Nate joined his friends.

Mink turned to Rachel defiantly, her blue eyes blazing, her gold hair a sodden tangle against her face.

"So you've come at last, armed with your weapons."

Khattak glared at her. "What are you doing here, Rachel?"

"It's what you're doing that concerns me, sir. I don't have any weapons," she said to Mink. "Were you expecting that I would? Did you expect me to arrest you?"

Harry Osmond jerked in his brother's hold.

"Rachel, I'm warning you—"

"I'm sorry, sir. You have to know the truth about her. You have to realize why it matters so much that Drayton was Dražen Krstić, the butcher of Srebrenica." A palpable shudder ran through the men behind her. "You knew this, didn't you? Not just you, Mr. Newhall, but the others as well. Avdo and Hakija Osmanović, the survivors of Srebrenica. You recognized Krstić from the base at Potočari. That's why you moved here."

Harry jerked his head back and forth in a strange repetitive motion. "No," he said. "Oh no."

Rachel spoke to Mink. "I thought it was Mr. Newhall—Damir Hasanović—but I was wrong, wasn't I? You sent the letters. It was you, all along. There is no Sable Norman studying at the Mozarteum University of Salzburg. And there's no Mink Norman either. But there was a Selmira once, wasn't there? That's who the girl in the photograph is, the picture you sent to Krstić. The girl who hanged herself—your sister, Selmira."

Esa turned toward her, shielding Mink from her questions.

"What in God's name are you talking about, Rachel? Do you have any idea what you're doing to your career? I took you on when no one would touch you!"

"I know, sir, and I'm truly sorry."

"Esa," Nate interrupted. "Krstić came here two years ago, the Bosnians came two years ago. And the plan for Ringsong was set in motion two years ago. Andalusia, Esa. What was Bosnia if not a second Andalusia?"

Cradling Mink closer under his arm, Esa pulled her back from the edge. Bright with fury, he turned on Nate. "If our friendship ever meant anything to you, you'll shut up right now. You'll take Rachel and you'll leave this to me."

"It's not just Andalusia, Esa. It's the music, the Adagio. She didn't just send him the photograph and the letters. She sent him the Adagio. Of course she knew what it was. She's literate in music."

"You don't know what you're talking about."

"They know," Rachel said desperately, pointing at the Osmond brothers. "Avdo and Hakija. They're from Srebrenica. I've been searching for my brother, sir, he was missing for seven years—that's when I understood what must have happened here. What happened to Krstić. It's the missing men, the missing boys. That's why they don't have families. That's why it's only Damir, only Avdo and Hakija, only Mink Norman. Nobody else survived, sir, you know this. It's about the dead of Srebrenica, the men Krstić ordered to their deaths. That's why she sent the letters and the photograph of Selmira. Tell him, Mink. Tell him your real name. He fought for your people, he's earned the truth."

"No one fought for us," Mink said tonelessly, drawing away from Esa. "Isn't that so, Damir? Let him tell you."

David Newhall shrugged, the rain on his glasses obscuring his eyes. "What do you want to know? I've told you the story of the base. I begged the Dutch for my brothers' lives, for my mother and father, but Mesha said, 'Don't beg for us, that's not how I want to live. There will be a prisoner exchange, that's what Mladić promised us. You see, he's given candy to the boys?'" David removed his glasses, studied the others through shrouded eyes. "He strode around the base, gave speeches to the refugees, some to us, some to others, dispensing chocolates to the children when all the time he knew there was never going to be a prisoner exchange. We didn't have any prisoners to exchange." He drew a ragged breath.

"Mink," Esa said. "Tell me what this is."

Rachel hated the hollow sound of his voice, the disbelief in it. It presaged an emptiness within her own heart as Mink Norman moved from the shelter of his arms without a qualm. She turned her face up to the rain and reached out a hand to hold Harry Osmond's.

"Selmira *was* my sister, your sergeant is very clever. I don't know how she identified Selmira from that photograph when the tribunal never could. She and I hid with the other girls inside the base on the day that the Serbs overran Srebrenica. Our parents were dead, our brothers had gone to the woods. We wouldn't learn for some time what had happened to them, and then only because of Damir." She nodded at the man whose gaze was fixed on her. "That night, Chetniks came to the factory looking for girls. They were dressed like the

Dutch, so I waved at them. That's how they noticed us. Nesib, my brother, told us to hide, to make sure we didn't attract their attention, but I was young, I didn't listen. They took us because I didn't listen. But I was lucky because Nesib had a friend in the Serb army. He warned my brothers to leave Srebrenica at once. And he rescued me from the Chetniks. I know he tried, but he couldn't rescue my sister. The others wouldn't let him."

Harry pressed his face into the back of her neck. "Don't," he sobbed. "Please don't tell them."

"We've come to it," she said gently. "Don't you see, Haki? We've come to it." She stared straight at Rachel. "What do you know of any of this, Sergeant Getty? All you've thought of is justice for Christopher Drayton." Rachel choked at the unfairness of this. It wasn't for Drayton she had shed her tears, sorted through testimony that would haunt her nightmares forever.

Mink continued her story in a monotone, rain beating against her head. "My sister told the Chetniks if they spared me, she wouldn't fight them. And Nole helped me escape from that room. 'Be clever,' he told me. 'I'll get Selmira.' And he did. When she came back to the base, she was covered in blood. They had torn away her clothes. One of our neighbors tried to clean her. Selmira said we were no longer girls—we would never be girls again. And then she stroked my hair and told me to rest. She said we would find Nesib—isn't that what she told me, Damir?"

"It is, Yasminka. You don't have to do this."

"I do. They need to understand." She drew a deep breath. If she was crying, Rachel couldn't tell her tears from the rain. "In the morning, the Chetniks came to take the boys from the base, all the boys, the young boys. While they were taking them, I lost sight of her. The Dutch were pushing us to the buses, it was a terrible crush. I was looking for Selmira, I was frantic. I forgot to look out for the boys, forgot to ask where they were going. Then our neighbor said, 'She's in the woods outside. Someone found her there. Don't go there.' But I went."

They had arranged themselves in a circle, the circle of survivors: Damir Hasanović, Avdo and Hakija Osmanović—and at its center, Yasminka Sinanović.

"She was hanging there. She had hanged herself with her own scarf, the scarf one of the Chetniks had nearly strangled her with. I couldn't recognize her face but I knew her scarf. I asked our neighbors to cut her down but they said we didn't have time. They said I had to get on the bus before the soldiers came back. It was my only chance or the soldiers would come for me again. Mrs. Obranovic— she rubbed dirt on my face to make me ugly. And I got on the bus. I didn't see my sister again. I don't know where she's buried. Her bones were never identified. All I have is the button from her sleeve and the sight of her body hanging in those trees." She rubbed her own sleeve self-consciously. "Why have you come here?"

Esa wiped the rain from his face with trembling hands. "Your name is Yasminka Sinanović?"

"Yes." She stared back at him with the eyes of a stranger.

"You wrote those letters to Christopher Drayton? It was you who sent them?"

"To Dražen Krstić, yes. There was no Christopher Drayton."

How little he had known her. How little he had understood the motivation behind her warmth, her instant closeness.

"Did you plant the lilies?" Rachel asked. "The Bosnian lilies in Drayton's garden?"

Aldo stepped forward, drawing Mink toward him. "That was my gift to Drayton. A gift from the Bosnian people. A reminder. That what he killed didn't die."

"Then which one of you killed him?"

They had drawn together in a little circle, sheltering each other from the cold gusts of the wind and the rain that slashed at them all.

Esa looked at Mink as if he were waking from a dream, a look composed of horror and betrayal. "You killed him."

Mink ignored him. She nodded at David Newhall.

"No," he answered. "He fell to his death."

"But you did something," Rachel said slowly. "For two years, you stalked Dražen Krstić. He must have felt terrorized."

Newhall laughed, a short, sharp bark. Crowded together in the darkness, the Bosnians arranged themselves like a crumbling wall.

"Terrorized?" he spit at her. "You don't know what terror is. Talk to me when you've spent three years strangled and starved by Serb guns, when every member of your family has been taken to an execution site, bulldozed into a grave, and then excavated to a secondary grave, their bones scattered over your homeland to disguise the monstrosities committed against them. Try a month in Banja Luka when your mosques are bombed back into history and your leaders are sent to a death camp to be murdered. Or a week subjected to every form of rape imaginable in Foča, or a day in Brčko where they toss the bodies of the people you love into a furnace. A few letters sent to a man like Krstić do not terrorize. He promised we would be knee-deep in blood. He reveled in it."

A sick feeling rose in Rachel's stomach. "You must have wanted him to feel the things you're describing to me," she said. "These two years of your campaign were leading somewhere, but what was the catalyst that brought about his death?"

Mink stared at Nathan, her gaze unflinching, and suddenly he knew.

"It was the opening of the museum, the opening ceremony for Ringsong. You never planned to take Drayton's money. It was the attempt he made to attach himself to the ideals of Andalusia, its culture of pluralism. It was too much for you to bear."

"I'm sorry, Esa," Mink said to him, abruptly. "You could never understand. Look at your position. You worship at any mosque you choose, and none of your neighbors would dream of saying to you that your minarets are a blight, the symbol of an execrable enemy. Your identity is a gift. It's a badge you wear with honor, and this girl"—she gestured at Rachel, then at Nathan—"and your friend, they respect you for it." She tried not to look at him and failed. "In

Bosnia, identity is a curse. In Srebrenica, it was a death sentence. So do not pretend to know us. Please, just do not pretend."

"Did you kill Christopher Drayton?" he asked, his voice tight.

"Dražen Krstić fell to his death." Despite the rain and the cruel roar of the wind, her voice was even.

Rachel slicked her wet hair behind her ears. "Why did you mention Foča, Brčko, and Banja Luka?" she asked David Newhall.

"I could name you a hundred other places," Newhall sneered. "Have you heard of Omarska, Trnopolje, Manjača?"

The Bosnians exchanged silent looks, huddled closer. A primal certainty electrified Rachel's nerves. She had guessed. Nearly everything, she had guessed.

"The night Drayton died, you went to see him. All of you. I couldn't understand the wax on the floor until I arranged the letters and photograph in a circle. The wax your candles left behind—they fell in a circle around Drayton's chair. It was a vigil—or maybe you saw it as a circle of justice. You must have planned that moment of confrontation, it was too well-rehearsed. But why was his gun on the floor? I've made sense of everything else—the lilies, the photograph, the letters—but I can't figure out the gun."

They looked at each other but didn't speak until Newhall took the lead.

"He was drunk. He was always drunk on Slivovitz in the evenings. It was easy to get him in the study. We told him the time had come to pay for Srebrenica. It was laughable in a way, how shocked he was when we told him our names, when we spoke in our language. We told him who we were and he sobered up quickly. He demanded we get out of his house. He pretended his chest was hurting."

"Maybe it was," Rachel argued. "Maybe he suffered an attack from the confrontation."

"He suffered nothing except our hatred," Mink said coldly. "We told him he was free to go at any time. We asked him if he wanted us to pronounce the sentence he had evaded for so many years."

"What sentence was that?"

"We knew he kept a gun in his drawer. We asked him to use it on himself. An execution. Like he had executed our families, our friends."

"The gun wasn't loaded," Rachel said cautiously.

"Yes." Her lips sketched the parody of a smile. "We knew a man like Krstić would never choose the honorable course. He told me I was a choice piece and that his men would have enjoyed me in the halls of Srebrenica. He said my sister killed herself because she wasn't good enough for them. He aimed the gun at me and pulled the trigger."

"And when the gun didn't fire?"

"He said his chest was hurting. He pleaded with us to go."

The smoke from the candles rose in spirals around him.

"Please," he gasped. "Acquit me."

The people gathered before his chair made no move to touch him. The gun fell from his nerveless hand to the floor, his eyes darting frantically about the circle, cowed by the pitiless faces.

They were chanting at him in Arabic, the language of the balija, *the prayers of the Turk. They were asking God to bring down His retribution. To chain him to the fire forever. His eyes searched out the lovely young girl. With a feeble effort, he reached out his hand to her. The girl with the soft face and kind eyes, surely she would acquit him, show him mercy. He would tell her—he would pretend he knew where the bones of her sister lay buried and what he would say would buy him absolution, a day, an hour, a moment to escape.*

His skin was clammy. He could feel the color drain from his face, the loss of motor control in his hands. The gun hadn't fired. Why hadn't the gun fired? What had been done to him?

"Please," he said again. "Absolve me. Let me go."

The girl raised her hand yet didn't touch him. She made the three-fingered Chetnik salute in his face, the salute Serb children gave the survivors of Srebrenica when they came to bury the bones of their loved ones.

"Absolve me," he cried piteously.

"So did our brothers plead before their murderers." Her cold eyes studied him. Had he ever thought her gentle, kindhearted? Had he fantasized about conquering her in bed?

"Beg," she said. "And remember them now."

The last thing he heard before the world went dark was the language of the enemy—Andalusia's golden idiom, the sacred name of Allah.

"He fainted," Mink said simply. "And so we left him there. If he chose to go to the Bluffs, it was God who held his reckoning at the last."

"You threatened him anonymously for years and then confronted an elderly man in a state of extreme agitation with a gun," Rachel contradicted.

David Newhall shook his head. "It was his gun. The only weapon in our hands was the truth. We asked him to admit his name, his nature. Did that endanger the butcher of Srebrenica?"

Rachel didn't argue. She hoped Khattak would say something. As a police officer she knew something needed to be said—this couldn't go unchallenged. He stood by, mute, silenced by the weight of so much deception.

"Come out, come out," Harry sang out. They turned to look at him. "Come out of the woods. Come to your families, your fathers. Come out of the woods."

But every man or boy who had ceded his hiding place in the woods had ultimately found his destiny in a ditch, in some cases after digging it himself.

His brother cradled him in his arms. "We didn't come down again, Haki. Remember? We stayed in the woods. We took the road to Tuzla. We found our mother."

"My brothers were not as fortunate," said Mink. "Neither was my sister. I am the sole survivor of my family. And he thought he could touch Andalusia, honoring not its glory but the calamity of its end. Tainting it with his name and his money. This from the man who destroyed Andalusia." She spit on the ground. "You take something beautiful, you raze it to the ground, and then you claim you didn't know what you had? You try to rebuild it and assure your status as a patron of things that are priceless and holy like the Sarajevo Haggadah, like the National Library of Sarajevo, when you burnt our history to ashes around us? Erasing us, erasing memory."

"You called it a memory palace," Rachel said. "You said the museum was a memory palace like the great cities of Andalusia."

"This is what we have now, the peaceful people of Bosnia. Palaces of memory. Everything else is lost or destroyed. A hundred thousand people are dead—and the women. Will you weep for the women of our country as we do? Will you help us? You couldn't even bring Dražen Krstić to justice." She broke free from the others to back away to the edge of the Bluffs. Rachel froze in place.

"Please," she said. "You can't give up."

Mink laughed, the sound acrid in her throat.

"I am not like these men who pretend to long for the country they destroyed. Momir Nikolić wants to serve his sentence and return to his home in Bratunac to live there in peace and harmony 'such as prevailed before the outbreak of the war.' Why don't they call it a slaughter?" She asked the question of herself, poised on the edge. "While my people are scattered across the globe, denied any semblance of justice."

"Mink, be careful!" She had been down this road before. In Waverley, where Miraj Siddiqui had died. That final moment when Rachel could have saved a life, could have foreseen the truth and had failed utterly at both. She still dreamt of it. She couldn't face that outcome again.

"Please," she whispered.

"Bratunac," Harry whispered, jerking at his brother's arm. "We stayed on the bus in Bratunac. They didn't take us into the school."

"No," Aldo said patiently. "We stayed on the bus in Bratunac, Haki. It saved our lives."

"The bus is life," Harry repeated, as if he had memorized it. "The school is death."

"Haki." Mink's voice broke. Harry covered his ears. A wild keening rose above the wind.

"They're shooting," he sobbed. "They're killing everybody."

"Don't." His brother covered his mouth. "Don't Haki, it's over. It's over. We found our mother in Tuzla, remember?"

Harry fought his way free. "Everybody is dead, everybody is dead." He chanted the words in a helpless rhythm. "Get them off me, Avdi! Get the dead ones off me! The ants, Avdi! I can't breathe—help me!"

Aldo drew in his breath, sheltered his eyes from the rain, let his brother break away perilously close to the edge of the cliff. There was resolution in his face.

"Lie still," he said to Harry. "Lie still and don't move until I give you the signal. Can you do that, Haki?"

"I can do it. I'm doing it, Avdi."

Harry fell to the muddy ground and lay flat, burying his face in the mat of coarse grass.

"I'm dead, Avdi," he said. His brother's strategy had worked. He'd removed himself from the edge of the cliff.

"You're dead," Aldo agreed. "We're both dead, Haki. That's how we make it." He looked at David Newhall. "Help me," he said.

"Mink," Rachel said again. "You're not safe there, please. Please move away."

Deaf to her words, Mink gathered her hair from around her face and twisted it into a rope. "Hold fast to the rope, Esa," she said. There was mockery in her voice, a mockery that sliced at his heart. "You thought we were the same, and we aren't. For you, Andalusia was an idyll, a golden dream. But it was real to us."

"Mink." Her name was a plea on his lips. Rachel saw the hopelessness on his face, the painful entreaty.

"My name is Yasminka Sinanović, and I am the last of my family. You cannot help me, Esa." She turned her attention to Rachel, stepping away from the edge. "I am a witness to genocide. My work is not done."

She took David Newhall's hand within her own. Together, they reached down to gather Harry Osmond's body from the ground, boosting him to his feet. As a group they shouldered past Rachel and Nate down the path toward Ringsong.

"Wait!" Rachel called. "How can you prove you didn't follow Drayton that night? How do we know you didn't take justice into your own hands?"

Mink answered her by turning up her hands. "We called a meeting for the museum that night. We were all there, well into the night. And so were Hadley and Marco."

David Newhall paused on the path.

"If there was one thing you should have learned from the letters, it is that we did not want what the fascists wanted. The destruction of all that we built together, the country that we shared. Our legacy isn't death." He shook his head at their inability to understand the simplest lesson in the world. Oblivious to Esa's pain, he kissed Mink's hand.

"Believe it or not, it's hope."

37.

Nothing can give me resolution. Nothing can give me consolation.

Nate passed Esa a towel. They were ensconced before the fire in his library, Rachel taking care not to drip onto the velvet sofa, despite Nate's reassurance.

"I'm all right." She warmed herself by the fire. "We're nowhere, sir. We're no further forward."

"Would you leave us for a moment, Rachel?"

He'd been too dignified to pursue Mink when her rejection was so complete. Something had broken between them; Rachel hoped it was irreparable.

"I'll help myself in the kitchen, shall I? How hard could your espresso machine be to work?"

"A fine mind like yours will solve the riddle in no time," said Nate. His face was serious despite the laughter in his voice. He watched her go. He stood by his friend's side before the fire, warming his frozen hands.

"Rachel told you?" Esa asked finally.

"She went back to the Bosnian mosque. She met with your friend Asaf, who told her about David Newhall's work—Hasanović's work, I mean. And he told her about the other survivors. He recognized the photo of Selmira. The rest was Rachel's doing. She kept talking about a circle and somehow—I don't know how—she deduced that a confrontation had taken place the night of Drayton's fall." He was afraid to test his friend, until the thought rose in his mind that if he couldn't say to Esa those things that had been natural and automatic in their friendship before, what point was there in continuing? "Do you believe what the Bosnians told us?"

Esa nodded. "I've no doubt of it. Hasanović isn't a killer."

"And Mink?"

Esa turned to him, rubbing the moisture from his hair with an absentminded gesture. "I want to ask you something," he said.

"Anything."

"I need to ask for your forgiveness. Because I didn't know. Until Mink, I didn't know the power a woman could hold over your thoughts. Over everything you knew of yourself. For me, it was black and white: myself or Laine Stoicheva, I couldn't see how you were torn. I didn't know a person could be torn like that." He laid the wet towel over the fireguard. "You tried to tell me, I know. You wrote *Apologia* and still—I couldn't find it in myself to let it go. I couldn't see how wrong I was until now."

He looked away from the pity in Nate's eyes, the warm compassion.

"Rachel was right when she accused me of having lost my objectivity. The clues were there for me to decipher—the letters, the lilies, the true identity of David Newhall. And yet it didn't occur to me that the others were acting a charade as well. Who better to have planted flowers than a gardener? How was I so blind to the connection between Andalusia and Bosnia? How could I have asked Mink nothing about her family, her history? She didn't need to lie to me. I gave her nothing to lie about. I was lost."

"You were caught," Nate corrected. "Don't blame yourself. I've lived with my neighbors for two years and never suspected that anyone was anything other than he or she pretended to be. As for Drayton, Mink had some sense that Hadley and Cassidy were in danger. I never did."

"Rachel made the connections."

"I can see why you chose her for your team. Her instincts are excellent. Be grateful she's on your side. Because she is. She's loyal to you. And maybe she guessed at all this because she knows what it means to lose a brother. She knows what a powerful driving force it can be. And since she didn't know any of these people, she could sense it was a charade. She knew it wasn't real. She also told me I should have read more as a child."

"Why?" Lightness tempered the grief on Esa's face.

"She said she finally made sense of the candles because of *Murder on the Orient Express.* It wasn't about a single person with a singular motive. It was something the Bosnians enacted together to serve a common end. Mink wrote the letters. David Newhall helped her. The Osmonds planted the lilies. And then they faced Drayton together."

"Because of the museum."

"Not just that." Nate pressed his friend's shoulder, aware that the reason would hurt him.

"Then what?"

"Because the Department of Justice didn't take them seriously. They must have felt they had no other choice."

Esa mulled this over. "Drayton would have disappeared," he agreed. "Before anyone could do anything."

"And that would have been too much. Much too much for Mink and the others."

The sound of rattling teacups drew their attention to the door. Rachel entered, bearing a tray of miniature espresso cups in their saucers. The room filled with a woodsy aroma.

"Don't ask me where I found these," she said.

"My sister's dollhouse?" Nate guessed.

"Just drink before you catch cold."

She said it lightly, her concern for Esa evident. Her hair plastered to her face by the rain, her soggy clothes bunched about her body, she was still the most interesting woman Nathan had met in years.

"Where does that leave us?" he asked. "Will you do anything further?"

"I'll advise Hasanović to leave the neighborhood. And I'll recommend that Tom release his statement immediately."

"You believe them, then," Rachel said.

"You don't?"

Rachel slurped her espresso, scowling when she scalded her tongue. "So much anger, so much hatred. Such practiced deception—I'm sorry, sir. I know you wanted her to be above this."

"I've no right to expect that of her," he said quietly.

"She had no right to lie to you. I can't figure out what it is that I haven't figured out."

Esa wasn't listening to her. He'd braced himself against the table, his thoughts abstracted. "Rachel," he said, "show me the photographs again."

Surprised, she retrieved the envelope from her bag and shook its contents out on the table. Esa sorted through them until his hand came to rest on the photograph of Drayton's study. The chair surrounded by puddles of wax.

She followed his gaze and his outstretched finger as he made his count.

She saw it too. And now what Damir Hasanović had told them on the Bluffs rocketed into place, fusing the pieces of the puzzle together.

"Great Holy God."

"I can't help but think that's appropriate."

They knocked on the door of his living quarters, sequestered behind the mosque, hidden from view by the overhanging maples.

He answered the door dressed in his customary long robes, his head bare, his beard neatly trimmed.

"Damir said you would come."

Under the wild rain on the Bluffs, David Newhall had told her about terror.

Banja Luka. Foča. Brčko.

"Why did you mention Banja Luka, Foča, and Brčko?" she had asked Newhall, oblivious to the answer.

They were the same cities Imam Muharrem had named. Rachel felt a momentary respite from horror as Nate squeezed her hand. Realization, sickeningly conclusive, tumbled through her thoughts. Why hadn't the imam told them about Damir Hasanović, the highest-profile member of their congregation? Why hadn't he mentioned the circle of Srebrenica survivors that had included Avdo and Hakija Osmanović, Yasminka Sinanović, and Damir? She had viewed photos of the genocide memorial online. She had read the long list of Osmanović dead, a list that seemed to trail down forever into history. So many men from one family dead, she had thought. And just these two boys to survive.

"Today no man from our family is older than thirty," Mirnesa Ahmić had said in her testimony before the tribunal.

Why had the imam told them the entire grand narrative of the Bosnian war, yet left out everything that made it so personal? The worst part was that she knew the answer to her question. Her previous scenario of the confrontation had been catastrophically incomplete.

Khattak had shown her the proof of it, counting out the number.

"There are five spots on the floor. Five places for the candles. Who else was there that night? Avdo, Hakija, Damir, Yasminka—that only makes four."

She saw their faces again in the rain, the silent exchange as they clutched each other's hands. Wounded as they were, none of the people poised at the edge of the Bluffs had set this plan in motion. And none of them had chosen to name him. The man who knew Srebrenica, knew Brčko, knew Banja Luka, knew Foča.

"You were there that night."

Muharrem led them inward to his rooms. A prayer rug was spread out on the floor, the Qur'an at its head balanced on a small wooden stand. One wall in the room was decorated, the wall in front of a comfortable chesterfield. Facing them was a poster of the sixteenth-century Ferhadija mosque. "Shall I make us tea?"

"We'd rather have the truth."

No one sat. After a moment, the imam gathered up his Qur'an and placed it on the coffee table.

"It was you," Rachel repeated. "You recognized Krstić from the moment you first saw him."

"And if I did?"

"You told the others."

"Was that a crime? Was it not a greater crime that Krstić was here in your country, safe and happy, thriving at every turn? Did you ask how he gained immigration? Can you explain why your Department of Justice did nothing when we reported who he was? Or why you ignored our pleas for assistance?"

There was nothing in his demeanour to recall the patience and forbearance of the man they had interviewed on two previous occasions. His bearing was proud, stiffly unapologetic. No suggestion of his former friendliness lingered about his eyes.

"We are investigating now."

"Now," he mocked them. "Two years later and only because the butcher himself is dead. We were prepared to wait for you to act. You chose to do nothing. And now you worry about your reputation, your government agencies, the black mark on your credibility as peace-keepers."

"Imam Muharrem—"

"You are the worst of all, Inspector Esa. You pretended solidarity, promised me an answer, and yet what did you have your colleague do? Did you tell the world about Dražen Krstić? Did your government admit its mistake? Were you even aware that a man known for sexual sadism had children in his care?"

"If you had told us what you knew, we would have been able to act more quickly."

"Well." The imam shrugged. "I didn't know there was such a person as the righteous Inspector Esa, defender of the Bosnians, did I? I knew of your War Crimes Commission, so we began there." His bleak gaze encompassed Rachel and Nate. "And nothing came of it."

Rachel swallowed noisily. "So what did you do about it, sir?"

"What did I do? What did I do? What did you expect me to do? I talked to you. I told you about Banja Luka, about Prijedor. I told you what happened in the rape camps of Foča. I told you what they did to my family in Brčko. Broken. Thrown into the furnace like refuse. What did *you* do?"

"We tried to find the truth. We followed every possible lead to prove that Drayton was Krstić."

"His gun, his tattoo—they were not enough? The tattoo I pointed you to. The JNA-issued military pistol. Not enough?"

"Then you were there that night," she breathed.

"Of course I was. It was my plan from the first. Did you think I would let my children face it alone? My poor Haki? My lonely lost Yasminka? Our beloved Damir, whose quest for justice has been blocked again and again? It is only because of Damir that Haki and Avdo made it to Canada. Why? Because when Avdi made it to Tuzla, he gave Damir his brother's tennis shoes. Mesha's body falling over Avdi was what saved him from the artillery fire. And Avdi—so young, so brave—made himself look at the body that saved him, made himself remember so he could tell one person what had happened to someone he loved. Damir will carry this debt all his life. And he saved Yasminka as well. Because of his efforts, she was able to bury her brothers and place their names upon the memorial. Did you think I would abandon these children to face the devil alone?"

"What happened that night?" Rachel asked him. "The others said they confronted Krstić and he fainted. They say they left him alive."

"Did they also tell you that he rose from his chair, threatening us with his gun? And that when he fell back drunk, he said our people had died because they were weak—too weak to fight, too worthless to live. He boasted about his accomplishments in Srebrenica. He said he would pull the same trigger again. He fired at Yasminka but his gun was empty. We had checked it beforehand—that seemed to surprise him. We weren't foolish enough to trust in his rehabilitation."

"Then where did you go that night? After the confrontation?

Yasminka didn't say you were at the meeting for the museum with the others."

"I wasn't."

"Where were you, then?"

He sat down in a single motion, balancing the Qur'an on his lap.

"Was I here in my rooms, offering prayers of gratitude and perseverance to the Almighty Protector? Or did I walk along the Bluffs in the dark to see what the butcher would do? He didn't have the strength or the humanity to point the gun at his own head, as we had asked him. Perhaps he chose another way."

Rachel bit back a gasp. "Are you saying he jumped? That Krstić committed suicide because you had tormented him for so long?"

"Would he do such a thing?" His smile was bleak. "Perhaps it was the ghosts of Srebrenica who haunted him. Perhaps they followed him wherever he went, the way they followed Avdo and Haki from the killing fields of Grbavici. Isn't that possible?"

Rachel's lips were stiff. "What did you really do, Imam Muharrem? Tell us the truth."

He caressed the Qur'an in his hands. "I did not begin hostilities."

"I'm asking if you finished them."

"Although he was a man who deserved death, I think you will find that my people are not murderers."

"And if you saw the men who murdered your family today? Marrying, having children? What would you do?"

"I would hunt each one of them down if I could."

"Were you on the Bluffs that night? Did you follow Drayton?"

"I'm very tired," he said. "This day has been a long time coming for my people. I would ask you to leave me to finish my prayers."

"We can't just leave it like this. Surely as an imam, you have a duty to the truth."

"No, my dear Sergeant. You had a duty to the truth and you failed it completely. I've fulfilled my responsibilities, one and all."

"With Krstić's death?" Esa asked him.

Imam Muharrem replaced the Qur'an on the table. He took up his stance on his prayer rug.

"How formidable is your desire for simple answers, Inspector Esa. Was I there or not? Did I follow Dražen Krstić? Did I send him to his death?" He raised his hands from his sides to his ears, to fold them over his stomach, oblivious to their urgency. "Allah knows the answer. Shall we leave it with Him?"

"If you're guilty of this, Imam Muharrem—"

"Then you will have to prove it."

They crowded together in the shelter of the mosque, its slender minaret backlit by the moon.

"Was that a confession?" Rachel asked. Her hands were trembling.

"I doubt we'll ever know." Nate said it, and Esa didn't contradict him.

"Then what do we do, sir?"

She wanted Khattak to know. She wanted to believe he had the bedrock certainty of right and wrong, truth and falsehood, that she herself lacked. There wasn't a single person who would mourn Dražen Krstić's death, whether murder, suicide, or accident. And yet, and yet—didn't they have a duty to the truth?

Khattak placed one hand on Nate's shoulder. "We call Tom Paley at Justice. The rest is up to them."

"Then come back to Winterglass."

She knew the invitation meant more than it seemed on the surface: it was Esa and Nate clearing away the wreckage of the past, the dross of Laine Stoicheva. It was Nate's warm eyes approving her as a person, a woman without artifice. It was the chance to sit by his fire and make a phone call to her brother without fear, without hopelessness, after he had helped her determine whether a girl named Sable Norman was a student at the Mozarteum.

Yet at this moment, it was the light of the minaret that seemed to hold the truth in the balance.

They had come full circle. Murder, suicide, accident, coincidence. There was no certainty to be had.

But Khattak thought he knew. He thought he knew what Muharrem had done. The man who had hounded Dražen Krstić and brought him to his knees would not have let him walk away at the last.

There had been a tussle in the dark on the edge of Cathedral Bluffs.

Justice had found the butcher of Srebrenica.

And the shadow of the mosque was no consolation.

Author's Note

This novel is based upon events that occurred during the 1992–1995 war in Bosnia, formerly a republic of the nation of Yugoslavia.

In 1991, Yugoslavia dissolved into its constituent republics, each of which was to wrestle with the question of independence. In 1990 and 1991, respectively, Slovenia and Croatia staged their referenda on independence from Yugoslavia. When Bosnia followed suit in 1992, it put forward a vision of the future that attested to its uniquely blended heritage. In Bosnia, Serbs, Croats, and Muslims spoke the same language, intermarried without controversy, and embraced each other's traditions in the fullness of history. In this vision of the future, the Bosnia that rose from the ashes of Yugoslavia was a nation of equal citizens, with rights guaranteed under a democratic constitution, in recognition of a centuries-old pluralism.

What came to pass instead was the vision of ultranationalists in the republics of Serbia and Croatia. In their formulation of Bosnia's future, a "Greater Serbia" or "Greater Croatia" could only be achieved by the annexation of a Bosnian territory rid of its non-Serb or non-Croat inhabitants. Thus followed a series of acts that began with the siege of Sarajevo in 1992, and culminated in the Srebrenica massacre of 1995.

For the first time since the Second World War, a genocide campaign of staggering ferocity and ruthlessness was unleashed against a civilian population in Europe, nearly in tandem with the international intervention that eventually became complicit in the suffering of Bosnia's people. In his influential work *Slaughterhouse*, journalist and author David Rieff calls the Bosnia of this period a "slaughter-house" and describes the conflict within its boundaries as a slaughter, not a war. Through Bosnia's many well-documented agonies, the terms *ethnic cleansing, cultural destruction*, and *rape camps* would also become commonplace.

The term *ethnic cleansing* first entered the parlance as a description of Serbian tactics that "cleansed" the land of its Muslim inhabitants. The substitution of this term for the actual crime of genocide went some distance toward undermining the international legal obligation to prevent the genocide while it was still under way. (See *Prosecutor v. Radislav Krstic* IT-98-33 [2 August 2001].)

Cultural destruction encompassed the deliberate campaign to eradicate mosques, Catholic churches, and countless other representations of religious and cultural identity—foremost among these, the architecture of Bosnia's Ottoman past. Finally, although an endemic part of the overall war strategy, it was for the widespread and systematic use of rape in the southeastern town of Foča that a historic legal precedent was set: rape was recognized as a crime against humanity under international law. (See *Prosecutor v. Dragoljub Kunarac and Radomir Kovac*, IT-96-23-PT [22 February 2001].)

For those who seek to learn how it was possible for the Bosnian enlightenment to be obliterated so swiftly and steadily, there are several key works I recommend. On the nature of the war crimes and cultural destruction that took place, see Roy Gutman's Pulitzer Prize–winning *A Witness to Genocide* and Michael Sells's *The Bridge Betrayed: Religion and Genocide in Bosnia*.

Rabia Ali and Lawrence Lifschultz's essay "In Plain View," in their edited book *Why Bosnia?*, remains a landmark in the study of the war, alongside *The Death of Yugoslavia* by Laura Silber and Allan Little. For perspective on the role the international community played, there is David Rieff's *Slaughterhouse: Bosnia and the Failure of the West*, Brendan Simms's *Unfinest Hour: Britain and the Destruction of Bosnia*, and Samantha Power's *A Problem from Hell: America in the*

Age of Genocide. Human rights reports, war crimes testimony, and UN reports are listed extensively in the notes section.

A comment on names used in this book. Although not based on actual persons, the characters Avdo and Hakija Osmanović were named for two Bosnians who did not survive the war. In 1993, Bosnia's vice president, Dr. Hakija Turajlić, was shot and killed by a Serb fighter while traveling with a United Nations Protection Force convoy. Surrounded by Serb forces on a road ostensibly under UN control, the French commander on the scene opened the armored personnel carrier transporting Dr. Turajlić, resulting in his immediate assassination.

Colonel Avdo Palić of the Army of Bosnia-Herzegovina defended safe area Zepa against Serb siege for more than three years, volunteering himself for negotiations with Serb forces during the fall of Srebrenica, so that the people of Zepa might escape a similar fate. Ordered to investigate and fully account for Colonel Palić's disappearance, the Palić Commission found that Avdo Palić had been held in a military prison until he was disappeared by Serb forces on the night of 4 September 1995. Avdo Palić's remains were subsequently located, exhumed, and returned to his wife, Esma, bringing her fourteen-year search for her husband to an end. He was buried with honors in 2009.

Though not based on any single individual, Dražen Krstić was named for two figures who were instrumental in the carrying out of the Srebrenica massacre. Dražen Erdemović was a soldier in the 10th Sabotage Detachment of the Bosnian Serb Army. He participated in the executions of hundreds of unarmed Bosnian Muslim men from the Srebrenica enclave and was the first person to enter a guilty plea at the International Criminal Tribunal for the former Yugoslavia (ICTY). General Radislav Krstić was the Deputy Commander of the Drina Corps. He took command of the Drina Corps on 13 July 1995, giving him direct command responsibility for the Srebrenica massacre and the forcible depopulation of the Srebrenica enclave. He was the first person to be convicted of genocide by the ICTY.

As to the tireless prosecutors and fearless investigators of the International Criminal Tribunal, who carry out such difficult yet necessary work: nothing has struck me more than the statement of the Chief War Crimes Investigator, Jean-René Ruez, when he said of Srebrenica, "It was a crime committed against every single one of us."

In that spirit, I wish to thank Professor Cherif Bassiouni, President Emeritus of the International Human Rights Law Institute. Professor Bassiouni took time out of his very busy schedule to educate a twenty-three-year-old law student about war crimes in Bosnia, at a time when he was investigating those crimes as Chairman of the United Nations Commission of Experts. His compassion and dedication have stayed with me all these years.

I worked briefly with the Bosnian Canadian Relief Association during the war and had the privilege of meeting many members of Bosnian communities and their imams. I particularly wish to thank Imam Muharrem, who shared his story with such courage and humanity. I have also had the opportunity to learn from the work of many Bosnian witnesses, activists, and scholars over the years, foremost among them Hasan Nuhanovic, whose efforts in the cause of justice have served so many without ever faltering.

I hope what couldn't be articulated at that time has been articulated in this book.

A last word on the people of Bosnia—Serb, Croat, and Muslim—who defended the Bosnian enlightenment in the face of the fascist drive for ethnic and religious uniformity. Their courage, perseverance, and dignity in the face of appalling carnage remind us why Bosnia was a place worth saving.

Notes

Chapter 1.

I will never worship what you worship. Nor will you worship what I worship. To you, your religion—to me, mine.
Sura Al Kafirun, "The Unbelievers." Qur'an 109: 4–6.

They are going to burn us all.
Paraphrased from the statement of Emil Čakalić, relating what he heard a soldier say to him and other prisoners at the Vukovar military barracks in 1991, after he narrowly escaped execution at Ovčara. He testified on 5 February 1998 in the case against Slavko Dokmanović; on 13 and 14 March 2006 in the case against the Yugoslav People's Army officers Veselin Šljivančanin, Mile Mrkšić, and Miroslav Radić; and on 16 July 2003 in the case against Slobodan Milošević. *Prosecutor v. Slavko Dokmanović*, IT-95-13a-T [5 February 1998], Witness Name: Emil Čakalić, page 908.

Chapter 2.

I keep wondering, where have all the good friends gone?
Letter of Muhamed Čehajić, former mayor of the Prijedor municipality, as read by his wife, Dr. Minka Čehajić, before the International Criminal Tribunal for the former Yugoslavia at the trial of Milomir Stakić. In its judgment of 31 July 2003, the Trial Chamber stated that it had no evidence at hand to establish beyond reasonable doubt the reason for Muhamed Čehajić's death. It said, however, that "even if Čehajić was not directly killed, the conditions imposed on a person whose health was fragile, alone would inevitably cause his death. His ultimate fate was clearly foreseeable." The Trial Chamber argued that due to Milomir Stakić's position as president of the Crisis Staff, the National Defense Council, the War Presidency, and the Municipal Assembly in Prijedor, and due to his close ties to both the police and the military, he could not "have been unaware of what was common knowledge around the town, the municipality, and even further afield." The Trial Chamber stated that "[i]t was Dr. Stakić himself [who] triggered the deplorable fate of this

honorable man." On 22 March 2006, the Appeals Chamber confirmed the convictions against Milomir Stakić and sentenced him to forty years' imprisonment. *Prosecutor v. Milomir Stakić*, IT-97-24-T [31 July 2003]. Minka Čehajić's complete "Voice of the Victims" statement is available through the International Criminal Tribunal for the former Yugoslavia at http://www.icty.org/sid/186.

Chapter 3.

He was a modest and reasonable man.
Minka Čehajić, a Bosnian pediatrician, speaking about her quest to find out what happened to her husband after she last saw him in May 1992. She testified on 14, 15, and 16 May 2002 in the case against Milomir Stakić. Čehajić's complete "Voice of the Victims" statement is available through the International Criminal Tribunal for the former Yugoslavia at http://www.icty.org/sid/186.

This is part of a cat-and-mouse game.
Letter dated 19 October 1992 from the Permanent Representative of Bosnia and Herzegovina to the United Nations, addressed to the president of the Security Council. S/24685, 19 October 1992.

You can either survive or disappear.
General Ratko Mladić, Commander of the Bosnian Serb Army (the VRS). Available online at *Justice Report*: http://www.justice-report.com/en/articles/interpreta tion-of-Mladić-s-words.

Because I tell you that the sky is too high and the ground is too hard.
Bosnian proverb.

Lo, with hardship comes ease.
Sura Ash-Sharh, "The Relief." Qur'an 94:5.

Chapter 4.

Father, take care of my children, look after my children.
Mehmed Alić, a Bosnian Muslim victim of the Omarska camp, speaking about how he tried to defend his son Enver from Serb soldiers who were about to beat him. He testified on 23 and 24 July 1996 in the case against Duško Tadić. Mehmed Alić was transferred to the Manjača camp on 6 August and released on 26 August 1992. Alic's complete "Voice of the Victims" statement is available through the International Criminal Tribunal for the former Yugoslavia at http://www.icty.org/sid /195.

Chapter 5.

I took my mother's head into my hands and I kissed her. I never felt anything so cold before . . .
Testimony of Indira Ahmetović, Srebrenica survivor. Her full statement is available through the Cinema for Peace Foundation at http://cinemaforpeace.ba/en/testi mony/indira-ahmetovic/46.

Chapter 6.

Do you still believe that we die only the first death and never receive any requital?
Sura As-Saffat, "Those Ranged in Ranks." Qur'an 37:58–59.

Muslims, you yellow ants, your days are numbered.
Old Chetnik war song.

Bend down, drink the water by the kerb like dogs.
Emir Beganović, a Bosnian Muslim man, was severely beaten and held under horrific conditions at the Serb-run Omarska detention camp, located just outside Prijedor, Bosnia and Herzegovina. He testified on 19 July 1996 in the case against Duško Tadić and on 4 and 5 May 2000 in the case against Kvočka et al. His complete "Voice of the Victims" statement is available through the International Criminal Tribunal for the former Yugoslavia at http://www.icty.org/sid/10120.

Give us some water first, then kill us. I was sorry to die thirsty.
Witness O (he testified with name and identity withheld from the public), a seventeen-year-old survivor of the Srebrenica executions, speaking about their perpetrators. He testified on 13 April 2000 in the case against Radislav Krstić. Witness O's complete "Voice of the Victims" statement is available through the International Criminal Tribunal for the former Yugoslavia at http://www.icty.org/sid/184.

Chapter 7.

Under a big pear tree there was a heap of between ten and twelve bodies. It was difficult to count them because they were covered over with earth, but heads and hands were sticking out of the little mound.
Ivo Atlija, a Bosnian Croat, speaking about killings that occurred in the area around his village in 1992 in the Prijedor municipality of Bosnia and Herzegovina. He testified on 3 and 4 July 2002 in the case against Milomir Stakić. His complete "Voice of the Victims" statement is available through the International Criminal Tribunal for the former Yugoslavia at http://www.icty.org/sid/190.

There's never any joy.
Saliha Osmanović, Srebrenica survivor, as quoted in "Srebrenica Memorial Day: Our Continuing Horror," *The Independent* (10 July 2013).

On Tuesday, there will be no bread in Sarajevo.
Letter dated 18 October 1992 from the Permanent Representative of Bosnia and Herzegovina to the United Nations, addressed to the president of the Security Council. S/24677, 19 October 1992.

The tragedy of Srebrenica will haunt our history forever.
UN General Assembly, *Report of the Secretary-General Pursuant to General Assembly Resolution 53/35: The Fall of Srebrenica*, 15 November 1999, A/54/549, paragraph 503. Available at http://www.refworld.org/docid/3ae6afb34.html.

It took some persuasion to convince my Serb neighbor with whom I had lived my whole life that I was suddenly his enemy and that I was to be killed.
Dr. Idriz Merdžanić, a Bosnian doctor who treated victims of the Trnopolje Camp, speaking about how he tried to have two injured children evacuated from the northwestern Bosnian town of Kozarac. He testified on 10 and 11 September 2002 in the case against Milomir Stakić. His complete "Voice of the Victims" statement is available through the International Criminal Tribunal for the former Yugoslavia at http://www.icty.org/sid/202.

I am aware that I cannot bring back the dead.
Momir Nikolić, "Statement of Guilt" (29 October 2003). Momir Nikolić was an assistant commander for Security and Intelligence in the Bosnian Serb Army. Nikolić was at the center of the crimes that took place following the fall of Srebrenica in July 1995. He did not raise any objections when informed of the plan to deport Muslim women and children and to separate, detain, and ultimately kill Muslim men. Nikolić did nothing to stop the beatings, humiliation, and killing of thousands of Bosnian Muslim men. He also personally coordinated the exhumation and reburial of victims' bodies. He testified in other proceedings before the Tribunal, including the trial of his two co-accused, Blagojević and Jokić. Nikolić was sentenced to twenty years' imprisonment. His complete statement is available through the International Criminal Tribunal for the former Yugoslavia at http://www.icty.org/sid/218.

Chapter 8.

All my life I will have thoughts of that and feel the pain that I felt then and still feel. That will never go away.
Witness 87 (she testified with name and identity withheld from the public), a Bosnian

Muslim girl talking in court about the effects of the rape and the abuse she suffered during the nine months she was held captive by Serb soldiers. During this period she was also raped by Dragoljub Kunarac and Radomir Kovač. She testified on 4, 5 April and 23 October 2000 in the case against Dragoljub Kunarac, Zoran Vuković, and Radomir Kovač. Witness 87's complete "Voice of the Victims" statement is available through the International Criminal Tribunal for the former Yugoslavia at http://www.icty.org/sid/10117.

Chapter 9.

I addressed one of the wingborn singers,
who was sad at heart and aquiver.

"For what do you lament so plaintively" I asked,
And it answered, "For an age that is gone, forever."

Ruggles, D. F., "Arabic Poetry and Architectural Memory in al-Andalus," *Ars Orientalis, Pre-Modern Islamic Palaces* (1993, Vol. 23), 171–78.

Chapter 10.

Easily predictable events have been proceeding inexorably in the cruelest, most atrocious fashion.
Ambassador Ahmed Snoussi, Representative of Morocco to the Security Council. *Provisional Verbatim Record of the Three Thousand and Eighty-Second Meeting, held at Headquarters, New York Saturday, 30 May 1992: Security Council.* S/PV.3082, 30 May 1992, p. 25.

Today a funeral procession was shelled. The whole city is without water.
Letter dated 28 September 1992 from the acting president of Bosnia and Herzegovina to the United Nations, addressed to the president of the Security Council. S/24601, 29 September 1992, p. 2.

Charred bodies lie along the street.
Letter dated 9 September 1992 from the Permanent Representative of Bosnia and Herzegovina to the United Nations, addressed to the president of the Security Council. S/24537, 9 September 1992, p. 2.

Chapter 11.

All my joys and my happiness up to then have been replaced by pain and sorrow for my son and my husband.
Srebrenica survivor Sabaheta, as quoted in Selma Leydesdorff, "Stories from No Land: The Women of Srebrenica Speak Out," *Human Rights Review* (April 2007, Vol. 8:3), 191.

Chapter 12.

Whoever was on the list to be killed would be killed.
Quoting Schefik, a thirty-eight-year-old construction worker taken to Manjača. Charles Lane, "Dateline: Croatia," *The Black Book of Bosnia*, ed. Nader Mousaviza-deh (New Republic, 1996), 84.

I have just been informed that the besieged city of Jajce has fallen to the aggressor.
Letter dated 29 October 1992 from the Permanent Representative of Bosnia and Herzegovina to the United Nations, addressed to the president of the Security Council. S/24740, 29 October 1992.

Massive air attacks continue in Bosnia today. We cannot defend ourselves yet no one is coming to our aid.
Letter dated 28 September 1992 from the acting president of Bosnia and Herze-govina to the United Nations, addressed to the president of the Security Council. S/24601, 29 September 1992, p. 2.

For having uttered a wrong word, people are taken away or killed.
Letter dated 9 September 1992 from the Permanent Representative of Bosnia and Herzegovina to the United Nations, addressed to the president of the Security Coun-cil. S/24537, 9 September 1992, p. 2.

The camps remain open.
Letter dated 4 November 1992 from the Permanent Representative of Bosnia and Herzegovina to the United Nations, addressed to the president of the Security Council. S/24761, 5 November 1992.

The enemy ring around the city is being strengthened with fresh troops.
Letter dated 22 June 1992 from His Excellency Mr. Alija Izetbegović, President of Bosnia and Herzegovina, to the United Nations, addressed to the president of the Security Council. S/24214, 22 June 1992.

For the past three days, Serb forces have been conducting a fierce offensive against the town of Bihac.
Letter dated 9 February 1994 from the Permanent Representative of Bosnia and Herzegovina to the United Nations, addressed to the president of the Security Council. S/1994/142, 9 February 1994, p. 2.

Today Serb forces shelled the city of Tuzla. While writing this letter, the city centre is under heavy mortar attack.
Letter dated 14 January 1994 from the mayor of the City of Tuzla to the United Nations, addressed to the president of the Security Council. S/1994/45, 14 January 1994, p. 2.

The famous National Library has been set on fire and is still burning.
Joint letter dated 26 August 1992 from the acting president of the Presidency and the Prime Minister of Bosnia to the United Nations, addressed to the Security Council. S/26500, 26 August 1992, p. 2.

Defend us or let us defend ourselves. You have no right to deprive us of both.
Alija Izetbegović, President of Bosnia and Herzegovina, before the Security Council. As quoted in Paul Lewis, "At UN, Bosnian Presses His Plea for More Land," *New York Times* (8 September 1993).

If Allah helps you, none can ever overcome you; but if He should forsake you, who is there after Him that can help you? In Allah, then, let the believers put their trust.
Sura Al Imran. Qur'an 3:160.

Chapter 13.

No one knows what will come tomorrow
and no one knows in what land he will die.
Sura Luqman. Qur'an 31:34.

Chapter 14.

Somewhere life withers, somewhere it begins.
Srebrenica survivor, from *Srebrenica: A Cry from the Grave*, directed by Leslie Woodhead ([distributor Thirteen/WNET PBS], 1999).

Chapter 15.

While the Serb soldier was dragging my son away, I heard his voice for the last time. And he turned around and then he told me, "Mummy please, can you get that bag for me? Could you please get it for me?"
Witness DD, a Bosnian Muslim woman, speaking about how she lost her husband and two sons in the July 1995 Srebrenica genocide. She testified on 26 July 2000 in the case against Radislav Krstić. Witness DD's complete "Voice of the Victims" statement is available through the International Criminal Tribunal for the former Yugoslavia at http://www.icty.org/sid/10124.

Chapter 16.

The National Library of Sarajevo is burning.
Joint letter dated 26 August 1992 from the acting president of the Presidency and the Prime Minister of Bosnia to the United Nations, addressed to the Security Council. S/ 26500, 26 August 1992, p. 2.

A radio broadcast instructed Muslims to put white ribbons around their arms, go outside, form columns and head towards the main square.
Emir Beganović, a Bosnian Muslim man. He testified on 19 July 1996 in the case against Duško Tadić and on 4 and 5 May 2000 in the case against Kvočka et al. His complete "Voice of the Victims" statement is available through the International Criminal Tribunal for the former Yugoslavia at http://www.icty.org/sid/10120.

Chapter 17.

I don't have a photograph of my child when he was small . . . I want to apologize for crying," Mrs. Čehajić told the court, "because you cannot compare this with what has happened, but this is also something that is important to many people.
Minka Čehajić, a Bosnian pediatrician. She testified on 14, 15, and 16 May 2002 in the case against Milomir Stakić. Čehajić's complete "Voice of the Victims" statement is available through the International Criminal Tribunal for the former Yugoslavia at http://www.icty.org/sid/186.

Chapter 18.

Simply, they left no witnesses behind.
Emir Beganović, a Bosnian Muslim man. He testified on 19 July 1996 in the case against Duško Tadić and on 4 and 5 May 2000 in the case against Kvočka et al. His

complete "Voice of the Victims" statement is available through the International Criminal Tribunal for the former Yugoslavia at http://www.icty.org/sid/10120.

I would like to appeal to you to ask, Mr. Krstić, whether there is any hope for at least that little child that they snatched away from me, because I keep dreaming about him. I dream of him bringing flowers and saying, "Mother, I've come." I hug him and say, "Where have you been, my son?" And he says, "I've been in Vlasenica all this time." So I beg you, if Mr. Krstić knows anything about it, about him surviving someplace . . .

Witness DD, a Bosnian Muslim woman, appealing to Judge Rodrigues at the Krstić trial. She testified on 26 July 2000 in the case against Radislav Krstić. Witness DD's complete "Voice of the Victims" statement is available through the International Criminal Tribunal for the former Yugoslavia at http://www.icty.org/sid/10124.

Chapter 19.

How is it possible that a human being could do something like this, could destroy everything, could kill so many people? Just imagine this youngest boy I had, those little hands of his, how could they be dead? I imagine those hands picking strawberries, reading books, going to school, going on excursions. Every morning I cover my eyes not to look at other children going to school and husbands going to work, holding hands.

Witness DD, a Bosnian Muslim woman, speaking about how she lost her husband and two sons in the July 1995 Srebrenica genocide. She testified on 26 July 2000 in the case against Radislav Krstić. Witness DD's complete "Voice of the Victims" statement is available through the International Criminal Tribunal for the former Yugoslavia at http://www.icty.org/sid/10124.

Collect your ammunition and let's go to the meadow to kill the men.

Gojko Simic, Commander of the Anti-Tank Platoon of the Fourth Battalion, 1st Zvornik Brigade, as quoted in *Srebenica: Reconstruction, Background, Consequences and Analyses of the Fall of a "Safe" Area* (Netherlands Institute of War Documentation, 2000): part 4, chapter 2, p. 72. Available online at http://www.srebrenica-project.com /DOWNLOAD/NOD/NIOD%20Part%20IV.pdf.

Chapter 20.

All wounds will be healed but not this one.

Bekir Izetbegović, Bosnian member of the Presidential Council of Bosnia and Herzegovina. As quoted in Markar Esayan, "Srebrenica, Cain's Sign and Poetry," *Today's Zaman* (10 July 2011). Available online at http://www.todayszaman.com /columnists/markar-esayan-250045-srebrenica-cains-sign-and-poetry.html.

Chapter 21.

I apologize to the victims and to their shadows. I will be happy if this contributed to reconciliation in Bosnia, if neighbors can again shake hands, if our children can again play games together, and if they have the right to a chance.
Dragan Obrenović, Statement of Guilt (30 October 2003). Dragan Obrenović was a senior officer and commander within the Bosnian Serb Army in July 1995. He was convicted for persecutions carried out through the murder of hundreds of Bosnian Muslim civilians, committed in and around Srebrenica. Under the plea agreement, he agreed to testify in other proceedings before the Tribunal, including those trials related to Srebrenica. Obrenović was sentenced to seventeen years' imprisonment. His complete statement is available through the International Criminal Tribunal for the former Yugoslavia at http://www.icty.org/sid/219.

Chapter 22.

Mr. Stakić is here. He's a physician just like I am, and he made decisions concerning the camps. He knew that we were there. He knew that his colleague Jusuf Pasic, who was facing retirement, had been taken to Omarska and killed there. He knew about dozens of doctors, physicians being taken to Omarksa and killed. Why? These people were the Muslim intelligentsia and they meant something. Is there an answer to all of this?
Dr. Idriz Merdžanić, a Bosnian doctor who treated victims of the Trnopolje Camp. He testified on 10 and 11 September 2002 in the case against Milomir Stakić. His complete "Voice of the Victims" statement is available through the International Criminal Tribunal for the former Yugoslavia at http://www.icty.org/sid/202.

Chapter 23.

Verily God will not change the condition of a people until they change what is in themselves.
Sura Ar-Ra'd, "The Thunder." Qur'an 13:11.

Chapter 24.

We heard it on the radio. They will send the airplanes now. They will save us now.
Witness DD, a Bosnian Muslim woman, appealing to Judge Rodrigues at the Krstić trial. She testified on 26 July 2000 in the case against Radislav Krstić. Witness DD's complete "Voice of the Victims" statement is available through the International Criminal Tribunal for the former Yugoslavia at http://www.icty.org/sid/10124.

I'm not going to any safe place. The Serbs are going to take me.
Hasan Nuhanović, translator at the UN base at Potočari, discussing the fall of Srebrenica. As cited in Joe Rubin, "Srebrenica: A Survivor's Story," *Frontline/World* (28 March 2006). Available online at http://www.pbs.org/frontlineworld/stories/bosnia502/interviews_hasan.html.

Chapter 25.

30 Dutch = 30,000 Muslims.
Note handed to a Dutch lieutenant by a Muslim officer in Srebrenica. Mark Danner, "What Went Wrong?" (PBS.org, 1999). Published online in conjunction with *Srebenica: A Cry from the Grave*, directed by Leslie Woodhead ([distributor Thirteen /WNET PBS], 1999). Available online at http://www.pbs.org/wnet/cryfromthe grave/aftermath/t2_essay.html.

Chapter 26.

It is a crime committed against every single one of us.
Jean-René Ruez, Chief War Crimes Investigator, Srebrenica. *Srebrenica: A Cry from the Grave*, directed by Leslie Woodhead ([distributor Thirteen/WNET PBS], 1999).

Chapter 27.

When I close my eyes, I don't see the men.
Srebrenica survivor. *Srebrenica: A Cry from the Grave*, directed by Leslie Woodhead ([distributor Thirteen/WNET PBS], 1999).

In fourteen days, Srebrenica will be gone.
A statement made by a VRS (Bosnian Serb Army) soldier to one of the military personnel trying to get through to Srebrenica on 4 July 1995. It is unclear if it was a DutchBat driver or a company medic who was warned. *Srebenica: Reconstruction, Background, Consequences and Analyses of the Fall of a "Safe" Area* (Netherlands Institute of War Documentation, 2000): part 4, chapter 5, p. 260. Available online at http://www.srebrenica-project.com/DOWNLOAD/NOD/NIOD%20Part%20IV.pdf.

When the Serbs took Srebrenica, they wiped from the earth three generations of men.
Mirsada Malagić, a Bosnian Muslim woman, speaking about the women whose husbands were killed in the Srebrenica massacres in 1995. She testified on 3 and 4 April 2000 in the case against Radislav Krstić and on 16 February 2011 in the case against Zdravko Tolimir. Mirsada Malagić's complete "Voice of the Victims" state-

ment is available through the International Criminal Tribunal for the former Yugoslavia at http://www.icty.org/sid/191.

The young boys were crying out for their parents, the fathers for their sons. But there was no help.
A survivor of the Srebrenica massacre, describing the preparations for executions. *Srebenica: Reconstruction, Background, Consequences and Analyses of the Fall of a "Safe" Area* (Netherlands Institute of War Documentation, 2000): part 4, chapter 2, p. 71. Available online at http://www.srebrenica-project.com/DOWNLOAD/NOD /NIOD%20Part%20IV.pdf.

I realized then that nothing good was in store for us in Potočari.
Mirsada Malagić, a Bosnian Muslim woman. She testified on 3 and 4 April 2000 in the case against Radislav Krstić and on 16 February 2011 in the case against Zdravko Tolimir. Mirsada Malagić's complete "Voice of the Victims" statement is available through the International Criminal Tribunal for the former Yugoslavia at http://www.icty.org/sid/191.

Chapter 28.

Any rape is monstrously unacceptable but what is happening at this very moment in these rape and death camps is even more horrific.
Semra Turkovic, women's rights advocate in Zagreb, Croatia. Quoted in Angela Robson, "Weapon of War," *New Internationalist* (vol. 244, June 1993). Available online at http://www.newint.org/features/1993/06/05/rape.

Chapter 29.

We saw them rape the hadji's daughter—one after the other, they raped her. The hadji had to watch too. When they were done, they rammed a knife into his throat.
Alexandra Stiglmayer, ed., *Mass Rape: The War Against Women in Bosnia-Herzegovina* (University of Nebraska, 1994), 82.

Chapter 30.

Mina was crying the most. She said, "We are not girls anymore. Our lives are over."
Stephen Kinzer, "Bosnian Refugees' Accounts Appear to Verify Atrocities," *New York Times* (17 July 1995).

Chapter 31.

It is inconceivable for me all of this that is happening to us. Is life so unpredictable and brutal? I remember how this time last year we were rejoicing over building a house, and now see where we are. I feel as if I'd never been alive. I try to fight it by remembering everything that was beautiful with you and the children and all those I love.
Last letter of Muhamed Čehajić to his wife, Minka Čehajić, 9 June 1992. Minka Čehajić is a Bosnian pediatrician who testified on 14, 15, and 16 May 2002 in the case against Milomir Stakić. Her complete "Voice of the Victims" statement, along with the translation of her husband's letter, is available through the International Criminal Tribunal for the former Yugoslavia at http://www.icty.org/sid/186.

Any of the following acts committed with intent to destroy, in whole or in part, a national, ethnical, racial or religious group, as such:
(a) Killing members of the group;
(b) Causing serious bodily or mental harm to members of the group;
(c) Deliberately inflicting on the group conditions of life calculated to bring about its physical destruction in whole or in part;
(d) Imposing measures intended to prevent births within the group;
(e) Forcibly transferring children of the group to another group.
Convention on the Prevention and Punishment of the Crime of Genocide (entered into force 12 January 1951), Article 2 (United Nations, *Treaty Series*, vol. 78, p. 277).

You Muslim women, you Bule, we'll show you.
Witness 50 (she testified with her name and identity withheld from the public), a teenage rape victim from Foča, speaking about how ICTY convict Zoran Vuković raped her. She testified on 29 and 30 March 2000 in the case against Dragoljub Kunarac, Zoran Vuković, and Radomir Kovač. Witness 50's complete "Voice of the Victims" statement is available online at http://www.icty.org/sid/188.

You will see, you Muslims. I am going to draw a cross on your back. I'm going to baptize all of you.
Witness 50 (she testified with her name and identity withheld from the public), a teenage rape victim from Foča, speaking about how ICTY convict Zoran Vuković raped her. She testified on 29 and 30 March 2000 in the case against Dragoljub Kunarac, Zoran Vuković, and Radomir Kovač. Witness 50's complete "Voice of the Victims" statement is available through the International Criminal Tribunal for the former Yugoslavia at http://www.icty.org/sid/188.

Chapter 32.

This was the city's still center, the very essence of Islam: in a walled courtyard, water, a tree, and the warm geometry of stone. In the deep blue velvet sky by the minaret hung a sliver of incandescent silver light: the first moon of spring.
Francis R. Jones, "Return," *Why Bosnia?*, ed. Ali Rabia and Lawrence Lifschultz (Pamphleteer's Press, 1993), 33.

We see
that things too quickly grown
are swiftly overthrown.
Ibn Hazm, *The Ring of the Dove*, trans. A. J. Arberry (Luzac, 1994, Rpt.). Available at Islamic Philosophy Online, Inc. at http://www.muslimphilosophy.com/hazm /dove/index.html.

Chapter 33.

We saw our sons and husbands off to those woods and never found out anything about them again.
Mirsada Malagić, a Bosnian Muslim woman. She testified on 3 and 4 April 2000 in the case against Radislav Krstić and on 16 February 2011 in the case against Zdravko Tolimir. Mirsada Malagić's complete "Voice of the Victims" statement is available through the International Criminal Tribunal for the former Yugoslavia at http:// www.icty.org/sid/191.

Today no man from our family is older than thirty.
Mirnesa Ahmić, Srebrenica survivor. Quoted in "Srebrenica Survivor: Today No Man from Our Family Is Older Than Thirty," *Today's Zaman* (8 July 2011). Available online at http://www.todayszaman.com/news-249880-srebrenica-survivor-today -no-man-from-our-family-is-older-than-30.html.

I seek refuge in the Lord of Daybreak, from the evil of that which He created. From the evil of the black darkness wherever it descends.
Sura Falaq, "The Daybreak." Qur'an 113.

Chapter 34.

I knew all of them who did it. They were my neighbors.
Eighteen-year-old rape survivor Ziba Hasanović, as quoted in Roy Gutman, *A Witness to Genocide* (Macmillan Publishing, 1993), 76.

Keep the good ones over there. Enjoy yourselves.
General Ratko Mladić during the fall of Srebrenica, July 1995, as quoted in Adam LeBor, *Complicity with Evil: the United Nations in the Age of Modern Genocide* (R. R. Donnelley, 2001), 44.

Everything around us is on fire and we ourselves are nearly smoldering.
Paraphrased from Abdulah Ahmić, a Bosnian Muslim man, testifying about the massacre in the central Bosnian village of Ahmići, one of the conflict's most brutal acts of ethnic cleansing. His brother and father were murdered in front of him by Croat soldiers and he survived attempted murder. Abdulah Ahmić testified on 10 and 11 June 1999 in the case against Dario Kordić, member of the Presidency of the Croatian Community of Herceg-Bosnia, and Mario Čerkez, commander of the Vitez Brigade of the Croatian Defense Council (HVO). They received their final judgment on 17 December 2004. Abdulah Ahmić's complete "Voice of the Victims" statement is available through the International Criminal Tribunal for the former Yugoslavia at http://www.icty.org/sid/10118.

Chapter 35.

The dead are not alone.
Paraphrased from "Remarks by High Representative and EU Special Representative Valentin Inzko at the Memorial Ceremony for Victims of Genocide, Srebrenica, 11 July 2009" (Office of the High Representative, 2009). Available at http://www.ohr.int/ohr-dept/presso/presssp/default.asp?content_id=43702.

Chapter 36.

I cannot find words for what happened there.
Slobodan Milošević speaking to the European Union President Javier Solana about Srebrenica. *Srebenica: Reconstruction, Background, Consequences and Analyses of the Fall of a "Safe" Area* (Netherlands Institute of War Documentation, 2000): part 4, chapter 2, p. 91. Available online at http://www.srebrenica-project.com/DOWNLOAD/NOD/NIOD%20Part%20IV.pdf

Your Honours, I feel that my confession is an important step toward the rebuilding of confidence and co-existence in Bosnia and Herzegovina, and after my guilty plea and sentencing, after I have served my sentence, it is my wish to go back to my native town of Bratunac and to live there with other peoples in peace and harmony, such as prevailed before the outbreak of the war.
Momir Nikolić, "Statement of Guilt" (29 October 2003), available through the International Criminal Tribunal for the former Yugoslavia at http://www.icty.org/sid/218.

Chapter 37.

Nothing can give me resolution. Nothing can give me consolation.
Hasan Nuhanović, translator at the UN base in Potočari. *Srebrenica: A Cry from the Grave*, directed by Leslie Woodhead ([distributor Thirteen/WNET PBS], 1999).

Acknowledgments

To the many people who deserve my thanks for contributing to a book that has been so personal to me. My deep gratitude to everyone at Minotaur Books and St. Martin's Press for taking a chance on *The Unquiet Dead* and bringing it to life. I am especially indebted to my exemplary editor, Elizabeth Lacks, who believed in this book so wholly, and who championed it with such unwavering commitment. Her many brilliant suggestions improved it in every way.

My thanks to Inspector William Ford (Retired) for his invaluable and very kind advice on policing in Ontario. And to Mir Ali, Director of the Amherst School of Guitar, for generously taking the time to explain how Albinoni's Adagio might be written and orchestrated. And my sincere appreciation to Professor D. Fairchild Ruggles, who graciously permitted me to use her exquisite translation of Ibn Arabi's Ringsong. And to Stephen Hirtenstein of the Ibn 'Arabi Society for his expert guidance on sources.

My warmest thanks to Faye Kennedy, Steve Bowering, Elena Kovyrzina, and Rob Hunter, who taught me so much about publishing, and whose values embody the Canadian spirit better than anyone I know. Just know—we'll always have Paris.

And I owe an immeasurable debt of gratitude to my family and friends, for their continual love and support. Especially my parents, whose lifelong example taught me the dignity, compassion, and human decency to be found in faith. I owe them more than I can possibly express, but I hope this book will speak for me.

And to my sister, Ayesha Shaikh, my first reader since childhood, my greatest friend in life, and the most ardent believer in all my dreams, including this book. Thank you for bringing my milk money to school, just the first in a lifetime of rescues. And to Omer Shaikh, big brother, for letting me tag along everywhere.

To my brother, Irfan Khan, for everything he contributed to Esa Khattak, and for making me think about Bosnia in much more rigorous ways. I'm more grateful than I can say for his love and generosity—it enriches every aspect of my life, and always has.

To my brother, Kashif Khan, co-founder of the Republic. For taking care of me for so long, and with such love, that I can't imagine anything else. For Pennygrams, phone calls, time-share vacations—and that constant stream of presents in the mail. (Send another one soon.)

To my niece, Summer Shaikh. For bringing so much love, laughter, and adventure into my life. And my nephew, Casim Shaikh, for being my champion from the beginning. Both, the most precious of all precious things. When you get knocked down, remember to get up again.

To Dr. Nozhat Choudry, reader of ragged manuscripts, keeper of writing timetables, and awe-inspiring, undisputed soul sister. For all the ways she encourages and guides me, and for the love of those beautiful girls, Zahra, Hanna, and Maariya.

To Hema Nagar, for taking this manuscript to India and nurturing it in a magical place, just as she's nurtured me. And for being my other, more wholesome and nefarious, half. The love and decency of her friendship mean everything to me.

To Farah Bukhari, for the most genuine love a dearly loved friend and sister can give while suffering heartbreak. She has the courage of the lionhearted, which perhaps she does not know.

To my adopted parents, Uncle Munir and Auntie Aira, for lifelong encouragement and love. And for the unmitigated belief of a feisty little Finn.

And to Mum and Baba and the Hashemi family, for all their love and faith. Especially Fereshteh, with whom I have shared such a deep love of books. And my companion in adventure, Noor Shaikh (allo, matey!).

To my family in Pakistan, Canada, and England, who transmit their pride and encouragement across oceans and continents, particularly my aunt, the distinguished novelist Shakila Khan, my devoted aunt Sameena Tahseen, and my unconquerable grandmother Niaz Fatima Khan.

And to my cousins Saad, Athif, and Akif Khan, and Zohaib Siddiqui, for helping in so many ways.

And to a deeply cherished group of friends, for the moments that have made up the whole. Farah and Saima Malik, Afshan Ahmad, Najia Usman, Haseeba Yusuf, and Seema Nundy: readers of early works, partners in memorable performances, and steadfast companions in various hijinks.

Afshan Javed, for incomparable letters from Arabia and friendship beyond measure.

Farah Choudhry and Nihan Keser, for those years of fearless joy and discovery in Ottawa. And all the times we skated at midnight.

Yasser Khan for being so much a part of those years.

Asma Amjad, for making me welcome.

Aysha Nusrat, for so much kindness in a strange city.

Wisam Karawan, the most beautiful girl from Gaza. With whom I crossed impassable borders.

Jennifer, for travels through Cairo and Jordan, and the Nuweiba crossing at dawn.

Lena Johansson, for *Samarkand*, dreams of Alamut, and so much else.

Yara Masri, for laughter and solidarity at the Dome of the Rock. And all the girls of Qasr al-Hamra.

Iram Ahmed, for larks. And for the love she gives to what is priceless to me.

Uzma Alam, my much-loved sister, for the conversations that have warmed the years and made us wise. And for reading the stories I write for Layth, Maysa, and Zayna, my light and joy.

Yasmin, Semina, and Kamran Ahmad, who grew up to make me so proud with their courage, grace, and boundless hearts.

And most of all, to my husband, Nader Hashemi, the love of my life. For the matchless faith that has made my dreams possible. For encouragement, advice, and the easing of every hardship. And for being who he is. How sweet this life has been with your love.

1. The original title of this book was *An Unsafe Area*. Now that you have finished *The Unquiet Dead*, consider why *An Unsafe Area* might have been an appropriate title. What themes, events, or settings in the book does it speak to? Do you prefer this title to *The Unquiet Dead*? Why or why not?

2. By the end of the mystery, we learn that Inspector Khattak is certain that Christopher Drayton was pushed to his death by Imam Muharrem. However, no independent corroboration of Khattak's conclusion is offered, as Muharrem never makes a direct confession. If Inspector Khattak is correct, should he have arrested Imam Muharrem? Has justice been served? What does the ending of the book tell us about our notions of what real justice is?

3. How do you interpret Mink Norman's statement to Khattak: "In Bosnia, identity is a curse. So do not pretend to know us." Why is Khattak so personally invested in the investigation? In what ways do his personal feelings cloud his judgment and/or help illuminate some of the facts that lead to the mystery's resolution?

4. The relationship between the two detectives, Esa Khattak and Rachel Getty, is sometimes an uneasy one. Although Khattak treats Rachel with respect, Rachel behaves as though she has something to prove to him. What factors influence Rachel's sense of inadequacy? What impact has Rachel's relationship with her father, retired police superintendent Don Getty, had on her career as a police officer? In what ways do Esa Khattak and Don Getty differ as superior officers?

5. Mothers play an important role in *The Unquiet Dead*. We see strikingly different manifestations of motherhood in the characters of Melanie Blessant and Lillian Getty. Tangentially, we also hear about the mothers of Aldo and Harry Osmond, Nathan and Audrey Clare, and David Newhall. How might our traditional expectations of motherhood be subverted by the relationship between Melanie Blessant and her daughters, Hadley and Cassidy? Or by Lillian Getty's relation-

Discussion Questions

St. Martin's Griffin

ship with her children, Rachel and Zachary? How might the deceased mothers of David Newhall and the Clares be more idealized by contrast?

6. One of the themes of *The Unquiet Dead* is loyalty versus betrayal, a theme that is both personal and political. In what sense might the Bosnian characters in the story believe that they have been betrayed? Is this betrayal personal or political? Does it apply to Mink Norman's relationship with Esa Khattak? If so, which of these two characters might claim to have been betrayed by the other, and why? What other examples of loyalty or betrayal in *The Unquiet Dead* can you think of?

7. The Bosnian lily, or *Lilium bosniacum*, is a plant native to the country of Bosnia. The *fleur-de-lis* symbol used on the coat of arms of the kings of Bosnia until 1463 may have been a representation of the Bosnian lily. It was revived on the Bosnian flag of independence in 1992, then removed in later iterations of the flag. Discuss the significance of the Bosnian lily as a personal and a political symbol in *The Unquiet Dead*. Why does it matter that this lily was planted in Christopher Drayton's garden? What impact does the discovery of the lily have on Christopher Drayton?

8. In *The Unquiet Dead*, the librarian Mink Norman alludes to the history of Moorish Spain or Andalusia. She sees this period of history as a "golden idyll," and later compares Andalusia to the country of Bosnia before the 1992 war. Is this a valid comparison? In his frequent visits to the Andalusia Museum, is Inspector Khattak drawn more to the history of Andalusia or to the librarian herself? What does Ringsong represent to Esa Khattak, and why might he identify so strongly with the museum?

9. Toward the end of the book, Rachel begins to focus on a series of clues: the music, the photograph, the lilies, the gun. What role does each of these clues play in the mystery? How does the association of these particular clues help Rachel understand what happened on the night that Christopher Drayton fell to his death?

Turn the page for a sneak peek at
Ausma Zehanat Khan's next novel

THE LANGUAGE OF SECRETS

Available February 2016

Esa Khattak was grateful for Martine Killiam's call. She was a superintendent with the Royal Canadian Mounted Police, and she had asked for a consultation in his capacity as head of the Community Policing Section, a request that was both courteous and unmistakably firm.

He was relieved to be getting her call, given the outcome of his last case. The hounds of the press were at bay for now, but the rumors of a pending inquiry were gaining traction. The conclusion of the investigation into Christopher Drayton's death had sparked a national outcry, leading the Minister of Justice to issue a personal reprimand.

You've bungled this, Khattak. And you've taken Tom Paley down with you.

Khattak knocked on Martine Killiam's door.

Tom Paley, the chief war crimes historian at the Department of Justice, had been a friend. When he'd passed away from a heart attack last month, his case file on Christopher Drayton had vanished.

And now the press was calling for Khattak's head, accusing him of delay, denial, and too close an association with the Bosnian community. No one was happy with the outcome.

Esa thought of Tom, often. Of the care he'd taken to ensure that the truth about Drayton's death would come to light. Tom couldn't have foreseen that Esa would be left alone to face the glare of the national spotlight. And it occurred to Esa to wonder if

Superintendent Killiam had been assigned the task of calling him to account.

At his knock, the superintendent rose from her desk to greet him. Her smile was tempered by the reticence of her manner as she shook Khattak's hand. A woman in her late fifties with a strong, square face, Killiam had spent her life in the RCMP, forging a respectable path for herself through narcotics and organized crime. The second half of her career had focused on human resources, with a portfolio that encompassed thousands of employees. With Killiam's appointment to the role of human resources officer, there had been a change in the wind for women who joined the Force. She'd originated a mentorship program that paired senior female officers with promising new candidates, alongside wider latitude and opportunities for promotion. But Killiam's most telling achievement was her strictly enforced zero-tolerance policy on sexual harassment.

Khattak respected Killiam's methodical approach to police work. It lacked imagination perhaps, but it could not be faulted on thoroughness. Behind the rimless glasses Killiam wore, he sensed she was making a similar evaluation of his background. And his current troubles with the Department of Justice.

"I asked you here because a man has been murdered in highly sensitive circumstances. I need your help as a liaison with INSET."

Khattak glanced past the glass doors of Killiam's office to a space beset with human traffic. A small team was shifting through a thoroughfare of computer terminals and whiteboards, listening to a technical consultant explain a new operating system. A second group was gathered around the coffee machine. A few heads had nodded at Khattak in recognitionas he passed. He'd raised a gloved hand in response.

Martine Killiam had asked him to meet at the Toronto base of operations for INSET, the Integrated National Security Enforcement Team. Khattak had once served as core personnel with INSET,

THE LANGUAGE OF SECRETS

before he'd been asked to head up CPS. Many of the men and women in the room were former colleagues.

"You're working something big," he said. "Is it terrorist activity? Cross-border?"

He'd noted the presence of officers from the Canada Border Services Agency.

"Sit down, won't you? What you see out there—we're at the tail end of an operation that's been running for two years. We simply didn't foresee this turn of events."

"The murdered man was part of your operation? Is that where you need my assistance?"

If Killiam was asking for Khattak's help despite what had happened with the Drayton investigation, the INSET operation would have to be at a critical point.

"I need you to investigate the murder. The victim's father is well-known, both in the national media and in your community. He plans to use his platform to obtain justice for his son. If we don't stop him, we'll lose everything we've achieved to this point." She rubbed her forehead, easing the deeply etched line between her brows. "It's much worse than you can imagine. To be frank, you're the only person I could think of who stands the slightest chance of shutting him down."

"Who is he? Who are you talking about? What happened to his son?"

"His son infiltrated a terrorist group that runs a training camp in the woods. He was found at Algonquin Park. He'd been shot twice, and left to bleed to death."

She surprised Khattak by reaching across the desk to take his hand.

"Esa," she said. "I'm sorry. The man they killed is Mohsin Dar."

He shrank away from the words, recoiled from her touch, flattening his hands against her desk.

"No," he said. "No, it's not Mohsin."

Her face crinkled with a sympathy he couldn't bear.

He made his own face a blank in response.

There was supposed to be time to work things out with Mohsin, to meet at the mosque again, to embrace like long-lost brothers, to admit they missed each other.

Instead of Mo pointing the finger when Esa had been recruited to INSET.

You're making a mistake, brother. You can't come back from this.

Think what it means for the community.

You think about it. Every mosque in the city will shut its doors to you. You'll become a pariah, a resident spy. Is that what you want? To be the house Arab? To see your face in the papers as the inside man?

It's not what you're making it out to be.

You don't spy on those you call your own, brother. You work with them, for them.

They'd had many similar conversations during the volatile period after the September 11 attacks.

With the obstinacy of a younger man still uneasy with his Pashtun roots, Esa had answered, *You should be careful who you claim as your own.*

The ummah, *man, the* ummah. *We belong to it. You don't remember the paper?*

This had been Mohsin's favorite refrain. He believed in the Islamic nation, a supranational community whose faith transcended language, sect, ethnicity, and borders, tied together by a spiritual commonality.

For a brief time, Esa and Mohsin had been contributors to the newspaper at their university. Khattak's inclination had been for poetry, Mohsin's a highly emotional form of reportage. He'd taken the global Muslim community as his subject.

An article Mohsin had written to honor Afghan warriors in the aftermath of the Soviet withdrawal praised the simplicity of mujahideen worship, evoking the image of a solitary figure praying at the summit of a mountain fastness.

This was the weapon that won the war.

So Mohsin had believed.

The article had revealed a gaping ignorance of global politics. Of the future prospects of an illiterate society flush with weapons and drugs and rife with the divisions the Soviet occupation had suppressed, Mohsin had had little to say.

Khattak had found no fault with Mohsin's critique of the Russian invasion, but he'd wondered at his friend's refusal to see beyond that singular moment in history. Afghanistan's tribal past, its uncertain future, with decades of war still to come. The oft-named graveyard of empires, with many of its dead yet to be counted.

Mohsin's view of the world had been naive: friends versus enemies, *ummah* versus outsiders, the pain of the now measured against the sweet reward of the afterlife, though he'd never flung the word "infidel" as an accusation. When he looked for common ground, he usually found it. But as with other members of their community, Mohsin's grievances had multiplied with time.

Khattak's eyes searched Killiam's face.

"He was an agent of the RCMP? When did that happen?"

And what did it mean that Mohsin had made such a choice when he'd broken with Esa for doing the same?

Killiam cleared her throat. "Mohsin came to us through the Canadian Security Intelligence Service. We developed him as an agent. I'm not at liberty to say for how long."

"But this camp you mentioned in the woods—that was your operation?"

Martine regarded him gravely.

"The operation is not over, Esa. It's moving to the tactical stage soon." She passed him a folder across the desk. "We've penetrated two cells that are working together on a bomb plot. They've designated four targets." She counted them off on her fingers. "Union Station, the CN Tower, Queen's Park, the SkyDome. They're calling their attack the 'New Year Nakba.'"

Khattak's head came up from his perusal of the file.

"Nakba" was a word freighted with history.

It was the Arabic word for "catastrophe."

A catastrophe taken to heart by an undivided Muslim world—a match to light a tinderbox.

Yawm an-Nakba, the Day of Catastrophe, commemorated the day after Israel's Independence Day. It linked the founding of the state of Israel to the loss of the Palestinian homeland, when 700,000 Palestinians had fled or been expelled during the 1948 war. Settlement construction, home demolitions, and state-sanctioned violence in the West Bank were only superseded by the desperate human rights crisis in Gaza. They kept the memory of Palestinian suffering fresh in the minds of the *ummah*.

The men behind the Nakba plot would have chosen the name for its symbolic value as a Lydian stone of defeat.

The mighty against the weak.

The occupier against the indigenous.

The colonizer against the lost and defenseless.

But was Palestine still a touchstone after so many years? After Afghanistan, Syria, Lebanon, Iraq?

Khattak closed the file with a snap. He couldn't bring himself to look at the photographs of Mohsin. Just as he couldn't bring himself to imagine that any of this was real.

"Is this serious, Superintendent? Are you telling me that Canadians are training at a camp in Algonquin, with the intention of carrying out a terrorist attack?" He pushed the folder back across the desk. "How are they coordinating it? Where are they getting the weapons? Is there any operational legitimacy to this?"

Killiam's eyes narrowed at Khattak's implication.

"We've put two years into this investigation, so you can trust that it's not a hoax. These people may be amateurs, but they have know-how and materials, and they've coordinated a plan. We've been detailed and thorough. It's just as well that you don't know how thorough."

The words gave Khattak pause. Killiam was hinting at the broad net cast by the Anti-Terrorism Act, known at its controversial inception as Bill C-36. It wasn't a subject he intended to debate with her. His reservations at the time of the introduction of the legislation had been noted in his personnel file. And he'd participated in debates about the recent, far more serious encroachment on civil liberties—the hammering home of Bill C-51, the new legislation with its unchecked surveillance powers and lack of civilian oversight.

He feared what they were becoming.

Killiam knew all this.

"And the takedown?" he asked.

Killiam's eyes narrowed. "Sometime between Christmas and New Year's Day. That will be my call. What I need to know is whether you can handle Andy Dar, Mohsin's father."

Khattak spread his hands helplessly.

"Do they have the bombs?" he asked.

"If Mohsin hadn't warned us in time, they'd have had everything they need to detonate four fertilizer bombs on location. We'll be taking over the delivery, switching out the fertilizer with inert material. We're in the setup phase of that operation now."

Khattak didn't ask for details about the plan. Martine Killiam was Officer in Charge of a critical national security operation. She wasn't about to tell him anything that didn't directly relate to Mohsin Dar's murder. But he did worry that the takedown had yet to occur.

"You said you've run this operation for two years now. You don't have to answer, but by that I presume you mean surveillance. Do your intercepts indicate premeditation? Had the group in the woods planned to kill Mohsin at the camp?"

"There's no evidence that anyone in the group had uncovered Mohsin's agenda."

"What about the second cell you mentioned? Is it possible they know their communications are being monitored?"

"It's quite clear that they don't."

"So the tactical strike is on schedule."

"Yes."

"Then isn't it possible that Mohsin was murdered for reasons unrelated to his work as an RCMP agent?"

Killiam gave him a quick nod. "That's exactly the line I want you to pursue with Mohsin's father. No one is to know anything about Mohsin's work with us. Not his father, not his wife. You're to treat this as a routine homicide investigation. You'll work your way through a list of suspects without tipping either your hand or mine."

"Do you know who these suspects are?"

"There were seven people at Algonquin with Mohsin. Two of them are women who may or may not have been involved in the activities of the cell. They may be hangers-on or partners; we can't be certain. It would help if you tackle them first. Ask questions, dig around, but stay away from the camp itself. Don't do anything that would compromise the operation."

"I can't work undercover," he pointed out. "Not after the press coverage I've received."

Martine Killiam shrugged. If she had bowed before the weight of ridicule directed at women when she was coming up in the Force, she'd still be deferring to men with half her abilities and none of her insight. She had very little patience for self-doubt. But given what she was asking of Esa, she seemed prepared to unbend a little.

She pushed the buff-colored folder back at Khattak. "You won't be undercover. You'll be there in your very well-known capacity as head of CPS, 'transparently and fully representing the rights of minority communities.'"

She quoted the CPS mandate back at Khattak with a scorn he knew was not directed at his work, but at the political maneuvering behind it. She was well aware of the risks inherent in Khattak's position. He would always be accused of failing some constituency or mandate—either the minority communities he'd been tasked to represent or the law he was meant to uphold. Only in rare cases would these objectives run together.

"I don't know that my history with Mohsin will make any difference to his father."

The words sounded strange on his tongue, as if he was distancing himself from his friend. Their lives had brushed up against each other without touching anything that truly mattered, at the end.

"I won't apologize for saying this, Esa. Use whatever you can with Andy Dar. Make a religious appeal, make a personal appeal—try anything that might work. You know his radio program. We can't have him using it to raise questions about the camp. His grandstanding could scuttle the entire operation. You have to be seen as committed to solving Mohsin's murder."

With a sense of genuine sadness, Khattak replied, "I am committed."

Killiam looked at him for a moment, but she left the comment alone.

"If you find you're not getting anywhere on the public front, send Rachel Getty in. You've been wise enough to keep her under wraps, but I've heard your partner is quite talented."

Khattak smiled. "More than talented," he said. "She's been a tremendous asset to CPS, and to me."

He watched Martine Killiam take note of this on a writing pad at her elbow.

"Then you've done well to protect her from the spotlight, which in turn serves my operation now. Get her in if you can, but no one—and I can't emphasize this enough—breathes a word about Nakba."

Khattak frowned. "Is there any chance the attack could succeed?"

She avoided a direct answer.

"I'll leave the Outreach Coordinator to brief you on the details. You'll work with her, and report to the Special Assistant, as I believe you've done in the past. Anything you find out, you convey to me through him."

But Khattak didn't know anyone with that rank in the RCMP.

"Inspector Ciprian Coale was promoted two years ago," she told Khattak. "And you already know the Outreach Coordinator."

Khattak turned around in his chair. Two people were waiting outside Killiam's office, one with a nasty smile playing about his mouth. As their eyes met, Ciprian Coale sketched a salute, the gesture just short of offensive. A dark-haired woman in a navy-blue suit raised her hand to knock at Killiam's door.

It was Laine Stoicheva, Khattak's former partner.